Susanna Gregory is   her
Ph.D. at the Universi   arch
Fellow at one of th   police officer in
Yorkshire. She has written a number of non-fiction books,
including ones on castles, catherdrals, historic houses and
world travel.

She and her husband live in a village near Cambridge.

A SUMMER OF DISCONTENT

Susanna Gregory

timewarner
paperbacks

A *Time Warner* Paperback

First published in Great Britain in 2002
by Little, Brown

This edition published by Time Warner Paperbacks in 2003

Copyright © Susanna Gregory 2002

The moral right of the author has been asserted.

A CIP catalogue record for this book
is available from the British Library.

ISBN 0 7515 3238 X

Typeset in New Baskerville by Palimpsest Book Production Limited,
Polmont, Stirlingshire

Printed and bound in Great Britain by
Clays Ltd, St Ives plc

Time Warner Paperbacks
An imprint of
Time Warner Books UK
Brettenham House
Lancaster Place
London WC2E 7EN

www.TimeWarnerBooks.co.uk

For the Pritchard boys –
Pete, Ed and Alan

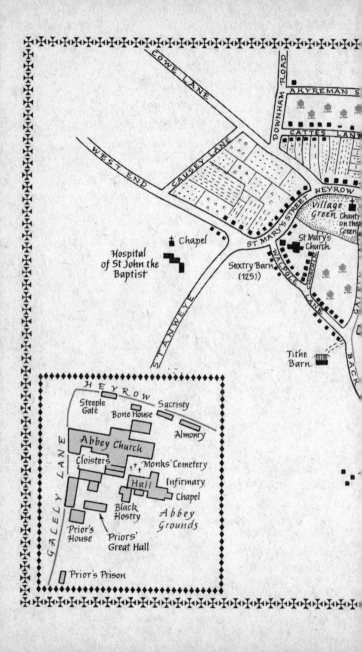

COWE LANE

DOWNHAM ROAD

AKYREMAN S

CATTES LANE

WEST END

CAUSEY LANE

HEYROW

Village
Green

Chantry
on the
Green

ST MARY'S STREET

Chapel

St Mary's
Church

Hospital
of St John the
Baptist

Sextry Barn
(1251)

WALPOLE LANE

CHURCH

STANWEYE

Tithe
Barn

BACK

HEYROW

Steeple
Gate

Sacristy

Bone House

Almonry

GALELY LANE

Abbey Church

Cloisters

Monks' Cemetery

Hall

Infirmary

Chapel

Black
Hostry

Abbey
Grounds

Prior's
House

Priors'
Great Hall

Prior's Prison

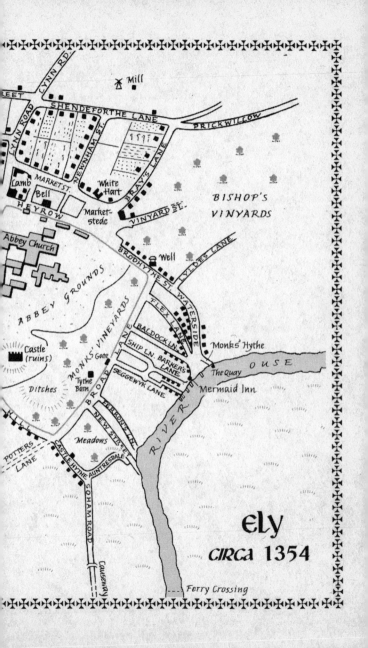

Mill

LYNN RD

SHENDEFORTHE LANE

PRICKWILLOW

STREET

LYNN ROAD

NEWNHAM ST.

FRAY'S LANE

White Hart

BISHOP'S VINYARDS

MARKET ST.

Lamb

Bell

HEYROW

Market-stede

VINYARD ST.

Abbey Church

BRODHYTHE ST. WATERSIDE

Well

TYLDES LANE

ABBEY GROUNDS

FLEX LANE

MONKS' VINEYARDS

LANE

BALDOCK LN.

Castle (ruins)

Gate

SHIP LN. BARKERS LANE

Monks' Hythe

O U S E

Tythe Barn

SEGGEWYK LANE

The Quay

Ditches

BROAD

Mermaid Inn

R I V E R

FERRON LN.

NEW STREET

Meadows

POTTERS LANE

CASTLE HYTHE AUNTRESDALE

SOHAM ROAD

ely
CIRCA 1354

CAUSEWAY

Ferry Crossing

PROLOGUE

Colne, Huntingdonshire; February 1354

THE PEOPLE WHO HAD THE MISFORTUNE TO LIVE IN THE tiny Fenland village of Colne led miserable lives. Their homes were little more than hovels, with walls of woven hazel twigs that had been plastered over with mud from the nearby river. The crude thatching on the roofs leaked, allowing water to pool on the beaten-earth floors and to deposit irregular and unpleasant drips on the huts' inhabitants. Winter rain and biting winds had stripped away some of the walls' mud, so that Ralph could see the orange flicker of a hearth fire through them in the darkness. He shifted his position, uncomfortable after the long wait in the frigid chill of a February night. In one of the houses, a dog started to bark. Its yaps were half-hearted, as though it, like its owners, was too dispirited to care much about someone lurking suspiciously in the shadows outside.

Ralph huddled more deeply into his cloak, grateful that he worked for a man who provided clothes that kept him warm through the worst of winter and boots that were equal to wading through the thick, sucking muck of the country's roads. The same could not be said of the people who lived in the cottages he watched. These were villeins, bound by law for their entire lives to the estates of Lady Blanche de Wake. If their own crops failed and they had not stored enough food for the winter, then they would starve. Blanche was not obliged to help them, and they were not permitted to leave their vermin-infested homes to seek a better life elsewhere. Ralph sniffed softly, thinking that what he was about to do might even help the poor wretches in their cramped, stinking huts, shivering near meagre fires lit with stolen wood.

He had been watching them for the best part of a week now, and knew their daily routine: they trudged home from labouring in Lady Blanche's stony fields, ate whatever they had managed to poach or steal from her woods – the grain saved from the last harvest had long since gone – and then fell into an exhausted slumber until the first glimmer of light in the east heralded the beginning of another dreary day. Ralph's careful observations had yielded a great deal of information about the people of Colne and their lives. For example, he knew that the folk in the cottage to his left had feasted on a pigeon that night; the inhabitants of the other two had made do with a thin stew of nettles, a handful of dried beans and some onion skins that had been intended for Blanche's pigs.

Lady Blanche's manor house stood in a thicket of scrubby trees some distance away, near the swollen stream that bubbled through the dull winter-brown fields. Ralph had managed to slip inside it earlier that day, when the reeve was out overseeing the peasants at their work. Although Blanche was not currently in residence, the house was always kept in readiness for her. There were clean rushes on the floor, sprinkled with fresh herbs to keep them sweet smelling, and the kitchens were well stocked. Blanche liked her food, and the reeve saw no reason to let standards slip just because his mistress was away. He and his family had certainly not eaten onion skins and nettles that evening.

Ralph turned his attention back to the cottages. The occupants had been sleeping for a while now and Colne was well off the beaten track: no one was likely to come along and disturb him. It was time. Stiffly, because he had been waiting for some hours, Ralph stood and brushed dead leaves and twigs from his cloak. He flexed his limbs, then made his way to the nearest of the three hovels, treading softly. The dog whined, and Ralph grimaced, sensing that he would have to be quick if he did not want to be caught red-handed.

He had thought carefully about what he was going to do,

painstakingly planning and making preparations. He had already packed the thatched roofs with dried grass, and had placed small bundles of twigs at strategic points around the backs of the hovels. He would have used straw, but was afraid one of the cottagers would notice if he made too many obvious changes.

The dog barked again when he struck the tinder, but he ignored it as he set the tiny flame to the first clump of dry grass. It caught quickly, then smoked and hissed as the flames licked up the damp thatch. When he was sure it would not blow out, he moved to the second bundle of kindling, and then the next. The dog barked a third time, more urgently now, unsettled by the odour of smoke and the snap of gently smouldering roof. Someone swore at it, there was a thud, and its barks became yelps. Hurrying, Ralph moved to the next cottage, where he set the dancing flame to a bundle of tinder-dry sticks.

He did not have time to reach the third house. The dog would not be silenced and, as the occupants of the first hovel were torn from their exhausted slumbers, they became aware that the top of their home was full of thick white smoke and that the crackle of burning was not coming from the logs in the hearth. A child started to scream in terror, while the adults poured out of the house, yelling in alarm. Their shouts woke their neighbours, who tumbled into the icy night air, rubbing the sleep from their eyes.

By now, the fire had taken a good hold of the first home, and the roof of the second released tendrils of smoke: already it was too late to save it. Sparks danced through the darkness to land on the roof of the third, and soon that was alight, also. Ralph ducked away from the peasants' sudden fevered, but futile, attempts to douse the flames, watching from a safe distance. No amount of water would save the houses now, and any pails or pots that might have been used were inside, being consumed by the very flames they might have helped to quench.

The cottagers milled around in helpless confusion. The

men poked and jabbed desperately at the burning thatches with hoes and spades, but their efforts only served to make the fire burn more fiercely. The women stood with their children clinging to their skirts and stared in silent dismay. For them, life had been almost unbearably hard. Now it would be harder still.

Ralph watched them for a while longer, savouring the sharp, choking stench of burning wood and the crackling roar of the flames that devoured the last of the thatching. The people were silhouetted against the orange pyre, breath pluming like fog in the bitter winter night. The reeve and his family came running from the manor, woken by the shouts of alarm and the fountain of glittering sparks that flew into the black sky, but there was little they could do to help. Ralph heard the reeve demand to know which household had left a fire burning while they slept, and saw two families regarding the third in silent reproach. He smiled in satisfaction. The cottagers who had warmed themselves with stolen kindling, and had rashly fallen asleep to its comforting heat, would be blamed for the mishap. No one would suspect foul play. Ralph was now free to leave.

The Isle of Ely, early August 1354

Tom Glovere finished his ale and wiped his lips with the back of his hand. He was aware that the atmosphere in the Lamb Inn was icy, despite the warmth of the summer evening, but he did not care. The inhabitants of Ely were too complacent and willing to believe in the good in people. Glovere intended to cure them of such foolery.

'So,' said the landlord, turning away from Glovere to address another of his patrons. 'It is a good summer we are having, Master Leycestre. Long, hot days are excellent for gathering the harvest.'

'Do not try to change the subject, Barbour,' snapped Glovere nastily, as he set his cup on the table to be refilled. 'We were discussing the spate of burglaries that have plagued our city for the last few days: the locksmith was relieved of six groats last night, while the Cordwainers Guild had three silver pieces stolen the day before.'

'We know all this,' said Barbour wearily. 'My customers and I do not need you to tell us the story a second time. And we do not need you to make nasty accusations about our fellow citizens, either.'

Glovere smiled. It was not a pleasant expression. 'Then you should expect these thefts to continue. Whoever is breaking into our homes and making off with our gold is a *local* man. He knows which houses are likely to contain the most money, the best way to enter them, and even how to pacify the dogs. The locksmith's hound is a mean-spirited brute, and yet it did not so much as growl when its home was entered in the depths of the night. That, my friends, is because the dog *knew* the burglar.' He sat back, confident that he had made his point.

The landlord regarded Glovere with dislike. It was growing late, so most of his patrons had already gone to their beds, but a dozen or so remained, enjoying the cool, sweet ale that made the Lamb a popular place to be on a sultry summer night. The sun had set in a blaze of orange and gold, and the shadows of dusk were gathering, dark and velvety. The air smelled of mown hay, and of the ripe crops that waited in the fields to be harvested. It was a beautiful evening, and Barbour thought Glovere was wrong to pollute it by creating an atmosphere of distrust and suspicion. He turned to Leycestre again, and enquired politely after the health of his nephews in the hope that Glovere would grow bored and leave.

'Why would an Ely citizen suddenly resort to burgling the houses in his own town?' asked Leycestre, ignoring the landlord's attempt to change the subject and addressing the gleefully malicious Glovere. 'Your accusations make no sense. I keep telling you that it is *gypsies* who are responsible for these thefts. The burglaries started the day after those folk arrived, and that speaks for itself.' He folded his arms and looked around him belligerently, sure that no one could fail to agree.

Barbour sighed heartily, wishing that Leycestre would keep his unfounded opinions to himself, too. The gypsies liked their ale just as much as the next man, and the landlord did not want to lose valuable customers just because Leycestre had taken against them.

Glovere sneered. 'The gypsies would not burgle us. They come here every year to help with the harvest, and they have never stolen anything before. You just do not want to face up to the truth: the culprit is a townsman who will be known to us all. You mark my words.' He tapped his goblet on the table. 'Another ale, Barbour.'

'No,' said Barbour, angry with both his customers. 'You have had enough of my ale.'

Glovere gazed at him, the scornful expression fading from his face. He was not an attractive man – his complexion was florid and flaky, and the uneven whiskers that sprouted from his cheeks and chin made him appear unwashed and unsavoury, despite his neat and expensive clothes. 'I am not drunk. Give me another ale.'

'I did not say you were drunk,' said Barbour coolly. 'I said you have had enough of my ale. You have a vicious tongue and I do not want you wagging it any longer in my tavern.'

Glovere glowered at the Lamb's other patrons, his eyes bright with malice. He held the lofty position of steward, after all, while they were mere labourers, and it galled him to think that they should be served Barbour's ale while he was refused. 'I am not the only one who tells what he knows. Leycestre revealed that it was Agnes Fitzpayne who raided the Prior's peach tree last year, while Adam Clymme told us that Will Mackerell ate his neighbour's cat.'

'That is not the same,' said Barbour firmly. 'Your gossip is dangerous. You have already caused one young woman to drown herself because her life was blighted by your lies.'

There was a growl of agreement from the other drinkers, and Glovere at least had the grace to appear sheepish. 'It was not *my* fault that she killed herself before it could be proven that she was not with child,' he objected sullenly. 'I only told people what I thought. And it was not *my* fault that her betrothed went off and married someone else, either. Was it, Chaloner?'

He stared archly at a burly man who sat alone in one corner of the inn. Others looked at Chaloner, too, and none of the expressions were friendly. Chaloner was a rough, belligerent fellow who cared little for what people thought. But he knew the good citizens of Ely had neither forgotten nor forgiven the fact that he had too readily abandoned poor Alice to marry another woman when Glovere made his accusations – accusations that turned out to be wholly false. People had liked Alice; they did not like Chaloner and he often found himself at the receiving end of hostile glances or comments. Usually, he ignored it all, and certainly did not permit his neighbours' priggish disapprobation to influence the way he lived his life. But it was late and Chaloner was too tired for a confrontation that night. He drained his cup, slammed it on the table and slouched from the tavern without a word.

'Why Alice killed herself over him is beyond me,' said Glovere sanctimoniously, after Chaloner had gone. He was well aware that a conversation about the detested Chaloner might induce Barbour to forget his irritation with Glovere himself. 'I did her a favour by saving her from marriage with him.'

'A favour that killed the poor lass,' muttered Leycestre under his breath.

'It would not surprise me to learn that Chaloner is the thief,' Glovere went on. 'We all know he has a penchant for the property of others. Perhaps he has become greedy.'

'And the reason we all know about his weakness for other people's goods is because he keeps getting caught,' Barbour pointed out. 'Chaloner does not have the skill or the daring to burgle the homes of the wealthiest men in Ely.'

'The gypsies do, though,' said Leycestre immediately.

'I do not know why we tolerate men like Chaloner in our town,' said Glovere, cutting across what would have been a tart reprimand from Barbour. 'None of us like him, and Alice is better dead than wed to him. More ale, landlord!'

Barbour's expression was unfriendly. 'You can have more when you can keep a decent tongue in your head. And it is late anyway.' He glanced around at his other patrons. 'You all need to be up early tomorrow to gather the harvest, and so should be heading off to your own homes now.' He began to collect empty jugs and to blow out the candles that cast an amber light on the whitewashed walls.

Glovere glared at the landlord, then stood reluctantly and made his way outside. There was a sigh of relief from several customers when the door closed behind him.

'He is an evil fellow,' said Leycestre fervently. 'And Chaloner is not much better.'

'There are a number of folk in this city we would be better without,' agreed Barbour. He gestured to a lanky, greasy-haired man who lurched to his feet and clutched at a door frame to prevent himself from falling. 'Haywarde is drunk again, which means his wife will feel his fists tonight. If there was any justice in the world, someone would take a knife to all three of them.'

Leycestre frowned, watching the other patrons give Haywarde a wide berth as they left. Haywarde was scowling angrily, and no one wanted to be on the receiving end of his quick temper. 'What do *you* think of Glovere's claims, Barbour? Do you believe that a townsman – like Chaloner – is responsible for these burglaries?'

The landlord shrugged as he set a tray of goblets on a table and began to dunk them in a bucket of cold water; he was relieved when Haywarde finally released the door frame and staggered away into the night. 'Possibly. These are desperate times.'

'But it is the gypsies, I tell you,' insisted Leycestre. 'The thefts started the day after they arrived in Ely. It is *obvious* that they are to blame.'

'It is late,' said Barbour flatly. He was tired, and had not silenced Glovere's malicious diatribe in order to hear one from Leycestre. 'And if you see Glovere on your way home, you can tell him that I meant what I said. You know I like a bit of gossip myself – what taverner does not like news to entertain his guests with? – but Glovere's chatter is spiteful and dangerous, and I want none of it in my inn.'

He ushered Leycestre unceremoniously out of the door and barred it from the inside, walking back through his inn to exit through the rear door. He stood for a few moments, savouring the silence of the night before deciding he was too unsettled for sleep, and that he needed to stretch his legs. When he reached the main street, he saw that Leycestre and several of his fellow drinkers had also declined to return home when the night was too humid and hot for comfortable sleeping.

Meanwhile, Glovere was still angry as he slouched towards the river. Unlike the others, he was not obliged to rise before the sun was up to spend the day labouring in the fields. As steward to Lady Blanche de Wake, his only task was to watch over her small Ely manor while she was away. It was scarcely onerous, and he often found himself with time on his hands, and he liked to pass some of it by speculating about the private lives of his fellow citizens. He had risen at noon that day and was not yet ready for sleep. He reached the river and began to stroll upstream, breathing in deeply the rich, fertile scent of ripe crops and the underlying gassy stench of the marshes that surrounded the City in the Fens.

A rustle in the reeds behind him caught his attention and he glanced around sharply. Someone was walking towards him. He stopped and waited, wondering whether he had gone too far in the tavern, and one of the patrons had come to remonstrate with him or warn him not to be so outspoken. It was too dark to see who it was, so he waited, standing with his hands on his hips, ready to dispense a taste of his tongue if anyone dared tell him how to behave. A slight noise from behind made him spin around the other way. Was someone else there, or was it just the breeze playing among the waving reeds? Suddenly Glovere had the feeling that it was not such a fine evening for a stroll after all.

chapter 1

A LIGHT MIST SEEPED FROM THE MARSHES, AND WRAPPED ghostly white fingers around the stunted trees that stood amid the wasteland of sedge and reed. In the distance, a flock of geese flapped and honked in panic at something that had disturbed them, but otherwise the desolate landscape was silent. The water, which formed black, pitchy puddles and ditches that stretched as far as the eye could see, had no ebb and flow, and was a vast, soundless blanket that absorbed everyday noises to create an eerie stillness. Matthew Bartholomew, physician and Fellow of the College of Michaelhouse at the University of Cambridge, felt as though his presence in the mysterious land of bog and tangled undergrowth was an intrusion, and that to speak and shatter the loneliness and quiet would be wrong. He recalled stories from his childhood about Fenland spirits and ghosts, which were said to tolerate humans only as long as they demonstrated appropriate reverence and awe.

'This is a vile, godforsaken spot,' announced his colleague loudly, gazing around him with a distasteful shudder. Brother Michael was a practical man, and tales of vengeful creatures that chose to inhabit bogs held no fear for him. 'It is a pity St Etheldreda decided to locate her magnificent monastery in a place like this.'

'She built it here precisely because it was in the middle of the Fens,' said Bartholomew, glancing behind him as a bird fidgeted noisily in the undergrowth to one side. The causeway along which they rode ran between the thriving market town of Cambridge and the priory-dominated city of Ely, and was often used by merchants and wealthy clerics. Thus it was a popular haunt for robbers – and four travellers comprising a richly dressed monk, a physician with a well-packed medicine bag, and two servants would provide a tempting target. 'St Etheldreda was fleeing a husband intent on claiming his conjugal rights, and she selected Ely because she knew he would not find her here.'

'Did it work?' asked Cynric, Bartholomew's Welsh book-bearer, who sat in his saddle with the ease of a born horseman. Tom Meadowman, Michael's favourite beadle, rode next to him, but white-knuckled hands on the reins and his tense posture indicated that he was unused to horses and that he would just as soon be walking.

Bartholomew nodded. 'The legend says that she fled from the north country to the Fens almost seven hundred years ago. Her husband, the King of Northumbria, never found her, and she built her monastery here, among the marshes.'

'She is one of those saints whose body is as perfect now as when it went into its tomb,' added Meadowman, addressing Cynric but looking at Michael, clearly intending to impress his master with his theological knowledge. 'Her sister dug up the corpse a few years after it was buried, and found it whole and uncorrupted. A shrine was raised over the tomb, and some Benedictine monks later came and built a cathedral over it.'

'I know the story,' said Michael irritably. 'I am a monk of Ely, after all. But my point is that Etheldreda could equally well have hidden in a much nicer place than this. Just look around you. That we are riding here at all, and not rowing in a boat like peasants, is a testament to my priory's diligence in maintaining this causeway.'

'It is a testament to the huge tithes your priory demands from its tenants,' muttered Cynric, casting a resentful glower at the monk's broad back.

Since the Great Pestilence had swept through the country, claiming one in three souls, there had been fewer peasants to pay rents and tithes to landowners. Inevitably, the landowners had increased their charges. At the same time the price of bread had risen dramatically but wages had remained low, so there was growing resentment among the working folk toward their wealthy overlords. Cynric sided wholly with the peasants, and seldom missed an opportunity to point out the injustice of the disparity between rich and poor to anyone who would listen.

Meadowman shot his companion an uneasy glance, and Bartholomew suspected that while he might well agree with the sentiments expressed by Cynric, he was reluctant to voice his support while Michael was listening. Besides being the Bishop of Ely's most trusted agent, a Benedictine monk, and, like Bartholomew, a Fellow of Michaelhouse, Brother Michael was also the University's Senior Proctor. He had recently promoted Meadowman to the post of Chief Beadle – his right-hand man in keeping unruly students in order. Meadowman enjoyed his work and was devoted to Michael, and he had no intention of annoying his master over an issue like peasants' rights. Cynric, on the other hand, had known Michael for years, and felt no need to whisper his radical opinions.

'Between the Bishop and the Prior, the people in Ely are all but bled dry,' he continued. 'The Death should have made the wealthy kinder to their tenants, but it has made them greedier and more demanding. It is not just, and the people will not tolerate it for much longer.'

Bartholomew knew that his book-bearer was right. He could not avoid hearing the growing rumble of discontent when he visited his poorer patients, and believed them when they claimed they would join any rebellion that would see the wealthy strung up like the thieves they were seen to be. Personally, he believed such grievances were justified, and thought the wealthy were wrong to continue in their excesses while the peasants starved.

Michael chose to ignore Cynric, concentrating on negotiating a way through one of the many spots where the road had lost its battle with the dank waters of the Fens. The track, for which 'causeway' was rather too grand a title, was little more than a series of mud-filled ruts that barely rose above the bogs surrounding them. Reeds and long cream-coloured grasses clustered at its edges, waiting for an opportunity to encroach and reclaim the barren ribbon of land that stood between Ely and isolation.

The route through the Fens was an ancient one, first established by Romans who did not like the fact that there were huge tracts of their newly conquered empire to which they did not have easy access. They built a road that ran as straight as the flight of an arrow across the marshes and the little islets that dotted them. In places, this ancient trackway could still be seen, identifiable by the unexpected appearance of red-coloured bricks or cleverly constructed drainage channels that kept the path from becoming waterlogged. There were bridges, too, which took the track higher in areas that regularly flooded, and from the top of these the traveller could look across a seemingly endless sea of short, twisted alder trees and reed beds that swayed and hissed in the breeze.

The people who lived in the Fens – and many considered the risk of flood and the marshes' eye-watering odours a fair exchange for the riches the land had to offer – made their living by harvesting sedge for thatching, cutting peat to sell as fuel, and catching wildfowl and fish for food. Legally, any bird or animal that inhabited the marshes belonged to the priory, but the Fenfolk knew the area much better than their monastic overlords, and it was almost impossible to prevent poachers from taking what they wanted. Punishment, in the form of a heavy fine or the loss of a hand, was meted out to anyone caught stealing the priory's game, but it was not often that the thieves were apprehended.

'There is certainly a growing unease among the people,' said Bartholomew, his mind still dwelling on Cynric's comments and the hungry, resentful faces he had seen hovering in Cambridge's Market Square the previous day.

Men and women had come to buy grain or bread, only to find that prices had risen yet again and their hard-earned pennies were insufficient. 'These days, a loaf costs more than a man's daily wage.'

'It is disgraceful,' agreed Cynric, his dark features angry. 'How do landlords expect people to live when they cannot afford bread? There is talk of a rebellion, you know.'

'And "talk" is all it is,' said Michael disdainfully, finally entering the conversation. 'I, too, have heard discussions in taverns, where men in their cups promise to rise up and destroy the landlords. But their wives talk sense into them when they are sober. However, you should be careful, Cynric: not everyone is as tolerant as Matt and me when it comes to chatting about riots and revolts. You do not want to be associated with such things.'

'It may be dangerous *not* to be associated with an uprising,' muttered Cynric darkly. 'If it is successful, people will know who stood with them and who was against them.'

'In that case, you should bide your time and assess who is likely to win,' advised Michael pragmatically. 'Keep your opinions to yourself, and only voice them when you know which of the two factions will be victorious.'

'I see you will be on the side of right and justice,' remarked Bartholomew dryly. 'Cynric is right. The people are resentful that the wealthy grow richer while the poor cannot afford a roof over their heads or bread for their children. The King was wrong to pass a law that keeps wages constant but allows the price of grain to soar.'

'Cynric is not the only one who needs to watch his tongue,' said Michael, giving his friend an admonishing glance. 'When we arrive at Ely, you will be a guest of the Prior. He will not take kindly to you urging his peasants to revolt.'

'You mean you do not want me to embarrass you by voicing controversial opinions,' surmised Bartholomew. 'You were kind enough to arrange for me to stay at your priory so that I can use the books in the library to complete my treatise on fevers, but you want me to behave myself while I am there.'

'Exactly,' agreed Michael. 'Prior Alan is a sensitive man, and I do not want you distressing him with your unorthodox thoughts. And while we are on this subject, you might consider not telling him what you think of phlebotomy, either. He has all his monks bled every six weeks, because he believes it keeps their humours balanced. Please do not disavow him of this notion.'

'Why not?' demanded Bartholomew. 'In my experience as a physician, bleeding usually does more harm than good. If a man is hale and hearty, why poke about in his veins with dirt-encrusted knives and risk giving him a wound that may fester?'

'The monks *like* being bled,' replied Michael tartly. 'And they will not want you encouraging Alan to deprive them of something they enjoy.'

Bartholomew regarded him uncertainly. 'Why would they be happy to undergo unnecessary and painful surgery?'

'Because afterwards they spend a week in the infirmary being fed with the priory's finest food and wine. You will make no friends by recommending that the practice of bleeding be abandoned, I can assure you.'

Their conversation was cut short by a warning yell from Cynric. Meadowman fumbled for his sword, then fell backwards to land with a gasp of pain on the rutted trackway. Cynric whipped his bow from his shoulder and nocked an arrow into it, looking around wildly. As a crossbow bolt thudded into the ground near the horses' hoofs, a stout staff miraculously appeared in Michael's hand and Bartholomew drew his dagger. When a second bolt hissed past his chest, perilously close, Bartholomew's horse panicked and started to rear and buck. Knowing he would be an easy target in his saddle, the physician abandoned his attempts to control the animal and slipped to the ground, anticipating the sharp thump of a quarrel between his ribs at any moment.

*   *   *

It was all over very quickly. Cynric drew his long Welsh dagger and spurred his pony into the undergrowth. Moments later he emerged with the crossbowman held captive. Meadowman sat up and grinned sheepishly, indicating that it had been poor horsemanship that had precipitated his tumble, not an arrow. Michael held his staff warily, ready to use it, while Bartholomew tried to calm his horse.

'And the rest of you can come out, too,' growled Cynric angrily, addressing the thick bushes that lined one side of the causeway. 'Or I shall slit your friend's throat.'

Evidently, Cynric's tone of voice and gleaming dagger were convincing. There was a rustle, and two more men and a woman emerged to stand on the trackway. Still clutching his knife and alert for any tricks, Bartholomew studied them.

They were all olive skinned and black haired, and their clothes comprised smock-like garments covered in a colourful display of embroidery. Bartholomew imagined they were itinerant travellers from the warm lands around the Mediterranean, who drifted wherever the roads took them, paying their way by hiring out their labour in return for food or a few pennies. They looked sufficiently similar to each other for Bartholomew to assume they were related in some way, perhaps brothers and sister.

The three men were heavy-set fellows who sported closely cropped hair and a week's growth of beard that made them appear disreputable. One of them stared at Cynric, his eyes wide with childlike terror, and Bartholomew saw that although he possessed the strong body of man, his mind was that of an infant. The woman moved closer to him, resting a comforting hand on his shoulder to silence the beginnings of a fearful whimper. She was tall and, although Bartholomew would not have described her as pretty, there was a certain attractiveness in the strength of her dark features.

'There is no need for further violence,' she said in French that held traces of the language of the south. 'You can see we are unarmed. Just take what you want and let us be on our way. We have no wish to do battle with robbers.'

Michael gaped at her. 'It may have escaped your notice, madam, but *you* were shooting at *us*, not the other way around.'

The man who was still perilously close to the tip of Cynric's knife turned angry eyes on the monk. He was the largest of the three, and had a hard-bitten look about him, as if he was used to settling matters with his fists. He wore a peculiar gold-coloured cap that was newer and of a much higher quality than his other clothes. Bartholomew wondered whether he had stolen it, since it seemed at odds with the rest of his clothing.

'That is a lie!' Gold-Hat shouted furiously. 'We heard you coming, so we hid in the undergrowth to wait for you to pass. Then your servants spotted us and immediately drew their weapons.'

'That is *not* what happened!' exclaimed Michael, astonished. 'We were riding along in all innocence, when you started loosing crossbow bolts at us.'

'You fired first,' said the woman firmly. 'We are not robbers.'

'You look like robbers,' said Meadowman bluntly. He inspected their clothes with the uneasy, disparaging curiosity of an untravelled man encountering something with which he was unfamiliar.

'I will not stand here and listen to this—' began Gold-Hat angrily, and rather rashly, given that Cynric's dagger still hovered dangerously close to his neck. The woman silenced him with a wave of her hand – although the prod of Cynric's weapon may also have had something to do with the sudden cessation of furious words – and turned to Michael, addressing him in a controlled and reasonable tone of voice.

'We are respectable folk, who have come to Ely to hire out our services for the harvest. The priory owns a great deal of land and casual labour is always in demand at this time of year. We are not outlaws.' She looked Michael up and down as if she thought the same could not be said for him.

'Do *I* look like the kind of man to rob fellow travellers?' demanded Michael, tapping his chest to indicate his Benedictine habit. 'I am a monk!'

'Why do you imagine that exonerates you?' asked the woman in what seemed to be genuine confusion. 'In my experience, there are few folk more adept at stealing from the poor than men of the Church.'

'That is certainly true,' muttered Cynric, sheathing his weapon. Gold-Hat immediately moved away from him, rubbing his neck where the blade had nicked it and glowering at the Welshman in a way that indicated he would be only too willing to restart the fight.

'No harm has been done,' said Bartholomew quickly, seeing Michael bristle with indignation. Arguing about who was or who was not a robber in the middle of the Fens was a pointless exercise, and the longer they lingered, the greater were the chances that they might all fall victim to a real band of brigands. 'There was a misunderstanding: few people can hide successfully from Cynric, and he mistook your caution for hostile intent. I suggest we acknowledge that we were lucky no one was hurt, and go our separate ways.'

'Very well,' said the woman stiffly. 'I suppose my brothers and I can agree to overlook this incident. As I said, we are honest folk, and only want to go about our lawful business.'

'And what "lawful business" would see you skulking all the way out here?' demanded Michael tartly. 'The priory has no fields to be harvested so far from Ely.'

'We are only a mile or two from the city,' protested Gold-Hat, still rubbing his throat. 'And we are not obliged to explain ourselves to you anyway.'

Michael regarded him coolly. 'Four people in the Fens with a crossbow? It seems to me that you were thinking to fill tonight's cooking pot with one of my Prior's ducks. Or perhaps a fish.'

Gold-Hat pursed his lips, but said nothing, and Bartholomew suspected that Michael was right. There had been no need for people with honest intentions to hide in the undergrowth, and doubtless it had been Michael's Benedictine habit that had prompted them to make themselves scarce. Had the sharp-eyed Cynric not been with them, Bartholomew and Michael probably would have passed by without noticing anything amiss, and the encounter would never have taken place.

'Walk with us to Ely,' the physician suggested pleasantly, determined to avoid any further confrontation. The Fens were full of fish and fowl, and he was sure the Prior would not miss the few that ended up in the stomachs of hungry people. However, he saw that Michael could hardly leave the gypsies where they were, knowing that they fully intended to steal from his monastery.

The woman regarded him soberly for a moment, then nodded reluctant agreement, apparently accepting this was the only way to terminate the encounter without either side losing face. She turned to stride along the causeway, indicating with a nod of her head that her companions were to follow. Bartholomew took the reins of his horse and walked with her, more to ensure she did not antagonise Michael than for the want of further conversation with her. Meanwhile, Cynric placed himself tactfully between the three brothers and Michael, leaving the monk to mutter and grumble with Meadowman at the rear.

'Where are you from?' Bartholomew asked the woman, thinking it would be more pleasant to talk than to stride along in a strained silence. 'Spain?'

She glanced at him, as if trying to determine his motive for asking such a question. 'I was born in Barcelona,' she replied brusquely. 'You will not know it; it is a long way away.'

'I spent a winter there once,' he replied, thinking back to when he had been a student and had travelled much of the continent in the service of his Arab master, learning the skills that would make him a physician. 'It is a pretty place, with a fine cathedral dedicated to St Eulalia.'

She gazed at him in surprise, and then said thoughtfully, 'I see from your robes that you are a physician, so I suppose you may have travelled a little. But, although I was born in Spain, my clan do not stay in one city for long. I have moved from place to place all my life.'

'Do you like that?' Bartholomew asked, certain that he would not. While life at Michaelhouse could be bleak, and Cambridge was often violent and always dirty, he liked having a room that he could call home. He recalled from his travels that he had loved the summer months, when he had wandered through exciting and exotic places, but that the enjoyment had palled considerably once winter had come. Sleeping in the open was no fun when there was snow in the air and hungry wolves howled all night.

She shrugged. 'It is all I know.'

Bartholomew glanced behind him, where her brothers slouched three-abreast more closely than was comfortable. The slack-jawed lad seemed contented enough, but the other two were sullen and brooding, and clearly resented being deprived of their illicit dinner. Behind Cynric, Michael rode with his stout wooden staff clutched firmly in one meaty hand, as though he did not trust the would-be robbers to refrain from further mischief.

As they walked, the final wisps of mist disappeared as the summer sun bathed the marshes in a clean, golden light. The bogs responded by releasing a malodorous stench of baked, rotting vegetation, so strong that it verged on the unbreathable.

'No wonder so many Ely folk complain of agues in July and August,' said Bartholomew, taking a deep breath and coughing as the stinking odour caught in his throat. 'This fetid air must hold all manner of contagions.'

The woman agreed. 'We visit Ely most summers, and I have never known an area reek so.'

'How big is your clan?'

She shot him another suspicious glance. 'There are twenty-one of us, including seven children. Why do you ask?'

'Because I have not set foot outside Cambridge since last summer, and it is good to meet new people,' replied Bartholomew with a smile. 'Did you say your three companions are your brothers?'

She jerked a thumb at the man with the gold hat. 'He is Guido. He will become king soon.'

'King?' asked Bartholomew uncertainly, hoping he was not about to be regaled with details of some treasonous plot. There was always someone declaring he had a better right to the English throne than Edward III, but few lived to press their claims for any length of time.

The woman smiled for the first time. 'It is not a word that translates well. He will become the leader of the clan when our current king dies.'

'You sound as though you think that will not be long.'

She nodded sadly. 'Our uncle is becoming more frail every day, and I do not think he will see the harvest completed. Then Guido will take his place.'

Bartholomew glanced at Guido, thinking that the surly giant who glowered resentfully at him would make no kind of 'king' for anyone, and especially not for a group of itinerants who needed to secure the goodwill of the people they met. Guido seemed belligerent and loutish; Bartholomew imagined the clan would do better under the rule of the more pleasant and intelligent woman who walked at his side.

'The others are Goran and Rosel,' she continued. 'Rosel is slow-witted, but, to my people, that means he is blessed.'

'Does it?' asked Bartholomew, intrigued. 'Why is that?'

'He has dreams sometimes, which we believe is the way the spirits of our ancestors communicate with us. They have chosen him to voice their thoughts, and that makes him special.'

'What is your name?' asked Bartholomew, becoming more interested in the gypsies' customs.

'Eulalia.' She smiled again when she saw the understanding in his face. 'Yes, I was named for the saint in whose city I was born.'

They continued to talk as they neared Ely. Michael's staff was still at the ready, and the three brothers were tense and wary, evidently trusting the monk no more than he did them. Cynric began to relax, though, and leaned back comfortably in his saddle with his eyes almost closed. To anyone who did not know him, he appeared half asleep, but Bartholomew knew he would snap into alertness at the first sign of danger – long before anyone else had anticipated the need for action. Next to him, Meadowman had followed Bartholomew's example and was leading his horse, relieved not to be sitting on it.

Michael took the lead when they reached a shiny, flat expanse of water that had invaded the causeway. His horse objected to putting its feet into the rainbow sheen on its surface, and disliked the sensation of its hoofs sinking into the soft mud. It balked and shied, and only Michael's superior horsemanship kept the party moving.

Finally, they were on firm ground again – or at least ground that was not under water – and the causeway stretched ahead of them, a great black snake of rutted peat that slashed northwards. Ahead of them stood the bridge that controlled access from the south to the Fens' most affluent and powerful city. It was manned by soldiers in the pay of the Prior, whose word was law in the area; they were under orders to admit only desirable visitors to his domain. However, because Ely was surrounded by marshes and waterways, anyone with a boat could easily gain entry, and although guards regularly patrolled, there was little they could do to bar unwanted guests.

As they approached the bridge, Bartholomew had a clear view all around him for the first time since leaving Cambridge. There was little to see to the south, west or east, but to the north lay Ely. The massive cathedral, aptly called 'the ship of the Fens' by local people, rose out of the bogs ahead. Its crenellated towers, distinguished central octagon and elegant pinnacles pierced the skyline, dominating the countryside around it. It looked to Bartholomew to be floating, as if it were not standing on a small island, but was suspended somehow above the meres and the reeds. He had been to Ely several times before, but this first glimpse of the magnificent Norman cathedral never failed to astound him.

'Ely *is* a splendid place,' said Michael, reining in his horse to allow them time to admire the scene in front of them. Ely was his Mother House, and he was justifiably proud of it. 'It is the finest Benedictine cathedral-priory in the country.'

'Peterborough is also splendid,' said Bartholomew, who had been educated there before completing his education at Oxford and then Paris. 'But the surrounding countryside is not so distinctive.'

'Barcelona is more impressive than either of them,' stated Eulalia uncompromisingly.

'Ely's setting is its one sorry feature,' said Michael, ignoring her. 'I cannot imagine why St Etheldreda's followers did not grab her corpse and move it somewhere more conducive to pleasant living. They must have been deranged, wanting to continue to live in a place like this.' He cast a disgusted glance around him.

'It allowed them to live unmolested,' Bartholomew pointed out. 'If the causeway were not here, Ely would be difficult to reach. The monks wanted isolation for their religious meditations, and the Isle of Ely provides just that.'

'But it puts us so far from the King's court and influential institutions like the University in Cambridge,' complained Michael. 'When I first came here, as a young novice, I very nearly turned around and headed for Westminster instead. I was not impressed by the Fens. Then I saw the cathedral, and the wealth of the priory buildings, and I decided to stay. Given that I am now indispensable to the Bishop, I am confident I made the right decision.'

'Why has de Lisle summoned you?' asked Bartholomew, falling back to walk with him while the gypsies moved ahead. He saw that some kind of muttered argument was in progress – evidently, Guido was objecting to the fact that Eulalia had agreed to return to Ely, rather than continue to try to catch something for the cooking pot. 'You have not told me.'

'That is because I do not know myself,' said Michael. 'Two days ago I received a message asking me to visit Ely as soon as possible. The summons sounded important, but not urgent, and I decided to wait until you were ready, so that we could travel together. Then, late last night, I received another message ordering me to come at once.'

'So you packed my bags, hired horses and I was obliged to leave for Ely a day sooner than I had intended,' said Bartholomew, not without rancour: he had not been pleased to return to Michaelhouse after a long night with a querulous patient to learn that the monk had taken control of his travel plans. 'Despite the fact that today is Sunday – our day of rest.'

'It makes no sense for us both to make such a dangerous journey alone,' said Michael, unrepentant. 'Your students were delighted to be rid of you for a few days anyway, and you will have longer to work on that interminable treatise on fevers. You should thank me, not complain.'

'What could be so urgent that the Bishop could not wait a day to see his favourite spy?'

'Agent,' corrected Michael. 'And I cannot imagine what has distressed de Lisle. His second note was almost rude in its summons, and contained none of the fatherly affection he usually pens in missives to me.' He prodded his horse gently with his sandalled heels to urge it forward. 'But he will despair of me ever arriving if we delay much longer.'

With some reluctance, Bartholomew tore his eyes away from the spectacle of the cathedral and followed Michael to where a group of soldiers were dicing in the bridge's gatehouse. One dragged himself to his feet when he heard visitors approaching, although his eyes remained firmly fixed on the far more interesting events that were occur-ring in the gloomy shadows of the lodge.

'Business?' he asked curtly, not looking at them. He wiped his nose on his sleeve and gave a sudden grin as, presum-ably, the dice rolled in his favour.

'We have come to set fire to the cathedral,' said Michael mildly. 'And then I plan to rob the Guildhall of St Mary's and make off with as much gold as I can carry.'

'Enter, then,' said the guard, pushing open the gate that led to the bridge, craning his neck so that he could still watch his game. 'And go in peace.'

'Well, thank you,' said Michael amiably. 'Perhaps when I have finished with the cathedral and the guildhall I shall pay a visit to your own humble hovel and see whether you have any wives, daughters or sisters who might warrant my manly attentions. What is your name?'

'I said you could enter,' snapped the guard, becoming aware that the travellers were lingering when he wanted to return to his game. 'What are you waiting for?'

'Your name,' snapped Michael, with an edge of anger in his voice that suddenly claimed the guard's full attention. Aware that a confrontation was brewing, his comrades aban-doned their sport and emerged into the sunlight to see what was happening. Eulalia and her brothers edged away, unwilling to be part of the argument.

'Stephen,' replied the guard nervously. 'Why?'

'You are worthless,' said Michael coldly. 'You should not be allowed the responsibility of gate duty. I shall recom-mend that my Prior replaces you as soon as possible.'

Stephen sneered insolently. 'The Prior will have more important things on his mind than the likes of me, Brother. Like how he can help Bishop de Lisle evade the hangman's noose.'

'What are you talking about?' demanded Michael testily. 'Do not try to divert me with lies.'

'Not lies, Brother,' replied another guard, who had straw-coloured hair and thick lips that did not cover his protruding front teeth. 'De Lisle stands accused of murdering a man called Glovere. The Bishop claims Glovere killed himself, but Glovere's folk say he is lying. They accused him on Friday – two days ago now.'

Michael stared at them, while Bartholomew saw in Stephen's triumphant, spiteful smile that his comrade was telling the truth. Stephen appeared to be genuinely delighted that a powerful and probably unpopular landlord had been accused of so serious a crime.

'I do not believe you,' said Michael eventually.

Stephen shrugged. 'Believe what you like, Brother. But de Lisle is accused of murdering the steward of a woman he disliked – and that is as true as you are standing there in front of me. The whole town is agog at the news. Go ahead, and see for yourself.'

Once they were through the gate, it was a short ride along the remaining section of causeway to the city of Ely. Michael said little as they hurried past the outlying farmsteads and strip-fields, although Cynric and Meadowman muttered piously to each other about the ruthless and undisciplined behaviour of bishops who considered themselves above the law. Bartholomew sensed Michael's unease, and left the monk alone with his thoughts. The gypsies, who confirmed the soldiers' claim that Ely was indeed buzzing with the news of the Bishop's predicament, slipped away to their camp on the outskirts of the city as soon as they could, the three men clearly relieved to be away from the monk and his companions. Eulalia hesitated before giving Bartholomew a brief smile and darting after them.

Bartholomew glanced at Michael as they drew near the first of the houses. The monk had clearly been appalled to hear that his mentor had been accused of a crime, but Bartholomew noted that he did not seem particularly surprised. The physician knew, as did Michael, that Thomas de Lisle had not been selected for a prestigious post like that of Bishop of Ely by being nice to people, and imagined that a degree of corruption and criminal behaviour was probably a requirement for holding a position of such power. However, most churchmen did not allow themselves to become sullied by accusations of murder, and Bartholomew suspected that the Bishop had miscalculated some aspect of his various plots and machinations. While grateful that *he* would be spending his time in the priory library, well away from the webs weaved by men like de Lisle, the physician was worried that Michael's obligations as de Lisle's agent would lead him into something sinister.

He pushed morbid thoughts from his mind, and looked around him. Ahead, on a low hill, stood the grey mass of the cathedral. At its western end was a vast tower, topped by four crenellated turrets. To either side were smaller turrets, separated by a glorious façade of blank arcading that Bartholomew knew was at least two centuries old. The section to the north-west was clad in a complex system of ropes, planks and scaffolding, and the physician recalled hearing rumours that it was ripe for collapse. The bells were ringing, an urgent jangle of six discordant clappers calling the monks to the office of sext – the daily service that took place before the midday meal.

At the cathedral's central crossing, where the north and south transepts met the nave, was Ely's best-known feature, and one of the most remarkable achievements of its day. Thirty years earlier, the heavy tower erected by the Normans had toppled, taking with it a good part of the chancel. The monks had hastened to repair the damage, and one of their own number had designed an octagonal tower. More famous architects had scoffed at the unusual structure, claiming that it would be too heavy for the foundations. But the gifted monk knew his theories of buttressing and thrust, and the octagon stood firm.

Clustered around the base of the cathedral, and almost insignificant at its mighty stone feet, was the monastery. This was linked to the cathedral by a cloister, and included an infirmary, a massive refectory, dormitories for the monks to sleep in, a chapter house for their meetings, barns, stables, kitchens, and a large house and chapel for the Prior. There was also a handsome guesthouse for the exclusive use of visiting Benedictines, known by the rather sinister name of the Black Hostry. All this was enclosed by a stout wall, except for the part that bordered an ancient and ruinous castle, which was protected by a wooden fence liberally punctuated with sharpened stakes.

At first, the only people Bartholomew saw were distant figures bent over the crops in the fields, but as he and his companions rode closer to the cathedral, the streets became more crowded. Besides the drab homespun of labourers, there were merchants, clad in the richly coloured garments that were the height of fashion in the King's court – hose and gipons of scarlet, amber and blue, while their wives wore the close-cut kirtles that had many prudish clerics running to their pulpits to issue condemnations. Personally, Bartholomew liked the way the dresses showed the slender – or otherwise – figures of the women, and he thought it would be a pity if fashion saw the return of the voluminous garments he recalled from his youth.

For Ely's lay population, the heart of the city was the village green. This grassy swath was bordered by St Mary's Church, the cathedral, and the usual mixture of fine and shabby houses: the merchants' large, timber-framed buildings that boasted ample gardens for growing vegetables; the poorer ones comprising shacks with four walls and a roof of sorts, clinging to each other in dishevelled rows.

The green was busy that Sunday morning, and a band of itinerant musicians played to a large gathering of townsfolk. Drums thumped and pipes fluted cheerfully, interrupted by bursts of laughter as a group of children watched the antics of a brightly clad juggler. A man was selling fruit from a barrel of cold water, shouting that a cool, juicy apple would invigorate whoever ate it, that it was more refreshing than wine. Bartholomew stopped for a moment, enjoying the spectacle of people happy on a summer day.

'Come on, Matt,' Michael grumbled. 'I do not want to linger here while the likes of those guards are spreading malicious rumours about their prelate.'

'At least you now know why de Lisle summoned you so urgently.'

'We have only the claims of those incompetents on the bridge to go on,' said Michael. 'And I do not consider *them* a reliable indication of why my Bishop might need me.'

'I see the crows have begun to gather,' hissed a soft voice from behind them. Bartholomew turned and saw that they were being addressed by a man of middle years, who wore a green tunic with a red hood flung over his shoulders. He had shoes, too, although they were badly made and more to show that he was someone who could afford to buy them than to protect his feet from the muck and stones of the ground. 'When a noble beast lies dying, a carrion bird always stands nearby, waiting for the end.'

'What are you talking about?' snapped Michael irritably. 'There are no crows nesting on this village green – they would find it far too noisy with all the unseemly merry-making. Do none of these folk have work to do? I know it is Sunday, but no one should be at leisure when there are crops to be harvested.'

The sneer on the man's face quickly turned to anger at Michael's words. 'Everyone has been in the fields since long before daybreak, Brother. They deserve a rest before they return to toil under the hot sun until darkness falls. But I am wasting my time explaining this – I cannot imagine *you* know much about rising before dawn.'

'I rise before dawn every day,' replied Michael indignantly. 'I attend prime and I sometimes conduct masses.'

'Prayers and reading,' jeered the man. 'I am talking about *real* work, using hoes and spades and ploughs. But why have you come to Ely, Brother? Is it to help the good Bishop escape this charge of murder? Or have you come to drive the nails into his coffin?'

'You are an insolent fellow,' said Michael, half angry and

half amused at the man's presumption. 'My business here is none of your concern. Who are you, anyway?'

The man effected an elegant bow. 'Richard de Leycestre. I owned land here before the price of bread forced me to sell it to buy food. So, now I am a ploughman, in the employ of the priory.'

'And clearly resentful of the fact,' observed Michael. 'Well, your reduced circumstances are none of my affair, although I know there are many others like you all over the country. But you should not make a habit of slinking up to monks and insulting their Bishop, unless you want to find yourself in a prison. If you are a wise man, you will keep your thoughts to yourself.'

'That is hard to do, when harsh landlords drive men to take their own lives because they cannot feed their families,' said Leycestre bitterly. 'And do not give me your sympathy, Brother, because I am certain *you* cannot recall the last time you were faced with an empty table at mealtimes.'

'Not this morning, certainly,' muttered Bartholomew, aware that Michael had fortified himself for the twenty-mile journey from Cambridge with a substantial breakfast of oatmeal, fruit, bread and some cold pheasant that had been left from the previous evening.

'Who has taken his own life?' demanded Michael. 'Are you talking about this steward – Glovere – whom those rascally guards told me the Bishop is accused of killing? However, they also happened to mention that de Lisle maintains Glovere's death was a suicide – which I am sure we will discover is the case.'

'Not Glovere, although they died similar deaths,' said Leycestre obliquely.

Michael sighed. 'I have no idea what you are talking about.' The way he kicked his sandalled feet into the sides of his horse indicated that he had no wish to find out, either.

'I am talking about Will Haywarde, who killed himself yesterday,' said Leycestre, keeping pace with Michael's horse. 'Like Glovere, Haywarde died in the river.' He waved a hand in the general direction of the murky River Ouse, which meandered its way around the eastern edge of the town.

'I see,' said Michael, uncomprehending, but not inclined to learn more.

'You should not listen to tales spun by the likes of those guards, though,' Leycestre advised. 'I do not believe that Bishop de Lisle has killed anyone. I think Glovere was a suicide, just like the Bishop says.'

'I am sure he will be relieved to know he can count on your support,' said Michael, digging his heels into his horse's flanks a second time to hurry it along. It was no use – Leycestre merely walked faster.

'The gypsies killed Glovere,' said Leycestre. He cast a contemptuous glance to a group of people wearing embroidered tunics similar to Eulalia's, who were watching the musicians on the green. 'They say they came to help with the harvest, but since they arrived houses have been burgled almost every night.'

'Do you have evidence to prove that these travellers are responsible?' asked Bartholomew curiously, thinking that it would be very stupid of the gypsies to indulge themselves in a crime spree as soon as they had arrived. It would be obvious who were the culprits, and his brief encounter with Eulalia told him that she had more sense.

Leycestre rounded on him. 'The fact is that the day after these folk arrived, a house was broken into. And then another and another. Is this *evidence* enough for you?'

Bartholomew did not reply. He suspected he would be unable to convince the man that the spate of burglaries need not necessarily be related to the arrival of the gypsies, and knew it was simpler to blame strangers in a small town than to seek a culprit among long-term acquaintances.

'And while these vagabonds strut openly along our streets, honest men like me are forced to labour like slaves in the Prior's fields,' continued Leycestre bitterly.

'Go back to work, Master Leycestre,' said Michael, making another attempt to leave the malcontent behind. 'And I advise you again: take care whom you approach with your seditious thoughts, or your land might not be all you lose. The King is weary of demands by labourers for more pay.'

'And labourers are weary of making them,' Bartholomew heard Cynric mutter as Leycestre finally abandoned his quarry and went in search of more malleable minds. 'And soon they will not bother to ask, when the answer is always no. So they will take what they want, permission or not.'

'You be careful, too, Cynric,' warned Bartholomew, looking around him uneasily. 'This is a strange city for us, and we do not know who might be a spy. I do not want to spend my time arranging your release from prison because you have voiced your opinions to the wrong people.'

'I am always careful,' replied Cynric confidently. 'But you should heed your own advice, because you are not a man to ignore the injustices we see around us either. I will keep my own counsel, but you must keep yours, too.'

He gave the physician a grin, which broke the mood of unease, and they rode on. Eventually, they reached the Heyrow, where the largest and most magnificent of the merchants' houses were located. It was a wide street, with timber-framed buildings standing in a proud row along the north side and the stalwart wall of the cathedral-priory lining the south side. Two inns stood on the Heyrow – the Lamb was a huge, but shabby, institution with a reputation for excellent ale, while the White Hart was a fashionable establishment with two guest wings and a central hall.

Opposite the White Hart was the entrance to the priory called Steeple Gate, so named for the small spire on the half-finished parish church that was little more than a lean-to against the north wall of the cathedral. The Gate was located near the almonry, where food, and occasionally money, was distributed to the city's poor. A cluster of beggars hovered there, jostling each other to be first to grab whatever the priory deigned to pass their way. Michael dismounted, pushed his way through them and hammered on the door.

Moments later, a pair of unfriendly eyes peered through the grille, and the door was pulled open with distinct reluctance.

'Oh, it is you,' said the dark-featured monk who stood on the other side. His face was soft and decadent, like an Italian banker's, while a sizeable bulge around his middle indicated that he should either do more exercise or eat less at the priory's refectory. 'I thought it would not be long before *you* came to help the Bishop get out of the mess he has made for himself.'

'I was summoned,' said Michael haughtily, pushing open the door and easing his bulk through it. 'And what are you doing answering gates, Brother Robert? I thought almoners were far too important to perform such menial tasks.'

'It is Sunday sext – one of the times when we distribute alms to the poor,' replied Robert, unpleasantly churlish. 'I can hardly do that with the door closed, can I?'

'This is Robert de Sutton, Matt,' said Michael, turning to Bartholomew and indicating the monk with a contemptuous flick of his hand. 'He is a famous man in Ely, because he demands a fee of three pennies from anyone wanting to pray at St Etheldreda's shrine.'

Bartholomew gazed at Robert in disbelief. 'You charge pilgrims to pray? But some of them have no money to give you. They are poor folk, who make their way here on foot because they are desperate, and can think of no other way to improve their lot.'

'Then they do not gain access to St Etheldreda,' said Robert with finality. 'Maintaining an edifice like that is expensive, and pilgrims will wear it out with their kisses and their knees rubbing across its flagstones.'

'Come on, Matt,' said Michael, giving Robert a withering glance. 'We have no time to waste in idle chatter.'

'Wait!' ordered Robert. He nodded to Bartholomew and

the two servants. 'Who are these people? We do not let just anyone inside, you know.'

'They are with me, and that is all you need to know,' said Michael importantly, turning to leave. Robert dared to lay several plump fingers on the expensive fabric of Michael's gown to detain him, which earned him an outraged glare.

'The Bishop's house was burgled a few nights ago,' said Robert, withdrawing his hand hastily. 'The Prior says that no strangers are to be admitted to the monastery unless they are accompanied by one of us.'

Michael gave a hearty sigh at the almoner's slow wits. 'They *are* accompanied by one of us. Me.' He started to walk away, but then turned again. 'What is this about the Bishop being burgled? What was stolen, and when did this occur?'

'It was about ten days ago,' replied the almoner, reluctantly yielding the information. 'Nothing much was stolen. I expect the thieves anticipated gold, but de Lisle is deeply in debt, as you know, and there is little in his house worth taking.'

Michael poked his head back through the gate and gazed at the handsome house on the Heyrow, where the Bishop resided when he was in Ely. De Lisle could have stayed in the cathedral-priory, but the Bishop no more wanted a prior watching his every move than the Prior wanted a bishop loose in his domain. De Lisle's renting of the house on the Heyrow was an arrangement that suited everyone.

'He may be in debt, but he is not impoverished,' said Michael defensively. 'He still owns a considerable amount of property.'

'Well, none of it was in his house when the burglars struck,' argued Robert. 'They took a silver plate and a ring, but nothing else. The rumour is that the gypsies, who are here to help with the harvest, are responsible.'

Bartholomew wanted to point out that the travellers would have to be either very rash or very stupid to start stealing the moment they arrived in the town, but he decided to hold his tongue, since he would soon be a guest in Michael's Mother House. Meanwhile, the monk thrust the reins of his horse at the bemused Cynric, then shoved past Robert to the sacred grounds of the priory beyond.

As always, when he entered Ely Cathedral-Priory's grounds, Bartholomew was astonished at the difference a wall could make. On the city side, Ely was all colour and bustle. The houses were washed in pinks, greens and golds, and the gay clothes of the merchants and their apprentices added brilliance to a scene already rich with life and vitality. People ran and shouted, and horses and carts clattered. The streets possessed thick, soft carpets of manure and spilled straw, and the atmosphere in the heat of midday was a pungent mixture of sewage, the sulphurous stench of the marshes and the sharper smell of unwashed bodies and animal urine.

But the priory side of the wall was a world apart. Monks and lay-brothers were dressed in sober black or brown, and no one hurried. Hands were tucked reverently inside wide sleeves, and heads were bowed as the monks spoke in low voices or were lost in their meditations. Bartholomew knew the kitchens would be alive with noise and movement, as the cooks struggled to prepare meals for more than a hundred hungry men, but in the carefully maintained grounds the scene was peaceful and contemplative.

In front of them, the cathedral rose in mighty splendour, with rank after rank of round-headed arches. Its smooth grey stones formed a stark contrast to the riot of colour in the houses in the Heyrow, and although there was a faint scent of cooking bread from the ovens, the predominant smell was that of newly mown grass.

'I take it you do not like Brother Robert,' said Bartholomew conversationally, as he followed Michael towards the sumptuous house the Prior occupied. Michael had decided to see Bartholomew introduced to the Prior and settled in the library before beginning what promised to be a lengthy interview with de Lisle.

Michael grimaced. 'As almoner, Robert thinks that

dispensing a few scraps of bread to the poor – that would have been destined for the pigs anyway – makes him more important than the rest of us. And he has taken an irrational dislike to the Bishop.'

'And why would that be?' asked Bartholomew, unsurprised. While he did not actively dislike de Lisle, he certainly neither trusted nor admired him. The Bishop was too grand and haughty, and far too vindictive a man for Bartholomew's taste.

'Probably because Robert is devious and petty,' replied Michael dismissively. 'And because he is jealous of anyone better than him – which is most people, as it happens.'

'I see,' said Bartholomew. 'You do not think Robert's dislike is anything to do with the fact that ten years ago Ely's Prior – Alan de Walsingham – was chosen by the monks here to be the Bishop of Ely? Alan was ousted in favour of de Lisle, because de Lisle happened to be at the papal palace at Avignon at the time, and the Pope had taken a fancy to him. So Alan remained a mere prior, while de Lisle was made Bishop.'

'I hardly think it happened like that,' objected Michael testily. 'De Lisle was appointed by the Pope, because the Pope thought he would make a better bishop than Alan. And he was right: de Lisle is an exceptional man.'

'He is also a murderous one, if these rumours are to be believed. You should be careful, Brother: it could be dangerous to ally yourself with de Lisle when he has been accused of committing unforgivable crimes.'

'Those accusations are malicious lies, probably put about by the likes of that Robert,' said Michael.

'I hope you are right. Do you think it is significant that the Bishop was burgled, and then finds himself accused of murder?'

Michael stared at him. 'Should I?'

Bartholomew shrugged. 'Perhaps de Lisle sent one of his spies to discover who had the audacity to steal from him, and then dispensed his own justice to the culprit.'

Michael grimaced. 'You are quite wrong.' He frowned

uneasily. 'At least, I hope so. There is always someone who would like to see a bishop fall from grace, and it is possible that whoever burgled de Lisle's house was looking for something that might do just that. Finding nothing, this accusation of murder was fabricated instead.'

'You do not have any evidence to jump to that sort of conclusion,' said Bartholomew. 'Do not try to make this case into one of your complex University plots, Brother. We are miles from Cambridge here.'

'True,' said Michael with a grin. 'But clerics are just as good at creating webs of lies and intrigue as scholars, you know.'

Bartholomew caught the monk's sleeve and pointed to a tall, silver-haired man who was hurrying towards them with a significant retinue of servants at his heels. 'Here comes de Lisle now. He looks agitated.'

'Of course he is agitated,' said Michael. 'So would you be, if half the town believed you guilty of murder.'

Michael stepped forward as the Bishop approached, smiling a greeting. Bartholomew stood back, to allow Michael to speak to de Lisle in private, although the great man's retinue showed no such consideration. They pushed forward to surround him and his agent, some elbowing others so that they might better see and hear what was happening. There were pages, clerks and retainers, all dressed in the sober livery of the Bishop's household. They changed each time Bartholomew saw them, and there was only one face among the crowd that he recognised – that of de Lisle's steward, Ralph. De Lisle was not an easy man to work for, and it was to Ralph's – and Michael's – credit that they had survived in his service for so long.

De Lisle had aged since Bartholomew had last met him, and the austere, arrogant face that the physician remembered was lined with worry and fatigue. His hair was greyer, too, with no trace of the dark brown of his earlier years. De Lisle was a man in his fifties, with a tall, upright bearing and a confident swagger. His hair was neatly combed around a small tonsure, and his black and white Dominican robes were made of the finest cloth money could buy. Not for de Lisle the sandals worn by most monks and friars; his feet were clad in shoes made from soft calfskin. Several rings – so large they verged on the tasteless – adorned his fingers, and a large cross of solid gold hung around his neck.

'Michael! At last!' exclaimed de Lisle, extending one beringed hand to be kissed. He gave Bartholomew a cool nod of recognition, then his attention returned to Michael. 'Where have you been? I expected you yesterday.'

'I was detained by pressing business in Cambridge,' Michael replied vaguely, giving the proffered ring the most perfunctory of kisses, and indicating that while he might be the Bishop's spy, he was a cut above the sycophantic ranks that clustered around him. Michael was an ambitious man, and it was promises of future promotion and power that induced him to remain in the Bishop's service, not financial necessity.

'I needed you here,' said de Lisle sharply. 'And when I want my people, I expect them to come to me at once.'

'Well, I am here now,' replied Michael, a little tartly. 'How can I be of service?'

De Lisle took a deep breath and when he spoke his words came out in a rush. 'I have been accused of the most heinous of crimes!'

'So I have heard,' said Michael expressionlessly.

De Lisle nodded a dismissal to the servants who crowded around him. Reluctantly, they moved away until only one man was left: Ralph, the steward, who looked rough and unkempt with his lousy hair and unshaven face. It was said that Ralph would do almost anything for his Bishop, and certainly anything for money. He sported a mouth full of black, broken teeth, and even cast-off clothes from a fashionable dresser like de Lisle failed to render him more attractive.

Bartholomew edged away with the others, having no

desire to hear any secrets de Lisle might want to divulge to Michael. He was surprised, and not terribly pleased, to feel Michael's restraining hand on his sleeve. He fought against it, but the monk's grip intensified, and Bartholomew saw he would have to stay unless he wanted to tear his shirt. De Lisle hesitated before beginning his story, glancing uneasily at the physician.

'Do not worry about Matt,' said Michael. 'He is as good a man as you will ever hope to meet, and has been my right hand in many a nasty case.'

'Oh, no!' muttered Bartholomew in dismay. 'I came here to read, not to become embroiled in one of your investigations.'

'Of course, none of these stories about me are true,' said de Lisle, ignoring him. 'They are lies, put about by my enemies to discredit me.'

'Of course,' said Michael smoothly. 'What stories are being told and by whom?'

'Do you know Lady Blanche de Wake?' asked de Lisle. 'She is the widow of the Earl of Lancaster and a close relative of the King. Her estates border mine, and she is constantly trying to steal a field here and a sheep there.'

'Typical of the Lancasters,' announced Michael. 'They are a greedy, grasping brood. But how does she relate to this charge of murder?'

'She has accused me of burning her tenants' houses,' said de Lisle indignantly. 'At Colne.'

'And did you?' asked Michael casually.

Bartholomew glanced uncertainly at his friend, anticipating that de Lisle would not take kindly to such blunt questioning. But the Bishop apparently realised that he needed Michael's good graces, and he bit back what had doubtless been a crisp response.

'Yes and no,' he said, exchanging a guilty glance with his steward. 'Ralph and I had a slight misunderstanding one evening. He took something I said literally, when I was speaking figuratively.'

'Oh,' said Michael flatly. 'One of *those* misunderstandings.'

'But she has no evidence to prove I did it, and Ralph was very careful,' de Lisle continued. 'The case came to the courts, and the King ordered me to pay a fine of ninety shillings. He listened with great care to his kinswoman, but refused to hear my side of the story at all.'

'He would,' said Michael sympathetically. 'He is well known for showing partiality to his favourites. Did you pay the money?'

'I did, even though I can scarce afford such a monstrous fine, but worse was to come. About ten days ago, Lady Blanche's steward died here, in Ely, and she has accused *me* of killing him!'

Michael gazed at his Bishop, and Bartholomew held his breath, half expecting the monk to demand to know whether de Lisle had added murder to the crime of arson. But Michael merely regarded the prelate with sombre green eyes, rubbing the bristles on his chin as he did so.

'And the Bishop had nothing to do with the death, before you ask,' put in Ralph nastily, apparently believing that Michael hesitated only because he was searching for the right words to phrase the question. 'In fact, there is no evidence that Glovere met his end by violence at all. It is obvious to me that he was in his cups and he fell in the river.'

'He drowned, then?' asked Michael. 'Did anyone see him drunk or walking near the water?'

'That is what I want you to find out,' said de Lisle. 'And then, at dawn yesterday, another man was found dead, floating near the hythes in the same river.'

'Haywarde,' muttered Bartholomew, recalling what the malcontent Leycestre had told them. 'A suicide.'

'Quite. But it is only a matter of time before that vile-minded rabble in the city claim that my Bishop killed him, too,' said Ralph indignantly. 'That is why he sent word for you to come *yesterday*.' His stress indicated that he strongly disapproved of Michael's tardiness.

'Your task is to exonerate me from these malicious and wholly untrue charges,' said de Lisle to Michael. 'You must begin immediately; there is not a moment to lose.'

'Very well,' said Michael. 'But is there anything else I should know about this case? Have you and Blanche's steward argued in public at any time? Did any of your household issue threats against the man?'

'Glovere was a vile specimen of humanity,' said de Lisle with distaste. 'I have never known such a misery. All he did was complain; he was even unpopular among Blanche's retinue.'

'That is true,' agreed Ralph. 'He was hated intensely by anyone who knew him. Blanche loathed him, too, and she is only showing concern for him because he is dead.'

'I see,' said Michael. 'But neither of you has answered my question. Was Glovere the subject of threats from the Bishop's household?'

'I doubt we were any more hostile to him than the unfortunates in Blanche's employ who were obliged to work closely with the fellow,' said de Lisle ambiguously.

'So, you did threaten him,' surmised Michael thoughtfully. 'That could prove awkward. What did you say, exactly?'

De Lisle gave a sigh. 'It all happened two weeks ago – four days before his death. I happened to meet Blanche, here in the priory – she stays here when she visits her Ely estates, because it is more comfortable than the shabby manor house Glovere maintained for her. Naturally, I told her that I was disappointed with the King's verdict over the burning of her tenants' houses, and we started to argue.'

'Glovere took part in the disagreement, even though it was none of his affair,' elaborated Ralph. 'He became abusive, and claimed that my Lord Bishop was the kind of man to father children and then abandon the mothers.'

'Really,' said Michael flatly. He kept his voice neutral, as though he did not know for a fact that the Bishop had indeed fathered children, and that Michael and Bartholomew had encountered one of them fairly recently.

'I wonder what gave him that impression.'

'The monks were appalled, both by the foulness of Glovere's language and by his unfounded accusations,' continued Ralph hotly, outraged on de Lisle's behalf. 'The only way my Bishop could shut him up was to threaten him with dire consequences if he did not.'

'So, the entire priory heard you promising him harm,' mused Michael, regarding the prelate gloomily. 'This is not looking good at all.'

'Even the most dim-witted Benedictine must have seen that the threat was made purely to silence him,' said de Lisle testily. 'No sane person could imagine it was issued in earnest.'

'It is not the dim-witted and the sane I am worried about,' said Michael. 'It is the sharp-witted and the *in*sane, who may well use this nasty little incident against you. Not all the monks here like you, and one may well have capitalised on the enmity between you and Blanche to have you accused of this crime.'

'If it *is* a crime,' suggested Bartholomew tentatively. 'Ralph said that Glovere had simply fallen in the river. If that is true, then any threats to kill him are irrelevant.'

'True,' agreed de Lisle approvingly. 'If Michael can prove that the man died in his cups, then there is no way Blanche or anyone else can substantiate this charge of murder.'

'What about the man who died yesterday?' asked Michael. 'Did you quarrel with him, too?'

'I had never heard of him before he was carried dripping to St Mary's Church,' said de Lisle. 'I do not even recall his name. I have no idea what is happening here, but I do not like it at all.'

'Will Haywarde,' said Ralph. 'He was a suicide, but you know how people let their imaginations run away with them. Mark my words, it will not be long before one of these silly monks puts two with two to get six.'

'What about the theft from your house ten days ago?' asked Michael of de Lisle. 'Do you have any idea what happened there?'

De Lisle did not seem particularly interested. 'The rumour is that the gypsies did that – the burglaries started in the city the day after they arrived, you see.'

'If everyone is so convinced of their guilt, then why are they tolerated here?' asked Bartholomew curiously. 'Why are they not driven away?'

'Because we need them for the harvest,' explained de Lisle. 'They undertake the heaviest and least popular work, and it is in no one's interests to send them away now. People will just have to lock their windows and doors, and be a little more careful until they have gone.'

'What was stolen from you, exactly?' pressed Michael. 'Were any documents missing?'

De Lisle smiled wanly at him. 'I know what you are thinking: the burglary was political, rather than a case of random theft. But, fortunately for me, you are wrong. I had a number of sensitive documents on my desk, but these were ignored. I lost a silver plate and a ring – things that an opportunistic burglar would snatch because they are saleable and easy to carry.'

Michael rubbed his chin thoughtfully as he considered the information.

'You will prove me innocent of any involvement in these unfortunate deaths,' instructed de Lisle when the monk did not reply. 'And do it quickly. I cannot leave Ely until this is settled and I have business elsewhere that needs attending.'

Michael nodded. 'Very well. I—' But he was speaking to thin air. The Bishop had swung around and was stalking across the courtyard towards the cathedral, with his sycophants strewn out behind him as they hurried to catch up.

'And this is the man to whom you have tied your ambitions?' asked Bartholomew doubtfully. 'He does not seem to be the kind of person who would remember favours done. In fact, I imagine he would expect loyalty, but then slit your throat when you have outlived your usefulness to him.'

'You have not seen him in his best light,' said Michael

defensively. 'He is a good man at heart. He was one of few bishops in the country who visited the sick during the Death, and he does pen a remarkable sermon.'

'It occurs to me that he might be qualified to give one on his personal experience of murder,' said Bartholomew nervously. 'I hope you know that he may not be innocent of this crime, Brother. He denies it, but so do most killers, and I do not see him offering any good reasons as to why he could *not* have killed this Glovere.'

'That is what I must find out,' said Michael, turning to steer Bartholomew towards the Prior's house. 'I do not imagine it will take me long. I shall inspect the corpses of these drowned men this afternoon, assuming they are still above ground, and will lay the matter to rest once and for all.'

'I suppose you want me to go with you,' said Bartholomew heavily. 'To see what clues might be found on the bodies.'

'No,' said Michael, opening the door that led to the Prior's private garden and pushing his friend inside. 'I want to introduce you to Prior Alan, and then I want you to spend your few days here reading about fevers. That is why you came, after all.'

Bartholomew gazed at him in astonishment. 'You do not need the help of a medical man?'

Michael shook his head. 'I have watched you often enough to manage perfectly well alone.'

Bartholomew regarded him askance. 'I am coming with you.'

The monk gave a humourless smile. 'Thank you, Matt. I only wish you were as forthcoming in *all* the murders I am obliged to investigate. But this is a simple matter, and I do not need you.'

'You do not want me involved,' said Bartholomew, trying to read what the monk was thinking. 'You are as suspicious of de Lisle's protestations of innocence as I am, and you think you will protect me by not allowing me to help.'

'Nonsense, Matt,' said Michael brusquely. 'You travelled

to Ely to indulge yourself in your unhealthy fascination with diseases, not to traipse around the city's inns to learn how much these dead men had to drink before they stumbled into the river. You do your work and I shall do mine.'

'I *am* coming with you,' repeated Bartholomew, this time with determination. 'You might need a good friend.'

Michael's smile became gentle. 'You were right the first time, Matt; I do not want you involved in this. It may lead to places you would not like, and it is better that I investigate alone.'

'It is better that you investigate with me,' said Bartholomew firmly. 'I am not afraid of de Lisle. The worst that could happen is that I lose his favour and he tries to make my life uncomfortable at Michaelhouse.'

'No, Matt,' said Michael softly. 'Discrediting you is not the worst he could do at all.'

CHAPTER 2

THE PRIOR OF THE BENEDICTINE MONASTERY AT ELY WAS an important man, and his living quarters reflected that fact. Set aside for his personal use was a handsome house with its own chapel and kitchen, while at right angles to it was the Prior's Great Hall, a sumptuous building with a lofty-ceilinged room that was almost as large as the one that served the entire community. The house itself was roofed with baked red tiles imported from the north country, and its plaster walls were neat and clean. Real glass in the windows allowed the light to filter into the rooms where the great man worked, slept and ate, although these were thrown open so that a cooling breeze whispered through the documents on the tables and billowed among the gorgeous hangings on the walls.

Originally, Ely had been an abbey, with an abbot to rule and a prior as his second-in-command. But when the post of Bishop of Ely had been created by Henry I, the position of abbot had been abolished – an abbot and a bishop in the same diocese would have been impractical. The Bishop then ran the diocese, while the Prior controlled the monastery. Without an abbot, Ely became a 'cathedral-priory', with the all-important 'cathedral' denoting the fact that although the foundation boasted no abbot, it was a cut above the average priory.

Prior Alan de Walsingham was sitting in his solar, a light and airy room that afforded a pleasant view over his private gardens. The sweet scent of ripening apples and newly mown grass drifted through the windows, along with the sounds of the priory – the chanting of a psalm in the chapter house, the distant voices of lay-brothers hoeing the vineyards, the clatter of pots from the kitchens and the coos of birds roosting in the dovecote.

Bartholomew had seen Alan officiating at masses when he had visited Ely on previous occasions, but he had never met him in person. From afar, Alan had given an impression of frailty, and his voice had barely been audible in the massive vaults of the cathedral. But as he glanced up from his work, Bartholomew could see that Alan was not frail at all. He was a slight man in his mid-fifties with a head of thick, grey hair and the kind of wiry strength that came from clambering over scaffolding and supervising the building work for which he was famous. He was generally regarded as one of the most talented architects in the country, and had personally overseen the raising of the cathedral's new tower and the splendid Lady Chapel. It was not easy keeping a band of masons and their apprentices in order, and that Alan had done so over a period spanning more than thirty years said a good deal about the strength of his character, as well as his body.

'Ah, Michael,' said Alan, presenting his ring for Michael to kiss. 'I imagine you are here because Thomas de Lisle has landed himself in trouble again?'

'He says Lady Blanche de Wake is responsible for these accusations,' replied Michael, making another perfunctory obeisance. He was never keen on acts of subservience, even to the Prior of his own monastery. 'He assures me that he is innocent, and has ordered me to prove it.'

Alan regarded Michael worriedly. 'I sincerely hope you did not accept such a commission. You have a reputation for tenacity, and if you explore this matter too closely, you will almost certainly discover that de Lisle did have a hand in this steward's death.'

'*You* believe the Bishop is guilty of murder?' blurted Bartholomew, alarmed that even the Prior should consider the accusations a matter of fact. Michael dug him in the ribs with an elbow, but it was too late. The Prior had already fixed Bartholomew with keen blue eyes.

'I know harsh words were exchanged between Glovere and de Lisle, and I know that de Lisle is not a man to allow such insults to pass unpunished. If de Lisle decided that the world would be a better place without Glovere in it, then it is not inconceivable that Glovere's days would have been numbered.' Alan's expression was sombre.

'But he is a bishop,' said Bartholomew, ignoring Michael's warning prods and persisting in trying to learn why everyone was so willing to believe de Lisle capable of the most violent of crimes. 'I do not think that bishops merrily indulge themselves in murdering people they do not like.'

'No,' agreed Alan. 'They pay someone else to do it for them. But you seem to believe these accusations are unjust – which is encouraging. I do not like de Lisle personally, but no monk wants to see a man of the Church in this kind of trouble, because it reflects badly on the rest of us. I should be delighted to see him exonerated. Do you have information that might help?'

Bartholomew shook his head uncomfortably. 'Forgive me, Father Prior. I should not have spoken. I was merely surprised that even you believe a high-ranking churchman could be capable of murder.'

Alan's smile was gentle. 'You must forgive my manners, too. Michael told me to expect you this week: you are Doctor Bartholomew from Michaelhouse, who is writing a treatise on fevers.'

'A treatise that will shake Christendom to its very foundations,' said Michael dryly. 'A more fascinating and thought-provoking work you could not hope to match – and I should know, because I have been treated to lengthy extracts from it over the last three years. The details regarding different types of phlegm defy description.'

'Really?' said Alan warily. 'I hope there are no sacrilegious sections in this work. Medical men are occasionally driven to present their views on matters best left to monastics, and I do not want my priory associated with wild and heretical theories.'

Michael grinned. 'There is a physician in Salerno who claims that God's removal of Adam's rib to make Eve would be a fatal operation and therefore impossible.'

Alan was visibly shocked. 'Lord help us!' he exclaimed, crossing himself. He gazed at Bartholomew. 'If you want to write that sort of seditious nonsense, please do not do it here. This is a holy place, where every thought and deed is dedicated to God.'

'Even murder?' muttered Bartholomew.

Alan did not hear him. 'I am lucky in my own physician. Brother Henry de Wykes is a god-fearing and sensible fellow, who would never offend our holy Church. *He* harbours no irreverent notions.'

The priory's physician sounded dull and tedious, and Bartholomew was surprised when Michael smiled fondly. 'Henry was kind to me when I was a novice. You will like him, Matt.'

'Michael tells me that you wish to read books in Ely that are unavailable in Cambridge,' said Alan to Bartholomew. 'However, I should warn you that while you are here you will almost certainly hear de Lisle criticised by my monks. He is not popular in the priory.'

'Why not?' asked Bartholomew. He immediately wished he had not spoken, suspecting that a good part of their antipathy was due to the fact that the Pope had appointed de Lisle as Bishop of Ely when the monks themselves had elected Alan.

Alan looked modest. 'No particular reason,' he said, 'although his personality does not help. He is arrogant and condescending, and that kind of attitude does not win friends. He is no better and no worse than most bishops I know, although I wish one of my monks had not taken it upon himself to throw in his lot quite so fully with such a man.'

He turned his piercing gaze on Michael, who shuffled his feet uncomfortably. 'I have been in de Lisle's service for five years, and during that time I have done nothing more than keep the University in order on his behalf,' said Michael defensively. 'It is important that *someone* is working for the Church there.'

'I agree,' said Alan softly. 'And you have done well. But now de Lisle has asked you to exonerate him from a charge of murder: that has nothing to do with the Church or your beloved University. I will not prevent you from acting as his agent, Michael -- although as your Prior, I could -- but I do not want my monastery associated with any fall from grace de Lisle might take.'

'De Lisle will not fall—' began Michael.

Alan raised a hand that was calloused and scarred from years of working with stone. 'I know you hope your fortunes will rise by aligning yourself with de Lisle, and your success may well reflect favourably on our Order. But the Bishop might equally prove to be a dangerous ally. Be vigilant, and do not allow him to drag you down with him, should you fail to prove him innocent.'

'I shall do my best,' said Michael stiffly.

'It is a pity you responded to his summons in the first place,' Alan went on with a sigh. 'It would have been better if you had avoided the issue altogether, and remained safely in Cambridge.'

'But I did not know what he wanted,' objected Michael. 'All I received were two messages, each instructing me to come immediately.'

Alan did not seem impressed. 'Really, Michael! I expected more guile from you! You should have guessed that there was something amiss when de Lisle carefully omitted to mention the reason for these abrupt summonses.'

'Well, it is done now, and I shall have to do the best I can,' said Michael, a little sulky at the reprimand. 'If he is innocent, I shall prove it for him.'

'I suppose stranger things have come to pass,' said Alan enigmatically. He turned to Bartholomew with a smile. 'But let us talk of more pleasant things. What do you hope to find in our meagre library, Doctor?'

'It is not meagre,' said Bartholomew enthusiastically. 'It has all the works of Avicenna, as well as Serapion's *Brevarium*, Pietro d'Abano's fascinating *Conciliaton*, Isaac Iudeaus's *Liber Febrium*—'

'A lot of books on medicine,' interrupted Michael, seeing that his friend was quite prepared to present Alan with a complete list of the priory's medical texts. 'But Lord, it is hot today! Do you have any bona cervisia, Father, to slake a burning thirst?'

Alan rang a small silver bell that was on his table. 'I wondered how long it would be before you asked for a jug of our famous ale.' Before he had finished speaking, a servant entered. 'Summon the Brother Hosteller,' he instructed. He smiled at Bartholomew. 'The priory makes four kinds of beer, and bona cervisia is the best of them.'

After a few moments, during which time Michael waxed lyrical over the delights of Ely's ale compared to other brews he had sampled all over East Anglia, the door opened a second time. The most distinguishing feature of the man who entered was his shock of grey hair, which had been sculpted into a bob around his tonsure. Bartholomew thought it made him look like an elderly page-boy. Around his neck he wore a cross made from a cheap metal, rather than the gold or silver favoured by most Benedictines of his elevated station. Bartholomew wondered whether the Brother Hosteller was one of those men who wore their poverty like badges, openly and ostentatiously, for all to see and admire.

The Brother Hosteller's small eyes glittered with hostility when he spotted Michael reclining in the Prior's best chair, and Bartholomew saw a similar expression cross Michael's face. He supposed that Robert the almoner was not the only Ely monk with whom Michael had crossed swords.

'William de Bordeleys,' said Michael heavily, looking the monk up and down as he might a pile of dung. 'You have been promoted, have you?'

'I am now the Brother Hosteller,' replied William grandly.

'I am responsible for both guesthouses and the monks' dormitory. It is an important post, and I am answerable only to Prior Alan and Sub-Prior Thomas. So, if you do not like it, you can go back to that stinking hell you seem to prefer to your own monastery.'

'Michael will be with us for a few days,' said Alan quickly. Bartholomew sensed he was adept at preventing arguments among his subordinates. 'He will stay in the Black Hostry, where all our visiting Benedictines are quartered. I wanted Doctor Bartholomew to sleep in the Outer Hostry. However, we are anticipating a visit from Lady Blanche de Wake soon, and her retinue will require every bed we have there, so he cannot.'

'But Blanche has accused de Lisle of murder,' said Michael in surprise. 'She cannot stay here!'

'It may prove awkward,' admitted Alan. 'But we have no choice. We do not want to anger the King by refusing hospitality to his kinswoman.'

'Since de Lisle prefers to stay in his own house when he is in Ely, he and Blanche may not even meet,' said William. He spoke wistfully, as though he hoped they would, so that he could amuse himself by observing the consequences.

'In a town the size of Ely?' asked Michael in disbelief. 'Do not be ridiculous, man! Of course they will meet.'

'Then you should advise your Bishop to control himself,' said William tartly. 'He will do himself no favours if he storms up to her and calls her names—'

'When is she due to arrive?' asked Alan. 'Soon?'

'Probably not for some days,' replied William, a little annoyed by the interruption, 'although you stipulated that we must be ready for her at any time. She says she wishes to be in the city when de Lisle is hanged, so she will not be long.'

Alan turned to Bartholomew before Michael could respond to William's provocative statements. 'Because of Blanche's impending visit I am afraid the only available bed is in the infirmary with our physician. Will that be acceptable? It is near the library.'

'I shall see to it,' said William, without waiting for Bartholomew's answer. He regarded Michael coolly. 'And I imagine *he* will be wanting a jug of bona cervisia, given that the sun is shining and he always claims a thirst if the day is warm – or if it is cold, come to that.'

'He does indeed,' said Michael, meeting the hostile gaze with a glare of his own. It was William who looked away first. The hosteller glanced at Alan, who gave a nod of dismissal, and stalked out.

Michael regarded Alan with questioning eyebrows.

'William was the most senior monk when the last incumbent passed away,' said Alan defensively. 'He was not my choice as hosteller, either, but it was his right and I had to appoint him.'

'He wants to be Prior when you die,' said Michael bluntly. 'He is ambitious.'

Bartholomew stifled a laugh. Michael had no small ambition himself.

'I must be very wicked for God to give me men like William *and* Robert in my flock,' sighed Alan. He glanced at Michael in a way that indicated he might as well add *him* to the list of undesirables, too.

'Perhaps God does not like the designs of your buildings,' suggested Michael rudely. 'That octagon is a peculiar thing; I have never seen anything quite like it.'

'That is the point,' said Alan, offended. 'It is unique.'

'It is a masterpiece,' said Bartholomew warmly. 'You must have a remarkable understanding of the properties of force and thrust to invent such a fabulous—'

'William is devious,' interrupted Michael, still agitated by his exchange with the hosteller. 'And Robert is a snivelling liar, who is mean with the alms intended for the poor.'

'They are not popular,' agreed Alan, reluctantly giving his attention to Michael. It was clear he would rather discuss his octagon. Bartholomew did not blame him. 'The other monks do not like them much.'

'Your sub-prior, Thomas de Stokton, is hardly destined for a place in heaven, either,' remarked Michael, raising his bulk from the chair and strolling to the window, where there was a bowl of nuts. He took a handful and slapped them into his mouth. 'He is a selfish glutton, who would benefit from a few weeks away from the dining table.'

Bartholomew glanced at Michael, whose own girth was by no means modest. He imagined the sub-prior must be of almighty proportions indeed to attract that kind of criticism from the monk.

'We finished painting the octagon last week,' said Alan, smiling hopefully at Bartholomew and eager to talk about his life's work to an appreciative listener. 'What do you think of it?'

'Very fine,' said Michael flatly, although Bartholomew knew he had not yet been inside the cathedral to see it. The monk rifled carefully through the Prior's bowl, selecting the best nuts with a concentration and attention to detail he would never lavish on any aspect of architecture.

Alan ignored him, and turned to Bartholomew. 'Do you know the story of the octagon? The original cathedral tower was too heavy for its foundations, and it collapsed in 1322. Something lighter and smaller was required, but it had to be a design that was both impressive and elegant. The octagon was my solution.'

'What will you do now it is finished?' asked Michael, jaws working vigorously as he rooted in the bowl. 'Will you shore up the foundations on the unstable north-west transept? I saw the scaffolding around that when we arrived. It looks as though it is ready to tumble down at any moment.'

'But it is not,' said Alan. 'It is more stable than it appears, although I do not mind people believing it is about to collapse.'

'Why?' asked Bartholomew, failing to see the advantage in making people think their cathedral was about to fall around their ears.

Alan was wistful. 'Because then they might ask me to

rebuild it. But as things stand, I am now obliged to devote my energy and resources to completing the parish church. Have you seen it? It is that uninteresting half-built lean-to structure against the north wall of the cathedral. The parishioners have been demanding that we finish it soon, so that they have a place of their own, and no longer have to use the cathedral. They do not like saying their prayers in the nave while we are in the chancel.'

There was a perfunctory knock on the door and William entered, followed by a servant who carried a heavy pewter jug and three goblets on a tray. The jug was filled to the brim with frothing ale, and the sweet, rich scent of it had Michael leaning forward in eager anticipation, nuts forgotten. William poured it, then infuriated Michael by deliberately presenting him with the cup that was only half full. Smiling maliciously, the hosteller gave Alan a brief nod and left again, closing the door behind him.

'Bona cervisia,' said Michael, taking a deep draught of the ale and sighing in appreciation, foam clinging to his upper lip. 'A drink fit for the angels.'

'Only ones with very strong stomachs,' said Bartholomew, wincing at the power of the brew in his cup. 'I could render patients insensible for amputations with a goblet of this.'

'It is wasted on you,' said Michael critically. 'You are too used to the watery muck served at Michaelhouse to be able to savour a fine brew like this.'

'I cannot help but worry about what de Lisle has asked you to do,' said Alan, taking his own cup and walking to the window, where he stood looking in dismay at his depleted nut bowl. 'I am sure it will not end well.' He turned to fix Bartholomew with his intense blue eyes. 'Can you not persuade Michael to return to Cambridge, Doctor? You can say he has marsh fever. There is a lot of that about at this time of year, and the Bishop would never suspect that Michael had removed himself for his own safety.'

'We could do that,' acknowledged Michael, draining his cup and refilling it – this time to the brim. 'But de Lisle is not the only one with a cunning mind. I have a little cleverness myself.'

'You do,' agreed Alan. 'And your success in solving the most perplexing of crimes is known in Ely, as well as in Cambridge. But that worries me, too. De Lisle knows you are clever and he knows you are likely to uncover the truth.'

'So?' asked Michael, draining his cup a second time. 'I do not understand your point.'

'I mean that if de Lisle knows you are likely to reveal him as a murderer – if he is guilty – then why did he send for you? Why not appoint a lesser investigator instead – one of his own creatures?'

Michael raised his eyebrows. 'Because he *is* innocent, and he wants me to prove it?'

Alan remained uneasy. 'Perhaps. But the murder of this servant is not the only thing that has happened to the Bishop recently. There was a burglary, too.'

'He was a victim,' Michael pointed out. 'No one has suggested *he* is the thief!'

Alan inclined his head in acknowledgement, although the anxious expression did not fade from his eyes. He was about to continue, when there was another knock, and William entered a third time.

'I thought you should know, Father Prior, that a messenger has just arrived. He informs me that Lady Blanche is a short distance from Ely, and will be here within the hour. She says she wants to ensure that the murder of her steward is investigated in a proper and thorough manner.' He shot Michael an unpleasant glance, as though he thought the matter well beyond Michael's capabilities.

'Damn it all!' muttered Michael. 'This case will be difficult enough to solve without the likes of that woman demanding to know my every move and trying to pervert the course of justice.'

While Alan de Walsingham and William hastened to make ready for the great lady's arrival, Bartholomew and Michael were left to their own devices. The physician wanted to go to the library, to begin his reading, but it seemed that the Prior and hosteller were not the only ones engaged in the preparations for Lady Blanche: Brother Symon, who was in charge of the books, was also unavailable, and sent a message to Bartholomew informing him that he would have to wait until the following day.

'But I only need him to unlock the door,' Bartholomew objected to the messenger, a cheerful novice with freckles, whom Michael introduced as John de Bukton. 'I do not require him to fetch books or carry them to a table. I can do that myself.'

Bukton looked apologetic. 'Symon does not like people reading his books. He would rather see them on the shelves, and considers their removal for education anathema.'

'That is not a good characteristic in a librarian,' Bartholomew pointed out, ignoring Michael's snigger of amusement. 'Books were written to be read.'

'That is not what Symon believes,' said Bukton with a grin. 'And there is another thing: he does not know what books we own anyway. He classifies them according to their size, so that they look nice on his shelves, but if you were to ask him for a specific volume, he could not tell you where it was unless you also told him how big it was.'

Bartholomew sighed. 'I was looking forward to a few quiet days among books. Now I learn that the librarian is a man who would rather his collection was never used, and that my friend is to investigate a murder for which his Bishop stands accused. What kind of place is this?'

Bukton was offended by the criticism. 'You have just caught us on a bad day.'

'I should say!' muttered Bartholomew, watching the young man speed away as he went to help his elders ready the Outer Hostry for Lady Blanche and her followers. He turned to Michael. 'No wonder you like Cambridge, Brother. It is a haven of peace compared to this.'

'As he said, you are not seeing us at our best,' replied

Michael, also unwilling to see his priory regarded in an unfavourable light. 'But I can take you to the infirmary, where you can settle yourself for your stay, and then we can go to view the body of the man whom my Bishop murdered.'

'Is *accused* of murdering,' corrected Bartholomew uneasily. 'You should watch what you say, Brother. One slip like that in front of the wrong people might see de Lisle condemned.'

Michael said nothing, and Bartholomew shot him a side-long glance, alarmed that Michael, like so many others, had accepted as fact the Bishop's guilt. The monk's task, there-fore, would not be to prove de Lisle's innocence, but to ensure that he escaped the charges. The physician felt a knot of anxiety forming in the pit of his stomach, aware that his friend was about to begin something that could lead him on to dangerous ground. Michael was a clever man, and his inventively cunning mind often surprised Bar-tholomew, but, nevertheless, the physician wished neither of them had come to Ely in the first place.

'We have been here for an hour, and we are already embroiled in something sinister,' he grumbled, following Michael along the well-kept path that led from the Prior's House in the direction of the infirmary.

Michael turned to face him, his expression sombre. 'I would not have let you come had I known what de Lisle wanted me to do. But it is not too late. Leave now, and take Cynric and Meadowman with you. You will be back in Cambridge before nightfall.'

Bartholomew shook his head. 'The horses are tired and Cynric is already showing Meadowman the taverns. It will be far too late by the time I find them. Besides, how can I leave you here alone?'

'I am in my own priory, Matt. I am surrounded by friends.'

'Hardly!' snorted Bartholomew in disgust. 'Prior Alan seems decent enough, but the almoner does not like you and neither does the hosteller. You are not among friends here.'

Michael smiled and slapped him on the shoulders. 'Then allow me to introduce you to Henry de Wykes, the priory's physician. He is a good and honest man, and there is hardly a soul in the town who does not like him. He is a little immodest, perhaps, but that is no great fault when you compare him to the rest of my brethren here.'

The hospital was a substantial building adjoining the Black Hostry. It boasted a large, airy central hall, its own chapel, and a pair of chambers for treating patients and preparing medicines. Another two rooms at the opposite end of the hall served as living quarters for the infirmarian and his assistants. The library occupied the rooms on the floor above. The building overlooked gardens on two sides, the cathedral on the third, and, rather disconcertingly for a place dedicated to the sick, the monks' graveyard on the fourth.

There were two entrances to the infirmary. One was via a covered walkway known as the Dark Cloister, which allowed the monks to reach it from the chapter house without exposing themselves to the elements; the other was through a small door in the north wall, which was reached by walking through the monks' cemetery. Michael chose the latter, strolling along a path that was almost obliterated by long meadow grass, and opening a small, round-headed gate that led directly into the hospital's main hall.

Bartholomew followed him inside and looked around, admiring the carvings on the arches that had been executed by Norman masons two hundred years before, and the dark strength of the oak beams that supported the ceiling. The floor comprised smooth slabs of stone that had been scrubbed almost white, while large windows allowed the light to flood into the sickroom. A row of beds ran down each of the walls, so that about twenty men could be accommodated at a time. However, the priory's infirmary was not only a place for monks who were ill; it was also home to elderly brethren who were too ancient or infirm to look after themselves. Bartholomew glanced down the hall, and saw that there were currently five such inmates, each tucked neatly under covers that were crisp and clean.

Michael walked between the rows of beds, to where voices could be heard in one of the chambers that stood at the far end of the hall. He knocked briskly on a door that was half closed, before pushing it open. An older monk was evidently teaching two novices some aspect of medicine, because he was holding a flask of urine to the light, and was in the process of matching its colour to examples given in Theophilus's *De Urinis*. The monk was too engrossed in his explanation to notice that his charges were bored and restless.

'I hope that is wine you are regarding with such loving attention, Brother Henry,' called Michael, leaning nonchalantly against the door frame.

'Michael!' exclaimed Henry in delight, immediately abandoning his teaching. He was a sturdy man in his fifties, who was burned a deep nut-brown by the sun. His forearms were sinewy and knotted, indicating that the large hospital garden they had passed on their way in, with its neat rows of herbs and vegetables, was probably tended by him personally and that he was no stranger to hard work. He had twinkling blue eyes, wiry grey hair and a large gap between his two front teeth.

'Good morning,' said Michael, taking the proffered hand and shaking it warmly. 'Why are you keeping these young fellows inside, when the rest of the priory is busy making ready for the impending arrival of Lady Blanche?'

'He wanted to show us this urine,' said one of the novices resentfully. He was a sulky-faced youth, with an unprepossessing smattering of white-headed spots around his mouth. 'Its colour is unusual, apparently.'

'It is,' said Bartholomew, who had noticed the orange hue from across the room. 'If you were to use Theophilus's guidelines, you would diagnose whoever produced this as having a disease of the kidneys.'

'Precisely!' exclaimed Henry eagerly. He turned to his

charges, who remained unimpressed. 'You see? Urine is a valuable tool for us physicians. It tells us a great deal about our patients and should never be disregarded or forgotten.'

'But I do not want to be a physician,' objected the youth. 'I am only working here because Prior Alan ordered me to.'

'Then you should not have tied the cockerel and the cat together, Julian,' said the other youngster, regarding the spotty-faced lad with cool dislike. 'It was a vile thing to do. I cannot imagine what possessed you.'

Julian's sigh suggested he was bored by the discussion. He placed his elbows on the table, plumped his pox-ravaged face into his hands, and stared ahead of him in silent disgruntlement.

'I thought we had agreed to say no more about that unfortunate incident, Welles,' said Henry admonishingly to the other lad. Unlike Julian, Welles had a pleasant face, with fair curls and a mouth that looked far too ready for laughter to belong to a novice. 'Julian has apologised to the Prior for committing an act of such cruelty, and we are all hoping he learns some compassion by working with the sick.'

Julian said nothing, but cast Henry a glance so full of malice that Bartholomew saw the physician would have his work cut out for him if he thought he could instil a modicum of kindness in a youth who was clearly one of those to whom the suffering of others meant little. It was clever of Alan to send Julian to the hospital, where he might be moved by the plight of the inmates, but Bartholomew suspected the plan would not work. He did not usually jump to such rapid conclusions, but there was something hard and cruel about Julian that was obvious and unattractive, even to strangers.

'What particular ailment would you predict, judging from the colour of this urine?' asked Henry of Bartholomew, bringing the topic of conversation back to medicine.

'I would not make a diagnosis on the basis of the urine alone,' said Bartholomew. 'I would want to speak to the patient—'

'To make his horoscope,' agreed Henry, nodding eagerly.

'No,' replied Bartholomew, a little tartly. He did not believe that the stars told him much about a person's state of health, and he certainly did not base his diagnoses on the movements of the celestial bodies, although many physicians did precisely that and charged handsomely for the privilege. 'I would ask him whether he had experienced pain in his stomach or back, what he had eaten recently, whether he drank water from the river or ale that was cloudy—'

'What does ale or the river have to do with his urine?' asked Welles, intrigued.

'In this case, probably nothing,' said Bartholomew, holding the flask near his nose to smell it. The two novices exchanged a look of disgust. 'I would say, however, that whoever produced this should not be quite so greedy with the asparagus, and that next time he should use a different dye to prove his point. Theophilus said that redness in the urine is caused by blood, but this is orange and was caused by the addition of some kind of plant extract.'

Henry gave a shout of excited laughter, and clapped his hands in delight. 'Excellent! Excellent! That is indeed my urine, and I did add a little saffron to make it a different hue. I wanted to show these boys that the colour of urine is vital knowledge for a physician. I see now I should have used a little pig's blood instead. I am not usually so care- less, but none of us is perfect.'

'Did you really eat asparagus?' asked Michael distastefully. 'Why?'

Henry laughed again. 'Not everyone loathes vegetables, Michael. And your friend is right: asparagus does produce a distinctive odour in the urine. You should have smelled the latrines this morning! He would have known at once what we all ate last night.'

'There is very little about urine that Matt does not know,' said Michael drolly. 'I knew you would like him. And that is just as well, because he will be staying here with you for the next week, since Blanche is going to hog all the beds in the priory guesthouse.'

'Lady Blanche is generous to the priory, so we are obliged to give her the entire Outer Hostry when she visits,' Henry explained. 'But this time I stand to benefit – by having a fellow physician to entertain. I am sure I shall teach him a great deal.'

'Oh, good!' muttered Julian facetiously to Welles. 'Now there will be endless discussions about piss and how to puncture pustules every time we move.'

'I am glad *I* do not have to sleep here, like you do,' replied Welles in an undertone. 'Listening to them would give me nightmares.'

'Matt is from Michaelhouse,' said Michael to Henry, pretending not to hear their complaints. 'He has some strange notions about medicine, so you should find a lot to talk about.'

'We will,' said Henry, grasping Bartholomew's hand in welcome. He turned to Michael. 'But what brings you to Ely, my friend? Have you come to rest from your onerous duties in Cambridge?'

'Unfortunately not,' said Michael. 'De Lisle sent for me because he is accused of murder.'

Henry's brown hands flew to his mouth in horror. 'No! Do not tell me that you have agreed to investigate on his behalf? Oh, Michael! How could you do such a thing?'

'I am his agent,' replied Michael irritably, growing tired of hearing this. 'I have no choice but to do what he asks.'

'I admire de Lisle,' said Henry sincerely. 'He was not afraid to visit the sick during the Great Pestilence, and he gives fabulous sermons – but powerful men have powerful enemies. Let de Lisle clear his own name. He is innocent, so it should not be difficult.'

'You believe de Lisle is innocent?' asked Bartholomew, wondering why he was so surprised to hear this from a monk.

'Of course,' said Henry, as though it were obvious. 'He is proud and arrogant, but he has a gentle heart. This charge has been invented to harm him by someone who is strong and resourceful, and Michael should not become embroiled in it. De Lisle can always petition for the Archbishop's support if matters grow too hot for him, but Michael has no such luxury. Do not accept this commission, Brother. Go home.'

Michael smiled gently. 'I cannot. But I am no longer the youth you protected when I first came to Ely, Henry. I can look after myself, and I have good friends in you and Matt.'

Shaking his head in disapproval, Henry turned to his apprentices. 'Tidy this room, and then you can join your friends preparing to receive Lady Blanche. Meanwhile, Michael and I have much to talk about. It has been months since I last saw him.'

'Free at last!' mumbled Julian, leaping to his feet. 'These duties are like a sentence of death. Who wants to spend all day wiping up old men's drool, and helping them to the garderobe every few moments? I would rather work in the kitchens.'

'I am sure you would,' said Henry tartly. 'There are dead animals and sharp knives in the kitchens, and I imagine it would suit you very well. But you have been committed to my care to learn how to care for the sick, and I shall do everything in my power to ensure that you do.'

Julian cast him another dark look, and then began to help Welles with the tidying, although Bartholomew noted that he left the more unpleasant messes for his classmate.

'Julian does not seem to appreciate what you are trying to teach him,' he remarked, as he followed Henry through the infirmary towards the other end of the hall, where the physician had a small bedchamber that also served as an office.

Henry agreed. 'I fear he will never be a physician. I do not think there is a single shred of compassion or kindness in him. Alan gave him to me as a last resort: if he fails here, he will be released from the priory, but I do not think that will be a good thing.'

'Why not?' asked Michael. 'It seems to me that he has no business being in a monastery.'

'I do not like to think of a cruel and vicious lad like that loose in the town,' said Henry. 'At least while he is here we can control him. He would commit all manner of harm without someone like me to watch him.'

He gave a cheerful wave to an old man who occupied one of the beds. The inmate waved back, revealing a battery of pink gums. The other four were either asleep or did not seem to be aware of anything around them. All were ancient, some perhaps as much as ninety years, and Bartholomew supposed that life as monks had been kind to them. It was not a bad way to end their days, although he personally did not relish the prospect of lying in a bed while he slowly lost all his faculties.

'Roger is deaf,' explained Henry as they walked. 'Two of the others are blind, and most have lost their wits. They are our permanent residents. Usually, we have half a dozen monks who are recovering from being bled, but the Prior has suspended bleeding for this month.'

'Why is that?' asked Bartholomew. 'Is it because he is aware of new evidence from French and Italian medical faculties that indicates bleeding is not always healthy?'

'Certainly not,' said Henry stiffly, indicating that he disapproved of such notions. 'It is because Blanche is coming, and we will be too busy to have monks resting in the infirmary. But *I* believe bleeding is a very healthy thing to do. You only need to compare the monks, who are bled regularly, to the townsfolk, who are not, to see the difference.'

'That is because the monks' food is better than that of the townsfolk,' argued Bartholomew. 'And they probably have more sleep, better beds, cleaner water—'

Henry grinned in delight, and slapped Bartholomew's shoulders. 'You are quite wrong, but I can see we shall enjoy some lively debates on the subject. It is always refreshing to converse with another medical man. And I anticipate we shall learn a great deal from each other.'

'I am sure you will,' said Michael. 'But I do not want to be present when you do it. Julian and Welles are right: you

can keep your pustules and your flasks of urine to yourselves!'

Michael found it impossible to drag Bartholomew away from
Henry once the two physicians had started to talk. Seeing
he would be unable to prise them apart until they had been
granted at least some time to exchange opinions, he left
them to their own devices, while he wandered around the
priory renewing acquaintances and listening to the latest
gossip. When the afternoon faded to early evening, and the
sun was more saffron than the hot silver-gold of midday, he
brought his socialising to an end and turned his mind to
the Bishop's problem.

Daylight in August lasted from about five-thirty in the
morning until around eight o'clock at night, and Michael
sensed there was probably a little more than two hours of
good light left in which to inspect bodies. Since he had no
desire to do it in the dark, he hurried towards the infirmary, intending to remove Bartholomew from his discussion with Henry and complete the unpleasant task of
corpse-inspecting as soon as possible. Briefly, he entertained
the notion of going alone, but, despite his blustering confidence when he had spoken to Bartholomew earlier that day,
he knew he would miss vital clues that would be obvious at
a mere glance to his friend. Reluctant though he was to
involve him in the enquiry, Michael knew he needed the
physician's help.

'Perhaps I should come, too,' offered Henry uneasily. 'I
have little experience with corpses – as a physician I prefer
to deal with the living – but I may be able to help.'

'No,' said Michael immediately. 'I do not want both my
friends involved in this. And anyway, although you know
nothing about corpses, Matt is very good with them. He
peels away their secrets as one might the layers of an onion.'

'Hardly,' began Bartholomew in protest, not liking the
way Michael made him sound so sinister. Although he had
discovered that he and Henry disagreed about many aspects

of medicine, he liked the man and wanted to make a good impression on him. This description of his skill with corpses would be unlikely to raise him in anyone's estimation.

'Come on,' said Michael, taking his arm and steering him towards the door. 'The sooner we examine this body, the sooner we shall have this case resolved and the Bishop's name cleared.'

'Then God go with you,' said Henry, sketching a benediction at him. 'If I cannot persuade you to leave Ely, then I urge you to prove de Lisle's innocence quickly, so that we can all be done with this unpleasant situation.'

Promising to bring Bartholomew back as soon as they had finished with the body of Glovere, Michael set off to the Bone House, where Prior Alan had said the corpse was being stored until Lady Blanche came to bury it.

'We have been told that de Lisle was accused of this murder two days ago,' said Bartholomew, walking with Michael along the path that wound through the monks' cemetery towards the cathedral. 'But when did the victim die? I thought the Bishop said ten days, but that cannot be right – if he died that long ago, he would have been buried by now, and we would not be going to look at his body.'

'Luckily for us, Glovere is still above ground, or we would have found ourselves obliged to do a little midnight digging.'

'We did that once, and I have no intention of doing it again,' said Bartholomew shortly. 'But why so long between Glovere's death and this accusation against de Lisle?'

'Lady Blanche was at her other estates near Huntingdon, and it took some time for the news to reach her about her servant's death. When she did hear what had happened, she sent a missive to Alan, informing him that de Lisle was responsible for Glovere's death. It arrived on Friday.'

'So, de Lisle summoned you the day he was accused – Friday – and then sent a second summons the following day,' said Bartholomew, trying to understand the order of events as they had occurred.

Michael nodded. 'It was the second death by drowning – Haywarde, on Saturday morning – that really alarmed him. He is afraid Blanche will accuse him of that, too, and while the good citizens of Ely may overlook one suspicious death, they will certainly not disregard two of them.'

'What was Glovere doing here without Blanche anyway?' asked Bartholomew. 'If he was her steward, why was he not with her in Huntingdon?'

'I asked Prior Alan that when you were gossiping about boils to Henry. Apparently, Glovere was employed to protect Blanche's Ely estates – she owns farms nearby, and he oversaw them for her. By all accounts, he was a proficient steward, but not likeable, and she was always relieved to be away from him when she left Ely.'

'Ten days is a long time for a corpse to be above ground in this hot weather,' said Bartholomew disapprovingly. 'Why was he not buried a week ago – before Blanche made her accusation?'

'Apparently, no one was willing to pay. His requiem mass is Blanche's responsibility, so I suppose she will provide the necessary funds when she arrives.'

'It does not cost much to dig a hole.' Bartholomew was still disgusted. 'It would have been better to bury him immediately, rather than leave him lying around until Blanche deigns to arrive. Supposing she refuses to pay? Then what happens?'

Michael waved a dismissive hand, uninterested in the logistics of burial. He felt it was fortunate that Glovere was still above ground, given the circumstances, and was hopeful that Bartholomew would be able to produce a verdict of death by drowning while drunk, and thus put an end to Blanche's machinations. He thought about what he had learned from talking to his brethren that afternoon.

'According to Alan, Glovere was universally disliked because he was a gossip. When he and de Lisle had that very public argument two weeks ago, it did wonders for de Lisle's popularity – everyone was delighted to see Glovere on the receiving end of some eloquently vicious insults. Now it seems that very same disagreement is leading people to believe de Lisle guilty of murder.'

'It is not just the public row, Brother,' Bartholomew pointed out. 'Even *you* think he may have done it, and you were not even a witness to this squabble.'

'Whatever,' said Michael impatiently. 'But suffice to say that Glovere was loathed by all, and no one is prepared to pay a few pennies for a hole for his corpse.'

'Because he told tales?' asked Bartholomew doubtfully. 'I can see that would make him unpopular, but I cannot see that it would lead to such heartlessness regarding his mortal remains.'

'Apparently he was a liar, too, whose uncontrolled tongue caused a lot of unnecessary heartache. Alan told me that his malicious stories resulted in a young woman committing suicide last winter.'

'How?'

'He started rumours that she was with child, which led her intended husband to marry someone else. It transpired that Glovere's accusations were wholly unfounded, and were based on the fact that he had seen the girl sewing clothes for a baby. The clothes were for her sister's child.'

Bartholomew regarded the monk uncertainly. 'But if Glovere was a known liar, why did this husband-to-be believe him in the first place?'

'Because he was a foolish man with too much pride and too little trust. It was one of those silly affairs that would have righted itself, given time. Unfortunately, the intended groom acted immediately, and Glovere's spite thus brought about a tragedy. But the city has not forgotten the story and Glovere remains friendless and graveless.'

'And the body is in a church somewhere?' asked Bartholomew, wishing he had not agreed to help Michael after all. The last ten days had been gloriously hot, and a corpse of that age was not going to be pleasant company.

'Lord, no!' said Michael. 'No sane parish priest would

agree to hosting a corpse for that length of time in the summer. Glovere resides in the Bone House.'

'What is a bone house?' asked Bartholomew dubiously. 'It sounds horrible.'

Michael started to explain. 'When the foundations of the Lady Chapel and the Church of the Holy Cross were laid, we kept unearthing bones. The whole area to the north of the cathedral – where these buildings were being raised – is the lay cemetery, you see.'

'I hope plague victims were not buried there,' said Bartholomew immediately. 'I do not think it will be safe to unearth those bodies for a long time yet.'

'Most were found thirty years ago. But there were so many remains that it was decided a bone house should be erected to store them until they could be reburied.'

'Why not inter them straight away? Why keep them above ground at all?'

'Because we did not want to lay them to rest only to dig them up later when more foundations were needed. It is better to stack them safely, then bury them with due ceremony when we are sure they will not be disturbed again. Look – there it is.'

Michael pointed to a two-storeyed lean-to building near the north wall of the priory, between the Steeple Gate and the sacristy. It was sturdily built, but was little more than a long house with one or two very small windows and a thick, heavy door. It was evidently anticipated that the occupants would not require much in the way of daylight, because the shutters had been painted firmly closed, giving the whole building a forlorn, secretive appearance that did not encourage visitors. For some peculiar reason, the Bone House had also been provided with a chimney, although Bartholomew could not see why. He could not imagine anyone – living, at least – tarrying inside for long enough to warrant the lighting of a fire.

'It is obvious it was built for laymen, and not monks,' said Bartholomew, critically eyeing its crude lines and unprepossessing appearance. 'It is hardly the grandest edifice in the area.'

'It is a storeroom, Matt,' said Michael irritably. 'It is not intended to be a final resting place.'

'I hope I do not end up in a place like this,' said Bartholomew, as Michael took a hefty key from his scrip and fitted it to the lock on the door. 'My skull at one end of a room and my feet at the other, all mixed with someone else's limbs, and my ribs still buried in the churchyard.'

'I shall see what I can do to prevent it,' said Michael, evidently anticipating that he would last a good deal longer than his friend. 'You should approve of Glovere being stored here, Matt. It means he is well away from living people.'

'But he is also out of sight and therefore out of mind. Perhaps the Prior is hoping that he will turn into bones if left long enough.'

'Good God!' exclaimed Michael, leaping backwards as he opened the door. 'What a stench!'

'I am not surprised the monks do not want this in their cathedral,' said Bartholomew, recoiling, despite the fact that he had prepared himself for the olfactory onslaught. 'Such a vile smell cannot be good for the health of the living.'

'It does not say much about the health of the dead, either,' muttered Michael. 'I have never known a corpse to stink so.'

He took a step forward, but then hesitated when he became aware that flies buzzed within. Pulling a face, Michael produced from his scrip a huge pomander stuffed with lavender and cloves, placed it over the lower part of his face, and indicated that Bartholomew was to precede him inside. Bartholomew obliged, taking care to breathe through his nose. It was a popular belief that inhaling through the mouth was the best solution for dealing with foul odours, but Bartholomew had learned that did not work for especially strong smells: he ended up being able to taste the foulness as well as smell it.

It was dark inside the Bone House, and the two scholars

waited a few moments for their eyes to adapt to the gloom. Someone had placed a lamp on a shelf to one side, and as Michael lit it, Bartholomew looked around curiously.

A row of shelves in front of him was stacked with grinning skulls, most with missing teeth that lent them rakish expressions. To his left was a pile of long bones – arms and legs – in various states of repair, while to his right lay a heap of broken coffins. Some revealed a glimmer of white inside, while others had apparently been emptied of their contents. An old barrel near one shuttered window was filled almost to the brim with bone fragments – flat pieces of cranium, and tiny carpals and tarsals that had once been living hands and feet.

'I suppose this must be him,' said Michael, stepping forward to a human shape that lay on the bare stone of the floor. It had been covered with a filthy piece of sacking, but that was all. Glovere had no coffin, no shroud, and no one had performed even the most basic cleansing of his body. The sacking was too small for its purpose: a bristly stack of hair protruded from one end, and a pair of legs from the other. Michael grabbed the material and pulled it away, backing off quickly when the movement aroused a swarm of buzzing flies.

'This is horrible!' he choked through his pomander. 'Why are we doing this?'

'Because you promised your Bishop you would,' replied Bartholomew, flapping at the insects that circled his head as he knelt next to the bloated features of the dead man.

In the summer months, most corpses were laid in the ground within a day or two of their deaths, and it was unusual to see one that had been left for so long. The face was dark, with a blackish-green sheen about it, and was strangely mottled. The eyes were dull and opaque, half open beneath discoloured lids, while the mouth looked as though it had been stretched, and gaped open in a lopsided way that Bartholomew had never observed in the living.

He studied Glovere for a moment before beginning his

examination, trying to see the man who had lived, rather than the corpse that lay mouldering in front of him. He saw a fellow in his middle thirties who had been well nourished, and who had sported a head of brown hair and a patchy beard. His skin was puckered in places, as though his complexion had been spoiled by a pox at some point. His clothes were dirty and stained, but of decent quality.

'He drowned,' pronounced Michael with authority. He reached out a tentative hand, and plucked something from Glovere's hair. 'See? River weed.'

'There is more of it in his clothes, too,' said Bartholomew, pointing. 'And that smear of mud on his cheek doubtless comes from the river bank. His bloated features also indicate that he spent some time in water, along with the fact that you can see a stain on the floor, where some of it leaked from him and then dried.'

'Nasty,' said Michael, backing away quickly when he saw his sandalled feet were placed squarely in the middle of one such stain. 'But, if he drowned, then the Bishop is innocent of murder. Come away, Matt. It is unpleasant in here with all these flies. I will ascertain from the inns in the city that Glovere was in his cups, and we will have an end to the matter.'

'He fell in the river while drunk and then drowned,' mused Bartholomew, turning Glovere's head this way and that as he examined the neck for signs of injury. 'It is possible, but we should be absolutely sure, if you want to lay this affair to rest once and for all.'

'Even I can see there are no marks of violence on the body,' said Michael, too far away to tell anything of the kind. 'I appreciate your meticulousness, Matt, but do not feel obliged to linger here on my account. Cover him. I will see you outside.'

Flapping vigorously at the winged creatures that swarmed around him, the monk was gone, leaving Bartholomew alone in the Bone House. The physician did not mind; he had found Michael's commentary distracting in any case. He moved the lantern to a better position for a thorough examination, and began to remove the dead man's clothes.

Just when he was beginning to think that Michael was right, and that Glovere had simply drowned – although whether by accident or deliberately was impossible to say – Bartholomew's careful exploration of every inch of mottled flesh paid off. His probing fingers encountered a wound at the base of Glovere's skull, just above the hairline. Bartholomew turned the body and studied it, noting that the injury was a narrow slit about the length of a thumbnail, and that it appeared to go deep. If it had bled, then any stains had been washed away by the river. Because it was hidden by Glovere's hair, Bartholomew realised that he might well have missed it, had he not been in the habit of inspecting the heads of corpses very closely when examining them for Michael.

He took one of the metal probes he carried in his medicine bag, and put one end into the hole to test its depth. He was startled when it disappeared for almost half the length of a finger before encountering the solid resistance of bone. He sat back on his heels and considered.

He knew that damage to the whitish-coloured cord that ran from the brain down the spine was serious, and it seemed that the injury to Glovere's neck was sufficiently deep to have punctured it. Since Glovere was unlikely to have inflicted such a wound on himself, the only explanation was that someone else had done it. It was very precisely centred, and the physician doubted that it could have happened by chance. He rubbed his chin thoughtfully, and then called out to Michael. The monk entered the Bone House reluctantly, but listened to what Bartholomew had to say without complaining, flies forgotten.

'Lord, Matt!' he breathed when the physician had finished. 'Glovere was murdered after all? And worse, someone committed the crime with considerable care, so that his death would appear to be an accident?'

Bartholomew nodded. 'It is impossible for me to say what happened, but it seems reasonable to assume that a blade of some kind was inserted into Glovere – perhaps while he lay drunk and insensible on the river bank – and then he was pushed into the water so that it would look as though he had drowned.'

'And would he have drowned? Or did this tiny wound end his life?'

'Probably the latter,' said Bartholomew. 'Injuries to this part of the neck often result in the loss of the ability to breathe. I do not think he drowned. If I lean hard on his chest, the water that emerges from his mouth is clear – it contains none of the bubbles that I would expect if he had breathed water.'

Michael shuddered. 'You really do know some unpleasant things, Matt. Thank God I am a theologian, and do not have to acquaint myself with how to squeeze water from dead men and where to stab them so it will not show.' He gazed at Bartholomew in sudden alarm. 'Would de Lisle know about these things?'

'What do you think? You know him better than I do.'

Michael was silent for a while, but then said slowly, 'I imagine he might. Cunning ways to commit a murder and then conceal the evidence are no secret to men in positions of power.'

'Then you will find it difficult to prove that de Lisle did not kill Glovere. Shall we look at the body of the other fellow who died? It was his death that resulted in de Lisle sending you a second summons, after all.'

'As yet, no one has accused de Lisle of killing anyone but Glovere,' said Michael. 'And I do not want to put ideas into people's heads by going straight from Glovere's body to Haywarde's, so we will examine him tomorrow. But this is all very cold-blooded, is it not? I can imagine de Lisle striking out in anger and perhaps knocking a man into the river, but I do not see him leaning over his victim and deliberately slicing through his neck.'

'So, you think the manner of Glovere's death means that de Lisle is innocent?'

Michael's eyes were large and round in the dim light from the lamp. 'I did not say that.' He gave a huge sigh. 'Damn it all, Matt! I was hoping this would be a straightforward case of Glovere taking a tumble into the river, and Blanche using the death to discredit her enemy. Now we are faced with a cunning killer. I wish we had never left Cambridge!'

'So do I,' said Bartholomew fervently.

There was nothing more they could do in the Bone House, so Bartholomew re-dressed Glovere, and covered him again with the piece of sacking. Michael watched him, now oblivious to the flies that formed a thick cloud in the air around his head as he thought about the implications of their findings. Then they walked out into the golden light of a summer evening. The bells were ringing for vespers, and the sounds of people walking and riding along the Heyrow on the other side of the priory wall were welcome reminders of normal life.

'What will you do?' asked Bartholomew, as he watched the monk lock the Bone House door. He could not imagine why the monks felt the need for such security, when no one in his right mind would have willingly entered the grim little house of the dead.

'I have no idea,' replied Michael gloomily. 'What do you recommend? Shall I visit de Lisle and ask to see any sharp knives he might own? Shall I enquire whether he knows that a man can be dispatched with a small jab to the neck or that there are ways of killing a man that all but defy detection?'

'Not if you do not want to find yourself with a cut neck in the river,' advised Bartholomew. 'I would concentrate on Glovere, if I were you. It seems that de Lisle was not the only person who did not like him. Perhaps the relatives of the woman who committed suicide killed him.'

'True,' said Michael, cheering up a little. 'I shall spend a few hours in the taverns tonight, asking questions of the local folk, and we shall see where that leads us. And there are also the gypsies to consider. Richard de Leycestre, who sidled up to us with his malicious tales when we arrived in Ely, seemed to think that they, and not de Lisle, were to blame for Glovere's death.'

'Only because the travellers are outsiders,' said Bartholomew. 'It is easy to pick on strangers and hold them responsible for inexplicable happenings.'

Michael studied him with an amused expression. 'You seem very defensive of these people, Matt. It would not be because you are stricken by the charms of Mistress Eulalia, would it?'

'It would not,' said Bartholomew tartly. 'It is because I do not like the way crowds are so willing to turn on people who cannot protect themselves. Leycestre said the gypsies were responsible for the burglaries, too, but he had no evidence.'

'No evidence other than the fact that the burglaries started the moment the gypsies arrived in the city,' said Michael. 'It seems that Glovere died a few days later. Perhaps he saw them committing their thefts and was killed to ensure his silence. That trick with the knife in the neck is the kind of thing a gypsy might know.'

'It is the kind of thing anyone might know. Soldiers, butchers, courtiers, medical men, scholars who might have read it – anyone, really.'

'Well, our enquiries will tell us whether your faith in these gypsies is justified,' said Michael, unruffled by his friend's annoyance. 'If they are guilty, I will find out.'

Suddenly, the serene stillness of the priory was shattered by the sound of running footsteps. Monks emerged from all sorts of nooks and crannies, aiming for the Steeple Gate. Robert the almoner was there, jostling the bob-haired William and the surly Julian to reach it first, the pending office of vespers clearly forgotten. There was an unseemly tussle for the handle, during which Robert used the bulge of his stomach to force his rivals out of the way. Eventually, he had cleared sufficient space to drag open the door and turn an ingratiating smile on the people who waited on the other side.

Michael chuckled softly as the almoner effected a sweeping bow that was so deep he almost toppled. Hosteller William had managed to elbow his way through the crowd of grovelling monastics to stand next to him; his bow was less deep but far more elegant than Robert's. Bartholomew and Michael stood well back as a cavalcade entered the priory grounds, content to watch those monks who enjoyed indulging in servile behaviour take reins from ungrateful courtiers and offer haughty maids-in-waiting cool cups of wine. That high-ranking clerics like Robert and William were prepared to submit themselves to such indignities told its own story: here was Lady Blanche de Wake and her retinue, arriving in Ely to see the Bishop convicted of the murder of their steward.

Bartholomew had never seen Lady Blanche before, despite her fame in the area, and he studied the King's kinswoman with interest. She was a short, dour-faced specimen in her early fifties. Her clothes were made of the finest cloth, but she clearly allowed none of the latest fashions of the court to influence what she wore. Her voluminous skirts were gathered uncomfortably under her large bosom, and were rather too short, so that a pair of stout calves poked from under them. Her wimple was viciously starched, and red lines around her face showed where it had chafed. There was a determined look in her pale blue eyes, and the strength of her character was evident in the way her bristly chin jutted out in front of her.

Her retinue was almost as impressive as the Bishop's. She was followed not by clerks and monks, but by grooms and squires and tiring women. However, while their mistress may have abandoned fashion thirty years before, her retinue certainly had not, and Bartholomew had seldom seen such a gaudily dressed crowd. All wore the flowing cote-hardies and kirtles that were currently popular, and sported the shoes with the peculiar pointed toes and thin soles that were so impractical for walking. One woman uttered an unmannerly screech of delight that was directed at Michael, and with a sinking heart, Bartholomew recognised the dark features and expressionless eyes of Tysilia de Apsley.

Tysilia was a close relative of Bishop de Lisle, and had been lodged at a convent near Cambridge for much of the previous year, but had been removed when the nuns had failed to prevent her from becoming pregnant for the third time. She was one of the least intelligent people Bartholomew had ever met, and certainly one of the most licentious. She was not a person whom he liked, nor one with whom he wished to associate in any way. He gave a groan when she started to come towards them, while Michael diplomatically arranged his fat features into a smile of welcome. Unfortunately, her energetic progress was hampered by the fact that her riding cloak caught in her stirrup as she started running, and for some moments she was a mess of trailing sleeves, long skirts, loose straps and agitated horse. William rushed to her assistance, and was rewarded with a leering smile and some unnecessarily revealing flashes of long white legs that had him blushing furiously

'Lord help us, Matt,' Michael muttered through clenched teeth, watching the scene with rank disapproval. 'What is *she* doing in Blanche's retinue, when Blanche and de Lisle are such bitter enemies? And anyway, I thought de Lisle had foisted Tysilia on the lepers at Barnwell Hospital, so that they could cure whatever ails her mind.'

'There is no cure for her,' replied Bartholomew in an undertone. 'She was born stupid, and no amount of "healing" will ever change that.'

Michael gave a soft laugh. 'And this was the woman you thought was a criminal mastermind earlier this year!'

Bartholomew grimaced. 'I was wrong. But I was right about one thing: her appalling lack of wits makes her dangerous to know. She should be locked away, but not with lepers.'

'Why? Because she might catch the contagion?'

'Because she puts them at risk. On one occasion, she seized someone in an amorous embrace that relieved him of three fingers and part of his nose, while on another she set the chapel alight by putting the eternal flame under the wooden altar.'

'Why did she do that?' asked Michael with appalled curiosity.

'To keep it warm during the night, apparently. After that, the lepers decided that they would rather starve than accept the Bishop's money to care for her. I wondered what he had done with her when they ordered her to leave. But here she is, overcome with delight at meeting her old friend Michael.'

'Brother Martin!' exclaimed Tysilia joyfully, flinging herself into the monk's ample arms. 'And Doctor Butcher the surgeon, too! You both came here to visit me!'

'We did not know you would be here,' said Michael, hastily disengaging himself before Blanche and her retinue could assume he was one of Tysilia's many former lovers. Bartholomew ducked behind the monk's sizeable bulk, before he could be treated to a similar display of affection.

'My uncle, Thomas de Lisle, suggested that I spend time with Blanche,' said Tysilia, smiling as vacantly as ever. 'I am now her ward. I did not like being with the lepers, anyway. Their faces kept falling off, so it was difficult for me to remember who was who.'

As she spoke, Blanche broke away from the obsequious grovelling of Robert and William and approached Michael, curious about the man who was acquainted with her charge.

'De Lisle lied to me,' said Blanche without preamble, regarding the monk as though he were responsible. 'He told me that Tysilia was a sweet and gentle child, who could benefit from a motherly hand. She is not, and he can have her back again.'

Tysilia's face fell. 'But I have had such fun with you and all your charming young courtiers!'

'I assure you I know,' said Blanche grimly. She turned to Michael. 'You are the Bishop's agent. Are you here to help him escape from the charge of murder I have brought against him?'

'I am here to see justice done,' replied Michael. 'I do not want to see an innocent man convicted of a crime any more than I want to see a murder go unpunished. We men of God have strong views on such matters.'

'Not in my experience,' retorted Blanche. 'Your Bishop is a wicked man. I know he killed poor Glovere, and I am here to ensure that he pays the price. And he can have this little whore back again, too. She has seduced virtually every man on my estates, so she will be looking for new pastures soon, anyway.'

'But I am not ready to leave yet!' wailed Tysilia in dismay. She was about to add details, but Blanche took her arm and hurried her away, leaving Bartholomew and Michael bemused by the encounter.

'Did you know that de Lisle had managed to foist his "niece" on Blanche?' asked Bartholomew. 'No wonder she loathes him! Looking after Tysilia would not be easy.'

'I did not know,' said Michael, smiling wickedly. 'Although it was a clever ploy on his part. By giving Blanche a kinswoman to watch over, he is indicating that he trusts her and that he wishes a truce. However, Tysilia is capable of driving anyone insane, and I imagine he derived a good deal of amusement from the fact that she would lead Blanche a merry dance.'

'Prior Alan!' Blanche's strident voice echoed across the courtyard and the hum of conversation between her followers and the fussing monks faltered into silence. Alan had emerged from his lodgings, and was hurrying towards her, a slight, wiry man converging on a squat, dumpy woman.

'Lady Blanche,' Alan replied breathlessly, as he reached her. 'Welcome to Ely.'

She inclined her head to acknowledge his greeting. 'I have come on grave business,' she announced in tones loud enough to have been heard in the marketplace. 'I accuse Thomas de Lisle, Bishop of Ely, of the most heinous of crimes: the murder of my steward, Master Glovere.'

Alan nodded. 'As a churchman, de Lisle is subject to canon, not secular, law, and this matter will be investigated accordingly. When I heard news of your imminent arrival, I dispatched a messenger to fetch the Bishop of Coventry and Lichfield – Roger de Northburgh – to examine the case. As luck would have it, he is currently visiting Cambridge, and I expect him here in two or three days.'

'Northburgh?' breathed Michael in horror. 'Alan has engaged Roger de *Northburgh* for this?'

'What is wrong with him?' whispered Bartholomew, puzzled by Michael's reaction. 'It would not be right for de Lisle to be examined by someone who is not at least a bishop.'

'I know that,' snapped Michael testily. 'But Northburgh is ninety years old, if he is a day, and is only in Cambridge because he has been pestering the canons of St John's Hospital to give him tonics and remedies to prevent his impending death. Like many churchmen who see their end looming large, he would rather stay in this world than experience what might be in store for him in the next.'

'Then look on the bright side: you will not have a rival investigator breathing down your neck. Northburgh will spend his time with Brother Henry.'

'True. I suppose Alan chose him because he is the only bishop within reach at such short notice. But no one in his right mind would bide by any conclusions drawn by Northburgh.'

'No one in his right mind would bide by any conclusions drawn by Northburgh,' announced Blanche to Alan, although she was too far away to have heard the muttered conversation between Bartholomew and Michael. 'I knew this priory would not select a suitable man, so I have appointed my own agent – a man whom the King and the Black Prince recommended to me.'

'Who?' asked Alan uneasily. 'I am not sure it is wise to have too many investigations proceeding simultaneously. De Lisle has engaged Brother Michael to look into the matter, too.'

Blanche shot Michael a disparaging glance. 'You mean de Lisle has instructed his creature to hide the evidence and allow him to weasel out of the noose he has knotted for himself.'

'He ordered me to uncover the truth,' said Michael indignantly, although as far as Bartholomew recalled de Lisle had done no such thing. Michael had been charged to prove de Lisle innocent, which was not necessarily the same. 'I am no one's creature, madam, and I am only interested in the facts.'

Blanche turned back to Alan. 'I have ordered Robert Stretton to come to my aid. He, too, will arrive in a day or two.'

Michael gave a sigh of relief. 'Thank God for small mercies!' he whispered to Bartholomew. 'Stretton is no more capable of investigating a murder than Northburgh. The royal family like him, but their confidence is misplaced.'

'Why?' asked Bartholomew uneasily, feeling that Blanche was not a fool, and that she would not have appointed Stretton if he were a total incompetent.

'He is virtually illiterate for a start,' said Michael. 'He was collated to the canonry of St Cross at Lincoln Cathedral earlier this year, and has ambitions to be a bishop. I doubt he will ever succeed, given his intellectual shortcomings.'

'I should hope not, if he cannot read. The days of prelates who do not know one end of a bible from another are mostly over.'

'I imagine the Black Prince encouraged Blanche to appoint Stretton.' Michael smiled complacently. 'But she will soon learn not to take advice from relatives, no matter how well meaning. Stretton will present *me* with no problems.'

'This investigation promises to be a farce,' remarked

Bartholomew. 'The principal for the Church is an aged malingerer; the principal for Blanche is a man who cannot read; and the principal for the Bishop is you, who has been charged to "find de Lisle innocent". I can already see the way this will end.'

'Yes,' agreed Michael comfortably. 'Matters *are* looking up. But now that Blanche's accusation is official, we have work to do. Come with me to the taverns, and we will see what more we can learn about Glovere that may help to exonerate my Bishop from the charge of murder.'

Traipsing around every tavern in Ely that evening was not Bartholomew's idea of fun, although Michael seemed to enjoy it. Scholars were not permitted to enter inns in Cambridge: such places were obvious breeding grounds for fights between students and townsfolk, so any drinking in the town needed to be conducted with a degree of discretion. No such restrictions applied in Ely, however, and Bartholomew and Michael could wander openly into any establishment they chose.

Ely's taverns varied enormously. Some were large and prosperous, like the Lamb and the Bell, while others were little more than a bench outside a hovel where the occupants brewed and sold their own beer. Some of it was surprisingly good, although Bartholomew found that the more he drank, the less discriminating he tended to be.

As evening turned to night, they finished with the respectable inns on the Heyrow and reached the less respectable ones near the quay. While the Heyrow taverns were full of visiting merchants and the occasional cleric, the waterfront hostelries were frequented by townsfolk and the beer was generally cheaper.

Michael's Benedictine habit caused one or two raised eyebrows, but most people accepted the fact that monks had a talent for sniffing out the most inexpensive brews and so their presence at the riverside taverns was not uncommon. Michael eased himself into conversations, pretending to be a bumbling brother from one of the priory's distant outposts, and earning confidences by making the odd disparaging remark about the wealth of the Benedictines. The ploy worked, and he soon had people talking to him about Glovere, Blanche, de Lisle and Alan.

It seemed that none was especially popular in Ely. The Prior was disliked because he was a landlord; Blanche was arrogant and unsympathetic to the plight of the poor; de Lisle was criticised for his love of good clothes and expensive wines; while Glovere was deemed a malicious gossip. The gypsies, who had been in Ely for almost two weeks, were also the object of suspicion, although Bartholomew did not think this was based on more than a natural wariness of outsiders. He sympathised with the travellers: once on his travels he and his Arab master had been on the receiving end of some unfounded accusations, because it was easier to blame misfortune on passing strangers than to believe ill of friends. He and Ibn Ibrahim had barely escaped with their lives, despite the fact that they had had nothing to do with strangling the local priest's lapdog.

When Bartholomew and Michael entered an especially insalubrious tavern named the Mermaid, they found the patrons sitting at their tables listening to a rabid diatribe delivered by the disenfranchised farmer Richard de Leycestre. Leycestre stood on a bench, waving a jug of slopping ale, his face sweaty and red from the drink and his passion.

'Anyone who cannot see that there is a connection between the gypsies and the burglaries is blind,' he raved. 'The thefts started *the day after* that crowd of criminals arrived. That is all the evidence *I* need.'

'I am sure it is,' muttered Bartholomew, regarding the man with disapproval as he waved to a pot-boy to bring them ale.

Michael nudged him hard. 'Watch what you say, Matt. Rightly or wrongly, these travellers are not popular, and it is not wise to be heard speaking in their defence.'

'Why not?' demanded Bartholomew, rather loudly. One or two people turned to look at him. 'Are you saying that no one should speak up for what he believes, for what is right?'

'Yes. There is no need to court problems. We have more than enough of those at the moment without you going out on a limb to protect the reputation of people you do not know.'

Michael turned to the man who stood next to him, and began a conversation about Glovere and the woman who had killed herself. The man only reiterated what they already knew – that young Alice had committed suicide when Glovere's tales had caused her betrothed to marry someone else. Alice had been pretty, sweet-tempered and likeable, and it seemed that Glovere was generally regarded as the Devil incarnate.

Bartholomew took a deep draught of the rich ale. It was stronger than anything available in Cambridge, and he felt his head swimming. He had been tired and thirsty, and had drunk too much too quickly when he and Michael had started their round of the taverns. He was well on the way to becoming intoxicated. Someone bumped into him, and a good part of the jug spilled down the front of his tabard. The culprit regarded the mess in horror, and then released a chain of impressive oaths.

'I am sorry,' she mumbled eventually, seeing that Bartholomew was regarding her warily. 'Nothing has gone right today, and now I drown a scholar in his own ale. Allow me to buy you more – although I can ill afford it. Haywarde's suicide will cost me a pretty penny.'

'I do not need any more ale,' said Bartholomew, trying to make sense of her seemingly random statements. 'Haywarde?'

'My sister's husband,' explained the woman. 'Damn the man for his selfishness!'

'Selfishness for committing suicide?' asked Bartholomew, bewildered by the conversation's peculiar twists and turns.

The ale slopping around inside him did not help.

The woman gave a tired grin. She was a large lady, who wore a set of skirts around her middle that contained enough material to clothe half the town. Her face was sunburned and homely, and she possessed a set of large, evenly spaced beige teeth. She was as tall as any of the men in the tavern, and a good deal wider than most, and Bartholomew supposed it was this that allowed her to thrust her way into a domain usually frequented by males.

'Forgive me. You are a stranger, and so cannot know what is happening in our town. My name is Agnes Fitzpayne, and my sister had the misfortune to be married to that good-for-nothing lout Haywarde, may God rot his poxy soul! His death will cost me a fortune.'

'I see,' said Bartholomew, who did not.

'It is not as if I even liked him,' continued Agnes bitterly. 'He was a bully, and my sister and their children are glad to see him gone.'

'I heard a man had killed himself yesterday,' said Bartholomew, trying to clear his wits. 'Leycestre said it was because it is difficult for folk to feed their families these days. If that is why Haywarde died, then his suicide will not help them either.'

'If Haywarde committed suicide, then it was not for selfless reasons,' said Agnes harshly. 'He was far too fond of himself to think of others. Leycestre wants to see everything in terms of the struggle between rich and poor. But then perhaps he was thinking of Chaloner. He committed suicide, too.'

'Chaloner? Who is he?'

'He drowned five or six days ago.'

Bartholomew gazed at her. 'So there have been *three* deaths in Ely over the past ten days? I thought it was just Glovere and this Haywarde.'

'Then you thought wrong. The river has claimed three souls recently. But I cannot see Chaloner killing himself to benefit others, either. He was no better than Haywarde in that respect.'

'Why?' asked Bartholomew, rubbing a hand through his hair and wishing he had never started the discussion. 'What had he done?'

'He married where he should not have done,' said Agnes mysteriously. 'And he caused a sweet angel to die of a broken heart.'

'Chaloner was the intended husband of Alice – about whom Glovere told lies?' asked Bartholomew in sudden understanding.

Agnes regarded him in surprise. 'I see you already know our local stories. Chaloner broke Alice's heart by wedding another woman, and it brought about her death. People would not have taken against Chaloner so, if he had been even a little remorseful. But he was not. Like Haywarde, he will not be missed.'

'Except by Chaloner's wife,' said Bartholomew.

'She died in childbirth a few weeks ago,' said Agnes with grim satisfaction. 'It was God's judgement on her for taking the man promised to another.'

'How did Chaloner die?' asked Bartholomew, sipping the remains of his drink.

'He was found floating face-down in the river, opposite the Monks' Hythe. You can see it from here, if you look through the window.'

'And Haywarde?'

'The same. But, as I said, his wife and children will be glad to be rid of *him*. He did no work, and drank away any pennies they earned. And he was violent to them.'

'He sounds unpleasant,' said Bartholomew absently, thinking that it had been a long day, and it was time he was in his bed. He hoped Henry would not insist on a lengthy medical discourse before he went to sleep.

'No one liked him,' said Agnes fervently. 'He was an animal!'

'It seems that Ely is inhabited by quite a number of nasty people,' remarked Bartholomew tiredly. 'Glovere was not much liked, either.'

'He was not. But we have decent people, too. There are a handful of folk we would be better without, but which town does not have those? I am sure Cambridge has its share.'

'It does,' agreed Bartholomew. 'More than its share, if the truth be known.'

Agnes finished her ale and set the empty jug on the table, impressing Bartholomew with her ability to quaff the powerful brew as if it were milk. 'I must go. My sister expects me to pray with her for that vagabond's soul tonight – and he needs all the prayers he can get. Goodnight.'

Bartholomew watched her leave, then settled on the bench next to Michael. A cool breeze wafted through the window, and the gentle sound of the river lapping on the banks was just audible above the comfortable rumble of voices in the tavern: normal conversation had resumed because Leycestre had slipped into a drunken slumber and was no longer ranting. Bartholomew glanced at Michael, and saw that his friend had abandoned his attempts to prise information from the good people of Ely, and was merely enjoying his ale. He appeared relaxed and contented, and Bartholomew sincerely hoped the Bishop's machinations would not bring him to harm. He closed his eyes. But that would be tomorrow. And tomorrow was another day.

CHAPTER 3

THE FOLLOWING DAY WAS CLEAR AND BRIGHT, AND THE SUN had burned away the odorous mist even before the office of prime started at six. Bartholomew stood in the nave, listening to the chanting of the Benedictines in the chancel, closing his eyes to appreciate the singing as it washed and echoed along the vaulted roof. The first rays of sunlight caught the bright glass in the windows, and made dappled patterns in red, yellow and blue on the smooth cream paving stones of the floor.

While the monks completed their devotions in the privacy of the chancel, which was separated from the nave by an intricately carved stone pulpitum, Bartholomew wandered through the rest of the church, admiring the soaring vaulting above the vast emptiness of the nave, so high that he could barely make out details of the ribs in the dusty gloom above the clerestory. Although every available scrap of wall space was covered in brilliantly hued paintings, and every niche boasted a statue of a saint or a cleric, the flag-stones were bare and, apart from a rather cheap-looking altar that stood at the east end of the nave, there was not another piece of furniture in sight. Walking alone, with his footsteps echoing, Bartholomew began to feel oppressed by the great emptiness. Of Lady Blanche and her retinue there was no sign, and Bartholomew assumed they were not in the habit of rising early.

At the heart of the cathedral was the shrine to St Etheldreda. It was a box-shaped structure with a wooden coffin in the middle, covered with a dazzling mass of precious stones, so that it glittered and gleamed with its own light. A number of pilgrims lined up nearby, each ready to present three pennies to a hulking lay-brother with hairy knuckles, who had evidently been selected for his ability to intimidate. One barefoot, ragged woman was sobbing bitterly, and Bartholomew supposed she did not have the necessary funds to buy access to the shrine. Bartholomew felt a surge of anger towards Almoner Robert for demanding payment for something that should have been open to all.

At the west end of the nave were a pair of matching transepts, each decorated with intricate designs in a riot of colours, and adorned with so many statues of saints and biblical figures that Bartholomew felt overwhelmed by the presence of the silent host that gazed down at him with blank eyes. Everywhere he looked was another face. Some were familiar, and he saw that clever masons had used monks in the priory as models for their creations. William was St Edmund, while Robert was an evil-looking green man.

The south-west transept contained a font for baptisms, and a group of lay-brothers who had gathered there were taking advantage of the monks' period of prayer by chatting in low voices. The north-west transept, however, was another matter. A half-hearted barrier in the form of a frayed rope suggested that people would be wise not to venture inside, although cracked flagstones and pieces of smashed masonry provided a more obvious deterrent. Bartholomew walked towards it and gazed upwards, noting the great cracks that zigzagged their way up the walls, and the peculiar lopsidedness of the wooden rafters above. A statue of an animal that looked like a pig leaned precariously overhead, as if ready to precipitate itself downward at any moment, while a couple of gargoyles seemed as though they would not be long in following. He recalled Alan saying that the building looked worse than it was, and thought the architect might well be underestimating the problem: to Bartholomew, it looked ready for collapse.

He was admiring the impressive carvings around the great door in the west front, when a crash preceded a string of people traipsing in. Some were rubbing sleep from their eyes, clearly having just dragged themselves from their beds, while others had hands that were stained dark with the peaty blackness of the local soil, having already started their day's labours. There were peasants wearing undyed homespun tunics, with bare arms burned brown by the sun; and there were merchants, in clothes of many colours with their tight-fitting gipons, flowing kirtles, and fashionable shoes.

Among them was a small, bustling character wearing the habit of a Dominican friar. He had black, greasy hair that was worn too long, and eyes so close together that the physician wondered whether either could see anything other than his nose. The priest spotted Bartholomew and strode purposefully towards him.

'Are you visiting the city?' he demanded without preamble. 'Or are you a priory guest?'

'The latter,' replied Bartholomew, startled by the brusque enquiry.

'Then you are the priory's responsibility and none of mine,' said the priest curtly. 'You may attend my service, but you must behave yourself in a fitting manner.'

'Behave myself?' asked Bartholomew, bewildered. Had the shabbiness of his academic tabard, which should have been black but was more charcoal due to frequent washes, and the patches on his shirt made him appear more disreputable than he had imagined? He decided to invest in a set of new clothes as soon as he had enough money to do so.

The priest sighed impatiently. 'Yes, behave: no swearing, no fighting and no spitting.'

'I shall do my best,' replied Bartholomew, wondering what kind of congregations the priest usually entertained with his morning masses.

'I hope so,' said the priest sternly. 'My name is Father John Michel, and I am the chaplain of the parish of Holy Cross – this parish. I am about to conduct mass, so take your place among my congregation, if you want to stay.'

'Here?' asked Bartholomew, as the priest struggled into an alb and made for the rough altar at the end of the nave.

'You plan to conduct a mass here, in the nave of the cathedral, while the monks are still singing prime in the chancel?'

'They are a nuisance with all their warbling,' agreed John, evidently believing that Bartholomew's sympathies lay with the mass about to begin rather than the one already in progress. 'Their strident voices tend to distract my parishioners from their devotions. Still, we do our best to drown them out.'

'Why not use St Mary's Church, on the village green?' asked Bartholomew, intrigued by the curious arrangement the priest seemed to have with the priory. 'Then you and the monks would not disturb each other.'

John gave a hearty sigh, and glared at Bartholomew in a way that suggested the physician should keep quiet if he did not know what he was talking about. 'Because St Mary's Church is in St Mary's parish,' he explained with painstaking slowness, as if Bartholomew were lacking in wits. 'I am the priest of Holy Cross parish, and the nave of this cathedral is Holy Cross Church.'

'I see,' said Bartholomew. 'I wondered why there was such a thick screen separating nave and chancel.'

'You may have noticed that a new structure is being erected against the north wall of the cathedral,' said John, gesturing vaguely to a spot where a half-finished building could be seen through the stained-glass windows. 'When that is completed, it will be our parish church, and I shall be disturbed by the monks no longer. I wish the builders would hurry up, though: I complained to the Archbishop of Canterbury about the situation years ago, and the monks have still not finished my new church. It is the fault of that damned octagon.'

'The cathedral's new central tower?' asked Bartholomew. 'How can that be responsible for your church being unfinished?'

The patronising tone crept back into John's voice. 'Because the monks took the builders away from my church to raise that monstrosity instead. Then the Death came, and many masons died. It was all most inconvenient.'

'Especially for the masons. I am sure most of them would have preferred to work on your church than to die of the plague.'

'They were a lazy crowd, anyway,' said John, apparently unaware of the irony in Bartholomew's voice. 'They would go to any lengths to avoid an honest day's work. It would have been quicker for me to raise the damned thing myself. But I have a mass to conduct. Stand there, next to that pillar, and stay well away from those three men near the altar.'

'Why?' asked Bartholomew, turning to glance at the people whom the priest indicated with a careless flick of his hand. As far as he could tell, they were perfectly normal, and had no obvious infectious disease that might be passed from close contact. Two were young men, who wore sullen expressions and exuded the impression that they thought the world owed them a good deal more than they had been given; the third was Richard de Leycestre.

'Just do as I tell you,' said John irritably. 'Stay by the pillar and keep quiet until I finish. However, in future I would rather you attended mass with the monks. My parishioners do not take kindly to having the priory's spies in their midst.'

'Spies?' echoed Bartholomew, startled. 'I am not a spy. And anyway, what could there be to report to the monks – or anyone else – about a mass held so close to them that they will be able to hear every word anyway?'

'I am sure you do not require me to elaborate on that,' replied John obscurely. 'And now you must excuse me, before my parishioners decide they have better things to do than watch me chattering to you.'

He bustled away, leaving the physician feeling like an unwelcome interloper. Bartholomew saw he was the subject of several curious gazes, not all of them friendly. The three men he had been forbidden to speak to regarded him with unreadable expressions before turning away to watch Father John.

Flinging a few tawdry receptacles carelessly on to the altar, John took a deep breath and began to bellow the words of his mass at the top of his lungs. Immediately, the volume of the monks' singing increased, so John yelled louder still. In reply, the monks notched up the volume once again, so that it was difficult to concentrate on either. The air rang with noise, frightening two pigeons that had been roosting among the rafters; the sounds of their agitated flapping, and the shrieks of a woman as one flew too close to her, added to the general racket. The lay-brothers, who had been talking quietly in the transept at the end of the nave, began to speak more loudly in order to make themselves heard, and John's congregation, unable to understand the priest's abominable Latin, started to converse among themselves. Bartholomew watched open-mouthed from the base of his pillar.

And so it continued, with John abandoning the usual format of the mass in favour of repeating those parts that would provide him with the opportunity to shout. He crashed the chalice and patens so hard on the top of the altar that Bartholomew was certain they would have broken had they been made from anything other than metal. That the sacred vessels made such satisfying clangs reiterated the fact that the dispute between monks and parish was not a new one, and Bartholomew wondered whether John had ordered iron vessels specially manufactured for the express purpose of allowing him to use them like gongs.

Eventually, the monks completed their devotions, and their unnecessarily loud footsteps could be heard leaving the chancel and stamping towards the cloisters. Doors were slammed, wooden pews banged and bumped, and psalters and prayer books snapped shut in one of the noisiest exits from a church Bartholomew had ever witnessed. He was surprised that Prior Alan, who had not seemed to be a petty man, permitted such churlish behaviour among his monks.

John's mass was completed as soon as the door to the vestries slammed for the final time and the last of the monks had left. Bartholomew had expected that John would merely lower his voice and complete the service at a more reasonable volume, thus instilling at least some degree of reverence into his restless, bored parishioners. But John merely devoured the Host, gulped down some wine, and gathered his iron vessels together in anticipation of a speedy completion. He raised his hand to sign a benediction over his assembled flock, although Bartholomew saw that the priest was more interested in the doings of the lay-brothers who were lurking among the shadows of the north aisle than in blessing his people.

'Did you enjoy our mass?' came a soft voice at Bartholomew's shoulder. The physician turned to see Richard de Leycestre; the two young men were at his side.

'It was an interesting experience,' replied Bartholomew guardedly. 'I am used to masses conducted a little more quietly.'

Leycestre chuckled. 'I imagine there are few who are not.'

'I have been instructed not to speak to you,' said Bartholomew, looking to where Father John's determined advance on the chattering lay-brothers had been brought to a halt: Agnes Fitzpayne, the prodigious drinker in the Mermaid the night before, had intercepted him and had his arm gripped in one of her powerful hands. Thus occupied, John had not yet noticed that his earlier command was being ignored, and that Bartholomew was conversing with Leycestre and his companions.

'By Father John, I suppose,' said Leycestre, shaking his head. 'He is always trying to prevent us from speaking to the strangers who pass through our city.' He indicated the two young men with a wave of his hand. 'These are my nephews, Adam Clymme and Robert Buk. They are of the same mind as me as regards the pitiful circumstances our peasants have been forced into by greedy landlords, but Father John dislikes us spreading the word.'

'I imagine he is trying to protect you,' said Bartholomew. 'You are very vocal about your beliefs, and he probably does not want you telling one of the King's spies that Ely is a hotbed of insurrection.'

'Unfortunately, it is not,' said Leycestre bitterly. 'I wish it were, because then we might be able to set about rectifying the unjust situation that prevails here. But although everyone complains about high taxes and crippling tithes, no one is prepared to do anything about them.'

'And you are?'

Leycestre regarded him warily. 'That is a blunt question. Perhaps Father John was right to try to prevent us from speaking to you.'

'Perhaps he was. Not everyone feels the same way as you do.'

Leycestre went back to his preaching. 'All the folk here resent the heavy taxes and the fact that they owe at least three days' labour each week to the Bishop or the priory – depending on who owns the land – before they can even begin to see to their own crops. But no one except us has the courage to speak out.'

'Father John is certainly vocal in his way,' said Bartholomew with a smile. 'He must have spoiled the monks' morning mass.'

Leycestre did not smile back. 'It is a matter of principle that we do not allow those fat, wealthy clerics to gain the better of us poor folk. It is a pity, though: I used to find prime in the cathedral a restful time, and now it has become a battle.'

'Then do not take part in it,' suggested Bartholomew. 'I am sorry if I offend you, but competing to see who can shout the loudest is no way to behave. It is very childish.'

'That is because you do not understand what is at issue here,' said one of the nephews, pushing forward and thrusting his heavy, ruddy face close to Bartholomew's. The physician was startled: he had forgotten the youths were there. 'You only heard a lot of shouting, but—'

'That is enough!' came a sharp voice from behind them. Bartholomew turned to see that Agnes Fitzpayne had abandoned John, and was approaching them. She glowered menacingly at the hapless young man. 'I have warned you about this kind of thing before, Adam!'

Adam fell back, reddening in embarrassment at the admonition.

'Mistress Fitzpayne,' said Leycestre pleasantly. 'Good morning.'

'A "good morning" for talking rebellious nonsense, you mean,' she snapped. 'Go on! Be off! All three of you have work to do in the fields, and making nuisances of yourselves in the cathedral will not get the crops harvested.'

'Priory crops!' spat Adam in disgust. 'The monks have no right to force us to work in their fields for no pay. We have families to feed and bread to earn, and we have no spare days for labouring just so that the likes of them can get fat on our sweat.'

'That may be so, but it is not for you to try to change things,' said Agnes briskly, cocking her head meaningfully at Bartholomew in an unsubtle warning that strangers were present. 'Go away before I take a broom handle to you.'

Reluctantly, the nephews slunk away, casting resentful glances over their shoulders to show their displeasure at being dismissed like schoolboys. Leycestre lingered, although he was evidently not in Agnes's good books for spinning his disaffected thoughts to the priory's visitors, because she turned her back on him when she addressed Bartholomew. She looked the physician up and down before speaking, as she might examine a fish she was considering buying.

'I am surprised to see *you* here so early this morning,' she began rudely. 'You and your fat Benedictine friend trawled every tavern in the town last night, asking about Glovere. I did not expect to see you until at least noon, given that Ely ale is stronger than that pale stuff served in Cambridge.'

'We did not drink that much,' said Bartholomew, blithely ignoring the fact that he had felt less than lively when he had awoken that morning. 'We wanted information, not ale.'

Agnes nodded. 'I know what you wanted. You are trying

to find evidence that Thomas de Lisle did not drown Glovere in the river.'

'Much as I despise the man for oppressing the people he is supposed to care for, I do not think de Lisle killed Glovere . . .' began Leycestre.

Agnes said tiredly, 'No, we all know what you think, Leycestre. You blame Glovere's death on the gypsies. Personally, I do not know what to believe, so I suppose we will just have to wait and see what the official investigators – Brother Michael, Bishop Northburgh and Canon Stretton – discover.' She turned her penetrating gaze on Bartholomew. 'But meanwhile, I would be obliged if you would forget what you just heard.'

'And you would be wise to oblige *her*,' Bartholomew thought he heard Leycestre murmur.

'Forget what, precisely?' asked Bartholomew. 'The fact that I have just witnessed the unedifying spectacle of rival clerics trying to yell each other hoarse? Or the fact that Ely's young men, like those in Cambridge, do not like harvesting crops?'

Agnes put her hands on her hips and regarded him closely. 'You are one of that rabble of scholars from the University in Cambridge. I hear that the masters there engage in unnatural acts with animals, and that the students practise satanic rites in the churchyards after dark – when they are not murdering townsfolk, that is.'

'Only when they are not roasting babies on spits in the Market Square,' replied Bartholomew, wondering what scholars had done to earn such a peculiar reputation. From what he had observed during his brief sojourn with the residents of Ely, he thought they should concentrate on improving their own image before launching attacks on those of others.

'Come, Leycestre,' Agnes ordered, apparently uncertain whether or not the newcomer was jesting with her and not inclined to stay to find out. 'We should make sure those feckless lads go to the priory's fields and do their duty, or there will be trouble.'

As Bartholomew watched them hurry away, a sharp voice made him turn. It was Father John, his face dark with anger. 'I told you not to talk to Leycestre and his nephews,' he snapped, seizing Bartholomew's arm angrily.

The physician pulled away, irked that the man should manhandle him. 'You can tell me whatever you like, but I am not obliged to follow any of your orders. And they spoke to me first, not the other way around.'

'They came to ascertain whether you are one of them,' said John bitterly. 'Foolish men! It is the surest way to place a noose around their necks – and mine, if they implicate me in their plans. It was lucky Agnes arrived when she did. Doubtless she stopped them from saying anything that might have been dangerous.'

'What are you talking about?' asked Bartholomew testily, weary of the threats and assumptions that Ely's citizens seemed happy to bandy about. 'What is so dangerous about a conversation in a church?'

'Rebellion,' said John in a whisper, glancing around him as if the King's spies might be lurking behind the cathedral's pillars. 'Sedition and bloody uprising. The people have grown tired of bending under the yoke of harsh landlords, and they are ready to rise against them. Leycestre and his nephews are the leaders of the movement in Ely. I am not with them, of course; I shall have to wait to see which side will win before I choose one faction over the other.'

'Very wise,' said Bartholomew dryly. 'But I am no rabble rouser, and I do not want to become involved in any such venture. You can tell your trio of rebels to leave me alone.'

'Not *my* trio,' said John hastily. 'But you will say nothing of this to the monks, especially Almoner Robert, or he will have them imprisoned. So, the matter is closed. Are we agreed? I see you carry a medicine bag. Are you a physician?'

'Yes – I am here to read in the monks' library; I have no time to work on horoscopes,' Bartholomew said quickly before he was inundated with requests in that quarter.

'I do not believe in such nonsense,' said John dismissively.

Bartholomew warmed to him a little. 'I am interested in acquiring your services on another matter. I will pay you for your time; I know how physicians like their gold. Are you interested?'

'It depends what you want me to do,' said Bartholomew warily. 'I do not cut hair or shave beards like a surgeon, and I certainly do not bleed people.'

'I want you to give me your opinion,' replied John mysteriously. 'I want you to tell me whether a man died from his own hand or by accident. Can you do that? I know University men use dead bodies to further their knowledge of anatomy, so you must be familiar with corpses.'

'Ask a local physician,' said Bartholomew, reluctant to spend his precious time examining bodies when he could be in the library. 'What about Brother Henry?'

'Henry is a good man, but he knows nothing about the dead,' said John.

'Then what about a surgeon? There must be one in Ely.'

'Barbour, the landlord of the Lamb, bleeds us and cuts our hair while we recover. But I do not trust a surgeon who is better with hair than he is with veins. I would rather hire you.'

'Who do you want me to look at?' asked Bartholomew uneasily. 'I have already examined Glovere in the Bone House.'

'And what did you find?' asked John with keen interest. 'Did he drown by accident, was it suicide, or did someone do away with him, as Lady Blanche would have us believe?'

'Why do you want to know?' asked Bartholomew, wishing Michael were with him. He did not like the fact that the priest already seemed aware that Glovere's death was not all it seemed, and he did not like to imagine how.

'Because Glovere's demise may be relevant to the deaths of my two parishioners. Ely is a small town, and we have had three deaths by drowning within the last ten days. Do not tell me that is not a little odd!'

* * *

Bartholomew did not want to begin an investigation into the other two suspicious drownings without Michael present, so he asked Father John to wait while he went to fetch the monk. Michael was in the refectory, enjoying a substantial breakfast with the Prior and several other high-ranking Benedictines. Not for the brethren the grey, watery oatmeal that most people were obliged to consume: each of their tables was laden with fresh bread, smoked eels and dishes of stewed onions. The Prior and his officers, as befitted men of their superior station, also had coddled eggs and a baked ham.

'Is it a feast day?' asked Bartholomew, astonished by the quality and quantity of food that was being packed inside ample girths all around the refectory. No wonder Michael was so large, he thought; there seemed to be an informal competition in play to see who could eat the most. People often joked about the amount of food that was available to Benedictines, and Bartholomew had always put this down to a natural jealousy of an institution that treated its members well. However, he realised that he had been wrong to dismiss the popular claims as wild exaggerations when he saw what was being devoured by the men in black habits.

'I must apologise for the paucity of the fare today,' said the swarthy Almoner Robert, as he rammed a large piece of cheese into his mouth. 'It is a Monday, and we always breakfast lightly on Mondays.'

Bartholomew studied him hard, but the intent expression on the almoner's face convinced him that the man was perfectly serious.

'Yes, there is almost nothing here,' agreed Michael, casting a critical eye across the table. 'I shall be ready for my midday meal when it comes.'

Bartholomew had no idea whether he was being facetious. Aware that Father John was waiting for him, he opened his mouth to ask Michael to accompany him, but he had hesitated and the conversation at the breakfast table suddenly took off. Bartholomew realised that besides having ample food with which to start the day, the monks also enjoyed talking, and there was none of the silence he had observed at mealtimes in other abbeys and his own College.

'These are hard times,' said Robert, still looking at the table in a disparaging manner. 'We are reduced to eating much smaller portions, and I sometimes wonder how much longer we will be able to continue dispensing alms to the poor. They are *always* hungry.'

'They are always hungry because they work hard,' said Henry sharply, giving the almoner a disapproving glance. Bartholomew saw that he and Alan were the only ones who were not snatching and grabbing at the breakfast fare as if they would never see its like again. Alan seemed to possess the kind of nervous appetite that did not allow him to eat rich food, while the infirmarian took only bread and ale. They were by far the slimmest members of the community.

'I cannot say I enjoyed prime this morning,' said Michael, loading his knife with coddled eggs and transporting the quivering mass to his mouth. So much of the implement disappeared inside his maw that Bartholomew thought he might stab the back of his throat. 'There was far too much noise. Can you not ask that parish priest to lower his voice?'

'I do not attend prime, for exactly that reason,' said Prior Alan. 'I cannot hear myself think with all that yelling, let alone pray. I am obliged to delegate prime to Sub-prior Thomas, while I celebrate the office in my private chapel.'

'I do not mind,' said a vast man, whose jowls quivered with fat as they munched on his smoked eels. Bartholomew had never before seen a man of such immense proportions. He noted that the sub-prior had been provided with a sturdy seat of oak, probably so that his enormous weight would not tip the bench and precipitate the others on to the floor. His Benedictine habit was the size of a tent, yet was still stretched taut across his chest and stomach, and a series of wobbling chins cascaded down the front of it. Even the process of sitting and devouring a monstrous meal seemed too much exercise; beads of sweat broke out across his red

face and oozed into the greasy strands of hair that sprouted
from his neck.

'Personally, I have always felt there is far too much
mumbling at prime,' Sub-prior Thomas went on, slicing
himself a slab of ham the size of a doorstop. 'I like a bit of
noise myself. All that soft whispering gives people the
impression that we are still half asleep, and prime is much
more rousing when we can put a little enthusiasm into it.'

'There was certainly a good deal of that,' muttered Michael,
repeating the operation with the knife. This time, several
monks watched with evident fascination, probably anticipating that he would either stab himself or choke, Michael
did neither, and when he spoke again, it was through a mouth
full of eggs. 'Young Julian yelled himself completely hoarse,
while the altos in the choir were screeching, not singing.'

'I am glad Julian can do something worthwhile,'
Bartholomew thought he heard Thomas mutter as he
reached out and grabbed a loaf of bread. The physician
expected him to cut a piece and replace the rest, but the
sub-prior proceeded to tear off lumps and cram them into
his mouth with the clear intention of devouring the whole
thing himself. As he ate, he cast venomous glances at the
back of the hall, where the novices were seated. The young
men did not seem happy to be the object of the sub-prior's
hostile attention, and Bartholomew had the impression that
there was no love lost between Alan's deputy and his young
charges. Julian gazed back with brazen dislike, although the
others seemed more cowed than defiant.

'De Lisle *never* bothers with prime when he is in Ely,'
observed Robert sanctimoniously. 'I imagine he is too busy
counting his money.'

'I sincerely doubt it,' said Hosteller William. He had
washed his hair that morning, presumably because Blanche
was visiting and he wanted to make a good impression. He
kept running his hands through it so that it would dry, and
it sat around his head like a giant grey puffball. 'He does
not have any. That is his problem.'

'How is Lady Blanche this morning?' asked Alan of his hosteller, tactfully changing the subject so that Michael would not be obliged to hear his fellow monks denigrating their Bishop. 'I invited her to celebrate prime in my private chapel, but she informed me that she does not like to rise while the dew still lies on the ground.'

'Her retinue follow her example,' said Robert disapprovingly. He helped himself to a chunk of cheese that would have fed an entire family of peasants. Bartholomew tried hard not to gape at him. 'Bartholomew was the only one of our guests in the cathedral this morning. However, I did not like the fact that he chose to sit with the town rabble, in preference to us.'

'I did not expect that to be an issue,' said Bartholomew, indignant at the criticism, when no one had bothered to forewarn him. 'I assumed the townsfolk would attend St Mary's, or listen to your offices from the nave. I was not anticipating that two masses would be celebrated in the same church at the same time.'

'There is something of a rivalry between priory and city,' explained William. 'And Father John is always looking for opportunities to exacerbate the problem. I saw him whispering secretly to you after he had finished howling his miserable Latin. What did he want?'

'He was not whispering and his request was not secret,' said Bartholomew, resenting the implication that he was engaging in subterfuge. He wondered whether the monks were in the habit of making inflammatory remarks to all their guests, or whether he had been singled out for that particular honour.

'I imagine he was telling you that the town needs more alms from us,' said Robert angrily. 'Well, we are poor ourselves and cannot afford to give more.'

'So I see,' said Bartholomew, his eyes straying to the piles of food that were rapidly disappearing inside monastic mouths.

'There is always something more we can do for the poor,'

said Henry softly. No one took any notice of him.

'Or was he complaining that we have spent too much time on the octagon, when we should have been working on his miserable parish church?' demanded Robert, working himself into a fever of righteous indignation. 'We are not made of money: we cannot pay every last mason in the country to work for us, and the cathedral is more important than any parish church.'

'Not to the people of Holy Cross,' said Bartholomew. 'And not to you, either, unless you happen to like shouting at prime.'

'Father John does have a point,' said the ever-reasonable Henry, appealing to Prior Alan. 'We started his church thirty years ago, and it is still nowhere near completion.'

'We had the octagon to build and the Lady Chapel to raise,' Alan pointed out. 'Those were large projects that took all our resources.'

'But the parish church *is* more important than a lady chapel,' argued Henry. 'Our first duty is to our fellow men, not to erecting sumptuous buildings that we do not need.'

'Our first duty is to God,' retorted Alan sharply. 'And I have chosen to fulfil that duty by raising magnificent monuments to glorify His name.'

Henry said no more, although Bartholomew was uncertain whether it was because he was abashed by Alan's reprimand, or because he could see that there was simply no point in arguing.

'Or was Father John muttering to you because he thinks churchmen have been slaughtering townsfolk?' asked Subprior Thomas of Bartholomew in the silence that followed, his jaws still working on the remaining crusts of his bread. Bartholomew looked around surreptitiously, certain that the fat sub-prior could not possibly have eaten an entire loaf within such a short period of time. The crumbs on the table indicated that he had.

'He wants me to examine some bodies for him,' said Bartholomew.

'Oh, that is a relief,' said a tall monk with a bushy beard. 'I thought you might be waiting there for me to give you the keys to the library.'

'Are you Symon de Banneham, the Brother Librarian?' asked Bartholomew immediately. 'When can I make a start? There are many texts to read and I would like to begin as soon as possible.'

Symon blew out his cheeks and shook his head, intending to convey the impression that the request was an impossible one to grant. 'Not today. Come back next week.'

'Next week?' echoed Bartholomew in horror. 'But I will have gone home by then.'

'Pity,' said Symon, pouring himself a large jug of breakfast ale and downing it faster than was wise. 'We have some lovely books. I am sure you would have enjoyed them.'

'Why can you not oblige our visitor sooner, Symon?' asked Prior Alan curiously. 'There is no reason why he should not start work whenever he likes. No one else is reading the books he wants to see, and the library is meant to be used by people just like him.'

Symon shot his Prior an unpleasant look. 'It is not convenient to deal with him today.'

'Why not?' pressed Alan. 'You have no other pressing duties. And you do not need to "deal" with him anyway. Just show him the books and he can manage the rest for himself.'

Symon gave a long-suffering sigh, but was obviously unable to think of further excuses. 'This is a wretched nuisance, but I suppose I might be able to fit you in tomorrow. You will have to find me, though. I am too busy to be at a specific place at a certain time.'

'That will not be a problem,' said Bartholomew, deciding that he had better agree to any terms set by the unhelpful librarian if he ever wanted to see a book. 'I will find you.'

Symon's eyes gleamed with triumph, and Bartholomew suspected that the librarian would make tracking him down as difficult as possible.

'So, you can inspect corpses today and read tomorrow,'

said Alan sweetly to Bartholomew. 'It sounds a perfect two days for a medical man.'

'I would rather see living patients than inspect corpses,' said Bartholomew, determined that the monks should not consider him a ghoul who preferred the company of blackened, stinking remains of men like Glovere to engaging in normal, healthy pursuits like examining urine. He beckoned to Michael. 'We should go, Brother. Father John is waiting.'

'Why do you need Michael to accompany you?' asked William, fluffing up his bobbed hair fastidiously.

'Apparently, the priest believes that two of his parishioners may have died in suspicious circumstances,' explained Bartholomew, not certain what he should say. Since he and Michael were not yet sure whether someone had murdered Glovere for the express purpose of compromising de Lisle, he did not want to tell the assembled monks too much: given that de Lisle was unpopular in the priory, it would not be surprising if one of the Benedictines had decided to try to bring about the Bishop's downfall.

Michael rose from his feast, dabbing greasy lips on a piece of linen with one hand and shoving a handful of boiled eggs and a piece of bread into his scrip with the other. Meanwhile, his brethren began a spirited debate about the bodies that Father John wished Bartholomew to examine.

'John is concerned by the fact that a couple of his parishioners have had the misfortune to meet their maker recently,' said Almoner Robert with a smugly superior smile on his dark features. He leaned back against the wall and folded soft white hands across his ample paunch. 'However, someone should inform him that it is quite natural for people to die.'

'But even *you* must admit that it is unusual for three men to drown in such rapid succession,' replied William tartly, treating the almoner to a scornful glance. From the way Robert glared back, Bartholomew sensed that this was not the first disagreement the two men had engaged in.

'Three?' asked Henry, crossing himself in alarm. 'I thought there were two – Glovere and Chaloner. Who is the other?'

'That ruffian Haywarde,' replied Robert, tearing his attention away from William and addressing Henry. 'He is that lazy fellow who is related to Agnes Fitzpayne. He was found dead near the Monks' Hythe on Saturday morning.'

'Drowned?' asked Henry, horrified. 'Like the other two?'

Robert nodded with gleeful satisfaction, clearly enjoying the fact that he was in possession of information that the others lacked. Bartholomew thought him a thoroughly repellent character, and was not surprised that Michael preferred life in Cambridge to that in his Mother House, where there were men like Robert, Thomas and William to contend with. 'He was found floating face-down in the water – he took his own life.'

'But why would he do that?' asked Henry uncertainly. 'I do not like to speak ill of the dead, but Haywarde was too selfish and arrogant a man to do himself any harm.'

'I agree,' said Robert, who seemed the kind of fellow who would always find something negative to say about someone. 'But that is what is being said in the town. As almoner, I am told these things, whereas you will hear little, locked in your hospital all day.'

'I have Julian,' said Henry, a little bitterly, as he cast an unreadable glance towards Alan. 'He more than compensates for any gossip I might miss. I have never met anyone with a more spiteful tongue.'

'I have,' muttered William, directing another glance of rank dislike at Robert. 'Even the reprehensible Julian could learn some tricks from the likes of our Brother Almoner.'

'Haywarde was a pig, and does not deserve to be buried in consecrated ground anyway,' announced Robert sanctimoniously, apparently unaware of William's murmured comments. 'Suicide or not, the potter's field is the best place for him.'

'That is a fine attitude for a man whose task is to care

for the poor,' said Michael coolly. 'Does it not touch your sense of compassion that the man felt compelled to risk his immortal soul rather than continue to live?'

'No,' said Robert firmly. 'And we paid him a perfectly fair wage, so do not listen to any seditious chatter put about by that Leycestre. He claims the priory does not care for its labourers.'

'We could have paid Haywarde a little more,' said William reasonably. 'The man had six children, and what we gave him was barely enough to feed them all.'

'It was, actually,' argued Thomas, reaching for the empty ham platter and proceeding to scrape up the grease with his spoon. 'Or it would have been, had he chosen to buy bread, rather than squandering it on ale at the Lamb.'

'He did enjoy his ale,' admitted Henry. 'And his drunkenness did not make for a happy life for his wife and children. He was altogether too ready with his fists – I cannot begin to recall the times that I have dispensed salves to heal his family's bruises.'

'Too many offspring,' proclaimed Thomas, licking the fat from his spoon with a moist red tongue. 'That was the essence of Haywarde's problems.'

'He should have thought of that before he rutted with his woman, then,' snapped Robert nastily. 'I have no patience with men who breed like rabbits and then decline to accept their responsibilities. Haywarde chose to have six children, and his death has condemned them to a slow death by starvation.'

'I am sure no one here will allow that to happen,' said Bartholomew, loudly enough to silence the hum of chatter that buzzed around the refectory. He felt Michael plucking at his sleeve, encouraging him to leave before he could embroil himself in an argument with the people whose hospitality he was receiving. Impatiently, he moved away. 'This man was one of the monastery's servants, and I am certain none of you will be so callous as to allow his children to starve.'

'That is unfair,' snapped Robert angrily. 'It is not our fault that Haywarde is dead, and we cannot afford to take every hungry child into our care; we would be bankrupt in no time at all.'

'We would have every peasant in the Fens clamouring at our doors for succour,' agreed Thomas, who had finished the fat and was eyeing the last of the cheese, indicating that the plight of Haywarde's children was not something that would affect his own appetite. 'Robert is right.'

'Robert is wrong,' declared William promptly, delighted with an opportunity to show his rival in a poor light. He turned to Alan, still raking his fingers through his peculiar hair. 'Bartholomew has a point, Father. It would be wicked of us to ignore this stricken family. I will donate my break-fast to Haywarde's children from now on.' He shot Robert an unpleasant smile, indicating that he thought he had won some kind of point.

'You will not, my lad,' said Thomas fervently, looking up from his feeding. 'That would place an obligation on the rest of us to do the same thing, and I can assure you that I shall allow nothing to come between me and my food. I am a large man, and I need sustenance to conduct my life in a manner that is fitting to God.'

'I am sure God would condone a little abstinence in the name of compassion,' said William, surveying Thomas's girth critically. 'And *I* shall undertake to ensure that Haywarde's children are cared for. You can do as you will.'

Bartholomew saw the novices smiling among themselves, apparently delighted to see the fat sub-prior opposed so energetically. It seemed that Thomas was not a popular man with the youngsters.

'I shall look into Haywarde's case,' said Alan wearily; it was not the first time he had acted as peacemaker between his senior monks. 'However, I took it upon myself to visit the family the day he died, and the widow assured me that she would fare better without him. I confess I was shocked, but she told me that the funds spent on Haywarde's ale would pay for the children's bread. She seemed rather delighted by her change of fortune.'

'She would,' said Henry. 'Haywarde cannot have been an easy man to live with.'

'A brute,' agreed Thomas wholeheartedly, gnawing the remnants of cheese from a rind. 'And I, for one, am glad he is dead. He will not be mourned in the town for a moment.'

Bartholomew gazed at him, astonished to hear such sentiments from a monk.

'Our visiting physician should be about his business,' said Robert, watching his reaction critically and showing that he thought it high time the outspoken interloper was gone.

'True,' said Thomas. 'There are three bodies awaiting his attention, after all.'

'Three,' mused William thoughtfully. 'Perhaps Father John is right to be concerned.'

'What do you mean?' demanded Robert, regarding the hosteller with open hatred. 'I have already pointed out that it is not unusual for men to die.'

'To die, no,' said William smoothly. 'But it is unusual for three to drown within such a short time. You should beware, Robert, because I have a hunch that it will only be a matter of time before a *monk* is found face-down in the river.'

'That was unpleasant,' said Bartholomew, as he followed Michael out of the refectory towards the Steeple Gate, where he could see the priest still waiting. 'Was William threatening Robert?'

'Lord knows,' sighed Michael. 'It would not surprise me. Robert and William have loathed each other for as long as I can remember.'

'Neither of them are especially appealing characters,' remarked Bartholomew, trying to determine whether he was more repelled by the superior, unreadable William or the vicious-tongued Robert. And the sub-prior was not much better, either. 'I cannot say that I am impressed with your Benedictine brethren, Michael.'

'Not those particular ones. But Henry is a kindly soul, and so is Alan.'

'I am not so sure about Alan,' said Bartholomew. 'He seems gentle and good, but he permits this silly feud with Father John, and he does nothing to curb the excesses of his monks. Robert, William and Thomas would benefit if he did not allow them so much freedom.'

'Alan really *is* a good man, but thwarted ambition has made him careless.'

'You mean because he should have been Bishop and the Pope selected de Lisle instead?'

Michael rummaged in his scrip and presented Bartholomew with the food he had taken. 'You should not poke around with corpses on an empty stomach, Matt. I should have grabbed you some ham, too, but that greedy Thomas wolfed most of it before I could act.'

Bartholomew took the offering, a little warily: Michael was not a man who readily parted with food, and the physician wondered whether there was something wrong with it. 'Are you not hungry?'

'Breakfast is always a tawdry affair on Mondays,' said Michael carelessly. He is probably full, thought Bartholomew. 'But I shall survive until we find a tavern, and you need sustenance, since you are about to meddle in de Lisle's affairs on my behalf. How did you persuade the priest to let you examine the others?'

'He asked me. But these other two deaths put a different complexion on matters, do you not think? They mean that unless de Lisle also murdered them, then he is unlikely to have killed Glovere.'

Michael gave a grim smile. 'You are underestimating de Lisle, Matt. He is quite capable of deducing that the presence of two other corpses might exonerate him from the murder of the first. And you are assuming that these corpses are all related in some way. Robert is right: the waters in the Fens can be dangerous, and it is not unusual for men to die while fishing or fowling or cutting reeds.'

'I suppose there is only one way to find out,' said Bartholomew reluctantly, watching with heavy resignation as Father John came to lead them to the corpses.

The two bodies lay in St Mary's Church, an attractive building with a spire, which overlooked the village green. John explained that the monks refused to allow corpses in the cathedral while they awaited burial, and so the parishioners of Holy Cross were obliged to pay St Mary's to store them until a requiem mass could be arranged. The priest of St Mary's was well satisfied with the arrangement, and John informed Bartholomew and Michael that the twopence per day for each body went directly into the man's own purse.

'The monks should provide that twopence,' John muttered bitterly. 'Why should my parishioners pay, just because the priory refuses to allow them proper use of our parish church?'

'But it is primarily the priory's cathedral,' Michael pointed out. 'And it is the seat of the Bishop of Ely. Thomas de Lisle will not want to be falling over corpses each time he enters his own church, either.'

'You make it sound as though we have dozens of them,' said John accusingly. 'There are only two. Prior Alan put Glovere in the Bone House.'

'Why not store the others there, too?' asked Bartholomew.

John explained patiently, 'Since Glovere is a retainer of Lady Blanche he is technically not my parishioner, and I refused to find the twopence for him. Rather than pay himself, Alan made the Bone House available. But I could not avoid financing Chaloner and Haywarde.'

'The River Ouse can be dangerous,' said Bartholomew. 'Why do you think the deaths of these two men are anything more than tragic accidents?'

'I do not, actually,' admitted John. 'The river *is* dangerous, and these fellows liked a drink. But there is a rumour that they killed themselves, and if that is true, then I cannot bury them in consecrated ground.'

'God's blood!' swore Michael, backing away as John opened the door to the Church of St Mary. 'This place smells almost as foul as Glovere in the Bone House.'

'It is summer, Brother,' said John. 'Of course there will be some odour.'

'No wonder you *pay* for the privilege of storing your dead here,' said Michael, removing his pomander from his scrip and shoving it against his nose and mouth. 'It is the only way you would ever persuade a priest to allow you to do it.'

The bodies lay in open coffins in the Lady Chapel, covered with grimy blankets that were liberally scattered with horse hairs. Under each coffin, Bartholomew saw that the floor had been stained by water dripping from the bodies; he had noted a similar phenomenon on the floor around Glovere. Since neither John nor Michael made a move to help, he went over to the first corpse. He presumed it was Chaloner, who he knew had died a couple of days after Glovere, because the face was blackened and there was a whitish mass in the eyes and mouth, indicating that flies had been at work. It would not be long before Chaloner had a cloud of insects buzzing around him, just as Glovere had done.

'Why have you waited so long to bury this man?' asked Bartholomew, beginning his examination.

'He has no family to arrange matters,' said John, as if that explained everything. 'His wife died in childbirth some weeks ago.'

'Then why does the parish not pay?' demanded Michael. 'It is not seemly to keep the dead above ground for so long.'

John looked resentful. 'How can I bury them when I do not know where they might be laid to rest? I must know whether either or both are suicides or died by accident.' He drew himself up to his full height and did his best to look pious. 'I will not see anyone consigned to unconsecrated ground if I can help it.'

'Better unconsecrated ground than no ground at all,' said Bartholomew. 'And you can always exhume them later and rebury them in the churchyard, if you are uncertain.'

John glared at him. 'A final resting place is just that. I do not hold with tearing men from their graves once they have been interred. That is why I brought *you* here, so that you can determine where they should go.'

Bartholomew looked at the pair of corpses, hoping that he would be able to deduce enough to allow the removal of the bodies from a public place. While the remains of executed criminals often adorned the gates of cities or were abandoned at gibbets for weeks on end, leaving them in a building that people were obliged to use regularly was a wholly different matter.

'What happened to Chaloner?' asked Michael, while Bartholomew began his examination. 'Was he drunk?'

'He enjoyed an ale in the Lamb and left after sunset. The next time anyone saw him, it was the following day in the river. He was floating face-down in the water, opposite the Monks' Hythe.'

'Did he drink heavily?' asked Michael.

John shrugged. 'On occasion, when he had the money.'

Bartholomew listened while he worked. He saw that while the parish had stretched itself to provide a blanket, it had done little else. Chaloner appeared to be in exactly the same condition as when he had been pulled from the river, and no one had made any attempt to clean him. Mud still streaked his arms, and there was river weed caught in his hair and beard. No one had even washed his face and hands, and they were thick with dirt.

However, the fact that the body had not been touched provided Bartholomew with some clues. Chaloner's fingers were deeply caked in mud, which was also ingrained under his nails. That it had not washed away was a sign that he had probably not died in deep, fast-running water, but somewhere sheltered and boggy. He might have clawed at the banks in an attempt to pull himself out. But Bartholomew knew it was possible to drown in very shallow water, and the evidence on the hands alone did not allow him to ascertain whether Chaloner's death had been accidental or deliberate. It did imply, however, that he had probably known what was happening to him, which suggested that he had not wandered into the river in his cups.

Beginning at the head, Bartholomew made a careful inspection of the body, paying special attention to the neck. He said nothing when he had finished, and moved on to the next corpse.

'That is Haywarde,' explained John. 'He was found dead on Saturday. Like Chaloner and Glovere, he went to the Lamb for a drink before going home. He left the inn after dark, and—'

'Let me guess,' interrupted Michael. 'He was found the following morning floating face-down in the river opposite the Monks' Hythe.'

John nodded. 'All three were. So, what do you think, Doctor? Can we bury them in the churchyard? Or are they are suicides?'

'You can bury them in the churchyard,' said Bartholomew soberly, straightening from his examination of the second body. 'They have both been murdered.'

Michael gazed at Bartholomew in the soft shadows of St Mary's Church. Somewhere outside a dog barked and a child gave a brief shriek of laughter, and then it was silent again, except for the buzzing of flies. The sun had broken through the morning clouds and was blazing hotly through the windows. St Mary's did not boast much stained glass, but it had a little, and light pooled in occasional multi-coloured splatters on the nave floor.

'Are you sure, Matt?' Michael asked. 'Both murdered?'

'Oh, yes,' said Bartholomew. 'They were killed very carefully, using an unusual method, but the signs are there for anyone to see. Had you examined the corpses yourself, you would have drawn the same conclusion.'

'I *did* examine the corpses,' said John indignantly. 'But I found nothing to help me one way or another.'

'Oh,' said Bartholomew, not certain what else to say. He was astonished that anyone could have missed the clues that he thought were so obvious, even to the casual observer.

'Did they die in the same way as Glovere?' asked Michael.

'What?' asked John in sudden horror. 'You think Glovere, Chaloner and Haywarde were killed by the same person?'

'I cannot tell you that,' said Bartholomew pedantically. 'But I can tell you that they were all killed in an identical manner.'

'Explain,' ordered John. 'I want to know exactly what you have learned. Use Haywarde to illustrate your points. We will move away from Chaloner: he is too ripe for my stomach.'

'All three bodies have traces of mud on them,' began Bartholomew, pointing to smears of dirt on the inside of Haywarde's left ear. Someone had given his body a superficial wash, but it was insufficient to hide the fact that he had died out in the open.

'Of course they are less than pristine,' interrupted John. 'They were found in the river.'

'The river is not especially dirty in Ely,' said Bartholomew. 'And it is low at the moment and the banks are baked dry, because it is high summer and it has not rained for a while. I would not expect the bodies to be covered in mud.'

'But they are not covered in mud,' objected John. 'Haywarde has the merest trace of dirt in his ear, and you are using it to claim the man was murdered! I can see I made a mistake in securing your services for an honest verdict!'

'If you listen to him, and do not insist on interrupting with your own facile observations, you will learn why he considers the mud to be important,' snapped Michael. 'Matt and I have solved more murders than you could possibly imagine, and I can assure you that he has a lot more experience of what is and what is not important in these cases than you do.'

'Very well,' said John sullenly. 'Explain, then.'

'The first point to note is that you said the bodies were floating in the river near the Monks' Hythe,' replied Bartholomew. 'They were waterlogged, if the stains under the coffins are anything to go by, and they probably continued to drip for some time after being brought here.'

'They did,' agreed John reluctantly. 'I had to pay St Mary's thieving parish priest another penny, because he claimed they were fouling his church.'

'But this soaking failed to wash away the mud in their ears,' Bartholomew went on. 'Why should their ears be muddy, if they were found in the middle of a fairly large river?'

'It came from when they were pulled out, I imagine,' suggested Michael. 'Dirt caught in the ears when they were dragged up the bank.'

'No,' said John, thoughtfully. 'In each case, Mackerell the fisherman took his boat to fetch the bodies back to dry land. And it would have been disrespectful to drag them across the mud anyway – regardless of the fact that all three were miserable sinners who will not be missed. The bodies were taken from the boat, laid on a bier and brought here.'

'The next thing I noted was that on each body there is slight grazing on the right side of the head and face,' Bartholomew went on.

'Could that be from when they were rolled from the boat to the bier?' asked Michael.

'Unlikely,' said Bartholomew. 'John says the corpses were treated with respect – at least until they reached the church.' He shot an admonishing glance at the priest.

'Then they may have damaged themselves when they fell – or were pushed – into the water,' suggested John.

'I thought the same, but the grazing is in the same place on all three corpses,' said Bartholomew. 'It occurs on the right cheek and ear. And it is the *opposite* cheek and ear that show the traces of mud.'

'But what does that mean?' asked John. 'That they each

went head-first into the water and hit themselves on the bottom somehow?'

'Look at this,' said Bartholomew, ignoring the question and pointing to the cut at the base of Haywarde's skull.

'I hope you are not telling me *that* caused Haywarde's death,' said John in disbelief.

Bartholomew understood his scepticism. The wound was not very large, although it was deep. 'The cut may be tiny, but it has been made at a very vulnerable point. I think these men were forced to lie on the ground, probably some-where muddy, and their heads held still by something placed across one ear.'

'Like this,' said Michael, making a grab for the priest. John yelped in alarm, but he was too slight and far too slow to evade Michael's lunge. The monk, for all his ample girth, was a strong man with very fast reactions. He wrestled the priest to the ground, holding him there with a hefty knee in the middle of the back.

'Let me go!' howled John, struggling ineffectually against the monk's bulk. He turned his head to one side to relieve the pressure on his neck, so that one cheek rested on the smooth stone of the floor.

'Exactly,' said Bartholomew, nodding at the instinctive position the priest had taken. 'And while the head was turned one way, the murderer placed something across his head to hold him still, possibly a foot or a knee.'

Michael placed one foot gently across John's face. Bartholomew noted that it covered the arch of the cheek and the ear, which was precisely where the abrasions on all three victims had been located.

'And then, while the victim lay trapped and helpless, unable to do a thing to save himself, the killer took a sharp implement and drove it into that spot at the base of the skull. The wound occurs precisely between the top two neck bones, and the tip of the weapon would have been driven into the point where the brain meets the spine.'

'No!' shrieked John as Bartholomew knelt next to him,

one of his small surgical knives in his hand to illustrate the point. The physician touched the spot lightly, then indicated that Michael was to release the priest. John leapt to his feet and backed away from the Michaelhouse men in terror.

'You are insane!' he whispered. 'You could have killed me, right here, on the floor of my own church!'

'It is not your church,' Bartholomew pointed out. 'This is St Mary's and you are chaplain of Holy Cross. But you see how it might have been done? It would not need a very large implement to damage the delicate tissues in that area. In fact, a smaller implement is probably better, because then you would not be trying to force a blade through bone but into the gap between them.'

'And then I suppose the killer pushed the bodies into the river, so that any casual observer would believe that they had thrown themselves in,' mused Michael.

John was unable to repress a shudder. 'It is well known in the city that the river slows at the Monks' Hythe, and that anything dropped upstream will fetch up there, where it is shallow and full of weeds.'

'That explains the weed in the hair and clothes of all three victims,' said Bartholomew. 'And as long as people believed they committed suicide – or had an accident – rather than being murdered, there was no need for the killer to hide the corpses.'

'But why would these men warrant being murdered?' asked John in a low voice. 'What could they have done to inspire someone to slay them in so horrible a manner? I know they were not liked, but that does not mean they deserved to die.'

'The deaths *were* premeditated,' said Bartholomew thoughtfully.

'How do you arrive at that conclusion?' asked John suspiciously. He gestured to the two corpses. 'There is nothing here to allow you to speculate about that.'

Michael gave a hollow smile. 'But it is obvious nonetheless. Each of these men was last seen alone – walking home from a tavern. The killer lay in wait, and took them when they reached a spot where they could not call for help.'

'But why *these* men?' pressed John, as if they had all the answers. 'They all knew each other, of course, but they did not associate, as far as I know.'

'Did they have a common relative?' asked Michael. 'Did they frequent the same tavern?'

John shook his head, then nodded. 'Well, yes, but there are only a few taverns in the city, so that means nothing. The Lamb sells the best beer, so men tend to congregate there, if they have money. But Chaloner had an undiscerning palate, and usually opted for the cheaper brews at the Mermaid.'

'What about Richard de Leycestre?' asked Bartholomew. 'Were they friends with him?'

'Why do you ask about Leycestre?' asked John suspiciously.

Bartholomew sighed impatiently. 'Because he has been inciting the peasants to riot with his claims of injustice. We were barely through the gates before he approached us.'

'What has that to do with anything?' demanded John.

'Perhaps these three were killed because they disagreed with Leycestre,' suggested Bartholomew. 'He is a committed man and it is possible that Glovere, Chaloner and Haywarde thought he was wrong.'

'What did they think of Leycestre?' pressed Michael. 'Did they approve of his opinions?'

John shrugged nervously. 'Glovere did not, because he was well paid by Lady Blanche, and earned a comfortable living. Haywarde and Chaloner did not care one way or the other, and would only have joined a fight when they were certain which side would win.'

'That is what you said you would do,' said Bartholomew, raising his eyebrows.

'Are you sure these three deaths are unrelated to Leycestre?' asked Michael, ignoring him. 'He *is* determined to make Ely a centre for insurrection.'

'I do not think he will succeed,' said John. 'The Bishop's soldiers and the Prior's men will stamp on any rebellion when the time is right. At the moment, each side is waiting to see whether such an uprising will harm the other, and hoping that it will work to their advantage.'

'The feud between Bishop and Prior is that bitter?' asked Bartholomew.

It was Michael who replied. 'They do not like each other and they argue a good deal, but compared to most bishops and priors, de Lisle and Alan share a remarkably tolerant relationship.'

'The monks seemed pleased that de Lisle was accused of murder,' Bartholomew pointed out, recalling the glee with which the obnoxious Robert had reported the news to Michael.

'Some are, but that is because it is *only* an accusation at the moment,' said John. 'If de Lisle were arrested and tried, you can be sure that the Church would close ranks and forget past differences. And anyway, in their heart of hearts, they know de Lisle is innocent, just as I do.'

'Well, I am glad someone does,' muttered Bartholomew, still not at all sure that the Bishop had no hand in the deaths of the three men.

'So, your examination has proved that the Bishop is innocent,' said John thoughtfully. 'Because the method of killing is unusual, we know that all three were victims of the same person. De Lisle has no reason to want Chaloner and Haywarde dead – I doubt he knew they even existed – and so it stands to reason that he did not kill Glovere, either.'

Michael and Bartholomew exchanged a wary glance, realising that it did no such thing. Michael had already said that the Bishop was wily enough to have reasoned that for himself, and that he would not be above killing two more men in order to 'prove' his innocence in the death of the first. They said nothing, and John went on.

'This is good news. I hope you will credit *me* with this discovery. After all, it was *I* who suggested that you should examine these other two corpses. The Bishop should know that it was due to my initiative that he is acquitted of this charge.'

'We shall tell him,' said Michael.

'So, if the Bishop is not the killer, who is?' asked John. 'I am certain it is not Leycestre. He is not the kind of man who commits murder.'

'Well, someone is,' said Michael. He glanced at Bartholomew. 'Was it a quick end, do you think?'

Bartholomew raised his hands, palms upwards. 'I have never heard of anyone being killed like this before. But I doubt the victims lived long after the blade penetrated their necks. None of the wounds seems to have bled much, which indicates they did not die from loss of blood.'

'Did it hurt?' asked John, rubbing his own neck as if in sympathy.

'Yes, probably,' replied Bartholomew. 'The marks on Glovere and Chaloner are not quite as neat as the one on Haywarde, suggesting that the killer did a little prodding before he found his mark. And then it would take considerable force to thrust the blade between the bones until it did its damage.'

'But Haywarde's wound looks as if the killer knew exactly where to push,' said Michael, leaning forward to inspect the mark again.

'Yes,' said Bartholomew grimly. 'He is getting better at it.'

chapter 4

IT WAS AFTERNOON BY THE TIME THAT BARTHOLOMEW AND Michael had completed their examination of the bodies in St Mary's Church, and had put them back the way they had found them. John offered Bartholomew four grubby pennies for his pains, which the physician refused, asking that they be given to Haywarde's widow instead. Then he and Michael left the church, and stepped gratefully into the glorious sunshine outside.

Michael took a deep breath to clear his lungs of the cloying stench of death, and tipped his pale face back so that the warmth of the sun could touch it. Bartholomew removed his black scholar's tabard and stuffed it in his bag. In Cambridge, he could be fined for not wearing the uniform of his College, but in Ely he was free of such restrictions. It felt good to wear only shirt-sleeves in the warmth of a summer day, and he did not envy Michael his heavy Benedictine habit.

'All that prodding with corpses has done nothing for my appetite,' complained the monk. 'I am not in the least bit hungry.'

'You are not hungry because you ate like a pig this morning,' said Bartholomew critically. 'I have never seen so much food piled in one place. No wonder so many of your brethren are fat.'

'Thomas is fat,' said Michael huffily. 'But *I* am large-boned, as I have told you before. You are far too quick to accuse people of being obese these days, Matt. Making your patients feel uncomfortable about their physical appearance is not a kind thing to do.'

'You are not my patient,' said Bartholomew, laughing.

'I will be soon, if you drive me to my sickbed with your constant comments about my size,' declared Michael testily. 'I am not fat; I just have heavy bones.'

'I am sorry, Brother,' said Bartholomew, still laughing. 'I forgot.'

'Well, do not forget again,' admonished Michael. He sighed. 'What do you think, Matt? Where have these discoveries of yours led us?'

'Deeper into a mystery to which I can see no answer,' said Bartholomew, who would rather have been discussing Michael's girth than the perplexing case of the three dead men. 'As you said, your Bishop is certainly clever enough to kill two more people in order to "prove" he was innocent of the death of the first.'

'I hope I am wrong,' said Michael fervently. 'I keep thinking that de Lisle would not have brought me here to investigate if he really had had a hand in Glovere's death, but perhaps that is exactly his intention: to make people think he is innocent by ordering me to make enquiries.'

'But the Bishop is not the only man on our list of suspects. A number of your brethren give the impression they harbour an intense dislike for de Lisle and would not be averse to hatching a plot that would see him blamed for a killing.'

'Such as Robert,' agreed Michael. 'He is a nasty man – greedy and niggardly with the alms he distributes to the poor. Men like Leycestre would not be so vocal about the priory's harshness if Robert gave away all that he should.'

Bartholomew was unconvinced. 'But Robert only dispenses kitchen scraps. Why should he be niggardly with those? There is enough food at the table to ensure he is never hungry himself.'

'He can sell spare food to the lay-brothers and pocket the proceeds. The priory also grants him an allowance of gold that is supposed to be used for the benefit of the poor. Who knows whether that goes the way it should?'

'Surely it is Prior Alan's responsibility to ensure that it does?'

'All Alan's attention is absorbed by his building projects. He delegates most other matters to Sub-prior Thomas. Thomas also dislikes de Lisle, although he is far too fat to go around killing people.'

'He is not too fat to grab someone and immobilise them once he has them on the ground.'

'True,' admitted Michael. 'Thomas shall remain on our list of suspects, then.'

'William seems cleverer than the others,' said Bartholomew, thinking of the monks he had seen at the refectory that morning. 'He is the kind of man to damage de Lisle, then sit back to watch the consequences and only step forward to take advantage when he is sure it is safe.'

'That is a good analysis of him,' said Michael approvingly. 'I have never trusted him – mostly because he sports that ridiculous hairstyle. However, he does despise the snivelling Robert, which tends to raise him in my estimation, and he is genuinely concerned for the poor.'

'Meanwhile, Alan should have been Bishop, but was cheated of the post when the Pope elected de Lisle instead,' Bartholomew went on. 'Alan has every reason to want de Lisle to fall from grace, because then it is likely that he will become bishop.'

'A possible solution, but an unlikely one,' said Michael dismissively. 'Alan is not the kind of man to kill.'

'That is what Father John said about Leycestre, but we remained sceptical,' Bartholomew pointed out. 'If we elect to use a particular logic to name one suspect, then we must use that same logic to name others.'

'But I know Alan, and so it is reasonable for me to make such assertions,' said Michael defensively. 'Alan is not a killer, Matt. At least, I do not think so.'

'Then we will keep him on our list until you are sure. What about the others? Perhaps Symon kills anyone who wants to read the priory's books.'

Michael laughed. 'I am sure he would like to. We will keep him on our list, though, because he is always plotting and hatching plans that will see him promoted to a higher rank. They are usually unsuccessful, but it is possible that practice has made perfect. He must have engaged in serious subterfuge to secure himself the post of librarian – I cannot imagine he was appointed because he is a keen proponent of education.'

'What about Henry?' asked Bartholomew. 'He is a physician, and would know where to place a knife so it would kill.'

'Never,' declared Michael. 'He is one of the most gentle, kindest men I have ever known. Look how patient he is with that Julian.'

'Julian,' said Bartholomew immediately. 'Now there is someone with a murderous personality. He is nasty, enjoys the suffering of others, and has no compassion.'

Michael nodded slowly. 'And his work in the hospital may well have provided him with the kind of knowledge necessary to kill with stealth – not learned from Henry, obviously, but from studying and reading.'

'So, those are the churchmen,' summarised Bartholomew. 'Bishop de Lisle, Prior Alan, Sub-prior Thomas, Hosteller William, Almoner Robert, Symon the librarian and Julian. Then there are the townsfolk: Leycestre and his nephews.'

'And that Agnes Fitzpayne seems more angry about the inconvenience of Haywarde's death than grief-stricken. She is strong enough to overpower a man.'

'She is a heavy-boned lady,' agreed Bartholomew.

Michael shot him a sharp glance, then went on. 'We must not forget those gypsies, either. Leycestre believes they are the culprits. Perhaps we should pay them a visit: you look as though you need a little diversion after poking at those vile corpses, and I am sure you would be only too willing to spend more time in the company of the attractive Eulalia.'

'And finally, we cannot rule out the possibility that someone in Lady Blanche's household might be committing the murders, simply to wreak havoc and confusion in de Lisle's domain,' said Bartholomew, thinking that a visit to the gypsy camp would indeed be a pleasant way to pass an afternoon.

Michael sniggered. 'Like Tysilia, you mean? You placed her at the head of a list of suspects once before, and it led you nowhere. Do not fall into the same trap a second time.'

Bartholomew rubbed a hand through his hair as he tried to make sense out of the meagre facts they had accumulated. 'Most of these suspects are on our list only because we have made the assumption that they want de Lisle accused of murder so he will be discredited. However, it seems to me that someone has gone to a good deal of trouble to ensure that Glovere, Chaloner and Haywarde did *not* look as though they were murdered.'

'That is true. They were rolled into the river so that it would be assumed that they had had an accident or committed suicide.'

'And that implies that these men were not killed in order to have de Lisle accused of murder, but for some other reason,' concluded Bartholomew.

Michael pursed his lips and frowned. 'But what? Apart from the fact that no one liked them – Glovere was a malcontent, Chaloner married the wrong woman and Haywarde was an idle, drunken bully – we have uncovered nothing that links them together.'

'They were all townsmen,' said Bartholomew. 'Perhaps that is where we should start. We have become side-tracked by the accusation levelled at de Lisle by Blanche, but I think these deaths may have nothing to do with your Bishop or the priory. They may just be the result of some falling out between these three men and their drinking cronies.'

'Well, that will be easy enough to find out,' said Michael confidently. 'I am used to investigating very complex crimes, and no Ely resident will be able to outwit *me* for long.'

'That may be so,' said Bartholomew. 'But you are assuming that people will talk to you. These are folk in a small community, who are protective of each other, and they will not be given to revealing their secrets to outsiders. You may find yourself unable to gather enough information to deduce anything – no matter how clever you are.'

Michael sighed. 'So, you are telling me that I might never solve these murders?'

'It is possible,' said Bartholomew. 'You have enjoyed success so far, and have found a culprit for every murder you have looked into. But there may come a time when you fail.'

'No,' vowed Michael. 'I *will* solve this. Unless I come up with an answer, my Bishop will be stained with this charge for ever, and then what would happen?'

'You would remain a proctor for the rest of your life, and de Lisle would end his days in some remote friary, far away from the King and his court and the centre of power.'

'And that would never do,' said Michael with a grin. 'Come, Matt. Let us revisit these inns, and see what we can do to further my career and save de Lisle from a life of ignominy.'

The day had grown hot while they had been inside the church, and it was not long before Bartholomew's shirt began to prickle uncomfortably at his skin as he walked with Michael to the first of the taverns. He imagined that Michael must be on fire under the thick black folds of his habit. In the winter, he was occasionally jealous of the fine-quality wool of the monk's clothes, which were able to keep out all but the most bitter of the Fenland winds, but in the summer he was grateful he was not encumbered by the heavy garments the Benedictines were obliged to wear, and relished the touch of a cooling breeze on his bare arms and billowing through his shirt. It was so hot that he seriously considered a swim in the river, but the notion that three corpses had been pulled from it tempered his enthusiasm somewhat.

'A jug of beer would be very acceptable, do you not agree?' asked Michael as they passed the Chantry on the Green – a chapel established for the express purpose of saying masses for the dead – and headed towards the Heyrow. 'I need something to wash the taste of bodies from my mouth, and Ely has a reputation for fine ales. This notion of yours to continue our investigation by revisiting the taverns was a very good one.'

'I would rather start working in the library,' said Bartholomew wistfully, thinking about the literary delights that were so tantalisingly close.

Michael shook his head. 'Symon told you to find him tomorrow. He will not oblige you any sooner, and it is better that you help me investigate these deaths, rather than kick your heels idly while you wait for him.'

'We should visit the Lamb first, then,' said Bartholomew. 'The bona cervisia served there comes from the priory brewery, and is said to be the best in the city. The Bell sells mediocris cervisia – weak ale – and the White Hart is right at the bottom of the pile with debilis cervisia.'

'Debilis cervisia?' asked Michael, horrified. 'That is what the priory gives its servants at midday, so that they are not too drunk to complete their duties in the afternoons. But how do you know all this? You only arrived yesterday.'

'I was treated to a full description of the taverns and their ales last night from Henry,' said Bartholomew with a smile. 'He believes that the quality of beer a person drinks reflects directly upon the state of his health.'

'I wish you would develop ideas like that,' said Michael ruefully. 'They would be far more pleasant to discuss than fevers and boils and the other repellent things you seem to find so fascinating.'

'There are flaws in his argument, though,' said Bartholomew thoughtfully. 'On the one hand, drinking vast quantities of strong ale cannot be good for the brain, while drinking large amounts of weak beer will cleanse the kidneys. However, on the other, the weak debilis cervisia contains impurities, becomes cloudy more quickly than does the strong bona cervisia, and can distress the stomach.'

'Then let us put this hypothesis to the test,' said Michael.

'You can imbibe debilis cervisia and I shall partake of bona cervisia, and we shall see who feels better tomorrow.'

Bartholomew laughed. 'That is no way to conduct scientific experiments, Brother! The results would be questionable, to say the least. But do you really think we will learn anything more from a second trawl of the taverns? We were not particularly successful last night.'

'That is because our questions were undirected and general. Now we know we are looking for specific links between Glovere, Chaloner and Haywarde. Last night, we did not even know that we should be looking into three deaths, not one – until we met Agnes Fitzpayne at the Mermaid.'

'Father John told us that all the victims enjoyed a drink in the Lamb before they died,' said Bartholomew. 'So it is as good a place as any to start. How many taverns are there in Ely, Brother? I lost count last night.'

'Seven, plus alehouses,' replied Michael promptly. 'Alehouses tend to come and go, since they are places where the occupants simply happen to have the ingredients to brew a batch of beer, so we will leave those for now. But as for taverns, there are three big inns in the centre of the city, three on the hythes and one near the mill. The central ones tend to be frequented by merchants and the town's more moneyed visitors, while the others are used by working folk. The Lamb is the exception, and anyone who can pay is welcome inside.'

He took Bartholomew's arm and steered him to where the Lamb stood on the corner of Lynn Road and the Heyrow. A substantial building on two floors, it had stables at the back that hired out horses as well as looked after those of its guests, and a huge kitchen with one of the largest chimneys Bartholomew had ever seen. Smoke curled from the top of it, wafting the scented aroma of burning logs and cooking meat across the green.

'Perhaps I could manage a morsel of something,' said Michael as they opened the door and his keen eyes spotted a sheep that was being roasted in the hearth. 'A slice of that mutton should suffice, along with a loaf of bread. It is not good for a man to be without sustenance for too long.'

Bartholomew picked his way across a floor that was strewn with sedge and discarded scraps of food. Several dogs and a pig rooted happily. But as soon as Bartholomew and Michael stepped across the threshold, the animals abandoned their scavenging and came as a pack to greet the newcomers, winding enthusiastically around their legs and waving friendly tails, so that Michael almost tripped. He grabbed a table to save himself and glared at the offending animal, which slunk away. The others remained, however, pushing up against the scholars and pawing at their legs.

'Damned things!' muttered Michael, trying to push them away with a sandalled foot. 'What is wrong with them? Can they smell the eggs I put in my scrip earlier? I thought I gave all those to you.'

'They know we have been near corpses,' said Bartholomew, pulling a face of disgust when he raised the sleeve of his shirt to his nose. 'But you do not need the nose of a dog to tell you that. I imagine everyone from here to Cambridge will know exactly what we have been doing.'

'How horrible!' exclaimed Michael, shooing away a particularly demanding specimen that clearly considered itself in paradise. 'Dogs really are revolting creatures.'

Bartholomew looked around him as Michael selected a quiet bench near the rear door. The main part of the tavern comprised a large room with a low ceiling that obliged Bartholomew and Michael to duck as they walked. The walls had been painted, but not recently enough to remove all the traces of the food that evidently sailed through the air on occasion. The benches were polished shiny by the generations of seats that had reclined on them, and the tables were almost white from the number of times they had been scrubbed. In all, the tavern curiously managed to be both scrupulously clean and rather dirty.

The landlord came to see them, wiping his hands on an apron that was covered in a mass of cut hairs of various colours, lengths and textures. On one wall hung a fearsome array of knives and scissors, and Bartholomew recalled Father John mentioning that the landlord of the Lamb was also the city's surgeon. Like many in his trade, the surgeon also cut hair and trimmed beards, although most did not usually run a tavern, too.

'Brother Michael,' said the landlord, greeting the monk as he took his seat. 'And you must be Doctor Bartholomew.'

'How do you know that?' asked Bartholomew curiously.

The landlord smiled. 'I am an innkeeper – Barbour is my name – and I make it my business to know everything that happens in Ely.'

'One of his pot-boys also works in the priory kitchen,' said Michael, unimpressed by the landlord's knowledge. 'I imagine he informed Master Barbour about the two visitors from Cambridge. And, of course, I am well known in this town anyway. Ely is my Mother House, and I am one of its most important monks.'

'You are not well known, because you are not here very often,' contradicted Barbour. 'But, yes, you have correctly guessed the source of my information. And now I will tell you something else: this morning you have been looking at the two bodies in St Mary's Church.'

'Who told you that?' asked Michael, without much interest. 'Your pot-boy again?'

'You stink of the dead. If you have no objection, I shall open a door to allow the air to circulate. I do not want the stench of you to drive away my other customers.'

'I told you that is why we are so popular with these dogs,' said Bartholomew to Michael.

'Well?' asked Barbour, as he opened the rear door and stopped it with what appeared to be a lump of fossilised dung. Immediately, a pleasant breeze wafted in, filled with the warm scent of mown grass and sun-baked horse manure from the yard beyond. 'What did you learn from your examination of Chaloner and Haywarde? There is a rumour that Haywarde took his own life.'

'Why are you so keen to know?' asked Michael. 'And while you tell us, you can cut me a slice of that mutton. I am starving.'

Barbour selected a knife from the wall, spat on it to remove any residual hairs from the last haircut it had given, scraped it across the hearth a few times to sharpen it, and then began to carve thick chunks of the mutton on to a wooden platter. Michael watched critically, ready to step in and complain if he felt Barbour was being niggardly. The landlord, however, showed no signs of finishing, and the pile of meat grew larger and larger.

'Chaloner and Haywarde were my customers,' he replied. 'In fact, Haywarde liked to sit in the exact spot that you are in, Brother. Glovere came here from time to time, too. It is hard to lose three men who liked their ale within a few days – hard for my business, that is.'

'I am sure it is,' said Michael. 'Were they friends, then, these three men?'

Barbour shook his head, sawing vigorously as his blade encountered bone. Bartholomew glanced at Michael, wondering whether a man who wielded knives with such vicious efficiency should also be included on their ever-growing list of suspects. So far, the only thing that connected the three men was that they had all enjoyed their ale in the tavern run by Barbour.

'Those three had no friends,' the landlord declared. 'They were not likeable, and they were certainly not the types to tolerate each other. Haywarde owed me money; I doubt I will see that again. Agnes Fitzpayne would reimburse me if I asked, but I do not see why she should pay for her brother-in-law's pleasures.'

'That is an unusual attitude for a landlord to take,' observed Michael. 'Usually, they will take what they are owed from anyone.'

'Agnes still comes to *me* to be bled,' confided Barbour. 'It is said that Brother Henry washes his knives before he bleeds people, so many of my customers have shifted their allegiance. And somehow, he also avoids having the blood spray over people's clothes. I am not sure how he does it, but I do not like to ask for his professional secrets.'

'Ask,' recommended Bartholomew immediately. 'I am sure he will tell you, and it would be better for your patients. And you should consider cleaning your knives, too.'

'I do *clean* them,' said Barbour indignantly. 'I always spit on them and give them a good wipe on my apron first – although a bit of lamb grease in a cut never did anyone any harm – but Henry uses hot water and *washes* his blades with a cloth.'

'What can you tell us about Glovere?' asked Michael hastily, seeing that Bartholomew was ready to give the surgeon a lecture on the benefits of clean implements.

'He whined about Lady Blanche and his fellow servants, and he complained bitterly about the Bishop of Ely. Mind you, I do not blame him for that.'

'You do not, do you?' asked Michael coolly. 'And why, pray, is that?'

'The Bishop is not a nice man,' replied Barbour, caring nothing for the warning in Michael's voice. 'He probably ordered Glovere killed, just as Lady Blanche claims.'

'And why do you think she is right?' asked Michael, eyes glistening as Barbour laid the loaded platter in front of him. The landlord reached up to a shelf above the hearth and presented them with a bottle of pickled mint, then went to draw two pots of frothing brown ale. The fact that he was on the other side of the room did not prevent him from answering Michael's question.

'The Bishop and Blanche are always fighting with each other,' he yelled. 'Their servants join in, and it is likely that the Bishop ordered one of his henchmen to do away with Glovere. I heard that de Lisle's steward, Ralph, set fire to some cottages that belonged to Blanche a few months ago.'

'The ones at Colne, near Huntingdon?' asked Bartholomew, recalling the Bishop himself mentioning that incident, and then admitting responsibility.

'Yes,' agreed Barbour. 'The King himself heard the case, and deemed the Bishop guilty, so he must have done it. After all, the King could never be wrong.'

'Never,' said Michael dryly. 'But did anyone in de Lisle's household issue threats against Glovere, that you know of?'

'The Bishop himself,' replied Barbour promptly. 'They had a row in the priory a few days before Glovere died. That is why everyone is willing to believe the Bishop killed him.'

'People often say things they do not mean in the heat of the moment,' said Michael. 'De Lisle has a quick temper, and words spoken in anger should not be held against him. But did anyone else have a quarrel with Glovere? Ralph, the steward, for example?'

Barbour brought the ale to the table and then leaned against the door. Bartholomew wondered whether he had chosen that position so that he could have access to a source of fresh air, away from the stench of death that hung around his guests. The physician took a piece of the mutton before Michael could eat it all. It did not taste as good as it looked, and was tough and dry. He suspected that the landlord was only too glad to see it go to a good home, and wondered whether the shortage of cash of which everyone complained meant that Barbour's customers did not have spare funds to spend on treats like good ale and extra meat.

'Ralph did not quarrel with Glovere, as far as I know,' replied Barbour. 'Although he is a man to slit a fellow's throat if he thought it would benefit his master. But a number of people wished Glovere dead. Including me. The night he died a number of my customers agreed that Ely would be a nicer place without him. You have to understand that these three men were like the scum on a barrel of beer – good for nothing and an offence to all. But I do not think any of my customers would actually go out and put wishful thoughts into practice.'

'Well, someone did,' said Michael. 'And I do not believe it was the Bishop.'

'Glovere was in here the night he died, trying to spread

rumours that one of *us* was responsible for the burglaries that have plagued Ely over the last two weeks. I had to ask him to leave.'

'Really?' asked Michael, interested. 'Why?'

'He was trying to stir up trouble and create an atmosphere of suspicion and unease in the town. He really was a despicable specimen. It was late and I was tired, and I refused to refill his jug, which did not please him. He was sullen and resentful when he left.'

'Where did he go?' asked Bartholomew.

'I have no idea,' replied Barbour. 'He lives on Flex Lane, so I assume he went home.'

'And no one followed him when he left?' asked Michael.

'I did not notice. I admit that when I first heard he was dead, I wondered whether Chaloner had done something to him. Glovere brought up the matter of Alice, you see, and suggested that Chaloner might be our burglar. But Chaloner died a week later, and so I dismissed my suspicions on that front.'

'Did you see Chaloner following Glovere?' asked Bartholomew.

'I did not. It was a hot night, and I recall several of my patrons lingering outside, reluctant to go to a hard bed and a prickly blanket. But Chaloner was not among them.'

'Who, then?' demanded Michael.

'I did not see – I only spotted shapes in the shadows. Then I went for a walk myself, because, as I said, it was an unpleasantly humid night for sleeping. But Ely is a respectable city – it is not like Cambridge, where killers lurk on every corner. I sincerely doubt that one of our citizens is our culprit, and *you* are the only strangers who have been here in the last two weeks. Other than the gypsies, of course, but they come every year.'

'Leycestre is spreading rumours that the gypsies killed Glovere,' said Michael.

Barbour nodded. 'But they had no reason to harm the man. Leycestre also thinks they are responsible for all these burglaries – there was yet another last night – and I think that is much more likely. Gypsies like gold.'

'As opposed to everyone else, who hates it?' asked Bartholomew archly. 'Who was burgled last night?'

'One of the cordwainers who lives on Brodhythe Street. He had sold a consignment of leather laces and had boasted about the high price he got. Then, the very next night, he lost it all when someone broke into his house.'

'So, whoever committed this theft must have known where to look,' surmised Bartholomew. 'The gypsies would be less likely to have that information than someone who lives permanently in the town.'

'Not true,' said Barbour. 'The cordwainer was celebrating his good fortune loudly, and virtually every man, woman and child in Ely – gypsies included – knew exactly how much money he had in the chest in his attic.'

'All this has nothing to do with these murders,' said Michael impatiently. 'I—'

'Murders?' pounced Barbour immediately. 'I heard Glovere was murdered, but was under the impression that Chaloner's death was an accident and Haywarde took his own life. Do you know different?'

'All three met their ends in the same way,' said Michael tiredly. 'You can ask Father John if you want details. Chaloner and Haywarde were stabbed in the neck, as was Glovere.'

'I was unaware that the Bishop even *knew* Chaloner and Haywarde,' said Barbour in confusion. 'Why would he kill them?'

'He did not,' snapped Michael. 'It is obvious that someone else dispatched all three. What can you tell me about Chaloner and Haywarde?'

'Not much,' said Barbour, eyeing the other patrons in his inn, as though already contemplating the enjoyment he would have when he revealed this particular piece of gossip. 'Chaloner died about a week ago. He was drinking alone – as usual, since no one much liked his company – and he left when it was dark. He was next seen when he appeared dead in the river the following day.'

'And Haywarde?' asked Bartholomew.

'He sat by the hearth and muttered in low voices to Leycestre and that pair of discontented brats, Adam Clymme and Robert Buk.'

'Agnes Fitzpayne said they are his nephews,' said Bartholomew.

'She was there, too,' added Barbour. 'Agnes Fitzpayne. The five of them huddled in the corner and mumbled. Then I told Haywarde that if he wanted to stay longer, he would have to give me a few pennies towards the debt he had incurred for past ales. He decided to leave.'

'That is interesting,' said Bartholomew. 'It sounds as though Agnes was happy enough with Haywarde to spend an evening drinking with him, yet she was disgusted that the cost of his requiem fell to her when her sister could not pay.'

'I confess I was surprised by the sight of a decent woman like Agnes deigning to converse with the likes of her idle brother-in-law,' said Barbour. 'But I suppose he was family. However, I can tell you that she never liked him. When he left the tavern drunk the night he died we all knew that his wife and children would feel the brunt of his temper. Only he never arrived home. Like Chaloner, Haywarde was next seen face-down in the river.'

'Could someone who liked Mistress Haywarde have stepped in and prevented him from returning home?' asked Michael, clearly thinking of Agnes.

'We *all* like Mistress Haywarde,' said Barbour. 'But her husband was a regular drinker – and a regular bully – and no one ever attempted to intervene before.'

'And once they had left your inn, as far as you know, no one set eyes on these men until they were found in the river the following day?' asked Bartholomew, wanting to be clear on that point.

'No,' said Barbour. 'Believe me, it was something that was

debated a good deal, both here and in the other taverns. We are all interested to know who was the last person to see them alive. It is generally agreed that it was me and my patrons, here at the Lamb. Other than the killer, of course,' he added hastily.

'Who found the corpses?' asked Bartholomew.

'Master Mackerell. When you talk to him, do not expect a pleasant discourse, such as you have had with me. Mackerell is another malcontent. He lives on Baldock Lane, but you may find him in the Mermaid Inn at this hour.'

'Right,' said Michael, finishing the mutton and rising to his feet. 'Let us visit the Mermaid Inn, Matt.'

Bartholomew declined to trawl the city's taverns again, claiming Michael could manage that on his own. Instead, he returned to the priory to seek out Henry and ask his opinion about the marsh fever that struck many Fenland settlements at certain times of the year. Henry professed to know a good deal about it, although Bartholomew decided his knowledge was anecdotal rather than analytical. Henry was the only physician covering a fairly large area, and Bartholomew supposed he had a rather inflated opinion of his skills because there was no one qualified nearby to contradict him. Henry was not as arrogantly dogmatic with his diagnoses as some medical men Bartholomew had encountered, but his immodesty was a flaw nevertheless.

'I see dozens of cases of marsh fever every year,' boasted Henry. 'Sometimes, it seems that there is not a soul in the entire region who does not want me for some ailment or other. I am famous for the efficacy of my treatments, so people travel considerable distances to ask my advice.'

'You must find it tiring,' said Bartholomew politely.

Henry smiled. 'Sometimes. But I like to help people, if I can. There is so much suffering in the world that it is good to be able to alleviate some of it. Julian claims we cause more than we cure, but he is a miserable boy who has nothing pleasant to say about anything.'

'That is certainly true,' agreed Bartholomew, glancing to where Julian and Welles were giving one of the elderly inmates a bath. Welles was being careful with the frail bones of the very old man, but Julian was rough and Bartholomew could see the patient wincing. Henry rebuked the novice twice, but was eventually obliged to oversee the operation. Personally, Bartholomew would have sent the boy packing, or found him a task that did not involve contact with anything living. He was torn between admiration for Henry's hopeful persistence with what was clearly a lost cause, and exasperation with him for wasting his time.

Meanwhile, Michael discovered that Barbour was wrong in his prediction that Mackerell would be at the Mermaid. The inn was deserted and locked, and a friendly bargeman told him that it tended to be closed during afternoons at harvest time, because most of its patrons were in the fields. The monk strolled back to the priory, where he spent the rest of the day in the chapter house, enjoying the pleasant chill of its shady stone interior and chatting to other Benedictines who knew that it was the best place to be on a day when the sun was hot enough to fry eggs.

Towards the end of the afternoon, Almoner Robert also arrived to take advantage of the chapter house's cool. He tripped over a step when he entered, blinded by the sudden darkness after the blaze of light outside, and Michael heard the distinctive jangle of coins bouncing together in his scrip. He suspected that the almoner was not carrying his small fortune to give to the poor, but that he intended to use it for some purpose that would benefit himself. Robert was that kind of monk. Hosteller William watched Robert carefully, and Michael saw that the clash of coins had not gone unnoticed by him, either.

Michael had disliked both men since they had all been novices together. Robert was self-interested and dishonest even then, while William had been secretive and difficult to understand. Their lives had not been improved by the vast, looming presence of Thomas, who rewarded those youngsters who told tales about the others, creating an atmosphere of suspicion and unease.

Then a young man called John de Bukton – who, like Welles, was always referred to by the name of his village, because there were so many Johns in the priory – chattered away to Michael, revealing that his own experiences as a novice at Ely were much the same as Michael's had been. Sub-prior Thomas's rule was still based on a system of favourites, and most youngsters were unhappy and uncertain about a future with the Benedictine Order. Michael was startled to learn that William was sympathetic to their grievances and that the novices turned to him, rather than to Alan or Robert, who tended to be dismissive of their complaints. The novices liked Henry, too, because he was patient and soft-hearted, and often shared with them the ale he brewed himself. Michael was not surprised that Henry was popular with the youngsters, recalling Henry's many acts of kindness when he had been a novice.

Once the sun had set and the day was cooler, Michael went to see whether Bartholomew wanted to visit the Mermaid Inn. Bartholomew, however, was deeply engrossed in treating one of Henry's patients who had a rasping cough, and the monk knew he would never prise him away for a mere murder investigation. He went to the Mermaid with Cynric and Meadowman instead, but although they passed an enjoyable evening, Mackerell did not appear.

The following day broke clear and bright, with the sun soaring into the sky and flooding the cathedral with light at prime. Michael noticed that Bartholomew deliberately avoided the office – he knew the physician had not over-slept, because that was impossible in a priory with dozens of bells chiming and clanging to announce each rite and a hundred monks hurrying around the precinct.

Cynric had somehow learned that Mackerell planned to take his breakfast in the Mermaid Inn that morning, and Michael was determined to speak to the man. He found Bartholomew in the infirmary, arguing about bunions with

Henry, and suggested they go to see him together.

'Who knows where he may disappear if he learns we want to question him?' he added.

'Why would he disappear anywhere?' asked Bartholomew. His early morning discussion had irritated him. Henry was very willing to dispense his own ideas, but was considerably less willing to listen to anyone else's, once he had had his say. It was a fault Bartholomew had encountered in other physicians, and was not a trait he admired. 'We only want to know what he saw when he discovered the bodies. We are not accusing him of putting them there.'

'That depends on what he knows,' said Michael. 'He is said to be another of Ely's less appealing characters. Perhaps a fourth malcontent murdered the other three.'

Bartholomew did not reply, feeling that Michael was grasping at straws in his determination to see the case solved, and they walked in silence through the priory grounds towards the Steeple Gate. They had not gone far when a commotion caught their attention.

'Now what?' muttered Michael, watching the new arrivals in disapproval. 'Is another Blanche arriving, to throw the priory into a state of emergency ingratiation? It made me sick on Sunday to watch the obsequious fawning by the likes of Robert and William.'

'I know him!' exclaimed Bartholomew, as a slightly hunched figure dismounted carefully from a donkey and brushed himself down fastidiously. When he took the cup of wine that was offered by the ever-ready Robert, he sniffed suspiciously at it and then wiped the rim with his sleeve before deigning to put it to his lips. 'He was at St John's Hospital in Cambridge when I was last there. He asked me if there was any hope of discovering a cure for death.'

Michael chuckled. 'That is Roger de Northburgh, Bishop of Coventry and Lichfield – the man Prior Alan has appointed to investigate the charges against de Lisle. And you see that fellow behind him, with his hair cut like a mercenary and the face of an ape? That is Canon Stretton, whom Blanche has chosen as her agent.'

'I know appearances may be deceptive,' mused Bartholomew, regarding the canon's pugilistic features uncertainly, 'but Stretton does not look very astute to me.'

'Look,' said Michael gleefully, pointing as Alan and de Lisle emerged from the Prior's house and Blanche strode purposefully from the direction of the Outer Hostry, all coming to greet the new arrivals. 'And listen. This should be entertaining, just as long as I am not seen and dragged into it.'

He pulled Bartholomew behind a buttress at the sacristy, and proceeded to observe the meeting of the protagonists with unconcealed merriment.

'Bishop Northburgh,' said Alan formally, his voice carrying across the yard. 'Welcome to our cathedral priory. I have asked you to come because a grave charge has been laid against Thomas de Lisle, and you were the closest prelate to hand. I hope my summons has not inconvenienced you.'

'It has, actually,' replied Northburgh peevishly. 'The priests at St John's Hospital were treating me for a debilitating disease.'

'I am sorry to hear that,' said Alan, sounding genuinely concerned. 'But we have an excellent infirmary here, should you need our medical services.'

'Oh, I shall,' vowed Northburgh, making it sound like a threat. 'I am a dying man. My heart beats quickly if I exert myself, my limbs are not strong, and my hair is brittle and dry.'

'That sounds serious,' said Alan sympathetically.

'It sounds like old age,' remarked Bartholomew to Michael. 'You said he is ninety, but he looks much younger. For his years, he appears to be in excellent health.'

Michael nodded. 'It is said that he has never had a moment of genuine illness in his life, although he has enjoyed a good many imagined ones.'

Northburgh had moved away from Alan and was gazing

at de Lisle. 'So, Ely,' he said, looking his fellow Bishop up and down contemptuously. 'I am informed that Lady Blanche de Wake thinks you killed her servant. Did you?'

'Of course not,' snapped de Lisle, treating Blanche to a hostile glower. 'She is deranged if she imagines me to be the kind of man to commit so base a crime as murder.'

'That was badly worded,' muttered Bartholomew to Michael. 'It sounds as though he is quite happy to commit crimes that he does not consider to be base.'

Blanche bristled with indignation, heaving her skirts up under her mighty bosom, as if girding herself for a fight. But before she could begin what promised to be an entertaining verbal assault on the haughty Bishop, Northburgh turned to her.

'There you have it, madam. Ely tells me he is innocent of this crime. The matter is resolved.'

Even Michael was startled by this assertion, and the wind was taken out of Blanche's outraged sails in an instant.

'Is that it?' she asked, aghast. 'That one question is the full extent of your investigation?'

'That one question is all I have been charged to find an answer to,' retorted Northburgh briskly. 'Now, if you will excuse me, I must visit the infirmary. I am a sick man, and it is not good for me to stand around for hours in draughty courtyards.'

There was a stunned silence as he stalked away. Even de Lisle seemed unsettled by the brevity of Northburgh's examination, and Bartholomew saw him looking around, obviously for Michael. The monk eased further into the shadows of the buttress, not wanting to play an active role in the uncomfortable scene that was unravelling in front of them.

'Well!' exclaimed Blanche, watching Northburgh stride across the yard with an agility men half his age would envy. 'I am glad I did not rely on *your* choice of investigators, Father Prior.'

'I will have a word with him,' said Alan nervously. 'Doubtless he was playing games with us when he claimed he had finished with the matter. Northburgh is noted for his sense of humour.'

Michael snorted with laughter. 'That is true! He is noted for being completely without one.'

'It does not matter, actually,' said Blanche smugly. 'I have no need of your ailing Bishop to investigate my accusation. As I told you, I invited Canon Stretton to act on my behalf.' She turned to the hulking figure who stood uncertainly to one side, regarding the proceedings with a puzzled expression on his thick features.

'Who, me?' asked the burly churchman, looking around him as though there might be another Canon Stretton present.

'Yes,' said Blanche impatiently. 'My kinsmen, the King and the Black Prince, recommended you to me. They say you are tenacious and that you will be a bishop one day.'

'I will, I expect,' said Stretton carelessly, as if he were talking about eating dinner or walking to church. 'But, at the moment, I am here. Ready to service you.'

Michael released a loud and wholly inappropriate snigger that caused Alan and de Lisle to stare curiously in the direction of the buttress.

'Right,' said Blanche, regarding Stretton uneasily. 'Then you had better begin.'

The canon turned to de Lisle, towering over the tall Bishop. Hairy hands protruded from sleeves that were too short, and Bartholomew noted that his knuckles were grazed, as though he had been brawling. His eyes were almost invisible under the thick ridge that spanned his forehead, and he had the kind of nose that had been broken so many times that it was barely nose-shaped at all.

'So, Ely,' Stretton said, looking de Lisle up and down in much the same way that Northburgh had done. 'Did you kill Lady Blanche's servant?'

'No,' replied de Lisle shortly. 'I have already said that I did not.'

Stretton turned to Blanche and spread his hands. 'It seems Ely did not—'

'For God's sake!' cried Blanche furiously. 'This will just *not* do! You do not merely ask the culprit if he has committed the crime and then accept his answer without demur.'

'You do not?' asked Stretton, puzzled. 'What more do you want me to do?'

'I thought you would know!' cried Blanche, becoming exasperated. 'You are supposed to be an experienced investigator, who always uncovers the truth.'

'He always uncovers the "truth" his clients want,' muttered Michael. 'That is why the Black Prince and King Edward like him so much.'

'You must examine witnesses and you must look at the body of the victim,' Blanche explained to the confused cleric. 'And then you must produce evidence to prove de Lisle's guilt.'

'Very well, if that is what you want,' mumbled Stretton reluctantly. 'I suppose I can do that. Who are the witnesses, and what will I see if I examine this body?'

Blanche's sigh of despair must have been audible all over the priory. 'That is for *you* to determine. I should have known better than to appoint a cleric to help uncover the truth!'

With a glower at her hapless agent, she hitched up her skirts a final time, then turned to stride back to the Outer Hostry, setting such a cracking pace that her retinue were obliged to run and skip to keep up with her. Bartholomew had expected that de Lisle would be delighted at the outcome of the 'investigations', but instead he was frowning anxiously.

'This is hopeless!' he said, more to himself than to the circle of monks who had gathered around him. 'Any evidence uncovered by the likes of Stretton *or* Northburgh will be questionable to say the least. Nothing they say or do is likely prove my innocence, and this charge may hang over me for the rest of my life. Michael is my only hope.'

'He is right,' said Michael soberly, turning to Bartholomew. 'No one will believe any conclusions reached by that pair, and having an unresolved charge of murder clinging to him will be almost as bad for de Lisle as being found guilty. We had better hurry up and see what we can learn from this fisherman in the Mermaid.'

Because Michael wanted to reach the Mermaid Inn as soon as possible, he and Bartholomew took the shorter route through the priory grounds to reach the wharfs. To one side, the ruins of an ancient castle poked through the long grass of the meadow like broken teeth, while mysterious bumps and humps in the turf told of a building once fine enough for kings to sleep in, but that had been destroyed after some forgotten war two centuries previously and subsequently plundered for stone by townsfolk and priory alike.

Near the castle ruins neat rows marked the monks' vineyard, where bunches of small, white grapes ripened and baked under the summer sun. The vines were not the healthiest specimens that Bartholomew had ever seen, and he supposed that the stony soil and west-facing slopes were responsible. The wine served with the meal the previous evening had been made from the priory's grapes, and it had been a sour brew that was dry enough to be unpleasant. He had learned from Hosteller William that the south-facing slopes of the Bishop's vineyards, a short distance away, produced a much sweeter and more palatable vintage.

They walked past a huge barn, where two lay-brothers were accepting the tithes that were owed by the farmers who rented the surrounding fields. The barn was already bulging at the seams, and Bartholomew wondered how the Prior could justify taking such large tributes when he obviously had plenty to spare. The barn was vast, but even so, the lay-brothers were having difficulty in finding space for the bags of wheat they were accepting from one thin, shabbily dressed man.

Near the barn was a small gate set into a sturdy wall. It was locked, but Michael had brought the key. He opened it, then locked it behind him. Bartholomew was not surprised that the monks felt the need for security, given the hostility of some of their tenants. And he was not surprised that Leycestre and men like him felt they had a valid grievance against the priory when it was stuffing its overfilled barns with grain that its farmers could ill afford to give.

The gate brought them out into Broad Lane, a spacious street that ran along the rear boundary of the monastery precincts. Several alleys lay at right angles to it, all of them leading towards the river and the hythes. Michael selected Seggewyk Lane, and Bartholomew found himself passing the grand homes of merchants and an assortment of warehouses for storing goods that had been brought to the city by river. In Cambridge, the hythes were seedy and populated by the town's poor, who were obliged to live near their place of work. In Ely, the hythes were an exclusive area, inhabited by the wealthy. The waterfront itself was wide and spacious, and a far cry from the scrubby grass and muddy footpaths that characterised the riverside at Cambridge.

The river that passed through Ely was wide and green, with a bottom fringed with weeds that waved and undulated in the current. The bank had been strengthened against flood by a stone pier, which ran the whole length of the river between Seggewyk Lane and Water Side. Sturdy bollards provided secure anchorage for the flat-bottomed barges that made their way through the shifting waterways of the Fens to the inland port. Jetties jutted into the river, like fingers, and a number had small boats moored alongside. One or two looked unseaworthy, but most were in good condition, and their owners obviously made a good living by transporting goods to and from Ely.

Flex Lane, Baldock Lane and Water Side converged to form a small square, which was kept neat, clean and clear of clutter, and was known as the Quay. It provided a spot where bargemen could meet with merchants and haggle over prices, and where samples of goods could be unloaded for critical inspection. Some good-natured shouting could be heard at one end of the Quay, as a barge laden with peat faggots and bundles of sedge prepared to get under way, while a group of bantering apprentices lugged caskets of spice towards one of the warehouses at the other end.

The eastern bank of the river was marshland and meadow, and a few straggly sheep grazed among the rushes. A swan glided majestically back and forth, the white of its feathers almost dazzling in the sunlight. It was watched with hungry eyes by a group of barefooted boys. Bartholomew hoped none of them would be rash enough to kill it and take it home to feed his family: swans were the property of the King, and the King was very jealous of the things that were his. It was not unknown for children to be hanged for stealing game.

'What did you think of Barbour yesterday?' asked Michael, as they walked towards a low-roofed house with a swinging sign that proclaimed it as the Mermaid Inn. It had been dark the first night they had visited it, and Bartholomew had not been able to examine the building or the sign properly. He did so now, noting the crumbling plaster and the dark patches of rot in the thatch. The mermaid painted on the sign was a lusty-looking wench with a scaly tail, whose leering presence above the door Bartholomew felt was more a deterrent than welcoming.

'I would not like to witness Barbour bleeding someone,' he replied. 'He uses his cooking knives to perform the operation, and it sounds as though spurting blood is common-place. It is supposed to drip or ooze, not spray out like a fountain.'

'I meant what did you think about what he told us?' said Michael impatiently. 'I am not interested in an analysis of his surgical skills.'

'He told us nothing we did not already know or guess,' said Bartholomew. 'There is no obvious connection between the three men; no one liked them; and they all enjoyed a drink in his tavern before someone decided they should not be allowed to waste any more good beer.'

'Do you think he was holding anything back?' asked Michael. 'You told me the Fenfolk would not be forthcoming with what they know, and that I might not be able to gather enough information to identify the killer. Was Barbour holding back on us?'

'I do not think so,' said Bartholomew. 'I had the impression that he wanted to provide you with a juicy snippet of information, but that he had nothing to tell.'

'That is what I thought. Of course, we may both be wrong. But we know for certain that all three men spent their last night at the Lamb, and that whoever killed them was not stupid enough to be seen by witnesses. This is a small town, and if the killer had been lingering outside, someone would have commented on it to Barbour. And I think Barbour would have told us.'

'So, we can conclude that the killer was careful,' said Bartholomew. 'His methods are precise, and he probably planned each murder carefully.'

'But how could he have known that his prey would be obliging enough to walk home alone after dark?'

'I imagine because they were in the habit of doing so,' replied Bartholomew. 'And we are assuming that the killer only stalked his victims once. Perhaps he did so on several occasions, but was always thwarted by something.'

'I suppose you could be right,' conceded Michael reluctantly.

'The wounds on his victims' necks are very small,' Bartholomew went on thoughtfully. 'They were not made by a knife with a wide blade, but with one that was thin and long.'

'Are you sure it was a knife?' asked Michael. 'Could it have been something else? A nail or some other sharp implement?'

'It is possible,' said Bartholomew. 'A nail would be about the right size, especially a masonry nail.'

'What is the difference between a masonry nail and a

normal nail?' asked Michael a little testily, considering it an irrelevant detail.

'The shafts of nails driven into stones tend to be oval, rather than round. I suppose it makes them easier to hammer into hard surfaces. Given that the church of Holy Cross is currently under construction, and that the octagon and Lady Chapel in the cathedral are barely finished, there must be a number of them lying around.'

'We should question any masons we come across, then,' said Michael. 'Perhaps our answer to these deaths will be as simple as that: a mason with a grudge against the city, who likes to spend his spare time randomly selecting townsmen to murder in his peculiar fashion.'

Instead of entering the Mermaid, Michael walked to the edge of the river and gazed across to the marshes on the other side. Bartholomew stood with him, staring down into the murky depths of the water. Michael pointed to the pier that was nearest to them, which stood where the river curved.

'That is the Monks' Hythe, where all three bodies were found. You can see that the water is deeper there, but that the current is sluggish. It is common knowledge that anyone falling into the river upstream will fetch up here sooner or later.'

'Then perhaps these men were murdered elsewhere, and simply floated down this way,' said Bartholomew. 'We shall have to take a walk, to see what we can find.'

'But not today,' said Michael, squinting up at the bright sun. 'It is too hot. We shall do it tomorrow, first thing in the morning. Or, better still, you can do it, while I stay here and question more people. You may enjoy paddling around in mud and traipsing through undergrowth in the heat of day, but I certainly do not.'

Michael pushed open the door of the Mermaid Inn and entered. The inside should have been cool, away from the morning sun, especially given that all the window shutters were sealed, thus allowing no warm air inside. But instead it was stuffy. A warm, sickly smell of stale grease mixed with the sharper tang of spilt beer. A number of men were being served by a filthy pot-boy, who constantly scrubbed his running nose on the back of his hand. Bartholomew thought he would rather go hungry than eat in the Mermaid. Apparently, Michael felt the same, because he ordered two small goblets of beer and no food.

'I do not like debilis cervisia,' Michael muttered to his friend as the beer arrived. 'It is virtually the cheapest ale money can buy, and you might as well be drinking water. It could be worse, I suppose: Ely also produces a brew called "skegman", but the priory usually issues that to its scullions or gives it as alms to the poor. No one would drink it if there was a choice.'

'This is not bad,' said Bartholomew, sipping the mixture. It was surprisingly cool, and its mildness meant that he could drink it quickly without running the risk of becoming drowsy or drunk. The priory's strong beer made him thirsty, and he decided the weak brew served at the Mermaid was perfect for a hot day, despite Michael's disparaging comments.

As the pot-boy passed, Michael caught his arm. 'Which one of your customers is Mackerell?'

The boy grinned, revealing yellow teeth encrusted with tartar, and pointed to the window. 'The one who looks like a pike,' he replied cheekily, before pulling away from Michael and going about his business.

Bartholomew could see the lad's point. The man they had come to see had a grey, sallow complexion that reminded the physician of fish scales. This was accompanied by large, sorrowful eyes and a mouth that drooped open in a flaccid gape, much like the carp in the priory's ponds. The fact that Mackerell was almost bald and wore an apron stiff with the blood and skins of the beasts that provided his living did nothing to dispel the piscine image. Michael took his beer and carried it across to the window. Bartholomew followed.

'Master Mackerell,' said Michael, sitting next to the man and favouring him with one of his alarming beams. 'I wonder if you would mind answering one or two questions.'

'I would,' replied Mackerell with naked hostility. 'Bugger off.'

'That is a pity,' said Michael, producing a bright coin from his scrip. 'I was willing to buy you a jug of ale in return for a moment or two of your company.'

'You can keep your ale,' replied Mackerell nastily. 'I have some already.'

'Debilis cervisia is not ale,' replied Michael dismissively, casually opening Bartholomew's medicine bag and removing the small skin of wine that he knew was kept there for medical emergencies. The physician tried, unsuccessfully, to snatch it back. 'I personally prefer the finest wine from southern France.'

'We are at war with France,' said Mackerell icily, unexpectedly patriotic. 'I would not allow any brew produced by Frenchmen to pass *my* lips.'

Michael sighed, and took a swallow of the wine before handing it back to Bartholomew. Then he quickly shuffled up the bench, so that Mackerell found himself trapped between the window and the sizeable bulk of the large-boned monk. Mackerell tried to back away, but there was nowhere to go. Michael favoured him with a grin that was neither humorous nor friendly.

'Come now, Master Mackerell,' he said in a soft voice that oozed menace. 'You cannot object to passing the time of day with a man of God. But neither of us is comfortable crammed together like this, so I will be brief. What do you know about the three bodies you found in the river?'

'They drowned,' replied Mackerell sullenly. 'Now leave me alone.'

'They did not drown,' said Michael firmly. 'They were stabbed. You found all three: should I assume that you had a hand in their deaths?'

Mackerell regarded him with open loathing. 'Leave me

alone, and go back to whatever vile monastery you come from.'

'Ely,' whispered Michael sibilantly. 'I hail from Ely Cathedral-Priory, and I will not be going anywhere. Now, someone has accused my Bishop of murdering one of those men, and I happen to know that he is innocent. I disapprove of innocent men being called to answer for crimes they did not commit, and that is why I want to talk to you.'

Mackerell shrank away from him, unsettled by the monk's persistence. 'But I know nothing! It has nothing to do with me!'

'What has nothing to do with you?' pounced Michael.

'Their deaths! I know nothing!'

'You know something,' Michael determined, regarding the fish-man intently. 'Behind all that arrogant bluster, you are a frightened man. If you tell me why, I may be able to help you. If you do not, then perhaps a fourth corpse will appear tomorrow, dripping river water over the church floor, dead by foul means.'

'Those three died of foul means, all right,' said Mackerell. 'There is nothing more foul than a death by water. First comes the shock of the cold, then the water grips you, and the weeds and mud suck at your legs. Then you realise you cannot breathe, so you struggle, but it is to no avail. The water closes over your head, and your ears are full of roaring—'

'Please!' exclaimed Bartholomew with a shudder. He had once had a narrow escape from drowning himself, not eight miles from where he now sat and Mackerell's vivid descriptions brought back memories that he would rather keep suppressed.

Mackerell gave a cold smile. 'All I can tell you is that the rumours about Haywarde are untrue: he never intended to take his own life. A man intent on killing himself would not choose the Monks' Hythe to do it. The water there is too slow-moving, and it would be too easy to lose courage and swim to safety.'

'So, all three were murdered elsewhere, and their bodies thrown into the river upstream,' deduced Bartholomew.

Mackerell glowered at him. 'I did not say that. You did.'

Michael sighed again, and eased even closer to the man, so that Mackerell's breath began to come in agitated pants. Bartholomew glanced uneasily at him, uncomfortable with the monk's ways of gathering information. 'Are you telling me that my colleague's suppositions are wrong?'

'No,' gasped Mackerell. 'I am saying that *I* was not the one who told you all this.'

'I see,' said Michael, easing the pressure a little and rubbing his chin with one fat hand. 'You are afraid that the wrong person may learn that you have been telling tales. Who?'

'I did not say that either,' said Mackerell angrily. 'You are like the Inquisition, putting words into people's mouths that they never intended to say! It is typical behaviour for a churchman!'

Michael regarded him sombrely. 'How did you come to find the bodies?'

'I am always the first to arrive at the hythes of a morning. Ask anyone here. They will all tell you that I am about my work long before anyone else bothers to stir a lazy limb. Of course I was the one to find them.'

'I see,' said Michael, regarding Mackerell in a way that indicated he had not completely accepted the man's story. Bartholomew supposed it was a ploy intended to make Mackerell nervous, and it seemed to be succeeding.

'I know nothing,' said Mackerell again. 'All I can tell you is that you may be right when you say they went into the water away from the town – either that or they were dumped in the Monks' Hythe very late at night, because no one here saw or heard anything as far as I know.'

'I see,' said Michael thoughtfully. 'Have you seen any strangers here recently? Folk you do not know, or who you consider dangerous?'

'The Bishop often strolls down here of an evening,' said

Mackerell slyly. '*He* is dangerous.'

'That is not what I meant,' snapped Michael, becoming angry. 'Have there been mercenaries or rough men, who might stab a man for his purse?'

'The gypsies,' said Mackerell immediately. 'They have been burgling their way around the town, and so it is possible that they have been murdering people, too.'

Michael sat back, finally releasing the fish-man. 'You have not been helpful at all. I have a good mind to arrest you, and see that you spend a few nights in the Prior's cells.'

'Arrest me?' asked Mackerell, the belligerence in his voice replaced by a sudden hope. 'You will put me in the prison near the castle?'

'Yes,' said Michael with grim determination. 'But the Prior's prison is not a place most sane men would want to be. Do not look as though you consider it a rare treat.'

'I would be safe there. It is a long way from the river, and the water-spirits will not be able to penetrate the walls. Yes, take me, Brother. Lock me away.'

Bartholomew regarded him intently. 'It was not water-spirits that murdered those men: it was a person. And this person must be stopped before he harms anyone else.'

'You know nothing,' said Mackerell contemptuously. 'The spirits are all-seeing, and they will know if I betray them. But the prison is a safe distance from the river, and no one would ever think to look there . . .'

'It would be more comfortable if we arranged for you to stay in the priory precincts,' said Bartholomew practically. 'I am sure a bed can be found in the stables or in the infirmary.'

Mackerell shook his head firmly. 'It will have to be the prison – at least until the water-spirits have had their fill of human souls and return whence they came. The prison has locks and thick walls.'

'What are you talking about?' demanded Michael impatiently, never a man interested or tolerant of the superstitions that governed the lives of many common folk. 'There is no such thing as water-spirits.'

'You are wrong,' said Mackerell. 'But I will not talk to you here. Put me in the cells first, and then I will discuss the spirits with you. If—'

He broke off as the door opened and Bartholomew was surprised to see the gypsies enter – Guido first, then the slack-jawed Rosel with Eulalia, and finally Goran, who wore a hood over his head to protect it from the sun. Eulalia smiled at Bartholomew and waved, earning a black glower from Guido.

Just as Goran was closing the door behind him, one of the stray dogs that lived on the streets rushed in, and there was a commotion as it ran around the tables barking at people and snapping at ankles. It was almost wild, and the foam that oozed from its mouth indicated that it was probably sick. No one wanted to touch it, and it was some time before it was evicted and calm was restored. When Bartholomew turned his attention back to Mackerell, the man had gone.

The pot-boy came to stand next to them. 'Mackerell says he will meet you at the priory gate on Broad Lane tomorrow after compline,' he said in his annoyingly cheerful voice. 'He told me that he wants to put his affairs in order first, but that he will tell you all you need to know then, in return for the favour you offered.'

'I see,' said Michael coolly, unamused that their witness had made his escape so easily. Seeing that there was nothing to be done about Mackerell, Bartholomew wandered across the tavern to talk to Eulalia, leaving the monk to the dubious pleasure of the pot-boy's company.

'He is a slippery one, that Mackerell,' said the boy, correctly deducing from the frustrated expression on Michael's face that the fish-man had ducked away in the middle of a conversation. 'Just like the eels he catches. What was he going to tell you? Perhaps I can help. You can give *me* the coin instead.'

'Tell me about the water-spirits, then,' said Michael tiredly.

The boy gazed at him, then burst out laughing. 'Is that what he was talking about? You should keep your money, Brother! Mackerell is a superstitious old fool! Water-spirits!'

Some of the men on the next table overheard him, and exchanged grins, shaking their heads in amusement.

'Mackerell grew up deep in the Fens,' called one of them, addressing Michael. 'They all worship water-spirits out there. In Ely, though, we are Christians and do not believe in pagan ghosts. Mackerell knows his eels right enough, but do not engage him on matters of religion.'

'Ask me something else,' insisted the pot-boy, plucking at Michael's sleeve in an attempt to regain the monk's attention. 'I will be a much better source of information than Mackerell. Mind you, I am more expensive, too. Quality costs.'

'Then what is the word about the three dead men?' asked Michael testily.

The pot-boy considered for a moment. 'Father John tells us that they were all murdered, but you will not find any tears spilled for them here. Personally, I think John is wrong, and that they just went the way of all evil men.'

'Meaning?' demanded Michael.

'Meaning that the river reached out and took them,' replied the boy simply. 'That river knows a wicked soul when it sees one, and it made an end of Glovere, Chaloner and Haywarde.'

'That sounds suspiciously like blaming water-spirits to me,' said Michael.

'It is not!' claimed the pot-boy indignantly. 'It is a completely different thing to believe in the power of the river and the existence of fairies.' He turned to the men at the next table to support him. 'Tell him I am right.'

'He is right,' agreed one of the men. 'There is nothing fairy-like about our river. But personally, *I* think that outlaws invaded the town and killed the three men for their purses. We will ask the Bishop's soldiers to mount more patrols until they are caught.'

Michael finished his ale and prepared to leave. 'I doubt patrols will do any good. What Ely has is a cunning and ruthless killer on the loose. All I can say is that I hope none of you will be his next victim.'

He turned on his heel and stalked out, leaving a lot of worried faces behind him.

It was noon when Bartholomew returned to the priory to hunt for Brother Symon. As Michael had predicted, the librarian had hidden himself in a last-ditch attempt to disobey his Prior's orders and prevent anyone from setting foot in his domain. Bartholomew searched the refectory, the dormitory, the cloisters and the cathedral, but the librarian seemed to have disappeared into thin air.

'What is wrong with the man?' asked Bartholomew, frustrated to think that there were books awaiting his attention, so close that he could almost see them, yet to which he was denied access because of a caretaker's idiosyncrasies.

'He is not a good librarian, and he does not want his shortcomings exposed,' said Michael with a shrug. 'His best strategy is not to allow anyone inside at all; thus his secret will be safe.'

'I do not care if he keeps his books in wine barrels,' said Bartholomew, exasperated. 'I only want to read them. I will even put them back the way I found them.'

'We will track him down,' said Michael consolingly. 'There are still one or two places you have not looked. We will check the infirmary, then the Prior's chapel and perhaps the almonry.'

'Why would he be in any of those?'

'Because he thinks you will not look in them,' replied Michael. He started to walk towards the infirmary, and Bartholomew fell into step beside him. 'I am annoyed that we allowed Mackerell to escape from us so easily.'

'You should not have stopped leaning on him. He could not have slipped away while he was pinned to the wall like a tapestry.'

'Did he strike you as an honest man, Matt? Or did he seem the kind of person who might commit burglary?'

Bartholomew stared at him. 'Do you think *he* is the man who is stealing from the merchants?'

'Why not? And he killed Glovere, Chaloner and Haywarde when they caught him red-handed and threatened to tell.'

'It is possible, I suppose,' said Bartholomew. 'Do you think he agreed to go to the Prior's cells because matters are getting out of hand? That what started as simple thefts have become murder, a far more serious crime? Or because he really does know the identity of the killer, and thinks the prison is the only secure place for him?'

'Well, I certainly do not believe in all that water-spirit nonsense. Still, we shall see when he appears tomorrow.'

'*If* he appears tomorrow,' said Bartholomew. 'It seems to me that the interruption caused by that dog was very timely.'

'What are you saying? That someone sent that wild mongrel into the inn to cause a disturbance and allow Mackerell to escape?'

Bartholomew thought it was possible. 'We were beginning to break through his barrier of silence, and I think it would not have been long before he told us what he knew – and he definitely knows something.'

'But that implies the gypsies are involved,' Michael pointed out. 'The dog was with them.'

'Their appearance may have been coincidental, and merely saved someone else the trouble of opening the door and ushering the dog inside.'

'But that means that this killer has eyes everywhere,' said Michael uneasily. 'I prefer to think of him slinking around the streets after dark – when we are safely in our beds – than following us around in broad daylight and preventing us from speaking to witnesses.'

'There was something else odd about that encounter, too,' said Bartholomew. 'Eulalia has three brothers, but there were only two of them with her in the Mermaid.'

'No,' said Michael immediately. 'There were three –

Goran had his hood over his face. Perhaps he does not like the sun on his skin. I do not, either, although it did not seem to bother him when we caught him poaching in the Fens.'

'But I do not think that *was* Goran,' said Bartholomew, frowning in thought. 'Goran is a different shape, and why should he feel the need to keep his face covered while he was inside?'

'Perhaps because there is some truth to these rumours, and it was indeed Goran and his brothers who have been burgling their way around the town,' said Michael promptly. 'He wore his hood so that he would not be recognised as the thief.'

'Then why were his brothers bare-headed? The more I think about it, the more that hooded figure seems familiar: short and squat, with a big chest . . .'

'Like Goran,' said Michael impatiently. 'Come on, Matt. We are confused enough as it is. Do not make matters worse by imagining things.'

'Lady Blanche!' exclaimed Bartholomew suddenly. 'That is who it was. I *knew* that figure was familiar!'

Michael gazed at him with incredulity. 'Blanche was in the Mermaid tavern with three gypsies? Yes, Matt. I can see why you came to that conclusion. Lady Blanche de Wake, kinsman of the King and widow of the Earl of Lancaster, is certainly the kind of woman who would enjoy an afternoon of rough company in Ely's seediest tavern.'

'It was her,' said Bartholomew firmly. 'I am certain.'

'Then we shall have to agree to disagree on this. I do not want to argue with you, but I have never heard a more ludicrous suggestion in all my days.' Michael pushed open the door to the infirmary chapel and changed the subject. 'I saw you enjoyed meeting Eulalia again. I am surprised you noticed anything when your attention was so securely riveted on her.'

'I did enjoy speaking to her,' admitted Bartholomew, looking around him. The chapel was empty, but he walked to the altar and peered behind it, just to ensure that Symon was not hiding there. 'I should have stayed with her longer. It would have been much more pleasant than wasting time chasing this silly librarian.'

'She is an attractive woman,' said Michael, regarding his friend slyly. 'And she likes you.'

'Probably because I am one of the few people who does not believe that she spends her evenings climbing through people's windows in order to burgle their houses. She knows a great deal about the curative properties of wild plants. She is fascinating to talk to.'

'I am sure she is, although I think you could have devised a more interesting topic of conversation with which to charm her than weeds.'

'She initiated it,' said Bartholomew defensively. 'And she said she would give me some black resin from the pine trees of Scotland. She has invited me to visit her and collect it.'

'Black resin!' said Michael caustically. 'I do not know how you can contain yourself with all the excitement.'

'She gathered it herself when she was in the north,' Bartholomew went on, ignoring his friend's facetiousness and following him out of the chapel and into the hospital's main hall. 'It is difficult to come by in England, but is a very good remedy for fluid in the lungs. I can think of a number of my patients who will benefit from a tincture made from black resin.'

'Henry?' called Michael. 'Where are you?'

'Did you mention black resin?' asked the priory's infirmarian excitedly, appearing from his workroom at the end of the hall. The sullen Julian was behind him. 'Do you have some? Will there be any to spare for a syrup to ease old Brother Ynys's cough?'

'I have been promised some,' said Bartholomew. 'What else do you use in such a mixture? I always find that—'

'Have you seen Symon?' interrupted Michael hastily. 'Matt is keen to begin his reading, but Symon has disappeared with the library key.'

Henry's mouth hardened. 'That wretched man! He is always running away when we have visitors who want to read our books. It is because he does not know where to find any of the tomes in his care, and he is afraid that Alan will deprive him of his post if he is shown to be incompetent.'

'He *is* incompetent!' muttered Julian.

'I have not seen him recently,' Henry continued. 'But I shall demand the key from him if I do, and send Julian to find you.'

'It is too hot for me to be chasing people,' complained Julian resentfully. 'I should not even be here, anyway. It is the time when us brethren are supposed to be enjoying a period of *rest*.'

Henry sighed. 'I have already explained to you that our day does not follow the same pattern as that of everyone else. We have patients to consider, and they are often uncomfortable and restless at this time of day. It would not do to sleep while they need us.'

'Why not?' demanded Julian insolently. 'You order me to read to them, but two cannot hear and the other three are too addled in their wits even to know that I am there. It is a waste of time!'

'It is *not* a waste of time,' admonished Henry crossly. 'They know you are close, even if they cannot understand what you are saying, and the presence of a visitor gives them comfort. That is all that matters. Now, take your psalter and go to sit next to Roger. He had bad dreams last night, and your reading may calm him.'

With very bad grace, Julian did as he was told, snatching up his book and marching down the hall to flop on to a stool by Roger's bedside. The old man smiled a toothless grin of welcome, which Julian ignored as he began to read in a bored voice, deliberately low, so that the old man was obliged to lean forward uncomfortably in a futile attempt to catch some of the words.

'He is a nasty youth,' remarked Michael, watching Julian's behaviour with distaste. 'I do not know how you have the patience to deal with him without boxing his ears.'

'That would not help,' said Henry tiredly, 'although I confess he tries my patience sometimes. He is in disgrace at the moment for putting worms in Brother Ynys's bed.'

'Why did he do that?' asked Bartholomew.

'Sheer malice,' said Henry. 'Roger, who is not as addled as Julian believes, saw him do it and told me, but not before poor Ynys became aware of the wretched things and threw himself into a panic. I do not understand this streak of cruelty in Julian.'

'Some people are just not very nice,' said Michael preachily. 'But if anyone can turn the lad into a saint, and save the town from having him set loose to follow his own devices, it is you.'

'I am a physician, not a miracle worker,' said Henry, although he seemed pleased by the compliment. 'But given a choice, there are others I would change before Julian.'

'There are?' asked Bartholomew, startled. 'They must be vile!'

'They are,' agreed Michael fervently. 'I would do something about that selfish Robert for a start, and that great fat Sub-prior Thomas, not to mention William.'

'William is not a bad man,' said Henry generously. 'He cares about the poor and he sold his gold cross last winter, so that I could buy expensive medicine for a novice with a fever. You must have noticed that the cross he wears is made of base metal?'

'Flaunting his good deeds,' said Michael in disapproval. 'Making the rest of us feel guilty for not doing something similar. But I do not want to spend a fine summer day talking about the likes of the Brother Hosteller. We have a librarian to locate.'

They took their leave of the physician and looked in the Black Hostry, where Michael had his lodgings. Northburgh and Stretton were there, lying next to each other and both snoring loudly, but there was no sign of Symon. Next, they walked along a pleasant path called Oyster Lane, heading

for the beautiful chapel that had been erected for Prior
Crauden, Alan's predecessor. It was a glorious building, with
long, delicate windows that allowed the light to flood inside.
The stained glass was exquisite, because the glazier had
abandoned the popular reds and greens in favour of blues
and golds. The result was a cool, restful light that lent the
chapel an appropriate atmosphere of sanctity.

But Symon was not kneeling at the altar, nor was he
crouching behind it. He was also not at the prie-dieu, or sitting
in the vestibule. Bartholomew was beginning to despair of
ever finding the man – or of finding him so late that the sun
would have set and the light would be too poor for reading.
But Michael was not ready to concede defeat, and together
they made their way to the almonry, checking the refectory
and dormitory a second time as they did so. The dormitory
rang with the snores and whistles of monks taking their naps.

On their way, they saw Sub-prior Thomas, who was walking
slowly towards the infirmary and looking as though the stroll
in the heat of the afternoon was not something he was
enjoying.

'Take this, will you, Brother?' he asked breathlessly of
Michael, passing a cloth-covered basket to the monk. 'Give
it to young Julian in the infirmary.' He closed his eyes and
fanned himself with one fat hand. In another man,
Bartholomew would have been concerned, but in the obese
Thomas the cause of his distress was obvious, and there was
nothing the physician could do to alleviate it – other than
to recommend a serious diet.

'What is it?' asked Michael, picking up a corner of the
cloth to peer at the basket's contents. 'A few pieces of stale
bread and a rind of cheese. Why would Julian want this?'

'It is for the old men,' explained Thomas. 'Julian always
prepares their dinner.'

'Is this what the priory provides for them to eat?' asked
Bartholomew, horrified. 'They have no teeth. How do you
expect them to cope with this? They need food like oatmeal
made with milk, or bean soup.'

'Their meals are none of your affair,' snapped Thomas angrily. 'They will eat what they are given, if they are hungry. If they are not, they can go without.'

'I am sure Henry does not know that his patients are being fed inferior fare,' mused Michael. 'But Julian is the kind of lad who would see old men starved in their beds.'

'The ancients give nothing back to the priory, so why should they have the best of everything?' demanded Thomas, still fanning himself vigorously. 'And they had a decent meal this morning, anyway. If we give too much away, there will not be enough left for those of us who work.'

'I do not think you need to worry on that score,' said Bartholomew dryly. 'No one at *your* table is likely to starve – only the poor old men who are no longer able to feed themselves at the communal trough are in danger of that.'

'There is no need to be abusive,' said Thomas indignantly. 'But it is too hot to stand around here arguing with you. I have important business to attend to.'

'Like dozing in the dormitory,' muttered Bartholomew, watching the man wobble away. He walked carefully, as though his ankles pained him. Bartholomew was sure they did.

'I will ensure Henry hears about this,' determined Michael. 'Those old men will have their oatmeal or bean soup from now on, do not worry, Matt. But let us search the almonry for Symon. Unless he is so desperate to avoid you that he is in the vineyard, squatting among the vines, there is nowhere else he can be.'

The spiteful Robert was leaving his domain as they approached. He had spent the morning outside, on some unspecified business he claimed would benefit the priory, and his naturally dark skin was more swarthy than ever. He saw that Michael carried a basket, and plucked away the cover to reveal its meagre contents.

'What are you doing with this?' he asked curiously. 'You, of all people, know that the kitchens are always open. The cooks will provide you with *fresh* bread and *new* cheese.'

'This was intended for the inmates of the infirmary,' Michael explained. 'Thomas gave it to us.'

Robert's expression became grim. 'That glutton! He volunteered for the task of fetching the ancients' food about a month ago, and I wondered what had made him so generous. He is eating it himself, and passing them scraps instead!'

'Why should he do that, when you have just said the kitchens are always open?' asked Bartholomew.

'Henry told Prior Alan that Thomas's size was dangerous for his health,' explained Robert. 'He is allowed to eat all he likes at mealtimes, but Henry recommended that he have nothing in between. This is Thomas's way of avenging himself on Henry and grabbing himself extra food at the same time. But I will arrange for the old men to have something better than this. The poor can have it instead.' He snatched the basket away from Michael.

'It is hardly nourishing fare for them, either,' Bartholomew pointed out. 'They need more than stale bread and the rinds of cheeses, too. And anyway, there is nowhere near enough in that basket to feed the crowd I saw gathering at the Steeple Gate earlier.'

'I have been cutting down on the amount I dispense,' said Robert. 'You see, the more food I give away, the more people come to receive it. *Ergo*, the less food I give away, the fewer recipients will come. It is simple logic.'

'But there are people who rely on the priory for their daily bread,' argued Bartholomew, becoming angry with the insensitive almoner. 'If they do not come, it is probably because they are too weak from hunger to do battle for a handful of scraps.'

'That is not my problem,' said Robert dismissively. 'I shall distribute this now. Thank you, Michael. It will save me a trip to the kitchen slops.' He took the basket to the Steeple Gate, and opened it. The crowd outside surged forward eagerly, although murmurs of disappointment were soon audible.

'Come on, Matt,' said Michael, as disgusted as was the physician. 'Let us see whether Symon is lurking in the almonry.'

They entered Robert's neat domain, with its piles of old clothes waiting distribution and its neatly stacked scrolls telling of the amounts given to the poor, and Bartholomew's heart sank: Symon was not there. However, knowing that the almoner was currently busy dealing with the poor, Michael decided it was a good opportunity to poke around, to see what he could discover to the detriment of a man he did not like. He was not the only one with such an idea, and he leapt back with a yelp of alarm when he bumped against a wall hanging and it swore at him.

'William!' exclaimed Michael in surprise. 'What are you doing here?'

'The same as you, I imagine,' said the hosteller coolly, easing himself out from behind the tapestry with some irritation. He patted his bobbed hair into place where it had been ruffled. 'I want to know whether Robert has been keeping accurate records of the goods he gives to the poor.'

'He has not,' said Michael, leaning over the ledger that lay open on Robert's table. The last entry was for the current day, which gave a list of the items that Robert was supposed to be distributing at that precise moment. 'It says that the poor were given two score loaves, twenty smoked eels and a barrel of ale. In addition, they are supposed to receive five blankets and various summer vests.'

'And what has he given them?' asked William eagerly.

'A few crusts of bread and a bit of stale cheese.'

William shook his head in disgust. 'I knew it! He has been cheating the poor and the priory ever since he was made almoner last year. Look at this.'

He tugged open a chest, and even Michael released a gasp of astonishment when he saw the number of coins inside.

'He is provided with a specific number of pennies to deliver to the poor each week,' explained William. 'I have suspected for some time that he has been hoarding them for himself. As you can see, I was right: he has amassed a veritable fortune.'

'I wonder what he plans to do with it,' said Bartholomew. 'He can hardly start spending it on new clothes or fine wines – even Alan would start to wonder where the money was coming from.'

William grimaced. 'I think he is preparing himself for every eventuality in his future. The poor are restless, and the cathedral-priory is a focus for their discontent. And there is a strong possibility that I will be appointed Prior in the not too distant future. Robert will not stay here as my inferior.'

'Why do you see that happening?' asked Michael uneasily. 'Has Alan said anything about retiring or moving to another House?'

'No,' said William. 'But de Lisle is in deep trouble, and Alan may become Bishop in his stead before too long. When that happens, I shall be made Prior. I am clearly the best man for the post, and I cannot conceive that it should go to anyone else.'

'I am sure you cannot,' said Michael, amused by the man's naked ambition and confidence. 'But do you think Robert also sees your advancement in the offing? I would have thought he would see himself as Prior.'

William sneered. 'For all his faults – and they are legion – he is not a complete fool. He knows the brethren will elect me, not him.'

'I see,' said Michael. 'Then I hope, for everyone's sake, that this nasty affair with de Lisle is resolved as quickly as possible. But unfortunately – especially for the poor – we can do nothing about this dishonest behaviour of Robert's for now.'

William gazed at him aghast. 'Why ever not? We have all the evidence we need to prove that the man is a thief. If we let him continue to deprive the poor of what is rightfully theirs, then we are as guilty as he is of shameful behaviour.'

'But if we go to Alan with this "evidence", Robert is certain to claim that he is saving the money for some secret project that will benefit the poor,' explained Michael patiently. 'He will deny any dishonesty and we will be unable to prove otherwise.'

'But he will be lying!' protested William, furious.

'Yes,' agreed Michael. 'But you know Alan is always loath to believe ill of people. I would like to see Robert fall from grace as much as you would, but it must be done with subtlety, when we are certain he will be unable to worm his way out of trouble with falsehoods.'

'Subtlety!' snapped William in disbelief. 'I just want to see a liar and a thief brought to justice. I shall tell Alan myself, if you will not. Right now.'

'You would be wiser to wait,' warned Michael. 'Now is not the time.'

William put his hands on his hips. 'And while we wait for a politically opportune moment the poor starve. How many people shall we allow him to kill, Michael? How many hungry children do you want to see crying at our gates?'

'It cannot be that bad,' objected Michael uncomfortably.

'But it is,' insisted William. He gestured around at the contents of the almonry. 'Robert has the power to relieve all that suffering, but he would rather line his own pockets. He told me the number of poor had decreased this year. Now I understand that they have decreased because they have despaired of receiving succour from us. He has driven them from our doors by ensuring that there is never enough for everyone.'

William was whipping himself into a frenzy of outrage, and Michael touched him gently on the arm, to calm him. 'Robert is a wicked man, and we will see him punished for this. But telling Alan now will not bring that about. We must—'

William made a moue of utter disgust. Pushing away from Michael, he stalked furiously across the room and into the grounds outside, slamming the door behind him.

'I do not think he agreed with you,' said Bartholomew mildly.

'He did,' said Michael tiredly. 'He knows perfectly well that telling Alan about this will do no good, because Alan will never believe anything unpleasant about any of his officers. He will no more accept that Robert is stealing the alms for the poor than he would accept that William is a sly power-monger who wants to be Prior himself, or that Thomas is an illiterate dictator who has no business being in charge of novices. William's anger was not directed at me – but at his frustration with Alan.'

'William is not a bad man,' said Bartholomew, leaning on the windowsill to watch the hosteller storm towards the cathedral. It seemed Michael had predicted correctly, because William was not going immediately to the Prior's House as he had threatened. 'He is not someone I would choose as a friend, but he has compassion, and he is able to see beyond his own selfish interests – which is more than I can say for most of your brethren.'

'Except Henry, of course.'

'Even Henry has his moments. He is a kind man and a decent physician, but there is a core of arrogance in him that means he is unable to accept that he is occasionally wrong.'

'I suppose you have been enlightening him with some of your controversial theories. You cannot say people are arrogant, Matt, just because they are not prepared to abandon their years of experience and learning to embrace your novel, and sometimes peculiar, ideas.'

'You should know me better than that,' said Bartholomew, a little offended. 'My assessment of Henry has nothing to do with the fact that we disagree about many fundamental aspects of medicine. He thinks his gentleness and compassion will eventually rub off on Julian – but he is overestimating his ability to influence people. He could keep company with Julian for a lifetime and it would make no difference. The boy is irredeemable.'

'You cannot criticise Henry for trying, though,' Michael pointed out reasonably.

'I am not. I am merely giving you an example of his arrogance in predicting that he will bring about a favourable outcome. Another example would be his assumption that he is a superb physician because dozens of people come to seek his medical advice each day. The reality is that he has lots of patients because he is the only physician available. His expertise, skill or even his success rates have nothing to do with it.'

Michael gave him a sidelong glance. 'I do not think this priory is a good place for you, Matt. You are already losing your powers of judgement. You see goodness in the reprehensible William and imagine faults in poor, dear Henry.'

'What shall we do about Symon?' Bartholomew asked, seeing that he and Michael were unlikely to agree and changing the subject. 'Has he left the city, do you think? Just to avoid lending me a book?'

'There is one more place we can look, although it is not somewhere I would linger, personally.'

'Where?'

'The latrines,' said Michael. 'Perhaps Symon has taken one of his books and is spending the afternoon in a place where he can be guaranteed solitude.'

chapter 5

ICHAEL WAS RIGHT: SYMON HAD SECURED HIMSELF IN one of the wooden cubicles that formed the priory's latrines. He claimed he had only just arrived, but Julian, who happened to be passing, announced with malicious glee that he had seen the librarian entering the place long before terce. Symon was slightly green around the gills, indicating that Julian was probably telling the truth, and that the librarian had indeed been hiding for several hours. Bartholomew thought the state of the library must be dire indeed to induce the man to resort to such extreme measures.

As it transpired, it was all Bartholomew could do not to exclaim aloud in horror when he entered the library and saw the careless stacks of texts, placed where leaks from the window would surely damage the parchment, and the over-loaded shelves that were thick with dust and neglect. Some shelves had collapsed under the weight, precipitating their contents on to the floor in chaotic mounds, while fragments of parchment scattered everywhere suggested that mice were allowed to enjoy the abused volumes, even if scholars were not. Books were precious and expensive, and how anyone could violate one was completely beyond the physician; it was beyond Michael, too: he surveyed the scene with large round eyes, then left without a word.

Symon's unique way of arranging the books with no regard for their content meant that medical texts rubbed shoulders with Arabic lexicons, and religious tracts were liberally sprinkled among collections of wills. Books with soft leather covers or scrolls, which did not stand neatly on shelves, were relegated to the floor, where they stood in unsteady, top-heavy pillars. Triumphantly Symon produced a copy of Theophilus's *De Urinis*, which chance had placed on the top of one of his unstable piles, and then quickly slunk away before Bartholomew could ask him to find anything else.

Once he had steeled himself to the distressing sight of crushed, ripped, gnawed and broken books, Bartholomew began to enjoy having the freedom of the library, delighting in the fact that every pile he excavated contained all manner of treasures that he had not anticipated. He spent the rest of the day refreshing his memory with parts of *De Regimine Acutorum*, then graduated to Honien ben Ishak's commentary on Galen, *Isagoge in Artem Parvam*. It was a pleasure to read with no interruptions from students or summonses from patients, although a drawback as far as his treatise was concerned meant that the experience of having a stretch of time to himself led him to explore secondary issues that he would normally have been forced to ignore. He decided he should make more time for leisurely reading, and determined to revisit the cathedral-priory and its treasure-store of knowledge at some point in the future – assuming, of course, that he would be welcome and had not played a role in the downfall of a bishop.

The library was an airy room, located above the main hall of the infirmary. Its thick, oaken window shutters were designed to seal the room's valuable contents from the ravages of the weather – although one or two of them had rotted and needed replacing – but Symon had thrown them all open, so that sun poured through the glassless openings and bathed everything in light. Desks with benches attached to them were placed in each bay window, affording the reader a degree of privacy, as well as permitting him to work in the maximum amount of daylight. Bartholomew, who was used to his shady room in Michaelhouse, found the light too bright, and its reflection on the yellow-white parchment of the pages was vivid enough to dazzle him. He found he was obliged to look up fairly frequently, to rest his eyes.

The desk Symon had cleared for him – by taking one hand and sweeping its contents to join the chaos on the floor – overlooked the monks' cemetery. The cemetery was a pleasant place, given its purpose, and comprised an elongated rectangle that backed on to a garden at one end and was bordered by the cathedral and various priory buildings on the other sides. Shielded from the worst of the Fenland winds, it was a comfortable haven for several exotic bushes and trees. Someone had planted posies of flowers here and there, some bright in the sun and others sheltered by the waving branches of willow and yew trees. The graves were mostly lumps in the smooth grass, although one or two monks had warranted something more elaborate, and there were a few stone crosses and carved slabs.

Bartholomew remained in the library until long after the sun had set, and did not leave until it was so dark that he could barely make out the shape of the book he was reading, let alone the words on the page. Disaster almost occurred when he heard the soft sound of the key turning in the lock, but he bounded across the floor and hammered until Symon returned to undo it again. Apparently, the librarian had forgotten about his visitor, and had only remembered that he needed to secure his domain when he was ready to go to bed. Bartholomew coolly suggested that in future he might like to ensure that it was empty before locking the door, but Symon was unrepentant, and informed Bartholomew that he should not have been there after dark anyway.

Symon followed Bartholomew down the stairs, so close that the physician felt Symon would dearly liked to have pushed him in order to prevent another invasion the following day, and then locked the outer door with a key of gigantic proportions.

'I would like to start work as early as possible tomorrow,' said Bartholomew, deciding he had better make that clear before he and Symon parted, unless he wanted to waste part of the next day exploring the latrines, too. 'A week is not long when a library is as richly endowed as yours.'

'You cannot come before prime,' warned Symon sharply. 'That would be ungodly.'

'It would also be too dark,' said Bartholomew dryly, seeing that Symon did not venture into his domain very often if he was unaware of such a basic fact. 'Immediately after would be good.'

'We shall see,' replied Symon, giving the door handle a vigorous shake to ensure it was properly secured. Without further ado, he strode away into the night, a tall, upright figure with a military strut and a lot of vigorous and unnecessary arm-swinging.

Bartholomew watched him go, and then turned to head for his own bed. It felt too late to venture into the town alone, and he imagined that Michael would be more interested in the priory's endless supplies of wine than in talking to him. But the physician did not feel like sleeping; his mind was buzzing with questions and ideas from the reading that he had completed, and he felt restless and alert.

Henry was just finishing his evening prayers in the chapel when Bartholomew strolled into the infirmary. He gave a grin of delight, making it clear that the physician should not expect to retire too soon, then walked with his visitor through the main hall, checking on the old men who were settling themselves down for the night as he went.

'Goodnight, Roger,' said Henry loudly to the most alert of the quintet. 'The posset I gave you contained a good deal of camomile, so you should rest well tonight.'

'I have dreams,' explained Roger to Bartholomew, his eyes rheumy in the flickering light of the candle. He gestured around at his companions, some of whom seemed aware that they were being discussed and others not. 'We all do. We were soldiers before we took the cowl, and sometimes the souls of the men we killed come to taunt us.'

'They do not,' said Henry sensibly. 'It is only the trick of a weary mind, and I do not allow tormented souls in my infirmary, anyway.'

Roger smiled. 'But I see them, nevertheless. It is an old man's dream, so you will not understand.'

'Sleep,' said Henry softly, helping the ancient monk to slide under the covers. 'Shall I fetch an extra blanket? The night is mild, but you can have one if you like.'

Roger shook his head, his eyes already closing as he huddled under the bedclothes. Bartholomew noticed that the blankets that covered the old men were made of soft wool, while the mattresses were feather rather than the more usual and cheaper straw. The floors had been scrubbed again that day, and the whole room smelled of fresh herbs and clean wood.

Henry moved to another of his patients, who had evidently been a giant of a man in his prime. Now he was little more than a skeleton, with massive-knuckled hands that shook uncontrollably as they plucked at his night-shirt. Henry straightened the covers and rested the back of his hand on the old man's forehead to test his temperature.

'Ynys fought for old King Edward at Bannockburn in 1314,' he whispered to Bartholomew. The physician thought he saw a glimmer of pride in the old man's sunken eyes, but was not sure how much Ynys was aware of his surroundings. 'They all did. And they were with him in France. And now they are here with me, dreaming of the days when they were full of life and vigour.'

'Do they know where they are?' asked Bartholomew, wondering whether he had imagined Ynys's reaction.

Henry shrugged. 'Roger does, although he is very deaf. Ynys is almost blind, and the others have failing memories. They recall the battles in which they were heroes, but they never remember Julian from one day to the next.'

'That is probably a blessing,' said Bartholomew.

Henry smiled. 'I have hopes that he will change. However, I pray that it will not take too much longer. There is a limit to how long I am prepared to inflict him on my old friends.'

He walked to the central aisle and began a long prayer; his Latin whispered and echoed through the darkened hall.

The old men seemed to sleep easier when he had finished, as though the familiar words had settled them. He sketched a benediction over each one, and then led Bartholomew out of the infirmary to the chambers at the far end. Henry occupied the smaller of the two, while the other was set aside for occasional visitors and Julian. The sullen novice was sleeping there now, lying with his mouth open and his breath hissing wetly past his palate. It was not an attractive sound.

Henry leaned down and retrieved something from the floor under Julian's bed, and Bartholomew caught the glitter of metal before the infirmarian turned away.

'What is that?' he asked curiously, seeing from the expression on Henry's face that the find had displeased him.

Reluctantly, Henry opened his hand to reveal a long silver nail. 'Sharp objects,' he explained in a whisper. 'Julian has a morbid fascination with them, and I am always discovering them secreted away. I am afraid he may use them to harm himself.'

'He is more likely to use them to harm someone else,' muttered Bartholomew, eyeing the sleeping novice in distaste.

Henry beckoned Bartholomew into his own room across the corridor, and closed the door so that their voices would not disturb those who were sleeping. He produced a bottle of raspberry cordial that he said he had made himself, and gestured for Bartholomew to sit on a bench, while he perched on the edge of the bed.

'How do you like our library?' he asked, seeming grateful to change the subject from that of his assistant's shortcomings. 'We have a splendid collection of texts, although I can never find anything because of the chaos. It is very frustrating at times.'

'Why does Alan permit Symon to be so slack in his duties? The priory's books are a valuable asset, and I am surprised he is allowed to abuse them so flagrantly. Alan should appoint someone who knows what he is doing.'

'Alan does not want strife in his monastery,' said Henry tiredly. 'If he forced Symon to resign and appointed someone else, Symon would make his successor's life very difficult.'

'It is a pity. Men like Symon should not be allowed near books.'

'I agree,' said Henry. He smiled. 'But let us not talk about Symon or Julian. Have you uncovered any new theories pertaining to the marsh fever that cripples us at this time of year? Michael tells me you speak some Italian, and I know we have books from Salerno. Tell me what you have read in them. Doubtless most of it will be wrong, but I should like to know what they say nevertheless.'

It was easy to lose track of time when discussing medicine with an opinionated man like Henry. The Benedictine physician disagreed with almost everything Bartholomew said, which resulted in a lively conversation. Bartholomew enjoyed it, despite the adversarial nature of the debate, and so did Henry, who relished pitting his knowledge against a man whose experience and learning equalled his own. The bells were chiming for the midnight mass before they realised they should sleep if they wanted to be fit for work the following day. Reluctantly, Henry allowed Bartholomew to go to his own bed, although the physician could see that questions and ideas were still tumbling through his mind.

The discussion had done more to rouse Bartholomew than to relax him, and the heat of the night did not allow sleep to come easily. The rough blankets were prickly against his hot skin, and the breeze that whispered through the open window was steamy-warm and stank of the marshes. Insects hummed high notes around his head, and flapping at them seemed to make them more interested in him than ever. They stung, too, and it was not long before he felt as though his whole body was covered in itching lumps from their bites.

Eventually, he slept, but it was to wake thick-headed and drowsy the following morning. The heat seemed more intense than ever, as though the night had done nothing to cool it down. When he looked out of the window at the slowly lightening landscape, he saw that a thick mist hung around the river, and wisps of it curled around the cathedral, obscuring the octagon and the towers from sight. He scrubbed at his eyes and sat on the bed, wondering what the day would bring.

It was late afternoon, and the sun was blazing with particular brilliance through the library window, when Bartholomew leaned back to stretch his stiff shoulders and look out across the cool, green grass for a few moments before returning to a complex problem regarding the relationship between fevers and standing water. He had been lucky that morning, because Alan had been nearby when Bartholomew had asked Symon to unlock the library door. The librarian was loath to refuse when the Prior was there, and so Bartholomew had been left to his own devices with the books for the entire day. Michael had put his head around the door at noon, to say that he was going to visit acquaintances of Chaloner and Haywarde, but he had waved away the physician's offer of company, claiming haughtily that he could interview peasants by himself.

Michael had not been alone in wanting to speak to those who had known the murdered men. Stretton had been ordered by Blanche to begin his enquiries. Reluctantly, the beefy canon abandoned the haven of the priory and ventured into the town to talk to anyone who admitted to knowing Glovere. It was not long before he found his way to a tavern, and was escorted back to the priory shortly after nones in no state to investigate anything for the rest of the day. Northburgh felt no such compunction to pursue his inquisitorial duties. Instead, he summoned Henry to his bedside, and quizzed him relentlessly on various symptoms and ailments, which Henry tolerated with a patience Bartholomew could never have emulated.

As Bartholomew flexed his cramped fingers and gazed

across the pleasant green sward of the cemetery, he saw a familiar figure hurry along one of the paths to stand under the shade of a particularly large tree, almost directly under the window through which he was looking. It was Tysilia de Apsley, the Bishop's wanton 'niece'.

Knowing Tysilia's reputation for securing lovers, Bartholomew supposed there was only one reason why she should make her way through the long grass to stand under shrubs when she could be somewhere a good deal more comfortable. The place she had chosen was a superb location for a tryst, because unless someone had spotted her making her way there, or happened to be leaning out of one of the library windows, she would never have been seen. Bartholomew smiled to himself, amused that she was already up to her old tricks. He supposed that the stern Lady Blanche was no more able to control the wilful young woman than the nuns at St Radegund's Convent in Cambridge or the lepers of Stourbridge had been.

Bartholomew was about to resume his reading when a flicker of movement among the bushes on the opposite side of the cemetery caught his eye. He watched in fascination as the branches parted and the priory's hosteller emerged, looking around him in a way that Bartholomew could only describe as furtive. William fluffed up his hair and ran nervous hands down his habit, to brush away twigs or grass, before gazing around slowly to ensure that he was alone. Then Bartholomew saw him take a circuitous route through the graves until he reached the tree under which Tysilia had taken refuge. Moments later, there came the hum of a muttered conversation.

Because both Tysilia and William had taken some care not to be seen, Bartholomew concluded that their meeting did not have the blessing of Lady Blanche or the Prior. He predicted that William was in for a good time, while Tysilia would be able to add a Benedictine to her list of conquests – assuming that she had not already notched up some of them already. He was surprised that William had succumbed to Tysilia's charms; he had imagined the hosteller to have more self control than that. But whatever their intentions, it was none of Bartholomew's affair. He gave his back a quick rub and turned back to his book, quickly losing himself in its subject matter and forgetting whatever was happening below his window. His work was interrupted by a voice that was raised in irritation.

'But I *am* acting normally! It is *you* who is acting oddly. How could you not, with that hair?'

This was followed by an urgent whisper by William, apparently ordering Tysilia to keep her voice down. Bartholomew leaned forward, and glanced over the sill. He could see the top of Tysilia's head, although William was concealed by leaves.

'And I will *not* be quiet!' Tysilia's furious voice went on. 'Why should I?'

William gave a heavy sigh and spoke in a loud voice himself, exasperation apparently winning over the need for silence. 'Because you do not want anyone to hear us here together, and neither do I. Think of your reputation.'

'My reproduction has nothing to do with you!' replied Tysilia indignantly. 'I can look after myself.'

'Then think of mine,' snapped William. 'My reputation, that is. What do you think people will say if they see us together like this?'

'Why should they think anything amiss?' demanded Tysilia petulantly. 'It is not as if we are doing anything wrong. We are only talking.'

'That is beside the point,' said William, and Bartholomew could hear the frustration in his voice. 'No one will believe we are here innocently.'

'Then I will just tell them that we are,' announced Tysilia, as if that would solve everything. 'They will believe me. Who are we talking about, anyway? Who knows we are here? I told no one we were meeting. Did you?'

'No,' sighed William wearily. 'Of course not. I was speaking hypothetically.'

'Speaking hypocritically is not nice,' said Tysilia firmly. 'Lady Blanche told me so. And if you intend to speak that way to me, I shall leave.'

'I was not being hypocritical,' said William, sounding bewildered. Bartholomew smiled. He had engaged in similar conversations with Tysilia himself, and he knew how frustrating the woman's slow wits and ignorance could be. He imagined that William was already regretting meeting her. 'But never mind that. Tell me what you have discovered.'

'Discovered about what?' asked Tysilia, sounding baffled in her turn.

'About what we discussed. About Glovere's death.'

'Oh, yes,' said Tysilia. 'I remember now. No.'

'No, *what*?' snapped William, sounding agitated. His voice was now louder than Tysilia's, all pretence at whispering abandoned.

'No, I have discovered nothing about Glovere's death,' said Tysilia slowly, enunciating every word as though she were speaking to a dim-witted child. 'I even asked Lady Blanche whether she had killed him, but she said she had not.'

'You did *what*?' exploded William. Bartholomew started to laugh, moving backwards so that he would not be heard, although he suspected that they were both far too engrossed in each other to detect any sounds of mirth from above.

It was Tysilia's turn to sound aggravated. 'You told me to learn anything I could about Glovere's death, so I asked people about it. How am I supposed to find things out unless I ask? And, as I have just told you, I demanded of Blanche whether she had killed Glovere herself, just as you told me she might have done, but she said she had not. So, she is innocent after all.'

Bartholomew heard a groan. The physician knew how William felt. Conversations with Tysilia did tend to make one wonder whether one was dreaming.

'I asked you to be discreet and to *listen*,' said William tiredly. 'I did not mean you to interrogate Blanche. You cannot begin to imagine the harm you have done. Now she will know that I suspect her, and she will be on her guard. She may even decide that I should go the same way as the servant she so despised.'

'But I did not tell her it was *you* who told me to ask,' protested Tysilia, with a pout in her voice. 'And I *was* discreet. I took care to lower my voice when I put my question.'

'Well, that is a relief,' said William heavily. 'And how did she respond to your clever probing?'

'Oh, she was a little annoyed,' said Tysilia cheerfully. 'She asked me who had put such an idea into my head, and I told her it had occurred to me all by myself, with no prompting from anyone. Then she told me I should never ask such a question again, and that I should leave the matter of Glovere well alone unless I wanted to end up in Abraham's bosom.'

'She said that?' asked William in alarm.

'Yes. I told her I knew no one called Abraham, but that if I met him I would take care that he did not embrace me. What did she mean, do you think?'

'She meant that your clumsy enquiries could result in your death,' said William flatly.

'Oh,' said Tysilia. There was silence as she mulled over this piece of information. When she spoke again, it sounded as though Blanche's words and William's translation had finally shaken her thick-skinned resilience. 'She was threatening to kill me?'

'I do not know,' said William. 'If she killed Glovere, then yes, she may well have been threatening to throw you in the river, too. If she did not, then she may simply have been warning you not to meddle in matters that might prove dangerous.'

'Well, that is all right then,' said Tysilia, sounding relieved. 'Blanche told me she did not kill Glovere, and so she cannot have been threatening to kill me.' Bartholomew could hear that she was pleased with her logic.

He rubbed his chin thoughtfully. What had possessed William to use the doubtful and dangerous talents of a woman like Tysilia as his spy in Blanche's household? And what had possessed Tysilia to agree to such an arrangement? Did William have evidence that Blanche had murdered Glovere and arranged for the Bishop to be accused of the crime, or was the hosteller merely speculating? Blanche had been at her estates in Huntingdon when Glovere had died. Was her absence deliberate, so that no one would think *she* was responsible for the death of her own steward? Glovere had not been one of her most prized servants by all accounts, and it was possible that she was delighted to be rid of him and strike a blow against her enemy the Bishop at the same time.

And what about the presence of Blanche with the gypsies in the Mermaid Inn the day before? Was the King's kinswoman more deeply embroiled in Glovere's murder than they had thought, and had she engaged the travellers to help her? Were William's suspicions justified? Bartholomew knew Michael did not believe that it had been Blanche wrapped in Goran's cloak, but Bartholomew knew what he had seen.

There was something distasteful in listening to others' conversation, even though it involved a discussion about the murder Michael had been charged to solve. So, when Tysilia started to regale William with ghoulishly intimate details of Blanche's private life, Bartholomew turned his attention back to his book, trying to ignore the embarrassing revelations that were being made below. Suddenly, there was an angry yelp from Tysilia, a sharp rustling of leaves and then silence. Bartholomew surmised that William had slapped one hand over her mouth and had dragged her deeper into the undergrowth. Puzzled, he peered across the cemetery to see what had alarmed them.

Michael, looking inordinately large in his flowing black robe, was ambling among the tombstones. His casual stance suggested that he was merely taking the air, although

Bartholomew knew the monk was not the kind of man to indulge in exercise without good reason. Occasionally he went for a walk when the weather was fine, but he complained bitterly if any distance was covered. Left to his own devices, Michael was far more likely to remain in his room, to work on University business or to enjoy the food and drink he invariably had stashed there.

So, what was he doing in the cemetery, looking as though he were taking a stroll? Fascinated, Bartholomew watched him saunter right past the tree where William and Tysilia were hiding, then cut across the grass to a box-like monument against the south wall of the cathedral. Carefully selecting the side that was hidden from casual observers – unless they happened to be hiding in the trees opposite or watching from the library window – he settled himself on a convenient ledge and turned his face towards the sun.

'Oh, look!' Bartholomew heard Tysilia sigh. 'It is that handsome Brother Michael!'

William's reaction to this description was much the same as Bartholomew's. 'Where? I can only see the Michael who lives in Cambridge.'

'That is the one,' Tysilia said wistfully. 'He is the most attractive man I have seen in this city. I wonder why I did not notice his charms before. I have only recently become aware of the fact that he is worthy of my affections.'

'Michael?' asked William, sounding as incredulous as Bartholomew felt. 'Are you jesting with me?'

'Why would I jest about such a thing,' said Tysilia, sounding genuinely puzzled. 'Michael is all a woman could ask for in a man, and I intend to have him.'

'Keep your voice down!' whispered William in alarm. 'He will hear you.'

'I do not mind,' said Tysilia dreamily. 'I would like him to know that I am fond of him.'

'Then you can reveal your unlikely infatuation at your peril, but not now. We do not want him to know we are here, having this secret meeting, do we?'

'No,' admitted Tysilia. 'Because then it would no longer be a secret, and that would be a pity. But I wonder why he is here. I hope he is not meeting another lover. I would not like that at all.'

Bartholomew also had no idea why the monk should choose to bask in the rays of the late afternoon sun while hiding behind a mortuary monument, until he spotted yet another figure walking among the graves. The physician grinned, wondering whether he would see half the priory and its guests emerging to engage in 'secret' assignations in the cemetery, if he watched long enough. This time, it was de Lisle.

The Bishop was a man imbued with plenty of energy, and he walked briskly and purposefully to the place where Michael waited. At the last moment, he stopped and spun around, gazing back the way he had come, looking for signs that he had been followed. Apparently satisfied that he had not, he quickly stepped behind Michael's mausoleum; pushing himself close to the monk, he leaned out around the wall and looked back a second time. Cynric, Bartholomew thought, would have been horrified at such a poor display of stealth. His book now completely forgotten, Bartholomew watched with interest.

'That is my uncle!' Bartholomew heard Tysilia whisper loudly. 'He is the Bishop of Ely, you know.'

'What was that?' demanded de Lisle immediately, gazing intently in her direction. 'Did you hear a voice, Brother?'

'A bird,' said Michael carelessly. 'Do not worry, my lord. No one else will be in the cemetery at this hour. My brethren are already massing outside the refectory to wait for the dinner bell, while Lady Blanche and her household are down by the river, where it is cooler.'

'Well?' demanded the Bishop. He made no attempt to keep his voice down as he addressed Michael. Bartholomew wondered whether de Lisle was as devious a plotter as he would have everyone believe, if he did not know that it was safer to speak quietly when meeting agents in graveyards – just because he thought he had not been followed did not mean that he could not be heard. 'What have you learned so far about Glovere?'

Bartholomew wondered what he should do, aware that anything Michael said would also be heard by the hosteller and Tysilia. If Michael felt the need to meet de Lisle in the cemetery, rather than openly at his house or in the cathedral, then the monk clearly wanted privacy. While he felt no particular allegiance to de Lisle, and cared little whether the Bishop revealed his innermost secrets while William and Tysilia listened, Bartholomew did not want the discussion to incriminate Michael. He picked up a small inkpot, and fingered it thoughtfully, seriously considering hurling it at Michael to warn the monk that he and de Lisle were not alone.

'I have learned very little, I am afraid,' replied Michael. 'A fellow named Mackerell spun some story about water-spirits snatching the souls of the three dead men.'

The Bishop nodded. 'Superstition is rife in the Fens, despite my attempts to try to teach otherwise. I am not surprised that ghosts have been blamed – but better them than me, I say!'

'True,' agreed Michael. 'Mackerell has agreed to meet me by the back door of the priory tonight, where he has promised to reveal all.'

'What could a man like Mackerell know?' demanded de Lisle disparagingly. 'He is a mere fisherman.'

'He is a mere fisherman who gave the impression he knew something that frightened him,' said Michael stiffly. 'We should not dismiss him without hearing his story.'

Bartholomew's grip on the inkpot loosened. The Bishop and his agent were not discussing anything incriminating or dangerous. He wondered why they had decided to meet in secret. Perhaps it was force of habit that encouraged them to be circumspect, even when there was no need.

'Very well,' said de Lisle, although he did not sound

convinced. 'You have more experience in these matters than I do, and I shall bow to your superior knowledge. What else have you learned?'

'I spoke to Haywarde's family today,' said Michael. 'And I also ascertained that Chaloner and Glovere had no kin – at least, no kin that would acknowledge them.'

'No family would ever admit to owning Glovere,' Bartholomew heard Tysilia whisper to William. 'He always smelled of horse dung, you see.'

'What?' William whispered back, evidently more interested in the conversation between Michael and de Lisle than in listening to Tysilia's deranged ramblings.

'I think he rubbed it in his hair,' explained Tysilia helpfully.

'Be quiet,' ordered William. 'And keep your hands where I can see them.'

'And?' asked de Lisle of Michael. 'What did the kinsmen of the unhappy Haywarde tell you?'

'Nothing,' Michael admitted. 'I was hoping to find some connection between him and the other two victims, but nothing was forthcoming. I thought they might be involved in the rebellion that seems to be fermenting in the town.'

'Leycestre and his silly nephews,' spat de Lisle in disgust. 'Nothing *they* discuss can be of sufficient importance to warrant murder.'

'Not everyone is as sanguine as you are,' Michael pointed out. 'Seditious talk may be considered treasonous.'

'What salacious talk is this?' demanded Tysilia in a hoarse whisper, sounding very interested.

De Lisle glanced sharply towards the tree in which she hid. 'Are you sure you can hear nothing, Brother? That sounded like a voice to me.'

'It was probably squirrels,' said Michael complacently. 'There are a lot of them around at this time of year, looking for nuts.'

'What about Northburgh and Stretton?' asked de Lisle, after a searching gaze revealed nothing amiss. Bartholomew could almost hear William holding his breath. 'Have they learned anything?'

'Hardly!' snorted Michael in disgust. 'Stretton had to ask me how to begin his enquiries, while Northburgh declines to leave the priory lest he contract some peasant ailment.'

'This is not good,' said de Lisle worriedly. 'My name will never be cleared as long as that pair is supposed to be uncovering the evidence. Everyone will merely assume I could not be proven guilty, rather than that I am innocent.'

'But you have me,' declared Michael, a little peevishly. '*I* will uncover the truth.'

De Lisle regarded him uneasily. 'I know. But this investigation is proceeding a good deal more slowly than it should. I dislike being accused of murder: it is not good for a bishop to be seen as the kind of man who commits earthly sins.'

'I imagine not,' said Michael. 'But this is not an easy case to solve, because there is very little for me to work on. I cannot see any link between these three men, except for the fact that they were all killed by the same unusual method. We may have to resort to using a tethered goat to draw the killer out – perhaps dangle some other malcontent in order to force him to strike.'

'As long as I am not the goat, you can do what you like,' said de Lisle. 'But do not linger over this, Michael. You have always been my faithful servant, and I am in your debt for the loyalty you have shown me in the past. But now my very life is in your hands. Prove me innocent of these charges, and I shall see you rewarded in ways that even you cannot imagine.'

Michael inclined his head in acknowledgement and the Bishop took his leave. Bartholomew was unable to prevent himself from laughing aloud when de Lisle strode quickly away without making the slightest pretence of keeping himself hidden, and then almost collided with Sub-prior Thomas and Almoner Robert, who just happened to be passing the end of the cemetery.

'Watch where you are going,' Bartholomew heard de Lisle snap.

'Why, my Lord Bishop!' exclaimed Robert in surprise, an unreadable expression on his foxy face. 'What brings you to our humble cemetery? It seems an odd place for a man like you to haunt.'

'I haunt wherever I like,' said de Lisle haughtily. 'I am the Bishop of Ely, and this is my See. And what I was doing in the cemetery is none of your affair.'

'It is often used as a place for meetings we would rather no one else knew about,' said Thomas, giving de Lisle a knowing nudge in the ribs. The Bishop spluttered in indignant outrage, but Thomas was unperturbed and his salacious grin merely grew wider. 'I have caught many a young novice here among the graves with the kitchen maids.'

'Well, I can assure you that you will find no kitchen maid here,' said de Lisle, giving the two monks an icy glare before strutting away, his bearing arrogant and determined.

Exchanging an amused smile, Thomas and Robert watched him go, then resumed their walk. When they had gone, Michael followed the route his Bishop had taken, before ducking quickly around the corner and heading in the direction of the Black Hostry, where a bell was ringing to announce that a meal was ready for any Benedictine guests who might be hungry. Bartholomew was sure Michael was hungry.

Moments later, Tysilia emerged from the trees, brushing leaves from her clothes. She gave William a conspiratorial grin, and announced in a loud voice that she hoped to hear from him very soon. Then she scampered away among the graves. As she reached the place where de Lisle had met the two monks a few moments before, someone appeared out of nowhere and all but sent her flying.

'Be careful!' she cried angrily, when she had regained her balance. 'You cannot take up *all* the path, you know. You must leave some of it for others.'

'I was not even on the path,' replied a bemused Thomas defensively. 'I was walking on the grass. Turf is easier on my ankles, you see, so I always tread on it, rather than the beaten earth of a trackway.'

'That is because you are fat,' declared Tysilia uncompromisingly. Bartholomew winced, recalling that the young woman had an unendearing habit of saying exactly what was in her mind.

She dashed on, leaving a startled Thomas gazing after her. Slowly, a grin of understanding spread across the sub-prior's porcine features, and Bartholomew could hear his delighted laughter. Clearly, Thomas had drawn his own conclusions about the sudden appearance of a young woman making her escape from the cemetery moments after the Bishop had left. Bartholomew heard an amused cackle from the tree below, as William also realised what the sub-prior had assumed.

William was the last to leave. He walked briskly among the graves, then peered around the corner to ensure that no one was watching, before turning towards the cathedral. And then the graveyard was silent and empty again. Bartholomew set down his pen and wondered what to make of it all.

The dinner served at the monastery that evening was excellent. It surpassed anything Michaelhouse was likely to produce, except perhaps at feasts or other special occasions. Considering that it was just a normal day, Bartholomew could not begin to imagine what was on offer when the priory had cause to celebrate. There was a pike in pear-flavoured jelly, the inevitable locally caught eels, a dish of turnips that had been roasted slowly in butter, and a bowl of thick pea pottage. In addition, there was bread made from the finest white flour, which was soft and delicious to eat with the creamy cheese from the priory's own dairy. Bartholomew ate his fill, and then retired to the infirmary to talk to Henry.

As sunset approached, Michael came to find him to ask if he wanted to take an evening stroll, carefully not mentioning the fact that it was almost time for their meeting with Mackerell. The monk was rubbing the sleep from his eyes, and Bartholomew assumed he had followed his own repast with a pleasant nap.

'What have you been doing today?' Bartholomew asked, as they walked towards the vineyards and the priory's back gate. 'Did you have a useful meeting with de Lisle?'

Michael smiled. 'I am glad you were not too engrossed in your studies to have missed that.'

'You mean you *wanted* me to eavesdrop on it?' asked Bartholomew, startled. 'Why?'

'Because I hoped he might say something important, and I wanted you to hear. But in the event, he said nothing of interest at all.'

'Perhaps he knew the discussion was not quite as private as it appeared,' suggested Bartholomew.

'No. We have met in the cemetery before. And although he is aware that you are working in the library, it would not have occurred to him that you might overhear anything he said.'

'But it did, Brother,' argued Bartholomew. 'He knew that someone might be spying on him, and kept gazing at the undergrowth below my window.'

'Then you should not have made all that noise. You were giggling and whispering to yourself like some half-mad crone. I was lucky he believed me when I said the racket was caused by birds or squirrels.'

'That was not me. William and Tysilia were already in the midst of their own meeting when you arrived. It was Tysilia you heard chattering.'

'Was it indeed?' said Michael, raising his eyebrows. 'Then it is just as well de Lisle said nothing incriminating. That William is a cold man, and I would not like him to be after the Bishop's blood. What were they talking about?'

'William has apparently charged Tysilia to discover whether Blanche was responsible for Glovere's murder. Needless to say, she was not a wise choice of accomplice.'

'Why do you say that?' asked Michael, amused. 'Did she march up to Blanche and demand to know whether she killed her own steward?' He chortled at the notion.

'Yes, actually. It is difficult to gauge Blanche's reaction from Tysilia's description of it, but she warned Tysilia that to probe further might be dangerous. However, it is not clear whether the harm would come from Blanche or someone else.'

'I wonder why William is meddling in this,' mused Michael. 'What can he have to gain from discovering who murdered Glovere?'

'A good deal. If he proves de Lisle guilty, he will be able to demand a high price for his silence. If he proves de Lisle innocent, then he will earn the Bishop's undying gratitude.'

'If he thinks that, then he is a fool. De Lisle will not take kindly to being blackmailed, and he gives his undying gratitude to those he trusts, not to those who interfere in his affairs. But this is all very revealing.'

'It is?' asked Bartholomew doubtfully.

Michael nodded. 'It means that William may have discovered something I have not.' He rubbed his hands in sudden glee. 'Now this is more like it! I was afraid I might be obliged to deal with some mindless butcher, who kills because the fancy takes him. Such a person might prove impossible to find – unless he grows so bold that he reveals himself by accident. But now I learn that no less a person than the hosteller – one of the priory's most important officers – is recruiting spies and asking questions.'

'I do not know why you consider that good news, Brother. William may be asking questions because he is the culprit, and his enquiries are merely to allow him to gloat as people speculate about his identity.'

'He will not outwit *me*,' boasted Michael. 'A clever man will have a certain method in his actions, which a man who kills by instinct will not. Patterns are revealing clues for us: we will be able to use them to trap him.'

Bartholomew laughed softly. 'A few moments after you left, Sub-prior Thomas doubled back on himself and bumped into Tysilia. I saw from his face that he thought *she* was the reason why the Bishop was in the cemetery.'

Michael's green eyes grew huge and round. 'Really?' he chuckled. 'It is not common knowledge that de Lisle has a "niece", and no one is likely to believe him if he conveniently produces one now. And no one will accept that it was William she was meeting, either. That sly, treacherous dog will never own up to meeting his doxy in the bushes.'

'There is nothing to suggest she is his doxy, Brother,' said Bartholomew. 'They stood chastely side by side, and the only physical contact was when William dragged her out of sight when you arrived. Anyway, Tysilia has set her heart on you.'

Michael glanced sharply at him. 'What are you talking about? She barely knows me, and I can assure you that I have done nothing to encourage her attentions.'

'Perhaps not, but it is you she admires. She was telling William how handsome and manly you are.'

'Then she has better taste than I credited her with,' said Michael, not sounding at all surprised that he had secured her devotions. 'However, she will be disappointed to learn that I am unavailable. She will just have to resort to William, or someone equally inferior.'

'She is a determined woman,' warned Bartholomew, smiling. 'You may find yourself powerless to resist her wiles.'

'But I am a determined man. Still, I am more interested in her relationship with William than her perfectly understandable attraction to me. That suggests a plot, sure enough.'

'We will see,' said Bartholomew. 'Perhaps Mackerell can throw some light on the matter. Come on, Brother. The sun is beginning to set and our fishy friend will be waiting.'

They had almost reached the priory's back gate, beyond the neat rows of vines, when Bartholomew spotted someone walking ahead of them. Normally, seeing another person in an area populated by about a hundred monks and their servants would not have been cause for comment, but there was something about the way this figure moved that set warning bells jangling in Bartholomew's mind. He grabbed Michael's arm and dragged him to one side. The vines were not tall, so the two scholars were obliged to crouch in undignified positions.

'It is Sub-prior Thomas,' whispered Michael, parting the foliage like a curtain and peering out. 'You were right to suggest we keep out of sight, because he is moving in a way that says he is up to no good at all. I wonder what he is doing.'

'Whatever it is, he must consider it important,' said Bartholomew. 'These vineyards represent a hard walk for a man of his girth, and I cannot imagine he is doing this for fun.'

Thomas stood gasping for breath, fanning his cascading chins furiously in a vain attempt to cool himself down. Even from a distance, Bartholomew could see the rivulets of sweat that coursed down the man's face and made dark patches on his habit.

They did not have to wait long to find out what had enticed Thomas to leave the luxury and comparative cool of the monastery buildings. Another figure emerged from the direction of the back gate. The person walked briskly towards Thomas, and they embarked on a hurried conversation, during which a neat white parcel was passed to the sub-prior.

'Who is that?' whispered Michael urgently, trying to push leaves out of the way. 'Can you see?'

Bartholomew eased himself forward. 'No. But it is someone who feels obliged to wear his hood pulled over his face. That in itself suggests something unusual, given the warmth of the evening. Should we try to get closer?'

'Well, there is not much point in spying if you cannot see or hear what is going on, is there?' snapped Michael irritably. 'Hurry up, or they will have finished their business before we reach them.'

On hands and knees, Bartholomew and Michael edged towards the fat sub-prior's trysting place. Crawling among the vines was such a ludicrously incommodious situation for a University Doctor and a Senior Proctor to put themselves in that Bartholomew started to laugh, thinking that he had not crawled around on all fours in the undergrowth since he was a child. Michael chortled, too, but his mirth was cut short by a litany of vicious curses when he put his hand on a thorn.

As they inched closer they tried to ensure they kept their heads low, so that they would not be visible above the stumpy bushes. Eventually, Bartholomew judged that they were within hearing distance, and risked a quick glance above the leaves. Neither Thomas nor the man he was meeting were where he expected them to be.

'Have you lost something?' asked Thomas coldly, the proximity of his voice making both Bartholomew and Michael jump violently. The physician was amazed that the obese sub-prior had been able to move so quickly and with so much stealth. His progress through the vineyard just a few moments before had indicated that he was incapable of speed or silence. Now he towered above the kneeling scholars, his large face flushed red from effort, anger and heat. He was still breathing hard, and the top half of his habit was soaked in perspiration. Bartholomew supposed that although Sub-prior Thomas could move with haste when necessary, the man's body was neither accustomed to nor happy with sudden spurts of activity. It was a physique that would reward its owner with a seizure if obliged to do it too often.

'My ring,' said Michael, thinking quickly and waving a hand sadly bereft of the baubles with which Benedictines usually liked to adorn themselves. 'I am so thin that it fell from my finger and Matt is helping me to look for it.'

'What were you doing here in the first place?' demanded Thomas, evidently unconvinced by such a flagrantly feeble excuse. 'I sincerely hope you were not following me.'

'Why would I do that?' asked Michael innocently, using Bartholomew to haul himself up from his knees. 'I am too busy to spend my valuable time stalking my fellow brethren through the bushes.'

'It is my understanding that you would go to any lengths to help de Lisle remove himself from this spike upon which he is impaled,' said Thomas accusingly. 'It would not surprise me if you intended to have one of *us* blamed for Glovere's death, merely to allow the Bishop to go free.'

'That is unfair,' objected Bartholomew, also standing and brushing dry soil from his hands. 'Michael has devoted his entire life at Cambridge to ensuring that justice is done.'

'Justice as *he* sees it,' said Thomas nastily.

'But that is what justice is, is it not?' pressed Bartholomew. 'It is someone's idea of fairness, be that person a proctor, a judge, or even a sub-prior.'

'I have no time to debate philosophical issues with you,' said Thomas. 'If I had wanted a university training, I would have gone to Oxford.'

'That would not have rendered you any less ignorant,' retorted Michael rudely. 'But since you feel the need to question me, I shall question you: what are you doing here, when it is approaching the time for compline?'

'That is none of your concern,' replied Thomas icily. 'However, I shall tell you, because I do not want to find my innocent actions turned into something sinister in order to allow de Lisle to blame *me* for the murder *he* committed.'

'Well?' asked Michael when Thomas paused, evidently casting around for an excuse he felt the monk would believe.

'I was taking bread to one of the town's children.' Michael's eyebrows shot up, but Thomas either did not notice or did not care. 'I meet him here often of an evening, when I give him food for his family. I do not make my actions public, because my acts of charity are between God and I.'

'You mean "God and me",' interjected Bartholomew.

'And did he give you anything in return?' asked Michael,

ignoring Bartholomew's grammatical pedantry and thinking about the white package that was safely packed away inside the sub-prior's scrip. Its outline could be seen, square and bulky, against the leather.

'Of course not,' said Thomas indignantly. 'What could a shepherd boy give me, other than his gratitude?' He poked at something on the ground with his foot. 'But here is your ring, Brother. It seems not to have rolled very far.'

'Thank you,' said Michael, leaning down to retrieve it from the dirt. 'I knew it would be here somewhere.'

'I shall wish you both good evening, then,' said Thomas, taking a deep breath as he contemplated the long incline that led towards the monastery buildings. 'I do not want to be late for compline because I have been dallying with you. Do not stay out here too long. It is not unknown for wolves to frequent these parts after dark, and I would not like to think of anything untoward happening to you.' He turned and began to huff his way up the hill.

'Was he threatening us?' mused Michael, replacing the ring as he stared thoughtfully after the sub-prior's wobbling progress. 'It sounded like a threat.'

'It was ambiguous,' said Bartholomew tiredly. 'I have no idea what he meant.'

'Wolves indeed!' muttered Michael. 'There have been no wolves here since the Conqueror's days. What did you make of his reason for being here?'

'I did not see the person he met properly,' replied Bartholomew, watching the sub-prior gradually lose speed. He was all but crawling when he crested the brow of the hill and disappeared down the other side. 'But it was no boy – unless it was a very big one.'

'A man, then?' asked Michael.

'It could have been a woman. And there is another thing, too.'

'Yes,' said Michael, nodding slowly as he anticipated what the physician was going to say. 'Thomas carried no bread with him, to give to a child or anyone else.'

'But this "boy" gave *him* something,' said Bartholomew. 'And it was certainly not bread.'

The daylight had all but gone by the time Bartholomew and Michael reached the gate where they had agreed to meet Mackerell. It was a pleasant evening, with a breeze that carried the scent of the sea that lay to the north. They propped open the gate, so that Mackerell would be able to enter, and then found a comfortable spot in which to wait. They leaned their backs against the wall of the great tithe barn, stretched their legs in front of them, and relaxed. They could see the gate from where they sat, and knew they would spot Mackerell when he came.

'Prior Alan agreed to my request for Mackerell to spend a few days in his prison,' said Michael. 'The man must be desperate, if he considers that foul place preferable to home.'

'He considers it safer,' Bartholomew pointed out. 'He said nothing about it being more comfortable. I wonder whether he really does have something to tell us or whether he is playing games.'

'I have been wondering that, too,' said Michael. 'The appearance of that dog – just when Mackerell's tongue seemed to be loosening – was rather too opportune for my liking.'

'I agree. In fact, I wonder whether he really left a message for us at all: that pot-boy may have been lying. I find it strange that Mackerell should be wary of us one moment, and then agree to meet us in dark and lonely places the next. And not only did he tell *us* exactly where to meet him, but he gave the message to that slack-tongued pot-boy, who, by his own admission, will tell anyone anything for a few pennies.'

Michael gazed into the twilight gloom. 'I have been thinking about your claim that Blanche was with the gypsies yesterday.'

'Yes?' asked Bartholomew. 'Do you accept that I could be right?'

'No, but I have been reconsidering the fact that the fourth gypsy declined to lower his hood the whole time he was in the tavern. It was hot in there, and wearing a thick hood like that cannot have been comfortable. So, the question is: who was he hiding from?'

Bartholomew blew out his cheeks. 'We seem to be making this unnecessarily complex, Brother. Why would Goran -- if indeed it was Goran -- go into a public place like the Mermaid, if he were trying to hide from someone? However, I am sure it was Blanche I saw. But it probably has no relevance to our case, anyway, so we should not waste our time by speculating about it.'

'If you are right, then it *is* relevant,' argued Michael. 'Blanche is here purely and simply to bring about the downfall of the man she hates. If she was dressed in rough clothes and lurking in seedy taverns with low company, then you can be sure that she was doing so to damage de Lisle in some way. But you are *not* right, and so all we can conclude is that Goran was probably up to no good.'

Bartholomew changed the subject, seeing they would not reach agreement on the matter. 'Where is Mackerell? It is dark already, and the dew is coming through.'

Michael shifted uncomfortably. 'True. I do not want to return to the priory with a wet seat. Then my brethren would really wonder what I had been doing!'

'We should look for him,' said Bartholomew, standing and offering Michael his hand. The monk grasped it, and Bartholomew only just remembered in time that Michael was very heavy, and that he needed to brace himself if he did not want to be pulled off his feet.

'I hope he is all right,' said Michael, growing anxious.

'He is probably in a tavern,' said Bartholomew, unconcerned because he had suspected the fisherman would not appear anyway. 'I will check the Mermaid. You stay here, in case he comes.'

But Mackerell was not in the Mermaid, and the pot-boy assured Bartholomew that he had not been seen since the previous day. Because he was out and felt like walking, Bartholomew glanced into the Lamb, the Bell and the White Hart, too, but there was no Mackerell enjoying his ale. Puzzled, but not yet worried, Bartholomew started to walk back to the priory, half expecting the man to have rendezvoused with Michael in his absence.

He was still on the Heyrow, deciding whether to return to the vineyard by walking through the priory grounds or by way of the town, when the door to the Lamb flew open and Guido the gypsy tumbled out. He was closely followed by his two brothers, all landing in a tangle of arms and legs in the street. Moments later, the door opened again and Eulalia emerged. A hand in the small of her back precipitated her outside faster than she intended, and she turned to glower at the person who had manhandled her. Bartholomew glimpsed Leycestre hurriedly closing the door, apparently unnerved by the glare of cool loathing shot his way by the travelling woman.

'What is going on?' asked Bartholomew, hurrying towards her.

'For some reason, Leycestre has taken against us this year,' said Eulalia, turning awkwardly and brushing her back. 'He has not been like this before. I cannot imagine what has changed him.'

'He accused us of taking wages that rightfully belong to Ely folk,' growled Guido as he hauled himself to his feet. His words were slurred, and Bartholomew supposed that he had been ejected before a drunken brawl could ensue. 'We have taken no wages from anyone: they cannot harvest their grain without our help and we are paid because they need us.'

'It is true,' said Eulalia to Bartholomew. 'We are hired as additional labour, not to replace local people. Usually, the folk here are delighted to see us, and always make us welcome. But it is different this year.' She turned angrily on Guido. 'And you did not help matters! We do not want to earn a reputation for brawling, or we will not be welcome here next year, either. You should not have risen to Leycestre's baiting.'

The door swung open again, and Bartholomew turned to see Leycestre framed in the light. There were others behind him, and some carried weapons. With a shock, Bartholomew realised that Leycestre's relentless claims that the gypsies were responsible for all manner of wrongs had finally come to fruition, and he now had a small army at his back.

'I suggested you leave days ago,' Leycestre said venomously, moving towards Guido. In the dim light, Bartholomew saw the dispossessed farmer's eyes were hot with anger, and the sweet smell of Ely's bona cervisia around him indicated that the gypsies were not the only ones who had been drinking.

'We have a right to be here,' objected Guido indignantly. 'We come every year.'

'Not any more,' hissed Leycestre. 'We have no room for liars and thieves in Ely.'

'*You* should leave then,' snarled Guido.

Eulalia put a warning hand on her brother's arm. 'We will be retiring to our beds now,' she said to Leycestre in a low, reasonable voice. 'We want no trouble.'

'Not so fast,' shouted Leycestre, making a grab for the slack-jawed Rosel as the lad made to follow his sister. Rosel should not have been given beer, because it made him unsteady on his legs. Leycestre's lunge did the rest, and Rosel took a tumble into the hard-baked mud of the street. There was an unpleasant crack as his skull hit a stone, followed by a frightened wail as the boy saw bright blood spilling through his fingers. Eulalia gave a cry of alarm, and rushed to her brother's side. Leycestre misinterpreted her sudden move as an attack, and his hand came up fast. In it there was a dagger.

The altercation might have ended in more bloodshed if Bartholomew had not stepped forward and knocked the dagger from Leycestre's hand, so that it went skittering across the ground. For an instant, Leycestre's expression was murderous, but then the fury dulled and he had the grace to appear sheepish. Even in his drink-excited state, Leycestre knew that there was no excuse for drawing a weapon on an unarmed woman who was doing nothing more threatening than kneeling next to her sobbing kinsman. Without a word, he strode away down the Heyrow. Someone retrieved the knife, and the small crowd quickly melted away into the darkness, as shamefaced as their leader.

'Thank you,' said Eulalia unsteadily, cradling Rosel's head in her lap. 'I think they might have killed us had you not been here.'

'They could have tried!' growled Guido belligerently, his own dagger in his hand now that the crowd had dispersed. 'But they would not have bested me!'

'I do not know about that,' said Goran uncertainly. 'There were an awful lot of them and only four of us. I, for one, am grateful the physician stepped in when he did.'

Guido's angry red eyes shifted to his brother, and he took a firmer grip on his knife. 'We do not need outsiders meddling in our affairs . . .'

'Help me, Guido,' snapped Eulalia. 'Do not stand there bragging like some great oaf when your brother lies bleeding.'

Bartholomew knelt next to her and examined Rosel's head in the faint light that filtered through the open windows of the tavern. It was only a scalp wound, which bled vigorously although there was little serious damage. He applied a goose-grease salve, and delighted Rosel by wrapping the boy's head in a bandage made from strips of white linen. Once the blood had been removed and he had an impressive dressing to show for his discomfort, Rosel made a miraculous recovery, and pulled away from Eulalia's anxious embrace to join his brothers.

'Goran is right,' Eulalia said, watching the three of them stagger unsteadily towards their camp. 'We would not have bested that crowd. Leycestre's blood was up, and he had encouraged his cronies to do us harm.'

'He thinks you are responsible for the burglaries,' said Bartholomew.

'And the murders,' added Eulalia ruefully. 'But I can assure you that we are not. Guido may seem like a fighter, but he is a coward at heart.'

'Is he a thief?'

She gave him a grin full of teeth that gleamed white in the moonlight. 'Who is not?'

'A good many people, I hope,' replied Bartholomew, rather primly.

'Then your understanding of human nature is sadly flawed. There is not a living soul – saints excluded – who has not taken an apple from someone else's tree or "borrowed" some unwanted thing that he has no intention of returning. Guido is no different from anyone else.'

Bartholomew stared at her, not sure what she was saying with her philosophical commentary. 'So, did he commit these burglaries or not?' he asked.

She smiled and shook her head, so that he did not know whether her answer was that of course he had, or whether the notion of burglary was so ludicrous that she could not even bring herself to reply to such a charge.

'Do you know Lady Blanche?' he asked at last, seeing he would gain no more information on that matter – at least, none that he was able to interpret.

'Of course I do,' she replied casually. 'She dines with us most Sundays on hedgehogs and acorns. What a ridiculous question, Matthew! How would *we* know such a person?'

'Because I saw her with you yesterday,' said Bartholomew, hoping that an honest approach would be more likely to gain honest answers.

She gazed at him. 'Do you mean in the Mermaid Inn? Are you talking about the person with the hood who was with us? That was Goran.'

'Then why did he look as though he was trying to disguise himself?' pressed Bartholomew, unconvinced.

'Because of men like Leycestre,' said Eulalia, her voice suddenly harsh. 'Like me, Goran is tired of being accused of things he did not do.'

'I am sorry,' said Bartholomew gently. He sensed he was wrong to question Eulalia about her brothers' affairs: he was only making her think that everyone in the town believed the accusations, even those who attempted to befriend them.

'You have not collected your black resin yet,' she said, smiling at him in the moonlight, her irritation apparently forgotten. 'Will you come for it now?'

Bartholomew gazed at the invitation in her dark eyes, and was already walking down the Heyrow with her when it occurred to him that Michael would be wondering why he had not returned.

'Damn!' he muttered, stopping in his tracks. 'Michael is waiting for me.'

'Let him wait,' suggested Eulalia. 'He does not look like the kind of man who would stand in the way of a friend's enjoyment.'

'He is not,' said Bartholomew. 'But there is a killer on the loose and a bishop who will grow more dangerous the longer he is cornered. I had better go.'

'Please yourself,' she said, clearly disappointed. 'But remember that you are always welcome at our fire.'

'Your brothers might not be so hospitable,' said Bartholomew ruefully, glancing down the dark road to where the trio lurched homewards. 'Guido dislikes me.'

'He will do as I ask,' said Eulalia confidently. 'He needs me a good deal more than I need him. I might have been king if he had not been my elder.'

'Can women be kings?' asked Bartholomew, surprised that rough men like Guido and Goran might be prepared to accept the rule of a woman.

'Of course,' she replied, as surprised by the question as he was by the answer. 'I told you that "king" is a poor translation of the word. But they will wonder what we are up to, if I linger here much longer. Do not wait too long before taking me up on my offer.'

'Black resin?' asked Bartholomew.

'Black resin,' she agreed as she walked away.

Bartholomew retraced his steps along the darkened streets, swearing under his breath as he tripped and stumbled over potholes and other irregularities. He had been some time, and hoped Mackerell had appeared in his absence and that Michael had the man safely ensconced in the Prior's cells. But Mackerell had not arrived, and Michael was fretting by the gate.

'I was beginning to worry about you, too,' the monk complained angrily, when Bartholomew reached him. 'What have you been doing? It only takes a few moments to run to the Mermaid and back.'

'It is too warm for running. Besides, I did not think there was any hurry.'

'Well, I have had enough of this,' said Michael irritably. 'We will go to the Quay, to see whether any of the bargemen there have seen Mackerell today, and then I am going to bed.'

'Good idea,' agreed Bartholomew, deciding not to mention the incident outside the Lamb while Michael was in such a bellicose frame of mind. The monk would assume Bartholomew had gone looking for Eulalia, blithely abandoning him to a lonely sojourn in a deserted vineyard. Since Bartholomew was not in the mood for an argument, he elected to tell Michael about the gypsies' altercation with Leycestre later, preferably after the monk had eaten and was in good humour.

They walked the short distance to the Quay, listening to the sounds of the night – the rumble of voices from the taverns, the barking of a dog and the faint hiss of reeds in the wind. The air had the distinct tang of salt in it, overlain with a powerful fishy odour. Gulls paddled silently in the river's shallows, ducking and pecking at the water as they ate their fill of the refuse that had been dumped there. When Bartholomew and Michael reached the Quay, a tiny prick of light implied that someone was working late near the barges. Michael strolled up to it.

'Has anyone seen Mackerell?' he asked.

What happened next was a blur. One of the figures turned slowly, then swung out viciously with what appeared to be a hammer. Michael jerked backwards, so that it missed his face, but he lost his balance and, after a few moments of violently whirling arms, toppled backward to land heavily among a pile of crates. With an almighty clatter, the crates fell and crashed around him, while the monk covered his head with his hands.

Bartholomew darted to his aid, but found himself confronted by three men, who seemed convinced that he was in their way. They rushed him in a body before he could reach into his medicine bag and draw one of the knives he carried. All four went thudding to the ground, and Bartholomew laid blindly about him with his fists, not really able to see and only knowing that anyone near him was not a friend. He grazed his knuckles several times, although whether his blows landed on a person or on the sacks of grain over which they struggled he could not tell.

The first of his assailants broke free and ran. The others followed, and Bartholomew leapt spectacularly on to the back of one in an attempt to prevent him from escaping. The man was larger than Bartholomew had anticipated; all at once he started spinning around, so that the physician lost his grip and went flying to land on Michael. He heard a hammering of receding footsteps as the last of them fled.

'Are you all right?' asked Bartholomew, climbing off the monk and peering into the darkness. There was little point in giving chase: he could not see, and he did not know the area well enough to guess where the three men might have gone.

'No thanks to you,' muttered Michael ungraciously,

reaching out and using Bartholomew to haul himself to his feet. His weight was enormous, and the physician almost fell a second time. 'You should have landed on those bags of wheat or the crates. You did not have to aim for me. You are heavy, Matt!'

'I needed something soft to fall on,' said Bartholomew, smiling at the monk's vehemence. 'But did you see their faces? They were not the gypsies, because I saw them only a few moments ago, heading in the opposite direction.'

'They could have doubled back,' said Michael. 'Are you sure it was not them?'

'No,' admitted Bartholomew. 'But Rosel has a cut head, and I do not think any of our attackers were swathed in bandages.'

'He could have taken it off since you last saw him,' Michael pointed out. 'And then they could have followed you here. There are three brothers, and three men attacked us.'

'But these people fought us because we disturbed them at something,' Bartholomew reasoned. 'They were not lying in wait for us.'

'They did not really fight, either,' said Michael thoughtfully. 'They pushed and struggled. No weapons were drawn, or you would have been a dead man. And they had all been drinking.'

Bartholomew stared at him. 'How do you know that?'

Michael tapped his nose. 'The smell, Matt. They had beer on their breath. They may not have been drunk, but they had certainly enjoyed a jug of ale.'

'That does not help,' said Bartholomew. 'Virtually every man in the city seems to have been in a tavern this evening. I even saw Almoner Robert and Symon the librarian in a secluded alcove of the Bell. Mackerell, you and I are probably the only ones to have abstained tonight.'

'So what were that trio doing among the reeds to have warranted all that belligerence?' asked Michael, walking to where the three men had been working, and peering into the inky darkness of the river. There was nothing to see. One of them had dropped the torch he had been using and it still burned. Bartholomew picked it up and looked around carefully, but there was nothing to suggest why they had been so reluctant to be caught.

'This may sound ridiculous, but when the first one lunged at me, I half supposed that we had stumbled on Mackerell's murder taking place,' said Michael.

Bartholomew stared at him. 'Why did you think that?'

'Because so many people know we are meeting him – the pot-boy at the Mermaid, Tysilia, William and the Bishop – that I wondered whether someone might try to reach him first and ensure that he follows in the footsteps of Glovere and the others: floating face-down in the river with a fatal slit in the back of his neck.'

Bartholomew shook his head. 'You will probably find that Mackerell had no intention of meeting us in the first place. Why should he? He will be safer hiding in the Fens.'

'I hope you are right,' said Michael gloomily. 'I would not like to think that Mackerell lies dead because we spoke to him.'

'He is not dead, Brother. If I raise this torch, you can see clear across to the other side of the river. There is no corpse floating here.'

'I have no idea what is going on in this town, Matt,' said Michael tiredly. 'But I intend to find out. No one gets the better of the Senior Proctor and his trusted associate. We shall solve this mess, Matt. You mark my words!'

chapter 6

THURSDAYS WERE MARKET DAY IN ELY, AND WORK STARTED early. The hum of voices, the rattle of carts along the streets and the whinnying of horses could be heard long before it was light, and Bartholomew had the sense that the city had barely slept the night before. He certainly felt as though he had not: old Roger in the infirmary had had a difficult night, and Bartholomew and Brother Henry had managed to sleep only in fits and starts. By the time the first glimmerings of dawn appeared, the infirmarian looked as heavy-eyed and weary as Bartholomew felt. With dawn came peaceful sleep for Roger, and the two physicians left Julian watching over him while they went for some fresh air. They strolled around the marketplace, watching the frenetic activity taking place in the half-light as stall owners struggled to raise bright awnings over their shops and arrange their offerings in a way that they hoped would prove irresistible to buyers.

Bartholomew looked around him. There were butchers' stalls with colourfully plumaged waterfowl hanging by their feet, and bloody hunks of meat already beginning to attract flies as well as paying customers. Hares were common at the Cambridge market, but they were rare in the Fens, and there was not one to be seen. There was plenty of fish, though, displayed in neat, glistening rows: the shiny black-skinned eels that were so famous in the area, trout and a grotesquely large pike hanging across one counter, its ugly head dangling just above the mud of the street.

Bakers and pie-sellers provided more sweetly fragrant wares, and baskets of loaves of all qualities and shapes were carefully stacked, along with cakes and pastries for those able to afford more than the basic necessities of life.

Food was not all that was for sale. Ely was a thriving city, and boasted its own pottery and a lucrative rope-making industry. Pots with a beautiful blue glaze were displayed by one proud craftsman, while others sold the unglazed, functional utensils that were present in every kitchen – large jugs for milk, great cauldrons for stews, and dishes for serving meat and fish. The rope-makers' stalls were piled with huge coils of cord in every thickness imaginable; some of extra strength were used by builders for their pulleys, while others were silky and delicate and were used to lace shirts and bodices.

There was livestock, too. Squealing pigs, frightened calves and milling sheep were locked in pens at one end of the marketplace, while flocks of geese, ducks and squawking chickens weaved in and out of the legs of the busy stall holders. Loud human voices added to the general noise and confusion. In one corner, spices from distant and little-known lands were on sale, and the exotic aroma of cinnamon and cloves almost, but not quite, dispelled the overpowering smell of warm manure from the animals. Dogs sniffed the soft mat of rotting straw and dung underfoot, occasionally excavating something they deemed edible.

Bartholomew bought some ink from a parchment seller in anticipation of the work he planned to do on his treatise on fevers, and then Brother Henry purchased some of the weak breakfast beer that was being sold by the priory's brewer. It was exactly how Bartholomew liked his morning ale: cool, sweet, pleasantly nutty and so clear that he could see the bottom of the jug. The ale served at Michaelhouse tended to be a brew that had been bought cheaply; it was already past its best, and invariably cloudy.

The physicians finished their ale and went to the cathedral to celebrate prime. A thin column of black-robed monastics was already winding its way into the chancel, each man pushing back his hood as he crossed from the cloister to the church proper. They walked in silence, their sandalled feet tapping softly on the flagstones. Henry nodded a farewell to Bartholomew and joined the end of the procession. The physician's heart sank when he saw a door open in the west end of the cathedral and Father John bustle in. Prime would not be a peaceful, contemplative occasion after all.

The monks began to chant their prayers, and Bartholomew closed his eyes to listen as the rich rumble of the basses acted as a drone for the higher notes of the tenors. Then Michael's pleasant baritone began to echo through the chancel, singing alternate lines with the rest of the monks acting as a chorus. Just when the physician began to lose himself in the beauty of the music, Father John's mass started.

Bartholomew opened his eyes to see Michael glowering in the direction of the nave, displeased that his singing was being spoiled by the priest's continuing battle with the priory. Bartholomew tried to concentrate on the words of the psalm, but found instead that he listened with horrified fascination to John's bastard Latin. Most of it was entirely nonsensical, but some bore enough resemblance to the original to be amusing. John's parishioners did not know, and probably did not care, that their priest's mass was incomprehensible, and were present in their usual numbers.

Bartholomew spotted Leycestre standing near the back with his two nephews. Feeling that it was unreasonable for anyone to expect him to pray under such conditions, he slipped out of the chancel and made his way to the nave, intending to ask Leycestre what had happened in the Lamb Inn that had resulted in the gypsies' undignified expulsion. Not surprisingly, given his state the night before, Leycestre looked fragile and his face was pale and unshaven.

'I trust you arrived home safely last night?' Bartholomew whispered.

Leycestre blinked stupidly for a moment, then rubbed his head as he understood what the physician was saying. 'It was you who prevented that fight. I am sorry. I was the worse for ale, and should have been better mannered.'

'Even to gypsies?' asked Bartholomew archly.

Leycestre smiled ruefully. 'Even to gypsies. They are thieves, and it is possible that they killed our three much-lamented townsmen, but we need their labour at this time of year, and we cannot afford to have them leave just yet.'

'That is not the position you held last night,' Bartholomew remarked. 'Eulalia told me that you accused them of stealing the wages from honest local folk.'

Leycestre edged around one of the great, thick columns, so that the priest would not see him talking during the mass. 'I should have kept my thoughts to myself. I do believe that *we* should have the money the landowners are willing to pay the gypsies, but it is not the gypsies' fault that the situation is as it is.'

'Will you apologise to them?' Bartholomew asked. 'It cannot have been pleasant to be accused of stealing in such a public place.'

'I will mention to Eulalia that I may have spoken out of turn,' said Leycestre, resentment thick in his voice. 'But I will not apologise to her loutish brothers – especially that Guido.'

'Was there a reason for all that drinking last night?' Bartholomew asked curiously. 'A large number of people were in the taverns, and they were all buying a lot more ale than usual.'

Leycestre gave him a puzzled glance, as though he could not believe the question had been asked. 'It was a Wednesday.'

It was Bartholomew's turn to look bemused. 'What of it?'

Leycestre gave a long-suffering sigh. 'We are paid on Wednesdays. It is the day before the weekly market, you see, and the landlords want us to spend all our hard-earned wages on the goods of other rich men. It is a cunning ploy.'

'I see,' said Bartholomew, wondering whether that was truly the reason for the choice of day, or whether it was to allow the women to make their purchases in the market-place before the men had time to squander all their earnings in taverns. If the previous night was anything to go by, such a policy might be well justified.

'Market days are always interesting occasions,' Leycestre

went on. 'They are excellent opportunities to discuss the heavy yoke of labourers with men who feel empathy with us.'

'I am sure they are,' said Bartholomew. He changed the subject, before Leycestre could start preaching. Like many men who burned with the fire of his convictions, Leycestre was tedious company once he had started holding forth. 'Do you know a man called Mackerell? He was supposed to meet Michael last night, but he never arrived.'

'He drinks in the Mermaid,' said Leycestre helpfully. 'You should ask there for him.'

'We tried, but no one seemed to know his whereabouts.'

Leycestre rubbed his chin thoughtfully. 'He is Ely's best fisherman, but the monks insist on buying all his eels for an absurdly low price. He is finding it increasingly difficult to manage on the wages they pay him, but they refuse to give him more.'

'He found the bodies in the river,' said Bartholomew, refusing to be side-tracked by Leycestre's biased assessment of fish economics – Mackerell was not that poor. He had been reasonably well dressed and had declined Michael's offer of free wine. 'We wanted to know whether he noticed anything that might lead us to the killer.'

'He might have done I suppose,' said Leycestre. 'He has certainly been acting a little oddly since he found them.'

'What do you mean?'

'Naturally, he was unsettled at being obliged to haul corpses from the river, but he makes his living by water and such men are used to drownings. However, I was surprised they bothered him as much as they seem to have done. He is a surly fellow at the best of times, but the discovery of these bodies has done nothing to improve his temper.'

'Other than the gypsies, who you believe are responsible for everything bad, is there anyone else who might have committed those murders?' Since Leycestre was a man who liked holding forth in taverns, Bartholomew wondered whether he had heard any rumours that he might be prepared to share.

'None of us know who else it could be,' came the disappointing answer. Bartholomew supposed he should not be surprised: Leycestre was rigid in his belief that the gypsies were the source of all evil.

'And none of the three dead men had any particular enemies?' he tried again.

Leycestre shrugged. 'They all had a great number of enemies. You must have heard by now that they were not popular. Haywarde drank heavily and was inclined to fight; Glovere was a miserable pig who wronged people with his vicious tongue; and Chaloner had an annoying liking for the property of other people.'

'A thief?' asked Bartholomew. 'No one has mentioned this before.'

'Well, I suppose no one likes to speak ill of the dead. We do not want them returning from Purgatory to wander among us because we have unsettled their souls.'

Bartholomew smothered a smile. While that might usually be true, few Ely citizens seemed to have any qualms about saying exactly what they thought of Glovere, Chaloner and Haywarde. 'And Mackerell?' he asked. 'Is he liked in the town?'

'Not especially,' replied Leycestre. 'He is an excellent fisherman, but he occasionally tops up his basket with the catches of others.'

'You mean he is a thief, too? When he does not catch enough eels for himself, he steals?'

'We all do it occasionally when we are desperate, but he does it frequently. I blame the priory, personally, for placing him in a position where he is forced into dishonesty on a regular basis.'

'Father John has warned you about discussing such matters during mass,' came a sharp voice behind them. Bartholomew turned to find he was facing the formidable Agnes Fitzpayne. Her words had been addressed to Leycestre, but it was Bartholomew she had in her beady gaze. Leycestre backed away a little, and some of his confident bluster evaporated.

'Leycestre was telling me about Mackerell,' said Bartholomew, hoping to placate her by revealing what they had discussed. 'He was supposed to meet Michael last night, but failed to appear.'

'Unreliable,' declared Agnes immediately. 'Do not read anything sinister into it. That man pleases himself whom he sees and when.'

'The landlord of the Lamb tells me that you recently had quite a conversation with the brother-in-law you told me you despised,' said Bartholomew, watching her closely for any reaction that might betray what she had been doing in the tavern with Haywarde the night he died. 'You, Leycestre and his two nephews.'

Agnes's eyes narrowed. 'What of it? Barbour is a shameless gossip, and had no right to tell you my personal business.'

'Perhaps not, but he did. What did you discuss? I was under the impression that you disliked him, but you still spent the last night of his life in eager conversation with him.'

'What we discussed is none of your affair,' snapped Agnes angrily. 'But I can see that if I leave it at that, you will tell your fat friend, and then he will spread lies that it was *us* who threw Haywarde in the river. If you must know, we were talking about money.'

'Money he owed you?' pressed Bartholomew.

'Money I gave to my sister and that he took for his own purposes,' said Agnes. 'Now, there is a mass in progress. If you are a heathen, who cannot bring himself to listen to Father John's pious words, then you should leave. If you are a Christian, you will stay and listen in reverent silence.'

The competition between chanting monks and yelling priest was reaching its customary crescendo and Bartholomew was finding it difficult to concentrate on his conversation with the seditious Leycestre and the aggressive Agnes anyway. He opted for the first choice, to the shock of Agnes, and nodded a brief farewell before walking outside.

But the discordant racket followed him so he walked more quickly, trying to escape the noise, and ended up racing past the cemetery and towards the infirmary. There, he ran head-long into Michael, who was making his way to the refectory.

'What are you doing here?' asked Bartholomew. 'You are supposed to be celebrating prime. In fact, you were a major part of it, the last I heard.'

'I could stand it no longer.' Michael glanced at the physician, breathless from his dash and with wind-blown hair, and smiled. 'You know exactly what I mean. But I left in a dignified manner, whereas you fled like a cat from water, with ears flattened and terror in your eyes.'

'It was nasty,' admitted Bartholomew. 'Where are you going?'

'Breakfast,' declared Michael, knowing that the tables would already be laden with the morning fare, and that an early arrival would allow him to select the best of it.

'And then what?'

Michael sighed. 'I really have no idea. Everyone tells me that Glovere, Chaloner and Haywarde were hated. That means that anyone from the city could have killed them. Meanwhile, certain factions in the town tell me that the deaths – and various burglaries – only started when the gypsies arrived in Ely.'

'Only Leycestre really seems to believe that,' objected Bartholomew. 'Others listen to his raving, but do not act on it.'

'They acted last night,' Michael pointed out, referring to the incident outside the Lamb that Bartholomew had described while the monk had devoured his final meal of the day the previous evening. 'You told me they were ready for a lynching.'

'They were drunk, and drunks are not noted for their powers of reason and common sense.'

'I do not know what to do next, actually,' confessed Michael gloomily, his thoughts returning to his floundering investigation. 'I could bribe a riverman to take me to

Mackerell's Fenland lair. I am even considering asking whether Stretton or Northburgh have learned anything of value – and I am certain they could not have done, so you can see how desperate I am.'

'Northburgh spent all yesterday pestering poor Henry about "cures" for old age. He is not interested in solving this case, only in cheating death. And Canon Stretton was far too drunk to have learned anything at all, other than that bona cervisia is a powerful brew.'

'Perhaps I should engage Tysilia to help me, as William has done,' grumbled Michael bitterly. 'I have never been quite so much at a loss in a case before.'

After breakfast, Bartholomew wandered outside, leaving Michael to the dubious delights of conversation with his fellow monks. It was unprepossessing company as far as the physician was concerned. Prior Alan was distracted and uncommunicative, because his clever mind was wrestling with some technical problem relating to his beloved octagon; Sub-prior Thomas was incensed that Michael had selected the best of the breakfast items before he had arrived, and was busily feeding in sullen silence with his vast jowls quivering in agitation; and Almoner Robert, who usually passed the time at meals by fighting with Hosteller William, was grim-faced and silent because William was not there. The only person who offered a potentially enjoyable discussion was Henry, but he was taking breakfast in the infirmary. Judging from his own experiences, Bartholomew did not blame Henry for preferring the company of deaf or senile monks to the bickering in the refectory.

Bartholomew hovered by the refectory's back door, then stretched out an arm to halt the urgent progress of Brother Symon as he shot out a few moments later. Displeased that his attempt to disappear had been thwarted, the librarian only agreed to open the door to his domain with very bad grace. While he waited for the monk to fetch the key from wherever he hid it each night, Bartholomew stared out across the graves in the cemetery and thought about the work he planned to do that day.

As he gazed, he saw a spot of colour among the leaves of the tree that William and Tysilia had used for their tryst the previous day. It was moving this way and that in an agitated manner; then he became aware of a peculiar noise, too. It sounded like sobbing. Curious, he walked through the dew-soaked grass and approached the tree.

Tysilia sat there, facing the wall and rocking back and forth as she wept in a most heart-rending manner. Bartholomew was used to Tysilia arousing a variety of emotions in him, the most common of which were dislike, exasperation and distrust, but he had never before experienced compassion for her. Wondering what could reduce the infuriatingly cheerful and ebullient woman to tears, he touched her gently on the shoulder.

'What is wrong? Can I help?'

She gazed up at him with eyes red from weeping, her face a streaked mess from the tears that had run down them. 'I want William,' she said in a wail. She began to cry again, this time much louder and more piercingly, so that Bartholomew glanced behind him in alarm, afraid that someone would hear them and assume he was doing her some harm.

'I will fetch him for you,' he said backing away. 'He is probably in the refectory, eating his breakfast.'

But he was not, Bartholomew realised. The seat usually occupied by William had been empty. But, the physician reasoned, William's absence at breakfast was an odd excuse for Tysilia's display of agitation.

'He is not in the refectory!' she howled. 'I have already been there, and he is not with the rest of the monks. He is taken, like the others.'

'What others?' asked Bartholomew. 'What are you talking about?'

'Glovere and the two peasants,' she screeched. 'We will find William dead in the river, like them.'

This notion brought on a renewed frenzy of grief, and

Bartholomew was hard pressed to calm her. Speaking was no use, because she was making too much noise to hear anything that was said, and the only thing he could think to do was to put his arms around her until she quieted herself. He hoped that her anguish had not attracted the attention of gossiping monks who might complain to Blanche or the Prior that one guest was seducing another. If so, he thought, Tysilia's reputation was such that he doubted whether *he* would be credited with the seduction.

'William will not be found in the river,' he said gently, when he was sure he could make himself heard. 'Glovere and the others were townsmen, and there is no reason to suggest that the killer would strike at a monk.'

'There is no reason to assume he would not,' she shot back, uncharacteristically astute. 'There is a first time for everything, as my uncle likes to say.'

'But no monks *have* been killed,' Bartholomew pointed out, helping her to stand. For the first time since he had known her, Tysilia was not pretty. Her eyes were red and swollen, and her usually clear skin was blotchy. Her appearance was not improved by twin trails of mucus that ran from her nose. He handed her a piece of linen, which she used to rub at a spot of mud on her sleeve. The mucus looked set to stay for the duration of the conversation. 'And you must remember that the victims so far have been unpopular people.'

'William is unpopular,' sniffed Tysilia miserably. 'No monks like him because he is harsh, and no townsfolk like him because he is a monk.'

'That may be so, but he is not hated, as Glovere was. Wipe your nose.'

'Almoner Robert hates him,' said Tysilia, snuffling wetly as she fiddled with the linen. 'They have loathed each other since they were children. I think it is because Robert is jealous of William's beautiful hair.'

'Please wipe your nose,' pleaded Bartholomew. 'But if William and Robert's antagonism is long-standing, there is no reason why one should harm the other now.'

She scrubbed at her face with the linen and then handed it back to him. 'I wish you were Brother Michael.'

'I am sorry,' said Bartholomew. 'He is having breakfast.'

'Will you fetch him? I am sure he will find William for me.'

'William will appear when he is ready,' said Bartholomew, determined not to deliver his friend into her hands. 'There is no need to disturb Michael.'

'Pity,' said Tysilia wistfully. 'A few moments with Michael would take my mind off my other worries. I am sure he knows how to make a woman forget herself.'

'I am sure he does,' said Bartholomew vaguely, not caring to speculate.

She turned towards him, and seemed to be regaining her composure. 'What shall I do?'

'Nothing,' said Bartholomew. 'William will come to you when he has finished whatever it is he is doing. And why do you care so, anyway? You have not been here long enough to have formed any serious attachment to the man.'

'He will *not* come!' wailed Tysilia with a fresh flood of tears. 'He was supposed to meet me this morning, during prime, but he did not come. He is dead, I tell you!'

'He is not,' said Bartholomew firmly. He took her elbow and guided her along the narrow path to the guesthouse, where he hoped he could deposit her with Blanche. She would doubtless know how to deal with the near-hysterical woman. 'But you have not told me why you are so upset about him. Is he your latest lover?'

She looked at him as though he had just committed the most frightful indiscretion. 'He is my brother! Do I look like the kind of woman who would sleep with my brother? Anyway, it is Michael who has my heart, not William.'

Bartholomew thought she looked like the kind of woman who would take anyone to her bed, but decided now was not the time to mention it. 'William is not your brother,' he said instead, puzzled as to how she had managed to come up with such a ludicrous notion.

She pulled away from him. 'He *is*,' she declared with

finality. 'And what would you know, anyway? You are only someone who mixes herbs – an apoplexy.'

'Apothecary,' he corrected, before deciding there was little point in trying to educate Tysilia. She would not remember what he had said by the next time she met him.

The door to the Outer Hostry opened and the burly Blanche bustled out, hoisting her skirts under her bosom and gazing around as if the world had done her a serious injustice.

'There is Lady Blanche,' he said. 'Wipe your nose again, before you go to her.'

'I do not feel like going to *her*,' said Tysilia sulkily, rubbing a sleeve across her face. 'She is worse than the nuns at St Radegund's Convent, and is always trying to keep me inside when I want to go out.'

'I am sure she is,' muttered Bartholomew, trying to attract Blanche's attention.

'It is very annoying, actually,' Tysilia went on with another sloppy sniff. Her acute distress was forgotten, and she was already sounding like her normal self. Bartholomew envied her ability to recover from inconvenient emotions. 'How can I make friends with charming men when she is watching me all the time?'

'What were you going to discuss with William?' asked Bartholomew. Blanche had her back to him, and did not see his energetic waving. 'Do you know anything more about these murders? Does he?'

'No,' Tysilia said aggressively, pulling her arm away from him. She thought for a moment. 'What murders?'

'Do not lie, Tysilia,' said Bartholomew softly. 'I overheard you and William talking yesterday. I know he has charged you to discover whether Blanche killed Glovere.'

She beamed proudly and took his arm again. 'William said it was a secret. But since you know, it is no longer a secret, so I can tell whoever I like. William trusts me. For some reason, some people think I lack wits, but he saw that I have quite a few of them.'

'And he set you to put them to use,' said Bartholomew, thinking that the hosteller was insane to have entrusted Tysilia with anything. At best, she had told Blanche that a member of the monastery thought her guilty of murdering her own steward to discredit de Lisle, and at worst, she might inadvertently reveal to the killer that William was on his trail.

'He said I am an intellec . . . inteller . . . clever woman, and could be of great use to him. He is right, of course. I may not have paid attention to my studies, and I have no patience with staring at silly marks on smelly pieces of parchment, but I have spent time at a University, you know.'

'You have?' asked Bartholomew doubtfully, still trying to catch Blanche's eye. As far as he knew, no universities accepted female scholars, and women who wanted a life of learning tended to do so in convents that had a reputation for their libraries. However, the notion that Tysilia had spent time in one of these was so improbable that it was humorous.

Tysilia nodded sagely. 'I have been to the University of Life.' She beamed her vacant grin, and Bartholomew wondered how, a few months earlier, he ever could have imagined that her slow-witted exterior hid a cunning mind. 'That is a clever phrase, is it not? I invented it myself. It means that while you have had learning from books, I have been living a life.'

'But you have spent most of your life in convents – or trying to escape from them – so how does that make you so worldly?' asked Bartholomew, amused.

'It just does,' pouted Tysilia. 'And do not wave your arm like that, or Blanche will think you are trying to attract her attention.'

'You have not answered my question. Have you or William learned anything about the death of Glovere? Why did he think Blanche might know about it?'

Tysilia looked around her quickly, and then leaned close to him, so that her breath was unpleasantly hot against his ear. 'William told me to keep my voice low when I talk about this, so that no one will overhear what I have to say.'

'But that is not necessary here,' Bartholomew said. 'There is no one close by.'

'Blanche is over there,' Tysilia pointed out, reverting to her normal bellow, so that the King's kinswoman turned around even though she was still some distance away. Blanche's eyes narrowed when she saw Tysilia clinging to Bartholomew's arm. She hoisted her skirts and powered towards them, her mouth set in a narrow, grim line. The physician was not sure whether the disapproval was directed at him or at Tysilia, and determined to extricate himself as soon as possible.

'Blanche has long, sharp ears, like a horse,' Tysilia went on. 'She hears all sorts of things.'

'A horse?' asked Bartholomew, before he could stop himself. He needed to ask about William before Blanche reached them, not allow Tysilia to side-track him with what would doubtless prove to be some asinine observation.

'Horses have long, sharp ears,' said Tysilia authoritatively. 'Although I suppose they are more pointed than sharp, really. In fact, I am not sure what is meant by a "sharp ear". But whatever it is, Blanche has them. William told me so, and he is my brother, so he must be right.'

'Why did he say that about Blanche? Has she overheard you and William talking?'

'She may have done. He told me that Ely is a dangerous place at the moment, and he thought it would be more dangerous with her in it.'

'Why did he think that?'

'He did not tell me,' Tysilia whispered, her voice confidential now that she knew she was speaking about William's secret matter. 'But he thinks there is a killer here, *in the monastery*! He said this killer will be watching me all the time, and that he has the power to look at my most secret thoughts.' She glanced around her fearfully. 'That means he is watching me now.'

'William was trying to frighten you into keeping quiet about what you discussed together,' said Bartholomew. 'The killer is a vicious man who owns a knife, but he has no super-natural powers or ability to read minds.'

'You do not know that for certain,' she shot back.

'Then tell me what William told you, and we may be able to expose this fiend and put an end to all the fear and suspicion,' Bartholomew reasoned.

She smiled her vacant smile again, her dark eyes empty of intelligent thought. 'He said the killer is in the monastery.'

'What did he mean? That the culprit is a monk?'

'I suppose so,' said Tysilia uncertainly. 'Monks do live in monasteries, after all. But then, so do other people. I have seen them myself – servants and tradesmen and visitors.'

Bartholomew stared at her. 'Blanche is a visitor at the monastery. And there are all manner of lay-brothers working in the grounds and the kitchens.'

'Oh, yes!' agreed Tysilia happily. 'I remember now. William did say that the killer could be just about anyone here. And he said that Glovere, Chaloner and Haywarde were not likeable men, and so someone relieved the world of them. That is why they died: because no one liked them.'

Bartholomew raised his eyebrows. 'William believes that someone is killing people just because they are unpopular?'

'Yes,' said Tysilia. 'And because William is unpopular, someone will want to kill him, too. Everyone who is nasty is at risk. That means that *I* am safe, of course.'

Blanche stormed up to Tysilia and Bartholomew and regarded them both with rank suspicion. 'What have you been doing?' she demanded. 'I hope you have not been romping in the cemetery again, Tysilia. I have already caught you doing that once, and have explained that a graveyard is no place for that sort of thing.'

'It was Julian's idea,' objected Tysilia indignantly. 'He assured me that all the monks used the cemetery for their—'

'Thank you, Tysilia,' interrupted Blanche. 'We do not need to know the details. Go and wait for me in the solar.

And leave my tapestry alone, if you please. You will ruin it again if you take a needle to it.'

'I can sew,' said Tysilia proudly, giving Bartholomew a bright grin before skipping away in the direction of the Outer Hostry.

'I cannot leave her for long,' said Blanche, looking after her. 'Wretched woman! She is a dreadful liability, and I never should have agreed to take her on. I was most shamefully tricked on that score – de Lisle again.'

'I heard he gave her to you as a symbol of your last truce – by placing a member of his own household in your care, he is demonstrating trust.'

Blanche gave a bitter laugh. 'And when she becomes pregnant again – which is only a matter of time, given her uncontrollable behaviour and undiscriminating tastes – de Lisle will claim that I have abused that trust. I should have known better than to accept such terms from him. He pretended to be reluctant to part with her, but I suspect he was only too glad to be rid of her.'

'Probably.' Bartholomew chewed his bottom lip, realising it was not wise to be agreeing with de Lisle's enemies that he was a devious schemer who might well use Tysilia as a weapon to inflict on his opponents. 'But the truce you had is surely broken, now that you have accused him of murder. Why does he not demand her back?'

Blanche gave a humourless smile. 'Declining to accept his niece is his way of wreaking revenge upon my household. You may have noticed that she is not pleasant to have around. But what was she doing with you? Did you catch her lying in wait for that William again? I cannot imagine why she has taken a liking to him – he is old enough to be her father.'

'Or her brother,' said Bartholomew. 'That is who she claims he is.'

Blanche regarded him in astonishment. 'They are not related! William is *my* cousin, actually.'

Bartholomew was certain that the claim of kinship was merely William's clever way of ensuring that he gained

Tysilia's willing services. Poor Tysilia was gullible and a little pathetic, and might well believe such a tale, no matter how improbable. However, Tysilia was actually the Bishop's illegitimate daughter, although few people, including Tysilia herself, were aware of the fact. William's claim might mean that he imagined *he* was de Lisle's kinsman, too. And if that were true, it could explain why he had gone to some trouble to investigate whether Blanche might have played a role in the murder for which his relative stood accused.

'Tysilia has an unbreakable habit of securing a man at any place we visit,' Blanche was saying, cutting across his thoughts. 'She is like an eel, slipping out of windows and past guards to reach the objects of her lust. Keeping her childless is one of the greatest challenges I have ever faced.'

'How do you like Ely?' asked Bartholomew, hoping to steer the conversation around to the fact that he had seen Blanche in the Mermaid Inn with the gypsies two days before.

Blanche looked around her disdainfully. 'Ely is a far cry from Huntingdon, which is as fine a town as ever graced the face of the Earth. But it has its good points, I suppose.'

'Such as the taverns?' asked Bartholomew probingly.

Blanche regarded him as though he were insane. 'How would I know about the taverns? I was thinking of the cathedral. Huntingdon does not have a cathedral.'

'Have you actually been in any of the taverns? Some of them are comfortable places, and offer decent accommodation for travellers.'

'I am sure they do,' said Blanche with distaste. 'And I can well imagine the kind of traveller who stays in them, too. I am sure the bedclothes are crawling with vermin, while one would share the straw mattresses with rats. It may suit Tysilia, but it would not do for me.'

'The Mermaid has that reputation,' said Bartholomew, watching her closely for any reaction. 'Although the Lamb is better.'

'Well, I would not be caught in either,' said Blanche firmly.

'Staying here is bad enough, but it is better than sharing an inn with the common folk. Glovere was fond of the Lamb before the Bishop murdered him. It just goes to show that my wariness of such places is justified.'

'Tysilia seems uneasy in the priory,' said Bartholomew, deciding to turn his attention to whether Blanche had heard any rumours regarding the murders, since his clumsy questioning regarding her appearance at the Mermaid seemed unlikely to lead anywhere. He considered asking her directly what she had been doing with the gypsies, but sensed that she would merely deny the incident and end the conversation. And then, if she had been up to no good in dubious company, his revelation of the fact that he suspected her might put him in line for a knife in the neck and a dip in the river.

'She should be,' said Blanche. 'The Bishop is busily killing folk he does not like. He killed my servant first and then – when he found he had a taste for murder – he dispatched the two peasants. And, since I am sure there cannot be any love lost between him and his shameless niece, she should watch herself.'

'I thought you only accused de Lisle of murdering your steward.'

'I did, but then I heard that whoever killed Glovere had also dispatched Chaloner and Haywarde. You were paid by Father John to determine the cause of death, so you should not need me to tell you that whoever killed Glovere killed the others, too.'

'But de Lisle has no reason to kill these men,' objected Bartholomew.

'Does he not?' asked Blanche smugly. She folded her arms and looked at him closely. 'Tell me, have you ever looked at a person you despise and wished there was something you could do to rid the world of him? Louts who steal? Men who beat their wives? Women who claim they attended the University of Life? Others with spiteful tongues?'

'I suppose so,' said Bartholomew, thinking of the times

when greedy and selfish acts had damaged or destroyed the
lives and happiness of people he had liked.

'Well, so has de Lisle. Only whereas the rest of us pray
to God to punish the wicked, he imagines he *is* God and
that he has the right to punish offenders himself.'

'I do not think—' began Bartholomew.

Blanche stopped him. 'You and that Brother Michael can
do all you like to prove de Lisle innocent, but you will fail.
And you should consider your next move very carefully,
because you do not want to be associated with the likes of
him when the good folk of Ely avenge themselves for the
unjust and wicked murders of its citizens.'

Bartholomew was unsettled by his conversation with
Blanche. He did not know what to think of William's suppositions as revealed by Tysilia: that there was a killer in the
priory; that Blanche was involved in something untoward;
and that he was Tysilia's brother. But there was nothing
Bartholomew could do about it for a while, because Michael
had already arranged to spend the morning reviewing
various scraps of evidence in the reluctant company of the
other two men charged with uncovering the truth behind
the deaths: the hypochondriacal Bishop of Coventry and
Lichfield and the oafish Canon of Lincoln.

Bartholomew worked in the library for a while, but the
questions about the killings that rattled around in his mind
would not be ignored, and he found it difficult to concentrate on the collection of writings on marsh fever. He left
the library, and wandered the grounds near the Steeple
Gate, until Michael emerged from his meeting exasperated
by Stretton's stupidity and disheartened by Northburgh's
lack of interest in anything except his health. As
Bartholomew told the monk about his encounter with
Tysilia, a bell started to ring, announcing that a meal was
about to be served. Michael immediately headed for the
refectory.

'But breakfast was not long ago,' Bartholomew

complained, staring after him. 'And it is only two hours until the midday meal.'

'Quite,' agreed Michael, turning to haul him along. 'Which is why we need a little something now, to sustain us for the rest of the morning. And when we have done that we will walk up the river, to see whether we can find the place where those three men were murdered.'

He pushed open the door to the spacious decadence of the monks' refectory, with its polished wooden floors and beautiful oak tables, each one laden with freshly baked bread, dishes of fruit and slabs of creamy cheese.

'Has anyone seen William yet?' asked Michael, as the priory's high-ranking monks took their seats and began grabbing the food that was laid out in front of them. No one bothered to waste energy in speaking when there was eating to be done, and shaken heads were the only response. As earlier, William's seat was empty, but Henry mentioned that the hosteller often ate alone, and that he did not always want a meal halfway through the morning anyway. His voice held a note of censure that was directed towards the obese Thomas, but the sub-prior did not even glance up from his trough-sized trencher as he gorged himself on bread and honey, his massive flanks spilling over the sides of his specially constructed chair.

In the main body of the refectory the other monks followed the gluttonous example set by their seniors, and Bartholomew could see that many of them were well on their way to matching the paunches, bulges and double chins that abounded on the high table. However, the back of the hall contained the novices – Julian sat with Welles and the lad Bartholomew recalled was named Bukton – who seemed less inclined towards unbridled greed. In fact, Bartholomew thought they seemed depressed and listless, and they picked at their food in a way that he did not think was healthy in lads who should have had good appetites. From the uneasy glances they shot at the high table, the physician supposed that one of the priory officers had upset them in some way.

Julian ignored his meal, and instead fiddled lovingly with a long, sharp knife, which seemed far too ornate and dangerous for use at the dinner table. Bartholomew wondered why Prior Alan allowed him to possess such an object. Welles, however, was using a lengthy masonry nail to spear the food he wanted, so Bartholomew concluded that the Prior was not too fussy about his novices' choice of dining equipment.

'I suppose William may be buying eels,' suggested Robert, rather plaintively. Although he and William openly detested each other, it seemed that when his protagonist was away, the almoner missed him. 'He always buys eels on a Thursday – it is market day.'

'But Mackerell also seems to be missing,' said Bartholomew. 'And I understand the priory obtains most of its eels from him.'

'Henry purchases fish from Mackerell, too,' said Robert, shooting an unpleasant glance at the infirmarian. 'He chooses nasty, evil-looking specimens that no normal man would eat.'

'I do not *eat* them either,' said Henry indignantly, ruffled by the almoner's comments. 'Some I dry and grind to a powder, while others contain valuable oils that are excellent for certain skin conditions. And I will need more of them than ever in the next few days: Bishop Northburgh has charged me with finding a cure for his wrinkled skin. He wants to look young again.'

'You will not succeed,' warned Bartholomew, supposing he should not be surprised that a man like Henry – supremely confident in his own skill and abilities – should consider himself equal to such a task. 'It is natural for a man to look like a walnut at ninety years of age.'

Henry shot Alan a resentful glance that made the Prior shuffle uncomfortably.

'You must try, Henry,' said Alan. 'Northburgh said he would pay for a new chapel if you were successful.'

'I see I shall be joining you in the library, Matt,' said

Henry ruefully. 'My knowledge of remedies is unparalleled in the Fens, but even *I* know of no treatment for an ageing skin. Agnes Fitzpayne told me she uses a paste made from raw sparrows' livers and the grease of boiled frogs, but she does not look especially youthful to me.'

'You could try—' began Bartholomew, feeling he had misjudged Henry by assuming the man was confident of success. The quest was an impossible one, and Bartholomew saw that Henry would need all the advice he could get.

'No!' said Michael firmly. 'No medicine while I am eating, please. You can discuss pastes and powders in the infirmary when you are alone. Meanwhile, we were talking about Mackerell.'

'That is not much of an improvement,' said Robert laconically.

'Mackerell is always wandering off alone,' offered Subprior Thomas. 'He knows the Fens better than he does the city streets, and he often takes himself away. I doubt his disappearance is significant – and it will certainly have nothing to do with William's absence.'

'I thought I saw Mackerell this morning,' said Symon, frowning thoughtfully, as he speared a lump of bread with military precision. 'I am certain it was his cod-like features and scaly clothes that I spotted near the castle.'

'What were you doing all the way down there?' demanded Robert immediately. 'Hiding from someone who wanted to use the library?'

'Checking the locks on the tithe barn,' snapped Symon huffily. 'I want wheat for bread this winter, even if you do not care whether the peasants steal it all because we are lax with our security.'

'I care,' said Thomas vehemently, helping himself to a loaf.

'Are you sure it was Mackerell you saw?' asked Michael of Symon. 'It would be good to know he is alive.'

Symon shook his head apologetically. 'Not really. In fact, I am almost certainly mistaken. Why would an eel fisherman be inside our grounds at all? He would have no business here.'

'Mackerell is a miserable soul,' said Thomas irrelevantly, stabbing half a cheese and hauling it across the table towards him. 'I am always under the impression that he finds the presence of his fellow men as taxing as we find his.'

'I do not like him, either,' agreed Robert, ever ready to say something unpleasant. 'He charges too much for his eels, when most of them are all bone and no meat.'

'Like me,' said Michael, piling his trencher high with nuts. 'I have become little more than skin and bone since I have been in Cambridge.'

'True,' agreed Thomas, assessing Michael's girth with an experienced eye. Next to his massive form, Michael appeared almost sylph-like. 'I pray to God that I will never be dispatched to such a place, if it means near-starvation.'

'You can rest assured that will never happen,' said Robert maliciously. 'I hear that the University likes its scholars able to read, and since you are all but illiterate, it would have no cause to extend any invitations to you.'

'I am *not* illiterate,' sighed Thomas, in a weary tone that indicated this argument was not a new one. 'I just find small words difficult to make out. It is a fault with the eyes, not the mind. Is that not so, Father Prior?'

'Have you discovered who killed these men yet, Michael?' asked Alan, apparently preferring to change the subject than to lie. 'You have had four days now, and I would prefer this murderer to be under lock and key, not free in our city.'

'Me too,' said Michael bitterly. 'But everyone I approach for information lies to me. I cannot catch a killer when I cannot sort out what is fact and what is fiction.'

'Who has been lying to you?' asked Alan in surprise. 'No one should have cause to tell you untruths. We all want this killer caught.'

'I am not so sure,' said Michael, eyeing his brethren meaningfully. 'Three detested men have been slain, and virtually everyone in Ely seems to have a motive for wanting them dead. Thus, there is little incentive for people to want to help me: they are all hoping that this killer will strike again, and rid them of someone else they do not like.'

'That is not a nice thing to say,' admonished Henry. 'You make it sound as though the whole city is looking forward to the next person's death.'

'I imagine a few of them will be fearing for their own safety,' said Robert gleefully. 'There are a number of people who are good candidates, if the killer is selecting his victims on the basis of their unpopularity. There is that seditious Leycestre and his two lazy nephews; there is that rude Agnes Fitzpayne; and there is that nasty Father John, whose Latin alone is good cause for *his* murder.'

'There will be another death,' warned Michael. 'And since no one seems prepared to help me, there is little I can do to prevent it, or to save my poor Bishop from these slanderous accusations.'

'We have helped you all we can, Brother,' began Henry, offended.

'Yes,' said Michael, turning to smile at him. '*You* have been both helpful and encouraging. But not everyone is as public spirited. Sub-prior Thomas is one such example.'

'Me?' asked Thomas, surprised to be singled out for such an accusation. 'I have not been obstructive. Indeed, I have taken some pains not to come anywhere near you.'

'I can well imagine why,' said Michael. 'There is clearly a great deal that you do not want me to know.'

'Such as what?' demanded Thomas, peevishness creeping into his voice. Michael's accusations were not disturbing enough to put him off his food, however; his jaws did not stop working for an instant.

'Such as what that person in the orchard gave you last night,' snapped Michael. 'And do not tell me false stories about alms for the poor. You carried no bread with you, and you were the recipient – not the giver – of a small white package.'

Thomas cast an agitated glance at the Prior. 'I do not see

that it is Brother Michael's business to interrogate me,' he began.

'No, it is not,' agreed Alan, regarding his sub-prior uneasily. 'But these are unusual times, and something peculiar is happening. The Bishop is obliged to remain in Ely until this murder charge is resolved, and I would just as soon he resumed his travels. Therefore, you will answer Michael's questions, so that we can be done with this business and be back to normal.'

'But my actions have nothing to do with the Bishop's affairs,' protested Thomas. His face was now white, and his breakfast forgotten. 'You should ask others, not me.'

'Such as whom?' demanded Michael.

Thomas licked nervous lips, aware that the refectory was silent and that everyone was listening to what he had to say. 'I did not mean . . . I did not—'

'No lies,' snapped Michael impatiently. 'What did you mean when you said we should ask others? What others? What do you know that you have not told me?'

Thomas was growing increasingly flummoxed, and his jowls were trembling and twitching in agitation. He ran a thick finger around the neckline of his habit, as if it were suddenly too tight. Bartholomew exchanged a quick glance of concern with Henry, aware that a grossly fat man like Thomas was the kind of person who might have a seizure if stressed too severely. 'It was a slip of the tongue. I will make no accusations against my fellow brethren—'

'They would doubtless make accusations against you,' warned Michael, giving the dark-faced Robert a sour glance. 'And I will learn what I want to know sooner or later anyway – with or without your help. But it will be quicker and easier if you are honest with me now.'

'I have instructed you to be of assistance to Michael,' said Alan, fixing his stern gaze on the hapless sub-prior. 'You *will* answer his questions. Who should he ask for information about this matter?'

'I do not know for certain,' said Thomas in a voice that

was suddenly frail and breathless. He pulled at his habit again and swallowed hard, as though his throat was bothering him. 'I am basing what I say on speculation and rumour, but William has been regularly missing his offices for the past two weeks or so.'

'Two weeks ago,' mused Michael. 'That is about the time when the first murder took place.'

Thomas gave a sickly, ingratiating smile. 'That is the connection I made, too. He has also been drawing heavily on priory funds. In fact, he has taken more in the last eighteen days than he has spent in the rest of the year put together.'

'Has he really?' asked Robert with unconcealed glee. 'He has been dogging my every move recently, trying to assemble "proof" that I have not been distributing our alms to the poor. Now we learn that the hypocrite has been stealing priory money for himself!'

'We have learned no such thing,' said Henry sternly, unimpressed by the way the almoner was so ready to believe the worst in people. 'We have been told that he has drawn on the hosteller's fund recently, but that is easily explained. Blanche is here: it is expensive to house her and her retinue, so of course he drew moneys to meet the costs.'

'William is not a thief,' said Alan. 'Self-righteous and irritating, yes; but dishonest, no.'

'The evidence speaks for itself,' said Robert smugly, sitting back and resting his swarthy hands across his paunch.

'How much has he had?' asked Henry reasonably. 'The amount will tell us whether he wanted this gold for funding Blanche's stay, or for other purposes.'

'About ten marks,' said Thomas unsteadily.

'Ten marks?' squeaked Alan in alarm. 'But that is a fortune! What has he been doing with it? And why did you not tell me this before?'

'Because, as hosteller, he is entitled to draw twelve marks a year,' said Thomas hoarsely. 'He has not actually done anything wrong – at least, as far as I know.'

'Where is he?' asked Alan, looking around the table, as if he expected William to be sitting in someone else's place. 'Why is he not here?'

'I thought we had already been through this,' said Michael wearily. 'Everyone claims they do not know where he is.'

'Brother Henry said it was not unusual for William to miss these additional meals,' Bartholomew pointed out. 'It is not surprising: breakfast and the midday feast are amply sufficient for the needs of most normal men.'

'True,' agreed Henry immediately. 'I do not believe that eating so much is healthy. It is why so many of us are large.' His gaze fell on Thomas.

'We will discuss the medical shortcomings of our dining system another time,' snapped Alan. 'What I want to know now is where my hosteller is. Robert! You and he seem to watch each other like hawks, waiting for the other to make a mistake that you can report it to me, so you must know of his whereabouts. Where is he?'

'He is probably in the Outer Hostry,' said Robert sullenly, no more happy with this public criticism than Thomas had been. 'He dines with the guests on occasion.'

'Go and find him,' Alan ordered. 'Tell him that I want to see him immediately, and I do not care what he is doing. Bring him here at once.'

'Me?' asked Robert in surprise. 'But I am eating. Send a servant.'

'*You* go,' said Alan, the ice in his voice making it clear that Robert would be wise to do what he was told. Wordlessly, the spiteful almoner left.

Thomas heaved a heartfelt sigh of relief, apparently believing that the search for William meant that he was safe from further interrogation. He was mistaken: Michael rounded on him again, just as the sub-prior was in the act of raising a honey-drenched slice of bread to his large lips.

'Who else?' Michael demanded of him. 'You implied that there was more than one person who might know more than he is telling.'

'Robert,' said Thomas, as soon as the door had closed and he was certain the almoner would not be able to hear. Bartholomew did not know whether Thomas was telling the truth, or merely picking on someone he did not like and who was no longer in the room to defend himself. 'He and William are the only ones whose habits and behaviour have been a little suspect of late.'

Alan sighed, and looked into the main body of the refectory for a suitable messenger. His gaze lit on Julian, who was watching the scene with unabashed delight, his spotty jaw dangling open to reveal a pink tongue. 'Go after Robert and bring him back. And then *you* can search for William.'

'Me?' asked Julian in surprise, echoing Robert's sentiments. 'But I have work to do in the infirmary. Ask Brother Henry.'

'He must clean the shelves and wash all the bottles in my storeroom today,' explained Henry to Alan. 'It is his punishment for hiding Brother Ynys's crutches last night.'

'I wanted to see if he could walk without them,' pouted Julian. 'It was a medical experiment.'

'It was malicious teasing,' said Henry coolly. 'And your additional duties today will warn you not to do it again. It is a tedious task and will take you many hours.'

'I do not care whether he is obliged to labour all night,' said Alan testily. 'Do as I tell you, boy. Fetch Robert back to answer the charge Sub-prior Thomas has laid against him.'

Reluctantly, because he knew he would miss what promised to be the most interesting meal for a very long time, Julian left, while Michael turned his angry glare on Thomas yet again. The sub-prior was sweating heavily, and his twitching jowls were beaded with perspiration. He pushed his trencher away from him, his appetite clearly ruined. Bartholomew thought a little abstinence would do him good, although he did not like the increasing pallor of the sub-prior's face.

'While we are waiting for Robert and William to appear, we will talk about you, Thomas,' said Michael unrelentingly.

'What were you doing in the orchard last night?'

Thomas swallowed, then glanced at the door. Bartholomew wondered whether the man imagined he could reach it and escape the uncomfortable interrogation, although he was deluding himself if he thought he could move his bulk faster than Michael, or even than some of the other monks who sat quietly eating but with their ears firmly trained on the happenings at high table. The novices made no pretence at disinterest, however. They sat in open-mouthed fascination, riveted to the drama unfolding before them, and Bartholomew saw they relished the opportunity to watch bullying seniors publicly castigated.

'I was meeting a friend,' Thomas offered in a strangled voice. Bartholomew exchanged another look of concern with Henry, and then laid a warning hand on Michael's arm.

'I know that,' said Michael, pushing Bartholomew's hand away impatiently. 'I am not a fool. I saw you meet someone, and I saw him pass you a package. Who were you meeting? What was in the package? And where is that package now?'

'I—' began Thomas, swallowing again, then pressing a hand to his head. His face was now drained of colour. 'It is hot in here. Can we open a window?'

Bartholomew stood quickly, intending to put an end to the inquisition before Thomas had a seizure. He recognised the signs that preceded a serious attack – the pallor, sweating and trouble in breathing – and he did not want Thomas to be ill because Michael was being aggressive in his questioning.

Unfortunately, Thomas misinterpreted Bartholomew's abrupt move as a hostile gesture. He rose to his own feet quickly, but then grasped at his throat and fell backwards, where he began to writhe and gasp for breath.

'Poison!' yelled young Bukton immediately, also leaping up. 'Someone put poison in his food because he was on the verge of betrayal.'

This caused great consternation. There was a rattle of pewter on wood as plates were shoved hastily away from diners. The deathly silence that had prevailed when Michael was conducting his inquisition was broken, and an alarmed chattering broke out.

'Do not be ridiculous,' snapped Bartholomew, struggling to keep the flailing Thomas from injuring himself. Henry knelt next to him, holding the sub-prior's head and trying to insert a rag into his mouth to prevent him from biting his tongue. 'He has been eating the same food as all of us, and no one else is showing these symptoms.'

'It is the wine, not the bread,' squealed Bukton in horror. There was another clatter as goblets were hastily set back on the table, and the murmur of frightened, confused voices suddenly turned into a roar, combined with the scraping of benches on the floor as some monks came to their feet. Alan silenced it by rapping hard on the table with a horn spoon. The monks sat again and the alarmed babble began to subside.

'What is happening, Matt?' asked Michael nervously, hovering over the physician. His face was almost as pale as Thomas's. 'Has he been poisoned?'

'He is a fat man who became overwrought with your questions,' said Bartholomew, waiting for Henry to prise their patient's teeth apart, so that he could drop a soothing syrup between them. 'There is nothing sinister in this – unless you count the fact that the man was so clearly involved in something unpleasant that he had a seizure at the prospect of admitting it.'

'Damn!' muttered Michael. 'I did not know this would happen. I dislike Thomas, but I did not mean to kill him with my questions. Why must everyone insist on being dishonest with me?'

'I do not know,' said Bartholomew, as Thomas's frenzied jerks and convulsions gradually died down and he became flaccid. He leaned down and put his ear against the fat man's chest. He half expected that there would be so much flesh that he would hear nothing, even though Thomas was still alive, but the heart could be heard loud and clear, beating fast and hard from its exertions. 'But he will not be telling you anything for a while yet – if ever.'

'Is he dead, then?' asked Michael in a whisper, crossing himself vigorously. 'Lord help me! I have killed him!'

'He is not dead,' said Bartholomew. 'But he has lost his senses. He may regain them again, but he may not. It is impossible to tell at the moment.'

Michael rubbed a hand over his face and slumped on Thomas's oversized chair. The other monks were silent as Bartholomew, Henry and three hefty novices struggled to lift the unconscious sub-prior on to a stretcher. Then the grim procession filed out of the refectory, and headed towards the building that overlooked the graveyard.

It was some time before Bartholomew and Henry finished working on Thomas. They removed several layers of very tight undervests, appalled when they realised that some of the garments had probably not seen the laundry for several years. Then the rolls of flesh spilled out, white and loose across the bed. Bartholomew felt queasy when his probing produced the stone of a peach that had probably lain hidden in one fold since at least the previous summer.

Once Thomas's clothes were removed, they sponged his burning limbs with cool water, then gave him drops of laudanum until his laboured breathing eased. Because the presence of a seriously sick man in their midst was distressing the infirmary's elderly inmates, Henry instructed that Thomas should be moved to Henry's own chamber. It was a good idea: the old men would be left in peace, while the physicians could do what needed to be done to Thomas without a horrified audience.

'Well?' asked Michael in a low voice, looking down at the pale, damp features of the stricken sub-prior. 'What now?'

'We wait,' said Bartholomew. 'There is nothing more we can do. He will awake – or not – when the time is right.'

'But when might that be?' asked Prior Alan, appalled. 'Today? Tomorrow?'

'It is impossible to say,' said Henry. 'I had a patient once who lay like this for a week, and it was a lack of water that carried him off in the end – he could not swallow and we were afraid we would drown him if we forced him to drink. Doubtless Matthew has encountered similar cases.'

Bartholomew nodded. 'But my Arab master showed me how a pipe might be passed down the throat, passing the entrance to the lungs, to allow water to be put directly into the stomach.'

'Really?' asked Henry, fascinated. 'Did you see this device in action? How long were you able to keep the patient alive?'

'Some weeks,' said Bartholomew. 'I saw two patients recover, although most do not.'

'This is horrible,' said Michael with a shudder. 'Medicine really is a ghoulish trade. I am surprised that vile Julian does not enjoy it thoroughly.'

'He enjoys inflicting pain, but he does not gain the same pleasure from easing it,' said Henry tiredly.

'You are exhausted,' said Bartholomew sympathetically. 'You were awake with Roger much of last night, and you will be busy now that Thomas is ill. Sleep, and I will sit with Thomas until you wake.'

'I could not sleep,' said Henry. 'But I would be grateful for an opportunity to visit the library, so that I can read about this illness that has stricken Thomas. I would hate to think that he died because there is a remedy about which I have never learned. Even *my* knowledge is occasionally lacking.'

'There is no remedy for this, other than time,' said Bartholomew. 'But searching the library for ways to keep him comfortable might prove helpful. However, you will be lucky if you can find Symon to let you in.'

'Symon is there,' said Michael, pointing out of the window to several monks who were milling around, pretending to be walking in the gardens or pulling weeds from the graves in the cemetery. They cast frequent and furtive glances towards the windows of the hospital, clearly intent on satiating their curiosity regarding the sub-prior's fate. Symon was among them.

Henry sighed and turned to Alan. 'Normally, it would be the sub-prior's responsibility to send these ghouls back to their duties. But since he is indisposed . . .'

'Of course,' said Alan, making for the door. 'How remiss of me. It shows how I have grown to rely on Thomas for this sort of thing. I shall order them back to work, and Symon shall open the library door for you immediately. If I send *him* away, the Lord only knows where he might disappear and for how long.'

Henry left with him, and moments later there were footsteps on the wooden floor in the library above. Bartholomew could hear Henry demanding specific books that he needed to consult, and Symon declaring that the priory did not possess them – although Bartholomew knew for a fact that it did. The conversation ended with Henry's exasperated voice asking whether Symon *wanted* to kill one of his own brethren by declining to produce the medical texts that might save his life.

Michael went into the infirmary's main room, where he flopped on to one of the spare beds and lay with his arms pillowing his head, staring at the ceiling. Having charged his nosy monks to be about their business, Alan retired to the table at the other end of the hall, where he sat with one hand cupping his chin as he gazed through the window to the cathedral beyond. Bartholomew drew a stool to the side of Thomas's bed and prepared himself for a long wait.

The five old men were unsettled, and Bartholomew could hear them muttering and whispering to themselves. Roger and Ynys seemed to understand what was happening, although Bartholomew could not be sure about the other three. They were all awake and sitting up in their beds, although at least two had the dull-eyed look of senility about them. Ynys barked querulous statements in an unsteady voice, and Michael went to sit next to him, holding a thin, blue-veined hand until the old man began to relax. The others also seemed comforted by Michael's burly presence, and peace was restored as they drifted into restless slumbers.

'Where is that wretched Julian?' Bartholomew heard Alan demand of Michael. 'I told him to bring Robert to me immediately, and then to look for William. The boy is totally untrustworthy – even the most simple of tasks seems too much for him.'

It was well past noon when Julian finally appeared. The old men had been fed their dinners, and had been settled to sleep away the afternoon. Young Bukton was washing the floor with a mop, and the only sound in the room was the faint hiss of its bristles on the flagstones. Julian burst into the hall, yelling for Henry at the top of his voice, careless that the elderly monks were dozing. Henry's other assistant, Welles, was with Julian, but his frantic attempts to silence his unpleasant classmate were ignored. Michael leapt in alarm at the sudden racket, and, anticipating more bad news, Alan rushed towards them, while Bartholomew heard the tap of Henry's footsteps on the wooden floorboards in the library above. Moments later, the infirmarian appeared, white-faced and anxious at the sudden commotion in his usually serene realm.

'What is it?' he demanded, darting to Thomas's bed. 'Has he taken a turn for the worse?'

Julian was breathless, and his face was flushed with excitement. He faltered when he saw the vast form of Thomas motionless on the bed, and took a sharp intake of breath when he realised why Henry had asked such a question.

'What happened to him?' he asked with fiendish fascination. 'He was fit and hearty the last time I saw him – before I was dispatched like a servant to fetch Robert and William.'

'The sub-prior was taken ill,' replied Henry shortly.

'Oh,' said Julian, sounding disappointed at such a mundane answer. 'Is that all? No one tried to kill him? He was not stabbed or struck with some heavy object.'

Henry gazed at him, and Bartholomew saw dislike creep across the infirmarian's usually placid expression. Julian's unsavoury interest in the macabre had gone too far.

'Why should you be interested in such things?' Henry asked, distaste clear in his voice. 'Here is a man ill and in need of help that you might be able to provide – I taught you about seizures last week – but you ask about sharp knives and blunt instruments.'

'Your obsession with weapons and their application is unseemly, Julian,' reprimanded Alan. 'I have warned you about your unnatural love of violence before, and if you persist, I shall have no choice but to ask you to leave this priory and make your own way in the world outside.'

'Then I will join the Knights Hospitallers,' declared Julian defiantly. With barely concealed loathing he stared at his Prior. 'They will find a place for a man like me, who is prepared to fight and kill for what he believes.'

'No!' cried Henry in alarm, appealing to Alan. 'Do not let him go to an Order of soldier-monks. He would be uncontrollable, and would commit all manner of atrocities in the name of God. Give me a few more weeks to work with him.'

Alan regarded Julian coldly. 'You are lucky to have a friend like Henry, although I can see from your sneering that you do not appreciate him. But I sent you to fetch Robert and William some time ago. Where are they? Why have you not carried out my orders?'

'William has gone!' said Julian, his voice ringing through the infirmary. Roger and Ynys twisted uneasily in their beds as Julian's shout penetrated their confused dreams. Meanwhile, Julian's gloating gaze passed from Alan to Henry, and then to Michael. 'He is not here.'

'Do not yell,' snapped Alan sharply. 'This is not a tavern. It is a cathedral-priory and a place sacred to God. And what do you mean by "gone"?'

'He is not in the guest halls, the chapter house or any of the outbuildings,' said Julian, enunciating each word slowly, as though Alan were a half-wit who needed to be addressed like a child. Bartholomew felt a strong urge to box the lad's ears, and thought Henry was a saint that he had so far kept his hands to himself. 'So, I went to see if he was in his cell, but some of his belongings are missing.'

'You mean someone has stolen them?' asked Alan in confusion.

'No, I mean that someone has carefully removed items from his cell – his spare habit and his cloak have gone.'

'So he has left the priory?' asked Alan aghast. 'But how? When?'

Bukton stepped forward and cleared his throat nervously, still holding the mop. 'I saw Brother William leave the priory near dusk last night, but I assumed he was just taking some short trip on the priory's behalf. He rode Odin, the black gelding.'

'He may well have taken a short trip,' Alan pointed out hopefully. 'He probably returned later. I want to know where he is now.'

Bukton shook his head. 'Odin was not in his stall this morning when I fed the other horses. I assumed William had left him somewhere else, or perhaps he had thrown a shoe and was with the blacksmith. But now it seems that Odin's absence and William's disappearance are connected.'

'Did William have any baggage with him when he left?' asked Michael.

Bukton nodded. 'Two saddlebags. I thought nothing of it then, but now I see they must have been crammed with his possessions. He has probably taken that ten marks from the hosteller's fund, too.'

'He probably has,' said Alan wearily. 'It would not be the first time a greedy monk has made off with his priory's treasure.'

'But I find it curious that he should choose now to do so,' said Michael, puzzled. He was about to add something more, when the door opened a second time, and Symon the librarian stood there, his chest heaving from a brisk run and his eyes wild with fright.

'I have just seen him,' he babbled. 'It can only just have happened – we all saw him not long ago.'

'Who?' snapped Alan, becoming tired of his monks' eccentric ways of breaking news. 'What are you talking about? Take a deep breath and tell us what has happened in a coherent manner. We have had more than enough hysteria for one day: look at what it has done to poor Thomas.'

'Robert,' gasped Symon. 'You sent him to search for William, if you recall. When I was in the library helping Henry, I glanced out of the window and saw him making off towards the vineyards, presumably as part of his hunt.'

'Presumably,' said Alan dryly. 'He had orders to do so. But then I learned that he, too, had questions to answer, and so I sent Julian to fetch him back.'

'I know,' said Symon, agitation making him verge on the insubordinate. He took a deep breath in an attempt to calm himself and tell his story slowly. 'I was present when you issued that order. And it occurred to me, as I stood in the library and watched Robert striking out towards the vine-yard, that Julian might have missed him, and that he had no idea he was wanted—'

'I *did* miss him,' declared Julian resentfully. 'I looked everywhere for him and William both. In the heat of the day, too!'

'Do not interrupt!' snapped Symon. He turned back to Alan and adopted a less cantankerous tone. 'When I finished providing Henry with the books he requested, I left the library and went straight away to the vineyard, intending to tell Robert to attend you in your solar with all due haste. Well, almost straight away.'

'You "provided" me with no books!' said Henry indig-nantly. 'We were obliged to sift through random piles in search for them.'

'What do you mean by "almost straight away"?' asked Alan, ignoring Henry.

Symon looked sheepish. 'Well, I made a detour first. In

all the excitement at the refectory that morning, I did not drink sufficient breakfast ale, and it was a hot day. So, I stopped at the kitchens to slake my thirst.'

'How long?' demanded Alan, making it clear that he disapproved of this dereliction of duty.

Symon shrugged. 'I was obliged to pass the time of day with the brewer – it is not polite to down your ale and leave without exchanging pleasantries. Then his assistant arrived . . .'

'So you were there for some time,' surmised Alan heavily. 'Very well. You eventually prised yourself from the congenial company of the brewer, and you went to the vineyard. Then what happened?'

Symon coughed to hide his embarrassment. 'Unfortunately, Robert was no longer there.' He ignored the exasperated sound Alan made and went on. 'So, I decided I had better expand my search to the Quay.' He paused, whether for dramatic effect or because he did not know how to continue, Bartholomew could not say.

'And?' demanded Alan testily, when the delay stretched to an unreasonable length of time.

'And I am sickened to say that I found him, but he will not be answering any questions from you or Michael or anyone else – except perhaps God as he knocks on the Gates of Heaven.'

'What in God's name are you saying?' demanded Alan. 'Where is Robert?'

'Dead,' replied Symon. 'He is floating in the river near the Monks' Hythe.'

chapter 7

ONCE SYMON HAD ANNOUNCED THE NEWS THAT ROBERT was dead, there was a concerted dash to the hythes. Alan was first, running in a lithe, sprightly manner that did not seem appropriate in a high-ranking cleric. Julian and Symon bounded after him with Henry hurrying at their side, although the older monk soon lagged behind. Michael huffed along with him, sweating and panting in the searing heat of the midday sun. Bartholomew was easily able to keep up with Alan, but was surprised when someone caught up with them and started to pass. It was de Lisle.

'I heard what happened,' the Bishop gasped to the Prior, as they sprinted past the castle ruins and Alan grappled with the gate that led through the wall and out on to Broad Lane. 'Your librarian told me.'

'He had no right,' muttered Alan, casting a venomous glance at Symon, who was bending over to try to catch his breath. 'It is priory business, and not for outsiders to meddle in.'

'I will not meddle,' said de Lisle breathlessly. 'I came to offer support and spiritual guidance, should you need it.'

'I will not,' said Alan firmly. 'And it is better that you are not seen with us. I do not want it said that my priory consorts with killers.'

'I am not a killer,' said de Lisle angrily, following him through the gate. 'I am your Bishop. And anyway, the man *you* appointed to investigate Glovere's murder has declared me innocent. You heard him yourself.'

'Northburgh!' spat Alan in disgust. 'I had not realised he had grown so eccentric, or I would never have asked him to come.'

'Then what about the venerable Canon of Lincoln?' demanded de Lisle archly. 'He has also failed to find any evidence of my guilt – and he represents my most bitter enemy.'

'Stretton is worse than Northburgh,' snapped Alan. 'The man could not even name the four gospels last night, yet he hopes to be a prelate one day.' He pushed past de Lisle and dashed out into Broad Lane. Bartholomew and the Bishop were at his heels, while Michael, Henry and the others followed more sedately.

Alan led the way down one of the narrow alleys that led to the river. On the Quay, a group of people had already gathered to view the unusual spectacle of a dead monk being dragged from the water. Leycestre and his nephews were there, manoeuvring a small boat towards the head and shoulders that broke the water near the opposite shore. Robert's dark robes floated out around him, so that his sodden hair reminded Bartholomew of the centre of a great, black flower. Leycestre tried to pull Robert into the boat, but it threatened to capsize, so he took a firm hold of the monk's cowl and towed him back to the Quay, where willing hands reached out to help. The landlord of the Lamb, who owned two of them, remarked critically that Mackerell was far better at removing corpses from the water.

Alan asked Bartholomew to inspect the body there and then, but the physician had done little more than identify one muddy ear, a slightly grazed cheek and a puncture mark in the neck before he sensed that it would not be right to conduct a thorough examination with half the town looking on. He glanced up at Michael, but the monk was busily scanning the crowd, obviously studying them for reactions that might reveal one of them as the guilty party. He had plenty of choice, for virtually all their suspects were there, with the notable exception of William.

First, there was Leycestre with his nephews, pleased to be the centre of attention and claiming in a loud, important voice that *he* had been the one to have spotted the body.

He was unflustered when Michael demanded to know what he had been doing near the river when he should have been in the fields, and claimed that he had supplemented his midday meal with a jug of ale in the Mermaid. Agnes Fitzpayne was there, too, leaning her mighty forearms on a peat spade and looking very much as though killing a man would be well within her capabilities.

The gypsies were hovering near the back of the crowd, and watching with intense interest. The slack-jawed Rosel was being held back by his brothers, or it seemed he would have elbowed his way to the front. Eulalia was with them, although the expression on her face was more troubled than curious. Bartholomew wondered why. Guido's face was unreadable, half shadowed by his curious gold cap.

Lady Blanche stood to one side. Her retainers clustered around her, as though they were forming a wall to protect her from the common folk who jostled and prodded at each other as they vied for the best vantage points. Tysilia was with her, and Bartholomew heard Blanche informing her that the body was Robert's, not William's. Tysilia began to hum happily, and Bartholomew wondered if she had already forgotten the fear she had expressed for William, or whether she imagined that the death of one monk rendered all the others safe. The strange logic in her mind was almost impossible for Bartholomew to penetrate, and he decided not to try.

And then there were the monks: Symon, Henry, Julian, Bukton, Welles and a number of others, gathered at their Prior's back like black carrion crows. De Lisle stood between them and the landlord of the Lamb.

'Michael,' said Tysilia softly, edging closer to the monk and gazing at him with doe-eyed adoration. 'How nice to see you.'

'Not now,' said Michael sharply, moving away from her. 'I am busy.'

'Later, then,' said Tysilia. 'I shall be waiting.'

'That body belongs to the almoner,' declared Agnes Fitzpayne with satisfaction, when the monk's robes had been pulled away to reveal his face. 'He was a sly devil.'

'He pocketed the alms that were supposed to go to the poor,' agreed Leycestre, looking around at his fellow citizens in sanctimonious indignation. There was a growl of agreement from the onlookers and Alan looked decidedly nervous.

'That is untrue,' he said, although his expression indicated the opposite. 'Robert always executed his duties with the utmost care and honesty.'

'No, he did not,' announced Tysilia, beaming at the crowd as though she were about to impart some good news. 'William told me that Robert stole from the poor *all the time*!'

'Tysilia, please,' said de Lisle with uncharacteristic gentleness. 'It is not kind to speak ill of the dead. Keep your thoughts and accusations to yourself, my dear.'

'I shall tell you later, then,' she said happily, evidently not noticing that she had been chastised. 'You always listen to what I have to say with great interest.'

'Yes,' said de Lisle, patting her arm, then moving away when he realised that proximity to his "niece" also brought him far too close to his arch-enemy Lady Blanche de Wake. He was not quick enough, however, and Bartholomew saw that one of Blanche's powerful hands had latched on to his arm. She gave a vigorous tug that yanked him out of Tysilia's hearing.

'Your niece is driving me to distraction,' she hissed furiously. 'Remove her from my presence before I throttle her.'

De Lisle gazed at her coldly with his heavily lidded eyes. 'That would be a terrible sin, madam. I shall send Ralph to collect her today, if that is how you feel. However, I must remind you that it was not *my* idea that you took her from me. I wanted to keep her, if you recall.'

'I made a mistake,' admitted Blanche reluctantly. 'I thought that having her would seal our alliance and prevent further aggravation, but it has made no difference. That woman is a vile harlot who has no place in the house of any respectable lady.'

'Madam!' exclaimed de Lisle, sounding shocked. 'Watch what you say. There is something wrong with her mind, and she requires patience and understanding, not censure.'

'There certainly is something wrong with her mind,' growled Blanche. 'Her behaviour is like that of an animal on heat.'

'Yes,' agreed de Lisle, casting a glance at Tysilia that was full of compassion. Bartholomew was startled to see the depth of emotion there, astonished that such love from the arrogant Bishop should be reserved for a person like Tysilia. 'But she cannot help it. I have sent her to the best physicians in the country, and have sought the opinions of medical men from as far away as Avignon and Rome, but no one has been able to help her.'

'You have?' asked Blanche doubtfully.

De Lisle nodded. 'I have been obliged to place her in convents for most of her life, although I would sooner have her with me. Unfortunately, her illness makes that impossible. When you offered to become her guardian, I had hopes that she would come to love you as a daughter might, and that such affection would go some way towards effecting a cure. I am deeply sorry that it did not.'

'Well?' demanded Agnes, breaking into the muttered conversation between Blanche and de Lisle. 'Did someone do away with the almoner or is his death natural?'

Bartholomew had been so engrossed by the Bishop's open admission of affection for Tysilia, that he had all but forgotten the soggy form of Robert that lay at his feet. He glanced at Michael, doubtful how he should reply. He did not want to tell an outright lie – there would be no point when he was so bad at telling untruths, especially in front of such a large gathering of people – but he was not sure it would be wise to announce that a fourth victim had been claimed. Fortunately for Bartholomew, de Lisle came to his rescue.

The Bishop looked imperiously down his long nose at the crowd, and then addressed them as though he was giving one of his famous sermons. 'You have all seen this sad sight now. Poor Almoner Robert has drowned, and there is nothing more to keep you from your business. Go back to your work, and let the monks bury their brother in peace.'

'There will not be much peace for the likes of Robert,' stated Agnes, folding her arms and making no move to obey the Bishop. 'He will be on his way directly to Hell.'

'Then we must pray for his soul,' said de Lisle firmly.

'Will we be praying for the soul of a *murdered* man?' asked Leycestre of Bartholomew with keen interest. Once again, the physician was conscious that the crowd was listening intently for any reply he might make.

'Yes,' replied Michael bluntly, deciding upon a policy of honesty after a brief exchange of glances with Bartholomew told him what he wanted to know. 'It seems that Robert has suffered a similar fate to Glovere, Chaloner and Haywarde.'

'And Robert is a monk!' breathed Barbour, the landlord of the Lamb. 'It is not just us any more; it is *them*, too.'

'What is being done to catch this killer?' asked Agnes conversationally to Alan, not in the least awed by his rank.

'A lot, now that a monk is a victim,' said Leycestre bitterly. He stood on tiptoe and glanced at Eulalia and her brothers. 'And there are these burglaries, too. The monastery is safe, inside its walls, but there was another attack on a town house last night.'

'Another burglary?' asked Michael. 'Who was it this time?'

'Me,' said Barbour ruefully. 'Wednesday nights are always good for the taverns – especially ones that sell good ale, like the Lamb – because it is the day men are paid. Whoever stole from me must have known that.'

There was a horrified murmur and many heads were shaken in disgust. Leycestre's eyes remained fixed on the gypsies and, slowly, others turned to look at them too.

'However,' Barbour went on, 'I am not the kind of man to leave my takings lying around for all to see. I had them well hidden.' He leaned forward confidentially and lowered his voice, so that only half the surrounding spectators could hear. 'I keep the money under a floorboard in the attic.'

'A good place to secure it from passing thieves,' said Leycestre, his gaze still fixed on the hapless gypsies. Eulalia was looking decidedly uncomfortable, although whether it was because she and her brothers knew more about the theft than they should have done, or because it was not pleasant to be the object of the hostile scrutiny of so many people, Bartholomew could not say. Several men began to mutter among themselves.

'Not this again,' said Bartholomew with a sigh. He was tiring of having to defend the gypsies. 'You have no evidence to identify the culprits for certain, Leycestre, or you would have acted already. Do not accuse the travellers simply because they are strangers and have a style of life that is different from your own.'

'There *is* evidence,' hissed Leycestre, still glaring in the gypsies' direction. Eulalia was more uneasy than ever, although Guido stared back defiantly. The dim-witted Rosel saw Leycestre gazing at him, and interpreted it as a sign of friendship. He gave an empty grin, full of misshapen teeth, and waved.

'Bartholomew is right,' said de Lisle firmly. 'There will be no hounding of innocent people in my See. There has been more than enough of that already.' Here he gave Blanche a meaningful look. 'Meanwhile, I shall go to the cathedral to pray for the soul of the unfortunate Robert, and any of you who can spare a few moments are welcome to join me.'

'*I* will not join you!' spat Blanche, unable to keep her loathing for the Bishop under control any longer. 'You probably put Robert in his coffin in the first place! Murderer!'

There was an expectant hush as the spectators anticipated with relish what promised to be a fascinating spectacle of Bishop and noblewoman hurling insults at each other in the street. Blanche's retainers gathered more closely around her, while de Lisle's steward Ralph came to stand behind his master with his hand on the hilt of his sword. Bartholomew saw Michael take up a position on the prelate's other side.

De Lisle remained unmoved. 'I know you believe me capable of all manner of crimes, madam,' he said in firm, measured tones, loud enough for everyone to hear. 'You are mistaken, and I swear before God that I have killed no one. But we will not debate this issue here, while a man's soul is crying out for our masses. You may visit me at my home later, should you wish, and there I will listen to anything you have to say.'

He bowed elegantly, and moved away. Seeing the excitement was over, the crowd began to disperse, although Bartholomew noticed that the Bishop's calm, sober manner and his reluctance to become embroiled in a public fight had won the admiration of many. As de Lisle walked up the hill towards the cathedral, a large proportion of the townsfolk followed him, evidently willing to take him up on his invitation. Blanche saw she had been bested, and surged away in the opposite direction, a much smaller train of people in her wake.

'That is one reason why I am in de Lisle's service, Matt,' said Michael, staring after him. 'He is a remarkable man.'

'He is a complicated man,' Bartholomew corrected. 'He is unpredictable.'

'He can be arrogant, overbearing and demanding,' agreed Michael. 'But other times, he demonstrates a compassion that I have rarely seen in a cleric. If we were to listen to his mass for Robert, you would not detect a single insincere word in it – which is more than could be said if any of the monks were to officiate.'

'Why does he care about Robert so?' asked Bartholomew. 'Do you think Blanche is right, and he did murder the man?'

'I do not believe so. But we should go to the cathedral, too, so that you can inspect Robert as soon as the mass is done.'

'Are you available now, Brother?' came Tysilia's voice from behind them. She gave a bright beam and sidled up to Michael, fluttering her eyelashes alluringly.

'Lord help us!' breathed Michael. 'If it is not one thing, it is another.' He moved away from her; she followed, aiming to stand as close as possible. He took another step, and they began a curious circular dance that gathered momentum as each was determined to achieve his objective.

'Not here, Tysilia,' ordered Michael, becoming hot with the sudden vigorous exercise. 'It is not seemly with one of my brethren lying dead.'

'Are you saying that it would be seemly if he were not?' asked Bartholomew, amused.

'If not here, then where?' demanded Tysilia, interpreting his words as a veiled invitation. 'I can meet you at any place, at any time.'

'Not at mealtimes,' suggested Bartholomew, struggling to keep a straight face. 'He has far more important business to attend then.'

Michael shot him an agitated glance, then quickly turned his attention back to Tysilia: his loss of concentration had enabled her to extend one lightning-fast hand towards his person. He yelped and looked more outraged than Bartholomew had ever seen him. When the monk's normally pale face turned red, the physician began to laugh.

'Tysilia!' The exclamation came from Ralph, the Bishop's steward. Like Michael, he was horrified by her behaviour in such a public place. 'What in God's name are you doing?'

Tysilia regarded him sulkily. 'I am having a privy conversion with Michael. Go away.'

'She means a private conversation,' said Bartholomew, when the steward looked bemused.

'Well, he does not look as though he wants to finish it, so make your farewells and come away. The Bishop has decided that you will be safer with him than with Blanche.' Ralph turned to Bartholomew and Michael. 'That comment about throttling has deeply worried him, and he wants Tysilia in his own quarters.'

'Good idea,' said Michael flatly. 'I imagine Blanche is at the end of her tether as caretaker. We would not want an accident, would we?'

'Blanche does not wear a tether,' supplied Tysilia helpfully. 'Her lap-dog does, though.'

'The Bishop would do well to invest in one, too,' said Ralph to Michael, casting a meaningful glance at Tysilia. 'And I do not mean a lap-dog.'

'You can inform the Bishop that any future meetings between him and me will be in the priory,' said Michael, moving away quickly as Tysilia advanced. 'I am not coming to his house.'

'But *I* will be at his house,' said Tysilia, surprised. 'If you do not come there, you will not see me.'

'No,' said Michael grimly.

'Well, I shall just have to come with Uncle to the priory, then,' said Tysilia, undeterred. 'But he said he was going to that big church to pray, so we have some time to ourselves before he returns. Come to his lodgings with me, and we will—'

'Go with Ralph,' ordered Michael brusquely, bringing the conversation to an abrupt end. 'And behave yourself.'

'Come with me,' she invited coyly. 'And then you can make sure that I do.'

'God's teeth!' muttered Michael, twisting away quickly as she lunged at him. Ralph seized her arm and hustled her up the hill, although she struggled and fought every inch of the way. It was as well Ralph was a strong man, because she was a tall, vigorous woman and would have escaped from anyone weaker.

'I do not know why you are not making the most of this,' said Bartholomew, laughing as he saw the alarmed expression on the monk's face. 'It cannot be every day that a pretty woman favours you with her undivided attention.'

'I am a monk,' said Michael, as if he thought that explained it all. It did not. The vow of celibacy was not one to which he often gave much regard, and he used it only when it suited him.

'What is the real reason for this aversion?' asked Bartholomew curiously. 'I have never known you run from this sort of situation before.'

'De Lisle would not be amused if he thought I had

tampered with one of the few people he feels any affection for,' said Michael. 'He is very protective of her, as you probably gathered from the conversation between him and Blanche.'

'It is not Tysilia who needs the protection,' said Bartholomew, laughing again. 'It is you, and the hundreds just like you who have passed through her pawing hands.'

'That is not how de Lisle would see it. And I will not risk his displeasure for a quick romp under the bedclothes with a woman like Tysilia. It would not be worth it.'

'I just hope you know what you are missing, Brother. It may never happen again.'

'It will,' said Michael, confident that he was every woman's dream. 'Only it will be with a lady of my choice, who does not have an uncle with an unproven charge of murder to his name.'

They walked slowly, to allow the monks time to carry the body up the hill and deposit it in the Lady Chapel, where it would be washed, dressed in a clean habit and prayed for until it took its final journey to the monks' cemetery. Bartholomew was certain that Robert would not be obliged to wait above ground like Glovere, Chaloner and Haywarde. No sooner had the thought gone through his mind than he spotted Father John. He decided to ask whether the parish of St Mary's was still blessed with two festering corpses.

The priest was walking with Leycestre, while Leycestre's nephews – Clymme and Buk – and Agnes walked some distance behind, as though intent on preventing anyone else from hearing what the priest and the disinherited farmer had to say to each other. Not surprisingly, given that their obsession was not with murdered monks, Leycestre and his cronies were among the few who had not followed de Lisle to the cathedral.

'Father John!' called Bartholomew, increasing his stride so that he would catch up with the priest. He was startled to find his arm grabbed, very firmly, by Clymme. He gazed at Leycestre's nephew, too astonished that he had been manhandled to do anything about it.

'I want to speak to the priest,' he said, trying to free himself. The grip was a strong one, and he saw that the other nephew was ready to add his own brawn to the struggle if Clymme proved unequal to the task.

'Let him go,' snapped Agnes sharply.

'But you said—' began Clymme.

'Release him!' repeated Agnes, this time more forcefully. 'He wants to speak to Father John.'

Bartholomew disengaged his arm from the bemused Clymme, and saw that his supposition had been right: the nephews and Agnes were indeed a sort of rearguard, whose duty was to prevent the discussion taking place between labourer and priest from being overheard. John, who had turned as soon as Bartholomew called his name, saw exactly what Bartholomew had deduced.

'Leycestre and I were just talking about what could be done for poor Robert,' he gabbled unconvincingly. 'The violent death of a monk is a terrible thing.'

'But no one liked Robert,' Michael pointed out immediately. 'And why should *you* do anything for him? You have done little enough for the other victims.'

'That was before a fellow cleric had died,' said John defensively. 'We will do something now. Flowers, perhaps. Or candles. We have some candles left over from Haywarde's mass.'

'Then they belong to *me*,' declared Agnes immediately. '*I* paid for his mass, God rot his soul, and any candles remaining are mine. They will *not* be used for Robert.'

'You would give one for the cause,' wheedled John, his eyes uneasy. Bartholomew had seldom seen behaviour that was more indicative that its perpetrator was up to no good.

'"Cause"?' Michael pounced immediately. 'And what "cause" would that be? Inciting the populace to riot?'

'No!' declared John, a little too quickly. 'But I am on my way to the cathedral to pray with de Lisle and cannot stand here talking all day. What did you want from me?'

'I wanted to make sure that the other bodies had been buried,' said Bartholomew. 'But Agnes said she paid for Haywarde's mass, which means that he, at least, is below ground, where he should be.'

'So are the others,' said John. 'Blanche gave me sixpence for Glovere, which only left Chaloner. And Bishop de Lisle provided the funds to get rid of him.'

'De Lisle?' asked Michael. 'Why did he do that? It is not his concern.'

'Blanche has been telling folk that he wanted his victims underground before the next new moon rises,' said Leycestre. 'Murdered folk walk abroad then, if there is no layer of soil to keep them down. But I think de Lisle was just being charitable.'

'He *was* being charitable,' insisted John. 'He has no ties to Chaloner, but no one else came forward and offered to take responsibility for his body, so the Bishop gave me a shilling.'

'Did you ask him for it?' said Michael.

'He was praying in St Mary's – it is quieter than the cathedral these days, which tends to be full of angry pilgrims who cannot pay Robert's entrance fee to St Etheldreda's shrine – when he became aware of the smell of Chaloner's corpse. He said a mass there and then, and we had the man buried in an hour.'

Leycestre smiled. 'De Lisle is often maligned because he is proud, but he has more goodness in his little finger than any of those wicked monks – present company excepted, of course.'

'Of course,' said Michael dryly.

'His kindness was a great relief,' said John. 'I was beginning to think that the parish would have to pay, and I am trying to save all our money to buy bread for the poor when winter comes.'

'John should be careful,' said Bartholomew, as the priest ushered his seditious parishioners away. 'He is terrified of being accused of fuelling this rebellion, but he does nothing to calm troubled waters.'

'No,' said Michael thoughtfully. 'Indeed, it seems to me that he is doing a good deal of splashing.'

Robert lay in some splendour in the cathedral's Lady Chapel, and by the time Bartholomew and Michael arrived the wet habit had been stripped from him and he had been covered with a clean white sheet. A coffin was ready, leaning against one wall, but Robert still dripped, and the lay-brothers did not want to spoil a fine box by having water leaking in it. So, Robert was draining: he lay on two boards balanced on a pair of trestles with several bowls underneath him. In the nave, the part of the cathedral that was deemed the town's, de Lisle was busy with his mass. Michael's prediction was right: the Bishop was praying with considerable conviction.

Michael dismissed the lay-brothers who had been charged with laying out the body, then indicated to Bartholomew that he should begin his examination. The physician leaned hard on Robert's chest, to see whether water bubbled from his lungs. It did not, so he deduced that Robert had been dead when he had entered the water: the wound on the back of his neck had killed him, not the river. Next, he rolled the body to one side and examined the small injury that was visible just above the line of the almoner's hair. It was slightly larger than that on the others, and had evidently bled, for the silken pillow under the corpse's head was stained red. Bartholomew supposed that either the killer had been in a hurry and had not been as careful as he might, or Robert had struggled, despite being held still with a foot or a knee on his head.

Next, he examined Robert's once-fine habit, which was now a sodden mess caked in mud and slime. The greenery that adhered to it was not just water vegetation: there were vine leaves, too. Bartholomew deduced that Robert had met his end in the vineyard, where he had been searching for William, and then had been taken to the water and pushed in.

Finally, he inspected Robert's hands. He saw that the

fingers were slightly swollen and that blood encrusted the nails. Robert, unlike the others, had struggled hard against what had happened to him. There were grazes on his knees, too, and one or two marks on his arms and body that might have resulted from some kind of skirmish.

Bartholomew did not want to linger in the cathedral, where he felt he was being watched by spectators who wanted to see a murdered monk for themselves; it would be better to discuss his findings in the infirmary, where he would also be able to help watch over the ailing Thomas. When they arrived, Henry glanced up from his position near the sub-prior's bed. He looked tired already, and Bartholomew suspected that the infirmarian would see little of his own bed until Thomas either recovered or died. He wanted to ease Henry's burden as much as possible, although he suspected that Henry would still want to undertake most of Thomas's care himself.

Henry informed them that Thomas had stirred from his unconsciousness when the bell had sounded for the after-noon meal, at around three o'clock – Bartholomew thought this was probably because of some deep-rooted instinct – but had found himself unable to talk. As he had been on the verge of confessing to being involved in something unto-ward, Bartholomew was sceptical about an illness that so conveniently deprived the offender of coherent speech. However, Thomas was so clearly terrified by the sudden impairment that his hysterical panic went a long way in convincing the physician that he was not bluffing.

Reluctant to go to his own room to rest while the sub-prior lay stricken and frightened, Henry agreed to lie on one of the infirmary's spare beds for a while. Almost imme-diately he fell asleep; the long night of nursing Roger, plus the energy expended in tending Thomas, had left him exhausted.

'Robert did not die easily,' said Bartholomew to Michael in a low voice, when they were seated in one of the rooms at the end of the infirmary hall. From it, he could see

Thomas in Henry's chamber next door, and could also watch the old men. 'He knew what was going to happen to him, and he fought hard.'

'The others did not,' said Michael. 'At least, you did not mention that they had.'

'They may have done, but there was no damage to their hands, as there is to Robert's. But the others probably did not know what was in store for them – the killer may have ordered them to lie still and quiet, and promised to release them if they complied. But Robert, like everyone else in Ely now, was aware of how the killer works. He knew he was going to die as soon as his assailant had him helpless on the ground.'

'That explains why the others died without a fight, and Robert did not. But it implies that the killer is no rogue stranger from outside the city; he is someone they all knew, if not trusted.' Michael pursed his lips. 'I wonder what Thomas was involved in? It must have been something dreadful, or he would not have had a near-fatal seizure when I questioned him about it.'

'Perhaps,' said Bartholomew cautiously.

'Then what do you think?' pressed Michael, aware of Bartholomew's hesitation. 'What was in that packet? And who gave it to him? It might have been a letter. Perhaps it was even the letter that resulted in William fleeing his priory with half its available cash.'

'It may have been a letter,' acknowledged Bartholomew. 'Although it would have been quite a long one. It was no single sheet of parchment that changed hands in the vine-yards last night.'

'Damn it all!' muttered Michael, pacing in the small room. 'I was so determined that Thomas should not believe we were spying on him in the vineyard that I neglected to ques-tion him when I should have done. If I had accused him of lying when he first did it, we would not have had that unpleasant scene in the refectory today.'

'No, we would have had it in one of the most remote

corners of the monastery, which would have been far worse. But the man was ripe for a seizure anyway – we saw that last night when he was sweating and panting over that short walk from the priory. I suspect that the strain of being involved in subterfuge set him off, not you.'

'That killer is growing bold, Matt,' said Michael sombrely. 'At first, he murdered secretly and in the depths of night, when all honest folk were in their beds, but today he struck in broad daylight.'

'It *was* in broad daylight, but it was also in the vineyard – parts of which are very isolated – where the killer knew he would be unlikely to be disturbed.'

'Not necessarily,' argued Michael. 'Robert was wandering about there, so why could others not have been, too?'

'That is an interesting point. I wonder whether the killer spoke to Robert first and learned *why* he was in the vineyard hunting for William, instead of gorging himself in the refectory.'

Michael mused for a moment. 'But that assumes that Robert knew the killer. It also assumes that the killer was someone from *outside* the priory – all the monks *inside* had been party to the unedifying scene in the refectory, and knew perfectly well why Robert was out and about.'

'William did not,' said Bartholomew. 'He was not eating his second breakfast when you interrogated Thomas, and would have no idea why Robert should be hunting for him.'

'No,' agreed Michael. 'He would not.'

'My explanation also supposes that the killer gained access to the vineyards with ease. They are surrounded by formidable walls on three sides and by priory buildings on the other. There are four gates, but all are kept locked and only the Steeple Gate has a guard who will undo it for you.'

'The culprit broke in, then,' said Michael. 'Perhaps the previous night.'

'Or he has a key. You borrowed one easily enough when you wanted to use it the other day.'

'Damn!' muttered Michael softly. 'There are a number of

the wretched things, and every monk here is aware that they are hanging on hooks in the chapter house. This is not a priory that restricts every movement of its members, and we all know that we are permitted to leave the precincts on occasion if necessary – as long as we do not abuse the privilege.'

'So, a count of the keys will tell us nothing, then?' asked Bartholomew. 'What about asking if anyone is aware who borrowed them recently?'

'That would tell us nothing, either,' said Michael gloomily. 'I know for a fact that Henry has had one for years, so that he can go out to hunt for medicinal herbs when he needs them, and there are others who also hoard them for their personal convenience – Robert for example, and Thomas and Symon.'

'Robert had one? Then perhaps the killer stole it from him,' suggested Bartholomew.

Michael sighed. 'If we start asking about keys, we will waste a lot of time and possibly end up accusing someone who is innocent. It is too difficult an avenue of investigation, and it will be too easy for the killer to lie.'

'I do not understand how the killer took Robert's body from the vineyard and dumped it in the Quay with no one seeing what he was doing,' said Bartholomew. 'It was not dark, and this is a busy city.'

'That is simple to answer, although I am surprised you need me to point it out. It is market day, and even if you have nothing to sell or to buy, it is the most important day of the week for Ely folk. Everyone gathers in the marketplace to chat and exchange information. It is safe to assume that the killer would be unlikely to meet anyone near the water.'

'But even so, it is a brave man who risks being seen by a merchant glancing out of his window, or by an apprentice on an errand for his master. This is a lively place, and to expect the Quay to be deserted at that time of the day is unreasonable.'

'Nevertheless, it is what happened. You examined the body yourself, and you were the one who pointed out the vine leaves. Since the corpse did not walk to the water itself, it must have been taken there.'

'I suppose it is possible that Robert was killed on the Quay – not in the vineyard – and then his body was rolled into the water,' said Bartholomew, casting around for plausible solutions.

'Why would Robert have been at the Quay? He was searching the priory grounds for William, not looking for fish. And anyway, what about the leaves you found on his clothes? They were from vines, and they mean he was in the vineyard.'

'But they do not mean that he was *killed* in the vineyard. And suppose he was not searching for William at all? Suppose he was at the Quay for some other reason?'

'Damn it all! I wish I had not questioned Thomas – then he would not be in the infirmary, and Robert would not be in the cathedral with a slashed neck.'

'How do you know that? Robert might have gone to his death today regardless of anything you could have done, while I have already told you that Thomas was ripe for a seizure.'

'God's blood, Matt! When I agreed to investigate this case, I had no idea it would lead to all this. I am tempted to grab my horse and ride back to Cambridge today, where at least I understand the scholars and their ways.'

'And what about de Lisle? He will not appreciate being abandoned while a charge of murder hangs over his head.'

'No, he will not,' said Michael. 'But I am at a loss as how to make any progress. There is Thomas, who declined to tell us whom he was meeting or what was passed to him in that white package. There is William, who convinced Tysilia she is his sister and then persuaded her to spy on Blanche for him. Now he has fled.'

'*If* he has fled, Brother,' said Bartholomew grimly. 'It would not surprise me if he turned up floating in the river at some point, and the missing money was nowhere to be found.'

'What are you saying? That someone packed away all William's belongings, and then pretended to be him riding away on a gelding last night?' asked Michael incredulously.

'Why not? His flight does not fit the evidence: he was investigating the murders on his own behalf, then, with no explanation, he left without a word to anyone. It is too odd.'

'You would leave without a word if you thought you were about to be murdered and were running for your life.'

'But why should he think such a thing? We have no evidence that he was afraid, or that he had discovered any dangerous secret.'

'Perhaps he fled because he *is* the murderer, and he felt the net closing around him.' Michael grimaced. While he did not much care for the bob-haired hosteller, he felt the man had some redeeming qualities, and did not like to think of him as the killer. He would have preferred the loathsome Robert or the gluttonous, selfish Thomas to be the culprit.

'William as the killer means that he made good his escape last night, then returned today to dispatch Robert,' said Bartholomew. 'That does not make sense, even bearing in mind that they were bitter enemies.'

'Perhaps William has not gone far,' pressed Michael. 'You are assuming that he has disappeared from the area, but perhaps he is close by, and intends to continue his deadly work until we can stop him. I have already sent Meadowman and Cynric to ask the people who live on the causeways whether they saw him leave the city.'

'Good idea. But to continue with our list of people who have demonstrated curious behaviour, we also have Robert, whom Thomas accused of being involved before he had his fit.'

'But obviously *he* is not the killer. Meanwhile, in the guest-house, we have Blanche and her retinue. Tysilia has some strange relationship with William and knows more than she will tell, while you think Lady Blanche was in the Mermaid in the presence of gypsies, although, not surprisingly, she denies it. I do not like that Father John, either, or his association with those rabble rousers.'

'Not liking someone is no reason to include them on our

list of suspicious characters,' said Bartholomew, smiling.

Michael grinned. 'But it is satisfying to see them there.'

'Going back to the priory, there are others we should keep an open mind about: there is Prior Alan, who must hate de Lisle for being appointed to the See he thought was rightfully his. There is Symon, who seems as feckless and shifty a man as I have ever encountered . . .'

'You do not like him because he is a dismal librarian,' observed Michael. 'But there is that snivelling Julian, too. Yesterday, I caught him filing a key into a viciously sharp point. Lord knows what he was planning to do with it.'

'Henry says he has an obsession with sharp implements, so we should definitely retain him on our list of suspects.'

'Could it really be that simple?' asked Michael. 'A boy with a deep-rooted desire to do harm and a love of sharp objects?'

'And then there is Henry,' said Bartholomew, lowering his voice as he resumed the list. 'Do not forget that he has access to sharp implements, too – a good many of them confiscated from Julian, I suspect, as well as his blood-letting devices.'

'Henry could not have killed Robert,' said Michael with a superior smile, knowing he could prove his point. 'He was in the library when that happened. I heard him moving around up there, and so did you, when Robert was in the vineyard having his neck slit.'

'True,' admitted Bartholomew. 'Henry can be discounted then. But your Bishop cannot. While he may not have wielded the knife himself, it would not surprise me if he knows who did.'

'But that does not explain why he instructed me to investigate,' said Michael. 'If he wanted the truth left undisturbed, he should have asked someone sycophantic to investigate for him.'

'Perhaps he did,' said Bartholomew soberly. 'I do not mean to offend you, Brother, but in the past you have made no secret of the fact that you might alter the truth in order to achieve the verdict you want, and your Bishop is always delighted when things work to his satisfaction.'

'But I am not prepared to overlook the murder of innocent people,' objected Michael.

'You might be if you considered hiding the truth was for the greater good. Both you and I have kept silent on matters in the past, when we thought it was better people did not know the truth. For example, no one but us knows that the martyred Simon d'Ambrey lies in Master Wilson's grave in St Michael's churchyard in Cambridge.'

'That was different,' said Michael. 'Justice had been served, and we were merely tying up loose ends. Four murders are not loose ends, and I would not be prepared to see a killer go unpunished for such crimes.'

'I hope not,' said Bartholomew noncommittally, still not certain that the monk would make public the facts of the case if he felt it was inappropriate to do so. While he generally trusted Michael to do what was right, he felt the monk was somewhat under the power of his Bishop, who might not do the same.

'And on top of all our suspects, we have a clan of gypsies who appear at peculiar moments; we have a missing fisherman who promised to tell us what we wanted to know but then fled; and we have talk of water-spirits and other such nonsense.'

Bartholomew stood. Henry was stirring in the hall. The infirmarian rubbed sleep from his eyes and went to kneel next to Thomas, indicating with a tired nod to Bartholomew that he was ready to begin his vigil and that the physician was free to go.

'There is only so much we can do by speculating,' said Bartholomew to Michael. 'We need some facts, and we will not find them here. We must go out.'

'Out?' asked Michael suspiciously. 'Now? In the full heat of day? It was bad enough when we had to chase to the Quay. I am not sure I am up to another foray under the blaze of the sun.'

'Oh, I am sure we will survive,' said Bartholomew. 'And we need full daylight for what we are going to do.'

'And what is that?' asked Michael warily.

'We are going to walk upstream along the banks of the river, to see whether we can find the place where Glovere, Chaloner and Haywarde were murdered. But first, we will look in the vineyard, to see whether we can determine where Robert met his end.'

'Very well,' said Michael, reluctantly heaving his bulk to its feet. 'The sooner we can uncover this murdering fiend, the sooner we can return to the safety of Cambridge. And believe me, that little town has never seemed so appealing.'

It was very hot in the late afternoon sunlight. Michael fetched a wide-brimmed black hat to keep the sun out of his eyes, while Bartholomew changed in the infirmary. He dispensed with hose and jerkin in favour of a loose tunic and some baggy leggings. Michael declared that the physician looked like a peasant, but at least he was comfortable. Michael was sweating into his voluminous habit, and complained that it prickled his skin and caused rashes.

Since he was there, Bartholomew asked Henry about the keys to the back gate, but the infirmarian merely confirmed what Michael had already summarised: that there was a number of spare keys, and that the brethren tended to help themselves as and when they needed them. No one took any notice of who took what and the chapter house was deserted for most of the day; anyone could enter and take a key without being observed.

Henry walked with them to the infirmary door, looking for Julian, so that he could dispatch the lad to fetch wine from the kitchens. He wanted to make a soothing syrup from cloves and honey for Ynys's chest, and he needed the wine as a base. Julian, however, had made the most of his mentor's uncharacteristic afternoon nap, and had disappeared on business of his own. Henry made an exasperated sound at the back of his throat.

'That boy is his own worst enemy! I am doing all I can to give him a trade that will earn him respect – and a living if he ever finds himself expelled – but he flouts me at every turn.'

'You should let Alan dismiss him,' advised Michael. 'You have done all you can, but there is clearly no good in him. You cannot make a beef pie from a weasel and a pile of sand.'

Henry smiled bleakly. 'I confess I am beginning to wonder whether all my efforts have been in vain. Still, I am not ready to concede defeat yet.'

'What kind of wine do you use for your syrup?' asked Bartholomew, ignoring Michael's bored sigh as the monk anticipated the start of a lengthy medical discussion.

Henry raised his hands in a shrug. 'Whatever the cooks give me. Why? Do you find one type makes for a better result than another?'

'Without a doubt,' said Bartholomew. 'For example, the vile vintage from the monks' vineyards will not be very soothing for Ynys. I use a rich red from southern France.' He rummaged in his bag and produced the small skin he always carried there for emergencies. 'Try this, and let me know what you think.'

Henry took it from him. 'That is very kind. I will replenish it with something of equal quality later. Do not forget to ask for it back. But here is Bishop de Lisle's steward, Ralph. What can he want? I hope no one was taken ill during the mass for Robert.'

'I have come for some cordial,' said Ralph, approaching and leaning against the door. He treated the three men to a confident grin. 'It is too hot for beer – even bona cervisia – and my Bishop wants some of that nice raspberry syrup you make.'

'But I do not have much left,' objected Henry indignantly.

There was a cold gleam in Ralph's eyes, which intensified when he straightened from his slouch. 'That is not a pleasant attitude to take, Brother. Do you want me to return to my Bishop and tell him that the infirmarian refused him a refreshing drink after he has spent all afternoon saying masses for the almoner?'

'Be off with you,' ordered Michael angrily. 'You are doing my Bishop a disservice by going about making demands like this.'

'It is all right, Brother,' said Henry. 'The Bishop can have the last of my cordial if that is what he wants.'

Ralph revealed ugly black teeth in a grin of victory, and followed Henry inside. Bartholomew eyed him with distaste, disliking the man's confident swagger and assumed superiority because he was a bishop's servant. He was dirty, too, and a sharp, unwashed smell emanated from his greasy clothes. He was not a good ambassador for a fastidiously clean man like de Lisle.

Michael shook his head. 'That is not de Lisle's errand, Matt. That is Ralph acting on his own initiative, and I will wager you a jug of bona cervisia that my Bishop will never see that cordial. Ralph has always been a selfish sort of fellow.'

'Why does de Lisle keep him in his service, then?' asked Bartholomew. 'Surely it is not good for a bishop to employ such a man?'

'He needs someone he can trust,' replied Michael, stepping from the shade of the hospital door into the brightness of the sun beyond. He winced as the heat hit him. 'Such trust is difficult to come by, and usually results only after years of service. I doubt de Lisle likes Ralph, but Ralph is loyal and that counts for a good deal.'

They walked slowly through the vineyard, each taking one side of the main path as they scanned for signs that a scuffle had taken place. Bartholomew smiled when he saw one area of disturbed soil: it was the spot where he and Michael had dropped to their hands and knees to spy on Thomas. He heartily wished Cynric had been with them, because the Welshman would not have allowed himself to be caught, and he would almost certainly have overheard the conversation without being detected.

'This is hopeless!' mumbled Michael, wiping his sweaty

face with his sleeve. 'We do not know that Robert used *this* path, and these vineyards are enormous. We are wasting our time. We should pay another visit to the Mermaid, and see what else we can find out about Mackerell.'

'We would learn nothing,' said Bartholomew. 'First, I suspect they have already told us all they intend to say, and second, they are Fenmen, who are a taciturn lot at the best of times. They will not surrender information to people like us.'

'And what they are prepared to tell us is nonsense,' agreed Michael in disgust. 'Water-spirits, indeed! I will give Mackerell water-spirits if I ever see him again.'

'I hope you will have the opportunity. I expected to see him dead this morning, washed down the river into the Monks' Hythe, like the others.'

'He is alive. Symon said he saw him this morning near the castle.'

'Symon was uncertain. Why would Mackerell be in the priory grounds, anyway? I think that if he is still alive, then he has done what Thomas said – disappeared into the marshes he knows better than anyone else.'

'Do you think we can discount Symon's sighting then?'

'I think so. It does not make sense – unless Mackerell killed Robert of course.'

'Why would he do that?' asked Michael tiredly. 'Mackerell was not a particularly poor man, and so would have no cause to deal with the priory's almoner. He could not have been resentful about miserly alms.'

'We do not know that,' Bartholomew pointed out. 'As we keep saying, there is a good deal we do not know about this case.'

'I had not expected Robert to be the next victim,' said Michael with a sigh. 'But we are getting nowhere with this, Matt. We should walk up this damned river, since you are so sure we will find something there.'

'In a moment,' said Bartholomew. 'I want to look along some of these smaller paths first.'

He ignored Michael's groan of displeasure, and concentrated on exploring a promising area near some scattered stakes. But the presence of feathers suggested that a fox had killed a bird there, and that the scuffed soil had nothing to do with Robert or his killer. Eventually, they had walked the entire length of the vineyard, and were near the rear gate. Behind them, the tithe barn loomed, casting a cool shadow across the path along which they walked.

Michael shuffled across to the barn and flopped against it, wiping the sweat from his eyes with a piece of linen. Bartholomew picked up a stick and began to prod around in the grass near the path, looking for he knew not what. It did not take him long to see that Michael was right, and that they were unlikely to discover anything that could help them by searching at random. And even if they did manage to pinpoint the place where Robert had died, it would probably tell them little that they could use in the tracking of his killer. Dispirited, he went to join Michael. He was hot and thirsty, and wished they had some ale with them.

As if he read his friend's thoughts, Michael rummaged in his scrip and produced a wineskin, showing that Bartholomew was not the only one who carried supplies for just such situations. It contained a rather robust white, which tended to increase Bartholomew's thirst rather than relieve it, but he took a hearty swallow anyway, grateful for the fact that it washed the dust from his throat. He looked up at the barn that towered above them.

It was a huge structure, designed to take grain from the people who worked the priory's land. There were two giant doors at the front, with smaller entrances piercing the sides about halfway down. Several substantial locks sealed them, and the whole thing was robust and rigid, intended to protect its contents from marauding flocks of rats as well as those people who might decide to repatriate some of the wheat within.

'Who has the keys to the barn?' Bartholomew asked, taking another swallow of the wine, then passing the skin back to Michael.

'A number of people, I imagine. The Prior will have his own set, as will sub-prior, hosteller, almoner and cellarer. I heard at the evening meal last night that this barn is already full, and that any tithes presented from now on will go to the sextry barn near St Mary's.'

'Another vast edifice,' said Bartholomew disapprovingly. 'Your priory certainly knows how to squeeze its money's worth from its tenants.'

'It owns a lot of land,' said Michael defensively. 'Of course it needs large barns. But I knew this one was full anyway, because I recall watching some lay-brothers trying to cram the last few sacks inside it a couple of days ago.'

'I remember, too.' Bartholomew looked thoughtfully at Michael. 'So, everyone knows it is full, and that it has been locked until the grain is needed at the end of autumn. There is no need to disturb it and risk rats getting inside until then, is there?'

'I imagine not,' said Michael, bored. 'I really have no idea about agriculture, Matt. You must ask a farmer if you are interested in that sort of thing.' He took another swallow of wine, tipping his hat back from his face as he did so, to run his sleeve across his wet forehead.

'You do not need to be a farmer to know that a full barn will not be disturbed for some weeks. It would make a perfect hiding place. And you just said that the hosteller has a key.'

Michael's eyed gleamed, and he scrambled to his feet, his lethargy vanished. 'You are right, Matt! We should have thought of this sooner.' He stepped back, and squinted up at the barn, scanning it for weaknesses. 'There is a window on the upper floor. You can climb up those beams and undo the latch.'

'I most certainly cannot,' said Bartholomew, laughing at the near-impossible feat Michael expected him to perform. 'I am not an acrobat. We should try the doors first.'

'They will be locked,' objected Michael. 'There is no point.'

'Locks can be forced,' said Bartholomew, producing a

hefty pair of childbirth forceps he had used in this way before. At one time, he would have been appalled to think of his handsome forceps being used for such a purpose – they had been a gift from a very dear friend, quite aside from the fact that he used them to grab a baby's head while it was still inside the mother – but no expense had been spared on the forceps, and they were the most resilient thing he owned. It was almost impossible to bend or dent them, and they had proved useful for all sorts of purposes.

Michael watched as Bartholomew inserted the arms of his forceps into the gap between door and frame. It was an easy matter to ease it open, and the physician wondered whether they should mention the fact to Leycestre, so that the would-be rebel could arrange for some of the wheat to be returned to the folk who probably had a better right to it.

With a creak, the door swung open, and Bartholomew and Michael peered into the dusty gloom. It was almost completely black, because all the windows were closed to keep out pests and any gaps in the timber sides had been sealed for the same reason. But, after a while, their eyes grew used to the darkness, and they could detect the vague outlines of heaped sacks within. They pushed open the door as far as it would go for light, and made their way inside.

At first, Bartholomew thought they had wasted their time. It was unpleasantly hot inside the granary, and dust from the wheat made his eyes scratchy and his throat tickle. Michael began to sneeze uncontrollably, and it was not long before he abandoned the search to Bartholomew, while he waited outside. There was a sudden eerie rustle, and the physician froze, half expecting a furious William to come leaping out of the shadows, incensed that his hiding place had been so easily discovered. But whatever had made the noise was still when Bartholomew inched his way over to investigate, and he could see nothing other than endless rows of wheat sacks. He decided the granary was not as rat-resistant as it appeared.

He was about to give up, when it occurred to him that he should try to climb as high as possible, and then inspect the entire barn from above, to ensure that no one was hiding on top of the piled bags. He peered around, and located the rough wooden ladder that led to the upper floor. He called to Michael, to tell him what he planned to do.

'Do not bother,' the monk shouted back. 'William is not in there. No one is. How could a normal person survive in it? It is as hot as a baker's oven and the air is thick with dust.'

'It will not take a moment,' said Bartholomew, putting one foot on the bottom rung and beginning to climb. 'And we do not want to miss something.'

Michael sighed heavily, but came to hold the bottom of the ladder. 'I suppose I had better wait here. Since you were afraid of falling on the outside, I should be prepared to catch you if you fall on the inside.'

Carefully, because the ladder was in a poor state of repair, Bartholomew began to ascend. At every step it grew hotter, so that it was almost impossible to breathe. Wheat dust caught in his throat, making him cough, and through his choking he could hear Michael sneezing in the darkness below. He supposed that it would not be so bad when the great doors were thrown open, or when the weather was not quite so hot, but that day it was a vile experience. Anxious to complete his task and return to the comparative cool of the sunlight outside, he climbed more quickly, ignoring the protesting creaks of wood that should have been renewed years before.

When he reached the top of the ladder and stepped cautiously on to the platform at its head, he found his way barred by sacks that were piled as high as the ceiling. There was no earthly way anyone could be hiding there – even a rat would have problems insinuating itself between the closely packed bags. Moving carefully, he turned to inspect what lay below.

Looking from above offered a radically different perspective. The bags were lumpy and uneven, although they appeared to be neat enough from the ground. Bartholomew could see Michael below him, wiping his nose on a piece of linen that gleamed very white in the gloom. There was something else, too. Directly beneath him, Bartholomew saw an indentation in a sack that would perfectly match the shape of a man: someone had recently been there.

Still moving cautiously, he climbed down a few steps, then leapt from the ladder to the top of the pile, landing on his hands and knees and releasing a choking cloud of chaff. He coughed hard, vaguely aware that Michael was demanding to know what he thought he was doing. Almost blinded by the whirling dust, Bartholomew groped around, trying to see whether the person who had been in the granary had left some clue as to his identity. It was not long before his tentative fingers encountered something hard. He took hold of it and discovered it was yet another grain sack, although a clanking sound suggested that something metal, rather than cereal, was contained within. Slinging it over his shoulder, he began to descend the ladder.

He was halfway down when the thing he had been afraid would happen did: one of the rungs gave way. Had he been using both hands to climb instead of one, he would have been able to save himself, but he was unbalanced by the heavy sack and the broken rung was the last straw. With a yell, he found himself precipitated downwards, arms and legs flailing.

He landed with a thump on more bags of grain. They were not as hard as the ground would have been, but the fall winded him nevertheless. He decided that wheat was a lot harder than it looked. His sudden weight had caused the cheap material of one sack to split with a sharp rip, and its yellow contents began to spill across the floor. Mixed with the grain was something darker, and when Bartholomew inspected it closely he saw it was gravel. He rubbed his elbow ruefully, and thought it was not surprising the sacks were so hard for a falling man if they were more than half full of stone.

'I caught it,' he heard Michael say. He turned to see that the monk had deftly fielded the bag he had dropped.

'Well, that is a relief,' he grumbled, standing stiffly and flexing his bruised arm. 'I am glad you decided to save the bag and not me.'

'The sack looked the lighter of the two, and I thought you would come to no harm on all that soft wheat anyway.'

'Most of it is grit,' said Bartholomew. 'No wonder so many people in Ely have broken teeth, if they eat bread made from this rubbish.'

Michael leaned down and ran a handful of the grain through his fingers, his eyes round with surprise. 'The lay-brothers should have been more careful with what they accepted. Alan will not be pleased when he learns that most of the tithes comprise gravel.'

'True. And he will never know who gave it to him, either.'

'He will if *all* the sacks are like this,' said Michael grimly. 'Let us hope that only one farmer has been so rash as to try to cheat the priory. But I do not like it in here, Matt. We should go outside to see what you have found.'

Bartholomew was grateful to be out in the sunshine. Michael's habit was covered in chaff, and no amount of brushing seemed to remove it. Bartholomew took off his tunic and gave it a vigorous shake, disgusted by the dust that billowed from it. He was even more disgusted to see how much stuck to his body, but supposed it would come off when he had cooled down.

He sat next to Michael in the shade and watched the monk struggle to untie the thongs that fastened the sack's neck. It was secured very tightly, and it was some time before it could be unravelled. When it was finally open, Michael up-ended it on to the ground. With a clank and a clatter, three objects rolled out. The first was a handsome silver chalice that appeared to have come from the high altar of a church.

'Has a theft of religious vessels been reported in the city recently?' asked Bartholomew, picking it up and polishing it on his tunic.

Michael shook his head and reached for the second object – a small pouch. He opened it, and bright coins rolled into the palm of his hand. They were gold nobles and he counted twenty of them – a total of ten marks.

'Ten marks is what William took,' said Bartholomew, regarding his friend soberly. 'Or it is what Thomas told us William requisitioned from the hosteller's fund.'

'Yes,' said Michael. 'That had not escaped my attention, either.'

The third object was perhaps the most puzzling. It was a neat white package, similar – if not identical – to the one they had seen Thomas secreting away the night before.

'Well,' said Michael, picking it up and turning it over in his hand. 'Is this Thomas's property, do you think?'

'It looks the same,' said Bartholomew. 'But does that mean Thomas took William's money and hid them here together?'

'Or does it mean that William took or was given this package before he decided to flee with all his belongings?'

'Then why did he leave them behind?' asked Bartholomew. 'I am sure ten marks would come in useful for a man on the run, especially if he does not intend to return.'

'I do see how he can return. Stealing monastery property is not something most priors look kindly on. No, Matt. If William has gone, and his missing belongings suggest that he has, then he will not be coming back.'

'But what about his gold? Why leave it? The barn was only a temporary hiding place, because the grain will be used by the end of the year. It is not as if he can come back for it whenever he likes.'

Michael shook his head. 'I wish Thomas could speak! A few sentences from him would probably solve all these mysteries.' He grabbed Bartholomew's arm suddenly. 'He may not be able to speak, but he can write! That will suffice – we shall have our answers after all!'

'You heard Robert goading him the other day,' said Bartholomew wearily. 'Thomas is virtually illiterate. I suggested he wrote down what he wanted to say as soon as we discovered he could not speak, and I tried very hard to make sense of his scrawl. I thought paralysis was causing the problem, but Henry told me that he barely knows his alphabet.'

'I forgot about his lack of skills in that direction,' said Michael, disappointed. 'It has always been something of a scandal, actually – that a man should rise so high in our Order and the Church without being able to spell his name. Damn it all! I thought for a moment that we might have had our solution.'

'Not from Thomas. But perhaps we can show him these objects, and see from his reaction whether they are his or William's.'

'Very well,' said Michael. 'At least we do not have to walk along the river today. It will be too late by the time we finish with Thomas.'

'What is in the parcel?'

Michael opened it carefully. It was tied with fine twine and sealed with a line of red wax. It was not large, perhaps the size of a small book. And once Michael had carefully removed the wrapping from the package, he saw that was exactly what it was.

'It is a book of hours,' he said, puzzled. 'Is that all? I expected a letter from the King, or something far more interesting.'

Bartholomew took it from him, and flicked quickly through it to see whether any passages had been marked that might be significant. But there was nothing.

'It seems very old,' he said doubtfully. 'Perhaps it is valuable.'

'It may be, I suppose,' said Michael, regarding it disparagingly. 'It is a little gaudy for my taste. I do not like bright colours in my books. That is for men who cannot read, like Thomas.'

But when they returned to the infirmary, Thomas was sleeping, and Bartholomew would not allow Michael to wake him. Still troubled by the notion that he was responsible for the man's condition, Michael deferred to his friend's opinion, and wandered away to spend the evening with Prior Alan. Bartholomew offered to spend the second half of the night watching over Thomas. Reluctantly, Henry acknowledged that he could not tend Thomas all night *and* his elderly patients during the day, and agreed to wake the physician at two o'clock. When he took Bartholomew's shoulder and shook it, the bell was ringing for nocturns. Henry's eyes were heavy and he seemed grateful to be going to his own bed.

Bartholomew went into the hall and lit a candle, intending to pass the night by reading Philaretus's *De Pulsibus.* The infirmary was as silent as the grave. One of the old men occasionally cried out, and Roger and Ynys were sleepless and gazed into the darkness, lost in their memories. Thomas's sleep was unnaturally deep, but his breathing was little more than a whisper, not even enough to vibrate the mounds of fat that billowed around him. Bartholomew studied the grey, exhausted face and wondered whether the sub-prior would see another morning.

When dawn came, it was with a blaze of colour. The sky lightened gradually, then distant clouds were painted grey, orange and pink, and finally gold. Henry awoke and came hurrying to Thomas's bedside, smiling a prayer when he saw the fat sub-prior still lived. There were lines under Henry's eyes that suggested he had slept badly, but he was still cheerful and patient with the old men. Bartholomew offered to sit with Thomas while Henry attended prime, not at all disappointed to miss another volume competition in the cathedral.

When Henry returned, Julian and Welles were with him, carrying the dishes and baskets that contained the old men's breakfasts. There was a large pot of warm oatmeal, enriched with cream and enough salt to make an ocean envious, the inevitable wheat-bread, some tiny cubes of boiled chicken and a bowl of candied fruits thick with honey from the priory's beehives. Bartholomew saw Julian slide a slice of peach into his own mouth when he thought no one was looking.

'Your own meal will be ready soon,' he remarked, suspecting that the sickly fruits were the most popular item with the old men.

Julian treated him to a hostile sneer. 'These are wasted on those old corpses in there! You might as well give them dung – they would never know the difference.'

'Julian!' exclaimed Welles, his normally smiling face dismayed. He was busy spearing chicken with the masonry nail Bartholomew had seen him use in the refectory before Thomas was taken ill, arranging the cubes in an appetising pile on one side of a platter. 'That is a vile thing to say.'

'But I would know the difference,' said Henry sternly, as he ladled oatmeal into wooden bowls. 'And if I catch you trying to feed my old friends anything unpleasant, you will have me to answer to.'

'He would not really try to feed them dung,' began Welles, loyally defensive of his classmate. His words petered out when he saw from the expression on Julian's face that he might.

A loud thumping from the library above made them all glance upward.

'Goodness!' exclaimed Henry in astonishment. 'Symon is at work already, and the sun has only just risen. That is unusual.'

'I expect one of the priory's guests has demanded to use the books, and he feels obliged to make at least some pretence at caring for them,' said Welles.

Bartholomew was unimpressed to see that even the novices knew about and condemned the appalling state of the library, and yet Prior Alan was still not prepared to replace the man with someone competent.

'Bishop Northburgh, actually,' came a voice from behind them. They were all startled to see Symon framed in the doorway. 'And I will thank you to keep a civil tongue in your head, Welles, or I shall tell the Prior about your insolence.'

'Why does Northburgh want to use the library?' asked Henry. 'He is supposed to be dedicating his time to solving these murders.'

'I imagine he wants to scour the medical texts to learn about elixirs that will make him young again,' said Bartholomew. 'In case you fail to provide him with one.'

Henry grimaced. 'Prior Alan should never have agreed to those terms. He has put me in an impossible situation.'

'You should let me try a few things on him,' offered Julian, selecting a knife used for paring fruit and fingering the blade meaningfully. 'I am prepared to use more imaginative methods than you are.'

'Perhaps so, but Northburgh wants to survive the treatment intact,' said Henry wryly. 'He does not want to lose his wrinkles by having his skin pared from his bones.' He glanced upward as another thump sounded from above. 'Is that him now?'

'That is Bukton,' said Symon, insinuating himself into the infirmary and choosing one of the candied fruits to eat. 'I do not perform menial tasks like cleaning. That is why we have novices.'

Welles and Julian exchanged a glance, then turned back to their preparations wordlessly. Bartholomew was suddenly aware that the paring knife had disappeared.

'Where is that blade?' he demanded, looking hard at Julian. 'It was here a moment ago.'

Julian stared back at him insolently, and did not reply.

Henry sighed. 'Put it back, Julian. You know you are not allowed knives.'

'I do not have it,' said Julian, in a way that made Bartholomew sure that he did. 'I finished using it and I replaced it on the table. You can search me if you like.' He raised his arms above his head, inviting any interested parties to run their hands down his person. No one took him up on the offer.

'I expect it will reappear after breakfast,' said Henry, eyeing Julian minutely. 'And then we shall say no more about it. But we must give my old friends their food, before it goes completely cold.' He watched Julian and Welles carry the bowls of oatmeal to the hall, and then turned to Symon. 'Did you want anything in particular, Brother, or are you here to avoid watching Bukton labouring in the library, lest you feel compelled to help him?'

Bartholomew glanced at the infirmarian in surprise. Henry was not usually sharp-tongued. Indeed, he had the patience of a saint when dealing with people Bartholomew regarded as unworthy of such courtesy. Symon did not appear to notice the insult, however.

'I came to see Thomas, actually,' he said, reaching out for another fruit, but having second thoughts when Henry wielded a ladle at him in a rather menacing fashion. 'Is he still with us?'

'As you see,' said Henry, gesturing to the monstrous mound of flesh in the chamber at the far end of the hall. 'He needs all our prayers, but it is best that we restrict visitors for now. Do you want to pray for him in the chapel?'

'No, thank you,' said Symon, sounding disappointed. Bartholomew was unsure if the librarian was sorry that he was not allowed to pass the time of day with the ailing sub-prior, or sorry that Thomas was still in the land of the living. He found himself speculating on why Symon should wish the obese Thomas dead, when an illiterate sub-prior and a secretive and elusive librarian would probably have had little cause for contact.

Another bang from upstairs made the librarian wince, although he made no move to leave.

Henry picked up a tray containing five small dishes of the honeyed fruit and a basket of bread. 'You should see to your books, Brother,' he recommended as a third crash rattled the bottles on his shelves.

Symon nodded reluctantly. Still casting curious backward glances at the sub-prior on his sickbed, he left and

Bartholomew heard his footsteps ascending the wooden stairs that led to his domain. Henry heaved a sigh of relief that his voyeuristic guest had gone, then smiled when Bartholomew took another tray containing jugs of breakfast ale.

'I imagine Symon will not be the only one to come here today, anxious to see for himself the miserable state of our poor sub-prior. Thomas is not a kind man, and few monks who were novices here have cause to remember him fondly.'

'So Michael mentioned. And Bukton told me that little has changed since then. Thomas is still unpopular with the priory's youngsters.'

'Sometimes grave sicknesses change men's lives,' said Henry, walking into the infirmary to supervise Julian and Welles as they distributed the oatmeal. 'Perhaps that will happen to Thomas, if he recovers.'

'Perhaps,' said Bartholomew, who thought Thomas too thoroughly reprehensible to be a candidate for Damascus Road life changes. When he happened to glance back at the workbench, he saw the paring knife had been replaced.

When the old men had been fed – and Bartholomew had ensured that Henry had eaten a little, too – the physician went to the refectory to join the brethren for his own breakfast. He almost collided with Symon, who was hovering near the chapel door, craning his neck to see Thomas and apparently unable to resist the attraction of seeing a mighty man felled. Bartholomew made a point of waiting for him, unwilling to allow the man's macabre presence to distress either Henry or the old men, and they made uncomfortable, desultory conversation as they walked together to the refectory. They were overtaken by Welles, Julian and Bukton, released from their duties by the ringing of the breakfast bell. The three lads pushed and shoved each other playfully as they raced towards their meal.

When Bartholomew arrived, Michael was already there, rolling up his sleeves in anticipation of some serious snatching and grabbing, although the competition had been severely reduced at the high table that morning. Empty spaces gaped where Thomas, Robert and William usually sat, while Henry had asked to be excused so that he could remain with his patients. Alan presided, but was distracted and careworn, and ate little of the sumptuous meal provided by the kitchens.

'Is Thomas awake?' the Prior asked anxiously, seeing that Bartholomew was to join them for the meal. 'Has he regained his speech yet?'

'Not yet,' replied Bartholomew. 'Although he rested well last night, which is a good sign.'

'But he has not spoken?' pressed Symon, very interested. 'He remains mute?'

Bartholomew nodded. 'But he may regain that power today. Why do you ask?'

'No particular reason,' said Symon, with a careless shrug. 'I was merely voicing concern for one of my brethren.'

Alan mumbled a hasty grace, and Bartholomew turned his attention to some of the best oatmeal he had ever consumed, despite the fact that the cooks seemed to have ladled salt into it with a shovel. He wondered whether the monks liked it salty because it made them want to drink more ale.

In contrast to the unease and awkwardness among the few remaining occupants of the high table, the main body of the refectory exuded an atmosphere of relaxed jollity. It was not only the novices who appeared to be happy and hopeful, but many of the older monks, too, and Bartholomew sensed that the trio of sub-prior, almoner and hosteller had done little to create a pleasant environment in the monastery and much to repress one. Welles and Bukton smiled and laughed, while Julian was positively jubilant. Bartholomew watched Julian closely as he ate, thinking that there was something unsettling about the lad's bright eyes and flushed cheeks. He wondered whether it had anything to do with the incident regarding the paring knife, or whether Julian, like the other monks, was merely grateful to be free of Thomas's looming presence for a while.

After the meal, which seemed unusually protracted that morning – mostly because he wanted to escape the uncomfortable company at the high table – Bartholomew walked with Michael back to the infirmary, to see whether Thomas was awake. Now that the day was wearing on, Michael was anxious to ask him about the contents of the grain sack they had discovered the night before.

Symon had left the refectory before them, and set off in the direction of his domain, arms swinging and feet stamping with military precision. Because Bartholomew had spent some time over the past few days tracking Symon in order to be admitted to the library, he was familiar with the man's habits. He knew Symon always took the longer path, through the gardens and around the eastern end of the hospital chapel. This route was invariably deserted, and he guessed that Symon preferred it because he was unlikely to run into anyone who might ask him for a book.

However, that morning Symon's ghoulish fascination with Thomas led him to abandon custom and stride instead towards the Dark Cloister, which would mean a diversion through the infirmary itself. Bartholomew saw him disappear inside, presumably to walk through the hall and then leave via the rear door in order to reach the library from the cemetery.

Michael grimaced. 'There is nothing like the downfall of an unpopular man to bring out the worst in people. Symon *never* uses the infirmary as a shortcut to the library, and is only doing so today so that he can gloat over Thomas's predicament.'

'I hope no one ever views any illness of mine as an excuse for entertainment and celebration,' said Bartholomew distastefully.

'You would have to go a long way before you attained Thomas's standards,' replied Michael. He stopped suddenly, and Bartholomew saw that de Lisle was hurrying towards them from the chapter house, his steward at his heels like a faithful hound. He sighed. 'Damn! I hope he does not detain us for long. I want to question Thomas as soon as possible.'

'Then you can deal with de Lisle and I will talk to Thomas,' said Bartholomew, starting to walk away. De Lisle, however, had other ideas, and his haughty summons clearly included the physician, and well as his agent.

'Any news?' asked the Bishop immediately. 'What do you plan to do today to bring about my release from these charges?'

He listened intently while Michael described their findings in the granary and their plans to walk upriver to see whether they could find the place where Glovere and the others were murdered. He seemed disappointed by the lack of progress, while Ralph was openly disgusted by it. He bared his blackened teeth in a sneer of contempt, and Bartholomew turned away, so that he would not have to look at the man. As he did so, he saw Julian slinking into the infirmary, dragging his heels and evidently reluctant to resume his daily duties. Welles was not long in following, although he seemed more enthusiastic than his friend. He waved cheerfully to Bartholomew as he disappeared inside.

De Lisle had no more idea how to speed up the investigation than did Michael, but that did not prevent him from making all manner of impractical suggestions. Michael listened patiently while the Bishop recommended arresting Blanche's entire household and holding them until one of them confessed, followed by an illogical analysis of the reasons why the missing William was at the heart of everything, aided and abetted by the now-dead Robert.

The interview came to an end when the agitated prelate abruptly spun around and began to stalk towards the cathedral, muttering under his breath that since Michael did not seem able to prove his innocence, he would have to petition the help of St Etheldreda. A handsome ruby ring, he claimed, would be hers if she came to his rescue. Prior Alan overheard as he passed them on his way to the infirmary, and shook his head to show what *he* thought of the notion that saints could be bribed with baubles. Bartholomew and Michael were about to follow Alan, when the monk became aware that Ralph had fastened his dirty claw on to the fine fabric of his habit.

'You need to do more than stroll up the river today,' said the steward unpleasantly, not relinquishing his hold even though Michael glared angrily at him. 'My Bishop is not a wealthy man, and he cannot afford to stay in Ely much longer. He needs to visit other people, so that they are obliged to house and feed his retinue. You must dismiss this case so he can go about his business before he is bankrupt.'

'I assure you, I know that,' said Michael, knocking the filthy hand from his sleeve in distaste. 'And I am doing the best I can. He – and you – must be patient. The truth is not something you can just summon to appear. It must be teased out carefully, and each fact properly analysed.'

'Bugger the truth,' said Ralph vehemently. 'I said you should dismiss the case, not mess around with irrelevant details.'

Michael regarded the steward disapprovingly. 'You are an ignorant man, and so you cannot know what you are saying. The Bishop must be totally exonerated from these charges, or they will haunt him for the rest of his life. The verdict must be the truth. Nothing else will do.'

He turned away, but Ralph was not so easily dismissed. He delivered his own little lecture about loyalty and trust, to which Michael listened with barely concealed astonishment at such impudence. When Ralph saw that his homily was not inspiring Michael to go out and declare the Bishop's innocence by any means necessary, he gave up in disgust and followed his master to the cathedral.

'He is a nasty little man,' said Michael, watching him go. 'He thinks he is the only one capable of serving de Lisle, just because he has done it for longer than anyone else.'

'Yes,' agreed Bartholomew. 'He must be a saint.'

'Which of them?' asked Michael. 'De Lisle for putting up with that horrid little worm, or Ralph for selling his soul to de Lisle? But come, Matt. We cannot stand here all day chatting to whoever happens to come past. We have a killer to catch.'

But before they reached the door of the infirmary, Henry emerged and started to walk towards the cathedral. His shoulders slumped with tiredness, and he grimaced at the brightness of the sun in his eyes.

'How is Thomas?' asked Bartholomew, puzzled that the infirmarian should leave when he had a seriously ill patient to tend.

'He slipped away in his sleep – between the time you left and a few moments ago,' said Henry with a catch in his voice. He saw Michael's face fall, and mistook the monk's dismay for grief. 'I am sorry, Michael. Bartholomew and I did all we could, but old, fat men are prone to such attacks, and death is not infrequent. In my experience this appeared to be a serious episode, and I doubt he would ever have recovered his faculties fully. It is better this way.'

'Damn!' swore Michael vehemently. 'If we had not dawdled here, listening to de Lisle and Ralph ranting on about nothing, we might have been able to talk to Thomas before he died.'

'I do not think he ever woke,' said Henry wearily. 'And even though you are my friend, and I know how hard de Lisle is pushing you to prove him innocent of murder, I would not have allowed you to disturb Thomas with potentially distressing questions.'

'I am surprised he died this morning, though,' said Bartholomew. 'When he survived the night, I thought he was through the worst.'

'I hoped so, too,' said Henry. 'But yesterday's seizure was long and violent. To be frank, I thought he would slip away in his sleep last night. I was astonished that he still lived when I relieved you of the vigil at dawn.'

'This is a sorry business,' said Michael, defeated. 'Were you with him when he died?'

Henry's eyes filled with tears and he turned away. He

tried to speak, but no words came.

'What is the matter?' asked Bartholomew, alarmed.

'I fell asleep,' said Henry in a muffled whisper. 'I did not work on the accounts while I watched over him, because I thought I might doze off with the heat and the lack of recent rest, and so I decided to mix Ynys's medicine instead. But as soon as I sat down, I must have fallen into a slumber. Even if God sees fit to forgive me for this, I will never forgive myself!'

His voice cracked and he put both hands over his face as his shoulders shook with anguish. Michael turned him around and guided him through the hall, where he sat the distraught infirmarian down in his workshop. The old men slept fitfully, although Roger seemed to be watching what was happening. In the chamber at the far end of the hall, Bartholomew could see Prior Alan kneeling at the bed where Thomas lay. Julian and Welles were nowhere to be seen. Bartholomew's wineskin still lay on the table, its contents untouched, so he poured some into a goblet and urged Henry to drink. After a few moments, Henry regained control of himself. His shuddering sobs subsided, and he was able to give them a wan smile.

'I am sorry. I hate to lose a patient. It is not why I became a physician.'

'You cannot blame yourself for falling asleep,' said Bartholomew. 'I knew you were exhausted; I should not have left you.'

'I wish you had not,' said Henry bitterly. 'I hope to God that poor Thomas did not wake to find he was alone in his last few moments of life.'

'What happened?' asked Michael.

'I sat here and began to grind the cloves,' continued Henry unsteadily, 'and the next thing I knew was that my head was on the table and Prior Alan was shaking my shoulder, asking whether I was unwell. I leapt to my feet and ran to Thomas, lest he had been calling for me, but he was dead. I hope it was a peaceful end.'

Bartholomew patted his shoulder, then went to look at the sheeted form that lay in Henry's bed. While Alan continued to pray, and Henry and Michael looked on, Bartholomew pulled back the cover, and saw the still features of the sub-prior beneath, layers of fat already waxy white as they rippled away from his face. Bartholomew thought Henry's diagnosis had been right, and the sub-prior had indeed slipped away in his sleep. But his stay in Ely had made him cautious: he slipped one hand under the back of Thomas's neck and then withdrew it in alarm. Something cold and metallic was there.

Alan leapt to his feet in horror when Bartholomew tugged the inert figure on to its side, revealing the short blade that protruded from the base of its neck. The bed-covers below were stained red, and when Bartholomew touched the knife he found it was firm and unyielding under his fingers. Someone had forced it in very hard. However, there was no grazing of Thomas's ears or cheeks, because the killer had not needed to secure his victim this time: Thomas had been powerless to defend himself.

'No!' cried Henry at the top of his voice. In the hall, the old men started to call out, frightened by the sudden clamour in their usually serene environment. 'Not in my infirmary!'

'My God!' breathed Alan, crossing himself slowly. 'My God!'

'Well,' said Bartholomew, meeting Michael's eyes. 'Our killer *is* growing bold. Now he is taking his victims in broad daylight *inside* the priory itself, while Henry was only a short distance away.'

'But I saw no one,' whispered Henry. 'I do not know how long I slept, but it could not have been more than a few moments. What have I done?'

'*You* have done nothing,' said Alan grimly. 'It is not you who is prowling around killing sick men as they sleep.'

'I shall never forgive myself!' whispered Henry, his face as white as snow. 'If I had not been so weak, I would have stayed awake and this would never have happened.'

'You are assuming you would have been able to prevent it,' said Bartholomew kindly. 'Your exhaustion probably saved your life, because the murderer is a ruthless man who would have killed you, too. You would not have been able to save Thomas, even if you had been awake.'

'And I would have had a good deal more to grieve about,' said Michael bluntly. 'Thomas was not one of Ely's better monks, but you are. The priory would have lost a far greater prize in you than in Thomas.'

'No!' objected Henry, distressed. 'You cannot say such things! Thomas occasionally gave me wine from his own cellars for my patients. He was not all bad.'

'And why did he do that?' demanded Michael archly. 'Because it was past its best and he could not bring himself to pour it down the drain?'

Henry swallowed miserably. 'That is not the point. He thought of the sick when he had supplies to share. But I cannot believe this has happened. I heard nothing and saw nothing.'

'I am sure you did not,' said Michael grimly. 'This killer is too good to leave witnesses or clues.'

CHAPTER 8

WHILE HENRY WENT TO CALM HIS ELDERLY PATIENTS, AND Alan redoubled the fervour of his prayers over Thomas's bloated corpse, Bartholomew and Michael sat in the infirmary chapel, their thoughts in turmoil. They talked in low voices, so that no one could hear.

'We were virtually present when this happened,' whispered Michael, his green eyes huge in his white face. 'This monster took his fifth victim while we were right outside the building!'

'I wonder whether we saw him,' mused Bartholomew, trying to recall what he had seen as they had lingered with de Lisle and Ralph in the Dark Cloister. 'I spotted Symon, then Julian, then Welles and finally Alan. What about you?'

Michael shook his head slowly. 'No killer would have gone about his grisly business knowing we had actually watched him enter the hospital. He would have crept in through the back door, not through the Dark Cloister.'

'Do not be so sure,' said Bartholomew. 'He killed Robert and carried the body to the Monks' Hythe in broad daylight. He is not a timid fellow, and he seems oblivious of the fact that he might be caught.'

'There is a difference this time, though,' said Michael, staring down the hall to where Thomas's mammoth form could just be seen, swathed in a white sheet, with Alan kneeling next to it. 'He left the murder weapon. He did not do that with the others. That must help us.'

Bartholomew had noticed. 'It was the paring knife I saw earlier, when Henry, Julian and Welles were preparing the inmates' breakfasts. It disappeared briefly, and I assumed

Julian had stolen it, but it had been replaced on the work-bench before we left for the refectory.'

'Julian,' said Michael thoughtfully. 'We have always agreed he was a good suspect. He has a fascination with sharp objects, and now you say you saw him in possession of the murder weapon not an hour before this crime was committed.'

'The only problem with that notion is that the paring knife is not what killed the other victims.'

Michael regarded him doubtfully. 'How can you tell?'

'Because the injury on Thomas is a different shape. You may recall I told you that the others' wounds were made with something long and thin, perhaps rather like a nail.'

'So, what are you saying? That Julian killed Thomas, but not Glovere, Chaloner, Haywarde and Robert?'

Bartholomew spread his hands. 'Julian saw Robert's corpse, if not the others, and may have overheard us discussing how these men were killed. It is not wholly beyond the realm of possibility that he wanted to try it out for himself, and used the much-detested sub-prior for his experiment.'

'Should we arrest him, then?'

Bartholomew was uncertain. 'The problem with doing that is that we have no incontrovertible proof that he is the killer. Do not forget that we also saw Symon enter the infirmary. In fact, the librarian was the first of a number of people to wander in, and he would have had plenty of time to kill his sub-prior – he was all alone with him while Henry slept and before Julian and Welles arrived for work. He has been lurking near Thomas's sickbed all day, and he also was in the work-room when I first noticed the presence of that paring knife.'

'Welles?' suggested Michael. 'What about him as our cunning criminal?' He rubbed his face hard. 'Lord, Matt! What am I saying? Welles is a nice lad – cheerful and hard-working. Why would he suddenly turn killer?'

'Perhaps some of Julian's personality wore off on him. It is not inconceivable that spending day after day in company like that may have a polluting effect.'

'There is Alan, too,' said Michael softly, looking over at the Prior, who was shifting uncomfortably next to Thomas, finding the stone floor hard on his knees. 'He was the last person to enter the hospital, and the one who woke Henry. We must not leave him off our list of suspects.'

'He was the last one you *saw* enter the hospital,' corrected Bartholomew. 'You said yourself that the culprit may have reached Thomas by going through the back door.'

'Damn!' breathed Michael, disheartened. 'We are no further forward now than we were *before* this maniac claimed a fifth soul to add to his collection. We have another victim who was disliked by most people who knew him, and we have a knife conveniently available. How am I supposed to discover who did this, when virtually anyone in the entire monastery could be responsible?'

'Not just in the monastery, Brother,' said Bartholomew. 'There are townsfolk who may have heard of Thomas's vulnerable state, too. There are at least a hundred layfolk employed here – one of them may be the killer, or may have helped the killer gain access to Thomas. And do not forget that the Outer Hostry is bulging at the seams with visitors, too.'

He stopped speaking when Alan entered the chapel, his sandalled feet tapping softly on the worn flagstones. The Prior genuflected in front of the altar, and gazed at it for a moment, his thin face haggard.

'Tell us what happened, exactly,' said Michael, watching him. 'Did you see Thomas dead and go to rouse the slumbering Henry?'

'Good gracious, no!' exclaimed Alan, seeming appalled by that notion. 'I glimpsed Thomas lying still and silent through the open door of his chamber, but assumed he was sleeping. I was actually looking for Henry – to ask him for a report on Thomas's health. When I saw Henry dozing in the room next door, I went to shake his shoulder. I did not think he had fallen asleep intentionally, and imagined he would prefer to be awake when Thomas was so ill.'

'It is that cure for wrinkles you promised Bishop Northburgh,' said Bartholomew, rather accusingly. 'Henry is working feverishly on it, and it is too much for him with his other duties, too.'

'Perhaps you are right,' acknowledged Alan sheepishly. 'I thought he could manage – he is an excellent physician, after all. Anyway, I touched him on the shoulder and he jolted upright, looking as confused and startled as a scalded cat. He sat for a moment blinking and staring, then seemed to recall that he was supposed to be caring for a sick patient. He all but shoved me out of the way in his haste to reach the next room. It was clear he had been dozing for some time.'

'Why do you say that?' asked Bartholomew curiously. 'Because it took him a few moments to gather his wits once you had woken him?'

'Because there was a sizeable puddle of drool on the table, where his head had rested,' replied Alan, rather proud of his powers of observation. 'It is still there, actually. You know how that happens when you doze heavily in an awkward position.'

'I do not,' said Michael primly. 'I never drool. But what happened after that?'

'Henry fussed around with Thomas's bedclothes for a moment, and wiped his face with a cloth. Then it seemed to occur to him that all was not well. He held a glass in front of Thomas's mouth, then put his ear to Thomas's chest.'

'And Thomas was dead,' concluded Michael.

'But still warm to the touch. Henry told me that was because Thomas had only just died, combined with the facts that he has a large body for retaining heat, and because the weather is hot.'

'He is right,' agreed Bartholomew. 'Those factors would combine in making a corpse cool more slowly.'

'I started to pray,' continued Alan. 'There was no reason to assume Thomas had not slipped away in his sleep at that point. Meanwhile, poor Henry stumbled to the door for some fresh air. He hates to lose a patient. Then you came in.'

'Was there anything unusual about the sickroom that you noticed?' asked Michael hopefully. 'Anything that might suggest the identity of the killer?'

Alan shook his head. 'I saw Symon enter the infirmary a little while before I did; you might want to ask him whether he saw anything strange. You can also question Julian and Welles: they were also in the vicinity.'

'We shall,' determined Michael. He rubbed his hands across his flabby cheeks, making a rasping sound that was loud in the peaceful chapel. He was about to add something else when there was a commotion in the hall, and he poked his head around the door to see that de Lisle had arrived, demanding to know what had happened. It seemed that bad news spread quickly.

'This will reflect badly on me,' the Bishop declared, marching into the chapel and addressing his agent. 'People will say that *I* had the sub-prior murdered, as well as a couple of peasants and the servant of a woman I detest.'

'And that would never do,' said Alan, watching de Lisle with some dislike. Bartholomew noted that the prelate was unusually mercurial in his moods. The previous day, many people had been impressed by his graciousness and poise, and by his genuine compassion for Robert, but now he was back to the selfishness that made him so unpopular. It was all very well for Michael to say he found his Bishop remarkable, but for a good part of the time the Bishop was remarkable only for his arrogance, self-interest and ambition.

'People will say no such thing about you,' said Michael soothingly, if probably untruthfully. 'If anything, they will begin to see that you had nothing to do with the death of Glovere, because you have no reason to wish any of these other people harm.'

'As I told you, not an hour ago, I want this criminal caught,' shouted de Lisle furiously. 'It is bad enough being accused of murder, without the people in my See being dispatched by some monster who feels it incumbent on himself to slaughter monks in broad daylight on holy ground.'

'We were—' began Michael.

'You have always been excellent at solving this kind of mystery,' snapped de Lisle, pacing back and forth. 'Yet, when the outcome is important to me personally, you seem to be dragging your heels.'

'I am doing nothing of the kind,' said Michael, his eyes dangerously cold. 'You know very well that I have been working hard. This case is just more complicated than I anticipated, that is all. I told you all this earlier.'

De Lisle sensed that he had overstepped the mark, and that if he wanted Michael's continued services then he would need to adopt a more conciliatory attitude. Bartholomew supposed the prelate was frustrated because Michael was the only person who could clear his name to everyone's satisfaction. Bishop Northburgh and Canon Stretton were worse than useless; Michael was his only hope. De Lisle's face softened, and he laid an apologetic arm across the monk's shoulders.

'Forgive me, Brother,' he said. 'I am not myself today. That wretched Blanche has been aiming to damage me and my reputation ever since I had the misfortune to cross her path twenty-five years ago. Of course, Tysilia is at the heart of it.'

'Tysilia?' asked Bartholomew, startled into blurting an interruption.

'She is my niece,' said the Bishop, smiling fondly. 'But, of course, you know her from that business that took you to St Radegund's Convent earlier this year.'

Bartholomew knew that Tysilia was far more closely related to the prelate than that, although how someone as brazenly dim-witted as Tysilia could be the offspring of the wily Thomas de Lisle was completely beyond Bartholomew's comprehension.

'Why would she be at the heart of your quarrel with Blanche?' he asked curiously.

The Bishop shot him a look that indicated that if he could not use his imagination, then he should not speak. The physician glanced at Michael, who obliged him with an almost imperceptible wink. Bartholomew's mind whirled. Were they saying that the mother of Tysilia was Lady Blanche, and that the first meeting of churchman and noble-woman had resulted in something more permanent than a nodding acquaintance? Michael saw the understanding dawn in his friend's eyes, and smiled to show that those suppositions were correct. Bartholomew stared down at his feet, so he would not have to look at de Lisle.

'I do not understand what you are talking about,' said the less worldly Alan. 'Why should your niece be at the root of your problems with Blanche?'

'Blanche foisted the child on me a long time ago,' said de Lisle, walking to the window to gaze out across the grave-yard. 'I was an innocent young man then, and when Blanche came to me with an unwanted child and asked me to give it a home, I obliged. I felt sorry for it.'

'But why should she ask *you* such a thing?' pressed Alan, failing to put together the clues that stared him in the face – although Bartholomew was certain the Bishop would be content if the Prior remained blissfully ignorant. 'You were a churchman, not a landowner with a family of your own. You seem an odd choice of guardian to me.'

'I imagine she detected my kind heart, and decided to use it to her advantage,' said de Lisle smoothly. 'She was about to be married to the Earl of Lancaster, and could hardly present him with a recently born child from an illicit liaison. I helped a woman in distress, and my act of charity has plagued me ever since.'

'I see,' said Alan, although his eyes remained puzzled. 'She feels guilty about abandoning the child, and feels anger because she is in your debt. It is often the way that a kind-ness eventually produces resentment on the part of the bene-ficiary. It is one of the reasons why I am reluctant to be overly indulgent to my peasants.'

'It is hardly the same—' began Bartholomew, who thought Alan could afford to be a little more generous in that direction. Then men like Leycestre would not be plotting a rebellion.

De Lisle cut him off. 'Suffice to say that Blanche will do all in her power to harm me. It is most unjust.'

'It is unjust,' agreed Alan. 'A selfless act should never culminate in merciless persecution.'

'Let us return to these murders,' said de Lisle, who at least had the grace to be disconcerted by Alan's misguided sympathy. 'You must arrest this killer, Michael. And the sooner the better. We shall meet again this time tomorrow, when I want to hear that the wretched man is in a prison cell.'

'I shall do my best,' said Michael. 'This morning we will speak again to Henry, Symon, Welles and Julian.' His glance at Alan implied that the Prior should not consider himself immune to further investigation, either. 'And I will ask whether any of my brethren recognise that book of hours and the chalice we retrieved from the granary yesterday.'

'Ask about those gold coins, too,' suggested Alan. 'I would like to know how they got from the priory coffers to a sack in the storehouse. They are definitely ours, because I recognise one or two irregularities in their minting.'

'But it is obvious why they were in the granary and who put them there,' stated de Lisle uncompromisingly. 'William demanded payments for various expenses he claimed he had incurred as hosteller, then secreted the coins away for his own use.'

'Then why did he not take them with him when he fled?' asked Bartholomew, sure the explanation was not this simple.

De Lisle did not like his opinions challenged. 'Perhaps he forgot them. Or perhaps he intends to collect them later.'

'No,' said Bartholomew. 'William will not return to the priory he abandoned in such mysterious circumstances. And I doubt whether a well-organised and efficient man like him would have forgotten the small fortune carefully stashed away.'

'Then perhaps he did not have room in his saddlebags for all his possessions,' said de Lisle, becoming exasperated. 'He seems to have taken virtually everything else he owned.'

'He does not own much anyway,' said Alan. 'Like me, he prefers to live a simple life, and has not accumulated a lot of personal goods.'

Bartholomew glanced at the rings on Alan's hands, and recalled the rugs and wall-hangings that decorated his chamber, before turning his attention back to de Lisle. 'I do not think that William would take a spare habit and a clean undershirt, but leave a fortune in gold because there was no room for it. He would dispense with the clothes and take the gold instead.'

De Lisle glowered at him. 'Well, *you* tell us what happened, then. You repudiate anything I suggest, so *you* explain how William's gold came to be in the storehouse, apparently abandoned.'

'I cannot,' said Bartholomew. He saw de Lisle's triumphant expression. 'But I do not accept any of your reasons, either. Perhaps William packed his possessions, then realised that he did not have time to retrieve the granary gold. Perhaps Thomas was near the barn, receiving or delivering packages from unknown benefactors, and William was unable to enter it without being seen.'

'He would have waited,' said de Lisle immediately, determined that Bartholomew's explanations should not escape criticism either.

'Perhaps he did not have time,' suggested Michael. 'But Matt is right: we are missing an important piece of this puzzle regarding William and his coins. When we know *how* they came from William's hands into the granary sack, I suspect we shall be on our way to solving that particular mystery. And Alan is right, too: William really does not own much.'

Bartholomew and de Lisle both regarded him doubtfully.

'He is a Benedictine,' said de Lisle eventually.

Michael glared. 'Not all of us flagrantly dispense with the rule of poverty, you know. And William, for all his faults, is a man who is genuinely uninterested in material wealth.'

'Robert was very interested in it, though,' said Alan. 'It pains me to tell you that since his death I have uncovered more than enough evidence to demonstrate that *he* was stealing from the priory. But I do not believe that William is dishonest.'

'How do you explain Thomas's book being in company with William's money?' demanded de Lisle of Bartholomew, ignoring Alan now that he had focused on someone to argue with. 'And where did that chalice come from? Was it stolen from a church? I hope it was not one in my See.'

'I have no idea,' said Bartholomew. 'We should ask the other monks, to see whether any of them recognise it. Did you, Father Prior?'

'I did not,' said Alan. 'But, as you know, I was a gold-smith before I took the cowl, and I appreciate fine work. That chalice is exquisite. Whoever owns it should be proud.'

'What about the book?' asked Michael.

'Again, it shows excellent workmanship, but I have never seen it before.'

'I wonder if it is from the library,' mused Bartholomew.

Alan smiled apologetically. 'Unfortunately, our librarian's records are poor in some areas, and just because something is not listed does not mean we do not possess it. It could well be ours.'

'Symon de Banneham,' said de Lisle heavily. 'Why you put a fellow like that in charge of your precious tomes is beyond my understanding. The man can lay his hands on nothing I ask for, and invariably hides in the latrines when he thinks someone might want to gain access to his territory.'

'But he takes good care of our texts,' argued Alan defensively.

'Actually, he does not,' said Bartholomew. 'He only likes the ones that sit neatly on shelves.'

'Can none of your other brethren identify that book Michael found in the granary?' asked de Lisle of Alan, impatient with the digression. 'It is a beautiful thing, and surely one of them must have come across it in his studies.'

'Symon tends to restrict our access to the library, too,' confessed Alan uneasily. 'He says there are too many delicate volumes that might be damaged by the casual or careless reader.'

'What a crime!' said Michael fervently. 'Monks should be encouraged to study, not barred from it by the likes of Brother Symon.'

'I would send them to you in Cambridge, if any of the community revealed an academic bent,' said Alan mildly. 'But Thomas told me that no one warranted that sort of treatment.'

'That is because Thomas was illiterate,' said de Lisle bluntly. 'He could barely write his own name, and how he managed the business of sub-prior is totally beyond me. I suppose he had scribes to work for him. But still, some good will come of this. You can now appoint a good man as your deputy.'

'Lord!' muttered Alan in alarm, as though fearful that he would not be able to meet such a challenge.

'We should make a start, before anyone else dies,' said Michael, raising his large arms in a weary stretch. 'I will ask the brethren about these treasures.'

'I am not sure I fully understood everything that passed in there,' said Bartholomew, walking quickly to catch up with Michael, who was heading for the refectory, where he knew the monks would be massing. It was approaching the time for the midday meal, and black-robed figures were already emerging from every nook and cranny. The deaths of Robert and Thomas, and the mysterious absence of William, were apparently not matters that warranted any loss of appetite for or devotion to the priory's rich fare for most of the brethren.

Michael chortled at his friend's confusion. 'You understood a good deal more than Alan did. What do you think you missed?'

'Are we to understand that the basis of this feud between de Lisle and Blanche is an ancient love affair that turned sour?'

Michael chuckled a second time. 'It did more than turn sour, Matt: it produced Tysilia. Apparently, Blanche did all she could to rid herself of the brat before she married the Earl of Lancaster, but nothing worked. She produced a baby girl, despite her best attempts not to do so.'

'I wonder if those attempts resulted in the impairment of Tysilia's mind,' mused Bartholomew, intrigued by the possibility. 'It would certainly explain why she is not normal.'

'Blanche foisted the child on de Lisle as soon as she could, then went about her business with the Earl.'

'And the Earl did not notice that his allegedly virgin wife had recently been delivered of a child?' asked Bartholomew incredulously. 'I know that most courtiers dwell in worlds of their own, and that their views of reality are somewhat different from those of the rest of us, but it would be astonishing if that little detail slipped past him.'

'The union between the Earl and Blanche produced no heirs,' replied Michael ambiguously, giving Bartholomew a meaningful wink. 'And we know that was no fault of Blanche's, given that she was able to produce healthy babies for amorous clerics.'

'You think she did not produce any heirs for Lancaster because he discovered she had already provided someone else with one?'

Michael sighed, impatient with his slow wits. 'No. You must remember that Lancaster was a member of the court of Edward the Second, and that Edward preferred men to women. It is generally believed that Lancaster never consummated his marriage with Blanche. When he died of the plague, all his possessions went to his sister. That partly explains Blanche's bitterness.'

'The fact that her marriage was unconsummated, that she

lost her husband to the pestilence, or that she lost her posses-sions to her sister-in-law?' asked Bartholomew, bewildered.

'The last, of course,' said Michael scornfully. 'Blanche went from being the wife of one of the richest landowners in the country to being a widow with little property of her own – and that is why what she does own is important to her. De Lisle should not have set fire to her cottages at Colne.'

'Well, all this is irrelevant anyway,' said Bartholomew. 'What the Duchess did with the Bishop more than two decades ago can hardly have any bearing on this case.'

'Never dismiss anything, Matt,' lectured Michael. 'Who knows where this trail of murders may lead us? But the cooks are only just carrying the food from the kitchens, so it will be some time before it is ready for eating. Walk with me to the cathedral.'

'Why?' asked Bartholomew suspiciously. A long queue was forming outside the refectory, and Michael was usually not a man who walked away from a meal that was about to be served.

'Because I want to think more about Thomas's death before we tackle any suspects. And because I want to see whether pilgrims are still being charged three pennies for access to St Etheldreda's shrine. It was Robert's idea, and I was wondering whether his death has resulted in the lifting of the levy.'

'It is grotesque,' said Bartholomew angrily. 'I know it is customary for pilgrims to leave gifts at shrines, but they are for the saint, not for the monks who tend them. And I have never heard of a fixed fee imposed before.'

'Nor me,' said Michael. 'I was surprised that Alan allowed it. But then I saw the amount of money the priory makes from the levy, and I suppose natural greed stepped in. Alan is a good man, but he is blind to everything when it comes to financing his buildings.'

They entered the cloister, where the shade and coldness of stone was a welcome pleasure after the heat of the noonday sun. Delicate tracery cast intricate patterns of shadow and light on the flagstones, while in the centre of the courtyard the gurgle of water from the fountain that supplied the lavatorium was a restful and pleasing sound. A dove cooed on the tiled roof above, and Bartholomew caught the scent of baking bread wafting from the kitchens. It seemed inconceivable that murder should have entered such a haven of tranquillity and beauty.

'You know, Matt, even our exalted ringside view of Thomas's murder has not left us with any decent clues.' Michael sounded exasperated and dispirited.

Bartholomew understood how he felt. 'Although we saw Alan, Symon, Welles and Julian enter the infirmary via the Dark Cloister, anyone else could have entered through the rear door, knowing that we were being detained by an irate prelate and his grubby steward.'

'Well, at least we know de Lisle is innocent of Thomas's murder. He was with us when Thomas died, and so could not possibly be the culprit.'

'That is not necessarily true, Brother,' said Bartholomew wearily. 'We have no idea when Thomas died. For all we know, Henry could have dropped off to sleep the moment we left for the refectory, leaving all of breakfast time free for the killer to strike. De Lisle may have killed him while we ate, then returned later to the Dark Cloister to berate you for sluggish investigating.'

'So, it may be wholly irrelevant that we saw various monks enter the infirmary?' asked Michael despondently.

'Yes. Thomas's breathing was shallow – so shallow that Henry was obliged to fetch a glass to see if he lived, while I had to press my ear against his chest at least twice during the night. A casual glance would not tell anyone whether he was dead or alive, and so we cannot read anything into the fact that Symon, Alan, and the novices failed to raise the alarm.'

'Damn!' muttered Michael. 'I was hoping we might be able to eliminate at least someone from our list of suspects.'

'We can. Henry.'

'He was never on my list,' said Michael. 'Henry is no killer. But why are you suddenly so sure? I would have thought he was suspect in your eyes because he was alone with Thomas for a good part of the night and this morning.'

'True. But if Henry were the killer, he would have chosen a time when he would not be the obvious suspect.'

'So, what convinces you of his innocence now?'

'The saliva Alan mentioned, basically. Drooling often occurs when someone is in a particularly deep sleep or an awkward position – and Henry was in both. Also, the amount of saliva present on the desk suggests that Henry was dozing for some time. It is not the kind of detail anyone would think to fabricate – even a cunning fellow like our killer. I might have suggested that Henry feigned sleep in order to excuse his presence in the infirmary when Thomas was murdered. But the drool is a fairly iron-clad alibi.'

'Thomas was definitely alive after prime – we have your testimony for that. Henry would not have needed to risk dispatching Thomas this morning, with all these visitors traipsing in and out of the infirmary, when he could have selected a safer time at his leisure.'

'He probably would not have stabbed Thomas, either,' Bartholomew pointed out. 'There are other ways to kill that are far easier to conceal, not to mention the fact that no physician likes to lose a patient in his own hospital.'

'We will ask the old men whether they saw anything,' said Michael. 'They will know whether Henry was asleep or prowling around.'

'Then you had better hope Roger was awake. You will not get much from any of the others. Another thing you need to bear in mind is that Thomas's murder may have been someone copying the killer's methods. Remember how I said I thought Julian might well want to test how it worked? Even if we solve Thomas's murder, it may not give us the identity of the man who killed the others.'

Michael swore softly under his breath.

The cloisters ended in the beautiful carved door that

opened into the cathedral. It was silent inside the great building, with no monastic offices in progress, and the nave abandoned by the parishioners of Holy Cross. Sunlight created patterns in the dust of the clerestory high above, and the blind eyes of saints gazed at them from every direction, as if disturbed by the footsteps that echoed as Bartholomew and Michael walked.

In contrast to the rest of the cathedral, the area surrounding St Etheldreda's shrine was a hive of activity. People clustered around it, some kneeling, some standing, and prayers of all kinds were being spoken. Some pilgrims were awkward and self-conscious, whispering their entreaties almost furtively, as if they imagined that the great saint would never bother to listen to them and that their mere presence was presumptuous. Others had no such qualms, and their prayers were more akin to demands, often delivered with ultimatums.

De Lisle's were among the latter. He knelt on a velvet cushion at the shrine's head, holding the jewelled ring that he promised would be St Etheldreda's if she would only free him from his predicament. Evidently, the deal was to be payment on delivery, because the Bishop replaced it on his finger before leaving.

Also among the multicoloured throng that surrounded the tomb was Guido, holding his gold hat awkwardly in his hands. Next to him Eulalia was kneeling on the floor with her hands pressed together in front of her and her large dark eyes fixed solemnly on the saint's wooden coffin. After a few moments, she rose and walked away, her brother at her side. When she saw Bartholomew her eyes lit with pleasure.

'I did not expect to see you today,' she said, coming towards him with a smile. 'I thought you would be busy investigating the death of the almoner.'

'We are,' said Michael, before Bartholomew could reply. 'But first, we wanted to see whether Robert's untimely demise has resulted in the lifting of the toll on the shrine.'

Eulalia nodded. 'It happened at dawn this morning – Brother Henry petitioned Prior Alan to abolish the charge at prime. Henry is a good man. I thought it would take weeks for something like this to come about, but he had it all arranged in a trice. Three pennies was a lot for many people to pay, and it is good to come here as often as we like with no thought for the cost.'

'And we need St Etheldreda at the moment,' added Guido pugnaciously. 'People keep accusing us of these burglaries, so I told her that she had better tell whoever is spreading these lies to stop. If she does not, then I will find out myself, and ensure that the culprit never utters another lie again.' His face was ugly with anger.

Eulalia sighed in exasperation. 'If you put our request like that, it would serve us right if she does not answer.' She turned to Bartholomew. 'There have now been at least ten burglaries in the city, and a lot of money has gone missing. I admit that some members of our group occasionally take a chicken or catch a fish when times are hard, but we do not arrive in a town and systematically burgle every house in it.'

'It would be obvious it was us, if we did that,' added Guido for Bartholomew's benefit, just in case he had not understood. 'And we are not stupid.'

'You have not collected your black resin yet,' said Eulalia, smiling shyly at Bartholomew. 'It is waiting for you any time you want it.'

'I cannot come today,' said Michael, as though the offer were being made to him. 'I am busy. But perhaps we could manage tomorrow. Keep a pot of stew bubbling over the fire, just in case. I will provide some wine, and we will drink a toast to the removal of Robert and his nasty fees.'

'You live dangerously, Brother,' said Eulalia, laughing at the way the monk had inveigled himself an invitation. 'I do not think you should be seen celebrating the deaths of your fellows, no matter how much you disliked them.'

She walked away, the cloth of her skirt swinging around her fine ankles. Next to her, Guido looked like an ape, with his thick arms and slightly stooped stance. Bartholomew wondered how their mother could have produced two such different offspring, but supposed it was easy enough if there were different fathers. He was so engrossed in watching Eulalia that Michael had to nudge him hard in the ribs to gain his attention.

'I said look at Father John,' whispered the monk crossly. 'It seems that the lifting of the toll has resulted in all manner of new supplicants.'

Bartholomew looked to where the monk was pointing. At the rear of the shrine, in a place where they probably imagined they were invisible to the casual observer, John and Leycestre were involved in one of their low-voiced discussions. Bartholomew looked around for Leycestre's nephews, and, sure enough, spotted them near the door, almost as though they were keeping guard. They were obviously unconcerned by the possibility that someone might enter from the priory side of the cathedral – or perhaps it was only townsfolk in whom they were interested.

'They are always muttering to each other,' said Bartholomew thoughtfully. 'John claims he wants nothing to do with the rebellion-in-the-making, but he seems to spend a lot of time in conversation with Leycestre, who seems able to talk about nothing else. I think John is involved a good deal more deeply than he would have us believe – especially since Leycestre's nephews seem to think these chats warrant privacy. Also, John ordered me not to speak to Leycestre when I first met him. He thought I might be a spy for the King.'

Michael agreed. 'If you were, and if Leycestre told you exactly what he thinks of the local landowners, then Leycestre would be deemed guilty of treason. He would name his accomplices and John would hang with him.'

Bartholomew turned away from the seditious plotting in the corner. 'We have done what we came to do, Brother. You will miss your meal if we wait here much longer.'

Michael started to follow him away, but footsteps striding resolutely down the nave caught his attention. As quick as lightning, he darted behind a pillar, so that Bartholomew suddenly found himself alone. Then he saw that the person who walked with such purpose was Tysilia, with Ralph scurrying in her wake. The steward did not seem pleased by the task of escort, and his red face and harried expression indicated that he was finding it a great deal of work.

'I have three pennies,' Tysilia announced happily, as she drew close enough to speak to Bartholomew. 'I am going to pray to the saint.'

'You no longer need your pennies,' said Bartholomew. 'Robert is dead, and the levy was his idea.'

'I shall buy a new dress, then,' she said, apparently unaware that she would need a good deal more than three grubby coins for that sort of item.

Next to her, Ralph sighed impatiently. 'Hurry up, Tysilia. You said your prayers would only take a few moments, but we have been out for more than an hour and we have not even reached the shrine yet.'

'I like to walk around the town,' said Tysilia, unperturbed by Ralph's bad temper. 'I might meet Brother Michael there. Where is he, by the way?' She began to look around eagerly, and Bartholomew saw a shadow easing further behind the stout pillar.

'Ready for some food, I imagine,' said Bartholomew ambiguously. 'I told you he is never available at mealtimes.'

'Yes, I suppose he would not like to miss his midday meal,' said Tysilia thoughtfully. 'He is a little fat, although it just lends him more charm, do you not think, Ralph?'

'Oh, yes. Very charming,' growled Ralph irritably. 'Now, pray at this damned shrine, and then let us go home. I promised the Bishop I would have you back ages ago.'

'I am going to ask St Earthdigger to give him to me,' she said confidentially to Bartholomew, making no attempt to obey Ralph.

'St Etheldreda,' said Bartholomew. 'And to give you who?'

'Brother Michael, of course,' said Tysilia. 'I shall pray to the saint to let me have him. I am sure she will oblige. After all, Michael is a monk, and so he is a holy man. The saint will want to make a holy man happy.'

'I do not think it works like that,' said Bartholomew, trying not to laugh. 'And Michael is a Benedictine. That means women are forbidden to him.'

'I heard that,' said Tysilia confidentially. 'Ralph explained it to me. It all sounds very silly, and it will not apply to me, anyway. I am not an ordinary woman. I am special. My uncle told me so, and he is a bishop, so he must be right.'

'Come *on*,' said Ralph, finally losing patience and taking her arm to drag her roughly towards the shrine. She continued to chatter as he led her away, and Michael stepped out from his pillar with a sigh of relief. She was informing Ralph – and anyone else who happened to be within a mile of her – that Blanche wore a wig, and that her front teeth were tied in place each morning with two small pieces of twine.

'That was close,' said Michael, puffing out his cheeks in a sigh. 'Come on, Matt. We will have to walk around the back of the building, to make sure she does not see us on our way out. It would be terrible to be accosted by her in a public place like this, and I do not think Ralph is strong enough to keep her under control.'

They walked briskly to the back of the cathedral, where the rope had been stretched between two stools as a frail barrier to prevent people from entering the north-west transept. Fresh rubble on the floor indicated that there had been another recent fall. Bartholomew glanced up and saw that an angel he had observed a few days before was leaning at an even more precarious angle, and that one or two gargoyles looked as though the merest breath would be sufficient to send them crashing to the ground below. Even as they watched, a shower of plaster and a few larger flakes drifted downwards, like a sudden flurry of snow.

'Come on, Brother,' said Bartholomew, pulling the monk away. 'It is not safe here.'

'You are right!' said Michael, casting a nervous glance back to St Etheldreda's shrine.

*   *   *

Bartholomew wanted to talk to Henry, Symon, Welles, Julian and the old men, to see whether anyone could recall any small detail about the death of Thomas that might allow them to trace the killer. However, Michael declined to do anything until he had eaten, claiming that the near encounter with Tysilia had unsettled him, and that he needed food to calm his nerves. It was still early, and the brethren milled around the refectory door, waiting for it to open. Looking critically at them, Bartholomew decided that a missed meal would do many of them a lot of good: Benedictines were a contemplative Order, and sitting around thinking about God did little for their waistlines. Because Ely was a wealthy cathedral-priory with a large number of servants and lay-brothers, few of the brethren were obliged to work in the fields, except as penance, and the effects of lack of exercise and a surfeit of rich food was very apparent.

Delicious smells emanated from behind the doors – freshly baked bread, roasted parsnips, fish (because it was Friday) and the obligatory pea pottage. These rich aromas mingled pleasantly with the scents of summer, and mown grass, flowers and warm earth reminded Bartholomew of the abbey school he had attended in Peterborough.

Henry was not among the men who thronged impatiently outside the refectory. The novices were there, however, and Julian, Welles and Bukton stood chatting together nearby. Julian informed Bartholomew that the infirmarian was taking his meal with Roger, because the old man had expressed a desire for company.

'I do not suppose it crossed *your* mind to dine with him?' asked Bartholomew archly.

Julian shook his head vehemently. 'It did not! I prefer eating here, with men of my own age. I have no wish to feed with dribbling ancients, who ask me to slice up their peas every few moments. But it occurred to Henry, and *he* offered my services to Roger. I was not pleased, I can tell you!'

'I am sure you were not,' said Bartholomew coolly. 'So what are you doing here, if you are supposed to be with Roger?'

'Roger said he would prefer Henry to me, actually,' said Julian, looking away, uninterested by the discussion. 'I cannot imagine why. All Henry wants to talk about is medicine, and what a good thing it is to make people well again. Boring!'

'Brother Henry is the best man in the priory,' declared Welles hotly, fists clenching. 'He is kind and sweet-tempered, and you have no right to say unpleasant things about him!'

'I agree,' said Bukton, equally angry. 'Henry cured me when I had marsh ague last year. He is like a father to us novices, so just watch what you say about him.'

Sensibly, Julian said no more on the matter. Bartholomew suspected that if he had, he might well have been punched. In a priory full of unkind men, the gentle Henry provided a much-needed haven and he was loved for it. Bartholomew glanced at Michael and saw that he entirely concurred with the novices' sentiments, and that he also owed a debt of gratitude to the man who had befriended him in his youth.

'I saw you two slipping into the infirmary after breakfast this morning,' Michael remarked casually to Julian and Welles.

'So?' demanded Julian insolently. 'We work in the infirmary – unfortunately. We are supposed to be there.'

'They dallied in the refectory after breakfast,' said Bukton helpfully. 'In the end, Prior Alan made them go to work.'

Julian shot him an unpleasant look for his tale-telling, then turned to Michael. 'I did not kill Thomas, if that is what you are thinking. I did not even go into the chamber where he was resting. I went straight to the workshop and started my chores.'

Bartholomew glanced at the faces of Julian's fellow novices and saw a gamut of emotions there. Some seemed impressed that Julian should be under suspicion for removing a much-detested member of the community;

others appeared to be uneasy at the thought that Julian might commit such a crime.

'I did not kill him, either,' said Welles, worried that Julian's denial might result in the accusation passing to him. 'I did not stay in the hospital – I collected a basket and then left through the other door to buy fruit in the marketplace.'

'That should be easy to check,' said Bartholomew to Michael. 'We can ask the lay-brother on gate duty when he saw him.'

Welles lost some colour from his face and swallowed nervously. 'But he was not there. I suppose he was either dozing or had gone to the latrines. I let myself out.'

'Really,' said Michael, sounding interested. 'How convenient. What about when you came back?'

'The same,' replied Welles, a curious mixture of defiant and fearful. 'He will deny leaving his post, of course.'

'Of course,' said Michael expressionlessly. He glanced around, and his eyes lit on another monk in the milling throng awaiting dinner. The novices were temporarily forgotten. 'Brother Symon! Just the man I wanted to see.'

'It is too late to use the library today,' said Symon, edging away from Michael in alarm. 'Apply in writing and I shall see what I can do.'

'It is not the library I want.' One powerful arm shot out to prevent the librarian's escape. 'It is you. Am I mistaken, or did I spot you entering the infirmary after breakfast this morning?'

'You just said that was Julian and Welles,' said Bukton, confused.

'I saw several people,' said Michael meaningfully. 'One of whom was the Brother Librarian.' He waited expectantly for Symon's answer.

Symon blustered and coughed for a moment as he collected his thoughts. 'I did cut through the infirmary hall,' he admitted. 'But I did not see any killers. I saw Henry dozing and Thomas fast asleep on his sickbed, but nothing else.'

'How do you know Thomas was fast asleep?' pounced Michael. 'How do you know he was not dead?'

Symon blustered even more. 'I suppose he may have been. The old men were watching me, so I did not go and prod him.' His reply made it sound as though he might have done if no one had been looking.

'Why did you go into the infirmary at all?' asked Bartholomew. 'You have been haunting it like a ghost ever since Thomas was taken ill, although you never set foot in it normally.'

'I was concerned for the welfare of my sub-prior,' replied Symon, looking pleased with himself for thinking up this reply. 'Is that all? I have other business to attend . . .'

'Just a moment,' snapped Michael, tightening his grip on the slippery librarian's arm. 'I have not finished with you yet. I want your expertise.'

'My what?' asked Symon nervously.

'Quite,' muttered Michael grimly. 'Bukton – run to the Prior's House and ask him for the contents of the granary sack I discovered yesterday. He will know what I mean.'

Bukton did not take long. He handed the bag to Michael, who withdrew the book of hours from its parchment wrappings. 'I found this recently. Do you recognise it?'

Symon regarded the tome suspiciously, then turned to Bartholomew. 'Is this a trick? Have you removed it from my shelves, and are testing to see whether I am able to identify it?'

'Of course not,' said Bartholomew scornfully. 'We merely want to know whether you have seen it before.'

'If I say yes, will you give it to me for my collection?' asked Symon craftily.

'No, I will not,' said Michael irritably. 'And I want you to tell the truth, not some lie that you think will earn you a gift. Do you recognise it?' He gave a hearty sigh when Symon glanced down and then away. 'You will not be able to give me your considered opinion if you do not inspect it closely, man! Take it and leaf through it.'

Symon opened the book, and even he could see that here was a script of considerable value. He turned the pages carefully, almost reverently, but then handed it back to Michael with clear reluctance. 'I am afraid I have never seen it before.'

'What about this chalice?' asked Michael, producing the fine cup that had also been hidden in the granary.

Symon shook his head a second time, although he seemed considerably more interested in the silver than he had been in the book. 'No, but it is very fine and should be in the Prior's coffers.' He took it from Michael, then held it and the book up to show the monks who stood in a curious circle around him. 'Do any of you know these?'

There was a chorus of denials and several shaken heads, although Julian said nothing. His silence did not go unobserved. Michael immediately homed in on him.

'Which of these is familiar to you?' he demanded.

Julian was startled to find himself suddenly the centre of attention again. 'Neither,' he said, nervously raising one hand to scratch at the smattering of spots around his mouth.

'Do not lie,' ordered Michael coldly. 'It is clear to me that you have seen one or more of these items before, and I want to know which one and where.'

'It cannot be clear to you,' blustered Julian. He had scratched one pimple enough to make it bleed. 'I have said nothing to give you that impression.'

'It is more a case of what you have *not* said,' replied Michael, showing off a little. 'You alone, of all these men, did not immediately claim ignorance of these items. You said nothing, and I could tell from your eyes that you know something. And now you are picking and scratching at yourself like a dog with fleas, which is a sure sign of an uneasy conscience. So, unless you want to find yourself on latrine duty for the next month, you had better be honest.'

'I know nothing,' said Julian in a small voice, close to tears. His continuing denials convinced no one, and here and there the monks began to murmur among themselves.

Bartholomew decided that the best way to make Julian speak was to appeal to their sense of self-preservation.

'There is a murderer in this city, who has already killed five men,' he said, addressing them. 'It is possible that William was so afraid that he took all his possessions and fled, while poor Robert was murdered in broad daylight in the grounds of your own priory. And the killer did not even take pity on Thomas, as he lay afflicted with a seizure that rendered him helpless. Is this the kind of man you want in your home?'

Heads were shaken fervently and there was a growing mumble of unease: Bartholomew's speech had visibly upset some of them. They looked around, as though they imagined that a killer might stalk up and slip his knife into their necks as they stood with their friends outside the refectory. Michael took up the argument.

'Then you will agree with us that it is imperative Julian tells us the truth, and reveals whatever secret he has learned that might have a bearing on this case?'

'Brother Michael is right,' said Bukton fervently, appealing to his friend. 'I do not want my neck cut as I sleep just because you are a selfish lout who cannot distinguish between truth and lies. Tell Michael what he wants to know.'

'Yes, or you will have me to deal with,' added Symon, although whether from genuine concern or merely for show, Bartholomew could not tell.

'I do not know what Brother Michael wants me to say,' said Julian, defiant to the last.

'Then tell him what you *think* he wants you to say,' growled Symon, taking a couple of steps towards the uneasy novice. Julian tried to back away, but Welles and Bukton had closed in behind him, and he found himself surrounded. He swallowed hard and turned to face Michael.

'Very well, but it will not help you.'

'I will be the judge of that,' said Michael pompously.

'I have seen that book before,' admitted Julian miserably.

'Where?' demanded Michael, when Julian faltered into silence again. 'Did Thomas or William own it? Did you see one of them reading it, or one passing it to the other?'

'No. I saw it in Robert's cell the day before he died.'

Bartholomew did not feel like devouring another monstrous meal, although Michael had no objection. They ate quickly, then left to go in search of Henry. Heat radiated from the yellow-grey stones of the priory buildings. Sparrows flapped and fluttered in the dust of the path, while a cat panted in the shade, too lethargic even to chase easy targets.

As they walked, the bell chimed to announce the end of the midday meal. Bartholomew glanced behind him to see the monks emerging from the refectory – more slowly than they had entered, and with considerably less urgency. Some had their heads bent, as though in contemplation, and all had their hands tucked inside their wide sleeves. Bartholomew noted that Michael had also adopted the priory style of walking: in Cambridge, the monk's hands were either guarding his scrip from pickpockets, or were ready to grab some student who was misbehaving. Julian walked with them, adopting a sullen slouch to register that he resented the fact that Michael had ordered him to accompany them, when it was customary for the brethren to take a period of rest in the afternoons.

'This mystery is becoming more opaque than ever,' Michael grumbled, careful to keep his voice low so that Julian would not hear what he was saying. 'Every time I think I have uncovered a clue that will lead me to new avenues of investigation, I learn something that confuses me even more.'

'You mean like the book of hours being in Robert's possession?' asked Bartholomew. 'We saw Thomas receive a parcel that looked very much like the one containing the tome, but we cannot even be sure that parcel and book are one and the same.'

'And the packet was most definitely part of the hoard

belonging to William,' said Michael. 'We know this because Alan said the gold was clipped in a distinctive way, and he is sure it is the same money given to William for his expenditure as hosteller.'

'But just because the book was found with William's gold does not mean to say that William put them together. Someone may have stolen the coins from him, along with the book from Robert, and hidden them in the barn.'

'And that someone may well have been Thomas,' said Michael. 'Damn the man! Why did he have to choose now to have his seizure? Had he remained healthy for a few more moments, we might have prised enough information from him to catch this killer – and Thomas himself would still be alive.'

'I am not sure Thomas put that sack in the granary,' said Bartholomew. 'The ladder broke when I climbed it, and I am a good deal lighter than Thomas.'

'Perhaps it was Thomas's weight that rendered the rungs weak in the first place,' suggested Michael.

Bartholomew frowned. 'I doubt a man of Thomas's girth could have hauled himself up those steps. I am not sure his arms would have been strong enough.'

'You would probably say the same about me,' said Michael, pushing back a black sleeve to reveal a meaty white arm, which he flexed proudly. 'But my strength has saved your life on numerous occasions.'

'But you do more than stroll between cathedral and refectory all day,' Bartholomew pointed out. 'You wrestle with students, and you ride. Thomas did nothing more strenuous than raise a spoon to his lips.'

Michael gave him an reproachful glance. 'That is unfair. He raised goblets, too. But, although we have a good deal of confusing information about the book, we know nothing about the chalice. England is a large country, and there are churches all across it that own attractive silver, so I suppose there is no reason for us to have heard if it was stolen from some distant place, like Peterborough or Huntingdon.'

'Is there any particular reason why you mention Huntingdon, Brother?'

Michael looked sharply at him. 'None. Why?'

'Because Blanche is from Huntingdon.'

'I was selecting places at random,' Michael said dismissively. 'However, you may have a point, and we must make sure we ask someone from her household whether they recognise it. A positive identification in that direction would give us something to work on.'

'But, as you have already pointed out, we do not need any more disjointed clues,' said Bartholomew. 'That has been our problem all along: we have a mass of small facts and scraps of information, but we are unable to make any sense out of them. The last thing we need is more.'

When they reached the infirmary, Bartholomew thought Henry did not look well. His face was pale, and his eyes were watery. He appeared to be on the verge of exhaustion, and Bartholomew decided he had better agree to sit with Roger that night, or Thomas might not be the only one to have a seizure.

'You should rest,' said Michael gently, when he saw the state the kindly physician was in.

'I feel responsible for what happened to Thomas,' said Henry in a low voice. 'If I had been more vigilant, then he would be with us now.'

'I doubt it,' said Michael brusquely. 'As I told you earlier, if you had been more vigilant, you might well be lying next to Thomas in a coffin. The murderer killed him because it was obvious that he was about to reveal information that would help us.'

'You did all you could,' said Bartholomew, seeing Henry was not much comforted by Michael's words. 'You made Thomas's last moments comfortable, and his death was probably quick and painless.'

'It is the "probably" that worries me, Matthew,' said Henry miserably. 'I have lost patients before, of course, but I have never had one murdered while I slept.'

'Just be thankful that you were *not* awake,' said Bartholomew. 'There is no one else in the priory with your expertise. What would happen to Roger and the other elderly men if the killer had taken you, too?'

'More to the point, what would have happened to the rest of us?' added Julian. 'You bleed us quickly and painlessly. If you were dead, then we would have to go to Barbour of the Lamb, and he makes a terrible mess.'

Julian's brazen self-interest brought a smile to Henry's face. 'You are a wicked boy,' he said mildly. 'I despair of ever filling you with compassion.'

'Never mind that,' said Michael. 'Since you will not rest, then you can answer my questions. Alan said you occasionally use the library. Do you recognise this book?'

Henry glanced at it, but then said, 'I am always too busy to read anything except medical texts on the rare occasions that I persuade Symon to allow me into his domain.'

'Could you have seen it outside the library?' pressed Michael.

Henry looked puzzled. 'Of course not. All the priory's books are locked up and Symon does not allow them out. Books are far too valuable to be left lying around, as I am sure you know.'

'Yes, I do,' said Michael loftily. 'I am a University scholar and well aware of the value of books. But could this particular tome have been in the dormitory, among the personal possessions of any of your fellow brethren?'

'I would not know that, either,' said Henry helplessly. 'I sleep here, with my patients, not in the dormitory. And I am not in the habit of rooting through my colleagues' belongings, anyway.'

'We are Benedictines,' said Julian piously. 'We do not have many possessions.'

'We can debate Benedictine wealth another time,' said Michael quickly, seeing Bartholomew ready to argue. He handed Henry the cup. 'What about this?'

'No,' said Henry, glancing at it without much interest.

'Does it belong to the cathedral?'

'Alan says not,' said Michael.

'He is right,' said Julian, taking the cup from Henry and turning it in his hands. His touch was more covetous than curious, and Bartholomew thought that if it went missing, Julian would be the first person to question about its whereabouts.

'How would you know?' demanded Michael, snatching it back from him.

'I was an altar boy before I became a novice,' explained Julian. 'But I have never seen this particular piece before.'

'All right,' said Michael, replacing the book and chalice inside the sack. 'Now, I want you both to tell me *exactly* what happened when Thomas died.'

'Again, Brother?' asked Henry, his voice husky with tiredness. 'It is a painful memory, and I would rather put it from my mind.'

'And I am sleepy from the heat,' added Julian. 'I need my afternoon doze. Can we not do this later?'

'Murder is not something that waits on sleeping times,' said Michael sternly. 'However, I shall allow you to tell me your story first, and then you can escape, since you seem more interested in that than in justice.'

Julian bridled, but began his story. 'I left the refectory with Welles and came here. He said he was going to buy fruit, while I went straight to the herb room. That is one of the two small chambers at the opposite end of the hall to where Thomas was lying and Henry was sleeping.'

'Yes, yes,' said Michael impatiently, seeing Henry wince. 'We all know what the infirmary looks like: there is the hall where the old men live; at one end is the workshop with the herb room beyond, and at the other end are the two chambers where you and Henry sleep.'

'Thomas was in one of those,' said Bartholomew for clarification. 'In other words, the hall *and* the workshop were between Julian and Thomas.'

'Yes,' agreed Julian. 'So I heard and saw nothing. I was

busy crushing saffron, anyway. I had the door closed, so that the noise would not disturb the patients.'

'I taught him to do that,' said Henry to Michael. 'We always keep the doors closed when we are making medicines. However, the door between my chamber and Thomas's was open so that I could hear him if he called out, but the killer must have come in stockinged feet. I do not sleep heavily.'

'But you were exhausted,' Bartholomew pointed out. 'Perhaps under normal circumstances you might have woken, but you had had several bad nights, and you had worked hard to try to save Thomas. In any case, the floor is stone, and so it is easy to walk silently.'

'That is usually a good thing,' said Henry ruefully. 'It would not do to have creaking floorboards every time I tend a patient during the night.'

'The killer must have felt himself blessed indeed,' mused Michael. 'Welles at the market, Julian in the herb room, and Henry in an exhausted slumber and uncharacteristically deaf. Perhaps one of the old men heard something.'

'You can try asking,' said Henry, although he did not sound hopeful. 'One is deaf, two are blind, and none is in his right wits. Even Roger's mind wanders from time to time, and he is the most lively of them all.'

'Matt can talk to them, while I visit Blanche,' said Michael. 'Continue with your tale, Julian. You were in the herb room, chopping saffron.'

'I was there from just after breakfast.' Julian showed them orange-stained hands. 'Henry did not need me to sit with Thomas, although I offered.'

'I could not trust you,' said Henry, for once critical of the novice he was determined to save. 'You are not good at anticipating a patient's needs, and you might have fallen asleep.'

'Unlike you, I suppose,' Julian shot back.

Henry fell silent.

'Did you hear or see anything that might help us?' asked Michael of Julian. He stepped closer, and there was more menace in the question than was necessary. Julian edged away, but Bartholomew moved behind him, deliberately making the lad feel there was no escape. Bartholomew considered Julian a wholly loathsome specimen, and hoped Michael's questioning would put the fear of God into him.

'No,' said Julian desperately. 'I told you. I was crushing saffron, which involves using a pestle and mortar and is fairly noisy. And the door was closed. There is a window, but my back was to it. I heard and saw nothing until Welles came. By then, Thomas had been declared dead and he and I were ordered to wash the body.'

'You did not hear me arrive and examine Thomas?' asked Bartholomew.

'No,' said Julian. 'To be frank, crushing saffron is so tedious that I had lulled myself into a sort of working drowse. I heard nothing.'

Bartholomew believed him. He was certain that the lad would have grabbed any opportunity to escape the boring task he had been set, and would have come running had he heard the commotion when it was discovered that Thomas's death had not been natural – unless, of course, he knew perfectly well the cause of the upheaval and elected to keep his distance from the scene of his crime.

'Welles,' said Michael. 'Did you see him leave the infirmary before you went to the herb room?'

'No,' said Julian. 'I went to the herb room first, while he poked about in the workshop looking for his basket. He was still searching for it when I closed the herb-room door.'

'Has anyone else visited the infirmary today?' asked Michael, exchanging a quick glance with Bartholomew. Welles, it seemed, should be questioned once again. 'Did anyone, other than us, come to see Thomas?'

'Doctor Bartholomew recommended that no visitors be allowed,' said Julian. 'But that is not to say that everyone would have obeyed him. As I said, my back was to the window, so I did not notice. But Thomas's illness caused much interest in the priory – lots of folk wanted to look at him. Who knows who may have sneaked in while Henry dozed?'

'Did you see Prior Alan come in?' asked Bartholomew.

'No!' cried Julian, becoming exasperated. 'How many more times must I tell you? I saw no one. The window is at an awkward angle for looking at either of the doors anyway – the main one leading from the Dark Cloister, or the back one.'

'Someone *could* have entered through the rear door,' suggested Henry. 'It is well oiled, because I do not want creaks and groans disturbing my patients, so it would have been easy to slip in. Poor Thomas!'

'All this does suggest that the killer is a monk,' said Bartholomew. 'Someone was aware that he had a very close call when Thomas was on the verge of telling what he knew, and that same someone was familiar with the layout of the infirmary, so he was able to kill Thomas without being seen or heard.'

'Not necessarily,' said Michael. 'News of Thomas's seizure and its implications spread through the city very quickly, and many Ely folk visit Henry in the infirmary. It is the one place in the priory that the townsfolk do know. Also, I think that a monk would have struck when Thomas was first taken ill. He would not have waited a day.'

'But there was no opportunity to do that until this morning,' said Bartholomew. 'A monk – or someone else – could have been waiting hours for the best moment to strike.'

'He did wait for the right moment,' said Henry bitterly. 'I had been sitting next to Thomas, holding his hand and praying for him. I whispered that I was just going to attend to some business, but that I would only be next door and would hear him if he wanted me.'

'Perhaps the killer heard you saying that, too,' mused Michael.

'How could he?' asked Henry in alarm. 'Do you think he was hiding under the bed all that time? Or in a cupboard?'

'No, but he may have been outside a window. The weather is hot, and all the shutters are open to allow a breeze to circulate. The killer could well have been crouching outside in the bushes, listening to you comforting Thomas, and biding his time.'

'And then I basically announced to the fiend that I was leaving, and that he could kill Thomas at his leisure,' said Henry in disgust. 'How could I have been so foolish?'

'You were not foolish,' said Michael gently. 'You just do not think like a killer – thank God! But the day is drawing on. Unfortunately, nothing you have told us throws any light on the killer's identity, although at least we know how he managed to commit his crime unseen. So, I will go to ask Blanche and her household whether this is her cup, while Matt can question the old men.'

'You should come with me,' suggested Bartholomew. 'They may have seen something, and you should hear what they have to say at first hand.'

Michael sighed when, without asking permission, Julian hurried away, presumably to take his nap. Henry came with them, trailing unhappily. Bartholomew supposed there was nothing they could say or do that would convince the physician that Thomas's death was not his fault and that the sub-prior had been doomed as soon as he had indicated he was party to some dangerous information.

Three of the inmates seemed barely aware that they were alive, and turned blank eyes on Bartholomew when he spoke to them. One of them was also blind, and his opaque eyes could not make out the bed next to him, let alone identify a murderer slipping through the shadows. Meanwhile, Ynys was having a bad day, and imagined himself to be at the battle of Bannockburn, desperate to know if the rumours were true that the English had been routed by the Scots.

'The Scots would never gain the better of an Englishman,' declared Michael uncompromisingly, conveniently forget-ting that the Scots had scored a significant victory over the armies of the English king some forty years previously.

Ynys was greatly relieved, but asked the same question again moments later, having already forgotten Michael's assurances. Michael regarded him warily, then turned his attention to Roger. The old man smiled when Bartholomew approached him, revealing pink gums and evidently anticipating a pleasant diversion from the monotony of his days in bed.

'How did Thomas die?' he asked in a voice that quivered with age. 'Did someone poison him at his trough? I saw his giant corpse carried away mid-morning.'

'He had a seizure,' said Bartholomew. Roger craned forward, cupping one hand around his ear. 'HE HAD A SEIZURE.'

'I wonder why Roger assumed someone had poisoned Thomas,' said Michael, frowning thoughtfully. 'I recall young Bukton saying the same thing when Thomas first became ill.'

'He had a seizure,' said Roger, nodding in what seemed to be satisfaction. 'It serves him right. Doubtless God struck him down while he gorged himself without a thought for others.'

'What do you mean?' yelled Bartholomew.

'He intercepted the cooks when they brought our meals from the kitchens, and took our food for himself. He was a greedy man. You will have to do a lot of praying if you ever want *him* to escape from Purgatory. I will not.'

'I know you caught him once, but I do not think that was a regular occurrence,' said Henry apologetically to Bartholomew. 'The poor man was probably hungry, and acted on impulse.'

'I am not sure—' began Bartholomew, not wanting to malign a man who was not in a position to defend himself, but certain Thomas's penchant for the patients' dinners had been fairly frequent.

'I saw him through the window,' interrupted Roger. 'I watched the cooks pass him steaming pots to bring to us. Those were the days we ate cheese rinds and stale bread.'

'But you did not tell me,' said Henry, agitated. 'Why did you not mention this before?'

'I told Julian,' said Roger. 'I did not want to bother a busy man like you with a trivial matter like our dinners. Julian did nothing, of course. The boy is worthless.'

'Never mind all this,' said Michael, casually overlooking the fact that *he* would not have been so sanguine had it been his own food that had been purloined by the sub-prior. 'I want to know whether Roger saw anything that might help us regarding Thomas. Ask him, Matt.'

'He is deaf, Brother,' said Henry reproachfully. 'That does not mean he is a half-wit. If you have questions, ask them yourself. Just speak loudly and clearly.'

'Did you see anything unusual around the time when Thomas was killed?' Michael shouted, loud enough to frighten Ynys, who demanded his horse and armour.

'Eh?' asked Roger.

'DID YOU SEE HOW HE DIED?' howled Michael, making his voice crack.

'Did I see his eyes?' asked Roger. 'I wish I had! I would have liked to have seen him aware that it was his Judgement Day. He would have known that there was not much hope for his soul after all his years of gluttony.'

'Thomas did have a reputation as a man who would do anything for his stomach,' admitted Henry. 'But I do not think that alone will send him to Hell.'

'Speak up!' snapped Roger. 'I cannot hear when you whisper.'

'I am sorry,' said Henry, patting the old man's blue-veined hand.

Roger smiled at him. 'I was glad you were not with Thomas when he died, Henry – you would have absolved him of all his crimes against us, and he did not deserve that.' He turned bright eyes on Michael. 'Poor Henry was so tired from all his nights of vigil that he slept in Julian's chamber while Thomas died. I saw him, drooling with his head on the table.'

'Please!' whispered Henry, mortified. 'You do not have to remind me of my negligence.'

Roger's sharp expression softened. 'I apologise, Henry. I have allowed my dislike of Thomas to overshadow my concern for your feelings. But I am still grateful you were not there to absolve him. I am glad it was someone else.'

'Someone else?' asked Michael immediately. 'You saw someone else with Thomas at the time of his death? Who?'

'Eh?'

'WHO WAS WITH HIM?' bellowed Michael.

'Armour! A sword!' hollered Ynys. 'The Scots are coming!'

'I do not know whether he was a Scot,' said Roger. 'I did not see the fellow clearly.'

'Was it a monk?' demanded Michael. 'A lay-brother?'

Roger scratched his head. 'I did not notice. I saw a fellow in a dark cloak leave the room where Thomas lay. Later – I am not sure how long, because time means little to me these days – Alan arrived, and he and Henry went to tend Thomas. Then Henry reeled from the chamber for some air, and I could tell from the expression on his face that Thomas had taken a turn for the worse.'

'Death *is* a turn for the worse,' agreed Michael wryly. 'It is a pity Julian had his back to the window, and saw none of these comings and goings. JULIAN SAW NO ONE COME THROUGH EITHER DOOR.'

'I can well believe it,' said Roger. 'The boy is not observant, and anyone intent on mischief would find it easy to elude him.'

'How did this cloaked man leave?' shouted Bartholomew, looking at Roger. 'Through the back door?'

Roger nodded. 'He was walking slowly, his head bowed in prayer, and he was making the sign of the cross.'

'Symon!' exclaimed Michael in satisfaction. 'We already have his confession that he cut through the infirmary hall to reach his library.'

'Did you see this figure enter the hall the same way?' asked Bartholomew loudly.

Roger gave one of his pink smiles. 'I saw no one arrive – I doze, you see, so I may have been sleeping – but I saw this fellow leave, after kneeling a while with Thomas. As I said, it appeared as though he was praying as he went.'

'You observed the way he walked, and yet you cannot tell me whether he was a monk?' said Michael, in disbelief.

'Not very often,' said Roger, answering whatever he thought Michael had asked. 'Few of the younger ones bother with us, and visitors are rare. Prior Alan comes occasionally, but apart from Henry, that vile Julian and young Welles, we seldom see anyone. That was why I noticed the fellow who came to see Thomas.'

'Can you describe him?' yelled Bartholomew. 'WHAT WAS HE WEARING?'

'I could not see whether he had an ear-ring,' replied Roger, puzzled by the question. 'Not that I would have noticed, given that his hood was up. He must be like me, and feels the cold.'

'He did not want to be seen,' said Michael. 'And he wore this cloak for the same reason.' He glanced at Bartholomew. 'I did not see Symon wearing a cloak.'

'But Alan's prior's habit is cloak-like,' suggested Bartholomew softly.

'All our robes would look cloak-like to Roger,' said Henry in a low voice. 'He does not see well. Besides, we are Benedictine monks, and all of us own dark cloaks with hoods that we could use for a disguise.'

'But it would be unusual to wear one today,' Bartholomew pointed out. 'It is hot, and anyone wearing a cloak would stand out as odd.'

'He probably removed it as soon as he left the infirmary via the rear door,' said Michael, disgusted. 'Damn it all! Here we have a man who actually *saw* this killer, and all he can tell us is that the fellow disguised himself.'

'Thomas was murdered,' shouted Bartholomew to Roger. 'Can you tell us any more about this person you saw? It is very important.'

'Thomas's mother?' asked Roger, confused. 'What does she have to do with this? I imagine she is long since in her grave.'

'THOMAS WAS MURDERED!' yelled Bartholomew.

'The Scots are here!' howled Ynys. 'Lock up your cattle!'

'Murdered?' demanded Roger. 'You told me he had a seizure. Which is it?'

'One led to the other,' shouted Bartholomew. 'Can you tell us any more about this visitor?'

'I saw him only for an instant,' said Roger. 'It is a pity: now I know what he did, I wish I had shaken his hand. But I have told you all I know: I glimpsed a figure leaving Thomas's room, and he was praying – probably asking God to reward him for the good he had done.'

'That is not kind,' said Henry admonishingly. 'And if you know anything at all, you should tell Michael so that he can prevent more people being harmed.'

'I know nothing more,' said Roger. 'I wish him luck in evading you, though. There are plenty more of our "sainted" brethren whom the priory would be better without.'

'Like who?' asked Michael curiously. Roger leaned forward in exasperation, pulling his ear to indicate that Michael should speak louder. 'WHO ELSE WOULD THE PRIORY BE BETTER WITHOUT?'

'Robert,' replied Roger immediately. 'He steals alms intended for the poor, and has been doing it for years. It is also a wicked sin to demand payment from the pilgrims who visit our shrine. And William is not much better.'

'He steals from the priory, too?' asked Bartholomew.

'He pits one man against another, so that their division will make him stronger. It would not surprise me to learn that *he* is behind this cruel slander against the Bishop.'

'Would it not?' mused Michael softly. 'Now that is interesting.'

When their questions showed that Roger knew nothing more, and that the list of monks he wanted to send to an early grave were those to whom he had taken a personal and frequently irrational dislike, Bartholomew and Michael left the infirmary and went to the Outer Hostry, to speak to Lady Blanche de Wake and her retinue.

Blanche was just sitting down to a meal, and her table was almost as loaded with food as were the ones in the monks' refectory. There were roasted trout, plates of boiled eel, a huge pot of parsnips and a dish of bright green peas. There was bread, too, in tiny loaves made from the priory's finest white flour. She glanced up when the two scholars tapped on the door, but did not stop her dining preparations. She rolled up her sleeves, so that grease would not spoil them, while a lady-in-waiting tied a large piece of cloth around her neck. A sizeable knife, the blade of which had been honed so many times that it had been worn into a sharp point, was presented to her, and then she was ready.

'Interesting knife,' said Bartholomew in an undertone to Michael. Since he had identified the killer's unique way of dispatching his victims, he had taken to inspecting people's weapons, to see whether any matched the length and width necessary to commit the crime. Blanche's fitted nicely.

'You think that could be the murder weapon?' asked Michael in surprise. 'And she is using it to eat her dinner?'

'Perhaps she does not know it might have been used for purposes other than culinary. Or perhaps she is not as squeamish as you are.'

'So, she or one of her retinue may be the killer,' muttered Michael. 'You suggested the killer was a monk. But you could be wrong, because the guests who stay in the Outer Hostry also have access to the vineyards and the hospital.'

'I was right when I said we did not need any more information, though,' muttered Bartholomew. 'The more we have, the further away seems the solution.'

'Can I help you?' asked Blanche, stretching her arms and flexing her fingers in anticipation. It appeared that, for her, eating involved a considerable amount of physical exercise. 'I would invite you to dine, but the monks have not been generous in their portions, and I would not like to go hungry because you have chosen to visit me now when it would have been more polite to defer.'

'Murder is a business that will not wait,' said Michael pompously. 'I will do whatever is necessary to catch this killer – even interrupt meals.'

'You already have your killer,' said Blanche wearily. 'The Bishop.'

'That is unlikely, given that other men have died since Glovere,' said Michael. 'I know for a fact that he did not kill Thomas. And if he is innocent of that, then he did not kill the others.' Glibly he omitted the fact that he knew no such thing, and that, as far as Bartholomew was concerned, de Lisle was still firmly on their list of suspects.

Blanche registered her irritation. 'I am not saying that he murdered them with his own hands; I am saying that he issued the instructions and that others obeyed them. De Lisle threatened to kill my steward, and I am sure De Lisle ordered Glovere's death. Pass me one of those trout, will you? It will save me standing.'

Michael produced the ivory-handled knife he used for cutting up his own food, and speared a dead fish on its point. Grease dripped across the table as he transferred it from the serving dish to Blanche's trencher. All around them, hands stretched and grabbed as the retainers began their own meal, although no one spoke. The conversation between Michael and Blanche was too interesting for that.

At that moment, the door opened behind them and Tysilia entered the room with Ralph at her heels. The Bishop's steward looked grey and tired, as though less than a day in Tysilia's company had already drained him of energy. When Tysilia saw Michael, she gave a squeal of delight.

'Michael! I did not expect to find *you* here, although I was going to persuade Ralph to make a detour to see whether we could find you a little later. It will be night, and fewer people will observe us.'

'What are you doing here?' demanded Blanche, none too pleased to see her charge back again. 'I hope the Bishop does not intend to foist you on me a second time. If so, he can think again.'

'He thinks you may try to strangle me,' said Tysilia brightly. 'That is why he has charged Ralph to remain with me at all times, to make sure that you do not.'

'Shall I step outside for a few moments?' Bartholomew heard Ralph mutter to Blanche. The physician was not entirely sure that the words were spoken in jest.

'Then why have you come?' demanded Blanche of Tysilia. 'If you seriously think I might throttle you, you should not be here at all.'

'She says she has left a doll,' said Ralph wearily. 'She claims she will not sleep until she has it. And believe me, I would very much like her to sleep.'

'A doll?' asked Michael doubtfully. 'You mean a child's toy?'

'It is a sorry-looking thing,' said Blanche. 'But she always has it with her in bed – at least, when she is sleeping. It is usually ousted when she has other company.'

'Three would be awfully crowded,' explained Tysilia sincerely. 'Especially if one of them was the size of Brother Michael.' She eyed him up and down in a way that made even Bartholomew feel uncomfortable.

'I can imagine,' said Blanche dryly. 'Your doll is in the window. I was planning to have it delivered to you tomorrow, along with all your other possessions, so that you would not think of returning to me.'

'I would not think of that,' said Tysilia guilelessly. 'I did not like living with you. You are ugly, and you drive away the most handsome men with your sharp tongue. I will have a much happier life with my uncle.'

'Fetch your doll,' snapped Blanche, taking hold of the trout and ripping it apart as if dead fish were not the only things she would like to dismember. Bartholomew thought de Lisle had been wise to remove the aggravating Tysilia from the King's kinswoman. Although Blanche doubtless knew perfectly well that Tysilia was her daughter, he imagined it would be extremely difficult to develop maternal feelings for her.

Tysilia skipped across to a shelf near the window, and began to toss things this way and that as she searched. Meanwhile, Ralph looked around him with interest, as though hoping to learn something he could use against Blanche for the benefit of his Bishop. Bartholomew saw his gaze linger on a pile of documents that lay on a table, but since the steward could not read, staring did him no good.

Michael edged as far as he could from the window where Tysilia was creating havoc among skeins of silk, packets of needles and sundry other objects, and spoke to Blanche's assembled household.

'Do any of you recognise these items?' he asked. He raised the cup so that everyone would be able to see it, and then produced the book of hours. 'Or this book?'

'That cup is mine!' exclaimed Blanche, standing up to snatch it back. 'I always insist that my own vessels are used for masses celebrated in my presence. I missed this two days ago – on Wednesday – and I wondered what had happened to it. I thought it had been stolen.'

She fixed Tysilia with a hard stare, and crammed a large piece of fish into her mouth. Tysilia beamed back at her, and hugged the doll she had finally retrieved. Blanche was right: it was a sorry thing with a painted head that had been chewed and a grubby gown that needed washing.

Bartholomew recalled that Tysilia had been known to steal the property of others in the past, although she had not been very good at hiding what she had taken and was invariably caught before she could profit from her crimes. It was entirely possible that she had taken the cup. But then how had it come to be in the granary with William's coins and the mysterious book of hours? Had she given it to William, perhaps in return for a promise that he would take her with him when he fled? Tysilia had not been happy with

Blanche, and might well have been seduced by a silver tongue that promised freedom in return for treasure. William had a reputation for plots and intrigues, and was perhaps the kind of man to promise something he had no intention of delivering.

'The chalice was hidden in a sack in the barn,' explained Michael. 'Do you have any idea as to how it might have arrived there?' He addressed his question to Blanche, although it was Tysilia at whom he looked.

'No,' said Blanche. 'But my chalice was stolen. It is valuable, so I suppose some thief took a fancy to it. It was a foolish thing to take, because it is not easy to sell church vessels for gold.'

This, too, was directed towards Tysilia, who seemed oblivious to their pointed comments. She stood clutching the doll to her chest, swinging this way and that as she whispered to it. Her eyes, however, were fixed on Michael, and were dark and unreadable.

'I imagine not,' said Bartholomew, declining to ask how Blanche would know that selling stolen church silver was difficult. 'But you noticed it gone on Wednesday, you say? That was when William disappeared.'

'I dislike all the yelling and shrieking as the monks compete with the parish priest in the cathedral, and I decided to hear mass from my own chaplain that evening. When he went to fetch the chalice, he found it gone. He assures me it was there at dawn that day.'

'So, it was stolen between Wednesday morning and dusk,' surmised Michael thoughtfully. 'Has anyone been lurking around here who looks suspicious?'

'Only de Lisle,' said Blanche, unwilling to allow an opportunity to pass without attacking her enemy. 'But I doubt he would muddy his hands by stealing my silver. He prefers to use them for murder these days, and theft is a paltry crime compared to that.'

'My Bishop has killed no one, and he is not a thief,' declared Ralph hotly, taking a menacing step towards her.

Immediately, there was the sound of daggers being whipped from sheaths and several of Blanche's retainers rose quickly to their feet. Ralph surveyed them and decided on a course of prudence, moving back towards the door. His face remained angry, though, and if looks could kill, then Blanche and her entire household would have been buried that day.

'The Lamb is a pleasant place for an ale,' announced Tysilia in the silence that followed, clutching the doll as she made her way towards Michael. She took hold of his arm. 'We shall go there first, then to somewhere more relaxing.'

'We shall not,' said Michael firmly, disentangling himself. 'I have not eaten yet, and I have no energy to romp with you.'

Bartholomew recalled that Michael had feasted handsomely in the refectory not more than an hour before. He supposed the sight of Blanche's repast had whetted the monk's appetite again.

'Do not expect me to give you any of this trout,' said Blanche with her mouth full. 'It is too good to be wasted on fuelling a romp with the Bishop's whore-child.'

'I will be gentle,' insisted Tysilia, reaching for Michael again, but missing when the monk side-stepped her with surprising agility. She snatched at him yet again, and the exercise was repeated several times before she realised she would not catch him. She gave a heavy sigh and folded her arms, pouting, while the courtiers and Ralph watched in open amusement.

'It is time you went home to de Lisle,' said Bartholomew, deciding to put an end to the spectacle. He took her arm and pulled her towards the door. 'He will be wondering where you are, and may be worried about you.'

'He knows Ralph is with me,' said Tysilia, trying to struggle away from him. 'And Ralph will allow me to come to no harm.'

'De Lisle would never forgive me if I did,' muttered Ralph resentfully. 'Although I do not think he has any idea about the enormity of the task he has set me.'

'Feign sickness tomorrow and let her spend a day in *his* company,' advised Blanche. 'That is all that will be necessary for her to be found floating face-down in the river at the Monks' Hythe.'

'Come on,' said Bartholomew, pushing Tysilia out of the chamber in front of him. She was thick-skinned and resilient and he did not like her, but even he felt uncomfortable to hear her murder discussed in such earnest tones.

'Why does Brother Michael not want to spend an evening with me?' pouted Tysilia, as she stood with Bartholomew outside the Outer Hostry. Ralph was with them, although he kept his distance, evidently deciding that every moment she was speaking to Bartholomew was a moment less he would have to deal with her. Sensibly, Michael remained inside with Blanche, asking more questions about the stolen cup and her knowledge of the monks who had been murdered. Bartholomew could hear Blanche declaring that she despised Robert for his obsequiousness, Thomas for his selfishness and gluttony, and William for his secret ways. Blanche, it seemed, had little good to say about anyone.

'Well?' demanded Tysilia, when Bartholomew did not reply. 'I am beautiful, so Michael has no reason to resist me. Why does he?'

'He is a monk,' said Bartholomew gently. 'Monks do not form liaisons with women; they swore sacred vows not to do so.'

'Michael swore such a vow?' asked Tysilia, wide-eyed, as if she had never encountered the notion of celibacy before. 'What is wrong with him? Does he have some disease that prevents him from enjoying himself with women? Or some physical difficulty?'

'No,' said Bartholomew, who was sure Michael had no problems whatsoever in that area. 'But you should not pursue him so brazenly. He does not like it.'

'How could he not like being pursued by me?' asked

Tysilia. 'I am a goddess: my body is perfect and I have a good mind. Blanche also says I am easy, which must also be a good thing.'

'Oh,' said Bartholomew, at a loss for words. He hated conversations with Tysilia: they rambled in whatever direction she chose and left him wary and bewildered.

Tysilia turned doe eyes on him, great black pools with no spark of life in them at all. 'Being easy is better than being difficult. My uncle says Blanche is difficult and no one likes her. Therefore, being easy is a virtue.' She smiled proudly, pleased with her reasoning.

'Did you take Blanche's chalice?' asked Bartholomew, feeling the need to take control of the discussion.

'Me?' asked Tysilia innocently. 'Why would I do that?'

'To give to William, in exchange for a promise that he would take you away from Blanche. Who told you he was your brother? Him?'

'Yes,' said Tysilia. 'But he has no reason to lie, and I have always wanted a brother.'

'He is not related to you,' said Bartholomew. 'He is too old, for a start.'

'He said that his family were obliged to part with me when I was infantile. He told me that de Lisle is not my uncle at all – just a family friend.'

'And why would a wealthy family like William's be obliged to pass one of its daughters to a family friend?' asked Bartholomew warily.

Tysilia sighed. 'I cannot remember the details now. He told me all this when we first arrived in Ely – days ago now – and facts slip from my mind after a while. I think he said it was because de Lisle was lonely. I forget why. Perhaps he has sworn one of these vows, like Michael.'

'He has,' said Bartholomew, feeling a surge of anger against William for taking advantage of someone so clearly short of wits. The only good thing was that it would not take Tysilia long to forget her fictitious brother, and that she would soon go back to her normal life – being placed with someone who tried hard to look after her while she made plans to escape that would never work. He wondered whether her sojourn in Ely would result in yet another pregnancy. To his knowledge, she had already been through three, and could not be made to understand the connection between inconvenient children and her promiscuous lifestyle. He was only grateful that Michael had taken fright at her determined wooing.

'Let us go back to the cup,' said Bartholomew, changing the subject. He knew he would not make Tysilia believe that she and William were not related when she had decided that they were.

'What cup?' she asked, looking around her as though she expected one to materialise.

'The cup Blanche claims was stolen,' he said, trying not to become exasperated. 'The one you stole to give to William. Did he ask you to take that particular item?'

'Of course not,' she said indignantly. 'But it was pretty and I thought he would like it.'

'Where is he? You were very worried about him yesterday, and now you do not seem concerned at all. Has he fled this area and gone somewhere safe?'

She clutched her doll tightly, as if she gained strength from it. 'I do not know where he is, but he has not fled, because he said he would take me with him. I am still here, so he must be nearby.'

'So, did you give the cup to William?'

'I *was* going to give it to him to prove my affection, but he did not arrive to meet me as he promised, so I hid it in the cemetery. But you know that, because you found me there.'

'I did not know you were hiding stolen property,' said Bartholomew. 'Did you tell William that you would secrete anything there that you managed to steal?'

'I was not stealing,' said Tysilia crossly. 'I took what *she* owed me for my company over the last few months. The good things in life are not cheap, as my uncle says.'

'Then someone must have seen you putting it there,' mused Bartholomew. 'I suppose it is possible that it was William – that he did not approach you because I was there, and he could not afford to be seen with you.'

He gazed at her vacant face as he thought about what she had told him. Was William the kind of man to relieve a silly woman of her property and then flee with it to save himself from the killer? Had he put the cup in the bag in the granary, along with the book and the gold? But then why had he left it? Did he plan to return, and take not only the treasure, but Tysilia, too? Or was he already dead, yet another victim of the killer's slim blade? Or could he be the one with the blade, who was even now fingering it as he considered his next victim?

'Is there any more you can tell me about William or Blanche – or anyone at all – that may help Brother Michael to help catch this killer?'

He did not hold much hope that any significant facts had lodged themselves in the peculiar mess of ideas and fantasies that passed as her mind, and was surprised to see her nod. 'I know a good deal. But I will only tell Brother Michael, since it is *he* who is looking for this killer.'

'We must go,' said Ralph, tired of waiting for her. 'I do not want to lose my job because you have kept me out all day. I like working for the Bishop.'

'What were you going to tell me?' asked Bartholomew of Tysilia. 'I promise to pass any information to Brother Michael.'

'I do not trust you,' said Tysilia. 'I will tell Michael or no one. Tell him to meet me here, at this door, at midnight tonight.'

'How do you think you will gain access to the priory at that hour?' asked Bartholomew, smiling at the ludicrous nature of her proposal. 'And what do you think the Bishop will say when he learns you wander the town at night meeting men?'

'He will not know,' said Tysilia confidently. 'My chamber

is on the ground floor, and I only need to climb out of the window. And I will do what William told me to do when I met *him* late at night. I will borrow my uncle's cloak, raise the hood and join the end of the procession of monks as they leave the cathedral after the midnight mass.'

Bartholomew considered her suggestion. Was Tysilia the cloaked figure who had wandered into the hospital and murdered Thomas while Henry dozed within hearing distance? He shook his head impatiently. He knew perfectly well that she was not sufficiently clever to carry out a careful and meticulous murder and leave no clues. But could she have done it if William had told her how? He rubbed a hand through his hair, but then decided that he could not be more wrong. Tysilia was exactly what she appeared to be, and she did not have the wits to pretend otherwise.

'Michael will not come unless he knows you have something useful to tell him,' he said. 'And I see nothing to suggest that is the case.'

'I will tell him about William,' said Tysilia.

Bartholomew gazed at her. People tended to dismiss her as a lunatic, and to ignore her presence when they were up to no good. Therefore, she often saw or heard things that were important and, occasionally, she even recalled some of it. It was just possible that she had something relevant to say about the hosteller.

'Midnight,' she whispered again, her breath hot on his cheek. 'Tell Brother Michael to come and meet me right here.' She paused, and then treated Bartholomew to a smile that was mostly leer, so that the physician was sure she had more in mind than an innocent exchange of information. 'And tell him to come alone.'

CHAPTER 9

'THE LAST TIME WE ARRANGED TO MEET SOMEONE AFTER dark in a quiet place, he never appeared, and we have seen neither hide nor hair of him since,' grumbled Michael, as he and Bartholomew sat together in the priory refectory later that evening. 'I cannot believe you allowed Tysilia to make the same arrangement with you. Especially on my behalf.'

They had missed the evening meal – Michael because he had been questioning the monks about Thomas's death, and Bartholomew because he had been in the library and had lost track of time – but Michael had learned that Symon had been inaugurated as temporary hosteller in the absence of William, and had hunted him out to provide him with a list of items he would consider devouring at a privately served meal. Too inexperienced to know how to deal with a demanding glutton like Michael, Symon had obliged to the smallest detail, and the repast that was set out in front of them was intimidating.

'This is enough to feed King Edward's entire army,' said Bartholomew, eyeing the spread in dismay. 'How do you imagine we will ever finish it?'

'Experience tells me that we shall make a respectable impact,' said Michael comfortably, tucking a piece of linen under his chin, and rubbing his hands together. He looked like Blanche, so sure she would make a mess that she took precautions before she began. 'And what we do not finish will be given to the poor, so we are doing them a favour, in a way.'

It seemed a peculiar way of viewing matters, but Bartholomew was in no mood for an argument. His mind was still fixed on Thomas, and how the killer had waited until the sick man had been left alone before slipping unseen into the hospital to do his deadly work. It did not make him feel easy, and a chilling sensation ran down the back of his neck. He glanced behind him, half expecting to see someone with a thin blade in his hand. He almost jumped out of his skin when he saw Bishop Northburgh there, with Canon Stretton at his heels.

'God's teeth!' he exclaimed. 'It is not wise to sneak up behind men when there is a killer on the loose, my Lord Bishop. You will cause them to have seizures, like Sub-prior Thomas.'

'I am not the kind of man to have seizures,' said Northburgh with a vague smile. Bartholomew stared at him. The Bishop of Coventry and Lichfield was persistently fluttery and irritable, and the mere mention of a disease induced him to imagine its symptoms, but now he seemed unnaturally calm. In fact, Bartholomew thought there was something not quite right about the man. He glanced at Stretton, whose heavy features were creased into a curiously beatific grin, and wondered what they had been doing together.

'How is your investigation coming along?' Northburgh asked pleasantly of Michael. 'Discovered anything new?'

'But *you* resolved the case the moment you arrived, Northburgh,' said Stretton fawningly to his companion, his voice rather slurred. 'De Lisle said he did not kill Glovere.'

'True, but someone did,' said Northburgh. 'And that is why we are here, Brother Michael. We are enjoying our sojourn in Ely, and Henry is working to find a cure for wrinkled skin for me, but I feel we should be doing something *more* about these charges laid against poor de Lisle.'

'You should not drive Henry to pursue pointless remedies,' said Bartholomew, nettled by the man's insensitivity. 'He is exhausted from looking after his old men and distressed by the death of Thomas. He needs to rest, not scour the library for literature on your behalf.'

'I have promised Ely Cathedral a chapel if Henry can oblige me,' said Northburgh, strangely unperturbed by Bartholomew's sharp reprimand. 'Alan will ensure he succeeds.'

'So, what do you want from us?' asked Michael warily. 'I know of no cure for gizzard neck, and Matt is too busy to start experimenting with animal grease and nut juice.'

'We have decided that we want *you* to investigate these murders, Brother,' said Stretton, sounding rather surprised by Michael's question. 'Northburgh thinks we should not leave until we have a culprit hanged, and we thought we should allow *you* to find us one.'

'Too many men making enquiries could cause problems,' elaborated Northburgh. 'So, Stretton and I have elected to let you do it.'

Michael regarded them through narrowed eyes. 'That is what I have been doing – while you have been pestering Henry or enjoying the ale in the city's taverns. What has changed?'

'There is no need to be defensive,' said Northburgh with a dreamy smile. 'We are only offering to stand back and give you full rein to do as you please. But I am weary. I think I shall retire to bed.'

He turned and walked away, with Stretton lumbering behind him. He tripped over the doorstep, and Stretton made a clumsy lunge to save him that had them both staggering. Their chuckles echoed across the courtyard as they made their way to the Black Hostry, arm in arm. Michael stared after them in amazement. Bartholomew laughed.

'Ely's bona cervisia is powerful stuff indeed, if it can turn that ill-matched pair into friends.'

Michael grimaced. 'Alan and Blanche were insane to hire either of them. That de Lisle chose *me* shows him to be a man of impeccable judgement. Unlike you. What were you thinking of by agreeing for me to meet Tysilia at midnight?'

'I am sorry, Brother, but she was intractable. I do not want to wander the priory in the dead of night with a killer on the loose, either, but she said she would only tell *you* what she knows.'

'What she knows!' snorted Michael in disgust. 'She knows nothing!'

'You cannot be sure,' objected Bartholomew. 'William may have let something slip about his plans. She will not know she possesses this important information, of course. It will have to be prised from her by someone who is an experienced and gifted investigator.'

'Perhaps,' admitted Michael, succumbing to the flattery as he reached for a dish of stewed onions. 'But I would be happier doing it tomorrow, in daylight. You should have tried harder to dissuade her from insisting on such an hour. How will you feel if someone murders us?'

'Dead, I imagine,' replied Bartholomew.

Michael ignored him. 'We have assumed the killer is a man, but what if it is a woman? It may be Tysilia herself, and here we are meeting her in a remote place at the witching hour!'

'First, there are two of us, and I am sure we can manage Tysilia. Second, the door to the Outer Hostry is not a remote place. It is relatively public.'

'Not at that time of night,' complained Michael. He finished the stew and snatched up a jellied eel and a slice of cheese, eating alternate bites. 'But what do you think of Tysilia as our killer, Matt? There is plenty of evidence to incriminate her.'

Bartholomew laughed in astonishment. 'There is not! I suppose you think that her clandestine meetings with William count against her?'

'They do,' agreed Michael. 'William disappeared after curious assignations with this woman. Meanwhile, she claims he is her brother, while we know perfectly well he is not. And you do not steal valuable chalices to give to your sibling, Matt: you steal them to give to your paramour.'

'You seem to know a lot about this,' remarked Bartholomew. 'What has she brought *you*?'

Michael made an irritable sound at the back of his throat. 'This is no joking matter. We questioned Tysilia's involvement in a case once before, unless you have forgotten. It is possible she is imbued with a certain animal cunning behind all that empty-headed prattling.'

'She is certainly imbued with feral emotions, but cunning is not one of them. She is an innocent, Brother, not capable of carrying out complex murders. William spun her some tale about kinship, and she believed it because she longs to escape from people who keep her wild behaviour under control.'

'Imagine what she would be like if they did not,' muttered Michael with a shudder.

'She is gullible and vulnerable, and easy prey for a clever man like William. He doubtless saw that seducing her would be far too simple——'

'It would not!' interrupted Michael fervently. 'He would never manage to seduce her before she had seduced him!'

'——and so he decided to adopt a different approach. By claiming kinship, he demanded a loyalty that she would never have afforded a mere lover. She spied on Blanche, and she stole for someone she thought was her brother. But that is all. She is not our killer, and if you think so, then you are as addled as she is.'

'You are the addled one – for agreeing to meet her in the dead of night. It is just an excuse to entice me out alone, so that she can force her attentions on me.'

'I am sure you can look after yourself,' said Bartholomew, trying not to laugh at the image of Michael as the besieged virgin.

'You suggested that William was the killer, and now you make arrangements for us to meet his accomplice in the dark,' Michael went on, unwilling to let matters lie. 'How do you know she has not been given the task of luring us out, so that he can kill us both?'

'It would be hard to kill two people at the same time. We will not lie down obediently while William murders one in front of the other. And it was only a passing suggestion as regards William as the culprit, anyway. I suspect he is already dead.'

'You have no evidence to support that,' warned Michael.

'No,' admitted Bartholomew.

'If I had any sense, I would send *you* to meet her alone. And then we will see how you feel.'

'I would not mind,' said Bartholomew with a shrug. 'But it would be a waste of time. She wants to speak to you, not me. But I do not think there is anything to fear in meeting her.'

Michael regarded his friend sombrely. 'I hope you are right, Matt. I really do.'

Bartholomew fell asleep while they waited to go out, and was woken some hours later by Michael shaking his shoulder. Blearily, not quite understanding why he was being pulled from a deep sleep, he reached instinctively for his medicine bag. Michael chuckled.

'I do not think you will be needing that, although you can bring those birthing forceps if you like. They are a formidable weapon, and we can always knock this woman over the head if she attempts to lay hands on my person.'

Bartholomew slipped the handle of his medicine bag over his shoulder. He did not feel quite dressed without it, and it seemed that he always wanted it if he did not have it with him. He followed Michael out of the refectory, and across the dark grass towards the Outer Hostry. Evidently, Lady Blanche and her household did not like early nights, because lights still blazed in one or two rooms. Laughter drifted across the courtyard, too; it seemed that she and her courtiers were enjoying themselves. It sounded to Bartholomew as though they were playing dice or some other gambling game, and Bartholomew wondered what Alan would say if he knew such activities were being carried out on the sacred grounds of his cathedral priory. On reflection, he supposed that Alan would say very little. Blanche was a generous patron, and Alan would never risk losing funds for his beloved buildings.

The hour candle had burned past midnight when Bartholomew and Michael reached the Outer Hostry. There was no moon and a film of clouds drifted across the sky, making the faint light from the stars patchy and unreliable. The clouds had turned the evening humid and thick; the still air stank of the fetid odour of marshes and carried the distinctive smell of sewage from the river.

Bartholomew led the way to the gate, and pulled Michael into the shadows when he detected a movement out of the corner of his eye. There was a soft murmur of voices, as those monks who had attended the midnight mass made their way to the dormitory. There were not many of them: the majority preferred a good night's sleep, and Alan did not insist on attendance at the midnight service. The other seven offices were a different matter, and Bartholomew had seen Thomas taking the names of anyone absent from those without a valid excuse.

'She is not here,' whispered Michael crossly, peering around him. 'Damned woman! She is probably tucked up in her bed enjoying her sleep – which is where we should be.'

Bartholomew called Tysilia's name softly, and was rather surprised when she suddenly materialised out of the darkness. Michael jumped violently and edged away in alarm.

'What are you doing?' he demanded, pressing a fat hand to his pounding heart. 'It is not nice to loom out of the darkness and startle innocent men.'

'Are you innocent, Brother?' breathed Tysilia huskily. 'Shall we find out?'

'We shall not!' said Michael firmly, and Bartholomew heard the distinctive sound of a hand being slapped away. 'Behave yourself! What would Blanche say if she found you here unescorted with two men in the middle of the night?'

'I imagine she would be rather jealous when she saw that one of the men was you,' gushed Tysilia. 'I think she has taken a liking to you herself. And anyway, she met a lot of young men alone in the dark when she was young. She told me so herself.'

'What do you mean?' asked Michael, interested, despite his nervousness.

'I mean that she had lots of lovers before her marriage,' explained Tysilia patiently. 'She told me about a churchman she wooed, because she said she did not want me to fall into the same pit. She said he gave her a child, and that it had almost ruined her life.'

'And what did you think of that?' asked Michael curiously.

'I told her that my lovers had already given me three children, but that the brats either died before I ever saw them, or someone kindly took them off my hands. She seemed rather shocked. I cannot imagine why, when all I did was tell her that we had shared the same experiment.'

'Experience,' corrected Bartholomew before he could stop himself. 'What else did she say?'

'She gave me lots of meaningful looks and kept holding my hands. I had no idea what she was trying to tell me. I do not know why she did not just come out and say whatever it was.'

'Did it ever occur to you that your mother might have been a lady like Blanche?' asked Michael. Bartholomew held his breath. Educating Tysilia about her parentage was not something for discussing at such a time or in such a place, and he was surprised that Michael was prepared to broach such a delicate subject.

'Of course,' said Tysilia carelessly. 'But she must have been a real beauty to produce me, so that takes Blanche out of the running. *She* looks like a pig.'

'De Lisle told me that Blanche was extremely pretty when she was young,' pressed Michael.

'But he has sworn one of those vows of celery, so he is no judge,' said Tysilia.

For the first time, it occurred to Bartholomew that in later life Tysilia might come to resemble the woman she

claimed to find so ugly. Tysilia would be a lot bigger than
the squat, buxom Blanche, and the combination would not
be an attractive one. He had always considered Tysilia's
claims of beauty rather exaggerated in any case. He felt a
surge of compassion for the bleak future she faced, when
her looks would no longer guarantee her the lovers she
craved.

'Anyway,' Tysilia went on, 'there is a very good reason
why Blanche cannot have mothered me. She is not William's
mother, so she cannot be mine.'

'Lord!' breathed Michael in exasperation. Bartholomew
heard him clear his throat, then adopt a more reasonable
tone. 'Tell us about William. How did you meet? Was he
ever your lover?'

Tysilia sighed heavily. 'Of course not! I am not a pervert,
you know.' She turned to Bartholomew. 'You should tell
Michael that decent women do not take their siblings to
bed.'

'I am sure he needs no tuition from me about suitable
bed-mates,' said Bartholomew. 'But why did you take
Blanche's cup?'

'I took it because William promised to spirit me away
from this place,' said Tysilia. 'I happen to know that staying
in clean taverns and hiring horses is expensive. I have travelled a lot while attending the University of Life.'

'Did you take the book, too?' asked Bartholomew,
ignoring the fact that most of the time she was locked up
somewhere fairly remote.

'No. I only removed things that would be easy to sell.'

'A chalice would not have been easy,' Bartholomew
pointed out.

'Any monk or friar would take it,' said Tysilia carelessly,
and Bartholomew could see the white gleam of her vacant
grin, even in the darkness. 'They spend all their lives in
churches, and so we could have sold a chalice to any of them.'

'Not many would buy one that they thought was stolen,'
said Bartholomew.

'Rubbish,' said Tysilia and Michael at the same time. Bartholomew saw Tysilia interpret this as a sign that they were made for each other, and she moved closer to him again. Michael stepped around Bartholomew, and the physician found himself in the middle of an unpleasant grappling contest until he pushed them both firmly away.

'Do you think one of Blanche's retinue might have owned this book?' he asked tiredly. It was very late, and he was growing weary of prising information from Tysilia. He began to acknowledge that Michael was right, and that she knew nothing worth telling after all.

'None of them can read,' said Tysilia. 'A book is no good if you cannot read it, unless it has a lot of pictures. Those are the ones I like.'

'Tell us about William,' said Bartholomew, electing not to mention that the book they had found was full of beautiful illustrations. That she seemed not to know was probably proof that she was not the person who had stolen it. He sensed Michael was as exasperated with the interview as he was, and decided it was time to draw it to a close. 'You said you knew a lot about him earlier. You were afraid that he might be in danger. Are you still afraid?'

'I had forgotten about that,' said Tysilia, glancing around her in agitation. 'You should not have reminded me. Now I feel frightened, and Michael will have to put his arms around me.'

'Michael will not,' said the monk firmly. 'Why did you think William was in danger?'

'Glovere was dead,' replied Tysilia. 'And William said that he and I would be the killer's next victims.'

'Why did he say that?' asked Bartholomew, feeling that they were finally getting somewhere.

'Because I was speaking too loudly,' said Tysilia sulkily. 'He said we would be next because I was shouting, and that people would see us together when we met in the cemetery.'

Michael made an impatient sound. 'He did not mean that

literally. It sounds as though he was just trying to make you understand the need for discretion.'

'Glovere died because he had enemies,' Tysilia went on, oblivious to Michael's frustration. 'When I was still with Blanche, he told me that someone might try to kill him. He did not appear to take it seriously. But it seems he should have done.'

'Who was going to kill him?' demanded Michael immediately.

'I do not know. Blanche said he was talking about the Bishop, but dear, sweet Uncle would harm no one. And then later, when I met William again, he told me there were dangerous people in Ely. He did not say who, though, before you ask.'

'I see,' said Michael. When he spoke again, his voice was more gentle; apparently he had decided he would learn more from her with kindness. 'We must catch the killer before more lives are lost, Tysilia. Can you think of anything – anything at all – that might help us? Did William give you any clues about the identity of the killer?'

'No,' said Tysilia. 'He talked about the places we would see together when we left Ely, but he said we would always come back here.'

'Did he indeed?' said Michael, surprised. 'I had assumed that his removal of some of the priory's property would have eliminated the notion of a triumphant return. Where did he say you might go?'

'Upriver,' said Tysilia. 'But only for a short time. He was going to be Prior when Alan died, then Bishop when my uncle dies.'

'How long have you known William?' asked Bartholomew.

Tysilia regarded him uncertainly. 'He is my brother. So I have known him since I was born, although I only met him a few days ago. But why are you asking all these questions when Michael and I could be doing something much more fun?'

'Did you notice any change in William's behaviour as time

went on?' asked Bartholomew, refusing to become side-tracked. 'Has he seemed different to you? Nervous or uneasy?'

'Of course,' said Tysilia. 'There is a killer on the loose. Who in his right mind would not be nervous or uneasy? That is why I am nervous and uneasy. I am in my right mind, you see.'

'Thank you,' said Michael. 'You have been very helpful.'

'I know,' said Tysilia confidently. 'Everything I say is interesting and useful. But you owe me something for all my time. What do you say to a little—'

'Matt will see you safely home,' said Michael briskly, stepping away from her exploring hands once again. 'I am too tired for anything you have in mind.'

'But that is not fair!' cried Tysilia in abject disappointment. Her voice was loud, and Bartholomew heard a lull in the chatter from the Outer Hostry above. 'I have helped you, and now you must give me what I want.'

'It is *not* fair,' muttered Bartholomew to Michael. 'I do not want to wander the town in the dark, either. I want to go to bed.'

'But I do not want *you* in my bed,' pouted Tysilia, mistaking his words for an offer. 'I want Brother Michael.'

'I am not available,' proclaimed Michael grandly. 'Go home, Tysilia, and take a cold bath.'

'That was a waste of time,' grumbled Michael when Bartholomew returned from seeing Tysilia safely back through the Bishop's window a little later. The monk was waiting by the Steeple Gate so that some officious doorkeeper would not lock the physician out. He need not have worried: the lay-brother who guarded the door was sleeping soundly in his small chamber, and Michael was surprised his snores could not be heard by the Prior in his quarters. He recalled that Welles claimed to have slipped past him around the time that Thomas was murdered. 'We should not have bothered to disturb our rest for that.'

'No,' agreed Bartholomew. 'So why did you tell her she had been helpful? She was not.'

'Tactics,' replied Michael, vaguely. 'If she is the accomplice of an evil killer, then he will be worried by my claim that she has assisted us. It may make him sufficiently anxious to do something rash, and may serve to flush him out.'

'Or it may tell the killer that we know more than we do and put our lives in danger. I am not sure that was a wise thing to do.'

'We shall see,' said Michael carelessly, as he closed the gate. 'But it is irrelevant anyway: she knows nothing of interest and my cleverness was wasted.'

'Do you think William is the killer?' asked Bartholomew. 'And that he is watching the city from a safe distance before selecting his next victim?'

'I have no idea what William is or what his motives were in leaving. How Tysilia could believe that he is her brother is wholly beyond my understanding.'

'She believes what she wishes were true,' said Bartholomew. 'Poor Blanche. It sounds as if she tried hard to communicate with Tysilia, but Tysilia was too stupid to understand what she was being told.'

'Well, we will find out more tomorrow,' said Michael. 'We shall go upriver and see whether we can find this spot where the townsmen were murdered. Perhaps we will learn something new then.'

'I hope so, Brother,' said Bartholomew soberly. 'Because if not, we have reached a dead end, and I do not know which way to turn next.'

Michael sighed. 'The annoying thing is that I do not feel like sleeping any more. That Tysilia has unnerved me. I am wide awake, and my mind is teeming with questions.'

'You will fall asleep once you lie down,' said Bartholomew, who was suffering from no such complaint and was extremely drowsy.

'I will not,' declared Michael with grim determination. 'I shall lie awake for hours. Then I shall disturb Northburgh and Stretton, who share my bedchamber. I feel like walking, to tire myself.'

'What, now?' asked Bartholomew, looking around unenthusiastically at the darkened buildings. 'It is pitch black, and you said yourself that the killer could well be at large in the priory grounds. Walking alone in the dark is not a sensible thing to do.'

'I was not thinking of going alone,' said Michael. 'I thought you would come with me. Besides, it is a hot and sticky night. You need to cool down before you head for your own bed.'

Bartholomew groaned. 'You are mad, Brother. But very well. Where do you want to go? Shall we risk breaking our necks on the graves in the cemetery, or shall we settle for a stumble among the roots of the vineyard?'

'We can keep to the paths,' said Michael testily. He gazed up at the sky. The clouds had parted, revealing a huge patch of sugar-spangled velvet. The stars seemed more bright than usual in the moonless sky, gleaming and flickering in their thousands. A white smear showed the presence of a belt of stars too small to be seen with the naked eye, although the ancient philosophers assured their readers that they were there.

Since they had met Tysilia, a light breeze had sprung up, rendering the night far more pleasant, despite Michael's grumbles regarding the heat. It fanned their faces, blowing cool air from the east. In it was the faint tang of salt, reminding Bartholomew that a vast boggy sea lay only a few miles away. The breeze carried other scents, too, which were less pleasant: the sulphurous odour of the rotting vegetation and stagnant water that were the cause of so many summer fevers, and the stench of the city itself. Bartholomew fell into step with Michael, allowing the monk to lead them in a wide circle around the north wall of the cathedral and then towards the almonry.

Bartholomew thought about Robert, who had died while looking for William. The almoner now lay next to Thomas in the cathedral's Lady Chapel, a great white whale of a corpse next to one that was darker and more swarthy in death than it had been in life. Both were due to be buried the following day, and the pomp and ceremony that was planned reflected the priory's indignation that two of their number had been mercilessly slain, rather than genuine grief. Only Henry had shown any emotion other than outrage.

The almonry was a two-storeyed building that overlooked Steeple Row, and that had contained Robert's lodgings as well as a dispensary for alms. Next to it was the sacristy, where the sacristan lived, along with all the sacred vessels and vestments that belonged to the cathedral and the monastery. Then there was a stretch of wall, and then the Bone House, where they had examined Glovere.

Bartholomew gazed at the Bone House with unease, thinking it a sinister place. He had encountered charnel houses aplenty, but these tended to be repositories for bones that were so ancient that they were all but unrecognisable. The Bone House contained rows of grinning skulls, many of them still boasting fragments of hair and patches of dried skin. One had even worn a hat – slipped at a crazy angle across one eye, but a cap, nevertheless.

'There is a light in the Bone House,' he said, startled out of his grim reverie. 'Did you see it?'

'No,' said Michael, peering through the darkness. 'You must have imagined it. No one is likely to be in the Bone House in the middle of the night.'

'There it is again!' exclaimed Bartholomew. There was a flicker, just under the shutter of the upper window. 'You must have seen it!'

Michael frowned. 'No one should be in there. Only a madman would want to be in the company of all those dead folk in the dark.'

'Perhaps a madman, like our killer,' said Bartholomew, gripping Michael's arm, as a way to solve the murders suddenly opened up to him. 'We should investigate this.'

'We should find Cynric and Meadowman,' said Michael, holding back. 'This killer is a dangerous man.'

'You are not afraid, are you?' asked Bartholomew, surprised by the monk's reluctance to investigate. 'He is only one man, Brother; we can tackle him between us.'

'How do you know he is only one man? We have always assumed it is a single person, but there is nothing to confirm that we are right. It could be a group of men, all armed to the teeth, and with a good deal more experience of fulfilling their murderous intentions than either of us.'

'I do not think so. Our killer works alone.'

'And how are you suddenly so certain, pray?'

'Simple logic, Brother. If there were two or more, working together, then one would hold the victim still while the other did the cutting. The grazing on the face and ear indicates that the victims were held down by means of a foot or a knee on their heads. There would be no reason to use feet and knees while there were hands to spare. *Ergo*, these murders look like the work of a single man.'

'And you are prepared to stake your life on this reasoning?' asked Michael doubtfully.

'We have no choice. At the very least we have to investigate. We have been bemoaning the fact that the mystery seems to deepen with every fact we uncover, but here is an opportunity to catch the man himself.'

'Of course, whatever we uncover in there might have nothing to do with the killer,' Michael pointed out. 'It could be someone with an unnatural penchant for bones in the dark.'

'True,' said Bartholomew. 'And in that case, we have nothing to fear.'

'Nothing much!' exclaimed Michael. 'I do not want to catch that sort of person red-handed, thank you very much. He would probably try to kill us just to keep his foul obsession a secret.'

Tapping Michael sharply on the shoulder to give him encouragement, the physician began to edge towards the

Bone House, taking care to tread carefully and to keep to the shadows. As they moved, he saw the flicker at the upper window a third time, and suspected that someone was walking back and forth, carrying a candle. It could not have provided much light, because the glimmer at the bottom of the window shutter was very slight and would not have been seen by anyone unless he happened to be looking at the Bone House at fairly close quarters. Whoever was inside doubtless imagined himself perfectly safe from discovery.

'How many doors does this place have?' whispered Bartholomew.

'One, of course,' replied Michael scornfully. 'It is not somewhere that requires multiple entrances and exits.'

'And how many windows?'

'I do not know,' whispered Michael crossly. 'Two, I suppose – one on the upper floor, and one on the lower. But you have been in there yourself. Why are you asking me?'

'It is your priory. You know it better than me.' Bartholomew stood back to assess the building, piecing together what he could see with what he remembered. 'Does it comprise a single chamber on the ground floor with a ladder leading to a single loft on the upper floor?'

'I have only been inside it once and that was with you,' grumbled Michael. 'But yes, I think so. The bones are on the ground floor, while the loft is probably empty.'

'Except for whoever is up there at the moment. I will go in through the door, while you stand at this corner and make sure that no one escapes through either window.' He unlooped his medical bag from his shoulder and removed his heavy childbirth forceps, holding them in his right hand, as he would a club. Then he stuck one of his surgical knives in his belt.

'Are you insane?' demanded Michael, eyeing his preparations in alarm. 'I was right in the first place: we should not do this alone. If we fail, the consequences do not bear thinking about. We cannot afford to let this man – or these men – escape and continue the bloody work.'

'But he may be gone by the time we fetch Cynric and Meadowman,' objected Bartholomew. 'And it would be a terrible thing to let this opportunity pass.'

'It will be no opportunity at all if we are the next victims!'

'But there may *be* no more victims if we can catch him,' argued Bartholomew. 'We cannot risk him escaping now we have him cornered.'

'Very well,' said Michael, clearly reluctant. 'But I am not staying out here alone. Hand me that spade. If I encounter anyone inside, who so much as moves, I shall knock his brains out with it.'

He grasped the stout spade that leaned against the wall of the Bone House, and prepared to follow Bartholomew inside. The physician reached out and silently unlatched the door. As it swung open to reveal the black maw of the charnel house, he began to have second thoughts himself about the wisdom of the plan. Michael was almost certainly right about the killer's cold ruthlessness, and they should have Cynric and Meadowman with them. He turned to admit as much to the monk, but Michael prodded him in the back, urging him to go ahead before he lost his nerve. Taking a deep breath that was tinged with the musty, wet smell of rotting bone, Bartholomew took a step forward into the house of the dead.

Inside the Bone House, the darkness was absolute after the starlight. Bartholomew and Michael waited for a few moments until their eyes became accustomed to the gloom. The skulls still sat in their eerie rows on shelves, and the dark mass of the pile of long bones could be seen on one side. To the other was the barrel that contained fragments of fingers, toes and crania.

Bartholomew peered around him, ignoring the dead inhabitants of the room and looking for its living occupant. He exchanged a glance with Michael, and then nodded to the ladder that ascended into the darkness of the upper floor. Michael shook his head vehemently, indicating that they should wait until whoever it was came down. Bartholomew hesitated, then nodded agreement. It would be difficult to climb a creaking ladder undetected, and the killer would merely strike at his head as soon as he was high enough. Michael was right: if they waited, then they would have the advantage. Treading silently, he eased into the darkest shadows with Michael next to him.

It seemed that whoever was upstairs had not detected their presence. They could hear his feet on the boards of the floor as he moved. Bartholomew shivered, suddenly chilled in the dankness. The walls were of wood, but they were thick, to keep their contents from the unwelcome attentions of dogs. The bones had been dug from damp earth, so there was a musty wetness in the atmosphere that was oppressive. Something dripped on his shoulder, and he imagined that while the walls were strong, the thatched roof was in a poor condition. Since the purpose of the Bone House was to deter animals that might make off with the bones, no one would be overly concerned about a leaking roof.

He and Michael waited in the shadows for what seemed like an age. The physician's legs and back began to grow stiff from standing, and the drowsiness he had experienced earlier returned. If he had been sitting down, he would have fallen asleep. Next to him, Michael shifted uncomfortably, and Bartholomew wondered whether he should send the monk to fetch Cynric and Meadowman after all. When he whispered the suggestion into Michael's ear, the monk shook his head vehemently. Although he sensed that they were making a mistake, Bartholomew was grateful for the reassuring presence of Michael at his side. A second drip of water from the roof above was loud in the silence.

Humans, living and dead, were not the only species that inhabited the Bone House. Tiny claws skittered across the floor and rustled in and out of the bones. While the thick walls kept out larger scavengers, rats had found gaps in the planking and had insinuated themselves inside. Bartholomew closed his eyes and listened, certain he could hear small teeth crunching.

After an eternity, there was increased activity from the floor above. The footsteps moved clear across the floor, and then someone began to descend the ladder. He carried a candle, and was moving cautiously, as if wary of falling. Bartholomew made out a pair of feet, then a swinging cloak that hid the clothes that were worn beneath. He strained his eyes, trying to determine whether he knew the person, and whether a monastic habit or secular clothes were being worn. But it was too dark, even with the candle, and Bartholomew could only make out the vaguest of shapes. When the person was halfway down the stairs, Bartholomew jumped in alarm as Michael issued a shriek of victory and dashed from his hiding place to make a grab for the mysterious figure.

If Bartholomew jumped in alarm, his reaction was mild to that of the man on the steps. He jolted violently, lost his grip and fell. The candle cartwheeled downwards and landed on the dirty blanket that had recently been used to cover Glovere's body. The cover began to smoulder, releasing an unsteady, flickering light into the gloomy room.

Michael had anticipated hauling the man down by force, and was not ready for the sudden release of weight. He tumbled to the floor with the man on top of him. Recovering from his fright, Bartholomew sprang to the monk's aid. The fellow on the ground struggled furiously, lashing out with his fists. Bartholomew heard the sharp crack of knuckles contacting nastily with bone, followed by a yelp of pain from Michael. He seized the man by a handful of his cloak and wrenched him away from the monk, who was on his knees with one hand fastened firmly to his nose.

The man stumbled over the pile of long bones, and when he straightened up again he held a femur. Bartholomew, his forceps at the ready, parried the first blow with ease, hearing the bone split as it met the metal. The man struck a second time, and the leg broke, so that the ball joint went cartwheeling away into the darkness. Using the same motion, the man struck upwards, attempting to use the jagged end of the shaft like a knife and catching Bartholomew a bruising blow under the ribs. The physician backed away but tripped over Michael, who was still crawling about on all fours.

Meanwhile, the flames had taken hold of Glovere's blanket and were burning furiously. They crackled and hissed as they consumed the filthy wool, sending sparks snapping across the wooden floor. Some sawdust caught light and started to burn. The Bone House began to fill with white, choking smoke.

The man grabbed a skull and lobbed it towards them. It hit Michael on the shoulder with a hollow crack, then bounced away across the floor. The next one was aimed at the physician's head, and he raised one hand to deflect it, dropping the forceps as he did so. He lunged forward again, aiming to grab the man and then hold him until Michael could help, but the man side-stepped quickly, and Bartholomew found himself with a grip that was inadequate. The force of his lunge caused him to lose his balance, and he fell.

With a dull roar, the fire took hold of something unidentifiable in a corner. As he tumbled, Bartholomew saw that flames were licking towards the pile of old coffins, too, and knew that the ancient wood would make excellent kindling.

He should not have allowed his attention to stray from his assailant. He felt a sudden pressure on his head. He struggled, but the man leaned his whole weight downward, and the physician found he was unable to move. And then he felt the prick of cold metal at the base of his skull.

Just when Bartholomew was certain it was all over, and that he would end his life on a filthy floor in a bone house with Michael soon to follow, the pressure was released. He heard a grunt and another crash, and flinched away as flames came too near his face. He saw Michael hovering above him. The man had gone, and the door was swinging open on its hinges.

'My God, Matt . . .' began the monk unsteadily.

'Where did he go?' demanded Bartholomew, scrambling to his feet.

'He ran through the door. I saw him with that knife at your neck, and I thought—'

'Which way?' Bartholomew made for the entrance. 'Did you see who it was?'

'No, I—'

'You mean he escaped?' shouted Bartholomew aghast, looking this way and that across the dark priory grounds. There was no movement anywhere, in any direction. Their quarry had bested them both and had slipped away into the night. 'But we had him in our clutches!'

'The fire!' shouted Michael. 'Quick! Help me before it takes hold.'

He flapped ineffectually at the flames that licked at the old coffins, making them burn more vigorously than ever. Bartholomew leaned hard against the barrel of bone fragments until it toppled, sending its damp, mouldering contents skittering across the floor. He threw handfuls of them at the sparks until they had been smothered. Shaking and breathless, he walked outside, where he took several breaths of clean night air. He wiped a hand across his face and looked at Michael, then swore softly, startling the monk with a sudden string of obscenities.

'It was not my fault,' began Michael defensively. 'When he fell on me, he knocked me all but witless for a few moments. When I came to my senses, I saw him kneeling on top of you with that nasty little blade gleaming in the firelight, and I thought I was already too late. I hit him with the spade as hard as I could, then came to see if you were still alive.'

'You let him go,' said Bartholomew flatly. 'You should have given chase.'

'I shall, next time,' said Michael stiffly. 'You must excuse me, Matt: I was sentimental enough to place concern for a friend over catching a criminal.'

'I am sorry,' said Bartholomew, relenting when he saw the monk's face was white, and that there was an unhealthy sheen of sweat on it. His nose was bleeding, too.

'*I* am sorry,' said Michael bitterly. 'I am sorry I listened to you in the first place. I *told* you we should have fetched Cynric and Meadowman, and that we would not be able to manage this man by ourselves. I was right and you were wrong.'

'We were careless. We should not have allowed him to defeat us.'

'We should not,' agreed Michael vehemently. 'But next time, we will do what *I* think is right. And I will concentrate all my efforts on catching him and *you* can fend for yourself.'

'Your nose is bleeding,' said Bartholomew, rummaging in his medicine bag and handing the monk a clean piece of linen. 'Sit down and tilt your head back.'

'Not out here, thank you very much,' said Michael stiffly, snatching the linen ungraciously. 'For all I know, that murderer is still close by, watching our every move. I will not sit down and present my throat to him like a lamb for the slaughter.'

'He has long gone,' said Bartholomew. 'He knew he was nearly caught, and will not be lurking around to see what will happen next. I suppose it was the killer, was it?'

'Of course it was!' exploded Michael furiously. 'How can you even ask such a thing, when you lay there with his knee on your head and felt the steel of his blade against your neck? My God, Matt! It is a sight that will haunt my dreams for years to come. I feel sick just thinking about it, and it makes the blood drum in my ears.'

Bartholomew took his arm and led him inside the Bone House. The smoke was dissipating, and the stink of burning was losing its battle against the more powerful odour of rotting bone. He indicated that Michael should perch on the overturned barrel for a few moments, to recover himself. The monk sat heavily, forcing Bartholomew to make a grab for it when it threatened to roll. On the shelf under the window was a small dish and a candle stub, apparently used by workmen when they brought their finds for storage. The physician struck a tinder, and filled the room with an unsteady, flickering light. Michael glanced up at him, and then gasped in horror.

'What is wrong?' demanded Bartholomew, looking around him in alarm.

'Blood!' muttered Michael, rubbing a shaking hand across his eyes. 'Lots of it.'

'Where?' asked Bartholomew, snatching up the candle. Then he saw what Michael meant. The floor was stained dark with congealing blood, much of it scuffed and spread by their feet during the skirmish that had taken place. 'Oh.'

'Not on the floor,' whispered Michael, raising fearful eyes to Bartholomew. 'On you. He must have stabbed you after all. I am having a conversation with a ghost!'

Bartholomew twisted, and saw that the shoulder and arm of his shirt were stained a bright red. Horrified, he felt the back of his neck, but there was no wound that he could find, and certainly no tenderness. He knew very well that some men were stabbed or shot and did not know pain until later, but he was certain he would be able to feel something. And then he remembered the drops of moisture that had dripped as he waited for the killer to descend the ladder. It was not his own blood that stained his shirt. His instincts told him to rush up the ladder immediately, to see if he could help, but the rational part of his mind informed him that there would be little he could do for anyone relieved of as much blood as lay pooled on the floor of the Bone House. His first duty was to the living, to Michael, who gazed at him with eyes that were wide with shock.

'Drink this,' he said, reaching into his bag and producing a phial. It was stronger than the brew he usually used for shocks, but Henry still had his other one. 'And then we will go upstairs and see what has happened.'

'What is it?' asked Michael, regarding the phial suspiciously. 'I do not like drinking medicine handed to me in the dark. You may make a mistake and hand me a purge.'

'Just strong wine.'

'Wine,' said Michael, taking it from him eagerly. 'That is more like it. I had forgotten you have taken to carrying a little something around with you these days.'

'It is not for me, and not for casual drinking,' said Bartholomew. 'It is for emergencies.'

'This *is* an emergency,' said Michael, putting his lips to the neck of the flask and all but emptying it in a single swallow. He took a deep breath and closed his eyes. 'That is better. Wine is indeed a good remedy for unsteady nerves.'

'Are you feeling better, then?' asked Bartholomew, holding the candle closer to Michael's face. He was relieved to see that some of the colour was creeping back into the monk's cheeks, and his eyes were losing their haunted expression.

'I do not know which was worse: having a killer land on me, or seeing him prepared to make an end of you. I thought my lunge with the spade was too late.'

'You hit him?'

'As hard as I could. However, it was not as hard as I would have liked – this is a small room, and there was no opportunity to swing the thing properly. I imagine it brought tears to his eyes, though.'

'Where did you hit him?'

'I was afraid he might duck if I aimed for his head, and then I would be off balance and he might succeed in stabbing us both. I aimed for his shoulders, but actually caught him on the back. Why do you ask?'

'Damn!' muttered Bartholomew. 'If you had injured his face, we might have been able to identify him tomorrow. But it will be difficult to see whether anyone has a bruised back.'

'I should have thought of that,' said Michael caustically. 'I seem to be slipping tonight. First, I let a killer go because

I was more interested in trying to save your life, and then I hit him in a place where you will not be able to see the wound.'

'I did not mean to sound ungracious,' said Bartholomew apologetically. 'I am just frustrated that we had the damned man in our clutches, but he still managed to escape.'

'It is too late to worry about that now. We did our best. It is not our fault we are not experts at wrestling in the dark with murderers, although we have done it often enough. Our performance tonight was not our finest hour. I am not a man for superstition, as you know, but I cannot help but think there was something diabolical about his strength.'

'There was not. We stumbled around like old ladies, and he merely took advantage of our ineptitude. He was not as diabolical as our performance.'

Michael smiled wanly.

'We should look upstairs,' said Bartholomew unenthusiastically. 'Something horrible is up there, and I think we should probably see what it is.'

'You go,' suggested Michael. 'I have seen enough vile things for one night. And anyway, I still feel unsteady around the legs.'

'Do you?' asked Bartholomew, concerned. 'Perhaps I should escort you back to your room, so that you can lie down and rest a while. I can always come back later.'

'We should get it over with,' said Michael, climbing stiffly to his feet. He drained the last of the wine, and handed the empty flask back to Bartholomew. 'That is a decent brew, Matt. I shall have to remember where you keep it.'

Bartholomew walked to the ladder and raised the candle to illuminate the darkness. He could see nothing, except that the rungs of the ladder were stained with red. Some had aged to a dark brown, but the most recent coat was a bright crimson.

'I do not recall seeing these marks when we examined Glovere,' he said. 'Do you?'

'No,' said Michael. 'But I did not look. This is not a

pleasant place, and I remember wanting to finish and be
out as soon as possible.'

'The ladder may have been discoloured before, but blood
was not dripping through the ceiling. I would have noticed
that.' Bartholomew raised the candle again, and inspected
the floor.

'Are you going up, or shall we just stand here and stare
at this mess all night?' demanded Michael peevishly.

'All right,' said Bartholomew irritably. 'I am going. Do
not rush me.' He placed the candle holder between his
teeth and prepared to climb.

With the candle wavering in front of his eyes, he climbed
slowly up the ladder, trying to ignore the unpleasant stick-
iness under his fingers. He wondered who the killer had
dispatched in the chill gloom of the Bone House. Was it
Mackerell or William? Or was it Mackerell or William with
whom they had wrestled downstairs? It had been impossible
to tell much in the dark. Or was the killer someone totally
different – one of the gypsies, perhaps, or de Lisle, or a
monk or one of the townsfolk?

He swallowed hard as he reached the top of the steps, to
fortify himself for the unpleasant sight he was sure he would
see. With his head and shoulders poking into the upper
floor, he took the candle-holder from between his teeth and
looked around.

'What can you see?' whispered Michael urgently. 'Is it
William or Mackerell's exsanguinated corpse up there?'

'Neither,' Bartholomew whispered back. 'No one is here.'

'What?' asked Michael, startled. 'That blood belongs to
someone.'

'Obviously. But its owner is not here.'

'Are   you   sure?'   asked   Michael,   unconvinced.
Bartholomew felt the ladder bend under his feet as the
monk began to climb. 'Let me see.'

Bartholomew clambered into the attic room, and waited
for Michael to heave his bulk up the ladder. Then both men
looked around them.

The attic was essentially bare, with a few shelves nailed to one wall, as if the original builders had anticipated that they would recover more skulls than the ones stored downstairs. Bartholomew suspected that the Bone House was not a popular place to visit, and that the workmen tended to dump their finds in the lower room, then leave as quickly as possible. None were keen to take the additional few steps to carry their finds to the upper floor, and so while the downstairs was crammed to the gills, the upper room was empty. And now, because the foundations for the parish church and the Lady Chapel were completed, and the finds were becoming infrequent, it was unlikely that the upper floor would receive any bony remains at all.

However, someone had found a use for it. A crate had been carried up the steps and placed upside down, so that it could be used as a seat, while two of the shelves had been pulled from the wall and balanced between the windowsill and a roof post, forming a kind of workbench. On it were pots and bottles, and a large vat of a red substance that Bartholomew knew was blood. He gazed down at the floor, revolted to see that it was deeply impregnated with the stuff, and that it felt sticky under his feet. It stank, too, the earthy sweetness of fresh blood overlying the bad odour of something rotten.

'What is that awful smell?' asked Michael, repelled. 'And what was the fellow doing here?'

'I have no idea,' said Bartholomew. He began to pick up bottles at random, sniffing at their contents and tipping them this way and that so that he could examine them in the candlelight.

'It looks like a workshop,' said Michael, peering into the farthest corners. 'Perhaps that is why you saw so little bleeding on the victims: perhaps he drained their blood when they died to use here.'

'It would not be easy to exsanguinate someone from a small puncture wound in the back of the neck. If you wanted to kill for blood, you would have to slit a major vessel, and keep the person alive as long as possible, so that it all drains out.'

'Like butchers with pigs,' said Michael distastefully. 'I have never liked blood pudding for exactly that reason. But is that what happened here – the killer wanted his victims' blood?'

'I cannot begin to imagine what he was doing, but there are pots of what appear to be different kinds of soil: here is peat, and this looks like the clay we have near Cambridge, while this small one seems to be powdered gold.'

Michael went to prod about under the eaves. He was silent for a moment, then gave a shrill shriek before leaping backward.

'What is the matter?' asked Bartholomew unsteadily, afraid the monk had finally found something truly repellent.

'There,' whispered Michael, pointing.

Bartholomew peered into the darkness and saw what had so alarmed the monk. In a piece of sacking, untidily wrapped, protruded the bloody end of a recently chopped bone.

'It is all right,' said Bartholomew, speaking in a voice that betrayed his relief as he studied the grisly object. 'It is only part of a pig.'

'A pig?' echoed Michael, his face pale in the candlelight. 'Are you sure?'

'You can tell by the shape. It is fairly fresh, and leads me to believe that the bucket of blood on the bench may belong to the same animal. There is nothing here to suggest it is human.'

'There is not a great deal to suggest it is not,' countered Michael, gazing around him with a shudder. 'I do not like being here, Matt. We have assumed the killer has gone, but he is not like other criminals we have encountered, and he does not do what we expect.'

Bartholomew followed him down the ladder, and then

into the comparative warmth of the night air outside, grateful to be away from the Bone House and its sinister contents. He walked with the monk towards the Black Hostry, taking deep breaths of air to clear the cloying odour of death from his lungs. He felt a certain unsteadiness in his own knees, and wished he had not allowed the monk to drink all his wine; a sip or two would be just the thing to calm his battered nerves.

'There is the call for lauds,' said Michael, as a small bell began to chime. 'It is almost morning, and we have been chasing shadows all night.'

'But we have learned little of interest,' said Bartholomew gloomily. 'We know that the killer collects phials of soil and pig blood, but we have no idea why. And we know he is an able fighter who bested us with ease.'

'Tysilia told us nothing of use, and we are still missing William and Mackerell. It would not surprise me at all to learn that they are both dead.'

'We will rest for an hour or two, and then walk up the river, to see what we can find. And while we are out, we can visit Mackerell's house. Perhaps he is in it, hiding.'

'We can try, I suppose,' said Michael without enthusiasm. 'But I have searched it twice already and found nothing to help us. Do you think *he* is the man who likes making blood pies in the Bone House?'

'Symon did say he thought he saw him in the priory grounds the other day,' said Bartholomew thoughtfully. 'But William is more my idea of a killer than Mackerell.'

'Mackerell is foul tempered, abusive and dishonest. And William is cunning and sly. Both possess qualities that may make them murderers.'

'Perhaps we will learn which one is our culprit tomorrow,' said Bartholomew tiredly.

'I do not believe that traipsing all over the countryside will achieve anything. Still, it is better than sitting here and dwelling on our failure. We will sleep until the breakfast bell rings, eat a little something, and then do as you suggest and wander upriver. If we leave early, it will not be too hot.'

Bartholomew went straight to his bed, then slept like the dead for three hours. He woke feeling sluggish and tired. He ate breakfast alone in the infirmary, while Henry fussed over his old men, and Julian and Welles were nowhere to be seen. Breakfast comprised more of the priory's delicious bread, a plate of smoked eels and a dish of apples. He considered visiting Ely more often, where he fared far better in the culinary department than at Michaelhouse. It was good to experience a change from watery oatmeal and cloudy breakfast ale, even if such luxuries did come attached to wrestling with killers in bone houses in the middle of the night.

When he had finished eating, he went to talk to Henry. The infirmarian seemed listless, and Bartholomew suspected he had spent much of the night in prayer, asking forgiveness for the neglect that had brought about the sub-prior's death. He gave Bartholomew a wan smile, and leaned back in his chair, putting down the pen with which he had been writing.

'It looks as though you slept badly again,' said Bartholomew sympathetically.

'I was in the cathedral until well after midnight, and then exhaustion overtook me. But, when I came to my bed, I found that every time I closed my eyes, the spectre of Thomas arose before me.'

'Spectre?' asked Bartholomew uncertainly. Somehow, he could not envisage the obese sub-prior in ghostly form. It would be more amusing than disturbing.

'Yes,' said Henry, pointing a finger in accusation. 'I think his spirit blames me for where it is.'

'Purgatory?'

Henry shook his head. 'Hell! A man like Thomas will not be in Purgatory: he was too selfish and greedy. But did you learn anything from your meeting with that woman? You told me you were going to meet the Bishop's niece, although how a good man like that can be related to such a wanton soul is wholly beyond me.'

'De Lisle is fond of her,' said Bartholomew carefully, not wanting the kindly infirmarian to know that the relationship was a good deal closer than everyone was led to believe.

'Yes, he is,' agreed Henry. 'He is complex: arrogant and condescending one moment, but capable of great acts of kindness and compassion the next. Did you know that during the Death he was tireless in his care of the sick? He visited the houses of the poor to grant them absolution before they died without a thought for his own safety. How many bishops did that?'

'Not many,' agreed Bartholomew. 'And his care of Tysilia shows him in a good light. He has taken her to all sorts of places in an attempt to find somewhere she might be happy. She even spent a short spell in a leper hospital.'

'Why there?' asked Henry, bewildered. 'That does not sound very safe.'

'Brother Urban is good with diseases of the mind, and de Lisle wanted him to observe Tysilia, to see whether anything could be done for her.'

'Nothing can,' said Henry confidently. 'The disease is permanent and incurable. She is a lunatic, and that is all there is to it. She is probably harmless, but she will never find a place in normal society.'

Bartholomew's own experiences with Tysilia led him to concur with Henry's diagnosis. 'She told us little of use last night. Everything she said was hearsay, and she knows nothing that can help us. But you say you left the cathedral after midnight. Did you see anything unusual?'

'Such as what?'

'Michael and I met the killer last night. He was doing something horrible with pots of dirt and what appeared to be the parts of a dead pig. We disturbed him at his work and wrestled with him, but he escaped.'

'You encountered him?' breathed Henry in horror. 'You had this man in your grasp and you let him go?'

'We did not do it intentionally,' said Bartholomew, slightly testily. 'But it happened just after midnight, so did you see anything?'

Henry shook his head slowly. 'Nothing that could be relevant. The gypsies were at St Etheldreda's shrine for a long time.'

'When, exactly?' Bartholomew pounced. 'And why?'

'They were kneeling at the altar. But they have as much right to be there as anyone else. Just because they are strangers, with a way of life that is different from ours, does not mean that we should persecute them.'

'Is that all they were doing?' asked Bartholomew. 'Praying?'

'I said they were kneeling,' corrected Henry. 'I might have taken some action if they were making a noise or looking suspicious, but they were not. They were kneeling very quietly and respectfully. I saw no reason to speak to them or to ask them what they were doing.'

'And it was about midnight?' pressed Bartholomew, wanting to be certain.

'I think so,' said Henry. 'I find it hard to judge time in the dark. I suppose it was an unusual hour for them to be in a church, but our doors are always open to those who need comfort.'

'The gypsies have prayed at the shrine before,' said Bartholomew, thinking about one of the times he had met Eulalia.

'Perhaps they had been working all evening. At this time of year, there is a lot to be done for the harvest and it is not unusual for people to labour until midnight.'

'We will find out,' said Bartholomew. He sincerely hoped Eulalia and her brothers were not the ones responsible for the strange happenings in the Bone House. He forced himself to think rationally, trying not to allow his fondness for the woman to colour his thoughts.

However, all the victims had been killed in an unusual way, and the gypsies could have heard of such a method of execution during their travels. It also required someone with a degree of strength – which Guido, Goran and Rosel possessed in abundance. And although he had insisted to Michael that there was only a single killer, Bartholomew saw that it was possible that one did the grisly work while the others kept watch to ensure the killer was not disturbed. However, he reasoned, there had only been one of them last night in the Bone House.

He wondered whether the fact that the killer had been inside the priory precincts was evidence that would exonerate the gypsies and put the blame instead on someone at the monastery – like the missing William, or Blanche and her retinue. But the gatekeeper had been sleeping, and Bartholomew himself had passed in and out with no questions asked. Someone from the town could easily have gained access. The Bone House was not a place to which most people willingly ventured, so someone could even have slipped into it during the day and hidden there until dark.

So, what did all this tell him? He rubbed a hand through his hair in exasperation when he realised that it told him nothing at all, and that his list of suspects was just as long as ever. The only people who were definitely innocent were the men who had already died. And there was nothing to say whether Eulalia and her clan were innocent or guilty, although Bartholomew thought it odd that they should choose midnight to pray to St Etheldreda.

'Was there anything else?' he asked.

'The Bishop was there, too, saying a mass for Thomas,' said Henry after a moment.

'At midnight?' asked Bartholomew, startled. 'Is that not an odd time for masses?'

Henry shrugged noncommittally. 'I am sure Thomas is grateful for all the masses he can get – regardless of the time they are said.' Bartholomew imagined that was true. 'But let us talk of medical matters. What do you prescribe for backache?'

'Backache?' asked Bartholomew, recalling Michael's blow

with the spade the night before. He gazed at the physician. But Henry could not be the killer! He had been eliminated as a suspect because he drooled when he slept.

'I have had two cases already this morning, would you believe,' Henry continued with a smile. 'It is not unusual to see such ailments: those who labour in their fields often have aching bones at the end of the day, while poring over scripts in the chapter house or the library sometimes gives rise to discomfort.'

'Who came to see you today?' demanded Bartholomew eagerly.

Henry was surprised at his interest. 'One was Bishop de Lisle, although I cannot imagine that *he* was harvesting crops or meditating on sacred scripts. And the other was Symon, who said he had been working in the library all yesterday.'

'He was not,' said Bartholomew. 'I was there in the afternoon, and I was alone.'

'He is rather given to exaggeration.'

'That is a polite way of putting it. He is a liar.'

Henry would not be drawn into agreeing outright. 'He is cautious with the truth. Perhaps he imagines that if he uses it too often, he will run out.'

'I think he has run out already,' said Bartholomew. 'But we should have a word with him. Maybe this mess will not be so difficult to resolve after all.'

'What has Symon's backache to do with finding your killer?'

'Michael struck the murderer hard as he was about to make an end of me. The man will now be nursing a bruised spine.'

At that moment the door opened, and Julian arrived to begin his daily duties. He nodded a greeting to Bartholomew and Henry, before placing both hands over the small of his back.

'Lord!' he muttered. 'Drying herbs is better than being assigned to mucking out the pigs or digging turnips, but leaning over them makes my back horribly sore!'

chapter 10

JULIAN WAS OUTRAGED WHEN BARTHOLOMEW DEMANDED TO inspect his back in the infirmary, and steadfastly refused to allow him, even when Henry added his voice to the argument. Bartholomew was on the verge of marching him directly to Michael for interrogation when the young monk relented, hauling up his habit to reveal silken hose and a fine linen undervest that Bartholomew suspected were well outside the proscribed regulations for novices. He inspected the young man's skin, but could see no abrasion, and was not sure whether a slight discoloration above the belt-line was bruising, or simply where Julian had been less than assiduous with his washing.

The evidence was inconclusive. Bartholomew reasoned that Michael's blow would not necessarily have caused a visible bruise, although it might still be painful. He was left not knowing whether Julian's reluctance to be examined stemmed from the fact that he did not want to be caught wearing clothes he ought not to have owned, whether he was merely exercising his right not to be manhandled by any physician who happened to demand to do so, or whether he had not known whether the spade had left a mark and did not want anyone else to find out either.

'Now what?' asked Bartholomew in frustration, as Julian marched away with a gait that was half-swagger and half-limp.

'It looks as though you will have to speak to Bishop de Lisle and Symon,' said Henry, watching Julian go. 'I do not envy you that task. De Lisle is not the kind of man who appreciates being a suspect for murder, and neither will Symon be.'

Bartholomew sat on the edge of Henry's workbench, not

knowing what to do next. Henry was right that de Lisle would not prove an easy man to interview, while the unhelpful Symon would object to being asked questions on principle. Meanwhile, what was Bartholomew to think about the gypsies being in the cathedral at an hour when most honest people were in bed? Had they been helping the killer, waiting for him to complete whatever grisly business he carried out in the Bone House?

'I am mixing a compound of camomile and borage for Bishop Northburgh's wrinkles,' said Henry, pointing to piles of freshly picked leaves on his table, along with a mound of garlic. 'Both are known to be good for the skin.'

'But they will not miraculously provide him with a youthful complexion,' said Bartholomew. 'And that is what he wants – not merely something that might help. He is demanding the impossible.'

'I suspect you are right, but I shall have to do my best. Alan is determined to have the chapel Northburgh promised, so I am under some pressure to do all I can. Anyway, there is always cucumber to experiment with, and garlic if I get desperate.' He sounded despondent.

'Surgery is the only solution for Northburgh's loose jowls,' said Bartholomew flippantly. 'You will need to take a knife to all that dangling skin and slice it off, just as Julian suggested.'

Henry regarded him aghast. 'That is a horrible idea, Matt! It makes you sound like a surgeon! I shall stick to my poultices and pastes, if you do not mind. At least in that way I will not kill him with my remedies.'

'Vanity has its price,' said Bartholomew, watching Henry add the leaves to a flask of water.

'Welles heard that there were yet more burglaries in the city last night,' said Henry conversationally, shaking the container to mix his ingredients. 'Agnes Fitzpayne first, and then poor Master Barbour of the Lamb Inn again. Obviously, the thieves decided they had not relieved him of everything the first time around.'

'He announced that the thieves were unsuccessful,' said Bartholomew, recalling Barbour's confidential bellow when they had found Robert's body at the Monks' Hythe two days before. 'He boasted that he had hidden his night's takings under the floorboards, and that the burglars had not found them.'

'Who heard him?' asked Henry curiously. 'Because whoever knew about his hiding place should be a suspect for this theft from him.'

'Lots of people. Many of the priory's monks, including Alan and Symon, de Lisle and his steward, Lady Blanche and her retinue, Leycestre and his seditious nephews, the gypsies . . .'

'The gypsies,' mused Henry thoughtfully. 'I wonder if that was why they were in the cathedral last night – praying for forgiveness for the thefts they had just committed, or for the success of the crimes they intended to carry out?'

'Or possibly neither,' said Bartholomew, more sharply than he intended.

Henry patted his arm with a self-effacing smile. 'I am sorry; I should not jump to that kind of conclusion. You have been warning the townsfolk against blaming strangers for all our misfortunes ever since you arrived, and you are right. I apologise.'

Bartholomew smiled, but Henry's comments had left a lingering doubt in his mind. Eulalia had been distinctly evasive when he had asked her about the thefts, and when she had given him a direct answer, he had not known whether to believe her. He took a deep breath and stood up.

'You look tired,' said Henry sympathetically, watching him. 'Take the advice of a physician, and do not overly exert yourself today.'

'But you seem better than you were a little earlier,' observed Bartholomew. 'You were lethargic and wan when we first started talking; now you have some colour and exude energy.'

'I took a tonic of boiled red wine with poppy juice and crushed hemp leaves not long ago. I give it to patients with nervous complaints, and it always works – now I have taken a dose myself, I can see why. I cannot afford to be listless and distracted when I have patients to tend. I do not want a second death on my conscience.'

'Hemp?' asked Bartholomew warily. 'How did you come by that? It is a powerful substance, and I seldom use it, because my patients always demand more. In large quantities it is dangerous.'

'I bought some from a merchant who said it came from the Holy Land. But if your patients come clamouring for more, then you use too much, Matthew. A tiny pinch mixed with wine and poppy juice is the best tonic I know – but, as you say, it is only to be used infrequently and certainly not in the quantities in which Bishop Northburgh quaffs it. Perhaps you should take some now. It will allow you to fulfil your duties today without making the mistakes that often stem from over-tiredness.'

'No, thank you,' said Bartholomew firmly. 'I do not want to develop a liking for hemp.'

'One dose will not result in a craving for more. You should try it, so that you understand why men like Northburgh praise its virtues.'

Reluctantly, Bartholomew accepted a minuscule amount of Henry's tonic, his bone-deep exhaustion making him disinclined to argue. He was surprised to find the infirmarian was right, and that it did indeed serve to dispel the sluggishness that had been dogging him since he had awoken. There was also a vague sense of well-being, which he supposed was why people tended to want more of it. He watched Henry seal the container, then replace it on a high shelf that was thick with dust. He hoped it was sufficiently high to evade the eager hands of the Bishop of Coventry and Lichfield.

'Northburgh drinks a lot of this, you say?' he asked.

Henry nodded. 'I have advised him to reduce the amount, but he will not listen. He has been dosing Stretton with it, too. He has his own supply, but I do not want him to fix greedy eyes on my little stash as well. I am obliged to hide it, as you can see.'

'No wonder their investigations have been so lax,' said Bartholomew, suddenly understanding a good deal about the behaviour of the visiting clerics. 'It explains why they were so mild tempered yesterday, when they spoke to Michael in the refectory. They are both drugged to stupidity.'

'Hardly that,' said Henry, smiling at the exaggeration. 'But I imagine it accounts for Northburgh's swings of mood between bonhomie and aggressive rudeness.'

'It probably works well for shocks,' predicted Bartholomew, a little thickly. 'I usually carry wine for that, although Michael finished mine last night after our encounter with the killer in the Bone House. He has developed an annoying partiality for my medicinal claret.'

Henry laughed. 'He is a large man with large appetites. Let him have his brew, if it makes him happy. But speaking of wine, I must refill your wineskin. I used what you gave me for Ynys's medicine, and you were right: good stuff is more soothing than a raw brew.' He reached for a large stone jug that stood in the corner.

'Did someone mention wine?' came a querulous voice from the infirmary hall. It was Roger.

Henry smiled at Bartholomew, as he poured a measure of deep red claret into the physician's battered wineskin. 'It is miraculous how words like "wine" and "dinner" seem to cure deafness. The others are the same. See how they are looking more lively now that they think they may be in for a cup of something special? But here is your flask. You must promise that you will not attempt to tackle this killer single-handed again: I do not want Michael to drink *all* the priory's best sack after the shocks of repeated encounters with murderers in the Bone House.'

Bartholomew took the container. The contents smelled strong and fruity, and he felt like taking a sip there and then. But he decided he had better not drink wine with the hemp he had taken, or he would be no good to Michael or anyone else. He put it in his bag, fumbling with the buckles and ties, and noting, but not really caring, that it took longer than usual to complete this minor task.

When he had finished, Henry was standing at his workbench with a chopping knife in his hands and a large pile of garlic in front of him. 'I cannot trust Julian to do this,' he said, looking down at his handiwork. 'He is incapable of cutting it to my satisfaction. Garlic should be chopped so fine that the pieces are all but invisible.'

'I always use a pestle and mortar,' said Bartholomew, thinking that chopping garlic was for cooks, not physicians. 'It is much quicker. But I must go. We have a lot to do today.'

He stumbled as he misread the height of the threshold, and Henry laughed softly. 'That floating sensation will pass in a few moments, and then you will feel the beneficial effects of the tonic. Remind me to give you some before you leave for Cambridge. It is excellent for soothing ragged tempers, and I recall hearing that there are one or two Fellows of Michaelhouse who would be better company if they were calmer.'

Bartholomew raised his eyes heavenward. 'That is certainly true.'

When Bartholomew reported to Michael that there had been a spate of complaints for backache that morning, the monk immediately decided they should speak to the sufferers, starting with Symon. He gave Bartholomew a rueful smile as they left the refectory together.

'I think it would be better to leave the Bishop until we have no other leads to follow. I am sure neither of us wants to travel along that line of enquiry except as a last resort.'

'Perhaps not even then,' said Bartholomew. 'There is enough evidence to imply that de Lisle had some kind of hand in Glovere's death, and if we find he also has a bruised back, then the case is more or less closed.'

'But I do not think the man with whom we fought last night was de Lisle,' said Michael. 'It did not feel like de

Lisle, and I do not think he was tall enough.'

'That is wishful thinking,' said Bartholomew. 'I recall thinking that it could have been just about anyone – it was too dark to see, and I do not think I ever saw him standing straight anyway. He was either climbing the ladder or grubbing about on the floor with us.'

'I do not like the way Symon's name keeps cropping up,' said Michael thoughtfully, deftly ending a discussion that made him uncomfortable. 'He was one of the people in the infirmary when Thomas died, by his own admission he was in the vineyard with Robert, and now he is claiming a sudden and suspicious back injury.'

'We do not know how he came by his backache,' warned Bartholomew. 'It is a common complaint, and one that is easy to develop – so it may be wholly irrelevant to this case. But it is certainly time that we had a serious discussion with him – his duties as librarian seem to afford him considerable freedom, both in terms of time and in allowing him to wander.'

'You mean he probably had the opportunity to kill Glovere, Chaloner and Haywarde, too,' surmised Michael. 'We shall bear that in mind.'

Predictably, Symon was nowhere to be found. Bartholomew and Michael scoured the monastery for him, but the elusive librarian seemed to have disappeared into thin air, just like William and Mackerell. Michael kicked at the Steeple Gate in frustration.

'I am growing tired of this!' he shouted. 'What is happening here? Is there a secret chamber somewhere, where people wanted for questioning can hide without fear of being discovered?'

'If so, then we shall find it. We will search the priory, from top to bottom.'

Michael gazed at him. 'Why do you have so much energy all of a sudden? Do you know something you have not told me? Or did you sneak away last night with the lovely Eulalia after our encounter with Death?'

'Neither. Henry gave me a tonic. Once the dizziness wears

off, it really does make you feel as though you have had a good night's sleep. I can see why people want to keep taking it, once they have started.'

'I have heard of medicines like that,' said Michael disapprovingly. 'Once the physician or apothecary is certain that his patient cannot manage without it, he increases the price. Well, you can tell Henry he can keep that sort of potion to himself. I want no fights in Cambridge because tired students can no longer afford the medicine that allows them to work.'

He stalked across the yard, and addressed a group of young monks who had been watching his display of temper with uneasy curiosity. One of them was Welles, Henry's assistant, who tried to back away before Michael reached him. The monk was having none of that. He put on a surprising spurt of speed, and had the alarmed youngster by the cowl before he could take more than two steps.

'Oh, no, you do not!' he growled. 'You will remain here and help me. First, I want to talk to Symon. He sleeps in the dormitory with you novices, so you must know where he is.'

'But I do not,' squeaked Welles in alarm. 'He is a senior monk and does not tell the likes of me his business.' With a shock, Bartholomew saw a glint of silver in the novice's fingers, and stepped forward quickly to knock it from his hand. A long, thin masonry nail tinkled to the floor.

Michael's eyes narrowed. 'And what, pray, is that?'

'Just a nail,' bleated Welles, his eyes flicking from Bartholomew to Michael and then back again. 'I found it in the octagon when the builders were working, and I always carry it with me. Prior Alan said we were not allowed knives as long as Julian was with us, but you have to have something sharp to use at mealtimes. I already had it in my hand when you grabbed me – I did not draw it to use as a weapon.'

'I see,' said Michael flatly, making it clear that he did not know what to believe. 'But I am not here to discuss you. I want Symon.'

'But I really do not know where he is,' protested Welles. 'I have not seen him since last night.'

'Last night?' pounced Michael. 'What are you telling me? That he did not sleep in his bed, and that you have not seen him this morning?'

Welles nodded unhappily.

'And where do you think he might be?' said Michael. 'Does he have a woman, or a particular friend in Ely to whom he may have gone?'

'Not that I know of,' said Welles, not seeming particularly surprised by the question, despite the fact that Symon was a monk. 'He does not have any friends.'

'That I can believe,' said Michael. 'Did he say anything to you last night before he left?'

'No,' said Welles. 'Only that he was going to confess his sins before it was too late.'

'What sins?' demanded Michael. 'His disgraceful treatment of books? His lies?'

'I suppose so. I do not know. Ask his confessor – Prior Alan.'

'I will,' said Michael grimly. He released Welles and headed towards the Prior's House without further ado. Bartholomew considered stopping him, but could see that the monk's temper was up and that nothing could prevent him from following the trail that had opened up before him. Michael strode across the yard, stamped up the stairs that led to the Prior's solar and burst in without knocking. He was slightly disconcerted to see that de Lisle was there, too, but not disconcerted enough to abandon his attack.

'Symon made a confession last night,' he snapped, addressing Alan. 'What did he say?'

'I cannot tell you that,' said Alan in surprise. 'And you know better than to ask.'

'He is missing,' said Michael angrily. 'He was last seen going to confession, and was apparently feeling guilty about his sins. That does not sound like the Symon I know, who is of the opinion that he does not have any. So, I conclude that something happened to make him see the error of his ways, and I need to know what he told you.'

'I am bound by the seal of confession,' said Alan calmly.

'As well you know. But, as it happens, there is nothing for me to tell. He may well have intended to come to see me last night, but he would not have been able to do so. I was out.'

'Where?' demanded Michael immediately, forgetting himself in his desire for answers.

'That is none of your affair,' said Alan, angry at the impertinence of the question. 'But I can assure you that it is irrelevant to your investigation. You asked about Symon's confession, and I am telling you that he did not make one to me.'

'So who else might he have seen, then?' pressed Michael.

'William, Robert and Thomas were also permitted to hear the monks' confessions, but none of them were available, for obvious reasons. Symon would have had to wait for me.'

'Well, if he does come, send for me immediately,' instructed Michael. 'It is imperative that I speak to him as soon as possible.'

'Am I to understand by your frustration and bad temper that this investigation is not proceeding as you would like?' asked de Lisle mildly. 'I hear that you almost had this killer last night, and I am disappointed by your failure.'

'So am I,' said Michael tartly.

De Lisle sighed, and then stood, wincing as he did so and pressing both hands to his lower spine. 'It has been several days since I charged you to exonerate me from the crimes of which I have been accused. Not only have you failed to do that, but there are now five corpses fresh in the ground, and at least two people missing – three, if you count Symon. I hope you will do better today.'

'Do you have an aching back?' asked Michael coolly, goaded into incaution by the Bishop's admonition. 'Matt has a way with aching backs. Perhaps you should let him examine it, and see what he can do for you.'

'No, thank you,' said de Lisle shortly. 'I have been plagued by backache for years, and physicians do nothing but make it worse. I would rather treat it myself with a poultice of ground snails and arsenic. That usually works.'

'I imagine it numbs the area,' said Bartholomew. 'But while it will ease the pain in the short term, you should not use it for long. It can result in slow poisoning.'

'That is what Henry said,' grumbled de Lisle. 'But it is only an excuse for him to get his hands on me and demand a high fee for a consultation, a horoscope and expensive medicines that will do me no good at all.'

'What is wrong with your back, exactly?' asked Bartholomew.

'I am not a physician, so I do not know,' snapped de Lisle, impatient with the discussion. 'But I spent a lot of time sitting yesterday, and I suppose that must have aggravated it. I shall have to walk today, or ride.'

'Ride,' recommended Michael sulkily. 'Walking is for peasants.'

'What do you think, Matt?' asked Michael tiredly, as he started to walk towards the river with Bartholomew a few moments later, in the hope of discovering the scene of the murders. 'Symon is missing, having apparently been about to confess his sins to Alan. That is suspicious in itself.'

'Something must have happened to make him want to see a confessor "before it was too late" to quote Welles,' agreed Bartholomew. 'Symon is arrogant, and not the kind of man to admit he has faults, unless something happened to make him believe otherwise.'

'What has he been doing and where is he now? His pains must be fairly serious, if he emerged from his hiding place to seek Henry's help.'

'Meanwhile, we also have de Lisle with a bad back that he declines to allow me to inspect.'

'And what was Alan doing yesterday that he refuses to tell us about? Playing in the Bone House with blood and soil? Lord, Matt! We have been here for seven days now, and the only reason my list of suspects has decreased is because some of them are dead. Give me that wine you have in your bag. I need a drink!'

'That is for medical emergencies,' said Bartholomew, moving away as the monk lunged. 'It is not for you to drink whenever you feel like it.'

It was a glorious day, with larks flinging themselves up from the grassy fields and flying high into the sky, their twittering songs sweet and piercing. It was a shame such a day had to be blighted by death and suspicion. Bartholomew and Michael walked in silence, thinking about the murders, and how they had changed the priory and the town within the course of a few days.

When they reached the river near the Monks' Hythe, Bartholomew shed his leggings to wade across it, so that they could examine both banks simultaneously. He enjoyed the sensation of the cool water on his skin, and Michael eyed him enviously before removing his sandals so that he could dabble his fat, white feet at the water's edge. He declined to go any deeper, claiming he could not swim.

The day grew steadily hotter, so that walking became uncomfortable. Bartholomew took to paddling along in the shallows, storing his shoes among some reeds to be collected on their return journey. Michael's complaints grew more and more frequent, and he began to make unsubtle demands for the medicinal wineskin in Bartholomew's bag. The physician remained unmoved, arguing that wine would only make the monk more thirsty, and that he would do better to drink some water from one of the many small brooks they passed. Bartholomew did not recommend the river on the grounds that it had already been through Cambridge, and he knew exactly what had been dumped in it there.

When they neared Chettisham, some two miles distant, Michael waved to Bartholomew that they had gone far enough. The physician agreed, knowing that Glovere, Chaloner and Haywarde would not have been killed too far away: it would not have been easy to make them walk far as prisoners, and the killer would hardly have carried them, knowing that they would fetch up in Ely anyway. He followed

Michael into a tavern called the Swan for a glass of cool ale, before beginning the return journey.

The tavern was dark after the glare of the sun, and Bartholomew could barely see where he was walking, even though its door and windows shutters were thrown open to allow the air to circulate. He stumbled to a table like a blind man, and listened in growing alarm to the extensive list of food that Michael was ordering from the taverner. When his eyes grew used to the gloom, he looked around him.

It was a large establishment for a remote location, with thick stone walls and a paved floor. It was virtually empty: the day was fine and there was work to be done in the fields. Two elderly men sat at a table near the empty hearth, staring at the ale in their cups with rheumy eyes. At another table, this one tucked in a corner, were Richard de Leycestre and Guido. Bartholomew gazed at them in surprise, wondering not only what had brought them together, but why they were so far from Ely when they should have been working. Once Michael had finished ordering his repast, he too watched the muttered conversation in the shadows, drawing his cowl over his head so that he would not be recognised. Bartholomew took Michael's wide-brimmed hat and wore it low, so that it hid his face.

The gypsy and the farmer seemed to be arguing, so intent on their own business that they were unaware of the interest they had attracted from the tavern's latest arrivals. Guido's gold hat bobbed furiously as he made some point or other, while Leycestre stabbed the table with a forefinger as he spoke. It was not an easy discussion. Eventually, Guido stood, glared at Leycestre and stalked towards the door, clearly furious. A few moments later, Leycestre also took his leave. Unlike Guido, who had headed straight to the door without taking the precaution of looking around him, Leycestre was circumspect. He saw two figures hunched over their ale with cowls and hats hiding their faces, and stared at them for some time, evidently unsure whether it would be safer just to leave or to approach them and find out who they were.

Apparently, he decided it would be better to know, and he tipped his hat in greeting as he edged closer to their table. Michael flipped back his cowl and beamed at him, enjoying the expression of horror that crossed the labourer's face when he recognised the Bishop's agent. Leycestre regained control of himself quickly.

'Good morning,' he said pleasantly. 'What brings you all the way out here? We do not usually have monks and priory guests in this small village.'

'It is a good place to meet fellow rebels, then, is it?' asked Michael, drawing his own conclusions about the meeting he had just witnessed.

Leycestre laughed nervously. 'Guido and I were just enjoying a drink. We have known each other for many years.'

'It did not look as though either of you was enjoying it to me,' said Bartholomew, flinging the hat on to the table. 'And I was under the impression that you disliked each other – you have accused his clan of burgling town houses and killing Ely's citizens.'

'That is because they are probably guilty,' snapped Leycestre, nettled. 'But it does not mean that I cannot share his table when we both happen to arrive for a much-needed ale.'

'I see,' said Michael, narrowing his eyes. 'You met by chance? You did not arrange to do so because you imagined it would be well away from anyone who might know you?'

'We met by accident,' replied Leycestre shortly. 'Why would I want to rendezvous with a man like Guido, anyway? What could he possibly have that would interest me?'

'You tell me,' said Michael, regarding the man intently. 'And why are you here, anyway, when there are crops to be harvested?'

'Every man is permitted to take a few moments away from his labours,' said Leycestre stiffly. 'Even the priory realises that we cannot work all day with nothing in our stomachs.'

'But ale is not the best thing to put in it,' said Bartholomew.

'I am not bound to the priory, so I am not obliged to answer your questions,' snapped Leycestre. 'I was merely taking a break from harvesting, and I happened to meet someone I know. There is nothing wrong or sinister in that. But I cannot spend all day lounging in taverns, like fat monks and wealthy physicians. I have work to do.'

He stalked away angrily, slamming the door behind him so hard that jugs rattled on the shelves and the two elderly men jumped in alarm. If Leycestre's intention had been to convince Bartholomew and Michael that his meeting had been innocent, then he had failed miserably. Both were now sure that the ill-matched pair had been discussing something of great significance.

'I suppose he was plotting his insurrection,' said Bartholomew. 'That is all he talks about, and it seems to be the thing that is most important in his life. Still, he usually does so only when his nephews can act as sentinels. I wonder where they are.'

'It is probably difficult for three strong men to leave the fields in the middle of the day,' said Michael. 'While Leycestre might slip away unnoticed, the whole trio certainly could not.'

'Was he trying to convert Guido to his cause, do you think? Guido is a traveller. He would be an excellent person to spread the news that discontent is brewing and that other peasants should be ready to act.'

'Guido is not the kind of man to engage in that sort of thing. Why should he? He is not tied to a landlord: this is not his fight, and I cannot see why he should become involved.'

'Then what *were* they discussing?' asked Bartholomew irritably. His head was aching, and he felt sick, as though he had had too much to drink the night before. He wondered whether it was the after-effects of Henry's tonic and assumed that there would have to be a down-side to such a marvellous potion.

'I do not know,' said Michael, rubbing his hands as the first of the food arrived. 'But it looked more like an argument than a discussion to me.'

'Perhaps they were debating who to murder next,' said Bartholomew, eating a piece of chicken without enthusiasm. He was more interested in the ale, although Michael claimed it was too weak.

'Did Leycestre look as though he was limping to you?' asked Michael. 'Go to the window and watch him. You are a physician, and are good at observing such things.'

Bartholomew obliged, watching the burly farmer walk towards the river. There was a distinct unevenness to his gait. He returned to Michael and reported his observations. 'I suppose he could always walk like that,' he concluded. 'It was not a limp so much as a stiffness. Perhaps working in the fields does not agree with him.'

'Or perhaps he is suffering from a spade blow to the back.'

'Our list of suspects for last night's débâcle includes everyone in the priory and everyone in the town. We cannot go on like this, Brother: we have to narrow it down.'

'But not by excluding Leycestre,' said Michael firmly. 'He was not on innocent business here in Chettisham.'

The landlord continued to bring dishes of meat, bread and pastries until Michael declared himself replete. Then he sat back with a sigh of pleasure, and made himself comfortable on the bench, leaning his back against the wall, and using his hat as a headrest as he prepared to take a nap.

'Guido and Leycestre,' mused Bartholomew. 'Men who dislike each other. They had a public fight in the Heyrow when Leycestre ordered Guido expelled from the Lamb, and Leycestre has been accusing the gypsies of all manner of crimes ever since we arrived.'

'Could they have committed the murders together?' asked Michael, sounding as if he did not care what Bartholomew thought, as long as it did not interfere with the doze he planned to take.

'No,' said Bartholomew. 'Their dislike of each other is too public. You would need to trust someone absolutely if you were going to use him as an accomplice to murder.'

'Perhaps their antipathy is a ruse,' suggested Michael with a shrug. His eyes were closed and his voice was slurred, as if his mind was already elsewhere. 'Perhaps Leycestre blames the gypsies so that people will not suspect that they *are* partners in crime.'

Bartholomew thought about that for a while, turning over the possibilities in his mind. He remembered the glittering malice he had seen on the faces of both when they had fought in the Heyrow, and the fact that weapons had been produced. He had no doubt that the crowd Leycestre had whipped into a frenzy might have done serious harm to the gypsies had Bartholomew not intervened, and there was only so far Guido would go for the sake of appearances. Being bludgeoned to death was definitely past the limit. And Leycestre's accusations were probably making it difficult for Guido and his clan to do his business in Ely, whether it was buying bread or securing work. It made no sense for Guido to agree to such conditions.

'You are wrong,' he concluded. 'They are not accomplices. Perhaps they met by chance after all.'

'Mmm?' murmured Michael, shifting slightly in his sleep.

Bartholomew thought about the other crimes that had been committed in the town. Although he and Michael had not been charged to investigate them, there had been burglaries almost every night since Guido and his clan had arrived in Ely. But, as Guido had claimed, the gypsies were unlikely to be the culprits, because it would have been obvious who was responsible. Justice in England tended to be summary and swift, and many sheriffs would regard the presence of travellers in a city plagued by a sudden spate of crimes evidence enough.

Were the murders and the burglaries related? Bartholomew tried to recall what he had been told about the thefts. They all occurred in the homes of the wealthy – merchants, Bishop de Lisle and finally Barbour the landlord. Bartholomew rubbed his chin as a thought occurred to him. No poor person had been targeted, and Leycestre was constantly pointing out that the rich lived well, while the peasantry seldom knew where their next meal was coming from. Was Leycestre the burglar, stealing from the rich people he so despised?

But how could that be right? One of the most recent victims had been Agnes Fitzpayne, who was a good friend of Leycestre's. The man would surely not steal from someone who seemed to hold the same views as he did. Or would he? Bartholomew frowned. Perhaps Agnes had agreed to claim she had been burgled for the express purpose of making Leycestre appear innocent. And Leycestre had certainly been present when Barbour had bragged about where he had hidden his money.

But Leycestre was not suddenly sporting new clothes or producing gold to buy back the land he had lost. Where were all his gains going? Bartholomew sat up straight when it occurred to him that rebellions cost money. There were weapons to be bought, and favours to be purchased from people in a position to dispense them. Messengers needed to be hired, with fast horses, to spread the word once it had started, and funds would be necessary to allow the leaders to meet in secret places and discuss tactics. Was that the reason for the burglaries? That Leycestre needed money to support his rebellion, and he had decided the rich should pay?

If that were true, then the gypsies' arrival had been a perfect opportunity to place the blame on someone else – people who would never join the revolution, because they were not tied to the land and were free to do as they pleased. They were excellent scapegoats; they had a reputation for stealing the odd coin or hen, and they were dispensable. Because they came every year, Leycestre had waited for their arrival before he put his plan into action.

The more Bartholomew thought about his solution, the more it made sense. Triumphant that he had made some headway, even though it probably had nothing to do with the murders, he prodded Michael awake.

'What?' demanded the monk crossly. 'I was sleeping.'

'I know what Leycestre has been doing,' declared Bartholomew, reaching for his jug of ale and taking a deep draught. 'His rebellion is more than wishful thinking. He is preparing to make it into a reality with funds stolen from the merchants.'

Michael listened to the explanation with wide eyes, saying nothing until he had finished. 'And you woke me to tell me this?' he demanded. 'I have never heard such nonsense! Where is your evidence? You do not have a scrap of it.'

'I do not,' admitted Bartholomew. 'But it makes sense.'

'It does not,' snapped Michael, rubbing his eyes wearily. 'I thought you had a headache. You would have done better to take a nap, rather than make it worse with all this false reasoning.'

'I feel better,' said Bartholomew, standing and stretching. 'The after-effects of Henry's tonic are not so serious after all. No wonder he keeps it locked away. If the general populace learns there is a substance that can make you happy and give you energy to work, and that the only negative is a slight headache and a little queasiness, then we would have no peace from demands for it, as Henry has discovered from Northburgh and Stretton.'

'Leycestre is not a burglar,' said Michael, eating a crust of bread he had missed earlier. 'He is too old for that sort of thing.'

'It was you who pointed out that he was walking stiffly this morning. It is probably because he had to climb the outside of the Lamb to reach Barbour's attic, and he is not used to it.'

'Well, even if you are right, this speculation does not help us. The burglaries and the murders have nothing to do with each other.'

But Bartholomew was certain he had solved at least one of the mysteries that besieged the little Fenland city. He finished his ale and followed Michael outside the inn to the bright sunshine.

*   *   *

The walk back to Ely was brutally hot. The sun was as fierce as Bartholomew had ever known it, and he was reminded of his travels in southern Italy and France, where the sun burned all the greenness out of the landscape. The river looked cool and inviting – if he did not think about what might be floating in it – and they had walked only a short distance before he removed his shirt and waded into the shallows to dive into the cool blackness of the deeper water.

Michael watched enviously from the bank, while Bartholomew urged him to jump in, expounding the virtues of a cool dip on a hot day. Michael demurred, and sat miserably in his heavy habit and wide black hat. His face was red, and he complained that the heat was making his skin itch. Eventually, the temptation became too great, and the monk removed his habit to reveal voluminous underclothes and monstrous white limbs. It was not a pleasant sight, and Bartholomew was glad they were not inflicting it on any passers-by.

Michael wallowed around like a vast sea creature, scowling and looking as if he were not enjoying the experience at all. He grumbled about the mud under his feet, and did not like the smell of the peaty water. After a while, when he had cooled down, he claimed he had had enough and was going home. He headed for a patch of sedge.

'You will never get out that way,' Bartholomew warned. 'It will be too boggy.'

Michael ignored him, then gave a sudden howl of alarm, splashing furiously in an attempt to push away from whatever had startled him. Water slapped into his mouth, and he began to choke, which increased his agitation. Afraid that the monk might have hurt himself on a sharp stone or a stick, Bartholomew went to his assistance. But it was not sticks and stones that had unnerved the monk.

Among the reeds, bobbing obscenely in the waves that Michael created, was a dead white hand. Bartholomew parted the stems to look at its owner, before turning to face Michael, who was treading water and gasping like a drowning man.

'It is William,' Bartholomew said softly, gesturing to the distinctive bob of grey hair, now sadly soiled and bedraggled. 'His body must have been caught in the vegetation, rather than washing downstream like the others'.'

Michael began to gag. His face was bright red, and he snatched at Bartholomew in panic when the physician went to his aid. It was not easy to haul him to the safety of the shore, and both were panting and exhausted by the time they had scrambled up the bank.

'Horrible!' exclaimed Michael, rubbing himself down with his habit. Water gushed from his massive underclothes, and ran down the flabby white flesh of his legs. 'I shall never swim in a river again. It is vile to share it with corpses – especially bloated and stinking ones like that.'

'William has not been dead that long,' said Bartholomew, pushing his way through the undergrowth that fringed the water to reach the body from the shore. He found it, and hauled it backward until it lay on the grass like a landed fish.

'How long?' demanded Michael, rubbing his habit across his hair, so that the thin locks stood in needle-sharp spikes across his head.

'I do not know. No more than three days – he went missing on Wednesday night, if you recall, and it is now Saturday.'

'And how did he die?' asked Michael. 'Is there a cut in his neck?'

'No.' Bartholomew knelt to examine the hosteller. 'But there is a serious dent in his head.'

'What are you saying? Was William murdered by the man who killed the others, or not?'

'I do not know,' said Bartholomew, turning the body as he assessed it in more detail. 'The method was not the same, but that does not tell us anything conclusive. From the damage to his hands, it seems that he struggled with his attacker. We saw the same thing on Robert, remember?'

Michael nodded. 'Robert knew there was a killer on the loose and fought with whoever grabbed him. Perhaps William was so afraid that he decided to leave the priory before he went the same way – he ran away, but the murderer found him anyway.'

'Not necessarily,' said Bartholomew. 'Where are his possessions?'

'The killer stole them, I imagine,' said Michael, as though it were obvious. 'If you have murdered someone, you may as well recompense yourself for your pains and make off with a couple of saddlebags of good robes and gold coins.'

'So, now we are looking for someone with a bruised back, who is wearing finest quality Benedictine robes and has a lot of money to spare,' said Bartholomew facetiously. 'He should not be too difficult to track down.'

Michael ignored him, and nodded instead to the dead man's hands. 'His nails are broken, and there are cuts on his arms. I assume the killer will also have scratches on him.'

Bartholomew shook his head. 'These are injuries caused while William tried to defend himself; there is nothing to indicate that he managed to inflict any harm on his assailant. The cuts show where he fended off a knife or another blade of some kind, and the broken fingernails could have been caused by his clawing at anything in his desperation to escape, even the ground.'

'But then his nails would be full of mud. And they are not.'

'He has also been in the river for an undetermined amount of time, and it may have been washed away.'

'His death was definitely a result of this blow to his head? There are no other fatal injuries? He did not drown?'

'I cannot really tell,' said Bartholomew. 'If I lean hard against his chest, some bubbles seep from his mouth, suggesting he breathed water into his lungs, but it is irrelevant anyway. What is important is that we know he fought against his attacker, and that at some point he was hit on the head – or perhaps he fell. He probably drowned while he was unconscious – his death was a result of the tussle, regardless.'

'So, now we have six corpses to avenge,' said Michael grimly. 'And Mackerell is still missing. Perhaps *he* is the killer.'

'William was not.'

'Not necessarily,' said Michael tiredly, trying to keep an open mind. 'It is possible that someone else discovered the identity of the murderer and took justice into his own hands. What we have here may be an execution, not a murder.'

Bartholomew was not so sure. 'The man we wrestled with in the Bone House last night was definitely our culprit, because of the way he tried to cut my neck. And, although I cannot be precise about the exact time that William has been dead, I can assure you it was not him we fought – unless his corpse was possessed by a water-spirit.'

'Please!' said Michael with a shudder, glancing around him uneasily. 'This is no place to make that kind of jest.'

'I was under the impression that you dismissed such stories as nonsense,' said Bartholomew, surprised by the monk's reaction. 'You have always been scornful of local superstitions and customs.'

'So I am, when in a busy town or the cathedral-priory,' said Michael. 'But things are different out here, among all this water and with that vast sky hanging above us. There are eerie rustles and strange sounds. I always feel I am entering a different world when I venture into the Fens.'

'We had better go home, then,' said Bartholomew, looking towards the path that would take them back to Ely. 'We should not linger here longer than necessary, when we have so much to do.'

'William will have to stay here. He is too heavy for us to carry without a stretcher and I do not feel like humping corpses all over the countryside, anyway.'

'We can cover him with reeds,' said Bartholomew, 'and hope he does not attract the attention of any wild animals. He has been all right so far, so a few more hours should not make a difference.'

'I will say a prayer and then we will be off,' said Michael, muttering something brief, then leaning down to touch William's forehead, mouth and chest. 'There, I am done.'

'I am sure that will make all the difference,' said

Bartholomew, hoping for William's sake that his other brethren were prepared to take a little more time over his immortal soul.

Michael took no notice, and put one hand on William's chest as he heaved himself to his feet. He withdrew his fingers quickly, then knelt again and peered closely at the front of William's habit. 'That is odd.'

Bartholomew crouched next to him, and looked at the cross that William still wore around his neck. His killer had evidently decided it was not worth stealing, because the metal was some cheap alloy, not the gold or silver usually favoured by high-ranking Benedictines. But it was not the cross itself that had attracted Michael's attention – it was something that had caught on one of its rough edges. Bartholomew took a pair of tweezers from his medicine bag and picked it up.

'What is it?' asked Michael. 'It looks like a strand of gold thread – not that gold-coloured thread you can buy in the market here, but the real stuff that courtiers use.'

'Not only courtiers,' said Bartholomew, thinking about Guido and his unusual hat.

It was noon by the time they had walked back to Ely, informed Alan that they had located his missing hosteller, and dispatched Cynric and five sturdy lay-brothers to fetch him back. Michael retired to the refectory, but had barely finished his repast when de Lisle summoned him, demanding to know the details of William's death and the implications of the discovery for the case. The Bishop was not pleased to learn that it meant little other than that the hosteller was probably not the murderer.

Symon was still missing, and it seemed no one had set eyes on him since he had visited the infirmarian early that morning. Alan was embarrassed to admit that he had no idea where his monk had gone, although Bartholomew sensed his concern did not yet stretch to actual worry. The Prior offered to open the library himself, so that

Bartholomew could use it, but the physician was unable to concentrate on work, feeling as though the case was gaining momentum, and that soon something would happen that would determine its outcome. He tried reading, but his attention wandered and he kept staring across the leafy cemetery instead of at the words on the page in front of him.

He went to bed early that evening, exhausted by the day's events and by the inadequate sleep snatched the previous two nights. He rose late, long after prime had ended, feeling refreshed but uneasy, as if he sensed that something significant would happen that day. He set out to find Symon, but then saw Welles emerging from the library. Henry had charged his assistant to hunt out Galen's *De Urinis* for a lecture he planned to deliver to his apprentices later that day, so Bartholomew seized the opportunity to slip inside. He suspected that Symon would never have granted him access on the Sabbath, and decided that at least some good had come of the librarian's continued absence.

According to Welles, no one was unduly concerned for Symon's safety: the man was permitted a considerable degree of freedom in order to purchase new books for the library, although Welles was unable to say whether the collection was expanding as a result. However, he did know that Symon seized with alacrity every opportunity to disappear for a few days. Bartholomew regarded the novice thoughtfully, wondering whether he and Michael should walk upriver again, to see whether they could find any more corpses to add to their collection. He suggested as much to Michael, who promptly sent Cynric and Meadowman on that particular errand, while Michael himself began routine interviews of each of the priory's monks, in the vain hope that one of them might know something pertinent that he was willing to share.

Freed from helping Michael, Bartholomew lingered in the library all morning, then helped Henry set a cordwainer's broken leg during the afternoon. He returned to his books at about four o'clock, when the day still sizzled under an unrelenting sun. Even the restless old men were sleeping soundly, exhausted by the heat, and Bartholomew found himself still unable to concentrate as the sun heated the room to furnace levels.

At last he gave up, and wandered aimlessly around the town in search of somewhere cool. Because it was Sunday, the town was busy with people walking to and from church. Officially, labour was forbidden on the Sabbath, but exceptions were made during harvest, so the atmosphere in the city did not feel much different from other days. He saw de Lisle leaving a meeting with Michael, limping heavily, as though in pain. Moments later, Julian walked past, both hands to the small of his back as though he were trying to rub away an ache. The novice dropped his hands to his sides as soon as he became aware that he was the object of Bartholomew's interested scrutiny, and hurried away.

Bartholomew met Eulalia, who was carrying an enormous pitcher of the weak ale called stegman, evidently intended for the men in the fields. She moved slowly, as though she had been working all day and was beginning to flag. Her face lit up when she saw Bartholomew, and her gait was suddenly more sprightly. She gave him a grin with her small white teeth, and her dark eyes sparkled with pleasure.

'Matthew! I have not seen you for a while. You still have not collected your black resin from me. It is in my cart, waiting for you.'

'I have been busy. But I am not busy now. Can I walk with you for a while, and carry your bucket?'

She shook her head. 'The priory may refuse to pay me if someone reports that you have been helping. But perhaps you can come this evening, when work is over. We cannot compete with the fine fare offered by the monastery, but we have strong wine, wholesome bread, fish caught illegally from the river this very morning by Rosel, and pleasant music.'

Bartholomew was startled when a hand placed firmly in the middle of his back shoved him forward so hard that he stumbled. When he regained his balance, he turned to see

Guido towering over his sister with an expression of black fury creasing his dark features. He thought about the gold thread – safely stowed in a box in Alan's solar – that he had recovered from William's body, but Guido was hatless. Bartholomew considered interrogating him about it, but decided he had better wait until he could inspect the garment properly and be sure of his facts. Guido was also angry, and Bartholomew did not feel like tackling the man without Michael or Cynric present.

'Get away from my sister!' Guido snapped. 'She does not want anything to do with you.'

'That is for her to decide,' said Bartholomew.

'It is for *me* to decide,' snapped Guido. 'Our king died on Friday night, and I have been elected in his place. And I say you should stay away from my sister.'

'Go away, Guido,' said Eulalia, casting her brother a withering look. 'You may intimidate Rosel, but you do not frighten me. Go back to your work, and earn an honest penny for a change.'

'For a change?' asked Bartholomew. 'Are the ones he usually earns dishonest?'

'Becoming king has gone to his head,' she said scornfully. 'He thinks it puts him beyond a hard day's labour, and he has been plotting with men in the city who mean us no good.'

'Like Leycestre,' said Bartholomew.

Both gypsies stared at him in surprise. 'How did you know that?' asked Eulalia.

'I saw them together at Chettisham yesterday.'

'You did what?' exploded Eulalia, rounding on Guido. 'I thought we decided that we would have nothing to do with Leycestre's proposition.'

'That was before I was king,' snarled Guido dangerously. 'Now *I* make the decisions, and *I* say Leycestre's offer is too good to turn down.'

'What offer is this?' asked Bartholomew.

'Nothing we will share with you,' shouted Guido, turning to the physician and adding emphasis to his point by jabbing a forefinger into his chest. It was like being stabbed with a piece of iron, and Bartholomew flinched backwards.

'Keep your hands to yourself,' flashed Eulalia. The humour that had danced in her eyes was replaced by a dangerous fury. 'It is because of your quick fists that we are in this predicament.'

'What predicament?' asked Bartholomew.

Guido took a menacing step towards the physician, but confined himself to waving a furious finger when Eulalia also moved forward. 'It is none of your affair. Mind your own business!'

Eulalia glowered at Guido, then turned to Bartholomew to explain. 'Leycestre offered to pay us if we would leave Ely tomorrow.'

Bartholomew stared at her, his mind whirling. 'How much did he offer you?'

'More than we would earn if we stayed here for another two weeks, and it means we can earn money elsewhere, too.'

'But the offer only stands if we leave tonight,' said Guido, sulky that Eulalia had told Bartholomew what he wanted to know. 'If we dither, he says he will give us nothing, and that is why I have decided we will go.'

'And it is why *I* have decided that there is something peculiar about this arrangement,' countered Eulalia. 'I do not trust Leycestre. Why does he want us gone, all of a sudden? And what will that mean for our return here next year?'

'It would mean that you would hang for theft and possibly murder,' said Bartholomew, knowing exactly why Leycestre was so keen for the gypsies to leave. 'Of course, that is assuming that there is a city here at all, and that his rebellion has not destroyed everything and plunged the country into a civil war.'

'What are you talking about?' demanded Guido. 'Leycestre is a man full of silly dreams. He does not have the authority to create that sort of havoc.'

'He is not alone,' said Bartholomew. 'There are pockets of unrest all over the country, and men like him are working to join them up. I am sure that *he* has been committing the burglaries around the town in order to raise funds for his cause. That is why he is able to pay you, despite the fact that he is little more than a labourer himself.'

Eulalia took a sharp breath. 'Is that why he has been so vocal against us this summer? He has always been friendly before, but this year he has accused us of all manner of crimes. We are to be the scapegoat for the crimes *he* has committed?'

'That is why he wants you to leave tonight: so that he can claim you burgled half the merchants in the city and then fled with your ill-gotten gains.'

'But why the urgency?' asked Eulalia. 'He told Guido the arrangement is only good until midnight.'

Bartholomew frowned. 'Perhaps it is because he intends to commit a particularly spectacular burglary tonight, and he knows it will result in a huge hue and cry. Unlike the offences committed against the merchants, this will be committed against someone more powerful and influential, who will have the resources to investigate the crime properly.'

'And their prime suspects will have gone,' said Eulalia, nodding. 'That is clever thinking on his part. The search will concentrate on us, and will allow him to dispose of whatever he has taken at his leisure and without suspicion.'

'This is all rubbish,' growled Guido. 'You are forgetting that the most powerful man in this area is de Lisle, and he has already been burgled.'

'He is also deep in debt and has little for a thief to take,' said Bartholomew. 'But there is someone a lot richer, and with a lot more resources at his fingertips, than the Bishop.'

'The cathedral-priory,' said Eulalia in a low, awed voice. 'He intends to burgle the priory and have us blamed for it. And he intends to do it tonight.'

Guido was not convinced by the interpretation of facts deduced by Bartholomew and Eulalia, and was becoming belligerent. The physician saw that his sister was having trouble controlling him and, since he did not want to make the situation awkward, he decided it would be better if he left. The gypsy hurled insults and threats after him as he walked away, causing more than one passer-by to stare.

Bartholomew went to find Michael, to tell him about Leycestre's offer to Guido, but the monk had gone in search of the elusive Symon, determined to interrogate him about his backache. Bartholomew scoured the priory for them with no success, then wandered through the town again. Finally, hot and tired, he retired to the cathedral, intending to sit alone for a while in its cool, stone interior.

As soon as he had entered the great building, he realised he should have sought sanctuary in it sooner. It was calm and silent, and a far cry from the hectic bustle of the town and the atmosphere of unease and distrust that pervaded the priory. Father John was conducting a short mass at his altar, but because there were no monks with whom to compete, he did little more than whisper his prayers. Bartholomew found a pillar at the rear of the church, and sat with his back to it, relishing the chill from the stone that seeped through his clothes.

John finished his mass, and Bartholomew was surprised to see Leycestre emerge from the shadows of the aisle and approach the priest. Agnes Fitzpayne was there, too, and Bartholomew grew more certain that his suppositions had been right and that the 'burglary' of her house had been fictitious, expressly designed to deflect suspicion from Leycestre and his nephews. The trio spoke in low, urgent voices for a few moments, before leaving to go their separate ways. Bartholomew had the feeling that Leycestre was spending most of his time organising his rebellion, because he certainly had not been in the fields much that day, nor the previous one.

John stumbled over Bartholomew's legs when he hurried past, then cast a furtive glance up the nave, presumably to assess whether Bartholomew could have observed his meeting with Leycestre.

'What are you doing here?' the priest demanded, staring down at the physician who sat comfortably at the base of his column. 'It is not nice to lurk in dark corners and startle honest men.'

'Not so honest,' said Bartholomew. 'I saw you with Leycestre and Agnes Fitzpayne, plotting how you will overthrow the landlords. You told me you would wait to see which side won before pinning your colours to a mast, but you seem to be very close to Leycestre.'

John glanced around him in alarm. 'I am advising him to caution, not encouraging him to engage in treasonous acts.'

'Of course,' said Bartholomew, who knew perfectly well that John had been agreeing with Leycestre, not remonstrating with him. 'But you should be careful, Father. I do not think this rebellion will succeed, no matter how many houses Leycestre has robbed to ensure its success.'

John clapped his hands across his face, and Bartholomew knew, beyond the shadow of a doubt, that all his reasoning had been correct. The priest gave a groan, and when he looked at Bartholomew again, his expression was haggard.

'I do not want to be mixed up in this, but how can I stop? All my parishioners are poor, and the landowners have made their lives even harder since the Death. Leycestre is right in that the wealthy will never listen to the peasants, and he is right when he says something must be done. But I am no rebel, and violence is abhorrent to me. What shall I do?'

'I do not know,' said Bartholomew, who could see the priest's quandary and was glad he had not been placed in such a position himself. 'But you should beware of involving yourself with men who break the law. It is one thing to be executed for treason over a cause you believe is just, and another altogether to be hanged for a common crime like theft.'

'I told Leycestre there were other ways,' said John miserably. 'I told him that King Edward would hear the voice of his people, and that we should allow more time to pass before he took such desperate action. He would not listen.'

'Fanatics rarely do.'

'What will you do with this knowledge?' asked John nervously. 'Will you tell the Bishop and Prior Alan? Or will you give me until sunset to leave with my few belongings? I know what they do to traitors, and I do not want to be an example for other would-be rebels. You would not wish the execution of a priest on your conscience, would you?'

'I think you will find that de Lisle and Alan already have some inkling of Leycestre's plans, although I doubt they also know about the burglaries. You must do what you think is right, but I will not tell the priory or the Bishop of your involvement, if that is what you want.'

'And what do you demand for your silence?' asked John tiredly. 'I have no money – anything I have goes to feed the poor these days. I could say a mass for you at St Etheldreda's tomb before I leave.'

'I would like some information,' said Bartholomew, gazing up at the priest. 'Does Leycestre intend to break into the priory tonight?'

John nodded unhappily. 'And now I am a traitor to both sides! If Leycestre ever learns I told you this, he will kill me.'

'Is he the kind of man who kills, then?' asked Bartholomew, very interested in this revelation. 'Is Leycestre the murderer who has been taking the lives of his fellow citizens?'

'I do not know,' said John in a whisper. He glanced around him fearfully. 'Really, I do not! The possibility has crossed my mind, because he is so determined that his rebellion will be a success, and the men who have died are folk who were not interested in joining him.'

'Chaloner, Glovere and Haywarde were against the rebellion?' asked Bartholomew.

'They just did not care one way or the other. And because of their apathy, I thought Leycestre might have decided they were better out of the way. But then monks died, and now I am not so sure.' He saw Bartholomew look sceptical, and he raised his hands in earnest entreaty. 'Please, believe me! I really do not know the identity of this killer.'

Bartholomew decided the priest was probably telling the truth, and supposed that Leycestre and his cronies did not confide in him because he was nervous and the kind of person to fall at the first hurdle – which was exactly what he had done. He charged John to say nothing to Leycestre about the fact that his plan to raid the priory had been anticipated. The priest nodded acquiescence, then informed Bartholomew that he was planning to leave Ely anyway, and that he would do better in another city.

'But you have been here for years,' said Bartholomew, surprised that the priest had made plans to abandon the people he professed to love, even before he knew his part in Leycestre's rebellion had been discovered.

'It is time for a change,' said John quietly. 'I shall be on the road by this evening and will not return.' He said farewell and then was gone, hurrying through the shadows towards the door, which he fled through without bothering to close it behind him. The sound of children playing nearby drifted in, along with the agitated bark of a dog, which was probably part of their game and wished it were not. Bartholomew stared at the gate for a long time before he uncoiled himself from the foot of his column and stood up.

Bartholomew walked slowly around the cathedral, thinking about what he had learned, and wondering when the legacy of the Death would loosen its grip on his country. The life of a peasant had not been easy before the plague, and there had been a shortage of land that had meant bread was expensive. But it was ten times harder after the Great Pestilence had swept through England, and now it seemed as though it would precipitate a rebellion that would plunge huge tracts of the country into a state of anarchy. Men like John saw that the cause was just, and were torn between siding with the people for whom they cared and staying on the right side of the law, while men like Leycestre were preparing for a war without considering the fact that their actions could make matters worse.

The sun was beginning to dip red in the afternoon sky when Bartholomew realised that he had been walking in circles for at least an hour, round and round inside the cathedral. He was at the rear again, near the pillar where he had met John, when he decided he had better stop and do something more productive than analysing his country's economic problems.

He glanced to one side, and saw that the transept was still in its chaotic state of disrepair, with the rope hanging between two stools to warn people to stay out. It seemed to Bartholomew that the ground was more littered with smashed flagstones and broken masonry than ever, and he noted that the angel, which had clung precariously to the beam high on the roof above, was now a pile of painted rubble on the floor. Only the angel's eyes were identifiable, gazing sightlessly upward as though admonishing the builders for giving her a niche that was not sound. The scaffolding that clung to the wall looked more unstable than the building it was supposed to support, and Bartholomew was surprised that the whole lot had not already crashed to the ground.

He was about to leave through the west door, when he saw two familiar figures walking slowly towards him. Tysilia and de Lisle were strolling arm in arm through the cathedral that was the centre of his See. Bartholomew had seldom seen a greater look of contentment on the haughty features of the Bishop, although Tysilia seemed bored with her father's company. Ralph was behind them, dogging their footsteps like a faithful, if reluctant, hound. Quickly Bartholomew moved behind one of the thick Norman columns. He did not want to meet Tysilia and have another conversation that revolved around Brother Michael's physical virtues in front of the Bishop. He listened carefully to their approaching footsteps, ready to edge further around the column if they came towards him.

'What is this?' he heard Tysilia ask, as she passed the ruinous transept.

'A broken angel,' came de Lisle's voice, tenderly patient. 'She must have fallen from the roof. This entire section is not as strong as the rest of the cathedral. One day it will tumble to the ground.'

Tysilia clapped her hands in childlike delight. 'Can I come to see it? I have never seen a church fall down.'

'I imagine few people have,' said de Lisle, reaching out to touch her hair in a rare sign of paternal affection. 'But I hope it will not happen for a while, because then the monks will insist on rebuilding it immediately, and they should finish the parish church of Holy Cross first.'

'But it will be much more fun to build a big church than a little one,' said Tysilia. 'I like large things. Like Brother Michael.'

'Michael?' asked de Lisle, somewhat startled. 'Do you mean my agent?'

'I do not know what he does in his spare time,' said Tysilia warmly. 'But he is a charming man and he has a fine physique.'

'Are we talking about the same fellow?' asked de Lisle, his voice wary. 'You mean Brother Michael from Michaelhouse in Cambridge?'

'That is the one,' said Tysilia dreamily. 'He is a perfect specimen.'

'I have always considered him rather fat, personally,' said de Lisle. 'But he has served me well in the past, although he is not doing a very good job as regards these murders.'

'Poor William,' said Tysilia. 'He was my brother, you know?'

Bartholomew saw de Lisle stare at her. 'He was not,' he said eventually. 'And I can assure you that I have a very good reason to know.'

'Well, you are wrong,' said Tysilia merrily. 'He said we were brother and sister because we both have black hair and dark eyes. It is a family resplendence, he said.'

'Resemblance,' said de Lisle fondly. 'But William did not have black hair – he had that puffy grey stuff that looked like a big piece of fungus, and eyes that were more pale than dark.'

'That is what I told him,' said Tysilia. 'But he told me that hair and eyes change colour when a person ages.'

'He was lying,' said de Lisle. 'But you and I both have dark eyes.'

'*You* cannot be my brother,' said Tysilia, pushing him playfully. 'You are far too old. In fact, you are so old that I would not even consider you as a bedfellow, and I do not usually mind a little maternity.'

'Maturity,' corrected de Lisle. 'They are not words you should muddle, my dearest one.'

He broke away from Tysilia when one of his clerks hurried towards him, holding some piece of parchment that had to be signed. De Lisle was not the kind of man who signed documents without reading them first, and Tysilia grew restless with the enforced wait. While the clerk and Ralph chatted, and de Lisle read his parchment, she wandered away to look at the damaged transept. Before anyone noticed what she was doing, she had stepped across the rope barrier and was poking around among the smashed statues on the floor.

With a sigh of annoyance, Bartholomew abandoned his hiding place and walked towards her. Much as he found her dim wits irritating, he could not stand by and see her in danger. He called her name, ordering her to leave the transept and move towards him. At the sound of his voice, de Lisle turned in alarm.

'Tysilia!' he cried, dropping his parchment and racing towards her. 'The physician is right. Come out of there at once!'

Tysilia half turned. 'But there are interesting things here,' she objected, stooping to lift a piece of painted wood to show them. 'Pretty things.'

'Come out!' de Lisle shouted. 'At once. That rope is to

stop people from entering that area, and you are not supposed to step over it.'

With a petulant pout, Tysilia started to slouch towards him. Then there was a rumble, a sharp crack and suddenly the whole of the north-west transept was full of falling stone and rising dust.

'Tysilia!' howled de Lisle, trying to run towards her but forced back by the veil of falling masonry and wood. Ralph darted forward to seize his Bishop's arm and prevent him from doing anything rash, but de Lisle was not a stupid man. He could see there was little point in dashing among the large clumps of debris that crashed in front of him.

After a few moments, the roar of falling rubble ceased and the cathedral was silent. De Lisle gave another wail, and tugged away from Ralph to rush towards his daughter. Bartholomew glanced up, afraid that he would be hit, too, but there was little more left to fall. He realised they had just witnessed the largest collapse so far, although most of the debris seemed to stem from the unstable scaffolding rather than the building itself. However, gaping holes had appeared in the roof, so that the golden sunlight of late afternoon caught the swirling dust and made patterns with it. Of Tysilia there was no sign.

'Here,' said Ralph, pulling ineffectually at a heavy slab of oak. 'She is under this.'

Bartholomew saw that one of the ugliest gargoyles he had ever seen had fallen virtually whole on top of the hapless Tysilia. It looked as though the artist had intended it to be a pig, but had lost interest halfway through. He turned his attention to Tysilia's body. Most of her was unscathed: it was only her head that had been caught under the carving.

'It has destroyed her clever mind,' Bartholomew heard the clerk mutter facetiously to Ralph. 'What a pity she will be giving no more of her erudite opinions on the mysteries of the universe.'

'Crushed by a pig,' said Ralph, who was fighting to adopt

a suitably sombre expression. 'What a way to go!'

Bartholomew crouched to examine her, although he knew she could not have survived under the tremendous weight of the gargoyle. De Lisle, however, pushed him away, kneeling next to her with tears running down his face.

'Tysilia!' he wept. 'How could the saints have allowed this to happen?'

'Perhaps one of them arranged it,' murmured Ralph to the clerk. 'St Etheldreda probably does not like being asked to deliver monks into the amorous clutches of women like that.'

'Let me examine her,' said Bartholomew, trying to ease his way past de Lisle. 'I may be able to do something.'

'You cannot,' said de Lisle, stricken. 'It is clear she is beyond any earthly help, and I do not want her poked at.'

'But we should be sure—' began Bartholomew.

'No,' whispered de Lisle, taking one of the lifeless hands in his and pressing it to his cheek. Bartholomew began to feel sorry for him. 'Someone will pay for this.'

'What do you mean?' asked Bartholomew, startled. 'It was an accident. She should not have wandered where she knew she was not supposed to be.'

'Someone caused this to fall deliberately,' fumed de Lisle, grief giving way to anger. 'The roof was unstable, but it was not that bad. Someone pushed something.'

Bartholomew was sure he was wrong, but there was a gallery running around the top of the transept, and so he supposed it was possible that someone had climbed up to it to launch a murderous attack on Tysilia, although he could not imagine who or why.

'Blanche,' snarled de Lisle, as if reading his thoughts. 'Blanche is responsible for this, to pay me back for Glovere.'

'I do not think so,' said Bartholomew reasonably. 'Murder is a grave sin at any time, but it would be even more so in a cathedral.'

'Blanche and her retinue are witches and warlocks,' ranted de Lisle. 'I will have them burned for heresy.'

Bartholomew stepped back as the Bishop came to his

feet fast, launching into a diatribe of hatred against the enemy he imagined to have killed the one person for whom he felt affection. As he moved away from the distraught Bishop, something yellow caught Bartholomew's eye. It was a coin. He picked it up, then spotted another. Ralph saw what he was doing, and within a few moments they had amassed a veritable treasure trove, including a number of coins and a selection of jewellery. De Lisle watched with a lack of interest, more concerned with the inert form of Tysilia.

'I know what these are,' said Ralph, gazing down at their hoard. 'They are items stolen during those burglaries in the town – there is the Bishop's ring and here is his silver plate. The thief has been storing them here, in the cathedral.'

'How ingenious,' said the clerk. 'Stolen property would be perfectly safe in this part of the building, because everyone is afraid that the whole thing will come down at the slightest touch.'

'I keep telling you that it is *not* that unstable,' said de Lisle testily. 'Alan is an excellent engineer, and he said the place would last for years yet. It is a little wobbly, but it is not about to tumble around our ears at any moment.'

'Tysilia would disagree,' muttered the clerk, staring at the dusty white legs that poked from under the gargoyle.

'But I have noticed fresh falls myself,' argued Bartholomew, not sure that he believed de Lisle. 'That angel, for example.'

But even as he pointed at the carving, he could see fresh marks on it, where it had apparently been chiselled away from its holding. He stared at it in confusion. De Lisle watched him.

'It seems to me that someone wanted people to believe the transept was dangerous so that they would stay out,' de Lisle surmised. 'And everyone was to stay out because here are the proceeds from those thefts.'

'Leycestre,' murmured Bartholomew to himself. 'So that is what he and John were discussing so furtively. No wonder

John knew about the burglaries – it may even have been his idea to use the cathedral as a storeroom.'

'What?' demanded de Lisle. 'What are you muttering about?'

'Nothing,' said Bartholomew, thinking of his promise to John. He supposed he would be justified in breaking it, given that John had kept a substantial part of the truth from him, but he did not want to see the priest suffer the kind of fate that might well be in store for Leycestre.

'Gather this treasure together,' de Lisle instructed his clerk and steward. He sighed impatiently when he saw them glance nervously at the ceiling. 'I have told you it is safe. Someone deliberately caused the fall you just saw, and it will not happen again.'

'It might,' said Ralph fearfully. 'Someone will not want us taking all this treasure.'

'No one is up there,' said de Lisle in a tone that brooked no argument. 'When you have collected it you can take it to my house, where we will arrange for the victims of these thefts to reclaim what is rightfully theirs.'

'What, all of it?' asked Ralph in horror.

De Lisle thought for a moment. 'Well, we will remove a little something as our reward for finding it. I shall need funds now that I have to pay for a requiem mass.' He looked back at the crumpled form beneath the statue. 'My fallen angel!'

'I think that is a pig, actually,' said Ralph, turning his head to inspect the gargoyle.

'I meant Tysilia,' said de Lisle in a strangled voice. 'My poor Tysilia!'

'Yes?' came a muffled voice from the ground.

Ralph and the clerk backed away in alarm, while de Lisle and Bartholomew gazed at Tysilia's body in astonishment. De Lisle crossed himself quickly.

'It is a miracle!' the Bishop whispered, awed. 'St Etheldreda has brought her back to us. I just hope she still has a head to claim as her own – life could be difficult without one, and the saints often forget this sort of detail when they perform their miracles.'

'She has managed without a brain so far,' muttered Bartholomew, kneeling to examine her. 'And she was not dead in the first place: this statue has fallen in such a way that I think she is unscathed.'

'But you told me she was dead!' shouted de Lisle accusingly. 'You are a physician, so I believed you.'

'I did no such thing,' retorted Bartholomew. 'You would not let me near her.'

He felt under the stone, then took Tysilia's feet and hauled her in an undignified manner from beneath the pig. When he released her, she sat up, her hair a dusty mess around her face and her clothes in ruins. She took a deep breath and shook her head, as though to clear it. Ralph and the clerk took a hasty step backward, as though they imagined she might shake it from her shoulders and they did not want to be nearby when it happened.

'That was not nice,' she declared. 'It was quite dark for a few moments, as though I was in my bed asleep. But of course I was not, was I?'

'Tysilia!' exclaimed de Lisle in delight, leaning forward to give her a heartfelt embrace.

'I am hungry,' she said, fending him off. 'And I do not like this church. What do you say to a visit to a tavern? There are lots of very nice young men in taverns.'

'Whatever you say,' said de Lisle fondly, helping her to her feet and taking her hand to lead her away from the rubble.

'I thought we were rid of her for a moment,' said Ralph, sounding deeply disappointed. 'But St Etheldreda stepped in and saved her, just as the Bishop said. It just goes to show that even saints can make mistakes sometimes.'

chapter 11

'AND SHE JUST SAT UP AND SHOOK HERSELF?' ASKED Michael, half amazed and half amused by Tysilia's reaction to her brush with death when Bartholomew gave him details of the miraculous escape as they sat in the refectory at sunset. An early evening meal had already been served, but Michael had managed to inveigle himself something extra from the kitchens. 'She did not complain of a headache or start to weep from fright?'

'She said she was hungry, and was bored by de Lisle's exclamations of delight and relief.'

'And the gargoyle had fallen in such a way as to leave her completely unharmed?'

'More or less. De Lisle thinks St Etheldreda intervened. But what shall we do about Leycestre? Shall we lie in wait and catch him red-handed as he relieves Alan of the monastic silver tonight?'

'Given our performance in the Bone House, I am not sure that is wise,' said Michael. 'And Leycestre's crimes are irrelevant to us anyway. It is the killer I want to catch, not a man with a penchant for other people's property.'

'But it is still possible they are one and the same,' said Bartholomew. 'John said Glovere, Chaloner and Haywarde all expressed no interest in Leycestre's rebellion, and it occurred to him that Leycestre had murdered them.'

'But he has no evidence,' Michael pointed out. 'John is a frightened man who realises that he cannot follow his conscience and the law at the same time. He is afraid of everyone. And how do you know he has not already told Leycestre that you have guessed what he intends to do tonight?'

'I think John will be halfway to Lincoln by now,' said Bartholomew. 'He was so terrified by his discussion with me that he will snatch the advantage he has been given and run away.'

'I am not so sure,' said Michael. 'He will have warned Leycestre, and there will be no theft from Prior Alan or anyone else.' He gave a sudden chuckle and changed the subject. 'De Lisle is a popular man at the moment. He took all that treasure to his house and displayed it for the merchants to identify and collect. It had all been returned to its owners in less than an hour.'

'Was everyone's property there?'

'Almost. Agnes Fitzpayne had listed various items that were not recovered.'

'I told you,' said Bartholomew triumphantly. 'There was nothing for her to claim, because nothing was stolen from her. And the fact that she was the only "victim" whose property did not reappear affirms it.'

'She was *not* the only one, though,' said Michael. 'A certain number of coins also remain missing, although all the jewellery was accounted for.'

'You should know where *they* went,' said Bartholomew, thinking that de Lisle would be very pleased with his unexpected windfall. No one would accuse him of keeping a small profit for himself when he had been to such pains to return the bulk of it to its rightful owners.

'I have had enough of the rebels and their petty crimes,' said Michael, obviously not wanting to hear that de Lisle was less than honest. 'But while you were busy pulling Tysilia from under pigs by her legs, I was also busy. I happen to know that Symon the librarian is currently lurking in his favourite hiding place – the latrines. He thinks he will avoid an awkward interrogation from me regarding the state of his back.'

'Then we should talk to him immediately,' said Bartholomew, taking the monk's sleeve and tugging it to make him finish his meal and leave. 'He is an elusive fellow, and if you have him pinned down, we should take the opportunity to speak to him before he disappears again.'

'He is an unpleasant piece of work,' said Michael, shaking Bartholomew off and returning to his food. 'I was thinking that if we left it long enough, the killer might come and relieve us of the bother of talking to the man.'

'I thought we were going to talk to him *because* he has a bad back, and we think *he* might be the one you hit with a spade.'

Michael shook his head. 'The killer is a clever man, and the only thing Symon is clever at doing is eluding people who want to see him. He blusters and brags, but when you press him it is obvious that he is nothing but hot air, and his knowledge is superficial and often erroneous.'

'But we should talk to him anyway,' said Bartholomew. 'We should at least learn how he came by his ailment. And do not forget he is one of our main suspects for the death of Thomas.'

Seeing that Bartholomew would not let matters rest until they had interrogated the elusive librarian, Michael sighed and stood, wiping the crumbs from his mouth as he followed the physician out of the refectory and into the soft gloom of a late summer evening. They walked to the latrines, looking at the monks who were still out for signs of limps or twinges. They passed Henry who emerged from his infirmary. He stretched both arms above his head, then clutched his back to give it a vigorous massage.

'How are you?' he asked of Bartholomew. 'What did you think of my tonic?'

'It worked well,' said Bartholomew. 'But I think it would be dangerous if taken too often.'

Henry nodded. 'I keep it only for emergencies. You will not take another dose, then? To see you through this unpleasant investigation?'

'He will not,' said Michael shortly. 'I do not want him exhausting me with excessive energy.'

As they talked, Prior Alan strolled towards them with a

distinctly uneven gait, and informed Bartholomew and Henry that his hip always ached when he spent too much time climbing on scaffolding – which he said he had been doing that day to oversee the work on Holy Cross Church. Henry offered him a poultice, and they disappeared inside the hospital together.

'I wonder if his climbs on scaffolding extend to pushing gargoyles on bishops' nieces,' muttered Bartholomew as they went on their way.

'No one tried to kill Tysilia, Matt,' said Michael. 'De Lisle was distraught, and was making unfounded accusations in his grief.' He looked thoughtful for a moment. 'Of course, it would have been difficult for Blanche to extricate herself from *that* indictment, given that she publicly threatened to kill Tysilia – the day we found Robert, remember? – and that she had a grudge against de Lisle because of Glovere.'

'Do you think de Lisle arranged to have the stone pushed himself, so he would be able to accuse Blanche of dirty tricks?'

Michael seriously considered the possibility. 'If so, then the pusher would have had to be a man he trusted, because he would not have wanted the pig to land on him by mistake. But Ralph was with you, and so I do not think that a likely scenario, Matt.'

'Is Ralph the only man he would depend on for such a thing?'

'Yes, I think so. But, unlikely though it sounds, de Lisle loves Tysilia and I do not believe he would risk harming her.'

'De Lisle is certain it was not an accident. It seems that the north-west transept was actually reasonably safe, but rumours were circulated that it was not. I asked Henry about it, and he thinks the rumours originated with John and Leycestre. Leycestre is obviously good at spreading tales that benefit him.'

'But it was not safe,' Michael pointed out. 'There were bits of broken stone all over the floor, and a pig dropped on Tysilia's head.'

'Then they were pushed deliberately, to maintain the illusion of instability. It was not so much the building that fell anyway – it was the scaffolding that was supposed to be shoring it up.'

'But why did Alan, who is an excellent engineer, say nothing to contradict these rumours?'

'Because he hopes some wealthy pilgrim will be so appalled by the state of the cathedral that he will donate funds for its restoration. He said as much when we first arrived. Alan seems as dishonest as Robert where money for his engineering is concerned.'

'He is obsessed with it,' agreed Michael. 'But here we are, at the latrines. This is a pleasant way to pass an evening. Why did I allow you to drag me from a perfectly good meal for this?'

'To catch your killer, Brother. And speaking of killers, if you look towards the Prior's House, you will see Agnes Fitzpayne meeting Alan. I wager you anything you choose that her presence here is the first stage in the plan to rob the priory. The theft is under way.'

'Is it my imagination, or is she limping?' asked Michael, peering through the gloom of dusk to where Bartholomew pointed.

'She is limping,' said Bartholomew. 'But she is wearing her best clothes for her assignation with Prior Alan, and it is possible that her shoes pinch. There is Welles. He is limping, too.'

'So he is,' said Michael. 'But he was not doing so earlier. The more I look around me, the more I realise that many folk walk in a way that is extremely odd. I have never noticed it before, but people really do have distinctive gaits.'

Bartholomew saw that Michael was right, and was aware of a slight throb in his own back, probably as a result of pulling William from the water the previous day.

'What will you do about that gold thread we found in William's cross?' asked Bartholomew, squinting up to where the first stars were beginning to gleam in a sky that was just turning from light to dark blue. 'Will you question Guido about it?'

'Yes, of course. But whoever killed William battered him over the head – no blades were inserted in his neck. This makes me suspect – rightly or wrongly – that William's killer is different to the others'. So, Guido can wait until tomorrow. Today, I want to catch the neck-stabber.'

'Guido may not be here tomorrow,' warned Bartholomew. 'He will have taken the money offered by Leycestre and left.'

'Then I will follow him. The clan owns a number of carts – his tracks will not be hard to find.'

'I am not so sure about that. Leycestre is unlikely to pay someone to disappear who will be easily found. Once Guido leaves Ely, you may never see him again.'

'That may be true elsewhere, but not here,' said Michael confidently. 'There are a limited number of paths through the Fens, and people with heavy carts can hardly load them all on to boats. They will not go far.'

Bartholomew thought he was wrong, but saw there was little point in arguing. He began to walk along the line of latrines, opening each door to see whether anyone was hiding inside. One or two people were there on perfectly legitimate business, but their outraged objections died in their throats when Michael leaned into the stalls to enquire whether they wished to make a complaint. The expression on his face made it clear that the best thing they could do would be to close the door and ignore whatever happened outside.

When they had reached the last stall, and there was no sign of Symon, Bartholomew began to think that the slippery librarian had eluded them yet again. But when he shoved the door open as far as it would go, it met with resistance, and when he pushed against it harder still, there was a small grunt of pain.

'Come out, Symon,' ordered Michael. 'I do not like latrines at the best of times, and I am not impressed that my search for you has led me here yet again. I am not in a good mood, and you would be wise to pander to my wishes.'

Reluctantly, Symon sidled from the stall, looking this way and that as though he imagined he might be able to run if the questions became too awkward. Michael grabbed him firmly by the arm and dragged him away. When he reached a place where the air suited him better, Michael stopped, but did not release his prey.

'You have a bad back,' he began without preamble. 'Would you care to tell us how you came by it?'

'No,' said Symon shortly.

'Then I suggest you reconsider, unless you want to spend all your time in the latrines for the next year. I am an influential man, and if I make a recommendation to Prior Alan that these buildings are filthy and need to be cleaned daily, he will comply with my suggestion regarding who is the best-suited man for the task.'

Symon blanched. Even his affinity with the latrines did not stretch that far, and he evidently knew Michael was the kind of man to carry out his threat. He began to bluster. 'I do not know how I came by my ailment. It just happened.'

'You did not engage in a fight of any kind or attack someone?' prompted Michael.

Symon regarded him as though he were insane. 'Are you mad? Of course I did not fight anyone! That kind of behaviour is for novices and men who are paid by the Bishop to chase criminals. *I* am a *librarian*!' He drew himself up to his full height and regarded Michael with disdain.

'Then how do you account for your bad back?' pressed Michael, unmoved. 'These things do not "just happen". You have to do something to aggravate them. Is that not true, Matt?'

'When you hide in the latrines, do you sit?' asked Bartholomew, deciding not to answer. Backaches were difficult complaints to diagnose, and came about as a result of a wide variety of causes. He had treated many patients who

claimed that a sudden pain in the back had started for no
apparent reason.

'That is a highly personal question,' said Symon, clinging
to the last vestiges of his dignity. 'But yes, I do. Sitting allows
me to rest my legs, whereas standing means I tend to lean
against the walls.' He shuddered. 'And no one should do
that in there.'

'Then your backache may be explained by your sitting
too long in one position,' said Bartholomew. 'There is not
much space for moving in those stalls. I recommend you
either stand more often or find another hiding place.'

'Thank you,' said Symon stiffly. 'I shall do that.'

'What have you been doing for the last two days?'
demanded Michael scowling at Bartholomew for allowing
the librarian to wriggle from the hook. 'Did you not hear
that we wanted a word with you?'

Symon's expression hardened. 'I have duties to fulfil, and
cannot abandon them just because you have decided to ask
me questions. For your information, I went to visit the nuns
at Denny Abbey yesterday, because they are selling a copy
of Matthew Paris's *Chronica Majora*.'

'You already have at least three copies of that,' said
Bartholomew, puzzled. 'Why do you want another?'

Symon glowered at Bartholomew, who assumed the
librarian had not known about the existence of duplicates.
'This one was illustrated,' he growled. 'My readers prefer
books with pictures. But suffice to say that I was engaged
with priory business, and that I have only recently returned.'

'I see,' said Michael, clearly not believing a word. 'What
were you doing at midnight on Friday? Were you here, trying
to avoid leaning on the walls, or were you out and about?
Near the Bone House, for example?'

'I certainly was not,' said Symon indignantly. 'And I was
in my library on Friday night, cleaning up the mess your
friend left with his reading. Henry may have heard me from
the infirmary, so you can ask him.'

'We will ask him,' said Michael, releasing the librarian's

arm. 'And if he does not support your claim, we will be back to talk to you again. Do not think that you will evade me: I know this priory as well as you do, and there is nowhere you can go that I will not find you.'

Symon scuttled away as fast as he could when released from Michael's interrogation, leaving the monk staring thoughtfully after him. Michael and Bartholomew began to walk back up the hill together, away from the odorous latrines. Michael professed himself unconvinced by Symon's story, and said he was going to ask Henry about the library's creaking floorboards. Meanwhile, the physician was concerned about the sudden presence of Agnes Fitzpayne in the monastery, and intended to do something about it. Prior Alan had been kind to him, and he did not want to repay the man's hospitality by allowing a theft to take place that might see some of the cathedral-priory's treasures permanently lost. He decided to ask his book-bearer to help him catch the thieves.

Cynric was more than willing to assist, claiming that he was bored in Ely with nothing to do other than help the cooks in the kitchen or wander the town's taverns. Meadowman was with him, and also readily agreed to a little thief-taking.

'What is the plan?' asked Cynric keenly, walking next to Bartholomew as they headed towards the Prior's House. 'Agnes Fitzpayne is already inside, you say?'

'I do not know the details,' said Bartholomew. 'I only know that it is already in action.'

'Not *their* plan,' said Cynric impatiently. 'Ours. What do you intend to do?'

Bartholomew regarded his book-bearer uneasily. 'How can we have a plan? We do not know what is going to happen.'

Cynric sighed in exasperation. 'But you have to have some idea as to what you want us to do! We cannot stand in a row outside Alan's house and wait for Leycestre to walk past.

Obviously our presence there would warn him that something was amiss.'

'We will hide, then,' determined Bartholomew. 'You can take the trees in the garden opposite Alan's house, Meadowman can stay near the end of the refectory, and I will find somewhere to disappear near the Prior's Great Hall.'

'And what are we looking for, exactly?' asked Cynric. 'Do you anticipate that Leycestre and his nephews will slip into the monastery unnoticed, creep up to Alan's solar, and help Agnes demand all his money? Now? Before all the monks have gone to bed?'

'Most of them have,' said Meadowman pedantically. 'I can see their lights in the dormitory and most of the precinct is deserted.'

Cynric sighed, 'But a few have not – Symon, Alan and Henry, to name but three. My point remains.'

'I suppose an evening crime would be a new venture for them,' admitted Bartholomew. 'Previously, they have entered and left their victims' property in the depths of the night. I do not know why Agnes asked for an interview with the Prior, but I am certain it is all part of their plot.'

'Perhaps she is aware that the rebels have been exposed, and she is asking Alan for his forgiveness while she still can,' suggested Meadowman charitably.

Bartholomew shook his head. 'They will be angry and desperate. They have worked hard and taken a lot of chances to burgle those houses over these last three weeks, but today saw them lose every last penny when their hoard was discovered in the transept. Leycestre has already bribed the gypsies to leave before tomorrow – to take the blame for the theft he plans to commit – so they have no choice but to act tonight.'

'But I thought you said that all the treasure Leycestre stole has been recovered,' Meadowman pointed out, always one to see flaws in the details. 'How will he pay the gypsies for their part of the bargain?'

'I do not know,' replied Bartholomew, becoming exasperated with the fact that the servants seemed more inclined to talk than to act. 'Perhaps they have already received their reward. Or perhaps he plans to pay them with some of whatever he takes tonight.'

'Very well, then,' said Cynric, apparently deciding the time was ripe for action. 'It is now dark, so I suppose they will be making their move soon. It is a pity for them that the night is clear and that there is a moon. Stay still and quiet, and be aware that they may carry weapons.'

They took up their posts, and Bartholomew watched the night settle cool and dark across the Fenland town. He was anticipating a lengthy wait, and was just moving into a comfortable position against the sun-warmed wall when he saw the familiar shape of Leycestre moving through the shadows created by the moonlight. The man was walking quickly towards the Prior's House from the direction of the vineyard. He was not alone; Brother Symon was with him, still limping from his aching back, and Leycestre's nephews were in their customary vanguard position. Bartholomew watched them in surprise. Surely Leycestre had not persuaded the librarian to rally to his cause?

The four men ducked among the trees of the Prior's garden, dangerously close to where Bartholomew knew Cynric was hiding. The physician was not unduly concerned. His wily book-bearer would not be caught by the likes of the rebel leader and the librarian.

Within a few moments, Agnes Fitzpayne emerged from the Prior's solar and stood speaking with Alan outside. Immediately, Symon left his hiding place and walked towards them, his casual saunter making it appear as though he had just happened to be passing. Bartholomew eased a little closer, so that he could hear what was being said.

'Good evening, Mistress Fitzpayne,' said Symon pleasantly. 'What brings you here?'

'I came to warn Prior Alan that some misguided people intend to break into the priory and rob it tonight,' she

replied. 'They will be looking for gold and silver. I suggested
that everything of value should be locked somewhere safe.'

'This is grave news,' said Symon, sounding concerned.
'But it was good of you to warn us.' He turned to Alan. 'I
am sure her fears are valid, Father, because a number of
houses have been burgled recently. We should secure all
our treasure in a place they will not think to look.'

'But where?' asked Alan worriedly. 'My chapel is the
obvious place, but there are no good locks on the doors –
and I do not want to be responsible for the violent fight
between monks and thieves that will surely ensue if I leave
guards with it.'

'I quite agree,' said Symon, rather too quickly. 'Bloodshed
must be avoided at all costs.'

'I would rather we just put the treasure somewhere they
will not think of looking,' Alan went on. 'It would avoid a
lot of unpleasantness – I have no grudge against desperate
people, and do not want to antagonise our peasants by being
forced to hang the leaders of this silly rebellion.'

'What about the library?' suggested Symon, as if the idea
had just occurred to him. 'It has strong locks, and only you
and I have the keys.'

Alan's worry evaporated. 'That is an excellent idea! No
one would ever think of raiding the library. We shall leave
one or two paltry items lying around to pacify these thieves,
so they will leave peacefully, but the valuable items we shall
hide away.'

'Good,' said Symon, sounding pleased. 'I shall make an
immediate start in moving it.'

'I will see Mistress Fitzpayne safely to the gate, then come
to help you,' said Alan. 'It is best that only you and I know
about this if we want to avoid trouble.'

Symon bowed to his Prior, then headed for the chapel.
Alan offered his arm to Agnes and walked away with her.

'Shall I fetch Brother Michael?' came a low voice at
Bartholomew's elbow. The physician jumped in alarm, horrified that Cynric could sneak up behind him and take him

unawares when he thought he was being watchful. He nodded, and the Welshman disappeared silently into the darkness.

Meanwhile, Symon emerged from the Prior's chapel staggering under a substantial armful of silver candlesticks, jewelled patens and heavy gold crosses. The moonlight illuminated him quite clearly, almost as clearly as if it were day. He could barely walk, but somehow managed to reach the library without dropping anything. Bartholomew followed cautiously, aware that he was not the only one dogging Symon's footsteps: Leycestre and his nephews had also left their hiding places, and intercepted the librarian near the infirmary. Fortunately, they were too intent on the treasure they anticipated would soon be theirs to notice Bartholomew behind them.

While the thieves made their way around the east end of the hospital to reach the library door via the cemetery, the physician ducked into the Dark Cloister and trotted quickly through the infirmary hall, aiming to slip through the back door, where he could creep through the bushes without being seen. The old men were dozing, but Henry watched his antics in bemusement.

'What are you doing?' he whispered, so as not to disturb his sleeping patients.

'Leycestre and his nephews are about to make off with the priory's silver,' Bartholomew explained, glancing over his shoulder. 'Symon is helping them.'

'Symon?' whispered Henry, aghast. 'You are mistaken!'

'Come and see for yourself,' Bartholomew invited. 'There is no mistake.'

Henry followed him through the rear door, then through the undergrowth that extended as far as the library entrance – near where Tysilia had met William. The infirmarian said nothing, but Bartholomew sensed his unease and distaste at what they were doing. Obviously Henry had not had much cause in the past to scramble among bushes in the dark to spy on his colleagues.

'Give it to me now,' Leycestre was saying to Symon. 'There is no point in taking it all up the stairs, only to carry it down again later.'

'True,' agreed Symon. 'But take half: I will have to put some in the library, or Alan will wonder what I am doing with it.'

There were clanks as the treasure exchanged hands, and moments later one of the nephews could be seen running away with it, aiming for the vineyard.

'I do not believe this,' whispered Henry, his voice cracked with distress. 'That is Symon, and I have just seen him pass the Lancaster Chalice – one of our most prized possessions – to Leycestre's nephew!'

'Here comes Alan,' said Bartholomew, as the Prior staggered towards them, laden down under a substantial chest.

'Do not tell me *he* is involved, too!' exclaimed Henry. 'He always seemed relatively honest.'

'Another trip each should see most of the treasure secure,' panted Alan, all but dropping the chest at Symon's feet. 'This is probably the most valuable thing, because it contains all our gold pieces and some precious stones. Some of them are worth a small fortune. Be sure to hide it well. Pile some books around it, so it is properly disguised.'

They disappeared up the library stairs together, the chest between them, and moments later came the sound of tomes being shifted around. Bartholomew also heard a cry of dismay from Alan, as he saw for the first time the state of the library; this was followed by Symon's loudly defensive claims that the mess was temporary. Leycestre and his remaining nephew stood patiently in the shadows, and did not move until Alan and Symon had left for the Prior's House to collect the last of the treasure, and had returned with it. Then Alan bade Symon a breathless good night, informing him that he had warned the guards to be on the alert for intruders without being specific.

'Not that it will do much good,' he added ruefully. 'The

guards tonight are lay-brothers – townsfolk – whose sympathies lie with the people they believe are being oppressed. That is another reason why it would be better for everyone if this plan to rob us were thwarted, and did not result in a physical confrontation. The guards might well fight on the side of the thieves.'

'I will make sure this door is locked,' said Symon. 'Go to your bed, Father. The priory's treasure will be safe with me.'

'It will not!' Michael's loud voice and the sudden flare of light as torches were lit made everyone jump. The flames immediately revealed Leycestre and his remaining nephew, who turned to melt away into the bushes but found themselves facing the tip of Cynric's sword. They regarded each other in alarm, and Leycestre turned accusingly to Symon, who was gazing around him in open-mouthed horror.

'You betrayed us, Symon! You promised to help, and now you have betrayed us!'

'He has done nothing of the sort,' said Michael tartly. 'He is every bit as guilty of this dreadful crime as you are.'

'This is not how it seems,' began Symon, appealing to Alan with a sickly smile. 'It is all a terrible misunderstanding.'

'You were assisting these men to steal our treasure?' asked Alan, bewildered and trying to make sense of the scene that was unfolding before him.

Symon glanced around surreptitiously, apparently considering possible escape routes. His eyes lingered on the dark cemetery, but Bartholomew and Henry climbed from among the undergrowth and blocked his path, and Meadowman and the imposing presence of Michael guarded the only other possible way out. The librarian's shoulders sagged in defeat.

'They made me do it,' he said in a low voice. 'I did not want to.'

'Yes, we made him,' said Leycestre harshly. 'We promised him a share of any treasure he helped us steal, and so placed him under indescribable pressure as he was forced to choose between loyalty to his priory and his natural greed. As you can see, greed won the day.'

'It was not like that,' said Symon unsteadily. 'I would have given my share back to the priory.'

'Then why steal it at all?' asked Alan, as unconvinced by Symon's desperate lies as everyone else who heard them.

'Because of you,' said Symon, taking a step closer to Alan and still smiling ingratiatingly. 'The Bishop is unpopular in the town, and men like him will be the first to go when the rebellion gets under way. Then *you* will be elected Bishop, and we will all be very much happier.'

'And I suppose you imagine *you* will be elected Prior in my place,' said Alan coolly. 'You will not. I would never appoint a man who spends half of his time devising ways to shirk his duties and the other half putting his ideas into practice. I had no idea you had allowed our precious library to sink to such an appalling state. What will our visitors think when they see it?'

'They do not think anything,' said Henry softly. 'They are seldom permitted past its portals – and now you know why.'

'And what do you think will happen to a cathedral-priory if this rebellion ever gains momentum?' asked Michael of Symon in disgust. 'It will not only be landowners like de Lisle who will suffer, but our monastery, too. You would never have been appointed Prior, because there would be no priory for you to rule.'

'We have no grudge against the Benedictines,' began Leycestre uneasily, trying to salvage what he could from the mess he had created.

Michael rounded on him. 'Do you not? That is not what you told me the first day I arrived in this miserable city, and I suggest that you have not been entirely honest with Symon about who will be safe and who will be attacked.'

'You promised me that the priory would not be harmed,' said Symon, taking a menacing step towards Leycestre, when the expression on the rebel's face proved that Michael was right. 'You promised that I would be Prior, and that Alan would be deposed because he would be held responsible for losing the treasure.'

'That sounds more like the truth,' said Alan bitterly. 'You did not intend to rid yourself of me by making me Bishop. You intended to have me disgraced.'

Symon glared at him. 'This is *your* fault.'

'Mine?' asked Alan, startled. 'Why?'

'I came to confess my role in this two days ago, and to warn you. But you were too busy dealing with your precious cathedral to have time for me. In fact, no one was available to hear my confession, so I decided to continue after all.'

'I was available,' said Henry. 'My doors are never closed to a monk in need, as you know.'

'And you cannot blame Prior Alan for your crime, just because he was out when you happened to want him,' Michael pointed out. 'You could have followed your own conscience with this: you do not need a confessor to tell you what is right and what is wrong.'

'This is a sorry mess,' said Henry, looking in disgust at the faces of the men who stood in a circle around the library door. 'I have never seen such treachery and lies. I am ashamed of and disappointed with you all.'

'It *is* a sorry mess,' agreed Michael. He looked at Alan. 'What do you want us to do, Father? Your librarian is a thief and a conspirator, while these others are plotting to rise up against the King himself.'

'Put them in the prison,' said Alan tiredly. 'I shall give the matter some thought and decide tomorrow what shall be done with them. I knew Leycestre and his kinsmen held rebellious beliefs, but I did not know they ran to burglary and the despoiling of monasteries, and I certainly did not imagine that one of my monks would stoop to consorting with them.'

'And arranging for others to be blamed,' said Bartholomew, thinking about Leycestre's agreement with Guido. 'Leycestre even apologised for fighting with the gypsies in the Heyrow, because he realised he needed them to remain in Ely long enough to play their part in his plot.'

Leycestre said nothing, knowing that any excuse would not be believed, and might even incriminate him further. His nephew was less sanguine about the accusations that were being levied.

'Yes, we did intend to have the gypsies blamed,' he declared defiantly. 'But their fate is irrelevant in the scheme of things, and God is on our side. Father John said so.'

'Did he now?' asked Michael coolly. 'And I suppose John allowed you to keep your stolen goods in the cathedral, too, in a place where no one would think to look?'

'It was John who convinced me to take up the battle against oppression,' said Leycestre wearily. 'He is an inspiration to us all.'

'John?' asked Bartholomew, startled. 'But he ran away at the first sign of trouble, and claimed he would only choose which side to support once the outcome was already decided.'

'John would never say that,' said Leycestre. 'He said God will help us when we finally lift the yoke from the shoulders of the people.'

'You will not be lifting any yokes,' said Michael firmly. 'Take them away, Cynric. I am weary of all this treasonous talk.'

When Cynric and Meadowman had gone, prodding their prisoners forward with the tips of their swords, Henry looked at Alan with sombre eyes. Bartholomew knew how the infirmarian felt. It was not pleasant to know that a monk had been responsible for attempting to strip the priory of its sacred vessels and crosses, and it was worse to think that the man had also conspired to have Alan deposed. While Alan might not be an ideal Prior, and often put his architectural projects above his other responsibilities, he had dedicated most of his life to the Church, and he deserved better than Symon.

'There is far too much evil in this world,' Henry sighed. 'Everywhere I turn it is staring me in the face. It is bad enough in the town, but I thought matters would be better here, in the sacred confines of a priory.'

'There will be sin where there are people,' said Alan pragmatically. 'And it will always be so.'

'I thought things would change after the Death,' Henry went on. 'The city saw God's displeasure when He sent a terrible pestilence, and I heard many confessions during those black times. But as soon as the disease loosened its hold, people went back to their old ways.'

'As I said,' replied Alan wearily. 'It will always be so. But this is no place to be. Come to my solar for a cup of wine, and we shall pray for the souls of these misguided people.'

Bartholomew declined, not wanting to talk any more about it, while Henry claimed that his patients needed him in the infirmary. Michael went, however, never one to refuse the offer of a goblet of wine. Since one of Leycestre's nephews had escaped with a decent portion of the monastic silver, Bartholomew decided to track him down before it was lost for good. He met Cynric and Meadowman near the prison. Meadowman was carrying a heavy sack.

'That looks like the treasure that went missing,' said Bartholomew, realising that he had been too slow and that the servants had already acted.

Cynric nodded. 'The other lad made off with it. He is in a cell, and this sack is about to be returned to the Prior.'

Bartholomew was amazed. 'Not much passes you, does it! The Prior owes you a casket of wine for your work tonight.'

Cynric grinned. 'Then just make sure he pays up. We have locked Symon in one cell, and Leycestre and his boys in the other. They were blaming each other for their predicament, and I did not want them to murder each other during the night.'

'They cannot escape?' confirmed Bartholomew.

'The doors are locked with a key and bolted from the outside.'

'Then you should deliver your treasure to Alan. I am sure he will be suitably grateful.'

Cynric and Meadowman walked away, leaving Bartholomew aimless and certainly not ready for bed. He saw the servants leave the Prior's solar a short while later, and the glitter of a coin that Cynric was tossing in the air. Alan had evidently paid them well for their troubles. They headed for the Steeple Gate, then crossed the road towards the taverns.

Bartholomew was half tempted to join them, but did not feel like sitting in a humid inn drinking copious quantities of ale. He wanted to do something active that would dispel the restlessness that was dogging him. He left the priory through the Steeple Gate, and began to walk towards the marketplace without much thought as to where he was going. The night had brought cooler air, and the fierce heat of the day had eased. Had he not been unsettled by the business with the burglars, he might have enjoyed the stroll in the velvety darkness of night from the cathedral to the quayside, past houses where candles gleamed in the windows and delicious smells still emanated from the kitchens.

More people thronged the streets than he had expected so long past dusk on a Sunday, and there was an atmosphere of anticipation. Some people were running, while others were chattering in excitement. Bartholomew wondered whether the news had already spread that their main rabble rouser was in the Prior's cells. He recognised the bulky form of Master Barbour of the Lamb, and went to talk to him.

'I trust your stolen gold was returned safely to you,' he said.

'Most of it,' said Barbour with a grimace. 'The thieves had already spent about a quarter, but better most back than none. The Bishop shall have my prayers for finding it, even if he did do so at the expense of a gargoyle landing on his niece's head.'

Bartholomew smiled, thinking that de Lisle had done well if he had taken that sort of percentage for himself. He nodded to the noisy streets. 'What has happened to make people leave their homes so late?'

'The Bishop's house was set alight,' said Barbour disapprovingly. 'That was an evil deed.'

'Was there any damage? Was anyone hurt?'

'No,' said Barbour. 'The alarm was raised by the gypsy folk before the blaze took hold, and there is only a scorch mark to show for her efforts. As you can see, the excitement is over and most people have gone home now.'

'Whose efforts?' asked Bartholomew. 'Tysilia's?'

'There are some who say they saw Lady Blanche,' said Barbour, puzzlement creasing his face. 'But she does not seem like the kind of woman who would sneak around at night and set light to people's homes.'

'She thinks de Lisle did exactly that to her cottages at Colne,' said Bartholomew.

'But she does not think he did it himself,' Barbour pointed out. 'She thinks he arranged for someone else – Ralph, probably – to do it for him. Anyway, that is what people are saying. But I must be back to my tavern, or I shall miss the pleasure of discussing this with my regular customers. They will be all but ready for their beds by now. Few linger in taverns too late when there is the harvest to be gathered at daybreak.'

'Except on Wednesdays, presumably,' remarked Bartholomew, 'when the men are paid. A good deal of late-night drinking takes place then.'

Barbour grinned. 'Wednesdays are different.'

Bemused by the story about the fire, Bartholomew watched him hurry away. He knew Blanche harboured a strong dislike for the Bishop, but he still could not see her setting light to his house personally. It seemed altogether an odd story. He turned to be on his way, but one of the buckles on his shoe had worked loose, so he stepped to one side and knelt to adjust it.

Moments later, he looked up to see Guido approaching, walking briskly as though he had business to attend. He wore his yellow hat, despite the fact that the evening was warm and that it must be uncomfortably hot. Straightening quickly, Bartholomew intercepted him and wished him goodnight. Guido glared at him.

'For some who never work, maybe,' he said, shoving past the physician to continue walking down the hill towards the Quay. 'Some of us are too busy to waste time looking at whether an evening is pretty.'

'Why are you busy?' asked Bartholomew. 'Do you plan to leave tonight after all?'

Guido rounded on him suddenly, seizing a handful of his shirt and almost lifting him off his feet. 'Stay away from my sister!'

Releasing Bartholomew with such abruptness that the physician stumbled, the scowling gypsy king went on his way. Bartholomew watched him go thoughtfully. The brief encounter had told him all he had wanted to learn from the man: Guido's hat was not as pristine as it had been. It was slightly muddy, and a peculiar bunching at one side indicated that a thread had been caught on something sharp and been pulled out. He wondered whether the local sheriff would consider it evidence enough to charge Guido with William's murder.

Bartholomew felt a surge of disappointment with the gypsy clan. It was easy to blame crimes and mishaps on strangers. He did not like Guido, but he had hoped the man's claims of innocence were genuine, and that he would not prove the bigoted accusations of narrow-minded townsfolk correct. The physician sighed, and wondered what to do. On the one hand, he wanted nothing more to do with the city's turmoils, but on the other, he suspected that Guido would not be an easy man to apprehend once he had left Ely, despite Michael's claims to the contrary. The monk would want to question Guido about William's death now that there was the evidence of the gold thread to consider.

He stared after the gypsy, noting again that the man was not walking for the pleasure of exercise, but striding along purposefully. What had he meant when he said he was busy?

Was he planning his departure that night, when he would disappear into the maze of ditches and dykes and islets with his people, never to be seen in the area again? After a few moments of hesitation, Bartholomew decided on a course of action: he would follow Guido to see where he went, and then he would drag Cynric from his revels if it appeared that the gypsy king intended to evade justice.

Taking a deep breath, not entirely convinced that he was doing the right thing, the physician followed Guido at a discreet distance, edging in and out of doorways to avoid being spotted – not that it was necessary, for Guido never once looked behind him.

He followed Guido to the Mermaid Inn on the Quay, then hesitated outside the door. Now what? He had done what he had set out to do, and knew Guido's intended destination. But the speed of the man's walk suggested that he had pressing business inside, and now Bartholomew decided he wanted to know what. He could hardly enter the inn and continue to observe Guido without being seen, and he did not want to linger outside waiting for him to come out – there were not many places to hide and he was sure his loitering would be noticed and reported to the occupants of the tavern.

Wiping sweat from his eyes with his sleeve, he ducked down a narrow passageway that led to the rear of the premises, uncertain of his plan, but determined to do something. He found himself in a small yard that had weeds growing between the cobbles and a generally derelict air about it, as though it was seldom used. In one corner was a large pile of sacks. Bartholomew had seen sacks like them once before: stacked inside the priory's granary.

He glanced around him, looking for a window or a back door through which he might enter unobtrusively. He saw a small window, and peered through it. It led to a pantry. Like the yard, it appeared to enjoy little regular use, and was piled high with crates and barrels, but none of them looked as if they had been moved recently. Bartholomew pushed open the shutter and eased himself inside, swearing under his breath when a sharp rip told him that he had caught his last good shirt on a nail that protruded from the neglected latch.

He stood on the tiled floor and listened, trying to detect the rumble of voices from the tavern's main room. But the walls were sturdy and thick, and Bartholomew could hear nothing, so he tiptoed across the floor and put his ear to the door. Again, there was nothing. He pulled open the door a little, but the silence remained absolute.

He reflected for a moment. There was little point in lingering in the pantry if he could see and hear nothing of interest. He needed to be nearer the tavern itself. However, he had no wish to be caught trespassing by the landlord and knew it would be difficult to explain why he was lurking in the private recesses of the inn. But, he decided, encountering the landlord was just a chance he would have to take. He grasped the handle and pulled the door open. He leapt in alarm when he saw that it was no empty corridor in front of him, but Guido. The gypsy held a knife in one hand and a candle in the other, and his ugly features were creased into a victorious smile.

Bartholomew backed away quickly, intending to dive through the window and escape into the yard beyond. He knew he could move more quickly than the heavier, slower Guido. But, even as he turned, a shadow darkened his line of vision, and he saw Goran framed in the window, wearing the same gloating grin as his brother. Bartholomew was trapped. He considered leaping for the window anyway, in the hope that his sudden move would take Goran by surprise and that he could make good his escape before the fellow realised what was happening. But there were other people in the yard, too – several of the clan were there, waiting for Guido to tell them what to do. Unfortunately, Eulalia was not among them.

Bartholomew turned back to Guido; he considered

shoving past him to reach the corridor, but Guido was watching him intently, and Bartholomew sensed a mad bid for escape would merely provide the gypsy king with the perfect opportunity to run him through. He let his hands fall to his sides to indicate that he was defeated, and waited to see what would happen next.

'I thought you Cambridge scholars were clever,' began Guido, in a tone of voice that suggested he considered himself cleverer. He set his candle on a shelf without taking his eyes off Bartholomew. 'You followed me, but you did not once glance behind to see whether anyone was following *you*.'

Bartholomew closed his eyes in disgust, aware that he had been unforgivably careless. It had not occurred to him that Guido might have charged his brother to watch his rapid progress down the hill.

'Goran was behind me,' Guido continued. 'And since my cousins and Rosel are here now, as well, you can be assured that you are well and truly outnumbered.'

'So I see,' was all Bartholomew could think to say.

'I suppose you thought you would eavesdrop. You wanted to overhear something that will prove that I am the killer you are hunting.'

Bartholomew was silent.

'You will learn nothing from us,' said Goran, climbing through the window. For some inexplicable reason, he was wearing an expensive-looking cloak and a woman's kirtle. There was padding around his middle, some of which had been arranged to provide him with a substantial bosom, and powders and paste had been applied to his face, so that at a glance he could be mistaken for Lady Blanche. Bartholomew gaped at him.

'It is a good disguise, is it not?' asked Guido, enjoying Bartholomew's confusion. 'Lady Blanche has just set fire to the Bishop's house. She failed as it happened, but a number of people saw her try.'

'Did the Bishop pay you to do this?' asked Bartholomew, thinking that de Lisle might well embark on a plot to clear his own name, since Michael seemed to be incapable of doing so. What better way than to arrange for Blanche to be 'seen' in the very act of venting her spleen against her enemy? Not only would it raise questions about her sanity and behaviour, but it would serve to increase the Bishop's popularity and add credibility to his claim that he was the victim of an unjust persecution.

'Ralph paid us two groats for what we did,' said Goran, pleased with himself. 'It was money honestly earned. No real harm was done, and Guido was ready to raise the alarm before the fire really took hold.'

'When I first saw you dressed as Blanche – here in the Mermaid Inn several days ago – were you demonstrating to the Bishop that you could achieve a reasonable likeness?' asked Bartholomew.

'Ralph wanted to see how good the disguise would be,' said Goran, still smiling in satisfaction. 'Apparently, several people mentioned to the Bishop that Blanche had been seen drinking with us in a tavern. You were fooled, too, I hear.'

'And when you were in the cathedral at midnight on Friday, was that to collect your pay?'

'No. Ralph would not pay us until the job was done,' said Guido. 'The meeting at St Etheldreda's shrine was to finalise details.'

'But the plan will not work,' said Bartholomew, surprised that they thought it would. 'No one will believe that a lady indulges in arson.'

Goran shrugged carelessly. 'That is not our problem. We were paid to do what we did, and what happens next is up to the Bishop and Ralph. But we came here to collect our grain, not to chatter with you.' He glanced at his brother. 'What shall we do with him?'

Outside the window Bartholomew saw Guido's cousins, dressed in their flowing skirts and embroidered hats. The yard was located at the end of an alley, well out of sight, so Bartholomew doubted that anyone knew they were there.

His only hope was that the landlord would see the strangers, and would fetch help. Guido seemed to read his mind.

'It is no good you expecting assistance from the taverner. Leycestre bribed him well to keep his eyes and ears closed regarding anything that happens in his yard tonight.'

'But what are you doing here?' asked Bartholomew, bewildered.

'We have come to collect what Leycestre promised us for leaving Ely,' said Guido. 'Father John is here to make certain that everything is done fairly. I insisted on him, because a man of God would not cheat us – I do not trust Leycestre.'

Bartholomew was not so sure his faith in John was justified, either. He could see the dark robes of the priest as he stood near the grain sacks. Guido's cousins were listening to him as he spoke in a low voice.

'John!' shouted Bartholomew, pushing past Goran. Goran stopped him from jumping through the window, but John glanced in his direction anyway. Bartholomew saw the priest recognise him, and then watched him register the fact that Goran held him in a grip that was far from friendly. For a moment, indecision reigned on John's face, then deliberately and slowly, he turned away.

'What these people choose to do with you is none of my affair,' he said, refusing to look in Bartholomew's direction. 'I will mind my business, and they will leave me alone. That is the arrangement we made.'

'You and I made an arrangement, too,' Bartholomew pointed out.

'True. But you are not in a position to threaten my safety now, and so I consider that particular agreement invalid,' replied John coolly. He moved away, clearly considering the conversation over. Bartholomew knew the priest would not reply if hailed again. He turned back to Guido.

'As I said, we are here to take possession of Leycestre's payment,' said the king of the gypsies, giving a malicious smile when he observed Bartholomew's despair.

'Eulalia suggested we should not accept gold,' added

Goran. 'She said we would only be accused of stealing when we tried to use it, and grain is the best currency anyway – we can use it to trade for anything we want, and if that fails, we can eat it.'

'Eulalia?' asked Bartholomew. He jumped sideways when he saw another person scrambling through the window, and felt a peculiar combination of relief and alarm when he saw the dark hair and eyes of his gypsy friend. 'I thought you were going to stay in Ely.'

'Guido is king now,' she said, with more than a trace of disapproval. 'He makes the decisions for the clan, and we are obliged to follow them. He has decided that we should accept Leycestre's offer and leave the city. All I did was recommend that we ask for wheat.'

'I imagine that suited Leycestre very well,' said Bartholomew. 'He lost all his gold today, thanks to Tysilia.'

'We heard about that,' said Eulalia. She did not smile, even though it was an amusing story.

'You do not have to leave,' Bartholomew said to her, his voice sounding more desperate than he would have liked. 'Leycestre and his nephews are under arrest. As we predicted, they planned to have you accused of stealing the priory's treasure, and your sudden departure tonight was to be evidence of your guilt.'

'If Leycestre is under lock and key, then it *is* necessary for us to leave,' said Eulalia. 'It will not be long before he tells people that we accepted stolen grain, and we will be fugitives anyway.'

'The authorities will track you if you go,' warned Bartholomew. 'They will do exactly what Leycestre intended – assume your guilt because you ran away.'

'No one will find us once we leave,' said Eulalia confidently. 'We know ancient route-ways that are barely above the water, and only a Fenman will be able to track us. None will, though, because they do not like the priory or the Bishop any more than we do.'

'But why are you allowing Leycestre to drive you away?'

asked Bartholomew, thinking they were making a serious mistake. Clerics travelled, too, and it was only a matter of time before the gypsies were recognised by someone from the priory and arrested.

'No one is driving us anywhere,' snarled Guido angrily. 'We are going because I have decided to leave.'

'It has not been pleasant in Ely this year,' said Eulalia, almost apologetically to Bartholomew. 'People have not been as kind as usual, and none of us has enjoyed being accused of crimes of which we were innocent.'

'But by leaving, it will appear as though you were complicit—'

'I know,' she said, raising a hand to his mouth to silence him. 'But that is part of the price we will have to pay for our grain. As I said, there is nothing for us here. You are virtually the only person who has not shunned us.'

'That is because he is lovesick for you, woman,' snapped Guido in disgust. 'It has nothing to do with the fact that we are innocent.'

'There is evidence that Guido killed William,' said Bartholomew, ignoring him and addressing his sister. 'Theft is serious enough, but the murder of one of the priory's most important officials will result in a much more vigorous search. You will not escape.'

Eulalia regarded him sombrely as she considered this new information. It was growing crowded in the small room with Eulalia, Guido and Goran there, and Bartholomew felt hot and hemmed in. He flinched when Goran accidentally bumped him, and his bare arm touched Guido's blade. He glanced at the weapon uneasily, wondering whether it was the one that had killed Glovere, Chaloner and the others.

'What evidence do you have?' sneered Guido contemptuously, when Eulalia said nothing. 'You cannot prove the clan had anything to do with that.'

'Not the clan,' said Bartholomew softly. 'You. Michael knows enough to hang you.'

Eulalia stood close to Bartholomew, gazing into his face.

'Are you telling the truth?' She nodded slowly, and answered her own question. 'Yes. I think you are. At least, what you perceive to be the truth. But you are wrong, Matthew: Guido has killed no one. I know he often says he will kill if anyone threatens the clan, but it is empty bluster. He is not a murderer.'

Guido's sneer deepened, and Bartholomew thought Eulalia could not be more wrong. Guido was a killer, and at some point he had translated his 'empty bluster' to reality. He pointed to the puckering on Guido's cap. 'The strand of gold thread that you see has been torn from the hat was found on William's body – caught on the cross he wore around his neck. William was engaged in a violent struggle before he died, and it is obvious that the strand was ripped away from the hat then.'

'Liar,' snarled Guido, his sneer instantly replaced by fury. Bartholomew thought he might have gone too far, and was surprised that Eulalia managed to stop her brother's sudden advance merely by turning to look at him and raising one imperious hand.

'Guido told me he had nothing to do with these deaths,' she said to Bartholomew. 'I know he would not lie to me: the clan is not given to telling untruths – at least, not to each other.'

'Then ask him again,' said Bartholomew, aware that Guido was looking decidedly uncomfortable. 'See then whether you still believe him.'

'I had nothing to do with the deaths of the townsmen and those monks – Robert and Thomas,' said Guido firmly, looking Eulalia in the eye as he spoke. She turned to Bartholomew and raised her palms upwards, indicating that she believed her brother.

'I did not say you killed *them*,' said Bartholomew, sensing that as soon as Guido had his sister's trust, he would take the grain and be away. And when Eulalia was out of sight, Bartholomew knew he could expect a knife between his ribs – for angering the clan king as much as to ensure his silence. 'I said you killed *William*.'

'Where is this so-called evidence?' spat Guido, snatching the offending hat from his head as though it were red hot. He shoved it into his shirt, in a gesture that spoke more for his guilt than anything Bartholomew could have said.

Meanwhile, Goran lunged for the physician and pinned him against the wall. Irrelevantly, Bartholomew heard a sharp rip as stitches in his shirt parted company. 'You have nothing against Guido,' Goran growled, forcing his face into Bartholomew's. The physician recoiled at the stench of his breath. 'You are making it up so that there will be distrust and dissension within the clan.'

'Where is this evidence?' repeated Guido. Bartholomew felt the gypsy claw at his medicine bag, supposing that the thread was hidden there. 'Give it to me.'

'You said you did not kill William, Guido,' said Eulalia immediately, regarding her brother through narrowed eyes. 'If that is true, then why are you looking for evidence?'

'We have the gold thread from his hat,' repeated Bartholomew.

Guido ripped the bag from Bartholomew's shoulder, up-ended it and began poking among the contents that rolled across the floor. He found the wineskin that contained the physician's remedy for shocks, and gave an insolent salute before draining its contents. He wiped his lips with the back of his hand, and slung it away. After a few moments, he saw that what he wanted was not in the bag. He lunged towards Bartholomew with his knife at the ready.

'Where is it? You might as well speak now, because you will tell me eventually. We know how to prise secrets from people.'

'I am sure you do,' said Bartholomew, sounding less afraid than he felt, and wishing he had never mentioned the hat. 'But I am telling the truth. The thread is secure in the Prior's solar, and I imagine he has already informed the sheriff about it. What will you do? Murder Alan, to ensure he tells no one what I gave him, then kill the sheriff and his deputies, too? And what about Michael and the other monks? Will you slaughter them as well?'

Eulalia watched the exchange with an expression of growing horror, understanding that Guido would not be so determined to locate the evidence if he knew it did not exist. His knife was dangerously close to Bartholomew's face when she stepped forward and pushed her brother's hand away.

'There will be no killing,' she said in an unsteady voice. She addressed Bartholomew. 'That thread means nothing. Someone put it there, trying to implicate Guido in a crime he did not commit.'

'Then why is he so intent on claiming it back?' demanded Bartholomew, struggling ineffectually against Goran's iron grip. He saw the doubt in her face, and pushed his point further. 'He has denied killing the others, and he may be telling the truth on that score, but he murdered William. Ask him. See whether he can look into your eyes and lie about William.'

Eulalia regarded Guido uneasily. 'Tell him he is wrong. We are not killers. Tell him.'

'You deliver a pretty speech, Eulalia,' sneered Guido. 'And you can stay here to give it to the sheriff if you like, but the rest of us are going. I am not staying here to be hanged for William.'

'You see?' said Bartholomew, appealing to Eulalia. 'He has all but admitted it.'

Guido's thick features became ugly with hatred. 'William deserved to die. He accused us of committing those other murders, and urged us to give ourselves up. He claimed he was riding to Norwich to fetch the King's justices, so that the whole clan would hang.'

Eulalia's face crumpled in shock and Bartholomew realised that convincing her of her brother's guilt had done nothing to extricate him from the precarious situation he was in. Now that Guido was a self-acknowledged killer, he suddenly appeared stronger and more dangerous. Eulalia seemed to shrink before him, while Goran was uncertain and wary. The balance of power in the clan had undergone a subtle shift, and it was in Guido's favour.

'William was travelling north?' asked Bartholomew. He sensed his predicament had just taken a definite turn for the worse, and that it would not be long before Guido decided to put an end to the conversation with the blade of his knife. He felt he was only delaying the inevitable, but some deep instinct drove him to keep talking, to grab every moment he could before his life was snuffed out. 'Is that what he was doing on the river path?'

'Yes,' said Guido. 'He was dressed in his finery, with his saddlebags bulging, to impress the authorities with his presence. He said everyone at the priory was putting too much faith in Michael, who was the Bishop's man and could therefore not be trusted to come up with the complete truth. He was going to fetch independent investigators.'

'So, that is what happened,' said Bartholomew. 'But why did he tell no one of his plans?'

'He said he informed a friend what he was going to do,' replied Guido. 'But I did not believe him. It was obvious that he was lying – claiming that people would come to look for him, just so that I would set him free. Well, he underestimated me. All monks believe the afterlife is more important than this one, so I helped him to Paradise. He was sick anyway. He claimed he had Fen cramps, so I did him a favour by releasing him from his agonies.'

'You knocked him on the head and threw him in the river,' said Bartholomew harshly. 'It was cold-blooded murder.'

'It was self-defence,' corrected Guido. 'He fought like the Devil – scratching and clawing at me, and trying to rake me with his nails.' He gazed around at his mute relatives. 'Do not look at me like that. You know I did it for you. How could I stand by and let him fetch men who would hang us all for something we did not do? It is my duty as king to protect you, so I did what I thought was best.'

'You were not king, though,' Goran pointed out. 'Not then.'

'And you committed murder!' whispered Eulalia in shock.

'Look!' shouted Guido, brandishing the coins he had been paid for the charade with Blanche and the fire. He bit one hard between his teeth to show that it was real, then pointed at the window. 'I got us money *and* grain. I will be a good king.'

'What about him?' asked Goran uneasily, still holding Bartholomew by the shirt. 'He knows what you did.'

'Leave him to me,' said Guido. 'Go and load the cart with the others. You, too, Eulalia.'

Brother and sister exchanged a glance, then Goran released Bartholomew and started to move towards the window. Eulalia was still hesitating when Guido began to advance on the physician with his wicked little knife. Bartholomew backed away, but stopped when there was a deafening bellow of pain and Guido doubled over. The weapon clattered to the floor.

Bartholomew looked at Eulalia, wondering whether she had taken a dagger to her brother when his back was to her, but she was still standing dazed and helpless, and her hands were empty. She appeared to be as puzzled by Guido's roar as everyone else. Guido crawled to a corner, and retched noisily. Eulalia and Goran gazed at each other in alarm, while Rosel leaned through the window and began an eerie keening. Eulalia moved to Guido's side.

'What is happening?' she cried in confusion. 'What is wrong?'

'Have you put a curse on him?' Goran asked of Bartholomew, appalled.

'No!' objected Bartholomew indignantly. 'I do not know any.'

'He has killed me,' gasped Guido, pointing an accusing finger at Bartholomew and pushing Eulalia away from him. 'He has filled me with poison.'

Everyone stared at the empty wineskin that lay on the floor.

*   *   *

The small pantry erupted into pandemonium. Rosel's keening wails grew louder, almost drowning Guido's groans of agony as he writhed on the floor. The cousins pushed into the room, too, so that there was barely space to move, and began talking in agitated, frightened voices.

'Do something!' Eulalia cried in anguish, her pleas adding to the mayhem. She gazed up at Bartholomew. 'Help him.'

Bartholomew tried, without success, to force the stricken man to lie still for long enough to be examined. He leaned close to Guido's mouth to smell his breath. The wine was there, along with something else: he was fairly sure it was a salt distilled from quicksilver or something similar. He was also certain that there was nothing he could do. Guido was already vomiting blood, from where the poison had eaten its way into his innards.

'I cannot help him,' he said, sitting back and turning to Eulalia. 'There is no cure for the poison he has taken. It is too late.'

Rosel scampered across the floor and snatched up Guido's knife, pointing it unsteadily in Bartholomew's direction. Tears streamed down a face that was twisted with despair and fear. 'If you do not make him well again, I will kill you,' he whispered in his childish voice.

'But there is nothing I can do,' said Bartholomew desperately. 'If I could help him, I would.'

'Guido was right!' Goran yelled, advancing on the physician with his fists at the ready. 'You are a liar! You are refusing to help him because we are different from you. Eulalia was wrong to think you are a good man.'

'No, I—' began Bartholomew.

'Kill him!' wept Guido weakly, clutching at his stomach. 'Give my soul the peace that vengeance knows. He has poisoned me.'

'I have not,' said Bartholomew, scrambling to his feet and backing away when he saw that Goran intended to fulfil his brother's last wishes with his bare hands. 'I never carry poisons in my bag, for exactly this reason. I do not know what has happened. But my wineskin is innocent. I—'

'Do not let him talk his way out of it,' whispered Guido. His face was now a ghastly greenish white, and his chin stained with vomit. 'Kill him, Goran, or I swear by all I hold holy that I will return and haunt you until your dying day.'

He began to convulse, heaving and shuddering as though possessed, while the clan gathered around him and tried to hold him still.

'Help him,' ordered Eulalia, turning to Bartholomew. Her face had lost the frightened, bewildered look, and was hard and determined. It also held an expression that made Bartholomew very uneasy. For the first time, he was the object of her fury. 'The poison came from you, so you must know how to counteract it.'

'It did not!' insisted Bartholomew. 'And there is no cure. All I can do is give him a potion that may dull his pain – although I doubt it will work well with mercurial salts – and advise you to fetch him a confessor as soon as you can.'

'Kill him, Eulalia,' hissed Guido between gritted teeth. 'Kill him, or I will send you mad with fear. I will curse you and all your children, and you will never know happiness again.'

Eulalia said something to her clan in a language Bartholomew could not understand, then snatched the knife from Rosel, and darted towards Bartholomew. He backed away, but Goran was ready for him and the physician felt himself bound by a pair of sturdy arms. Others rushed to help, and Bartholomew was wrestled to the ground, so that he could not move. An empty grain sack was pulled over his head, which turned his world completely black and muffled all sounds. He tried to shout, but the breath he took drew chaff into his lungs and almost suffocated him. He felt hands pulling at his limbs and tried to struggle free. But it was to no avail. He was helpless.

chapter 12

TIME LOST ALL MEANING FOR BARTHOLOMEW. IT COULD have been an hour or a good deal longer that he was bound hand and foot, with the sack pulled so tightly over his head that he could scarcely breathe, let alone hear or see. He felt himself bundled through the window, then dumped among the wheat that was being loaded on to the cart in the yard. A couple of sacks were placed on top of him, so that he would be invisible to anyone who happened to notice the procession of gypsies in the night.

They rattled along at a cracking pace, with the sacks lurching from side to side and threatening to topple. Bartholomew wondered whether the clan intended to travel to London with him trussed up like a Yuletide chicken, and was not sure that he would survive the journey. He could not feel his legs, and he was becoming dizzy and disoriented from the lack of air. He had no idea what they planned to do with him, but suspected that the murder of a clansman was regarded as a serious offence, and that they intended to dispense their own justice. He expected to be taken to some remote place deep in the marshes, where they would slit his throat and dump his body in one of the deeper bogs, where it would never be found.

Just when he was beginning to think that they merely intended him to suffocate slowly over a period of several hours, he felt someone fiddle with the knots that held the sack in place. When it was removed, he saw a blaze of fire-light. He began to cough, gulping fresh air into his lungs and feeling his eyes burn at the sudden brightness. When he could see properly, he glanced around him. He knew he was somewhere in the Fens: he could smell the marshes, and could hear reeds hissing softly in the gentle night breeze. He was in a small clearing, where the clan had made a camp for themselves. Some people were sleeping, huddled forms in the long grass covered with brightly coloured blankets, while others sat around the fire and talked in low voices. Eulalia was standing over him, her face creased with concern.

'Are you all right?'

He nodded, biting back an angrier and more truthful response. But he decided there was nothing to be gained from rudeness, and the last thing he wanted was the sack back in its place. 'Where are we?'

She began sawing at the ropes that bound him. 'At our camp. Do not worry; you are safe.'

'I do not feel safe,' he muttered, rubbing his arms as he glanced over at several burly cousins who seemed to be honing the blades of their knives or oiling the strings on their bows. Blood was beginning to flow back into his limbs, and the sensation was not a pleasant one. He knew he would not be able to run far should they attack. 'Where is Guido?'

'Dead,' said Eulalia, nodding to a large wicker chest on the ground nearby. It was the kind of box that was used to store clothes. Bartholomew supposed that coffins were not items that the clan carried as a matter of course, and that they used whatever came to hand as and when the need arose. The basket did not look long enough to hold Guido, and the physician did not like to imagine how they had prised him into it.

'I am sorry,' he said, looking away.

'He did not die easily, so it was fortunate that his suffering did not last too long.'

'I could not have saved him, but I might have been able to alleviate some of the pain,' said Bartholomew. 'You should have let me help.'

'But then you would never have proved your innocence to my people,' she replied. 'It was better for you that you did not try.'

'I do not understand. You asked for my assistance . . .'

'At first, yes. But when I saw that Guido was dying, I decided it would be best if you went nowhere near him. The kind of curses he was uttering are taken seriously by my people. The only way I saw to prevent one of them from killing you there and then was to suggest that we deal with you later. I said we should not leave blood and a body in the tavern.'

'Very practical,' said Bartholomew, glancing around him uneasily. 'How long do I have before they claim bloodstains in the Fens do not matter?'

She smiled. 'I have already told you that you have nothing to fear.'

'I do not understand,' said Bartholomew. 'You thought I poisoned him. Why are you helping me?'

She shook her head. 'You are not the kind of man to commit murder. However, de Lisle paid Guido two groats for pretending to be Blanche.'

'De Lisle?' asked Bartholomew, not seeing at all where her logic was taking him. 'What does he have to do with Guido's death?'

'Well, it was Ralph who actually gave Guido the coins, but they came from de Lisle's coffers.'

'Are you saying that Ralph killed Guido?' asked Bartholomew. His head throbbed from tiredness and tension, and he was finding it difficult to concentrate. 'But how? He was not in the Mermaid tavern, and Guido drank from *my* wineskin, not one provided by Ralph or de Lisle.'

'Think,' said Eulalia. 'What did Guido put in his mouth, other than wine?'

'The coins!' said Bartholomew, understanding at last. 'He bit the coins de Lisle paid him.'

In an age when forgers and coin-clippers were commonplace, only a fool did not inspect his money carefully before accepting it. Ralph and de Lisle would know that Guido would place any money given to him in his mouth. But a compound of mercuric salts – which Bartholomew thought was what had killed Guido – was an odd poison to employ. Still, Bartholomew supposed that they were unlikely to be spoiled for choice in Ely, and might well use any potion they happened to lay their hands on.

'But *why* should de Lisle and Ralph want Guido dead?'

'So that he would not tell anyone about Goran pretending to be Blanche,' said Eulalia, as though it were obvious. 'It would not look good for my brother to reappear in the future and claim that de Lisle had paid him to set fire to his own house.'

'But surely the whole clan was aware of the plan,' objected Bartholomew, unconvinced. 'And, as you say, it was Goran who pretended to be Blanche, but *he* was not poisoned.'

'It was Guido with whom Ralph negotiated. He will assume that Guido's fate will serve to silence the rest of us.'

'And you are prepared to ride away from Ely, knowing that de Lisle or Ralph took the life of your king?' asked Bartholomew doubtfully.

Eulalia gave her enigmatic smile. 'I have not left your side since Guido died, so *I* have taken no revenge. However, the night is dark, and who knows where Goran may have gone?'

Bartholomew felt a sinking sensation in the pit of his stomach. 'I hope he has not gone after de Lisle!'

'Personally, I doubt that de Lisle knew anything about the poisoned coins. I think Ralph was using his own initiative.'

'Then we must stop Goran,' said Bartholomew, trying to stand. His legs were like rubber, and he collapsed back on to the grain sacks. He gestured urgently to the men sitting around the fire. 'Send one of them after him. De Lisle will not look the other way while your brother murders his most loyal servant, and Ralph will fight. Ralph might end up killing Goran!'

She rested her hand on his knee, and pointed to where Goran's burly shape could be seen huddled on the far side of the clearing. 'It is already too late. Goran returned just before I released you, to tell the clan that the balance has been redressed. Ralph died in his sleep.'

Bartholomew regarded her in horror. 'You mean Goran climbed into his room and shoved a pillow over his face or some such thing? I thought you told me your people were not killers!'

'We are not,' she said indignantly. 'But we believe in natural justice. Ralph killed Guido, and Guido's spirit would not rest easy while Ralph lived. You heard the curses my brother screamed with his dying breath. They were strong words, and the clan does not want them travelling with us when we leave. You were lucky that Goran distinctly recalls Guido biting the coins *after* he had drained your wine, or *you* would have died to appease our brother's restless ghost.'

They were silent for a while, looking through the darkness to the trees that surrounded the gypsy camp. Dawn was still some way off, and the Fens were silent and still. A light mist curled out of the marshes, adding an eerie whiteness to the night. An owl hooted, and some creature gave a short, shrill screech. Bartholomew understood why men like Mackerell, and even Michael, thought the Fens different from the civilised world, and why the notion of water-spirits did not seem so far-fetched there.

'You were right about Guido killing William,' said Eulalia eventually. 'He seemed almost proud of the fact.'

'Thank you for helping me,' said Bartholomew, feeling the strength finally beginning to return to his legs. He started to stand, but Eulalia rested a hand on his chest.

'Do not go yet.' She went to the fire and came back with a steaming bowl.

'What is it?' The contents of the dish were mysterious and unidentifiable in the darkness, but Bartholomew detected herbs in it that he had not smelled since he had been in the southernmost parts of France many years before. For a moment, he felt he was there again, walking in the forests that tumbled down to little coves hiding secret beaches. It was a land of oranges and browns and emerald greens, with air that was always fragrant with flowers, earthy shrubs and the sea.

'Those are herbs I collected and dried myself on our travels,' she replied with a grin, her teeth white in the gloom. 'And duck from the priory's fields. Eat it. It will restore your strength.'

It was delicious, and Bartholomew felt a pang of regret that he would probably never again travel to distant places where the spices and flavours of the foods and wines were so different from those in England.

'Now we are even, you and I,' she said, watching him in the darkness. 'You helped us in the Heyrow, and I have saved you. Neither is in the other's debt.'

'I will always be in your debt. You risked a good deal to save me.'

'I did not! I merely told the truth. But what I said to you in that horrible tavern is right: we have not been made welcome in Ely this year, and it is time to move on to a place where the inhabitants might see us as something other than a band of vagabonds.'

'Even so, they should watch their ducks,' said Bartholomew.

She laughed, a pleasant, low sound that was a welcome change after all the misery and pain he had witnessed that night. 'We will take Guido with us and bury him in a secret place among the marshes, where the water-spirits will guard him.'

'Make sure he does not float,' advised Bartholomew, thinking that the basket might act like a raft, and bear Guido Moses-like on all manner of journeys. 'You do not want him sailing into Ely in a year's time.'

She gazed at him uncomfortably. 'What do you suggest? We cannot take him with us in this heat. And I do not want him buried in Ely. St Etheldreda might not like him near her after what he has done.'

'Punch holes in the basket and weigh it down with stones. It will not take long, then you can be sure that he will stay where you leave him.'

'Will you help me? I do not want my first command as

king to be such a ghoulish one. My people are superstitious, and that might be seen as a bad omen.'

'You are king?' he asked, surprised.

'The clan told me that I had been chosen as Guido's successor when Goran returned from . . . dealing with Ralph. I thought they would elect him, but they wanted me instead.'

'Then they are a wise people,' said Bartholomew. 'And you will be a wise leader.'

'I know,' she said simply. 'But filling my brother's coffin with stones is a distasteful task that should be completed quickly, before we have time to think about it. We should do it now while it is still dark.'

Stones were not a commodity that was in great supply in the Fens. Any rock that had littered the landscape had long since been gathered by local people for building; the rest had been imported at great expense. There were scraps of flint, but it would take a great many of them to make the coffin sufficiently heavy. They were beginning to think that they might have to fell a tree when Bartholomew's eyes lit on the sacks of grain that had given him such an uncomfortable journey.

'No,' said Eulalia. 'That wheat is valuable to us.'

'It looks like the cereal that was paid to the priory in tithes,' said Bartholomew, patting one of the sacks. It had a hard, dense feel, just like the one he had fallen on in the granary, which had split to reveal that it contained mostly grit. 'Symon probably arranged for Leycestre to steal it from the barn near the Broad Lane gate.'

'He did,' said Eulalia with a grin. 'Father John said the priory always demands the best grain from its tenants, and so this should be some of the finest in the area.'

'Unfortunately, you will find it is mostly sand,' said Bartholomew.

She gazed at him for a moment, then took a knife from her belt and slit one of the sacks. The top third or so contained a beautiful golden wheat, but the rest was full of gravel. She stared at it in dismay, before her eyes crinkled with laughter.

'We were cheated by a priest!'

'He is a priest who stole from the priory, and who is not averse to looking the other way while murder is committed. You should not be surprised.'

'I suppose not. But help me with this. The priory's gravel shall give Guido a decent grave.'

For the next hour, she and Bartholomew worked together, packing the gravel around Guido's corpse. Because the basket was too short, Guido's legs were bent, and he lay on one side, as if curled in sleep. He seemed curiously peaceful, devoid of the scowl that had marred his swarthy features in life. Bartholomew had seen some terrifying grimaces on the faces of poison victims, and was glad Eulalia's brother had been spared that indignity.

When they had finished, Eulalia sealed the coffin and nodded in satisfaction. Then she rummaged in one of the carts and emerged with a small bottle.

'Here is your black resin. I said I would keep it for you.'

Bartholomew took it from her and examined it in the faint light of the dying fire. 'I will think of you when I use it.'

'Come with us,' she said suddenly. 'You have travelled in the past, and I know you want to do so again. I saw your face when you tasted the herbs that were grown under the Mediterranean sun. You longed to go back there. And life as the consort of a gypsy king can be very pleasant.'

'I am sure it is. But my life is here, with my students and my teaching.'

She smiled sadly and touched his face lightly with her fingers. 'Pity.'

Much later, when dawn came and the sun cast pale shadows across the dark countryside, they still lay together in the tall grass, talking in low voices about their lives and their dreams. When the clan began to harness the horses and kick out the embers of the fire, Bartholomew slipped away, but did not return to the priory. He watched them pack the last of their belongings and heave Guido's coffin on to a cart. The last he ever saw of Eulalia was as she took the reins to lead her people out of the Fen glade and towards the road that led north.

'Where have you been?' demanded Michael, hurrying to meet him as the physician walked through the Steeple Gate. It was still early, but the sun was up and its rays were already warm, presaging another scorching day. 'Cynric and I have been looking for you everywhere.'

'With the gypsies. Guido is dead, and he confessed to William's murder. He said he did not kill the others, though, and I think he was telling the truth.'

'He was,' said Michael grimly. 'Our killer has been busy again, and last night he claimed yet another victim.'

'Who?' asked Bartholomew nervously. 'Where is Cynric?'

Michael gave a hollow smile. 'You need not worry about him; he is more than capable of looking after himself. The killer took Symon this time.'

'But he is locked in the Prior's prison. Or, at least, he was.'

'Keys and bolts do not deter our man. I am on my way there now, to ask Leycestre and his nephews whether they saw anything useful.'

'Our list of suspects is becoming smaller all the time,' observed Bartholomew, falling into step with him. 'Symon was near the top, as far as I was concerned, but now we know the gypsies are innocent and so was he.'

'Yes,' said Michael harshly. 'It is just a pity we know people are innocent only because they are dead, and not because we deduced it for ourselves. We must resolve this soon, Matt, or people will begin to say that I am waiting for *everyone* in Ely to die, and will only know the culprit when he is the last man left alive.'

Cynric came running to meet them when they reached the cathedral; he smiled in relief when he saw Bartholomew was safe. 'Ralph is dead,' he said conversationally. 'De Lisle found him at dawn, and is said to be rather peeved about it. The rumour is that Ralph had a fatal seizure when told he had to mind Tysilia for the rest of the summer.'

As they walked towards the prison, which was located near the castle ruins, Bartholomew told them exactly what had happened the night before, including John's role in the affair. Michael shook his head in disbelief, and said that the priest had been at prime that morning as usual, and had been more vocal in his prayers than ever. His congregation had been enormous, with people coming from every corner of his parish to direct sullen looks and rebellious muttering towards the monks who held their leader captive. Michael had tried to find him later, to ask whether he had seen Bartholomew, but the priest's house was already empty and his few belongings gone. As soon as the mass was over – and he had ensured his congregation were suitably aggrieved by the priory's arrest of Leycestre – he had apparently melted away into the Fens to bide his time until the uprising began – if it ever did.

When Bartholomew mentioned that de Lisle had commissioned the gypsies' services to pretend to be Blanche and set the fire under his house, the monk gave a grin of amusement.

'Ingenious, but flawed. It would certainly cast doubts on the validity of Blanche's accusations, and make her appear a few wits short of sane. But great ladies simply do not wander around at night setting fire to houses. People will not believe what they "saw".'

'Barbour was sceptical immediately.'

'I suppose it was worth a try, though,' said Michael. 'Poor de Lisle has had this charge hanging over his head for almost two weeks now, and it is crippling him financially. He cannot leave Ely until it is resolved, and his debts are such that he cannot afford to stay in one place for any length of time. He needs to visit people, so that they will feed his retinue and relieve him of the expense.'

'It was still an underhand thing to do to Blanche.'

Michael shrugged. 'But at least he did not murder anyone or steal.'

'He had no need to steal,' muttered Bartholomew. 'He now owns a sizeable share of the treasure he found in the fallen transept. And how do we know he did not murder? Guido would have something to say about that.'

'No,' said Michael firmly. 'Eulalia said *Ralph* paid Guido, not de Lisle. She believed it enough to condone Goran killing the man. De Lisle cannot be held responsible for the actions of an over-zealous servant.'

The glorious day belied the uneasiness Bartholomew felt. There was not a cloud in the sky, which was a fathomless pale blue. The sun bathed the countryside in yellow light, making the strips of barley and wheat a more brilliant gold than ever. It lit the cathedral, too, and, as they walked towards the castle and looked back, tendrils of pale mist hugged the base of the cathedral and gave the impression that it was sitting atop a bronze cloud.

The Prior's prison was an unpleasantly dank building inside the monastery walls. Made of thick, heavy stones from the demolished fortress, it comprised three small dark holes that passed as cells, linked by a narrow corridor. The ceilings were low and barrel vaulted, and the only light was from a tiny slit that was no wider than the length of a finger.

'I hope your priory does not keep people here for long,' said Bartholomew, watching Michael remove a key from his scrip to open the outer door.

'They are holding cells for people awaiting trials. No one is here for more than a few days.'

'There is no proper guard?' asked Cynric disapprovingly, as they entered a narrow, damp corridor. Water dripped down the walls, which were coated with a layer of green-black slime, and the little points of lime that jutted from the roof attested to the fact that leaks were continual.

'A lay-brother comes twice a day with food and water,' replied Michael. 'This is a secure place, and there is no need for constant vigilance.'

'But there is,' Cynric pointed out. 'The killer came and murdered someone here.'

'This has never happened before,' said Michael irritably. 'Prior Alan saw no need to do things any differently last night than he had done before. How could he – or anyone else – have predicted that the killer would strike in a prison?'

'How many people have access to these keys?' asked Bartholomew, thinking that the Prior's security and care of his prisoners left a lot to be desired. What happened if one of the captives became ill or needed attention? He supposed that the needs of a prisoner, who was doubtless deemed guilty of the crime with which he was charged by virtue of being in the cells at all, were not a high priority to the monastery, just as they were not to most other law-enforcing bodies.

Cynric answered. He was observant when it came to that sort of thing. 'The keys to the prison are on hooks in the chapter house – just like the keys to the back gate. Anyone inside the monastery is able to take them.'

'Usually, it is not an issue, because most monks do not want to converse with criminals,' said Michael defensively.

'But last night was different,' Bartholomew pointed out. 'A monk was captive here. What was to stop Symon's friends from coming to let him out?'

'His personality,' replied Michael tersely. 'No one liked him enough to help him evade whatever punishment Alan decides is just. He should have been safe here.'

Three stout wooden doors with heavy iron bars denoted the three cells. Each door had a grille set into it, which allowed anyone in the corridor to watch the captives. Bartholomew recalled Cynric mentioning that he had placed Leycestre and his nephews in one cell and Symon in another, so that they would not harm each other in their fury at being caught. He opened the grille of the first cell, and peered through it to see a trio of bedraggled specimens huddled on the floor.

'We made a mistake,' Leycestre said in a low voice. 'A

night in this foul place has given me time to reconsider, and I realise now that we were wrong. The landlords *are* oppressing the people, and it *is* unjust that some folk eat themselves fat while others starve, but now I see that attempting to steal from the priory was not the best way to rectify matters.'

'Tell Alan that,' said Michael, unmoved by the rebel's remorse.

'I would, but I am not likely to run into him here, am I?' There was a hint of anger in Leycestre's voice. 'Tell him for me. Ask him to be lenient with my nephews. They are boys and were only following my orders.'

'They are grown men, and perfectly able to see the difference between right and wrong,' said Michael sternly. 'However, I will petition the Prior on your behalf, but only if you tell me who killed Symon.'

Leycestre sighed. 'I was afraid you would ask me that, and you can be certain that I would tell you, since you have just agreed to speak to Prior Alan for us. But the truth is that we saw and heard very little. These doors are thick, and the grille can only be opened from outside.'

'I suppose a little is better than nothing,' said Michael, his voice conveying his disappointment.

'In the middle of the night – I cannot tell you when exactly, but it was dark – I heard the grille on our door open. I thought it might be Father John, coming to pretend to hear our confession, so that he could set us free, but then it closed again. Whoever opened it did not speak to us.'

Michael looked at Bartholomew. 'That means that the killer was looking for Symon specifically. He was not interested in the others.'

'I leapt to my feet and tried to peer through the bottom of the grille, where the wood is warped,' Leycestre continued. 'But all I saw was a figure in a dark cloak. I could not tell whether it was a monk or layman; I could not even tell whether it was a man or a woman.'

'Tall?' asked Michael. 'Short? Fat? Thin?'

'I could not see. He had a candle, but it threw out shadows, and I could only make out a shape. He unlocked the door of Symon's cell and I heard prayers. Mass.'

'We shouted to him,' added the nephew called Adam Clymme from his place on the floor. 'But he would not answer. He stayed with Symon for a while, then left, locking all the doors behind him.'

'Who found Symon?' asked Bartholomew of Michael.

'Julian the novice,' replied Leycestre at once, trying hard to provide as much information as possible to ingratiate himself with Michael. 'He opened our grille, and shoved bread and three cups of water through it, and then went to do the same for Symon.'

'What did he do?' asked Bartholomew. 'Did he yell out in shock when he saw Symon dead?'

'Not him,' said Leycestre bitterly. 'I heard the grille being opened. Then, after a moment, he unlocked the cell door, which I thought was an odd thing to do, given that Symon might have rushed him. It was not long before Julian came out again; he was grinning and, as he passed our door, he said "Symon will not be reading any more books". Then he left.'

Bartholomew gazed at Michael. 'I wonder if the nocturnal visitor was merely some kindly monk who came to offer Symon words of comfort, but the murderer is actually Julian. We have been suspicious of him from the start.'

Michael agreed. 'And if Symon was sleeping, then it would have been easy for Julian to slip into his cell and kill him.'

'Have you seen Symon's body?' asked Bartholomew.

'Yes. There was a grazed ear and cheek, and a small wound in his neck.'

'Any signs of fighting, like we saw with Robert?'

'None that I could see. It was as if Symon was taken completely by surprise. If you examine the body now, will you be able to tell whether he was killed in the night by this mysterious visitor, or an hour or two ago by Julian?'

Bartholomew shook his head apologetically. 'Leycestre is vague about the time this night visitor came, and it might have been only a short while before Julian. Had you called me immediately, I might have been able to tell by the warmth of Symon's body, but not now.'

'I would have done, but you happened to be off enjoying yourself with your paramour,' said Michael accusingly. He addressed Leycestre again. 'Is there anything else we should know?'

Leycestre swallowed hard. 'Only one thing. I apologise for knocking you into the crates on Wednesday night at the Quay.'

'I guessed that was you,' Michael said, although Bartholomew knew perfectly well that he had not. 'I suppose you were discussing which house you wanted to burgle?'

Leycestre licked dry lips, and the glance he exchanged with his nephews indicated that Michael had put his finger on the reason for their violent reaction to the interruption that night. 'But we did you no harm. We used no weapons, even though we all had daggers in our belts.'

'Most thoughtful of you,' said Michael stiffly. 'But Matt said you had been drinking heavily, and were on the verge of a brawl with the gypsies that night. Were you sober enough to break into houses?'

'The burglaries were becoming more difficult,' said Clymme ruefully. 'People were on their guard, you see, and each new house we robbed was harder than the last. We drank because we needed the courage ale brings. Eventually, we even had to pretend that Agnes Fitzpayne was also burgled, so that no one would think to blame us.' He unravelled himself from the floor and walked towards the door. His loutish face was streaked and dirty, and arrogance had been replaced by a pathetic misery. 'Will you chase the rats from the last cell before you go?' he pleaded. 'They kept me awake all night with their scratching and clawing.'

'That is not necessary,' said Leycestre to Michael, shoving his nephew away from the grille and shooting him an angry glance. 'We only ask one favour: speak to Alan on our behalf. We can put up with the rats, if you will do that.'

Bartholomew took the torch from Michael and went to investigate. Clymme's request was not difficult to grant, and the prison was grim enough, without having to contend with the sound of rodents scuttling around. The door of the third cell was not locked, so Bartholomew pushed it open, then held up the torch to illuminate the inside. He gasped in astonishment at what he saw.

The missing Mackerell was slumped against the wall, while a large brown rat hovered proprietarily in the background. When Bartholomew stepped forward it scampered away, but did not go far. The physician crouched down to touch the wound in the fish-man's neck. It had bled a little, and the side of his face was bruised, as if he had been held down hard. The body, however, was fresh, and Bartholomew concluded that Mackerell had been dead for a few hours at the most. He strongly suspected that the killer had dispensed with Mackerell at the same time as he had dealt with Symon.

'I will fetch a stretcher and arrange for him to be taken to the church,' said Cynric. He shot an arch expression at Michael. 'Do not worry about directions – I know where everything is. I am growing quite used to recovering the bodies of murder victims in Ely.'

'Did you hear this nocturnal visitor unlock *just* Symon's door?' the monk asked Leycestre, ignoring Cynric's facetiousness. 'Or could he have opened the third cell, too?'

'I could not tell,' said Leycestre. 'I thought I heard the scrape of a key in the lock once, but we were shouting to gain his attention and we were not listening to what he was doing.'

'I thought I heard Symon yell,' added Clymme. 'It happened just a few moments before the visitor left. It sounded frightened, as if he had suddenly realised that something terrible was about to occur.'

'I suspect Symon was dead before that,' said Bartholomew. 'The killer probably entered the cell and went about his business before Symon could fight him off. The shout you heard was probably Mackerell, when he realised that the Prior's cells were not so safe after all.'

'I cannot believe this,' said Bartholomew, as they left the oppressive dampness of the cells and stepped into the bright sunshine outside. He blinked at the sudden brilliance, and felt his eyes water.

Michael carefully locked the door behind him and shook it vigorously. 'Leycestre and his nephews should be safe in there. At least I hope so.'

'They are safe anyway. The killer is not interested in them. They are not nasty enough.'

Michael gazed at him, and then nodded slowly. 'I had forgotten that our killer only removes people who are unpleasant. All three townsmen were fellows whom the town was glad to be rid of; Robert was a thief who forced pilgrims to pay for the privilege of speaking to St Etheldreda; Thomas was a glutton who bullied the novices; and Symon was an indolent fraud who did harm to our priceless books.'

'And Mackerell had a reputation for stealing and lying,' said Bartholomew, looking away across the undulating ruins of the castle and the vineyards beyond. 'But this is beginning to make sense, and I can see at least some answers – such as the identity of the killer.'

Michael took his arm and they went to sit together on an ancient stone that had once acted as a lintel over the door of one of the fortress's finest chambers. It was now a moss-covered relic, half buried in grass and split down the middle, too heavy and damaged to be of use for building. A small oak tree offered welcome shade. Bartholomew gazed down at the moving patterns of leaves and sunlight that played and danced around his feet.

'Well?' asked Michael. 'Who? Prior Alan, because he has completed a beautiful cathedral and does not want it sullied by the presence of evil men? My Bishop, so that no one will think he killed Glovere? Blanche, because she is a lady and no one believes that a lady could set fire to a house, let alone commit murder? Henry, because he has been corrupted by that horrible Julian? Tysilia, because she does not like nasty people?'

'Julian,' said Bartholomew heavily. 'Because *he* does not like people with the capacity to be nastier than him.'

Michael nodded slowly. 'We have witnesses to confirm that he was alone with Thomas in the hospital, and now with Symon in the prison. He therefore had the opportunity to commit those two crimes. And then there is his penchant for sharp implements. We almost arrested him yesterday. I wish to God we had – then Symon would still be alive. But Henry will be distressed to learn that all his goodness has failed to save the boy from himself.'

Bartholomew stared at him, and the scraps of information and disconnected facts that swirled around in his mind started to snap into place. 'No!' he exclaimed vigorously. 'We are quite wrong. That is what we are *supposed* to think.'

'Explain,' ordered Michael impatiently. 'We have suspected Julian from the start. Why is he not guilty all of a sudden?'

'The killer is a clever man,' said Bartholomew, his thoughts racing ahead of him. 'Julian is cunning and inventive, but he does not possess a brilliant mind – not like our murderer.'

'You think it is Alan, then?' asked Michael. 'People say he has one of the most brilliant minds the priory has ever known. And he, like Julian, had time alone in the infirmary when Thomas was killed. Also he has his own copy of every key in the monastery – prison, back gate and so on.'

'Not Alan, either.'

Michael's eyes gleamed as he mulled over the remaining possibilities. 'There is one person left whom we have virtually ignored in our reckoning, but he also had the opportunity to kill all the victims. He is lowly and unimportant enough for us to have overlooked him completely.'

Bartholomew stared at him, thinking this description did

not match his prime suspect at all. 'Who do you have in mind?'

'Welles,' said Michael with satisfaction. 'The boy with the masonry nail. You said yourself that it was a long, thin blade that killed those men – such as a nail used by builders and left lying around the cathedral. I have seen him with one several times – and he was present when that paring knife went missing, then reappeared. Everyone blamed Julian, but perhaps we were all wrong.'

'I was not thinking about Welles. I was thinking of Henry.'

Michael gazed at him. 'Henry? But he is a physician, dedicated to healing people.'

'Physicians are as capable of murder as anyone else.'

'Henry is a good man,' objected Michael firmly. 'I have told you this before. Think about the patience and understanding he has shown Julian. The man is a saint: if Henry was the killer, Julian would have been dead a long time ago. Henry is also an intensely moral man. This killer has no morals at all.'

'He does,' argued Bartholomew. 'At least, morals as he sees them. He thinks he is doing good, and does not see himself as wicked or criminal. That is what makes him so dangerous. He is probably one of those people who thinks God is telling him what to do. They are the worst, because they cannot be made to see that they are wrong.'

'Henry is not a fanatic,' said Michael firmly. 'He is just a physician dedicated to healing the sick. You should appreciate that, Matt. It is what you do.'

'Clues have been staring us in the face all along, but we have ignored them,' Bartholomew went on, increasingly convinced by his own argument. 'First, we agreed when we inspected Glovere's body that the killer had a certain knowledge of anatomy. Henry is a physician.'

'That is not evidence,' snapped Michael. 'It is coincidence.'

'Then consider the death of Guido. He was poisoned, probably with mercurial salts. At first Eulalia blamed me, because he drank the wine from my medicine bag, but then she thought the poison was smeared on the coins de Lisle gave him.'

'We know Ralph did that,' objected Michael. 'And he has been executed for it.'

'But, on reflection, I think Ralph did no such thing. He was not stupid. He knew that Guido would tell the rest of the clan what de Lisle wanted him to do, so killing him would be futile. And they planned to disappear anyway, so de Lisle had nothing to worry about. Eulalia was right the first time: the poison came from my wineskin.'

'I do not understand,' said Michael impatiently. 'Are you now accusing yourself?'

'I gave Henry my own wine to make Ynys a tonic. And yesterday he refilled the wineskin for me. He dosed it with poison, because I mentioned to him that *you* were in the habit of drinking it. It was not Guido he wanted to kill: it was you.'

'Me?' asked Michael, startled and rather offended. 'What have I done wrong? I am not unpleasant and disliked by everyone.'

'But you are on his trail and likely to expose him as a murderer. And you are a large man who is used to sudden ambushes. Henry is quick and strong, but he could not hope to kill you in the way he has dispatched the others. He would never be able to wrest you to the ground and kneel on your head while he cut the back of your neck.'

'But what about you?' asked Michael, unconvinced. 'If he killed me, then you would take up the investigation in my stead.'

'Henry knows he can kill me in the same way as he has killed the others. He almost succeeded in the Bone House, remember? However, that did not stop him from considering alternative methods, too.'

'What do you mean?' asked Michael uneasily.

'He gave me his hemp tonic and watched its effects very carefully. It was at the same time that he refilled my wineskin. When I turned from putting it in my bag, he was holding a knife – to chop garlic.'

'So? That sounds innocent enough to me.'

'No physician ever chops garlic for remedies: we crush it with a pestle. I think he was seriously considering whether to kill me then, when I was sluggish from the hemp.'

'And he offered you more hemp later,' mused Michael. 'I declined it on your behalf.'

'He has also been dosing Northburgh and Stretton,' Bartholomew went on. 'Hemp produces a feeling of well-being, so Henry provided them with as much as they wanted, so that they would not bother to investigate the murders *he* committed. He claimed Northburgh was already addicted to hemp, but Northburgh did not seem affected by it when he first arrived in Ely.'

'Then why did Henry not give me hemp, too?' asked Michael, raising his eyebrows in rank scepticism. 'I was also investigating.'

'Because he knew I would have noticed any hemp-induced changes in your behaviour and would have looked into it. He might have managed to slip you a dose or two, but not enough to achieve the desired result.'

Michael was silent for a moment. 'There is a flaw in your logic, Matt. You say Henry gave you poisoned wine to kill me, but then you claim that he considered killing you with a knife instead of chopping his garlic. The wine would not reach me if you were dead.'

'I imagine that was what stayed his hand.'

'If he poisoned the wine, I suppose you think he poisoned Thomas, too,' said Michael flatly. 'Bukton claimed that Thomas had been poisoned when he first fell ill.'

'No, Thomas really did have a seizure. He had been on the verge of confessing something dreadful when he was stricken. But worse, as far as Henry was concerned, Thomas had been stealing the food from the old men. That is what sealed *his* fate.'

'But Henry was very distressed when Thomas died,' Michael pointed out. 'And do not forget he was asleep when that particular murder took place. We proved that beyond the shadow of a doubt – with drool, if you recall.'

Bartholomew saw his argument take a serious knock. 'Perhaps we were mistaken about that,' he said lamely. 'But, if I am right, then Henry's grief, bad dreams and pallor over the following days were not because he had let a killer make an end of Thomas – they were signs of a guilty conscience.'

'No, Matt,' said Michael, determined that his friend was wrong. 'Thomas was murdered in the infirmary the morning *after* Henry had spent a good portion of the night alone with him. Why would Henry kill the man during the day, when it would have been far safer and easier to do so during the night? Also, old Roger saw him sleeping when the cloaked intruder was prowling around.'

It was a valid point, and Bartholomew considered it for a moment. 'Whoever killed Thomas left the weapon behind – which had not happened before. I said at the time that someone might have been mimicking the killer's methods, and that may still be true. Perhaps Henry did not kill Thomas, but I am fairly sure he killed the others.'

Michael was unconvinced. 'And what would his motive be, pray?'

'The other victims were evil men who caused innocent people distress. As you have said many times, Henry is a man imbued with great compassion, and he looked around him and saw that wicked people were doing whatever they liked while God and His saints slept. He said as much when we caught Symon and his associates stealing the priory's treasure. Remember? He talked about the evil in the world, and how he was disgusted by it all. He decided to redress the balance.'

Michael remained dubious. 'In the past, you have often concocted unlikely solutions to various crimes, and I invariably dismiss them and later look foolish when it transpires that you were right. So, I do not want to abandon your theory completely. However, I must say that Henry is not only a good man, he is my friend. I have never known him do a selfish or an unkind thing, and this accusation of murder is so implausible that it is ludicrous.'

Bartholomew was well aware that the evidence he had presented was circumstantial, at best, but he was certain he was right. He pressed on with his argument. 'Then think about Symon's death. The librarian would not have been in a deep sleep – he had just been arrested, and no one sees time in prison as an opportunity for a good night's rest. He would have been frightened and wakeful. Clymme said he heard mass being said; that involves things being eaten and drunk.'

'You think Henry poisoned Symon with mercurial salts before kneeling on his head and cutting his neck?' asked Michael incredulously.

'He would not have used mercurial salts; they take some time to work, and death is painful and often noisy. I think he used a strong dose of hemp, which would have made Symon drowsy and relaxed. Then it would have been easy to take him by surprise, and cut his neck before he could do anything to prevent it. Bear in mind that the keys to the prison are in a place where any monk can take them – including Henry.'

'That proves nothing,' said Michael impatiently.

'Then consider what we know about Mackerell. Do you remember Symon claiming he had seen Mackerell near the castle the morning after we were supposed to meet him? He was right.'

'We discounted Symon's claim, because he said he was not certain,' Michael pointed out.

'Mackerell wanted to be in the Prior's prison, because he thought he would be safe there. The morning after he failed to meet us, he must have asked Henry to lock him in, and he has been hiding there ever since.'

'But that makes no sense at all,' said Michael impatiently. 'Why would Mackerell ask *Henry* to lock in him the cells? And why was he safe only until last night?'

'Because Henry had just killed Symon. Mackerell probably saw it happen.'

'I am not convinced by this at all,' warned Michael. 'You cannot even prove that they knew each other.'

'I can. Robert told us that Henry bought fish from Mackerell to make medicines. Henry is liked by everyone and universally trusted. *I* would have asked for his help, had I been Mackerell.'

'I am still not convinced,' said Michael, growing testy. 'What other "evidence" do you have that will see dear, gentle Henry accused of these vile crimes?'

'He owns a key to the back gate – he told us so himself – so could easily have slipped out at night to kill the towns-folk.'

'Then how do you think he managed to kill Robert?' asked Michael, his voice triumphant as he spotted another flaw in Bartholomew's logic. 'He was reading in the library when that happened. We saw him – and heard him – go there ourselves. Or, at least, I did.'

'Think about the order of events that day: Henry was exhausted, and I suggested he rest. He declined, and instead went to the library to read about treatments for seizures. He went there with Symon, and we heard them talking together. Then we heard their footsteps on the wooden floor, and then it was silent.'

'That was because Henry was sitting at a desk, reading. And Symon was with him, anyway.'

'Symon was not. He told us himself that he was not in the library for long, because he looked out of the window and saw Robert slinking off to the vineyard. He said he left fairly promptly to go in search of him, if you recall. Henry probably also saw Robert, and so knew exactly where his next murder would take place.'

'And how did he deal with the fact that Symon was also heading in that direction?' demanded Michael archly. 'Ask him to dally for a few moments, so that he could complete his grisly business undisturbed?'

Bartholomew sighed crossly, becoming irritated with Michael's refusal to see the facts. 'Think about what Symon told us, Brother. He did not go straight to the vineyard, did he? He went to the kitchens and spent some time chatting with the brewer and his assistant, probably telling them all that had happened in the refectory that morning. Doubtless he also mentioned to Henry that he was thirsty, and that he planned to visit the brewer before pursuing Robert.'

'But I *heard* Henry in the library at the time of Robert's death,' insisted Michael. 'He did *not* leave to go a-murdering in the vineyards.'

'That is what he wanted us to think. He made sure we heard him, then, as soon as Symon left, he tiptoed out of the library and went to the vineyard. Robert had no need to be afraid and Henry was able to get close to him. Then Henry must have lunged, at which point Robert knew he was fighting for his life. But it was too late: Robert's struggle was futile.'

'It was a while before Symon came to announce that Robert was dead,' acknowledged Michael grudgingly. 'I suppose there was time for someone to kill Robert and dispose of his body.'

'And plenty of time for Henry to return to the library, so that he could clatter noisily down the stairs and pretend to be horrified when Symon came with the news of Robert's death. Henry is a fit man – caring for his patients sees to that – but he could not keep up with Alan and me when we ran to the Quay; he lagged behind with you. That was because he was tired from having made the journey once already.'

'But if Henry is the killer, it means that he is the man with whom we struggled in the Bone House,' said Michael, as if he thought such a fact exonerated the priory's physician. 'Why would he tinker with pots of blood and buckets of soil in the depths of the night?'

Bartholomew sighed as the answer to that became clear, too. 'Because Alan has put Henry under considerable pressure to find a remedy for Northburgh's wrinkled skin. Every physician knows that no known herb or plant will work such a miracle, and so Henry was experimenting with other ingredients – blood – which is the essence of life; and earth – the substance from which all life springs.'

'But why the Bone House, when he has a perfectly good workshop for that kind of thing?'

'He would not bring pig's legs and buckets of blood into the infirmary, where their presence might distress his beloved old men. He would also not risk dabbling with those kinds of ingredients publicly, because all physicians are cautious of encouraging accusations of witchcraft. So, he chose a place where he thought he would not be disturbed.'

'It was unfortunate we happened to intrude, then,' said Michael tiredly. 'Most monks are in bed at midnight, not wandering the grounds near the Bone House, but I could not sleep and felt the need for a stroll.'

'By his own admission Henry was up and about that night, too,' said Bartholomew, as he recalled fragments of conversations with the infirmarian. 'He told me he was in the cathedral, praying for Thomas, and that he saw the gypsies there. They were meeting de Lisle and Ralph, who were to give them the final details regarding this silly business with the house burning. And then there is the fact that Henry also has a bad back. I have seen him rubbing it at least twice.'

'Half the town seems to be doing that,' Michael pointed out.

'Henry knew we would be looking for someone with an aching back after our encounter in the Bone House. That was why *he* raised the subject when I saw him the next day. By telling me that de Lisle and Symon had complained of similar problems, he was able to deflect suspicion from himself. And then there is William.'

'Guido killed William,' said Michael immediately. 'You heard him confess, remember? You cannot blame that on poor Henry.'

'But Guido said two things that should have made me realise Henry's role in this. First, William said to Guido that he had told a friend he was going to fetch another investigator; and second, Guido said William had some kind of stomach cramps.'

'I do not see how either of those incriminates Henry.'

'I think William told *Henry* that he was going to fetch another investigator. As we have said on numerous occasions, people like Henry and trust him. William may well have turned to the gentle infirmarian, to tell him what he intended to do. And then Henry poisoned him, which accounted for the cramps Guido noticed. Guido may well have knocked William over the head, but William was a dead man anyway.'

'You are quite wrong, Matt. Henry is the best monk in the priory, and he is also a dear friend. However, I have known you long enough to be aware that unless we prove Henry's innocence to your satisfaction, you will take matters into your own hands and set about investigating on your own. I do not want you to do that – not in my priory. So, we will go together and settle this matter once and for all.' He stood and put both hands to his back as he stretched. He realised what he was doing and gave Bartholomew a rueful smile. 'Now even I am doing it!'

They made their way up the hill in silence, thinking about what they were about to do. Bartholomew dragged his heels, as though by walking more slowly he could avoid a confrontation that he knew would be distressing. Michael was less reticent, since he was certain there was no truth in the allegations anyway. Even so, the prospect of asking his mentor to prove his innocence was not a pleasant one.

They reached the infirmary and gazed up at its carved windows and creamy yellow stones, bright in the sun. It was silent, and, for the first time, Bartholomew felt its peace was more sinister than serene. They entered through the Dark Cloister and walked along the rows of beds in the hall. Julian lay on one, fast asleep, while old Roger sat bolt upright in another, his hands clasped in prayer. The other old men slumbered, some quietly, others fitfully.

'You have no proof of anything,' said Roger. 'You will not convict him.'

'Why do you say that?' asked Bartholomew. Roger had guessed exactly why they were there. 'And what do you know about it?'

'Enough,' said Roger. 'I can see what has been happening, and I have ears.'

'Not ones that work, though,' muttered Michael.

Roger turned bright eyes on him. 'My hearing is not as dull as I would have you believe. It just suits an old man's pleasure to feign deafness. And it has served me well; I have been able to help Henry a good deal in his dispensing of justice.'

'What do you mean?' asked Bartholomew nervously. His jaw dropped. 'You mean *you* have been eavesdropping on secret conversations and passing information to Henry? Everyone believes you are deaf, and so no one minds what they say when you are near?'

Michael sat heavily on a bench, and Bartholomew saw the colour drain from his face. He had expected Henry to provide alternative interpretations of the evidence Bartholomew had presented, which would lead them to pursue other suspects. The fact that Roger admitted to helping Henry was a bitter blow.

Roger smiled, although it was not a pleasant expression. 'The young are always dismissive of the old. But we are wiser than you, and more clever. You might never have resolved this case, if it were not for Henry's imprudent use of that poison.'

'What poison?' asked Bartholomew. 'The one that killed William, or the one intended for Michael.'

'The latter. I told Henry that using such a method to dispense with Michael was unwise, when stabbing had worked so well on the others.'

'Why would he want to harm me?' asked Michael, hurt. 'I have done nothing to him.'

'But your investigation was leading you ever closer,'

explained Roger patiently. 'I told him he had to stop you before you learned too much. He was only spreading a little goodness in the world; I do not see why he should be punished for that.'

'Murdering people is not spreading good,' Bartholomew pointed out.

Roger rounded on him. 'Who says? Visit Mistress Haywarde, and tell me that her husband's death was not a good thing for her and her family. Speak to the novices, and ask them whether they preferred life with or without Thomas and Robert.'

Bartholomew walked across to Julian, and rested his hand on the young man's cooling forehead. His face was peaceful, as though he had experienced in death what he had never known in life, and the wound in his neck had bled little, which suggested a quick end.

'I absolved him before Henry killed him,' said Roger with satisfaction. 'He repented his sins, and so perhaps will not spend as long in Purgatory as he might otherwise have done.'

'But Julian was young,' protested Bartholomew, covering the assistant's face with a blanket. He glanced quickly around at the other patients, but Henry loved them and clearly intended them no harm. 'He might have changed.'

'Not him,' said Roger firmly. 'We gave him plenty of time to try, but he was irredeemable. Even you said as much. Julian was too firmly entrenched in his own wickedness to change.'

'Was that the criterion Henry used to select his victims?' asked Bartholomew. 'That they were people he did not like?'

'People who were selfish and rotten,' corrected Roger. 'People without whom the world is a better place. Just look around you. Pilgrims are thronging joyfully to pray to St Etheldreda now that Robert is not here to make them pay; my old friends in this hall are sleeping with full bellies, because Thomas has not stolen their food; and no one will deny that the library will fare better without Symon. The same goes for those townsmen – Glovere, Chaloner and Haywarde.'

'We should find Henry before he does any more harm,' said Michael heavily, standing up. It was not a task he anticipated with relish. 'Where is he?'

'I will not tell you,' said Roger, folding his arms and eyeing them defiantly. 'If you find him, you will have him hanged or imprisoned for the rest of his life. He does not deserve that, after bringing so much happiness to the world.'

'He did not bring much happiness to Guido,' said Bartholomew dryly.

'Cynric told me that Guido was poisoned,' said Roger. 'Henry and I guessed it was with the wine that was intended for Michael. But it does not matter. It will not take the clan long to realise that they are better without him, too. He was a killer himself.'

'Guido did strike William a fatal blow,' acknowledged Bartholomew. 'William was on his way to fetch another investigator, although I doubt he would have survived the journey. According to Guido's testimony, it sounds as though the poison was already working.'

'Why did William suddenly decide to fetch another investigator?' asked Michael. 'Did he discover something that made him realise that the case was more than I could handle?'

'William came here to tell Henry that he trusted none of the three official investigators to uncover the truth,' replied Roger. 'He wanted someone to know where he was going, you see, should he be missed. I slipped something from Henry's workshop into the wine he drank before he left.'

'*You* poisoned him?' asked Bartholomew, startled. 'I thought Henry had done it.'

'Henry prefers more compassionate methods of execution,' said Roger matter-of-factly. 'Poisons can be nasty.'

'A knife in the neck might be painful,' said Bartholomew. 'It would render the victim immobile, but he would know exactly what was happening to him. Henry's victims died in terror.'

'Thomas did not,' said Roger. 'Unfortunately.'

'Do not tell me that was you, too?' asked Bartholomew, horrified.

'It was,' said Roger with pride. 'I knew from Henry how it was done, and it was not difficult when the man was just lying there, so still and so silent. I did it while Henry slept so deeply that he drooled on his table – a small detail that did not escape Alan's attention, I remember.'

'So, there was no cloaked intruder wandering through the infirmary and praying as he went?' asked Michael.

Roger gave a wicked grin. 'You see how willing you were to believe a tale that made me look like some feeble half-wit? It never once occurred to you that if a killer really had entered my home, I would recall every detail about him.'

'That is because I did not think you would lie to me,' said Michael stiffly. 'You are offended now, because you think I imagine you to be some drooling ancient who can barely see. But you would have been even more offended if I had claimed I believed nothing you said.'

'So, Henry's shock at discovering that Thomas was murdered was quite genuine,' mused Bartholomew. 'He was right: Thomas probably would not have died if Henry had not slept.'

'Henry was distressed,' agreed Roger carelessly. 'He had hopes that Thomas's illness might make him repent of his wicked ways and render him a more pleasant person. Personally, I thought Thomas beyond that kind of salvation, and so I decided to remove him from this world while the opportunity was there.'

Michael shot Bartholomew a triumphant glance. 'You see? I told you Henry would not have killed a patient.'

'But he killed everyone else,' said Bartholomew.

'It is no more than they deserved,' said Roger, unmoved.

'And he intended to have *me* die from poison,' said Michael bitterly.

'True,' admitted Roger. 'But that was because the vigour of your investigation was unsettling him. He could not dose you with hemp like Northburgh and Stretton, because Bartholomew would have noticed. Poor Henry was at a loss to know what to do about you.'

'You admit Henry drugged the official investigators?' asked Michael, disapprovingly.

Roger shrugged. 'It has done them no harm. Indeed, it has made that miserable Northburgh much more amiable company.'

'William stole ten marks from the priory,' said Michael, abruptly changing the subject. It was disconcerting to hear his death discussed in such dispassionate terms, especially since Henry was involved. 'We found it in the granary. What do you know about that?'

'William did not steal that money. Robert lied to him, saying he did not have enough alms for the poor, so William drew on the hosteller's fund to help him. Robert, however, merely hid the coins away for himself.'

'That does not sound like William,' said Michael doubtfully. 'Why should he give his own funds to help the almoner – especially when that almoner was a man he despised?'

'Because William was not wholly wicked, like Robert,' said Roger impatiently. 'He was cunning and sly, but he did not allow the poor to go hungry. He genuinely believed that Robert really had run out of funds, but became suspicious later. That was why he watched Robert so closely all the time.'

'We found him searching the almonry once,' said Bartholomew, recalling that the hosteller had hidden behind a tapestry in Robert's domain so that he could search it for evidence that the almoner had been lining his own pockets.

'Henry caught Robert in the vineyards,' Roger went on, eyes gleaming, as though he was proud of what had happened. 'The man was not going to look for William, as Alan had ordered him to do, but was taking the opportunity to gloat over the hoard he had secreted in the granary. Henry said you found it and returned it to the priory coffers, so that ended well.'

'But why did Henry kill Robert?' asked Michael, rather plaintively. 'Or rather, since we already know why, why then? Why not later? Why did Henry take the considerable risk of slaying Robert in broad daylight and dumping his corpse in a very public place?'

'Because Robert was asking too many questions, and Henry had the impression that he was forming his own suspicions as regards the identity of the killer. It was simply not worth the risk. I told Henry to dispatch him as soon as the opportunity arose. And it did – when that reprobate went to the granary to pore over his ill-gotten gains.'

'So, Robert was killed for his greed,' mused Bartholomew softly. 'If he had not gone to a remote place to count his gold, then Henry could not have killed him. Well, not then at least.'

'What underhand business was Thomas involved in?' demanded Michael of Roger. 'We saw him in the vineyards and a package changed hands. What was that about?'

Roger smiled. 'You are right. Thomas *was* involved in underhand business. That lovely book of hours belongs to our library, as *I* would have told you, had you bothered to ask an old man. It is one of our most valuable possessions. Robert stole it, and that incompetent Symon did not notice it was missing. Robert gave it to Thomas in return for turning a blind eye to inconsistencies in the almonry accounts, which, as sub-prior, Thomas was obliged to check.'

'So it was Robert who met Thomas in the vineyard?' asked Michael.

Roger nodded. 'One thief paying another with stolen property. No wonder they met in such an isolated venue.'

'And Thomas was not about to reveal anything about the murders when he had his seizure in the refectory,' surmised Michael. 'He was about to confess his nasty little plot with Robert. He knew nothing that would have helped me track down the murderer.'

'No,' said Roger. 'Not a thing. He was too completely immersed in himself and his own world to have deduced anything about the murders. But Henry put an end to such wickedness. We will now have a good and honest sub-prior and an almoner who feels compassion for the poor.'

'And a librarian who will know how to look after books?' asked Bartholomew. 'Is incompetence on Henry's list of sins, too? Is that why he killed Symon?'

'Symon was more than merely incompetent,' said Roger, unperturbed by their patent disgust. 'He was responsible for suppressing learning and education among the monks. And he plotted with Leycestre to strip our monastery of all its treasure. Henry heard him confess. I urged him to deal with the man last night, lest the soft-hearted Alan set him free.'

'And Mackerell?' asked Michael coldly. 'Was he another man you consider steeped in sin?'

'He was not what you would call pleasant company,' said Roger. 'But he died because he saw Henry standing over Symon's corpse. Henry had said mass with Symon, then killed him quickly when he drowsed from the hemp in the wine. He had forgotten that Mackerell was hiding there, thinking himself safe from water-spirits. It was unfortunate, but some sacrifices have to be made.'

'I see,' said Michael coolly. 'But we need to find Henry, before he does any more mischief.'

'No,' said Roger. He rose from his bed on unsteady legs. From the next bed Ynys rose, too. Both held swords that had been hidden under the bedclothes.

'What is this?' asked Michael, backing away in alarm. 'Are all of you involved?'

'Roger and I are men who want to see justice done in our dying years,' said Ynys, clutching the bed for support. 'And we have no grudge against you, so sit down and behave and no one will come to harm. We were soldiers once, so you had better take us seriously.'

'But this is madness,' protested Bartholomew, moving away from Roger, whose grip on his sword was dangerous in its unsteadiness. 'Henry is not a dispenser of justice! It has gone beyond that. He is now a ruthless killer, and you must see that is not right or just.'

'Sit!' snapped Roger angrily. 'We will wait here until Henry comes, and then we will decide what is to be done. Perhaps he will agree to let you go. But then again, perhaps he will not.'

'The battle of Bannockburn,' said Michael harshly to Ynys. 'Were you really there, or are those memories as false as your act of senility?'

Ynys's eyes flashed. 'I was there, boy. And I am not senile, either. At least, not unless it suits me to be thought so, just as Roger's deafness serves him.' He gestured to his friends, lying restless and confused in their beds. 'I only wish I could say the same for these poor fellows.' His expression hardened when his glance returned to Bartholomew and Michael. 'Now sit down.'

Bartholomew prepared to argue, but the door opened, and Henry himself entered. The infirmarian surveyed the scene in front of him with open-mouthed horror, and the dish of fruit he was carrying as a treat for the old men clattered to the floor.

'We have been hearing all about how you have been removing some of the town's more unpleasant residents for the good of mankind,' said Michael coolly.

Henry sat heavily on Roger's bed. 'I did what I thought was right,' he said in a low voice. 'There is too much evil in the world, caused by men who have no thought for others and who are concerned only with their own well-being. They do cruel and unjust things, then go about their lives quite happily.'

'Vengeance is mine sayeth the Lord,' quoted Michael pompously.

Henry rounded on him. 'But it is not, is it? Evil people do evil deeds, then live to a ripe old age to enjoy the fruits of their wrongdoing. There *is* no justice in the world. Surely, you know people whom we would all be better without?'

'Who does not?' said Michael. 'But that does not mean I have the right to decide who should die and who should not.'

'But someone must,' argued Henry. 'Unless we take action to destroy wickedness, then the Death will return. And I, for one, do not want to live through that again.'

'The plague will not return,' said Michael with a conviction Bartholomew certainly did not feel. 'And I am becoming tired of people using it as an excuse to do whatever they like. I am hurt that you are the culprit, Henry. I loved you like a father!'

Henry shot Roger an agonised glance. 'I told you we should have stopped after you killed Thomas! There was no need to take steps against Michael. My life is not worth his!'

Roger disagreed. 'He will expose you as a killer. He has to die. We *need* you – we do not want another infirmarian to care for us as we approach our final days. Michael may love you like a father, but we are like fathers to you. You *owe* us our last little happiness.'

Henry looked from Roger to Michael in an agony of despair. It was clear he did not know what to think. Then, before they could stop him, he had leapt to his feet and darted towards the infirmary chapel.

'After him!' howled Michael to Bartholomew, starting to run.

'No!' yelled Roger, lunging with his weapon. It missed Michael by the merest fraction of an inch. The monk was still gaping at the gouge it had left in the wooden bed when Roger struck again. Michael ducked backward and snatched up a mop with a long handle to defend himself.

Meanwhile, Ynys advanced on Bartholomew, wielding a short fighting sword in a skilled manner that left the physician in no doubt of his expertise. The knives that were in his medicine bag were useless against such a weapon, and there was little he could do but back away and keep out of the range of the swinging blade. Henry was in the chapel, and they could hear his voice raised in pleading supplication.

'We cannot let you go,' said Roger to Michael apologetically. 'Despite Henry's affection for you. You would tell Alan what has happened, and he will send Henry away. And then what would happen to us?'

'Henry's motive may have been honourable, but you are only interested in your own welfare,' hissed Michael furiously, ducking away as the old man advanced. 'You have driven the poor man to despair, and he does not know which way to turn.'

'You saw his distress when you killed Thomas,' said Bartholomew, also moving backward. He knew he was in no real danger from Ynys as long as he kept out of range of the sword, which was not difficult given that the old man moved so slowly. 'You have confused him so much that he may do himself some harm. Put down your weapon and let me go to him.'

Ynys faltered, but Roger remained unconvinced. 'You are lying. Henry would never leave us.'

'You have pushed him too far,' said Michael. 'He is a good man, but you have corrupted him to the point where he does not know what to believe.'

'It is all Ralph's fault,' said Ynys, his sword shaking dangerously close to Bartholomew's chest. 'It was Ralph who came up with the idea – when he killed Glovere.'

'Just a moment,' said Michael, stepping quickly around a chest at the bottom of the bed as Roger edged closer. '*Ralph* killed Glovere?'

'De Lisle wanted rid of Glovere,' explained Ynys. 'So Ralph obliged. Then Roger here saw the good that stemmed from Glovere's demise – no more malicious gossip in taverns, poor young Alice avenged and her grieving family relieved of a heavy burden . . .'

'*Roger* saw the good in Glovere's death?' echoed Michael, bewildered.

'I did,' said Roger in satisfaction. 'I heard what people told me, and I saw I could spend my last summer helping people who deserved it. Then Ralph came to Henry to confess.'

'Henry is loved by all,' said Ynys fondly. 'Many townsfolk use him as their confessor. He is kinder and more lenient than the parish priests.'

'Ralph told Henry how he murdered Glovere with a small knife in the back of the neck. He made his confession here, in the infirmary, thinking that we were too deaf or weak-witted to understand.' Roger looked pleased with himself. 'But we did understand and it gave us an idea.'

'Henry was reluctant at first,' added Ynys. 'But when he saw the relief afforded to the townsfolk by Glovere's death, he killed Chaloner and Haywarde, too – two men who caused more misery to their fellow men than was their right.'

'So that explains why Ralph was so gloatingly smug when he came to demand cordial,' said Michael, as understanding dawned. '*He* knew that Henry had copied his method of execution. He understood that the culprit *had* to be Henry, because murder is not something one brays around all one's acquaintances – only to one's confessor. Henry was the only other man who knew how Glovere was killed, so Ralph reasoned that Henry killed Chaloner and the others.'

'Did de Lisle know what Ralph had done?' asked Bartholomew uneasily.

'No,' said Roger. 'And Ralph was delighted when de Lisle summoned Michael to investigate. He knew Michael's reputation as an investigator, and suspected that he would discover that Henry had killed Chaloner and Haywarde. He imagined that Glovere's death would be attributed to Henry, too. That would let him off the hook.'

'Henry,' called Michael, addressing the chapel. He tried to move forward, but Roger lunged with his sword and he was obliged to duck back again. 'Ralph is dead. He was murdered by the gypsies, because their king drank the poisoned wine *you* gave Matt.'

'No!' Henry's voice was anguished.

'So what?' demanded the more practical Roger. 'Ralph was a killer anyway – he murdered Glovere.'

Henry emerged from the chapel on unsteady legs. His

eyes were wild and his face was bloodless. Tears flooded down his cheeks and his hands shook. Bartholomew was concerned.

'Hemp,' he said. 'Take some hemp.'

'He does not have any more,' said Roger. 'He gave the last of it to Northburgh yesterday.'

For the first time, Bartholomew regarded Henry with the eyes of a physician, and was angry with himself for not being more observant sooner. Henry had been an amiable and placid fellow, seldom roused to anger, even when he had lads like Julian in his care. But now he was distraught and unstable. Henry had lied when he said his use of hemp was rare: Bartholomew recognised now that Henry was an habitual user, and that the sudden depletion of his supply was largely responsible for the emotionally ravaged figure who stood in front of them now. He saw that Henry might well injure himself in his current state. He stepped towards him, but Ynys was ready with his sword and barred the way.

'I am doomed!' cried Henry. 'I have committed grave sins.'

'Wait!' called Michael, as the infirmarian turned and darted out of the hall.

'Leave him,' ordered Roger, brandishing his weapon as Michael started to follow.

'He needs help,' shouted Bartholomew, trying to dodge past Ynys. Ynys, however, had not forgotten his military training, and came towards the physician with a series of hacking blows. The old man's face was strangely elated, and Bartholomew imagined that he saw himself young again, about to fell one of the King's enemies in Scotland or France.

Just when Bartholomew thought he might be struck, Ynys faltered, grabbing at his hip, and his ecstatic expression changed to one of agony. He groaned, then slumped to the ground, where he began to whimper feebly. Bartholomew kicked away the sword, and was about to go to the old man's assistance when he heard a yell from Michael. Roger had him pinned against a wall and looked determined to make an end of him. Bartholomew leapt towards them, grabbed Roger's arm and spun him around so that the weapon clattered from his ancient hand. Then he hesitated. He was a physician, and had never struck an elderly patient before. Michael had no such qualms, however. He gave Roger a shove that sent him stumbling on to the bed, then raced after Henry, dragging Bartholomew with him.

Outside, Henry was moving unsteadily in the direction of the cathedral. Bartholomew and Michael followed, with Michael wheezing and growing more breathless at every step. A group of young monks scattered as Henry barrelled through the middle of them. One of them was Welles, and another was Bukton.

'Stop him!' yelled Michael to Henry's assistant as he drew closer. His bulk was already slowing him down, and he was red-faced and gasping. 'Henry murdered your almoner.'

'What are you saying?' demanded Welles indignantly. 'Henry is no killer.'

'He is,' shouted Michael. 'Why else would he be running from me?'

Bukton snatched at Michael's sleeve as he ran past, pulling the monk off balance. 'Henry is not your culprit,' he cried. 'Leave him alone.'

'We have all the evidence we need,' said Michael, trying to extricate himself. 'Let me go! You are interfering with the course of justice.'

'I do not care,' said Bukton, maintaining his grip. 'Henry is a good man, and I will not let you hang him.'

'Nor I,' determined Welles.

Bartholomew edged around the group, eluding Welles's eager hands, and ran on. Welles detached himself from his friends and chased after him, leaving Bukton to wrestle with the outraged Michael.

'Where is Henry going?' Bartholomew yelled over his shoulder to Michael.

'The cathedral,' gasped Michael, trying to push Bukton

away. Normally, he would have used fists, but it was hard to strike a lad who was trying to protect a man like Henry. Bukton was permitted to take liberties that Michael would never have permitted in Cambridge. 'For sanctuary at the High Altar. Once he is there, we will not be able to touch him.'

Henry was making good time, and was heading for the cloister door. Bartholomew forced himself to run harder, determined to catch the kindly killer before he could reach it. Welles, however, was a good sprinter, and was gaining on Bartholomew. The physician felt a sharp tug as the young monk grabbed his shirt. He stumbled, losing valuable moments.

Welles leapt on him, trying to restrain him. Bartholomew struggled free and dashed on, leaving Welles gasping for breath on the grass, but by now Henry had disappeared inside the cathedral. Bartholomew dashed to the door and hauled it open, listening for footsteps that would tell him which way Henry had gone. He heard them in the south aisle – away from the High Altar, not towards it – and glanced behind to see Welles sprinting quickly towards him. In the distance he saw Michael ploughing forward, dragging Bukton along, as he made his more stately pursuit.

Bartholomew slammed the door hard, and looked for something to block it. The bolt was wholly inadequate, and was ridiculously delicate, obviously intended only to keep the gate from blowing in the wind and not to prevent access to people from the priory side of the cathedral. Bartholomew shot it closed, wishing there was a bar he could use to barricade it further. But there was nothing to hand in the vast emptiness of the cathedral. He heard a crash when Welles reached the door and thumped into it with his shoulder. The metal bolt bowed dangerously, and Bartholomew saw it would only be a few moments before Welles broke it and came in.

The physician started to trot down the south aisle, looking for Henry among the shadows. There was nothing. He stopped running and listened, but could only hear the crashes and thumps Welles made as he pounded on the door. Bartholomew jogged on, not understanding why Henry should choose the opposite direction from the place where he would be safe from pursuit. He ran harder then there was a booming sound and the door flew open against the wall. Welles uttered a yell of victory when he spotted the physician.

Bartholomew reached the end of the nave and skidded to a halt, gazing wildly around him. Then he heard a sharp crack and a patter, as some loose masonry fell to the ground in the crumbling north-west transept. Henry was climbing the scaffolding.

'No!' he cried, suddenly realising why Henry had not aimed straight for the sanctuary. 'Henry! There is no need for this!'

He darted forward. Voices echoing loudly in the aisle indicated that Michael and Bukton had arrived, too, and were coming towards him. Bartholomew rushed to the transept and looked up. A figure on the scaffolding was making its way higher and higher, aiming for the roof. Bartholomew started to climb after him, intending to bring Henry down. But with a triumphant cry, Welles reached him and grabbed one leg. Bartholomew found himself unable to move up or down.

'Henry!' he shouted, trying to kick free of the determined novice. 'You do not need to do this. Come down and talk to Michael.'

He could feel vibrations of movement through the scaffolding as Henry continued to ascend, and struggled to free himself. But with a monumental display of desperate strength, Welles swung all his weight on Bartholomew's foot and the physician lost his grip. He slipped to the floor, where Welles pinned him down. Bartholomew gazed up at the roof, disconcerted by the towering framework above him, which seemed to be swaying.

'It is going to fall!' he heard Michael yell. 'Matt, get out of there!'

Welles decided Michael was right. He released Bartholomew and scrambled away, and Bartholomew saw the entire structure begin to topple. He leapt to his feet, and ran with his head down, aware of falling spars, plaster and pieces of timber clattering all around him. He had only just cleared the transept when there was a tremendous crash, and the scaffolding came tumbling to the ground in a mess of broken planks, crushed stones and coils of rope. Dust billowed, making it difficult to see.

Michael surged forward, peering into the mess. 'Henry!' he shouted. 'Henry!'

But there was no reply.

Michael rounded on Welles, who was visibly shaken. 'Look what you have done! If you had not tried to stop us, we would have been able to catch him, and this would not have happened!'

'You would have hanged him,' said Welles, his eyes filling with tears when he realised that Henry was unlikely to have survived the fall. 'And he is a decent, kind man. I do not care what you say you have discovered.'

'He murdered people,' said Michael, trying to make them see reason. 'And then your interference allowed him to kill himself. I thought he came here for sanctuary, but the kind of sanctuary he had in mind was his own death.'

'If he did all that, then he only harmed wicked people,' said Welles loyally, white faced as a tear coursed its way down his dusty cheek. 'He loved the rest of us. He was patient with our faults, and he was gentle. He was the only man in the priory who tried to help that horrible Julian.'

'Julian is dead in the infirmary,' said Michael harshly.

'Then not before time,' said Bukton, defiant but shaken. 'If Julian had had no Henry to care for him, he would have been dead a lot sooner. I do not care what you say, you will never persuade *me* that Henry was not a saint.'

'I liked him myself,' said Michael tiredly. 'It is not pleasant to know that a man I have known and admired for years could do such terrible things.'

'He did not do terrible things,' wept Welles. 'He did things that made the priory better and made the town better.'

'All right,' conceded Michael. 'But he broke the law.'

'Then the law is wrong,' declared Bukton uncompromisingly. 'The townsfolk have a point when they claim the laws of the land are unjust. The law would have hanged Henry.'

'Henry has hanged himself,' said Bartholomew quietly. He pointed to the wreckage of smashed scaffolding, where the body of a monk swung slowly from side to side. A rope had caught around Henry's neck, suspending him in mid-air a long way from the ground. His hands hung limply at his sides, and the awkward angle of his head indicated that his neck was broken. Henry was dead, and there was nothing Bartholomew, Michael or the novices could do about it.

'Henry has hanged himself,' Bartholomew repeated softly.

epilogue

'T HAT WAS ONE OF THE LEAST PLEASANT CASES I HAVE
ever worked on,' said Michael two days later, as he
and Bartholomew sat quietly together near St
Etheldreda's tomb in the cathedral. 'I felt no sympathy whatsoever for the victims, and a great admiration for the killer.'

'Even after you discovered he was a murderer?' asked
Bartholomew.

Michael nodded. 'I have known Henry for years, and have
always respected and liked him. I am not surprised young
men like Welles and Bukton were prepared to do all they
could to save him.'

'They knew he would have hanged, had you caught him.'

'He would not,' said Michael tiredly. 'Alan would not have
permitted that, especially if you had provided evidence that
hemp had damaged his mind. He would have been sent
away from Ely, though, and would not have been allowed
near an infirmary again. But how did he die? Could you
tell, when you examined the body?'

'The rope broke his neck. He died instantly.'

'That is a mercy,' said Michael. He stood, and began to
walk out of the cathedral, pausing for a moment to glance
at the ruin of the north-west transept. 'I shall think of him
every time I come here. His sudden death means that he
did not have time to make a confession, and, according to
Roger, he always allowed the men he killed to repent.'

'That was good of him.'

Michael sighed, turning his flabby white face to the warmth
of the sun as they left the cathedral and walked through the
cloisters towards the Black Hostry. 'You knew Henry for only
a few days, so I cannot expect you to understand. He *was* a

good man. Welles, Roger and the others are right.'

'I suppose his pre-stabbing ritual partly accounts for the bruises on the victims' faces,' said Bartholomew thoughtfully. 'I assumed the killer was holding them to cut their necks, but he was also allowing them to make a final confession. I cannot imagine what was going through his mind at that point.'

'Nor me,' admitted Michael. 'But Roger revealed that he and Ynys helped Henry kill Chaloner and Haywarde. Then Henry took the bodies to the river to get rid of them.'

'They died late at night, Brother,' said Bartholomew. 'After they left the Lamb. What were two old men and Henry doing out and about at that hour?'

Michael regarded him with raised eyebrows. 'Patients come to you at all hours of the day and night, and Henry's were no different. Also, remember that these were selfish men, who thought nothing of waking a physician just because they happened to feel the need of one. One came to the infirmary with a sore thumb and the other an aching knee, apparently – both ailments that would have kept until a more convenient hour.'

'And so Henry copied Ralph's murder of Glovere by putting the bodies in the river? He, like Ralph, hoped to pass the murders off as suicides?'

'Yes. When Mackerell came to sell Henry fish, Roger asked him how and where to dispose of corpses in the river. This resulted in Mackerell assuming that Roger – not Henry – was the killer.'

'That explains why Mackerell was afraid,' said Bartholomew. 'He probably wanted to tell you what he knew, but suspected that you would not believe that a frail old man like Roger had killed strong and fit men like Glovere, Chaloner and Haywarde.'

'I would not have done,' said Michael. 'And neither did Mackerell, at first. Then he jumped to the conclusion that Roger was possessed by water-spirits, who have the strength to do whatever they like.'

'I suppose Mackerell thought Roger – and the water-spirits – would be unlikely to hunt for him in the Prior's prison, and so he asked Henry to lock him in. That was what Mackerell was doing when Symon spotted him in the monastery grounds.'

'Henry did as Mackerell asked, then murdered him at the same time as he killed Symon. Mackerell called out in terror when he realised that he had gone for help to the one person he should not have done. And that was the end of him.'

'What will happen to the old men?' asked Bartholomew. 'Roger and Ynys?'

'Nothing,' said Michael heavily. 'When Alan tried to speak to them, they went back to pretending they were blind, deaf and senile. He has decided to allow them to live out the rest of their lives in the infirmary. Henry did most of the killing, and I do not think they will resume where he has left off.'

'I am not so sure,' said Bartholomew, who thought Alan foolish to dismiss the determined old men who had allied themselves so readily to such a cause. They were soldiers, when all was said and done, and had wielded their weapons efficiently enough. However, he supposed that Ynys's damaged hip would keep *him* in bed a while at least.

'Nor am I,' said Michael. 'It was Roger who killed Thomas, after all, and who poisoned William, whose only crime was trying to fetch an independent investigator. But Alan thinks that spending their days being cared for by Bukton and Welles is punishment enough. They are good lads, but they will not coddle the inmates as Henry did.'

'Well, if I break a leg, please do not consign me to the priory's infirmary,' said Bartholomew vehemently. 'Roger or Ynys would have a knife in me the instant I closed my eyes to sleep. I only hope any other monk sent there knows the danger he might be in.'

'Blanche left this morning,' said Michael, after a moment of silence. 'Her "appearance" in the Heyrow a few nights

ago with a lighted torch is causing a good deal of speculation. People claim they do not believe that a lady would do
such a thing, but there remains a lingering doubt, and that
is enough to have driven her away.'

'Has she dropped her charges against de Lisle?' asked
Bartholomew.

'Yes. She now believes that Henry killed Glovere, because
we proved he killed the others.'

'You did not tell her that Ralph did it?'

Michael raised his eyebrows. 'I did not. She would have
accused de Lisle of ordering Glovere's death, and we would
have been back to where we started.'

'But de Lisle may well have ordered Ralph to kill Glovere,'
said Bartholomew.

'If my Bishop had known Ralph was guilty, then he would
not have appointed me to investigate.'

'Not necessarily. He appointed you after Chaloner and
Haywarde had died, remember? Perhaps he knew that Ralph
killed Glovere, but did not want him blamed for the other
two, as well.'

Michael declined to answer. He rubbed his chin, then
rummaged in his scrip to produce a thin piece of parchment. 'When I was going through Henry's possessions
yesterday I found this missive addressed to me, describing
his murderous rampage over the last few days. Everything
we reasoned is essentially correct. It concludes by admitting
that Ralph had given him the idea, when he came to be
absolved from Glovere's murder.'

'Why did he write this letter?' asked Bartholomew curiously. 'Was he planning to send it to you in Cambridge?'

'He had compiled a list of victims,' said Michael tiredly.
'When everyone on the list had been "removed", he was
going to leave Ely, to retire to some remote corner of the
country. He wrote that his work at Ely would have been
completed.'

'And how far through this list was he?' asked
Bartholomew, thinking that composing such an agenda was

a rather cold and calculating thing to do.

'Almost at the end. I suppose that was why the last few victims were killed in such rapid succession – he wanted to finish. The only one left was Father John. I thought Tysilia might be on it, but I am fairly sure her experience in the crumbling transept was just an accident.'

'Tysilia?' asked Bartholomew. 'Why would she be on such a list? She is not evil.'

'De Lisle thought someone had deliberately caused the fall, and with so many deaths it did seem suspicious for there to be a sudden accident. But I think that was all it was.'

'And why John?' asked Bartholomew. 'He has compassion for the poor, and is not one of those priests who cares only for his personal gain.'

'Henry believed that John is responsible for men like Leycestre plotting rebellion. He thought no good could come of it, and wanted to remove John before matters grew out of hand. He may have been right, but John has disappeared from Ely anyway. Doubtless he is being hidden by fellow rebels in the Fens.'

'John had a lucky escape, then,' said Bartholomew. 'Not only has he eluded Henry's sharp knives, but he has evaded justice for stealing the priory's grain and giving it to the gypsies.'

'It is ironic,' mused Michael. 'But one of the things that made Glovere unpopular in the town was his claim that one of Ely's citizens was the burglar. In the event, he was right: it was Leycestre.'

'But Leycestre and his thefts had nothing to do with the murders. They were separate and unrelated events. The burglaries were just that – and no one was killed when they were carried out.'

'So,' concluded Michael. 'We now know everything about this case: Ralph killed Glovere; Henry slew Chaloner, Haywarde, Symon the librarian, Almoner Robert – who was every bit as dishonest as his rival William believed – Mackerell the fish-man, and Julian the lout; Roger dispatched Sub-prior Thomas; and William's death was a combination of Henry's poison and Guido's aggression.'

'And Goran killed Ralph,' added Bartholomew. 'Do not forget that.'

'There is de Lisle,' said Michael, pointing to the Bishop, who was surrounded by his scurrying retinue, all rushing to pack their belongings on to the impressive herd of horses waiting in the courtyard. 'He plans to travel with us to Cambridge today, before heading south to give the Archbishop of Canterbury an account of the events that led to a prelate being accused of murder.'

'I hope he has his excuses all worked out,' said Bartholomew caustically. 'He would be wise to avoid the truth, given that it was his own servant who precipitated all this mayhem.'

'Are you ready to leave Ely?' Michael asked him, wisely ignoring the comment, since de Lisle was probably close enough to hear any response he might make. 'Tonight, you will sleep in your own room at Michaelhouse, and can rest assured that you are not in the same building as a killer.'

Bartholomew had lived in Cambridge long enough not to be so sanguine, but followed Michael to where the Bishop's household was packed and ready to go. Cynric and Meadowman also had ponies loaded with the few possessions the scholars had brought, and were mounted and waiting.

'Did you finish your reading in the library?' asked Cynric as Bartholomew scrambled inelegantly on to his mount. 'You did not spend much time there.'

'No,' said Bartholomew shortly. 'I have decided I would rather work at home. Prior Alan has given me two particularly valuable medical books as a donation to Michaelhouse, and I shall have to be content with what I learn in those.'

'And you have Henry's notes,' said Michael, pointing to a saddlebag that bulged with parchment.

'Right,' said Bartholomew, not sure whether he could bring himself to use them. It crossed his mind that, in addition to the cures the infirmarian had developed over the years, he might discover a list of good ways to kill people.

'Are you ready to go?' asked de Lisle, trotting up to them. His horse was a splendid black beast that had been groomed until its coat shone. Nearby, Tysilia slouched on a pony, a sullen expression on her face.

'What is wrong with her?' asked Bartholomew. 'She looks furious.'

'She is going back to the nuns at St Radegund's Convent,' said de Lisle. 'I cannot have her with me when I visit the Archbishop later this month; I do not think they would see eye to eye. And anyway, I do not have time to give her the constant attention she needs now that Ralph is gone.'

'I am sorry you lost such a faithful retainer,' said Michael insincerely.

'So am I. Tysilia let the gypsy into my house, thinking that she was being helpful. When Goran told her he had come to kill Ralph, she thought he was speaking metaphorically.'

'I doubt it,' mumbled Bartholomew. 'She would have taken Goran quite literally, and seen Ralph's death as an opportunity to escape from his protection for a night.'

De Lisle did not hear him, or gave no sign that he did. He continued. 'She found herself with hours to do as she pleased. She visited a number of taverns, and made various sorties to the stables, but I found her in the north-west transept the following morning.'

'I imagined her experiences with a certain gargoyle would have put her off that particular place,' said Bartholomew, surprised.

'She has already forgotten about that. I caught her tampering with the scaffolding. I have no idea what she did exactly, but I cannot help but wonder whether it might have been more stable before she got to it.'

Bartholomew gazed at him. 'What are you saying? That Henry may have died because that woman fiddled around with things she did not understand?'

De Lisle nodded slowly. 'I cannot be certain, but I know she had undone some knots and retied others wrongly. She told me it was like embroidery with large threads.'

'Are you sure she should be set loose on the nuns?' asked Bartholomew doubtfully. 'She is a danger to have around – as I have told you before. Look what she did to the lepers.'

'The nuns need the money,' said de Lisle, as if that was all that mattered. 'They will take her. But we should go, or we will be travelling after dark.' He grimaced. 'Damn! I was about to call for Ralph. I shall miss that man. He obeyed my orders without question, and I doubt I will ever find another servant like him.'

'Henry's letter said that Ralph was blackmailing him because he had guessed that Henry was the killer,' said Michael. 'So Ralph was not a good man for you to employ. You are better without him.'

Bartholomew was aware that de Lisle was looking at Michael strangely. '*Ralph* was blackmailing *Henry*?' he asked. 'Not the other way around?'

'Why should Henry blackmail Ralph?' asked Bartholomew, bewildered.

'For his silence, after Ralph was foolish enough to confess,' said de Lisle. 'At least, that is what Ralph told me. Clever old Ralph! He took money from me – which he said he was going to give Henry – and now I learn that he also took money from Henry. Both for the same thing. It just goes to show that you never know people as well as you think.' He gave them an absent smile, and spurred his horse away, down the road that led to Cambridge.

'He knew!' exclaimed Bartholomew, regarding the proud prelate in horror. 'He *knew* Ralph killed Glovere! He was even paying Ralph to ensure that Henry kept silent.'

'You are right,' whispered Michael, staring at the elegant figure of the Bishop astride his black horse as he rode away from Ely. 'De Lisle was guilty all along!'

hISTORICAL NOTE

THERE WAS A POWERFUL BENEDICTINE CATHEDRAL-PRIORY at Ely in 1354, despite the fact that at the time Ely was an isolated settlement in an area that was more water than solid land. The Romans had partly drained the Fens – some of their canals and dykes still survive – but it was not until the seventeenth century that this area came to resemble the landscape we know today, with its vast flat fields and the occasional farmstead or cluster of houses.

The monastery at Ely was founded by St Etheldreda in 673. Etheldreda was the daughter of a king called Anna, and she had been married twice in political unions, despite her objections that she wanted to live a life of contemplation and chastity. It was while fleeing from her second husband that she arrived in the mysterious marshes and islets that formed the Fens, and she selected the virtually inaccessible Isle of Ely as a suitably remote place for her abbey. She died six years later, and her bones were eventually translated into a shrine that formed the heart of the later cathedral. Many miracles were associated with her tomb, and it was an important site for pilgrims by the fourteenth century.

In the 1350s, the great cathedral at Ely was essentially as it appears today. Most of the building had been completed by Norman priors and bishops, although a collapse of the central tower in 1322 seriously damaged the chancel and necessitated further work. The cathedral-priory was fortunate that at this time its sacristan was the talented Alan of Walsingham. Little is known about Alan's early life, although it is recorded that he was a junior monk skilled in working with gold in 1314. In 1321 he was elected sacristan, and therefore was responsible for the fabric of the cathedral.

The story goes that the day after the 1322 collapse Alan gazed on the rubble in the chancel in despair, but then realised that here was a challenge worthy of his talents. The result was the octagon and its lantern tower, one of the most unusual and innovative designs in medieval ecclesiastical architecture. Instead of the usual four piers that carried the immense weight of a stone tower, Alan distributed the load by using eight piers, each extending back for the extent of one bay. This simple, but brilliant, design resulted in a structure that was extremely stable, and was later copied by other medieval architects. At the same time, Alan produced the exquisite Lady Chapel, with its beautiful tracery and niches for statues of saints, and rebuilt the damaged choir. He also oversaw the building of Prior Crauden's Chapel, which was raised in 1324. All still stand, a further testament to Alan's ability to design buildings that would last.

Originally, there were two parishes in Ely: Holy Cross and St Mary's. St Mary's had the splendid church that stands on the green, but the parishioners of Holy Cross did not have their own building until a lean-to was erected against the north wall of the cathedral. This was started in the early 1340s and was consecrated in the 1360s, although it was not completed until around 1460. Before that, parish services were conducted in the nave of the cathedral, although this suited no one, and letters of complaint were written to the Archbishop.

By 1373 the name Holy Cross had been changed to Holy Trinity, although no one seems quite sure why the dedication was altered. When this church was demolished in 1566, the parishioners used Alan de Walsingham's lovely Lady Chapel for their parish church, a tradition that continued until 1938, after which the parishes of Holy Trinity and St Mary's were amalgamated. Visitors to the lovely medieval church of St Mary, which still stands next to the mighty cathedral, will notice that the chapel to the south is named Holy Trinity Chapel. This was dedicated in 1941, and the intention was to provide a link with the lost parish.

The Benedictine monastery was also well established by the 1350s, although it lost its abbey status in the early 1100s, when the abbot was replaced by a bishop. Its proper title was Cathedral-Priory, with a prior in charge. The Ely Porta, through which visitors pass if they enter the cathedral through the back door, was not built until the 1390s, and so was not standing when Bartholomew and Michael visited the city. The almonry, Steeple Gate, cloisters, Prior's House, infirmary, Black and Outer 'hostries', chapter house and the beautiful Prior Crauden's chapel were all there, though. Some of the infirmary still stands, and forms part of the deanery buildings today. All these were surrounded by a sturdy wall that enclosed the vineyards to the east, and were bounded by the castle ruins to the south.

The cathedral-priory, being a wealthy landowner, had at least two barns in which to store the tithes it was paid by its tenants. One barn was near the junction of Back Hill, Walpole Lane (now Silver Street) and Galey Lane (now The Gallery), while the Sextry Barn (built in 1251) stood near St Mary's Church. The monks' vineyard did not produce good wine; the Bishop's vineyards, to the east of the town, were said to be a good deal better. Ely was famous for its ale, however, and it produced at least four types in various strengths and qualities. Bona cervisia, the best kind, was probably served to the monks and to their guests in the refectory. Skegman was the worst, and was brewed to be distributed as alms for those so poor they could not afford better. Mediocris cervisia was mild ale, while debilis cervisia was very mild ale that was issued to servants.

Thomas de Lisle was a controversial and complex figure. He was arrogant and overbearing, and ran up massive debts in equipping his court in a way he thought suitable for a man of his position. He antagonised the King on several occasions, forcing other churchmen to speak in his favour in an effort to prevent a rift occurring between Church and state. He could also be compassionate and selfless. He gave last rites unhesitatingly during the Black Death, and was known for excellent sermons. As with many powerful people of his time, records allow us only a glimpse of what must have been a fascinating and multi-faceted character.

Poor Alan de Walsingham really did lose a good deal to Thomas de Lisle. When Bishop Crauden died in 1344, the monks of Ely elected Alan as Crauden's successor. Unfortunately for Alan, the ambitious de Lisle happened to be in Avignon with the Pope at the time, and the monks' election was overruled in de Lisle's favour. When de Lisle died in 1361, Alan was elected by the monks a second time, but was passed over in favour of Simon Langham (later Archbishop of Canterbury). Alan never did become Bishop of Ely.

A Roll of Edward III (35 Ed III), dating to 1361, lists various monks at the priory with reference to a purchase of the Manor of Mephale. These monks allocated specific sums of money, all of which are meticulously noted. Among the names are: Alan de Walsingham, Sub-prior Thomas de Stokton, Robert de Sutton, William Bordeleys, Henry de Wykes, Roger de Hamerton, Symon de Banneham, John de Welles and John de Bukton.

Northburgh and Stretton also existed. Northburgh was a royal clerk by 1310, and was considered elderly when he attended a council of bishops in 1341. He was a favourite of Edward II (1307–1327), who regularly wrote to the Pope, begging favours on his behalf – including a request that Northburgh might be excused a trip to Rome when made Bishop of Coventry and Lichfield, because he was busy with other things. Northburgh held some very powerful posts, including that of Chancellor of Cambridge University from 1320 to 1326. However, he did little with his authority, and he is damningly summarised as a man 'whose ambition was greater than his ability' by one biographer.

Stretton was collated to the canonry of St Cross in Lincoln in 1353, and held several other prestigious posts before moving to Lichfield on 14 December 1358. A mere two weeks later Bishop Northburgh died, and Stretton became his successor on the direct orders of the Black Prince, eldest son of Edward III (1327–77). However, records state that Stretton was so illiterate that complaints were made to Pope Innocent VI. The Pope ordered an enquiry, during which Stretton was examined and found sadly lacking. Probably at the suggestion of the Black Prince, Stretton hurried to Avignon, where he demanded an audience with the Pope himself.

The Pope ordered a second assessment of Stretton's religious knowledge, but the verdict was the same as the first: *propter defectum literaturae.* However, the King refused to consecrate another bishop in Stretton's place, and kept the See vacant, seizing all the revenues for himself in the meantime. Two years later the Pope ordered yet another examination, this one conducted by the Archbishop of Canterbury. Stretton had not grown any more intelligent in the interim, and the Archbishop said so. In exasperation, wanting the whole affair done with, the Pope ordered the consecration anyway. The Archbishop refused to do it himself, but directed two of his suffragans to conduct the ceremony, which they did on 27 September 1360. Stretton enjoyed his position for twenty-five years, during which time most of his episcopal work was carried out by deputies. The Black Prince and Edward III were rewarded for their support with a chantry and a priest who was paid to pray for their souls.

The town of Ely was fairly prosperous in the 1300s, largely due to the presence of the cathedral and its priory. Ely was especially noted for its rope industry, and it also possessed a pottery. Trading was possible via the River Ouse, which linked it to Cambridge as well as the area to the north. The causeways were important, and, although the priory maintained them to a certain extent, they were liable to flood. There were also outlaws at large, who knew that the merchants and wealthy clerics who used the road were well worth the risk of robbing.

The motte-and-bailey-style castle had never been much of

a fortress. It saw some action during the anarchy in the reign of Stephen (1135–56), but some sources say there was already a windmill on the motte by 1229. No castle was recorded in documents dating to 1259, so it seems it had disappeared by then. By the 1350s it was probably little more than a few foundations, and the stone, a valuable commodity in the Fens, would have been spirited away for use on the cathedral, priory or town.

The map at the front of the book is based on references to street names used in the twelfth to fourteenth centuries. Some of these are still extant, and the names make more sense when viewed in their medieval geographical context. For example, Brodhythe and Ship Lane refer to ancient quay sites, while Steeple Gate refers to a steeple on the Church of the Holy Cross, which has long since disappeared.

The 1348–50 plague, which was not dubbed the Black Death until the nineteenth century, caused major changes in the social structure of England. Wages were kept artificially low by a bill passed in the early 1350s, but labour was scarce and the price of food was high. Rebellion was in the air. However, it was not until 1381 that the troubles came to a head. The Peasants' Revolt was far more violent in Ely than in the rest of the shire, and was sparked by a new poll tax. Its ring-leaders in Ely included a man named John Michel, who was a chaplain. Local men were Richard de Leycestre of 'Bocherisrowe', Robert Buk and Adam Clymme.

Clymme called on the local peasantry to decline to pay taxes and to behead lawyers, while Leycestre urged them to 'destroy traitors to the king and the common folk'. The revolt began on 15 June 1381, and within a few days Leycestre had given 'sermons' in the church and cathedral, and various officials had been executed and their remains placed on display in the town pillory. The rebellion spread like wildfire into the Fens, and the rebels marched to nearby Ramsey to continue their work. But the authorities were ready for them, and the leaders were quickly apprehended and executed.

A number of other characters in the book are also based on real people. Agnes Fitzpayne was mentioned in the mid-thirteenth century as a woman with money to donate to the priory, while records show that one Julian Barbour was landlord of the Lamb Inn at some point. Glovere, Chaloner and Haywarde also appear in medieval records as city residents. It is difficult to know how many inns were present in Ely in the 1350s, but there were probably several. Records show that the White Hart, the Bell and the Lamb are among the oldest.

And finally, Blanche de Wake and Thomas de Lisle really did have a serious feud. De Lisle was accused of firing some cottages on Blanche's estates at Colne near Huntingdon, and was tried (in his absence) and found guilty by the King. De Lisle refused to pay the fine, and the ensuing row threatened to spill over into a dispute between Church and state. A number of bishops and other churchmen intervened on de Lisle's behalf, but the King made de Lisle pay the fine anyway. By this time, de Lisle's lavish lifestyle had left him somewhat impoverished, and he spent the rest of his life trying to pay off his substantial debts. At some stage, the feud with Blanche resulted in a steward being murdered. De Lisle's steward, Ralph, was generally thought to be responsible, although de Lisle vigorously denied the charges. Was de Lisle complicit in the murder? It seems likely, although we shall never know for certain.